I0830412

Published by Hertfordshire Press Ltd © 2024
e-mail: publisher@hertfordshirepress.com
www.hertfordshirepress.com

Viktor Slipenchuk ©

ZINZIVER
Novel

Translated in English by Anton Kovalenko
Edited by Francesca Mepham, Laura Hamilton
Cover design & typeset by Aleksandra Vlasova

---

*British Library Catalogue in Publication Data
A catalogue record for this book is available from the British Library
Library of Congress in Publication Data
A catalogue record for this book has been requested*

ISBN:978-1-913356-86-6

Viktor Slipenchuk

ZINZIVER

Novel

London 2024

FOREWORD

Dear Readers,

I present for your consideration my novel "Zinziver," which I regard as a song of love. Aware of the subjectivity of my opinion, I refer you to the assessment made by the writer Vasil Bykov (a friend of V.P. Astafyev and V.V. Konetsky): "I have read your novel, which I enjoyed in every respect. The language and style are truly excellent, robust, Russian, literary... It reminded me of Remarque, his post-war novels with which we were once so enraptured, and this is the true hallmark of great literature, created on a national foundation."

Furthermore, dear readers, according to Velimir Khlebnikov, a zinziver is a large male titmouse which starts singing in the second half of March, when the winter chill is over.

With respect,
Viktor Slipenchuk

6

FROM THE TRANSLATOR

As a translator, it is not my role to evaluate "Zinziver" as a literary work. Professional reviewers and the author's colleagues will undertake that task. However, I must confess that the novel has brought me great pleasure, and the translation process was exceptionally engaging. The novel offers an excellent opportunity to glimpse the intricate world of late Soviet and early post-Soviet Russian culture—the era and society that may be relatively unfamiliar to Western readers.

The text is rich with cultural references expected to evoke memories and associations in Russian-speaking readers which may not be as evident and understandable to those unfamiliar with this period. These references encompass historical events and significant personalities, as well as an array of specific social norms and cultural "memes." To help Western readers bridge this gap, I have included many footnotes that provide context and explanations, enabling them to fully appreciate the depth and nuances of the text.

One particular challenge that Western readers may encounter is the Russian naming system, which includes a first name, a patronymic, and a surname. Each of these elements can appear in various forms and combinations, often carrying subtle emotional and social connotations. For example, diminutive forms of names can convey intimacy or affection, while the use of a patronymic alone almost always signifies respect and camaraderie. To help navigate these complexities, I have compiled a list of diminutive names used in the novel.

I encourage Western readers to delve even deeper into the historical and cultural context of "Zinziver" by consulting resources such as Wikipedia for additional information on the facts, events, and personalities mentioned in the book. This extra effort will undoubtedly enrich your reading experience, enhancing the sense of immersive exploration of Russian culture.

In picking up this novel, you have already shown a commendable interest in a world that may be quite different from your own. I sincerely hope that the additional context provided through footnotes and your own exploration of supplementary materials will enrich your understanding and enjoyment of this unique literary journey.

Happy reading,
Anton Kovalenko
Translator
2024

ЗДРАВСТВУЙ·И·ПРОЦВЕТАЙ

When the Pharisees saw this, they asked his disciples, "Why does your teacher eat with tax collectors and sinners?" On hearing this, Jesus said, "It is not the healthy who need a doctor, but the sick.
Matthew 9:11-12

Now the tax collectors and sinners were all gathering around to hear Jesus. But the Pharisees and the teachers of the law muttered, "This man welcomes sinners and eats with them."
Luke 15:1-2

The voice spoke from heaven a second time, "Do not call anything impure that God has made clean."
Acts 11:9

Wingletting with the golden scrawl
Of its finest veins…
Velimir Khlebnikov

…I closed my eyes and heard my mother's wailing through her sobs - she thought I was delirious again. I wasn't delirious… But so as not to frighten her, I buried my face in the flowers and immediately fell asleep, or rather dissolved into the fragrance of the garden. I don't know how long I've slept. When I came to my senses, I was still lying there with my face in the blossom, still engulfed by the fragrances of the May Garden.

I raised myself up. The windows were ablaze with such an extraordinary sunrise that I thought: the windows must be wide open, and I'm in a little white cottage, with the scent of roses wafting in from an enchanted garden. And indeed, I suddenly saw a neat little white cottage, paths covered in pink gravel, a low picket fence draped with flowering rose bushes and heard the approaching soft roulades of an accordion.

A thousand years, a moment's span,

A planet wide, a grain of sand.

In all the things God's face revealed,

The breath of light in all concealed.

I looked around. I expected to see my father or my mother, but instead I saw her. She was wearing white shoes and a golden polka-dot dress that made her look like a schoolgirl. She was smiling at me and calling, calling…

PART ONE

CHAPTER 1

One deep February night (I always wrote my poems and plays at night, sleeping during the day), a profound melancholy overwhelmed me. The cause was the hallucinations that initially amused me, alleviating the monotony of my solitary life. You'd stare at the yellowed, time-cracked tabletop, and suddenly, as if from its very depths, a vision would appear of a cafeteria tray laden with large plates of hot food, like that produced by a magic tablecloth[1]. There would be homemade cabbage soup, lamb simmering in tomato sauce, coffee with cream; all so vivid that in the soup you could see, as I did, those little brown onion rings floating and fresh green sprigs of parsley all over the lamb chop. (You must admit, quite a tempting illusion for a man starving not by choice but from abject poverty...)

Contemplating such magnificent gifts of the imagination, usually after midnight, caused me to start gradually preparing for them. Even before midnight, I would lay out a spoon, fork, table knife, and put an empty Borjomi[2] water bottle at the spot where my gaze most often fixed. A decanter and a little glass - those I did not set out. (I only allowed myself such a luxury once, on my birthday, regretting it bitterly the next morning: my head was

---

1   A magic tablecloth, or "skatert samobranka" is an artifact frequently mentioned in various Russian fairytales. It would produce all kinds of food for its user and make dishes and leftovers disappear after a feast.

2   Natural mineral water with a distinctive taste from springs in Georgia.

splitting, and my stomach was gripped by the sort of spasms that usually follow a terrible bender).

In general, I made my preparations with restraint, so as not to regret it later, but at the same time to feel free enough to choose both the menu and the musical accompaniment.

What is this - free choice… and music? It's a song! Yes, a song, because by selecting and combining these seemingly simple kitchen items, I, like a professor of magic, ultimately mastered the art of summoning almost predictable hallucinations.

Of course, I tried many variations before settling on certain ones most suited to my inclinations. By virtue of my profession, I am not fond of noisy company: there's always a kind of unrestrained revelry about them, an inner rowdiness. More often, I chose a private dining room, a table set with a snow-white tablecloth, two pieces of silverware, and a violinist in a black tailcoat and top hat. To tell the truth, the violinist entertained me more with his eccentricity than with his music. Performing Oginski's Polonaise, he would always thrust out his chest exaggeratedly, stalking my tablemate in such a way that the poor man had to keep dodging sideways to avoid spilling from his spoon. But my agile musician, not to be deterred, would deftly circle round to menace him from the other side.

In the end, the tablemate would lay down his spoon, pull a pink silk handkerchief from his chest pocket, hold it to his eyes and mumble emotionally: "I can't, I can't bear it, it's so heart-rending!"

Shifting my perspective just slightly, I'd move the violinist to the centre of the room, and the tablemate, glancing around nervously, would again take up his spoon.

"I can't, I can't bear it..." he'd keep muttering in my ear, but I paid no heed.

To keep my hallucinations under control, I always had to operate strictly within certain bounds. It may appear odd, but I never saw the faces of my tablemate, the violinist, or the server. And yet I knew for certain that my tablemate was an elderly prim Englishman, intelligent and very, very wealthy. (Sometimes he would leave the table before me, and I saw with my own eyes, the ample tips he left in US dollars.)

The setting, of course, was in the USSR, and not just because I remembered the factory stamp on the aluminium lampshade, and the waiter's obsequious servility toward foreigners was glaringly characteristic of that bygone era. Gangling and clumsy, in a show of supreme deference he would loom over the table as if to kiss the Englishman right on the crown of his head. Most unpleasant servility - I can still hear his syrupy, unctuous voice: "Comrades, what would you desire?"

I would not comment on the violinist, but I think that he and the server split the tips, with the latter, as boss, taking the bigger cut. At any rate, once I overheard this eloquent dialogue:

"But I say, where are mine, for the double polonaise?!"

"I don't know, I don't know, Comrade Goga, you got the lot. (sweetly but venomously) Look in the little hole under the lining."

"But I say, how can that be? It was a double polonaise!" (imperiously and indignantly)

"Well, even if it was a triple one, what about the instrument?!" (didactically admonishing) "Don't forget, Comrade

Goga, that for a Stradivarius like this I could easily find a new little musician…"

The private dining room suited me fine, for I had mastered the art of not only expanding its walls, but of transporting myself within it, as if in a time machine. Present in that room yet invisible to those around me, I could attend any celebration or even a wedding. I especially loved that between myself and Rozochka.

Most often it would happen like so: amid the raucous chanting of "Gorko! Gorko!"[3], clearly audible as if from the next room, I would concentrate on my wish to find myself there with every fibre of my being…A slight effort of will, just a slight one, and the wall to my right, directly opposite the Englishman, would fade as if by a wizard's wand; as if consumed by flickering motes of dust. Eventually, they would thin away, allowing the outlines of an unnaturally long table, occupying nearly the entire hall, to emerge. Seated guests densely lined the table, and at the far end, a snow-white lace veil revealed a radiant face glowing warmly beneath it, like a little candle flame.

But then the gauze would lift. The Englishman's left shoulder would shiver (especially noticeable with the pink handkerchief peeping from his chest pocket), and I would suddenly feel my life force flowing into the Englishman through that very pocket. Strangely, I somehow knew that in being transferred to the Englishman, I would not disappear but would present myself to those around us a kind of a figurehead.

And so, it happened. Adjusting the handkerchief, thus inhabiting his tuxedo, I would discover a substantial wallet in the right inner pocket, tightly stuffed with "green bucks" as they say

---

3 Guests shout this at Russian weddings, urging the bride and bridegroom to kiss, usually after a toast or even instead of one. It means "bitter" and implies that the newlyweds are called to sweeten the guests' vodka with their kiss.

nowadays, and an antique gold watch on a fire-flashing chain, adorned with diamonds, sewn into the lining of the left lower pocket. On the cover of that watch, inlaid with mother-of pearl, were engraved the Latin letters SVT. Incidentally, I instantly absorbed and read these in Russian as nothing other than "svat" - "groomsman" - which offered a certain natural quality to my presence at the wedding. In short, feeling myself a wealthy Englishman (at my own wedding, mind you!), with a pleasing sense of elderly leisure and primness, I would withdraw the gold watch and, having withdrawn it, capture everyone's attention with the mellow chime of opening its mother-of-pearl lid. The leisure and primness served me well in surveying the scene unnoticed and, within strictly defined bounds, in making my first, and most crucially, correct move.

Glancing at the dial, I would notice out of the corner of my eye that my physical, material "self" had vanished without a trace, evaporated, and while my private dining table with its white cloth merged with the unnaturally long wedding table, all faces turned toward me with an expression of respectful yet merry attention.

Here I allowed myself some grandstanding (ah, the years, the years!). I would struggle to my feet, nearly toppling my glass over and spilling my Borjomi, to offer a toast to the health and happiness of the newlyweds. Involuntarily abashed by my elderly infirmity, the guests would then rise as one, the groom and bride following suit. Sipping from the water-filled glass, I would begin my speech. I don't know if it was brief enough to be listened to while standing, but they listened. In my toast I would convey that I was there not by chance but through the good offices of, or more simply put, at the request of, the parents of the principals in this solemn celebration, who unable to attend, had charged me with delivering their sacred blessing.

Here, though without elaborating, I would intimate that the groom's mother, a lonely, retired woman, forsaken by her country, lived very far away somewhere near Barnaul. And the bride's parents, victims of a fire, lived even farther, near Manchester, where I, a former White Army[4] officer-émigré had met them in the Russian embassy.

Then, bestowing a broad Sign of the Cross over the newly-weds, I would convey my heartfelt hope that the dear daughter, a second-year medical student, would successfully complete her studies despite her marriage. And the dear son (I would add on my own) would not disgrace himself but would pass his final exams at the Literary Institute with flying colours and deliver his own input to the golden treasury of world literature within the next few years.

Finishing my speech, I would drain my Borjomi, and then a miracle would occur. Yes, a miracle, and always at the same juncture: just as I drained the last drops of the water but before I could set down the glass, someone would loudly and merrily announce: "Aren't our drinks bitter?!" in my mother's voice.

And then? The wedding would erupt in a concerted call, and the groom, shyness aside, would draw his bride toward him with such ardour that I could not help dropping my eyes, feeling the oblivion of his passion.

---

4   The White Army, as opposed to the Red Army, is an umbrella name for a group of monarchist armies and armed divisions opposing the Russian communist forces in the Civil War of 1917-1922.

Trying not to disturb him yet, no less stirred by those unforgettable moments, I would take out my tightly stuffed wallet and, quite the gentleman and on behalf of the parents, present the bride with her dowry.

I won't recount how exactly, but the hefty purse, folded to expose the dollars within, would be passed hand to hand over the guests' heads. I didn't watch it go. It would have been inappropriate for a cultured Russian raised in England to eye it greedily, yet with my suddenly keen hearing, I could not help but catch its wavelike trajectory through the air. No wonder: the merry chatter would die away, yielding to an awed hush as the purse approached.

I gave no sign. I would simply take out my watch again and, using my venerable leisure like a mask, open it precisely at the second when the bride received her dowry. Timing was crucial: I did not want to see, nor have others see, how and where Rozochka hid the wallet and, as expected, the mellow chime drew everyone's attention away from that private little ritual.

Not to be disingenuous, it didn't always work out according to plan. Sometimes, suddenly (please excuse me, but glitches do occur suddenly), from the middle of the table, or perhaps a bit farther down, a tight, rasping voice would pierce the silence:

"I'll bet anyone there must be ten thousand of those 'Georgies' in there!"

How could one not be flustered after that, and not break out of the strictly drawn bounds?! "Georgies"?! What kind of Englishman are you, if you've brought a dowry from Manchester not in pounds sterling but in dollars?! Indeed, what's with the dollars?! Truly it is all that quintessentially Russian vein: the warrior, unvanquished on the battlefield, ultimately ends his life's journey either taking monastic vows or, slipping on level ground, cracking his skull on a boulder.

And yet, like the naked emperor, exposed through my own thoughtlessness, I felt compelled to continue the pretence by taking out my watch and opening the mother-of-pearl lid to regain everyone's attention according to the established script.

And win I did! Delivering me from condemnation and disdain, the chime suddenly (yes, once again, suddenly) rewarded me with raucous jubilation. Yes, it was the jubilation of the revellers, inexplicably proving my kinship with the English queen, which in all modesty I had ostensibly concealed, but had now been most fortuitously clarified for all, thanks to the fabulous dowry.

It was so astonishing, so implausible, yet I was truly happy, truly happy…

CHAPTER 2

Returning to my den was always depressing, especially after the wedding. It wasn't because the poverty and squalor of my surroundings seemed harsher than usual. What tormented me were my feelings towards Rozochka. After we met, I was overwhelmed with loneliness and hopelessness, as if she had just left.

And yet, alas, I enjoyed my life.

The kitchen table served as both my writing desk and workbench for repairing household items. Overhead hung that same lamp with a bowl-shaped shade, wired to the radiator pipe. A kitchen stool was my office chair. An incredibly wide bed with no springs – the table-tennis top – peeked out from under the mattress, doubling as an ingenious bench. (anyone who sat on it couldn't help but compliment it: "Ingenious, quite ingenious!")

Just past the entrance in the left corner were stacks of books and piles of manuscripts, some tied with twine and some not, lying in heaps leaning against the side wall. On top of the books and manuscripts was my coat. A poncho of sorts, it was tailored from a dorm blanket at the time of the Gaidar[5] reforms and dubbed my "all-seasoner shocker." (Indeed, it shocked all passersby when I wore it. Not only did they stop dead in their tracks, but would gaze after me bewildered, as if at some South African ostrich.) Alongside the poncho coat sat other clothes and rags. In general, I kept them, the books, and various manuscripts, all neatly covered with a bed sheet in place of a closet.

---

5   Yegor Gaidar was a Russian politician who advocated for the rapid implementation of free market economic reforms. His major decision was to abolish price regulation by the state in 1992, which effectively amounted to officially authorising a market economy in Russia.

There was no other furniture, nor could there be. That is, there had been once, but Rozochka took it all. And rightly so! Why would I need a refrigerator, what would I keep in it? Same with the TV; I can watch "Before and After Midnight"[6] without one. No need for a wardrobe, and even less, a bookcase: the peeling, tattered wallpaper was far more convenient than any cabinet or shelf, safely covering newspapers, magazines, books, and all sorts of other things I might need close at hand. It became my rule for no overindulgence in my everyday life. Thanks to the multi-purpose nature of my belongings, it sometimes seemed I was living in luxury and could easily do with even less. Like that antique iron on the manuscripts, gaping open like a crocodile's maw. Judging by the old cigarette butts, pencils, and pens sticking out of it, one could safely conclude it was a multi-purpose item: a paperweight, an ashtray, stationery storage, and a formidable weapon of self-defence if need be. Besides, it was sometimes used for its intended purpose, albeit rarely.

In short, I experienced no poverty nor squalor whatsoever. Sometimes, admittedly, I was ravenously hungry. I felt on the verge of shouting out loud "Food, food!" and running away in my poncho coat wherever the road took me. But I had learned to control myself. Back in my student days, I conducted an experiment: I lived for exactly thirty days on little but salted water. I could have fasted even longer, but the word of my endeavour alarmed my dorm so much that the curious gave me no peace. They would crowd my room instead of attending their classes, waking me up again and again just to check if I was still alive. Even the leader of our writing workshop paid me a visit.

---

6   Popular TV show of the last years of the Soviet Union.

I displayed a talent for hypnosis and self-hypnosis… But that's another topic; now, going hungry from time to time paid me certain dividends in the form of "hot cabbage soup and lamb with parsley," which helped keep up my spirits to write my poems and plays. I was certain that one day society would take an interest in what I was writing behind closed doors. To write and to believe is the fundamental principle of a writer.

* * *

Rozochka dealt the first crushing blow to that fundamental principle: she left… Why?! She said nothing, gave no warning, just came one day in a truck with two Caucasian[7] highlanders (I learned later, though I tried not to listen) and took everything, leaving nothing behind. (She left only the table, manuscripts, and books, which she apparently piled hastily by the door in her hurry.) Where did she go, and why? Incomprehensible! There was a note on the table: "Don't look for me, you won't find me, I've changed my passport and last name."

It was so strange, so baffling. How could she just go and change them like that?! For what reason? Just a month earlier, when the judge suggested, "Think things over carefully before making the final decision to divorce," Rozochka had answered for both of us: "Okay, we'll think it over."

And now this?! Incomprehensible!…

---

7   Caucasian here means people from the Caucasus, the highland area between the Caspian and the Black Sea, the territory of Russia, Georgia, Armenia and Azerbaijan.

* * *

Back in my den, I tried recalling details of our life together. Our student wedding in a youth cafeteria. My successful final exams. Her academic leave (I got her the necessary medical papers from the writer's polyclinic[8] - there were concerns after Chernobyl). Our merry, noisy departure for this provincial town. My job as a literary consultant at the regional Komsomol[9] newspaper. (A cushy position, secured for me through the Literary Institute's solicitation. Yes, they had high hopes for me, but I'd rather not digress.)

We were provided with a room at the TV factory dormitory (bus line terminus, not too spacious but bright) - we had a roof over our heads. However you look at it, those first years we lived wonderfully. Of course, my salary wasn't enough, but as they say, with your sweetheart even a shack is paradise. I was writing around the clock and we had high hopes that the day would come when my plays would appear in a cascade, on many stages at once. The art director of the local drama theatre even paid us a visit, asking me to revise the play of a prominent Moscow dramatist that he was planning to stage, but for some reason never did, even though I made the required revisions and got paid a hundred roubles - money unheard of for us at that time.

Oh, how wonderfully we lived! Rozochka would sleep all day, while I wrote and wrote. I believed. I dedicated literally every one of my poems and plays to her, and she found them brilliant. Stretching languidly, her flawless little figure arched exquisitely, she would ask:

---

8 In the Soviet Union many professional unions and industrial facilities had medical facilities of their "own", even though not in their exclusive use.

9 Communist organisation for young adults.

"Do we have anything to eat?"

She would open the fridge door. I would feel terribly foolish, but she would reassure me:

"If not bread alone, then what…?"

Rozochka was hinting: a man does not live by bread alone. Slamming the door shut, she would take a "Rhodope"[10] from on top of the fridge, light up, and lie back down, ready to listen to my verses and play excerpts. I would read what struck me as the most successful, so wasn't at all surprised when she would suddenly burst into tears and say:

"You know, Mitya, in one sense, it's the work of a genius, but I don't deserve, I don't deserve even a crust of bread from your hands!"

I would race down the long dorm corridor hoping to borrow at least a little money from someone. Sometimes this process dragged on all day. I would show up at the editorial office under the guise of urgent business (I led a weekly literary union), and would surreptitiously scope out my colleagues, so as not to scare off a potential lender with a careless word.

After borrowing a hefty amount (they usually wouldn't lend me small sums), I would disappear in an unknown direction. That is, I would indicate my whereabouts in a notice: "Gone on a research trip (archival work), the literary union is postponed until the last Thursday of the month."

My frequent "archival" trips lent me the aura of a serious and intelligent literary heavyweight. I would head out briskly and confidently to the nearest grocery store and stock up on everything needed to celebrate my works of "brilliance," so to

---

10   Bulgarian cigarettes, very popular in the Soviet Union.

speak, with Rozochka. Understanding that they might be lending to me for the last time, I didn't stint. I would get several bottles of vodka and just as many of vermouth (Rozochka liked fortified wines). With food selected just as carefully, burdened with all these victuals, I would head home, joyful and blissful in anticipation of our regal feast.

Oh, how marvellously we lived! Later, thanks to Rozochka's ingenuity, we almost never ran short of funds. She suggested I borrow not from my colleagues, but from members of the literary union, and not repay the debts. That is, repay in another way, so to speak, with verbal critiques, praising each author not according to the literary merits of their work but for the amount I borrowed. At first, this felt awful, like trying to pass off sauerkraut as truffles. I probably would never have overcome my scruples if not for the vision of Rozochka. Luckily, at especially crucial moments her sweet face, full of reproach, would suddenly appear before my eyes as if shielding me from my own baseness. What's more, when I had to borrow from another hopeless graphomaniac, I would be seized by a kind of a mixed feeling of sadism and masochism. Stashing the money away, I would give the lender a conspiratorial wink and, clapping him chummily on the shoulder, recommend him to my literary elite without mincing words:

"Take a look, a new Lermontov!"[11]

I didn't misspeak about the "elite" - my operations were soon so successful that I presided over the most prestigious literary union in the world: a new Ostrovsky, a new Tyutchev, a new Chekhov, a new Blok... Every next "new" writer was determined

---

11   Michail Lermontov is considered to be one of the top geniuses of classical Russian literature and poetry, second only to Alexander Pushkin.

first by age and gender, and only then, by the genre of their submitted works. Among the poetesses, there was no shortage of new Akhmatovas, new Tsvetaevas, new Veronika Tushkovas, new Silva Kaputikians. When each of the more or less capable authors had abandoned the union, I really let myself go. With the help of the headman of the literary activists, one of the most hopeless cases, I inculcated a sort of price list into the minds of the fledgling literati. If, say, a novice prose writer offered me half his monthly salary, he could only aspire to be a new Herzen or Chernyshevsky. But if he handed over his entire paycheck, well, I didn't doubt I was dealing with none other than Fyodor Mikhailovich Dostoevsky himself, or Count Lev Nikolaevich[12]. I won't go into all the nuances of the pricing, I'll just say that the seventeenth century was the starting point, with fees rising incrementally from thereon in. Writers of distinction among the living commanded a particularly steep premium.

"You can surpass them while they're still alive," I would boldly tell one aspirant or another. Nobel laureates were no exception. "You have time, you can surpass them if you try," I would brazenly declare, seeing the sincere approval and even gratitude for my words in the eyes of the hopeful.

My enterprise went so smoothly that a day before the evaluation of their works the newbie authors themselves would approach me and flatly "lend" me money in anticipation of being anointed as Yesenin or Mayakovsky. At first, I would raise my eyebrows in feigned surprise, try to look bewildered and even offended, but I quickly realised that skipping the ceremony worked better. The only thing that gave me pause, considering the new

---

12   Lev Nikolaevich Tolstoy, author of "War and peace".

political winds, was that many of my Belinskys, Chernyshevskys, early Dostoevskys and Herzens started taking part in unauthorised protest rallies, environmental marches, and the like. To hold on to my remaining literary union members, I mocked the defectors, branded them deserters, unfrocked priests, warning that politics is a millstone around literature's neck - but all to no avail, the ranks were thinning catastrophically.

Once again, I was broke and forced into the harshest of Lent fasts, even more dreadful for having tasted the sweet fruits of sin. So as not to show my helplessness in the face of the circumstances, I began to write again. I wrote day and night in the Chekhovian sense, that is, until my fingers broke. Rozochka started looking for a job; I didn't dare dissuade her, only dedicating my writing to her with ever more ardour. On the days of the literary union meetings when she didn't show up, I would leave her love notes: "My darling Rozochka, a hundred kisses! Rozochka, kissing the tender tips of your fingers!; Oh, sweetest aroma of heaven, kissing you all over!" I wrote my notes large, on high-quality glossy paper, and posted them all over the room; on the wall, the TV screen, in the wardrobe, even in the freezer.

Once she came home looking especially fatigued and pale. She opened the empty fridge automatically. I remember it like it was yesterday - my note fluttered out: "Oh, the sweetest aroma of heaven, kissing you all over!" I won't lie, I was struck by the blasphemy and hopelessness of the situation. Not knowing what to say, I asked if she had eaten. In response, nearly choking with indignation, she cried out that she was fed up! And without even taking off her coat, she flung herself on the bed, with her back to me.

It was on that day that Rozochka demanded a divorce, leading me straight to the magistrate's court. Feeling guilty, and thus doubly unhappy, I was ready to agree to anything. It was from that day on, at her insistence, that I started calling her Rozaria Fyodorovna, while she called me Mister Slyozkin. Moreover, Rozochka strictly forbade me from reading my plays aloud, much less to her.

On that fateful night and for the first time, I slept huddled in the corner atop my manuscripts. Strangely enough, I slept like the dead. I awoke late, not to some external noise, but to the sound of my own laughter.

Just before waking, I had the most hilarious dream. All I can recall is that I was at another meeting of our literary union, but instead of the dyed-in-the-wool hacks, a tight circle of the greatest writers of all time and nations stood before me (an anthology of the world's classic literature coming alive, so to speak). Pushkin, Lermontov, Gogol, Dostoevsky and Turgenev were there amongst foreigners, Cervantes, Shakespeare, Dante, Goethe... Most of them, of course, were writers I saw for the first time, but they were all authentic luminaries, standing shoulder to shoulder in circles around me, like the rings of a tree trunk. I studied their faces: Sholokhov, Yesenin, Shukshin and, oddly, Gorky between Faulkner and Hemingway. Well, anything is possible in a dream. And I, Mitya Slyozkin, stood in the centre of this dense, multi-tiered ring, in a black top hat, wool coat with three crosswise stripes on its shoulders (I didn't actually own one then, but there you have it...), patent leather shoes with very high heels, and my hand holding a fine linen handkerchief. I was preparing to sing and dance some chastushki[13], searching with my eyes for Mikhail Afanasyevich Bulgakov, who just had to be there with a monocle on his right eye. I sought him out for moral support – it was rather daunting to sing and dance chastushki in such a serious company without one. (I hope you understand why I was so convinced of his support!) But instead of Mikhail Afanasyevich, my gaze landed on Lev Nikolaevich. His glare was fierce, his eyes blazing - the very Lord of Hosts, with a bundle of birch rods in his hand. I fell silent mid-stream, for I knew I would get a hundred lashes for every word I uttered incorrectly, right here, in front of the whole gathering. That would be it, the end of the show! And suddenly I realised that this gathering of writers of all ages and nations was not real, that they were merely my literary union members in disguise. Joy swept over me, a profound joy. And I burst into singing chastushki and dancing a jig, all verses with pictures[14] and a refrain after each: "I came as an ecologist, but I'll leave like a boss. Oy-li, oy-lu-loo, I'll leave like a boss!"

With this still vivid in my mind, I woke up laughing. I woke up and immediately remembered everything. And remembering it, I froze with a fear no less than before being lashed: Lord almighty, what nonsense, what will Rozochka think?! Fortunately, she had already gone to look for a job.

I quickly got myself in order (I had slept in my clothes on top of the manuscripts) and went to the editorial office. I confess, I didn't even think about breakfast, and not only because there was nothing to eat. The thing is, in Rozochka's presence, I

---

13   Russian folk quatrains, usually comic, satiric and/or bawdy.
14   "Chastushki with pictures" is an euphemism for the mentioned four-liners with obscene lexicon.

never felt the need for food, never. Just think about it: Rozochka and bread in my mouth—horrible, unbearable! Even now, being a totally different person, I find that back then I, or he rather, was largely right. In any case, his thoughts and actions at least deserved some indulgence, if not exoneration. Of course, I had to eat in Rozochka's presence, more than once a day at times, but it wasn't a purposeful action; it occurred mostly by chance, mechanically. It was quite different to feed Rozochka or to give her pleasure by eating myself; I hope the distinction is obvious.

Anyway, I showed up at the editorial office intending to borrow money. The excuse was the same (a business trip for urgent work at the archive). I hoped, and not without reason (it had been a long while since the last time I arrived in the morning), that my appearance would not be connected at all to my desire to borrow from anyone. I was wrong. As I stepped through the door, two reporters from the "Komsomol Life" department approached me briskly. Looking at me as if I were the richest person in the USSR, they asked to borrow ten roubles each. "At least," they insisted, "tell us who has money, we'll borrow from them." Of course, they were mocking me, but worse was the fact that these two were the most serious and well-off people in the editorial office, and it was precisely from them that I planned to borrow. Needless to say, this was their retaliation. I decided to stand my ground; my options were scarce anyway.

I sat down at my desk, and the first thing I did was write a notice: "I have money, but I won't lend it out of principle." I understood that by doing this, I was cutting off the editorial office as a source forever. But what could I do? There was still the editor of the newspaper, and I had to wait for him (as a rule, he came to the office just before lunch).

My suspicions were completely justified. Right after I displayed my note and pulled out a pile of manuscripts supposedly for reading, members of staff started approaching me one after another with the same purpose. Without saying a word, I pointed at the notice on my table. Inside, I was laughing hysterically at their frustrated expressions. I don't know how I even came up with this "I have money…" idea; it was a true epiphany. By the will of providence, I shuffled the cards: it wasn't me being humiliated, but me humiliating them. Moreover, I didn't need to engage in any dialogue. Question - answer. Alas, my jubilation proved premature.

After everyone had left me alone and everything had calmed down, those two from the "Komsomol Life" reappeared. I expected them to start pretending to reproach me, shame me, whining, "How could this be? You said you didn't have money, but you did," and so on. I was ready for this, but not for what was coming.

They came up to me as if for the first time and studied the notice silently for a very long time. Then, paying no attention to me at all, they started exchanging opinions, saying that principles should be respected, and that principled people should be revered and even indulged with money, if possible, for urgent work in the archives or a restaurant.

Their hints were too transparent to misunderstand… but all their taunting didn't bother me, didn't cause offence. On the contrary, it amused me to some extent, right until they pulled money from their pockets (crisp red ten-rouble notes). Only then did I feel as if I were falling into an abyss. The reporters engaged in a peculiar generosity contest: "You lend me twenty roubles, and I'll lend you thirty. You give me forty, I'll respond with a hundred."

I don't know how I managed to endure it. It was more than just torment. I stared unblinkingly at a manuscript, desperately trying to hide my feelings. I succeeded, they left, and I remained, waiting for the editor!

He showed up after lunch in a cheerful mood (he was going on holiday), saw me right away and asked cheerfully:

"What, Mitya, leaving on another business trip, urgent work in the archives?!"

I answered that no, that's not why I came: I urgently need-ed money. As I looked at him, all cheerfulness immediately disappeared from his face. At first, he pondered, as if suddenly remembering something, then somewhat fussily picked up the phone and in my presence, asked the accounting department:

"Give Mitya Slyozkin, - he corrected himself, - give the poet Slyozkin one-third of his upcoming salary."

And to prevent any dispute, he played his trump card:

"He has an urgent assignment in the archives. Yes, yes, in Peter."[15]

I don't know what the editor read in my eyes, but in ac-counting they also treated me with understanding and gave me not a third, but a half of my salary, when I asked them.

Everything inside me began to sing and dance as soon as I got the money. Involuntarily, I froze when walking up the stairs, trying to catch that melody, that dance resounding inside me, and

---

15   Colloquial for St. Petersburg.

recognised the words from the dream that repeated as a refrain: "I came as an ecologist, but I'll leave like a boss. Oy-li, oy-lu-loo, I'll leave like a boss!" Silly? Of course, it was silly, but I laughed, just as in the dream, and felt such an extraordinary lightness in my soul, as if I had shaken off the burden of all my previous and future humiliations down those stairs right at that moment.

CHAPTER 3

Rozochka greeted me magnificently. She set the bags of food on the table and allowed me to hug her. Oh Lord! In response, my every cell cried out in delight, inaudibly but with such languidness as if we hadn't seen each other for a thousand years. I held her tight in my arms, pressed against her, sobbed, and murmured in sweet agony:

"Ro-zo-chka!"

"Are you crying?" she asked sternly, but even more with satisfaction, and pulled her hand from somewhere under me to touch my eyes and make sure.

I don't know, maybe I did shed a tear from overwhelming happiness, only I didn't feel anything but the gentle lightness of her fingers. And even if I did cry, what of it?! I think Dostoevsky once said that everything comes to us through great suffering—and so did Rozochka. I realised, not through Dostoevsky but from my own experience, that happiness is like a gift to a soul for merely existing…

Rozochka's soul is amazing, amazing in how understanding it is: she always knew me better than I knew myself. And so again, deftly linking her hands in a lock, she ducked under me and, pulling away, pushed them against my chest as strongly as if with her knee.

"What's that, Rozochka?!" she mocked angrily and demanded that I let go of her immediately.

I let her go, of course, but in my mind, I still held her tight. It's like with a song: it may have long fallen silent, but if it truly touched your soul, its echo would still be with you, smouldering deep in your heart. So, I let her go and remained standing, overwhelmed, in some hypnotic state, afraid to move. And then she struck me as if with a skillet:

"What is it, comrade Slyozkin, got a bit carried away, let your hands run free?"

That should not have come as a surprise, for she had warned me back in the courthouse that from now on she was no Rozochka to me, but Rozaria Fyodorovna. And I was nobody to her either, just a physical entity, a stranger, comrade Slyozkin at best. So, there was no "skillet" on her part; it's just that everything she said at that moment was in such a terrible dissonance with my feelings that I just stood there, stupefied.

Tidying herself up after my embraces, Rozochka studied me intently, then laughed out loud as only she could, covering her mouth with her hand.

"I repeat: What is it, comrade Slyozkin, got a bit carried away, let your hands run free?"

And she laughed so heartedly, so infectiously, that I finally came to my senses and laughed as well, rejoicing in her merriment.

We cooked dinner together, frolicked, chased each other around the kitchen, and messed up the dishes. And it was even entertaining calling her Rozaria Fyodorovna and responding to Physical Entity or Stranger, as if to some suddenly bestowed prosecutorial or military rank.

I gradually got used to this innovation. It was only in bed when I found this prank inconvenient. (Rozochka allowed me to sleep with her again but under one condition: if comrade Slyozkin should ever cross the boundary and call her by the wrong name, he would only have himself to blame.) Even during the most intimate moments, when you're about to lose your mind, she would pre-emptively poke me in the stomach, signalling to keep myself in check and not get carried away. Once I consciously resorted to a ruse. Knowing that after lovemaking she would, much like myself, like to simply lie on her back, in a bit of a daze and without any thoughts, I moved closer to her and with sincere tenderness, characteristic of me at such moments, whispered: "My little blossom, Rozochka!" She sharply turned her head towards me, not even lifting it from the pillow, and said in a flat, cold, and clear voice:

"What is it, Stranger?"

Even now, two years later, I sometimes still hear that chilling voice. I didn't tempt my fate again. I always remained silent in bed, and if a conversation did occur, then by the force of my imagination I substituted Rozochka with some abstract Rozaria Fyodorovna, to whom I simply didn't exist in any way other than comrade Slyozkin.

I got used to that too. Moreover, in my thoughts I was still free and Rozochka still remained Rozochka for me, my life-saving radiant little flower. It was right around this time that she came up with a brilliantly simple way to revive our ailing literary union quickly: to replenish its ranks, or rather, to recruit new creditors.

* * *

At Rozochka's prompting, I delivered a passionate speech worthy of those I had listened to at the Literary Institute from famous and renowned masters of Russian literature. I did that in the presence of the headman of the literary union (he went by Lev Nikolaevich due to his age and beard) and his friend and assistant, who candidly admitted that he had never written anything but had honestly paid money at the known rate to be Nikolai Alekseyevich Nekrasov. The essence of my speech was that anyone could write a good work—a short story, play, novel, or poem—if they wanted to, the main thing was to really want to do it.

Thereby, I announced an intention to proceed urgently with compiling a collective anthology of local authors. I guaranteed special advantages in publication to all members of the literary union on the condition that each of those present would bring at least three new members to the next meeting.

Two unexpected questions arose from the listeners (there were two: the headman and his friend). The first was about the special advantages, asked by the headman. He said verbatim:

"How long will this introduced privilege remain in effect? The new members may want to bring three comrades of their own, and those of their own."

I thanked him for the question; it seemed to me worthy of gratitude. Switching to the headman's lexicon, I announced as if it had long been decided that the introduced privilege would be in effect for a month (the meeting was held late July).

The second question was asked by the headman's friend:

"In what city and at whose expense will the collective book be printed, or will it be under a state order?"

For all the friend's cluttered speech, one could not but admit that the question hit the nail on the head. A stray thought flashed through my mind: what if he really was Nikolai Alekseyevich, editor of "The Contemporary"[16] and "Notes of the Fatherland"[17]?! Then it would be quite logical that the head of the literary union was no headman at all but Count Lev Nikolaevich Tolstoy himself!

It took me some effort to dismiss this thought and I, hands trembling, began rummaging through my pockets in search of a handkerchief, just to buy myself time for a more or less coherent response. However, neither a handkerchief nor a response could be found. I began stalling, slowly removing various objects from my pockets, and laying them on the table where my worldly-wise classics were sitting.

The contents were nothing out of the ordinary: a key, a matchbox, a notepad, a quarter-folded sheet of standard paper with a commuter train schedule, and finally a graduation diploma from the one and only Literary Institute with an undisputable certification of me, Dmitry Yuryevich Slyozkin, as a literary worker.

I'll say right now in my defence that the diploma was never an ordinary object for me. I carried it only because at the dawn of my literary career in the City of N no one knew me, and the evening guards at the HAN (House of All Newspapers) would otherwise not give me the keys to my own editorial office, where

---

16   Russian literary, social and political magazine, published in St. Petersburg in 1836–1866.

17   Russian literary magazine published in St. Petersburg in 1818-1884

our literary meetings were held. The diploma served as a kind of ID and I got used to always having it on me. Thus, it was not like I hoped the diploma would answer everything so eloquently that it would settle all questions and answers for the foreseeable future once and for all.

Meanwhile, my worldly-wise observers were regarding the objects I was removing with undisguised interest, demonstrating the distinctive overdeveloped curiosity of writers and children. It was evident that it took great effort for each of them to restrain themselves from touching the objects laid out on the table. Finally, when the diploma hit the rest of the pile, the headman leaned his cane against a neighbouring chair with majestic grace, like a true Count, and decisively took the diploma, shielding himself from me with his eyebrows.

I don't know whether it was his eyebrows or his beard (or the head's majestic detachment from both me and his completely bald friend with an elongated goatee), but to me it once again seemed that I found myself in the company of the most real, genuine writers, to whom both I and their questions paled in significance compared to the diploma which had obviously disturbed them. I was present and absent at the same time, as some transcendental thing-in-itself, present in my absence and absent in my presence. I felt uncomfortable realising that Lev Nikolaevich and Nikolai Alekseyevich, despite their enormous literary merits, did not have such a diploma as I. Moreover, their eloquent stares betrayed an envy which they did not even try to hide.

This was a kind of derangement or hallucination, or rather both. In any case, I started to come to my senses only when Lev

Nikolaevich angrily rapped the floor with his cane and began to shame and even insult Nikolai Alekseyevich, apparently trying to win my approval:

"Hey you, you bumbler, at whose expense and where?! Not at your expense and not at the expense of your sponsors' roulette… Moscow will print it, by state order!"

He angrily rapped his cane again in the direction of the famous magazine's editor and, suddenly softening, turned to me.

"A little confidential letter from a literary worker would work… Am I correct?" he asked affectionately, rising.

Still spellbound by the genius seeking my support, I nodded in agreement.

However, with all my respect for the great writer, and even reverence for him, my imagination refused to picture Lev Nikolaevich allowing himself (to put it mildly) such liberty towards the editor of "The Contemporary," even to please me, the holder of a diploma which he sincerely envied. Moreover, the editor was none other than Nikolai Alekseyevich, with whom he had long been friends and whose poetry he often praised.

To finally dispel the fog of hallucination enveloping me, I rubbed my temples and immediately heard the receding tapping of the cane and the distinct bickering of my imaginary classics leaving through the open doors of the editorial office:

"Oh, you should not, you should not remain silent about the women's lot!"

"Well, it's the same as the men's."

"Don't say that, it's even harsher!"

For some time, the tapping cane alone broke the silence like a metronome. Then the same subtle apologetic voice came through again:

"As for the printing of the collective anthology, I was just inquiring about the general plan."

"Curiosity must have its limits," the bass voice, not so much low as rich, cut him off.

More silence and then a conclusion:

"Our plan is the same: bring three new members each."

Dissatisfied cane tapping became stronger, but the voices somehow abruptly faded: they must have reached the stairs. The last thing I heard was:

"As for the rest of it, it's not our business. Let our literary worker friend ponder it…"

I don't know how long I sat in front of my pocket treasure. I remember that on top of it, like some congratulatory address in recognition of undoubtedly heroic services to literature, there was my diploma upside down, exceedingly loathsome to me at that minute. Of course, it helped me, but at what cost? Yes, I had always been proud of it for being, so to speak, the evidence of my belonging to writers, the engineers of human souls, whose numbers never exceeded the number of Heroes of the Soviet Union, even in as huge a country as ours.

And here I had stooped low, fallen in my own eyes because of the diploma of which I had always been proud. I sat devastated, feeling like the lowest scoundrel possible. Oh, if only I could feel like a total drunk, but still a Hero of the USSR, who would at least be allowed to turn in empty bottles without waiting in line by virtue of his title! Alas, I was a hero of a different order: young, not drinking much and, even worse, knowing something about literature. There were no excuses for me, I had fallen, fallen, fallen!!!

I remembered how I used to enjoy casually showing off the comparison of the numbers of writers and Heroes to my listeners. Yes, this was my exquisitely subtle hint that since there were fewer writers, they were all the more important. Then, to demonstrate the full extent of a writer's generosity and respect for Heroes, I would descend from those heights and directly declare that literature was a battlefield where you would either fall an inglorious victim or demonstrate gallantry and earn your posthumous recognition and a monument in your honour.

Here, as a rule, I would make an impressive pause, awaiting the inevitable question: "Why necessarily after death?" I would soar again, staring at the ceiling and reaching upwards with my arms to follow my sardonic gaze. Just like our poetry workshop leader at the Literary Institute (I won't disclose his name to avoid being caught boasting) I wouldn't simply answer but respond as if before God himself: such has been the age-old custom in Russia that to be recognised you must first die.

I won't hide it, listeners' reaction was usually silence, that is, not a sound, not a rustle. Only my pacing back and forth. Stopping. Even I sometimes froze in shock myself, imbued with the injustice of the ever-belated recognition.

The Russian God knows the measure of talent allotted to each of us better than anyone, and therefore makes harsh demands. In our time it happened to Shukshin, Vysotsky, and now we... I never said "...will have to follow." I said: "And now we engage in literature." But the eyes of my scholarly comrades were already flickering with undisguised fear, and it spoke louder than any words: "Yes, yes, we will follow!"

I was vain and merciless but avoided baseness. And here was the finale, the finish line. Like no one else, I felt the full undisputable wisdom of the proverb at that moment: the longest day has an end. If I were to be so hugely defamed for my "loan extortion," then to fall as an inglorious victim now, this very second, would be a great joy for me, nothing short of salvation.

I grasped the edge of the table; a swarm of thoughts and feelings broke loose and was wreaking havoc in my head. A momentary weakness I had to overcome … And then, mocking the host of my feelings, shaping my thoughts into some new, unusual order, I heard a rhythmic tapping under my crown: "Let him pon-der, let him…" Yes, I recognised that cane. It grew and multiplied until I, shivering, squeezed out in response: "I'll ponder." I did not know whom I had agreed with and what I had promised. But my head cleared, bar one remaining thought: I should take care of the literary worker's diploma (the culprit of my downfall) first, and then of the worker himself. Yes, I decided to tear up, trample, destroy the diploma, and as the saying goes, take myself in hand.

Bubbling with hatred, I grabbed the ill-fated document impatiently with both hands as if it could slip away, and suddenly the key distinctly jingled under my hands, the key to the dormitory, to Rozochka's and my room. I froze—the key, the little key, the little jingle bell! A reviving joyful sound swept over me, washing away all bitterness, all shame, all fear. Truly a key to my head! Truly a wedge drives out a wedge!

Tucking the diploma into my jacket's inner pocket, I involuntarily pressed it to my heart and laughed, imagining how delighted Rozochka would be with me for having fulfilled her wish, or rather that it had fulfilled itself with the help of that wonderful diploma. Buoyant, I rushed home.

Oh Lord, I implore all those suffering: never turn away from life, do not lose heart, do not succumb to moods, life is beautiful!

Once on the bus, I suddenly giggled, recalling my despair, and in so doing, cheered up the girls, most likely kultprosvet[18] faculty students, clustered on the rear platform. At first, they laughed timidly, hiding behind each other, but then gave such free rein to their feelings when disembarking near the Palace Hotel that I too burst out laughing and waved to them from the window. I felt strengthened in my certainty that Rozochka was waiting for me with bated breath to delight me with some amazing gifts of hers.

---

18   "Kultprosvet" - Cultural education in the Soviet Union - was a country-wide complex of activities organised by the state to mass-educate citizens, foster creativity and cultural leisure within the framework of the communist ideology.

CHAPTER 4

My premonitions did not deceive me. Rozochka met me on the staircase, conversing with a young man who abruptly turned his back on me when I appeared and remained awkwardly standing and facing the wall until we left. I wanted to ask Rozochka who he was, but she distracted me by announcing that she had taken a job as a nurse at the Palace Hotel and would now be working on a sliding schedule with night shifts. To celebrate, we had dinner and everything was simply marvellous. I told her about the literary union, and Rozochka was absolutely delighted by my idea to make acquiring new union members a requirement for participation in the collective anthology. Yes, acquiring, she said!

Rozochka immediately took a pen and calculated that within a month, the number of "literary union members" would increase by exactly one hundred and fifty people. (Even she found that number unbelievable.)

"Borrowing a rouble from each will make one hundred and fifty. Thirty roubles above my salary, because there are deductions!"

For the first time, Rozochka looked at me for such a prolonged time and with such admiration, as if I were not myself but some genuine Nobel Prize contender.

"Now, Mitya, you'll be able to live without Rozaria Fyodorovna," she suddenly said in a sad voice.

Hearing my name from her lips, like in those carefree old times, moved me so much that I couldn't help but sob. She had to console me and even scold me for having drunk too much, otherwise, I would have realised: she simply meant nothing more than that she too would now have her own income at her disposal.

Two years later, I understand that even then, Rozochka had already made a difficult decision and simply let it slip out. Regardless, from today's perspective, I never cease to be in awe of her genius. Essentially, all her ideas regarding the literary union were nothing but ideas of a free market, which she anticipated long before Gaidar's reforms.

In general, Rozochka reassured me and insisted that I immediately abandon the tariff system. She convinced me that discussing the literary works as we used to do was no longer relevant. She proposed a one-off fee of seven roubles payable by each union member for technical expenses, so to speak: paper, retyping of manuscripts, editing... I remember objecting that it was too low, but she made her case:

"You'll be able to collect the money right away. Less is more. Besides, most of your writers haven't even written anything yet. Some will soon start bothering you about the progress of the anthology project, in three or four months maybe, and you can always blame unexpected financial issues and technical services for becoming more expensive. You'll see," said Rozochka, "no one will make a sound until you explain yourself, so, instead of rushing, just wait."

She also taught me to never ever, under any circumstances, take fees from the headman and his assistant. On the contrary, she demanded that I immediately repay them everything I had previously borrowed as soon as I got the money. Should they refuse, I must not insist or overdo it, so they wouldn't suspect me of looking to replace them.

The result exceeded even the boldest expectations. From meeting to meeting, the number of literary union members kept increasing in rapid progression. On one August day, our youth newspaper editor, who had just returned from vacation, met me on the steps of the Writers' Union building.

"Listen," he said, grabbing his head, "do they all really write something?!"

"They're trying," I answered evasively. "What's the matter?"

"Listen, what are they talking about?! There are so many of them, and not a single familiar face!"

He handed me the key to the auditorium, noting that I was now responsible for it (after the renovation, all seats had been upholstered in scarce red velour). Still under the impression of what he had seen, as if in a daze, he muttered:

"It's the end of the world, the end!"

He fled down the steps without looking back, mumbling something under his breath.

The editor's behaviour put me on alert. At first, I was quite aghast. His question - "Do they all actually write anything?"- caught me off guard. I even got chills from sensing the accusatory vibes of utter disbelief in the literary abilities of the people who had gathered for the meeting. This seemed suspicious to me.

I quietly passed through the entrance hall and entered the lobby, holding the heavy door to prevent its clattering slam. My arrival went unnoticed, and no wonder: the lobby was dense-ly filled with a mix of jackets, pullovers, and trench coats of a uniform worn-out grey colour, with elderly, mostly hunched, weathered backs beneath them. The crowd immediately carried me away from the door. If not for the editor, I would never have guessed these were my aspiring writers. I would have thought it was some kind of village reporters' convention, and they had spilt out of the auditorium for a smoking break. Judging by how they had clustered into separate groups, they continued to discuss their strictly assigned newspaper topics.

Particularly loudly and heatedly arguing by his desk under the stairs was the on-duty retired watchman Fatei Nikodimych (in his signature valenki boots with galoshes over them, rain, or shine). He was so seriously heated and stomping his feet that not just me but many others (as demonstrated by the hushed but distinct murmurs around) turned to listen to him, trying to grasp the subject of the dispute.

"I'm telling you once again," Fatei Nikodimych insisted in a booming voice, "a regular pension is higher, a hundred and thirty-two roubles, but a personal one is only a hundred and six, even a hundred and four!"

"Well, but it comes with benefits," several voices chimed in.

"And what did I say?" Fatei Nikodimych asked the whole crowd in an offended tone and concluded: "There are benefits, but he's being stubborn."

I couldn't see past the backs to discern who exactly was be-ing stubborn and didn't even try. The resumed friendly hubbub left no doubt: the topic of discussion was now common to all and truly burning.

Swinging between hot and cold, I understood that I needed to take control of the situation and start the meeting somehow, but had no idea how.

I slipped back out of the door and went out onto the steps to cool off. The sun was still high, but the overcast day was already preparing for a hazy dusk. Silence, warmth, and spaciousness embraced me. Suddenly I yearned to get somewhere far, far away from these hunched writers… well, at least as far as the ancient city rampart; I even found myself slowly going down the steps. I would probably have just left if not for the poplar tree: suddenly, it rustled its leaves affectionately and dropped a few random drops onto my face, as if lamenting me, Mitya Slyozkin. I sharply turned 180 degrees and, as though everything—my going down the stairs, the poplar's rustling, the random drops—absolutely everything was strictly within my plan for the upcoming actions, I resolutely headed inside the building.

This time, I intentionally slammed the door hard. I even overdid it a bit and nearly ran into an elderly man; the door caught up with me and literally pushed me into the lobby. It seemed that after drawing everyone's attention to myself, it would not be easy to get the literary talents to follow me. Nevertheless, almost no one noticed my noisy appearance. That is, the old man looked at me, as did his schmoozers, but without much attention, as if I were an annoying fly.

Never in my life had I felt so irrelevant and unnecessary to anyone. And where?! I was among the members of my own dear literary union, after all. I felt as dejected as the newspaper editor: "What are they going on about?! The end of the world, the end!"

And again, Rozochka came to my rescue. As soon as I mentally called out to her for a moment, trying to imagine what she would do in this situation, in a split second I already knew exactly how to act, and became one hundred per cent certain of success.

"Hey-hey-hey, comrades," I shrilled at the top of my lungs as if I had just stumbled upon something extraordinary. "So, these are the engineers of human souls for you?! Outrageous, outrageous!" I continued to ratch up the atmosphere of everyone's discomfort.

Sensing that the hubbub had subsided and people had noticed me, I boldly plunged into the very thick of the literary union members. I worked my way towards the stairs with my elbows, shoving everyone aside unceremoniously and indiscriminately.

"Who allowed it, who permitted it?!" I continued loudly with indignation, pouncing on the hunched backs like an enraged tiger. "No smoking, no littering, do you hear?" I protested with such passion, as if smoking and littering had been my personal bitter enemies from time immemorial. "Do you hear me? No smoking!" I repeated, choking with resentment, and froze for a second in bewilderment, having completely exhausted my vocabulary suitable for the occasion.

"Who is that?" I heard from behind.

"Our leader… hegemon, chief…"

I can't judge how the situation would have developed should the crowd not have split, but it did, revealing our watchman Fatei Nikodimych standing at the back.

He stood to attention, as much as his age and distinctly pensioner's attire - fur coat, dark woollen pants, and his famous valenki boots with galoshes -allowed. His whole demeanour expressed guilt, so it was no trouble for me to improvise.

"I didn't expect, never expected from you, Fatei Nikodimych, that you would allow smoking right at your post," I said sternly, in a party functionary style. Seeing the old man sheepishly smile, I softened and summed up: "Well, it's true, they're adults, they should know better."

"The fault is mine, of course, I've seen all sorts here, but it's the first time such remarkable people have arrived all at once in such numbers, so I couldn't resist, I thought, let them have a little smoke," Fatei Nikodimych confessed.

"Yes, remarkable they are indeed," I flattered in agreement, "but look, you can cut the smoke with a knife in here!"

I laughed, and in suit, Fatei Nikodimych laughed in relief, and then everyone else followed (thank God, the leader, the hegemon, pardoned us).

The leader, the hegemon?! I, Mitya Slezkin, am a leader and hegemon, such an important conclusion made by the literary union members, too important not to take advantage of it – and I did. Still standing beside the watchman's table under the stairs, I instructed Fatei Nikodimych to open the auditorium. Noticing three old members in the crowd, two Gorkys and one Mayakovsky, I called them over and charged them with standing by the door to keep things in order, and sent Mayakovsky (a pint-sized nimble man with a wrinkled face) to find the headman of the literary union and his friend.

My authority as the leader grew visibly by the minute; I felt like an actual hegemon giving precise military-style orders. My instruction to Mayakovsky yielded an impressive effect: he bellowed the names into the crowd in a totally unexpected deep bass voice, and the gasping, crowd immediately responded. Both Lev Nikolaevich and his friend Nikolai Alekseyevich were already elbowing their way towards me, and this blustering call gave them the strength to withstand the human flow streaming into the auditorium.

That evening, I did not make a single mistake or misstep. It seemed to me that I was participating in some majestic show, playing the lead role of either a chairman of some parallel Writers' Union or the head of an unknown political party with ties to a Masonic lodge, conducting highly secret operations somewhere in the backwoods. In any case, though my speech was brief, it was sufficiently imbued with subtext. Tapping my pencil on the decanter (seated with me at the praesidium were the literary union's headman, his friend, two Gorkys, and one Mayakovsky), I announced:

"Comrades, aspiring writers, perhaps today, among all of you seated here, there are future Dostoevskys, Tolstoys, Turgenevs, Leskovs, Goncharovs, Chekhovs, Aksakovs, and Gogols. Yes, yes, let's dream big! I would even allow for a future Pushkin, Lermontov, Nekrasov, Yesenin, Koltsov, Tyutchev, and Ivan Alekseyevich Bunin here among us. There are surely both Sasha Chorny and Andrey Bely here. There could be Omar Khayyam, Nazim Hikmet, and Hafiz of Shiraz—anything is possible. We need to seek, discuss, and publish the best in a collective anthology. Most importantly, do not get conceited and always remember - there is such a massive talent brewing within the populace that compared to it we are smaller than pygmies. Still, this is not a reason to underestimate ourselves. For literature, your age does not matter; what matters is what you bring to the table, for each person's experience is invaluable. And now let's think about a title for the collective anthology. Our Union's headman will speak on the second item on our agenda. We have already discussed his works and unanimously accepted him as our Leo Nikolaevich Tolstoy, so please love and appreciate him… Keep it down, comrades, the sooner we start, the sooner we'll be done."

My brazen assumption that the classics of world literature are likely here among us provoked a merry stir, precisely as I expected. The brazenness was quite justified. Yes, I was treading and leading the gathering on a razor's edge, so to speak. But a blunder was impossible, precluded by the very essence of the aspiring writers' vanity, which is much higher than that of accomplished writers. Besides, a narrow outlook usually results in an illusion of broad prospects. And one must not forget how flattering it is to be presumed to have something in common with a great writer. Even a purely outward similarity flatters, but the goal of the collective anthology was to find a professional resemblance through the works of my writers. These aspiring talents were not at all concerned about their secondary status, which gave me even more confidence. Moreover, I gave each of them a strong reason to look for their similarities not with celebrities, as most do, but with writers. You must agree that this would drive even unconscious thinking in the right direction. All this for a novice writer for a mere seven-rouble contribution to the collective anthology.

(The headman rather inaptly called this fee a "one-time quitrent" in his speech. At first, I wanted to correct him and point out the inappropriateness of this comparison, but the approving murmur of the audience made me hold off: let it be a quitrent, what difference does it make?!)

Just a bit more on my infallibility. When my assistants stepped down from the podium (the headman and his friend on one side, and Mayakovsky and two Gorkys on the other) to collect the money and write a list of the new members of the Union, I could hear and see from the stage how my Mayakovsky bellowed benignly to some writer eagerly limping from the hall without paying the quitrent: "Wait-wait, Byron, son of Lords, come on, come on, don't be stingy, dig out those subcutaneous[19] three-rubles[20]!"

19 This is a direct translation of the word used by the author in Russian. Not a common metaphor for a secret stash, it was not substituted by an English equivalent in this translation to preserve the spirit of the original. It is likely an allusion to subcutaneous fat, body's depot of energy and nutrients.
20 Three-ruble notes existed and were common in the Soviet Union.

CHAPTER 5

The literary union meeting lasted about four hours. No one wanted to leave. While my associates operated in the auditorium, I was compiling a list of potential titles for the future anthology. They showered down on me as if from a horn of plenty. Any other leader in my place would have easily slipped up, succumbing to either excessive acceptance or excessive rejection of the proposals, judging them on the spot. I, however, immediately declared that all the titles would be voted on at the next meeting, and the final one would be drawn from the pool of a shortlist of ten.

Titles such as "Living Springs," "…Sources," "…Roots," "…Rivers," "…Streams," "Sunrise" or "Sunset…," "Stars in the Sky," "…Above the Earth," "…Above the Roof," "…Above Us," "Lights Over the City," "…Over a Field," and again "…Above Us," "…Above the Roof" and so on I wrote down almost automatically, without lifting my hand from the paper. But amidst these painfully familiar, tediously repetitive titles, something would suddenly emerge that stopped my hand, made me pause to ponder, and even ask for an explanation. For example, "The Stars, You Know, Are Not of The Earth."

"Why 'The Stars, You Know,' and not just 'Stars'?" I asked carelessly, only to be immediately slammed by an exhaustive "clarification." The author smiled condescendingly and enlightened me, an ignoramus, by pointing toward the ceiling with his hand and repeating with profound pauses: "The stars, you know, are not of this Earth."

"So, you mean to say: 'Those are unearthly stars'?"

"Yes," he answered. "You grasped the meaning, but I ask that you keep the original wording: 'The stars, you know, are not of the Earth.'"

Hopefully, now you get the idea of how tough it was not to slip up. There were titles like "The Book of Books," "Hey Weeble, Go Wobble!" "To Each Their Own," and many others which, to put it mildly, provoked not just bewilderment but even apprehension. Thank God, the authors somehow decided to "clarify" the titles.

"The Book of Books" – this was meant to convey the comprehensiveness of works included in the anthology, the grandeur of a collection that could replace entire libraries. The author expressed his appreciation for my opening speech, especially the words: "There's no reason to underestimate ourselves." A former factory painter, he volunteered to write these historic words on red bunting and hang it above the stage here in the auditorium. The name "The Book of Books," he said, would be an excellent match to the slogan, and the slogan, which he was willing to put in writing for a mere seven roubles, would perfectly describe the book.

He then went on to explain that his factory rate was three roubles per word and all the materials he'd provide for free. My first thought was: is this a mockery or a prank? The second: have we, the entire literary union, already gone mad or are we going mad?! The third was for my protection: don't take anything seriously, it's just FYI, just FYI… My brain got stuck on that, like a needle on a scratched record. I don't know how the contemplation of the proposed title and slogan would have ended for me personally, if not for the intervention of the audience.

At first, the hall buzzed with indignation, then erupted in spiteful, sarcastic remarks: "What is this, payment in kind?! Why don't you pay in sauerkraut or pickles too? Look at this 'Smart Alec': 'The Book of Books,' but what is he trying to fob us off with?! A factory painter and a scoundrel are one and the same, let that stick in his head! ... 'The Book of Books' should be excluded from the vote and the factory guy expelled from the literary union!"

"Comrades!" I intervened, clattering on the decanter. "Don't forget that writers have always been humanists. 'The Book of Books' title implies enormous responsibility. It will enter the competition, but there will still be a chance to vote it out. And it's not charitable to exclude a comrade for proposing payment in kind. As clumsy as it was, it was done with pure intentions, no one is exempt from making an occasional blunder."

Mentioning "clumsiness" had a particularly positive effect on the audience, perceived as an adequate measure that nipped both "payment in kind" and "The Book of Books" in the bud.

"Hey Weeble, Go Wobble!" was a different matter. The reference to a famous toy was obvious, but, alas, the concept eluded me until the author explained:

"The essence of this title is that editors keep knocking us down, flooring us, hammering us down, and we keep ourselves on our feet by jabbing each other with our unconventional works: hey, get up, no time to loaf around, they are at us again!"

From the approving murmur of the gathering, to which I tuned myself like to a tuning fork, I understood that the explanation was found appealing, and "Hey Weeble, Go Wobble!" would surely make it to the top ten. The same happened with the title "To Each Their Own Hat."

"Anyone who takes the book will think: there's something bad in it, something unworthy. With 'To Each' in quotes, they'll connect it to the proverb[21], but for us that's good. Most people bite more eagerly at something bad. But then, after reading the book, they'll say: 'Oh, so that's what it's about, the cap on Senka is no ordinary one, but made of precious metals, encrusted with emeralds. And what about Senka himself?! Don't put your finger in his mouth... Yes, everything here is presented quite wisely, intellectually."

"Something like... 'A Fitting Hat for Every Senka,'" I prompted.

The author rebuked me:

"I'll repeat it once more for all the deaf here," he said, raising his voice in offence. "To Each Their Own Hat!"

The explanation was accepted unconditionally, the only correction being: even though the book is one, there are many authors, so there would be a discrepancy. They decided it would be more accurate to title it: "A Hat to Every Senka." But here, having learned from the misunderstanding and clash over the "unearthly stars," I baulked, refusing to correct the title.

"Authorship is sacred!" I said, raising my index finger. I don't know how to explain it, but I was adopting not only the vocabulary but also the profound gestures of my wards with astonishing speed. "Intellectual property is protected by law in all civilised countries. Only the author has the right to correct his creation,

---

21   The proverb in question is directly translated as "This hat is not for Senka" (Diminutive for Arseniy) and means "He's not up to the task" or "It's beyond his pay grade."

being the original title in this case," I said sternly.

My words caused the author to feel momentarily shy but then to grow so proud, that the literary union members had to make quite an effort to convince him to alter the title. Finally, someone from the audience shouted that they had persuaded the owner, that he agreed, so let it be "A Hat to Every Senka." I pretended not to believe what I had heard. Then the author himself stood up and, bashfully apologising, confirmed that the phrase may be altered because they were already calling him a "damned private owner" and claiming he had no business in a collective book.

"Well, in their own way they're right," I concluded, and announced that I had recorded "A Hat to Every Senka." The auditorium answered with a joyful murmur and sporadic rounds of applause.

In general, the meeting was so energetic that no one, myself included, noticed the passing of time. The strong rapport between the auditorium and the praesidium was not disrupted, even when my assistants operating in the auditorium were forced to distract me: they would come up on stage with pockets bulging with money and hand over the proceeds, so to speak, from pocket to pocket.

The thing is, the subcutaneous roubles, three-roubles, five-roubles (there were of course no ten-rouble, twenty-five-rouble, fifty-rouble, or hundred-rouble notes) differed greatly in their physical properties from normal money. To understand the difference, fold any banknote so that it is the size of a fingernail. Then insert this bill into a watch pocket or stick it under an inner sole of a shoe and take it out and unfold it after a month or two – this would be a subcutaneous banknote in its typical form, or rather deformity. Shaggy, bloated, bubbling, and twitching as if alive, they struck the imagination so strongly that even my world-weary writers were stunned, seeing them in such large quantities for the first time.

The culprit behind this was the headman, or rather, his meticulousness. When he ascended the stage to unload the money for the first time, he pompously put the money on the table, so that no one would have any doubts about his honesty. As he put the wad of cash on the table, this thick pack, released from his hand, transformed into a twitching pile that came alive and spread out in all directions, with banknotes outpacing one another.

"Well, look at that, crawling just like caterpillars," the headman marvelled. Someone in the audience blurted out in exasperation:

"For Pete's sake, grab them, they're crawling under the table already!"

About ten people jumped up from the front row and ran to the stage, but the headman stopped them.

"Stop!" he barked authoritatively, tossing his cane aside and diving face-first onto the table. He raked the spreading banknotes towards himself with both hands; it was a horrific sight. The money continued to twitch in his tousled beard, and it seemed as if he was chewing on the money. I rushed under the table, and just in time. Several subcutaneous three-rouble banknotes, pushing one another, were crawling onto the footlights, followed by a gaggle of "the tattered."[22], like ducklings, crossed the back of the stage and tried to slip away behind the curtain.

---

22 Old worn out one-ruble notes.

No one expressed displeasure when I had to occasionally interrupt and accept money after this nerve-racking incident. On the contrary, the listeners themselves fell into a tense silence, only breaking it to prompt how to avoid another blunder. Their prompts were especially useful when all my pockets were tightly stuffed, and I was at a loss as to where to put the incoming money.

"Let's get a pillowcase from the watchman," they helpfully suggested.

"A pillowcase isn't bad, but it's too conspicuous to be seen in public with it," Mayakovsky reasoned in a low, pressing bass voice.

He was standing on the stage next to me and saw with his own eyes that something had to be done, otherwise, the subcutaneous money might start crawling out of my pockets on its own.

"Then tuck it into your shirt."

Seeing my hesitation, the audience began to encourage me:

"You really better tuck it into your shirt, it will be pressed by your jacket, and no one will notice…"

"And you'll need to tie ligatures on your shirt cuffs," Nikolai Alekseyevich, the headman's friend, advised mindfully.

The medical term meaning a thread used to tie off blood vessels puzzled everyone.

"What is a ligature?"

To Nikolai Alekseyevich's great pleasure, it incidentally transpired that he, formerly a veterinary assistant who castrated pigs, had tied uncountable ligatures.

In short, Nikolai Alekseyevich had a little ball of silk threads, and he did indeed skillfully tie his ligatures on my cuffs and on the bottom of my trousers where they were tucked into my socks. Amazingly, the letters "N" and "A" could be clearly seen in his ligatures, or rather in the pattern of knots he made. Nikolai Alekseyevich also tightened my tie, just in case.

"If a button pops off, the tie will hold it," he explained.

I returned home surrounded by attention and honour. Nearly all the literary club members saw me off to the bus stop. We agreed that we would hold the next meeting on the last Wednesday of the month, August 28th. However, we decided not to linger as late as we did tonight, and to go home right after we vote on the titles. August 28th was a major Russian Orthodox holiday, the Dormition of the Holy Mother of God, and many of my listeners expressed a desire to spend the evening at home with their families and grandchildren.

I did not object, my soul was rejoicing, and now I too wanted to spend more time at home, with Rozochka.

CHAPTER 6

On the bus home, I sat in the corner, my rosy daydreams undisturbed. The money under my shirt didn't bother me either. It was when I got off the bus that the money was jostled by my walking. It swelled under my clothes so much that people started looking at me. A few young men, standing in a circle chatting, began asking each other loudly enough for me to hear:

"What is this?! Where's that mattress going?"

I quickly slipped into the shadows and made my way to the dormitory, avoiding the usual paths. Indeed, I felt like I was inside a straw mattress. The money got so unruly under my shirt and trousers that I just had to unbutton my jacket and raise my arms. I don't know what kind of creature I looked like, but I distinctly remember feeling like some angry bird of prey, like an enraged vulture.

I entered the dormitory unnoticed (luckily the back door was unlocked). On our floor's landing, I again encountered that mysterious young man who had made it an odd rule to turn away from me and face the wall whenever we met. This time too he turned away and stood like a statue until I entered the corridor. I heard rapid footsteps, like he was scurrying down the stairs. "Strange, very strange bozo," I thought, and somewhere deep down I appreciated his behaviour, which allowed me to keep my bird of prey appearance to myself.

The corridor was dark and deserted. I turned on the light. Most of the neon lamps were missing, and those that were lit flickered dimly; the shaking light made anyone walking down the corridor resemble a jumping kangaroo. All other visual cues were concealed. That was precisely why I turned on the lights: they were the best camouflage. Still, even that was not quite enough to completely prevent being recognised. The residents' hearing had become so sensitive that we all knew each other by our footsteps, coughing, and other individual sounds.

As I walked down the endless corridor, doors opened behind me on both sides, and I heard whispering behind the rustle of my trousers—they were checking if it was indeed me, Mitya the writer. I found this unanimous curiosity somewhat surprising and attributed it to the straw-like shuffle of my steps, alien to their keen ears.

The door to our room was wide open.

"Rozochka… Rozaria Fyodorovna," I called out, imagining her running out and perhaps throwing her arms around me (her actions were always unpredictable). The only answer was an echo briefly bouncing off the bare walls. I thought I had entered the wrong room: no bookshelf, no TV, no fridge, no wardrobe, not even chairs—nothing. "Just a table and books, dumped on the floor by the door with some bedding in a mocking heap. The lady's gone, all is lost. The lady's gone…" I had written those lines in one of my plays long ago, when I was still a student. Now those words suddenly came back to me so vividly that I shuddered, aghast to believe their prophetic meaning.

I dashed back into the corridor to check the number on the door, but even before that the abundance of bouncing marsupials coming towards me made me realise: the prophecy had been fulfilled, this was our room, mine and Rozochka's, and it was empty.

I stood and waited. That is, I wasn't waiting for anything or anyone, I stood fast because of the sudden painful weakness throughout my body, especially in my knees. I also felt nauseous and dizzy. I kept still, fearing to take a step, slide down the wall to the floor and end up sitting in the corridor by the empty room, which would be ridiculous. I didn't want to be ridiculous. Suddenly I was struck by the accuracy of the phrase "jelly legs." Whoever first called weakness in the knees "jelly legs" was undoubtedly a genius. I also recalled a professor from the Literary Institute claiming that prophetic words possess magnetism: they attract life, and life then unfolds according to the Word. Oh Lord, how much did I want to write prophetic poems back then, to instruct life itself on how to properly evolve. To be frank, I had always doubted that I could write anything of the sort. And yet I had written it, I had brought misfortune upon my own head. In that moment I would have given up all my present and future prophecies, and all the world's prophecies to boot, just for Rozochka to be with me, for what had happened to appear nothing but a dream or some absurd, entirely fixable misunderstanding.

Meanwhile, the residents approached, but not too close, stopping at a distance and blocking the corridor with a living wall, like a dam. Our fifth floor was listed with the housing manager as a family floor, although quite a few unmarried, mostly divorced men lived there. They stood before me in a row but stepped back when I swayed towards them, and all at once began recounting what had happened. Not a shred of genuine empathy could be felt in their supposedly sympathetic exclamations. On the contrary, the more they commiserated, recalling how the woman had sat in the corner on a chair while four Caucasians with Petka Ryaskin, those unwashed brutes, ran through the corridor with the furniture, their envy towards those unwashed fellows slipped through clearer and clearer.

"The bastards cleared out the room in just five minutes. And then that woman got up from her little chair and left with it right behind them."

"She's not just some woman, she's my wife!" I cried out in a thin, falsetto voice, covering my ears with my palms.

To tell you the truth, I could no longer see or hear anyone. I didn't even understand why I was standing there as if still listening and looking at the twitching faces of the residents. Nothing of the sort. I didn't recognise anyone individually in the hazy neon light. For me, all residents merged into some multi-faced being that agreed with me on everything, and even though I was silent now, my interaction with it still seemed uninterrupted. It was so strange to feel and understand that I took my hands away from my ears. The being really did agree with me, and now female tones dominated in its voice.

"That's right, the housing manager said Rozochka was his legal wife, and since she decided to move out their jointly acquired belongings, no one can order her what to do. The spouses can sort it out in court later. She's willing to provide a set of linen and whatever else is due to him, to Slyozkin, right away. She doesn't have any decent beds, but everything else he can obtain from the laundry downstairs."

"And who's this Ryaskin?" I asked.

For some reason I wondered if this wasn't that same young man who turned away from me whenever we met. (That was exactly right, I hit the bull's eye with the first shot.) It turned out that Petya Ryaskin had previously lived in the dormitory, and had brought a note from Rozochka and left it on the table right before I arrived. Lord, so that's what it was all about! I rushed into the room and began searching around on the table with my trembling, impatient hands. Then I saw the desk lamp and turned it on. The note was inserted into the iron[23]. I was astounded by it - "Don't look for me, you won't find me, I've changed my passport and last name." - that I just couldn't grasp why she had changed her passport and last name. When the meaning became clear, I suddenly felt so drained that I had to get down on the floor and lie on my back right where I stood. It was only then that I remembered the money under my clothes: it was soft to lie on, exactly like a straw mattress. The only thing that caused discomfort and even irritation was the presence of the multi-faced being, "a monster stout, wicked, huge, with a hundred maws," which squeezed into the room after me. Despite my silent protests, it continued our interaction on some subconscious level. In any case, I knew for certain that the beast had thoroughly familiarised itself with the note before me and was waiting for some important but entirely specific decision from me. It was this anticipation that explained its thoughtfulness in having a bed, a ping-pong tabletop, a mattress, a blanket, clean bedding, and even four glasses on a kitchen stool brought into the room.

I smiled, or rather, my pain smiled inside me, or more precisely, my soul smiled, suddenly exhausted by the superhuman efforts to cope with the loss of Rozochka. Incomprehensible?! Ridiculous?! "… Oh, laugh out, laughers! You who laugh with laughs…"[24], "… Oh, swanderful! Oh, dawnrises!"[25] I don't know

---

23   Antique coal irons were sometimes preserved as souvenirs or paperweights, or used as fancy boxes for small items, like mentioned here.
24   From "Invocation of laughter" by Velemir Khlebnikov.
25   From "Grasshopper" by Velemir Khlebnikov.

whether or not Velimir Khlebnikov would have understood me at that moment, but I understood his so-called mind-bending poems, which I had previously considered incomprehensible, as clearly as two and two make four. "Thus, on a canvas of some letters beyond dimension lived the face."[26]

I smiled, but nothing revealed my smile; I continued to lay there, on the mattress of money, my arms behind my head. I stared at the ceiling while the multi-faced being was no longer just interacting but persuading and negotiating what decision of mine would be the most acceptable for both of us. Something metallic, hidden by a bed sheet, clinked, and thumped solidly as it was carefully set in the corner behind the pile of books. Then the glasses tinkled. "Four glasses, four little flowers. A cyanide chapter in an intriguer's love story." "Well, I certainly won't let this prophecy of mine shape reality under any circumstances," I thought indignantly and abruptly got to my feet. My shirt's topmost button popped off, hit the floor, and ricocheted across it like a pellet, just as the vet had predicted.

"Get going, all of you, and take your glasses with you," I said angrily, involuntarily raising my arms vulture-like as if they were wings. The multi-faced being broke apart into three quite familiar characters, known to all the women in our dormitory, including Rozochka, as nothing but drunks from the TV factory.

One of them, nicknamed Doublenose, of rather puny build but with an exceptionally long nose on a very small face, had divorced three times, unlike his buddies. A funny rumour circulated about him that he had shot himself just as many times right in front of his former wives. There was a suspicion that he

---

26   From "Bo-beh-o-bi sang the lips" by Velemir Khlebnikov.

had used blanks. However, his actions left everyone bewildered so often that even though they didn't fear him, they still did not want to deal with him. Doublenose knew this and skilfully took advantage of the fact. Incidentally, he also spoke in an abnormal manner. He would fix his bird-like nose right between your eyes, then with each word he would jerk his head back and forth, so it seemed he wasn't talking but butting you in the forehead with his beak.

While everybody "got going" as I demanded, he fell back from his buddies, making a sour face, his nose protruding even further forward.

"Hey, we came with sympathy," Doublenose rattled, jerking his head. "Thought you were a good man, but you're a Mitya! What are you going to do without us?" he unexpectedly asked, as if we were long-time friends.

"Write," I lied.

"Write your will?! Go ahead, go ahead, if I were her, I'd have dumped a Mitya like you long ago," Doublenose jabbed spitefully, stepping over the threshold.

"What is it to you?!"

"It's that we feel for you. I even stashed some stuff for you in the corner behind the door, and you're all 'get going.' Not very friendly - what we need right now is a little vodka!" he summed up in an almost tender tone, snapping his finger at Adam's apple, which protruded from his throat just like the nose on his face. His buddies hurried away, as if on a signal. I gave each of them three roubles, not out of nobility or other high motives, I just stuck my hand in my jacket's inside pocket and, knowing the nature of subcutaneous money, took a small pinch. But when I pulled it out, it turned out to be a bouquet of three-rouble notes. I wouldn't have even minded fives, if only they'd leave me alone. And they did leave. They silently exchanged stunned glances and bounced down the corridor like kangaroos.

After slamming the door and sliding the bolt, I was finally alone, but once alone, didn't know what to do. I paced from corner to corner like a caged animal, not even noticing. It seemed like a demon had taken possession of me. Dozens of the most fantastic ideas flashed through my mind in one instant, only to disappear and give way to others even more fantastic in the next. I ran around the room as if in pursuit of imaginary chimaeras. Finally, I stumbled and fell. I became so enraged that I began pounding my head on the floor, feeling no pain, nothing but rage. Then, I suppose, I lost consciousness and fell asleep. But when I came to my senses, I recalled Doublenose's mention of having stashed something behind the door, along with my untrue promise to write.

Overcoming my battered condition, I got up, righted the overturned stool, and only then pulled back the crumpled, dirty sheet. Hidden beneath it was a double-barrelled 12-gauge shotgun, identical to the one I had hunted with in high school. My mother had at first been afraid and worried, but later she even took pride in her son hunting with his father's gun. I only remembered my father from photographs; my mother said he had died of galloping consumption[27]. She also said that my father composed folk rhymes and performed them so cheerfully to the accompaniment of a harmonica that he was often invited to local amateur talent shows. In the photographs, he always sat with a harmonica, and I sat on my mother's lap. My father must have

---

27   An obsolete name for progressive exhaustion as a result of a chronic disease, mainly pulmonary tuberculosis.

been quite a bungler; my mother sometimes reproached me for being all thumbs just like him. I was overwhelmed with pity for my mother, forgotten by everyone out there near Barnaul, alone her whole life, with me far away God knows where… Thanks to Rozochka's doing, we had concealed our address and forwarded letters through the Literary Institute. "Some son," I thought bitterly of myself, and broke open the shotgun by sliding the stop-button to the fore-end.

The brass bases of the cartridges peeked out from the barrels; I pulled them out and, weighing them in my palm, felt the lethal heft of the buckshot load. Putting the cartridges into the iron and returning the barrel, I sat for a long time, leaning on the gun by the table.

I envisioned our village, blue skies, my mother, my job as a cowherd, the handmade willow whistles decorated with intricate notches, the sun, the grass, the river, my first hunt with the adults, and suddenly felt a kind of jolt in my heart - poetry. That is, not poetry yet, but just the premonition, the mere possibility of it. It was as if something inside was lifting me up; I saw everything clearly and distinctly in all directions.

When I set the shotgun in the corner, I knew for certain that I was about to write a poem. Moreover, I could already feel the poem inside me; I just needed to extract it through those unique words that I had yet to locate in my memory and write them down in their proper order on a sheet of paper or white cuffs - it didn't matter which.

* * *

People whispered, "Can you fathom
Why he chose to end his life?"
When crimson moon over a cottage
Spilt its scarlet through the night.

The aspen tree remained bent low,
Man's body lay upon the grass,
A spot of clay, still moist and fresh,
Marked his crumpled sleeve, alas.

In distant, endless, starry skies,
A lonely aeroplane flashed its lights,
And molten hail like burning shot,
Rained down upon the earth all night.

Yet he, the one who took his life,
Paid no attention to it all,
As if his dreams were so profound,
That worldly matters were too small.

But those around him firmly said,
"Love is fine, but not this way!"
And someone thrice divorced declared,
"He was just a fool today."

I am aware that there is no limit to perfection. Any precious stone can be polished and cut, but you must agree: to get a finished diamond, you must at least have a diamond in the rough, which must first be found and extracted from the depths. I have no thoughts of justifying or exaggerating the literary value of anyone's works, including my own. What is, is, and what is not, cannot be considered. One may be Fet, but one must first be Shenshin[28].

* * *

My father's ammo belt well-stocked
With cartridges for geese, I head
To my hideout by the Ob
In hours when the skies glow red

Below, the river in the fields,
With spectral, solemn glow it shines,
It's like a highway to the moon,
Extolled by loud wild cranes' cries.

With cartridge chambered, moon in sight,
My aim is steady, calm, and clear…
But I don't dare disturb the night -
Can you hear the cranes so near?

And only when I'm back at home,
Recalling all that came to pass,
I'll see the moonlit path once more,
And hear my gun's resounding blast.

---

28   Shenshin was Afanasy Fet's family name at birth.

* * *

Roofs of cottages, lights, howling dogs,
I dreamt of them once, in the hollow they lie.
Though I run, it's like chasing fog,
No matter how hard I try.

Is it an owl that leads me astray,
Or the darkness lures me away?
Yet ahead I still see, clear and stark,
Roofs, lights, and dogs that bark.

Here I run through the snow so deep,
Chased by frost and night's dark might.
Will my running give some relief
To my longing for home tonight?

Roofs of cottages, lights, howling dogs,
Almost at hand, in the hollow, they lie.
I keep running, but grasp only fog,
No matter how hard I try.

I finished the last stanza out of inertia. Another poem, a major one, was already rumbling inside me, its breath, even though distant, throwing me into a chill, making me tremble like a candle flame. I started writing it down at once, without getting up from the table, without interruption.

* * *

Cursed be poetic words and rhyme!
I failed to find them, once she brought
all eloquence on earth to nought.
Oh, what a woman in her prime!

Let me be damned, I say!
Let mother forsake her son!
Such a woman, unique in her sway,
Like a harlequin's jolly song!

She had it all: love, praise, and more…
And hunger of dark passion's might!
The woman that I still adore;
My love was deep and outright!

If she had wished me to become
a perjurer so vile and crass,
I would have fallen and succumbed,
I'd have betrayed you, friends, alas!

I see no crime, feel no contrition.
Do I deserve your harshest curse?
The world was but a slight addition
To her, a spangle on her purse.

She had it all: love, praise, and more…
Just anything that one can get.
The woman that I still adore
And wish that we had never met.

CHAPTER 7

The sudden knock at the door shook me. Imperious and demanding, it burst into the room as if breaking through the ceiling. I jumped up, not fully grasping what had happened and surprised that the light bulb stayed intact and the walls did not crack. While I looked around trying to understand what was going on, the knock repeated. This time it was neither loud nor imperious, nor even demanding. An ordinary midnight knock, in a sense almost apologetic.

It was the neighbour knocking. When I opened, she did indeed apologize and asked me to return the double-barrelled shotgun. I handed it over without a word. Prepared in advance for refusal, fully resolved to get that gun by any means, she was spooked by how easily it came into her possession. Lost, she asked:

"Loaded?"

I said I had unloaded it, and to dispel any doubt, I went to get the shells.

"No, I don't need those." She cheered up noticeably. "Of course, Doublenose and all his gang are scoundrels! But you, Mitya, good on you, and your woman - what a bitch! Don't take it the wrong way, Mitya, I'm just being honest," the neighbour said, supporting the gun under her armpit with both hands, barrel back, and walking off lightly and quickly towards her room.

Upon closing the door, I went to the table intending to keep working, to write. Alas, I didn't feel like it. Chekhov's gun, always firing on stage, hadn't gone off, it was taken away, and inspiration seemed to have drained along with it. But at least the main poem was written, especially that last line where, however, you look at it, you agree that it would have been better if she, Rozochka, had never existed. You didn't even confront the neighbour, despite the direct insult. You didn't even think of challenging her. Strange conclusion…

I tried to resist, to oppose my own unexpected judgment, but I couldn't. I perceived both myself and Rozochka not for real, but as literary characters in some trivial play. I walked around the room, becoming more and more convinced that Doublenose's shotgun had fired after all, and whether I wanted it or not, I had slain us both, Rozochka and myself, with my major poem. How relieving it would be to cry, to sob, but nothing could penetrate my heart, its dead, empty space. I looked over and tested the new bed by doing a sort of belly dance on it. Huge and stable enough, it didn't remind me of my intimate times with Rozochka at all. The only thought that came to me was if we'd had a bed like this earlier, maybe I wouldn't have had to sleep on my manuscripts.

Suddenly I felt my entire body itching: the money! Disturbed by the belly dance, it was stirring again. Imagining myself as an enraged vulture, I laughed merrily. The residents had taken me for an angry bird not because of the money, but in the belief that anyone would become like that if their wife left them. It struck me as so funny that I had to bite my hand to stop laughing. Then, turning my pockets out, I started pulling out the money and throwing it at my feet. Soon the floor by the bed turned into a kind of cabbage patch, except for the growth of the heads happened in reverse. In slow motion, the heads swelled, broke apart, the leaves fell off and spread out, turning the open floor space into a living carpet.

Just as I stripped down to my underwear, picking out the last slithering banknotes from my clothes, there was a knock at the door. From the voices urging each other to keep quiet, I realised it was Doublenose and Co. They called out, inviting to join them for a little drink, while quietly discussing whether I had shot myself. And if I had, should they break the door or leave everything as it was until the morning? They agreed to wait. They were already leaving when Doublenose voiced an assumption:

"What if he's wounded, maybe put his eye out, and is bleeding to death?"

They got agitated out in the corridor and started calling to me again, knocking. Fearing they were about to break down the door, I coughed loudly and in an indignantly tearful voice demanded (I really did feel sorry for myself, wounded, bleeding to death) that they all immediately go away, and not disturb me while I concentrated on serious business.

"Mitya, we understand," Doublenose hastily answered for all of them. And pressing his lips to the keyhole, in a voice full of sympathy, consoled: "Don't worry, Mitya, we're here for you."

They sincerely wanted me to regain concentration quickly and considerately tiptoed away. I too, like a ham actor, tiptoed away from the door. I didn't know whether to laugh or cry. By force of circumstance, I had ended up in a kind of brotherhood of divorced men, a peculiar professional circle, and they had every right to expect some great sacrifice from me. Undoubtedly, by committing suicide I would have created an aura of great martyrs for them and in this time of hopeless poverty just by saying "We need to hold a memorial for poor Mitya" they wouldn't hesitate to get money out of any woman in the dorm. I was wondering at their persistence; "sharing a bottle for three" is always more convenient, and maybe they were eager to get rid of me so as not to have to take me into their well-established "party cell"? Scoundrels! The neighbour was right - a gang of scoundrels!

I took the iron off the table, sat on the floor, and started counting the money, using the iron as a paperweight. At first, I counted absent-mindedly, not even realising what I counted, roubles or simply bills. Then I thought to sort the bills by denomination: rouble notes, three-rouble notes, and five-rouble notes. But here too, I got muddled and made mistakes. In one of his stories, Andrei Platonov notes that a person needs inner happiness even for the simplest tasks. I had no happiness; I was counting money, amused by the thought that I was counting it when my wife left me, and in one of the rooms at the far end of the corridor, my well-wishers were contemplating scenes of me dispatching myself to a better world. I imagined them arguing, betting a bottle on how I would shoot myself: point the barrel at my young heart (Doublenose was good in rendering details) or clench the gun in my teeth and blow my skull to smithereens? Go ahead, go ahead, I mentally encouraged them, smiling merrily as I continued counting the money. Although I kept losing count and forgetting the totals; I counted with pleasure. This was my answer to Chamberlain[29].

The "party cell" crept up to my door almost silently the second time. I still detected them approaching because I was expecting them and was specifically planning not to miss the moment. I took the iron and carefully stood by the door. The

---

29   In 1927 Joseph Austen Chamberlain, at that time British Minister of Foreign Affairs, addressed the Soviet Union with an ultimatum, threatening to sever all relations for supporting the communist movement in China. "Pravda", the main Soviet newspaper, published the article titled "Greetings to Guandong! This is our answer to Chamberlain!", creating one of the iconic Soviet memes.

well-wishers stayed silent for a long time, listening. Obviously, they too had a plan. Our standoff lasted several minutes. Finally, shifting from foot to foot, one of them couldn't stand the tension any longer and carelessly let out a loud fart. The others hissed at him. The culprit, realising nothing could be fixed, cried out to vindicate himself somehow:

"Mitka, surrender, it's us, it's us!"

God knows why he said "surrender," it made no sense! However, it didn't matter to me how they revealed themselves, as long as they did.

"Ohhhh!" I groaned, as if my tooth had been pulled. "Disturbed again!" I cried out desperately and slammed the iron against the door with all my might for greater effect.

My plan was for the blow of the iron to be taken as a rifle butt strike, but I didn't expect that it would also click like a cocked gun. A lucky coincidence: the divorced gang took off running.

They ran down the corridor, and I, hearing toppled buckets clanging, doors opening, and the already familiar curses, knew it was time to put an end to this drunken gang of scoundrel marionettes. Why marionettes? That was always a mystery to me. Somehow, this word boosted the feeling of resentment.

Left alone for the first time, I felt no protest. "Scoundrel marionettes," me included—me even more so, me first, then them—seemed an ultra-precise definition at that moment, more than that, celestially precise. Indeed, all my actions resembled those of a puppet whose mechanism was out of its own reach. The only thing remaining of free will for me was the ability to explain my actions convincingly. Unfortunately, explanations could never convince Him or The Force holding all our strings since time immemorial. After all, first comes the tug on the string, and only then does our "thoughtfulness" follow.

I shook my fist at the ceiling and, spitting in anger, sat down to count the money. What's the point of shaking a fist if you already know it's foolish to wave your fists at someone's back?

The noise in the corridor subsided as suddenly as it had arisen. I counted the money, knowing that no one else would come, at least not that night. The counting went as smoothly as if throughout my whole life I had done nothing but count money at night, binding it with white threads and stacking it in bundles into the iron. I made notes and calculations on the back of the sheet with the major poem, without realising what I was writing on. I counted 408 rubles' worth of three-ruble notes, 335 rubles in fives, and 307 of "the tattered." After adding up all the numbers, I involuntarily tossed the sheet aside. The total sum of contributions from the literary union members, minus the 9 rubles gratuitously given to the gang of scoundrels, came to exactly 1,050 rubles, in other words, it had been brilliantly predicted by Rozochka—a genuinely fateful fact confirming that we are puppets, and life is nothing more than a theatre of marionettes.

Shaken, I slowly got up from the table and turned on the light. No matter how you look at it, from now on and forevermore, I knew for certain that Rozochka was far beyond me, far beyond! The significance of this prophetic coincidence was more convincing than any words: unlike me, she was closer to the Creator, closer!

Once again, the urge to weep overwhelmed me, and I felt the tears welling up. Out of habit, I flung myself face-down onto the bed and struck my face against the tabletop of the tennis table with such force that I involuntarily groaned, not so much from pain as from indignation. Could I have braced myself with my elbows, perhaps? "If only one knew where he would fall…" The desire to cry into a pillow, which I groped for far to the side, now echoed with annoyance. I wanted nothing, absolutely nothing. With my eyes closed, I crawled onto the mattress, turned on my back, and felt as though I had plunged into an abyss.

In the morning, I awoke with a swollen face. Traces of dried blood could be seen on the pillowcase. A new joyless day had dawned, but life had to go on somehow. While examining myself in the washroom, I couldn't shake the feeling that my reflection in the mirror didn't want to look my way and was outright turning its face away. The slightly twisted, puffy nose, the swelling on my forehead, and the swollen lips gave my face an expression of some persistent disgust. A strange grimace? Perhaps even an indirect association with the circle of the divorced inevitably reflects on the face with some mandatory branding. A peculiar seal, a stamp, both in the passport and on the mug – the last being especially astonishing. It seemed that my whole evening was spent avoiding the "divorcees," but upon closer inspection my face bore the same "landmarks" as theirs. A tempting thought flickered to send everything to hell and drown my sorrows in alcohol with my comrades.

I imagined entering with a bottle, the entire "party cell" already assembled and waiting. Finally, the first, most dreadful shot was overcome. Distorted faces cleared, smoothed out, and drunken camaraderie began with kisses and the inevitable spilling of wine and brine on the table, trousers, and even the bed. Cigarette butts and burnt matches were scattered on the floor, we dragged each other by the legs away from the table, faces insensibly mixed with the snacks, and someone, leaning against the wall, bitterly cried about his fate as an abandoned man, hitting himself so hard in the chest that he eventually fell backwards, ramming the table and toppling it along with himself into a feverish silence.

Everything inside me churned in a surge of disgust. I glanced in the mirror, and saw a face, a disdainful grimace brazenly staring back: eye to eye, not hiding its involvement in my daydream.

I remembered the money and immediately hurried, bustled about. Not that I aimed to seduce Rozochka with the money, no, I sincerely believed that all the money, or at least most of it, belonged to her. The reason to hand it over seemed so serious to me that it outweighed the doubts caused by Rozochka's note. I decided to go to the "Palace Hotel."

At the "Palace Hotel" no one knew anything about the nurse Rosa Fyodorovna Slyozkina, working on a flexible schedule. Moreover, the "flexible schedule" surprised the chief administrator (a middle-aged woman) so much that she didn't bother referring me to her staff, but accompanied me to the deputy director in charge of personnel. However, the deputy also knew nothing about Rozochka. And the "flexible schedule" elicited a mysterious smile from him, as if I were hinting at something indecent. They exchanged knowing glances with the administrator, and she suggested that maybe I was looking for one of those girls who offer their "services" on call?

"What services?" I didn't understand.

The deputy director intervened:

"Young man, if you are interested in women of easy virtue, you are at the wrong place. Contact the police. We don't have any Slyozkina working here and never did. A flexible schedule – that's quite something!"

He smirked disapprovingly and began talking to the administrator about hotel affairs, as if I had already left.

Of course, the deputy's smirk offended me, but even more so did the suggestion that I should look for my wife among women of easy virtue. Obviously, they had judged me by my face… "It's my own fault, I am overthinking this," I thought and decided that there was no need to go to the police, Rozochka would not approve.

That day, August 15th, I visited all hotels in the city, even the regional party committee's hotel—all in vain. No one knew anything about the nurse Rosa Fyodorovna Slyozkina. Instructed by experience, I did not mention her flexible schedule.

Back in the dormitory, I had an unpleasant conversation with Doublenose and his entire gang. I promised to hand over the gun only if I got Petka Ryaskin's address, that strange guy who made it a rule to turn away when meeting me.

"Keep in mind, you don't know me yet," I warned them. "I have nothing to lose now."

In the evening, I retrieved the gun and told the neighbour I would sell it. She happily returned it but expressed concern that terrible things happen out of jealousy—what if Rozochka repents and comes back in tears?!

Her suspicion didn't offend me. On the contrary, without realising it, she convinced me of something she could never have persuaded me of: I suddenly believed that Rozochka would come back and everything would be as before. I just needed to not change the address under any circumstances and wait, be ready to meet her, and write a lot in the meantime. Suffering tempers the soul, and work is the best fortress where one can and should take shelter from all misfortune.

I felt joy from the fact that, like Count Leo Nikolayevich Tolstoy, I was engaged in literary work. I would compile a collective anthology, and we, the literary union members, would publish it using our subcutaneous money. (One thousand and fifty rubles was a lot of money at that time.)

CHAPTER 8

I decided to redeem myself by dedicating a new poem to Rozochka. I thought of her with tenderness, in a pure, elevated way, but the poem was difficult to write; each word came hard, as if found blindly in a void. I was done long after midnight.

ANGELS OF LOVE
To Rozochka

Every love has its guardian angels,
Like villages calm and at ease,
Their wings are crackling like torches
Of cool and green canopies.

I saw them dancing in twilight
By the Swan Lake, serene and fresh.
They weren't a mere picturesque sight,
But real they were, in the flesh.

I started to cherish my dreams,
Fairytales and real entwined.
There glides to the lake in the moonbeams
The swan that is meant to be mine

Though I wasn't a prince in fine laces,
Life follows the same common principle:

Having found her among passing faces,
I myself became a prince invincible.

It's magic how fresh dill can seem,
From markets brought, like flowers bloom,
Her hands bring grace, a lovely dream,
Their scent now fills my humble room.

This can't be expressed by a language,
Angels are here, they exist.
But, without love, they languish,
So, in feelings, you must persist.

But even if you don't trust me,
Go see for yourself someday.
White-winged swans shall await thee,
They're always there to stay.

You'll have to endure some dangers,
Slain a wizard with love you can give.
Loving hearts are supported by angels,
And, like me, you will come to believe.

In the morning, I made a clean copy of the poem and went straight to the editorial, just to avoid indulging in fruitless guessing about whether it would be accepted or not. I had never desired to be published so much, neither before nor after. The poem could only appear in the next issue (on Tuesday, August 20th) as the best-case scenario, but I still had to convince Vasya

Kruzhkin, the Managing Editor (the editor only came in during the afternoons on Mondays and Fridays), that the poem was politically correct and wouldn't embarrass the newspaper.

Vasya Kruzhkin, nicknamed "Little Jew," used to oversee the sports section before becoming the Managing Editor. Long ago, he played volleyball with the Polytechnic Institute team and often brought in information about sports events as a freelancer. In one piece titled "Who Will Replace Uncle Grisha?" he directly raised the issue of finding a new coach for the Polytechnic Institute's volleyball team. After the legendary Uncle Grisha's retirement, volleyball fell out of favour at the institute.

The article garnered some public attention, getting noticed by the first secretary of the regional Komsomol committee. Thanks to his kind and, more importantly, influential hand, Vasya Kruzhkin was hired by the newspaper's sports department as a staff correspondent.

Two meters tall, blond, and snub-nosed, he could easily have doubled as the archetypal Russian hero and troublemaker Vaska Buslay. As the years went on and he grew stout, he could even have doubled as Ilya Muromets[30]. However, Vasya Kruzhkin completely denied having Slavic roots despite any spiritual or physical resemblance. He confided "secretly" at one of the Komsomol committee and editorial office parties that his mother's grandmother was a pure-blooded, highly intelligent Jewish woman who had lived her entire life in her historical homeland of Birobidzhan[31]. He, Vasya Kruzhkin, would have registered as a Jew too if not for facing discrimination.

---

30   Ilya Muromets, also known as Ilya of Murom, is a Russian folk hero, bogatyr – a man of extraordinary strength and high moral virtues.
31   The capital city of Jewish Autonomous Region, a failed attempt to create a Jewish enclave within the Soviet Union.

Soon Vasya was going to be fired from the paper for creative insolvency (being able to write news briefs was hardly sufficient even for a sports correspondent). However, he pre-empted this decision "from above." As soon as the head of the Komsomol life section had a talk with him, Vasya, without a second thought, went around all the editorial offices in the building, loudly declaring that they wanted to get rid of him because of the notorious "fifth line."[32]

"HR somehow found out I'm a Jew," Vasya would complain simply, throwing many staff members into agitation despite their own impeccable backgrounds and status as well-established talents. In any case, after a relatively short period of covert, subterranean, invisible shifts, tensions and fractures, Vasya "Little Jew" was unexpectedly appointed head of the sports section, and later managing editor of the paper. His latter appointment was directly linked to the successful transfer of the first secretary of the regional Komsomol committee to manage the Department of Culture and Propaganda at the regional Communist Party committee. One legend about Vasya had it that after his appointment the new department head gathered all the newspaper editors, including him, for a meeting. When the meeting ended, the department head casually asked:

"Well Vasily, are you keeping in touch with your historical homeland? Does your grandmother write to you?"

"She says things are bad," Vasya replied, lowering his eyes.

"What's the problem?" the department head enquired with interest.

"Discrimination. She may be the only one of the indigenous population left in all Birobidzhan."

---

32   A popular meme for ethnicity, which was the fifth line item in citizen's personal info card kept by Soviet passport authority.

"Is it so?!" the department head exclaimed in surprise. "Just the usual stupid overzealousness."

He abruptly changed the subject, saying that Vasily would soon be sent to the Higher Komsomol School in Moscow for managing editor training courses, so he should really apply himself. After Vasily left and all the editors had dispersed, the head of the Party's culture and propaganda department was heard loudly talking and laughing boisterously, so much so that the secretary-typist got up from her desk to close the door. She thought (according to her own account) that the department head was discussing Vasily Kruzhkin's candidacy for study in Moscow with someone on the phone. But no, he was just talking to himself, exclaiming: "That Vasya, what a Kruzhkin! He could give anyone a hundred-step head start, good for him!" Noticing the secretary, he first wanted to explain, but then waved his hand dismissively: "Go ahead and close it, close it—Vasya was just here!" And he broke into loud laughter again, pacing around the office.

Vasya displayed an outstanding talent for layouts and page composition, much to the surprise of many colleagues. Like a professional pianist feeling the music in his fingertips, he could flawlessly estimate the length of a piece of text. Vasya's only flaw was his total cluelessness regarding political issues, but here the editor and strict regulations bailed him out: the first and second pages were for Party and Komsomol committee announcements (unless there was urgent news from TASS), while the third page and especially the fourth were for sports, education, literature, arts, and so on. All of this somehow came back to me before meeting with Vasya, and I decided I would first ask if there was any free space on the fourth page.

There was no free space. I shuffled around Vasya's desk, which was completely covered with newspaper materials, and was about to leave when he stopped me:

"Who did that to you?" he said, pointing to my swollen nose.

"I fell," I said.

He handed me a sharply defined photo of a laughing high school girl in a white apron blowing soap bubbles.

"Evaluate it as a poet," he said.

"An excellent photo study, just wonderful!" I said, sincerely admiring it. (I was amazed by the reflections of buildings and cars in the soap bubbles.) "Who's the photographer?"

"Kolya Mishchenko, Nikolai Ivanovich. You know him?"

"I know who he is, but not personally," I replied.

"He put together a magnificent photo album about our city, but it got nixed."

"Why?"

"The usual thing - overzealousness."

Knowing that for Vasya "the usual overzealousness" meant discrimination because of the "fifth line," I objected that this couldn't be the case: first, he was an "Ivanovich" by patronymic, and second, his ethnic background was written all over his face, he was a pure-blooded Russian, no mistaking it.

Vasya Kruzhkin stood up from his desk, and when he picked up a cup of tea, I was immediately struck by his great height (the cup, which he held at chest level, hovered above the bridge of my nose).

"As it is well known, I'm "Ivanovich" too..."

Strangely, I had never heard that he was Ivanovich. In my memory, Vasily Kruzhkin was associated with Vasya "Little Jew," but never with the "Ivanovich"!

To avoid spilling his tea, Vasya carefully spread his arms, inviting me to take a good look at him. His Herculean physique, round face, blue eyes, freckles on his upturned nose—none of it matched his "Little Jew" nickname.

I had nothing to say, so I just mumbled, "Yeah…"

Agreeing with me, he repeated, "Yeeeaaah!"

It was an utterly absurd situation, and I protested indignantly trying to somehow defuse it:

"What 'overzealousness' do you mean when the entire press is in the hands of perestroika promoters?!"

Vasya smiled enigmatically and happily, took a sip of tea, and changed the subject. He made me explain my asking about the free space on the fourth page. I certainly never imagined that my mention of the perestroika promoters would be taken as a well-deserved compliment to himself.

When the typist retyped my poem at his insistence, he personally solicited reviews of it from all the section editors at our paper, and then asked me to come and see him (I was in the process of clearing out the drawers of my editorial desk, crammed with the literary union members' creations). The first thing he mentioned was indeed the perestroika promoters and that even with the press in their hands, things were not as simple as they seemed. (Vasya smiled, continuing to sip his tea, with that same smile, but this time instead of an enigma there was a flickering light of some significant knowledge.) Vasya went on to say that we were accustomed to living by the old ways and any innovation was like a knife to our throat. Yes, let him be known the "Little Jew." So what? He was proud of it.

Sitting down next to Vasya's desk, I saw that my poem had already been marked up for typesetting. It seemed unbelievable; everything in me rejoiced at the thought that on Tuesday Rozochka would read the dedication and, quite possibly, come back, and we would be reconciled!

I half-listened to Vasya's ramblings, as I had already decided to just agree with everything he said. Perhaps that's why, unexpectedly even to myself, I suddenly stood sideways and affirmed that I too was proud.

Vasya stopped (he had been pacing the room), and we stared at each other rather meaninglessly for a long while: I looked up at the ceiling, and he stared down, as if at the toes of his half-metre sneakers. That's when I realised that by half-listening to Vasya, I was overburdening myself. I shouldn't even be saying "uh huh," but instead stay silent. And I remained silent.

Meanwhile, resuming his pacing around the office, he started telling me about his grandmother in Birobidzhan, who, like Arina Rodionovna[33], had read him all of Samuil Yakovlevich Marshak's works in childhood.

He stopped again, dropped his head to his chest so as not to lose sight of me, and began to recite from memory:

> One little racoon
> Grew hungry by noon
> Give him porridge with milk.

---

33   Arina Rodionovna Yakovleva, nanny of Alexander Pushkin (1758-1828). The great poet loved her tenderly, devoted poems to her and mentioned her a lot in his correspondence.

With his tongue, he will lick,
Because racoons
Don't eat with spoons.

"Wonderful verses, as simple as truth!" I said admiringly, standing up and warmly shaking Vasya the "Little Jew's" hand. "Thank you!"

Then I sat down again and pretended not to want to embarrass Vasya, who did indeed seem flustered by my handshake, blushing with pleasure like a child. Propping my head up like Rodin's "Thinker," I could concentrate unhindered on my poem on the other side of the desk. Apart from the typesetting markings, the so-called editing stood out: the crossed-out lines.

What did the council of editors dislike about it? (After hearing about that little hungry raccoon, I was sure Vasya himself would have hardly dared to make any deletions.)

They must have influenced him, I thought, while he continued watching me from his towering height. Feeling his gaze, I deliberately scratched my head to let him think I too was deep in thought, overwhelmed by his grandmother, the "Arina Rodionovna."

The silence dragged on, yet I didn't want to look up. However, it was time to keep the conversation going. I scratched my head a second time and stated with all the profundity at my command:

"Marshak is Marshak!"

"And Osip Mandelstam, and Konstantin Simonov, and Boris Pasternak, and Joseph Brodsky for that matter!" Vasya chimed in, uncharacteristically quickly.

Amazingly, with that most banal of remarks, I had unexpectedly touched the core of Vasya's thoughts. I even felt a bit embarrassed, sensing that I had let myself down in Vasya's eyes—after all, it was I, not he, who was trying to be a poet. Forgetting the consequences, I stood sideways and said impassively, like a robot:

"Personally, I've always considered those poets Russian."

A shadow flickered in Vasya's eyes. He walked around the desk and sat down silently in an armchair. No, it wasn't a shadow of fear, more like a shadow of anxiety and something else that had no explanation, yet it stirred a feeling of pity in me. Yielding to it, I tossed Vasya a lifeline:

"Or what, were they too (I almost blurted out "from Birobidzhan" but caught myself in time), were they like your grandmother on your mother's side?" Vasya didn't say 'yes' or 'no,' he just nodded in agreement, his eyes closed. Then, switching to the polite 'you'[34], he asked:

"Have you ever wondered why they all (and Mandelstam never made a secret of it) wanted so much to become Russian writers? It was their cherished dream…"

"No," I said. "We have complete internationalism, a working-class and peasant interpenetration of all nations and ethnicities into one international community of Soviet workers."

Of course, my response was learned by rote, surfacing in my memory because Vasya's question seemed suspicious; I would have taken it as provocative, should someone else have asked it. But thank God it was Vasya the "Little Jew" asking, a man whose whole life blatantly demonstrated the said interpenetration.

---

34   Russian second-person pronoun (genderless) has an informal singular form, while a formal way to address a single person would be in plural.

After spouting off that answer, I marvelled at how sharply my self-preservation instinct had kicked in.

The phone rang, the typesetter called from the print shop. From the conversation, I understood that Vasya was planning to put the photograph of the schoolgirl and my poem in the remaining space on the front page.

I couldn't believe my ears—my poem and the photo of the girl blowing soap bubbles on the front page?! It seemed unbelievable.

But his musings about innovation… If he saw himself as a perestroika promoter, it was quite possible… Though there was still the editor… I tried somehow to rein in the joy rising from my depths, but in vain. My imagination eagerly conjured a delightful vision of Rozochka's return.

Vasya hung up and, as if answering my thoughts, said that until Tuesday, when the editor would be back, he was in charge and prepared to take the risk of publishing my poem on the front page on condition that I change the title and the dedication.

My joy evaporated. I was overcome with apathy, as the publication lost all its meaning. But Vasya kept arguing, insisting that all boldness has limits—angels in an atheistic Komsomol newspaper, and on the front page no less?! "They won't understand us," Vasya said heatedly. As for me, I didn't care anymore, I suggested just removing the title entirely. But he objected:

"The title spans five lines; if you remove it there will be a hole that can't be filled."

We settled on the title "By the Swan Lake."

"Of course, just 'By the Lake' would have been better," Vasya said. "But it will raise unwanted associations since there's an old film by Sergei Gerasimov with that title about Lake Baikal, and it would seem the poetic swan is the Baikal swan, and we don't want that."

Vasya was clearly demonstrating not his own knowledge, but that of the council of section editors.

"Of course not," I agreed. "Especially since the swan is from Manchester."

God knows why I said that! Vasya paid no attention to my irony, otherwise he probably would have refrained from making comparisons.

"To Rozochka! … You must admit, it sounds too frivolous! That dedication really must go."

"No way," I said irately, "As a last resort, let's replace it with initials: R.F.S."

Vasya rejected the initials, as they reminded him of the Gaidar[35] story titled "RVS." In short, the bargaining failed. We parted rather coldly, and I was sure they wouldn't print the poem. And thank God, I thought, I'll include it in the anthology. I had dragged almost a whole sack of manuscripts from the editorial office and decided to go through it without delay, selecting the best ones to include. Let me reiterate: a thousand and fifty rubles was a very large sum of money in those days, and having the collection published at the authors' expense seemed quite feasible.

---

35   Arkady Gaidar, famous soviet writer, grandfather of the previously mentioned politician Yegor Gaidar.

CHAPTER 9

I pored over the manuscripts for almost two weeks until the next meeting of the literary union. I lived on bread and milk. If anyone feels like sympathizing, don't bother—I was raised with bread and milk. Rozochka had left an almost untouched bottle of vegetable oil, and I would fry up stale bread, then crumble it into a bowl of milk, making something like soup with croutons.

I didn't want for food. Quiet and peace weren't a problem either; no one disturbed me. In fact, starting that Monday, something miraculous happened: the gang of drunkards would disappear in the mornings, and in the evenings literally everyone tiptoed around avoiding each other so as to not talk about anything. Truly a paradise on Earth, I was just left to sit and work without anyone getting in the way.

The only thing with which one could sympathize was reading the manuscripts. The piles I had dug up represented an archive that no human hand had touched in many years.

At first, I tried to sort the works by genre, but it didn't work out. The bulk of the writing didn't fit into any genres at all. Novels on three pages, novellas on four, and short stories retelling some cosmic events on planet Threa (Earth) among "literally headless people (without heads)" on a hundred and fifty pages would put me "in a state of such deep contemplation or short-term hibernation" that, coming to my senses, I would indeed feel like a headless Threaling for some time. Just to note, the brief explanations in parentheses were quite endearing in their unfailing ubiquity.

I sorted the prose by topics and found that in adventure pieces all the main protagonists were not only representatives of the creative class but also necessarily poetic personalities. This struck me so much that I set aside a separate folder for adventures. I was sure that careful reading would eventually provide me with quite a bit of amusement.

Poetry was completely impossible to make sense of. Not a single poem was really a poem, nor could a single verse be truly called a verse. The preference for secondary headlines was mainly from the spectrum of musical genres, ranging from barcarolles and intermezzos to oratorios and symphonies.

Especially confusing were librettos for totally unknown works that the authors presented as widely known and truly magnificent pieces, that just weren't written yet. One such work (an oratorio for an academic theatre) attracted my interest. In a letter (yes, a letter) preceding the future masterpiece "Song of Songs to the Dictatorship of the Proletariat" or "Duets of Leaders and Great Renegades," the author, the Invisible Incognito, informed his associate, that is, the presumed co-author, that this piece had come to him in a dream on his new bed. The author then asked the associate whether he possessed poetic and musical abilities, and most importantly, knowledge of musical score writing. If yes - read the libretto, otherwise pass it on to someone who has already mastered the required skills. (Mastery of score writing was essential.)

Of course, I had no moral right to read the libretto, but curiosity was irresistible and I turned the page.

ACT ONE

Scene 1. LEADERS AND TIME

The stage is a glade in a dark forest: century-old oaks, cedars and other mighty trees symbolise the proletarians of all countries. Some sparse shrubbery on one side - the audience. The sound of wind can be heard in the treetops. Ominous music emerges - write the score. The anxiety intensifies – again, write the score. Suddenly everything falls silent, waiting. The sun peeks out of the clouds. From afar, rousing music approaches, barely discernible – write the score. It grows closer and closer. Karl Marx and Friedrich Engels emerge from the thicket of other mighty trees (proletariat of Western Europe). They approach the sparse shrubbery and stop - the rousing music fades away. Write Marx's aria, lyrics, and score, then Engels' aria: "A spectre is haunting Europe - the spectre of Communism." After their solo performances, they sing a duet about the great gravedigger of capitalism - again words and musical score are needed. Their singing over, the leaders depart while glancing back (they want to see who will come to replace them). A glimpse of Plekhanov, then - Lenin. Plekhanov is almost unrecognisable. Lenin - recognisable. CURTAIN.

Scene 2. TIME AND LEADERS

A glade in a dark forest. Dawn - the sunrise. The song "Whirlwinds of Danger"[36] approaches - score needed. The forest rustles, especially the cedar grove, from where gallant lads march out in orderly ranks, dressed in whatever they have. It is clear from their firm tread that these are revolutionary sailors

---

36   Iconic Soviet revolutionary march, originally from Poland (Warszawianka 1905 roku)

and soldiers, daring deserters from all the ships and battlefields. They are led by Lenin in a proletarian cap, with a red bow on his lapel and a huge wreath of roses on his shoulders. Behind him the leader's favourite traitor Trotsky, Sverdlov, both in Bolshevik leather jackets, Dzerzhinsky in a long overcoat. Stalin is not yet visible. "Whirlwinds of Danger" gives way to the score of the "March of Enthusiasts."[37] The ranks take two steps forward, one back, concealing themselves again in the cedar grove. Again, two steps forward, one back. (as a hint)[38] The ranks approach the shrubbery in this manner. It is clearly visible that the ranks are somehow childishly and exaggeratedly leaning on the left leg. (Another hint.)[39] The march fades away. From the thicket of other mighty trees emerges an enormous panel with a reproduction of Goya's "The Naked Maja." (As a counterpoint - hints and half-hints, subtext on a global scale.) Lenin performs an aria about the idealist Berkeley[40], philosophically undressing the metaphysician Mach[41] and predicting the fission of the electron. He lisps slightly, a silvery song of the revolutionary nightingale reaches for the bottomless heights - write the words and score quickly. In the shrubbery, many are already weeping. Bring in Hegel and Feuerbach and use the cue: "The naked Maja and Mach were unaware of Feuerbach. They consorted with the wrong and had no clue about the electron." The aria ends but has not yet fallen silent. A swelling chorus emerges from the cedar grove, joined by the voices from the ranks. A cantata is

---

37 Iconic Soviet song from the motion picture "Bright Path" (1940). Both the movie and the song praise the Soviet Union as an ideal country and society where everyone is happy.
38 It is a hint to Vladimir Lenin's work titled "Two steps forward, one step back."
39 "Left-Wing Communism: An Infantile Disorder" is yet another Lenin's work.
40 George Berkeley, Bishop Berkeley (1685 –1753) - Anglo-Irish philosopher.
41 Ernst Mach (1838 –1916) – Austrian physicist and philosopher.

performed about how it was too early to rebel yesterday, too late tomorrow, that they must take the Winter Palace now[42], as the night falls. Lenin does not participate in the chorus, but one can see from his eyes he is listening intently, a joyful amazement shines on his face, he is happy - write the cantata. Everything falls silent. A cloud passes over the sun. Darkness. A pause. Suddenly traitor Trotsky steps forward, blocking the view of the leader of the world proletariat. He performs an aria in which he reveals the start of the uprising - write it. (The words and score are impossibly bad. The despicable performer sings out of tune again and again. Righteous indignation in the shrubbery.)

A sunbeam bursts onto the glade. It illuminates the man on the far right in semi-military attire. (Allegory) His moustache and Caucasian rendition of Lenin's squint are impressive. Without taking his eyes off the self-indulgent wretched soloist (now is the time to knock that foul head off the shoulders), the man on the right slowly draws his sabre. Then he sharply pushes it back into the sheath - no, this would be historically premature. The sunbeam disappears. The notes of the cacophony and the traitor's latest false note blend into one. There is no more strength to endure this, it must be put to an end. The saving shot of the "Aurora," perceived as a volley, comes from behind the dark cedar grove. The traitor's vile singing dissipates in it. A solemn drumroll - write it. Once more the sun shines over the glade, so much sun. Lenin is still at the head of the ranks; the ranks are waving crimson banners. The drumroll fades. The Revolutionary Nightingale sings the song that Marx and Engels sang as a duet. The ranks of gallant lads join in. The song grows louder. There is a stirring in the shrubbery, timid at first, then everyone stands up,

---

42   This is almost a literal quote from Lenin's speech.

all joining the song: "We'll build our new world!"[43] Thunderous applause. Apotheosis. CURTAIN.

ACT TWO had the overall title "Duets of the Leaders" and began with the scene called "Lenin and Stalin." After the scene named "Khrushchev and Brezhnev," the script abruptly ended, and the author addressed me as the presumed co-author:

"Dear Comrade! We are comrades-in-pen now. If you worked on my text wholeheartedly, then the oratorio should now have no less than thirty pages, count them!

Did you make less?! That's bad, you should have expanded my writing at least threefold. Put it back and get lost; you did not work wholeheartedly. I will only talk to someone who works wholeheartedly.

Dear Invisible Friend! You got more than thirty pages of text, well done! But it's too early to relax; there are still forty-five unwritten pages of the oratorio ahead, so roll up your sleeves. Are you angry at my prodding? Don't be. At the end of the oratorio, a sincere letter awaits you, and you shall understand my Great Selflessness once and for all. (Write the score of light music and aerobics. Why? Read on, join the creative process.)"

I didn't bother reading the duet scenes of Andropov and Chernenko, Gorbachev and Yeltsin. I was interested in the sincere letter to the "Invisible Friend" that would make me once and for all understand the author's "Great Selflessness." Leafing through the pages, I noticed that the duets of the great renegades were written for unknown names instead of famous historical figures. There were some Retirw and Tsicisyph (instead of Sis-

---

43   A line from "The Internationale"

yphus, perhaps?), whose arias in the epilogue the Lord himself listens to. The renegades' names seemed quite enigmatic until I figured out to read them right to left. I didn't understand why Solzhenitsyn and Sakharov had to be encrypted. However, answers were provided in the author's concluding letter.

"Dear Accomplice! You understood why I did not say 'Comrade-in-pen' or 'Invisible Friend'? Well done! If the oratorio turned out as it came to me in a dream on that new bed, it will be perceived as the crime of the century. Take pride, you are doomed to persecution: exile, prison, perhaps even a civil execution, should stars align. Yes, the glorious fate of the creative! (The best works of all times and peoples were initially met with nothing but hostility, only later did recognition come.)

Dear Accomplice, are you prepared to go all the way to the end?! Excellent! I never doubted it… and therefore completely renounce my text of the oratorio in your favour. Now you alone will go in shackles into the bright future. But don't get too full of yourself, the crime has ripened but not yet occurred. Writing the oratorio is less than half the deed. Staging the oratorio at an academic theatre - that is the culmination to strive for. Go ahead, you will succeed: I dreamed this too. I ask only one thing, if you feel like sharing the proceeds with me, know that I will be sitting at the premiere in the centre parterre, in the third row, third seat. When they pay tribute to you after the oratorio's conclusion (as it is always done), you can raise me from my seat with a slight nod, stretch your hand in my direction, and say for all to hear - here is the man who believed in my epic creation, let's applaud him! That will be my payment, the rest is yours, my

Wondrous Genius. See you at the premiere! Respectfully yours, the Invisible Incognito."

The Great Selflessness initially amazed me - imagine that, meet him at the premiere, he'll be sitting in the centre parterre, third row, third seat. Then it filled me with trepidation: so, what was this… a prophetic dream on a new bed? A prophecy of persecution? Some truly glorious fate of the creative - bright future in shackles!

A vision came to me: a howling February wind, a twisting blizzard whiteout cutting off the feet of the people in front of me, the rusty clanking of shackles in the slush of snow. I shivered: I haven't yet dealt with prophecies of my own, and am already being presented with the new ones, thank you very much.

I carefully set aside the oratorio: these Invisible Incognitos could bring misfortune upon anyone.

PART TWO

CHAPTER 10

We've all studied ancient history, the Middle Ages, and of course, modern history. The concepts of primitive communal society, slave-owning society, feudalism, capitalism, communism, and even the Asiatic mode of production were drilled deep into our heads. However, they somehow skipped the Asiatic mode, which, according to Marx and Engels, immediately followed the primitive communal society, and they were probably right to do so. Numerous stages and levels within the communist system alone, phases from lower to higher phase, could make your head spin. And spin it did…

In general, all these gradual transitions from one stage to the next became so convoluted that I inevitably started seeking some new ways to perceive the human essence that would help me put my modest knowledge in order, sort it on shelves, so that I could access it at any time for my own, shall we say, home use.

Strangely enough, it was the headmaster of our village school who helped me with this. He taught us Russian, botany, history, and geography. I can still picture his round, glistening glasses, his pelican-like chin with a beard wrapped in it. He would repeatedly scratch the tightly seated, button-like boils under it, cautiously turning his head as he did. This unhealthy habit often caused him to mispronounce vowels, which threw us into indescribable delight. I would just choke with tears from laughter.

"Slyozkin, get out of the class!"

His professorial absentmindedness, or rather, forgetfulness, convinced us of his extraordinary intellect better than any testimonial. For instance, he could teach Russian or geography in a botany lesson. In a history class, he might test our knowledge of botany. And sometimes he would mingle all four subjects so artfully that we no longer knew which one we were being graded on.

"Well then, you good-for-nothing Slyozkin, what can you tell us about Riga?"

We were working at the school's garden plot, most of us barefoot; we took no offence at his barbs, on the contrary, we perceived them as the height of wit.

"Riga is an agricultural building with an oven for drying unthreshed grain. Sometimes a simple shed is also called a riga."

"A stake[44], comrade Slyozkin."

"A stake is a sharpened thick stick or post to which planks are nailed, for example, in a fence."

"I meant not a stake in a fence, but the grade in your grade book, because Riga is the capital of the Latvian Soviet Socialist Republic."

In short, thanks to the school principal, I made three crucial discoveries that have defined my current understanding of not only world literature and art but also, the creative personality behind each masterpiece.

In childhood and youth, we feel eternal, as immortal as gods.

---

44   The lowest mark of 1 at Soviet schools was commonly called "a stake".

We hurry time, but "the mills of gods grind slowly; there's no need for the immortals to rush." Yet we rush to grow up quickly, to graduate from school quickly, essentially, to become adults. Hence the unshakeable conviction that with each day lived, the world changes from worse to better. There you have the first postulate: childhood and youth make you think that the world moves in a spiral, as if up a winding staircase, step by step, from lower to higher.

Then comes young adulthood, followed by, or accompanied by maturity. It seems that everything is within reach, and anything is possible; the only shortage is that of time, which goes fast and is hard to keep up with. But whenever you do keep pace with it, you suddenly notice that, in a sense, you're like a hamster in a wheel. No matter how briskly you run, you're running in a circle, and the whole world before you resembles a closed loop. You can't help but recall Ecclesiastes: "The wind blows to the south and goes around to the north; round and round goes the wind and returns to where it was." You too are caught in that vortex, and hence the realization: the world does not move in a spiral but in a circle - there's your second postulate. "What has been will be again, what has been done will be done again; there is nothing new under the sun."

But maturity, too, has its limits. And although "no one can fathom everything: eyes can never be done seeing, and ears can never exhaust all the sound," you come to realise that you are not eternal, that you cannot keep up with this frenzied passing of time. It seems like it was only yesterday when you were rushing time, striving to grow up quickly. Yes, yesterday a sunny day was filled with birds singing, and the stars at night were as big as apples! Yes, just yesterday the world shone with endless colours, but today it is grey and gloomy. Where, where has it all gone?! And now your retired neighbour is angrily rapping his cane and stomping his feet at the abhorrent youth who have no respect for their elders, and thus no shame nor conscience. In the end, we come to a melancholic conclusion: everything was better yesterday than today, youth, ourselves, and the forests were greener, and the rivers were cleaner. The conclusion is that the world does indeed move in a spiral, like a winding staircase, but not from the lower step to the higher, as we thought in childhood and our youth, but the opposite way, from the higher to the lower, from better to worse. Born angels, throughout our entire life, we descend from heaven to the ground, then even lower, into the ground itself. There is my final discovery, my third postulate: the world is moving towards its end.

Three postulates, three discoveries, three shelves on which I have arranged all the literature, all works of art, philosophy, and theology, in fact, the entire world of all times and peoples.

From the heights of the first postulate, as from the angel's heaven, I can understand "Ruslan and Ludmila," "The Girl on the Ball," and "The Love for Three Oranges," perhaps better than anyone. Of course, one must think for oneself: romanticism in literature and art is one thing, and eternal teaching is quite another. Only the Orthodox Church knows that as clear as day, evil is conquered by the absence of evil. Atheists have never believed and will never believe that the struggle for justice must be waged not against an evil person but the evil within a person, because

God creates humans in His own image.

Three shelves for everyday home use; I began to rearrange and reshuffle all my goods and chattels on them for the first time. I felt like entering a new period of life that did not hold anything for me: what has been, will be again, and what has been done will be done again…

Have you ever stood atop an aqueduct observing a river in spate, bursting its banks, when the flow of the heavens and the movement of the waters mingle, and it seems like you are flying like a bird? Or… have you ever stood at wide-open doors watching the festive May Day demonstration columns, the kaleidoscope of balloons and joyful faces, answering every cheer of the clamorous radio bells with a victorious cry of "Hooray!"

I have. It was in Barnaul. My mother took me to the hospital because I had a rapid heartbeat, but they wouldn't admit us. We had to walk a long way; I couldn't keep up, so my mother had to carry me. We climbed some hill, went through a pine forest, and crossed a stream. The bridge swayed springily, and I suddenly felt my heart flutter, and I flew, flew up into the height and depth of celestial waters. Of course, I clung tightly to my mother's hair, but I was flying, and my mother was flying with me. It was so terrifying, yet so wonderful, to just dissolve into the watery depths.

My mother told the lady in a red dress later that I had fainted again, and my nose was bleeding again.

Arming herself with a stethoscope, the lady listened to my chest, and tickled by the touch of the metal disc, I laughed. I laughed, but they watched me wide-eyed, listening to something

I could not hear.

"Those are just age-related murmurs; his left ventricle will normalise as he grows older," the lady reassured my mother, while I stared at the mosaic floor of the long corridor and felt the sadness of my life for the first time.

As a farewell, the lady doctor gave me a honey cake. We didn't have anything like that at home and I decided to bring it back to show to our mongrel Jack and our cow Zorka, so they would know I had been to the city.

That day we couldn't leave because all buses were over-crowded, so we slept on the floor at the railway station since the new bus station was still under construction. My mother made me a bed under a bench so no one would step on me, and I stayed there like Jack in his doghouse, pleased to be protected on all sides while my mother, though not beside me, also lay on the floor and could always see me with her big eyes, just as I could always see her. I also liked how strangers' feet kept passing close by as they hurried somewhere, and some would stop to tell me that they, too, were as tired as my little feet.

I awoke with a premonition of great joy. The sun peeked through the vast windows opening into the hall and strolled its glistening rays between the lofty columns. It was everywhere, so much of it that it seemed like my mother, and I were in an enchanted palace. It was not at all surprising that we were alone in it, that the sun had leaned over my mother and, without touching her face, released one of its sunny spots onto her palm. I reached for it; her hand responded affectionately, and the spot hopped onto her forearm. I felt merry, realising that although my mother slept, her eyes closed, her hand still remembered me and even urged me to sleep a little longer. I did not obey.

I crawled out of my little den and ran through the sunny halls toward the joyful hubbub to which I had awoken, which seemed to bubble within me. I already knew that the real music and laughter were outdoors.

The double doors, massive as cowshed gates, were wide open. I stopped at the opening and froze. Looking from inside the hall and over the heads of people standing on the steps outside, I saw a torrent of technicolour balloons and faces. Even if the people had been standing on the porch or even in the doorway, they still could not have obscured this flood of thousands upon thousands of radiant eyes.

"Peace to the world!" the radio bells rang out in unison.

"Hooray, hooray!" voices resounded into the azure heights.

Kettledrums and brass cymbals sang as if they were opening the gates to spring.

I stood facing the opening, forgetting everything. I had never seen so many green branches and garlands of white blossoms. I had never seen such a multitude of doves and balloons soaring into the sky all at once. And of course, I had never heard a brass band or voices thundering "Hooray!" together.

Yes, I had never seen this many joyful faces and eyes flowing past me in a single, swelling river.

"Peace to the world!" the radio bells boomed again, followed by "Hooray, hooray!" rising aloft.

"Peace to the world," I said aloud, for I had already learned to read those words in my ABC book.

I spoke these familiar words aloud, but they did not seem like words; more like the gates of heaven flung open.

"Hooray, hooray," I sang timidly, trying the marvellous word on my tongue, and suddenly I felt my heart flutter, and I flew, flew toward the balloons into the fathomless heights.

We arrived back in our village before dark. The bus stopped by the dairy farm, and as we walked home, people kept stopping my mother to ask about my health. No one asked me anything; I watched the puddles simmering in the sun and felt the familiar sadness of my life again. I did not understand my mother's worry over my fainting and nosebleeds, for I had already noticed that they always occurred when I felt terrified yet wonderful. So, I pitied my mother's conversations, and when the neighbours came by to have tea from the samovar to honour the holiday, I told them all that neither fainting nor nosebleeds hurt me at all; on the contrary, I flew high, high, like a lark or a merlin. Everyone looked at me very solemnly, while the hunchbacked old woman Korzhikha, whose crutches somewhat spooked me, cackled:

"That's right, my dear, one day you'll fly away for good..."

"Oh, come now, Evdokimovna, God forbid," my mother said disapprovingly, giving me a gentle, pensive look, the way she looked at photos of my father and pictures from her past life before I existed or when I was just a tiny baby.

I took the honey cake which had been in my mother's bag this whole time and went outside. The chickens paid me no mind, but Jack immediately emerged from his doghouse and happily rubbed against my knees. He even pretended to bite my legs as I crossed the yard to see our Zorka.

Zorka rested on fresh straw, facing the door. She was chewing her cud but stopped, heaving a loud sigh, and grew pensive as I squatted beside her and offered her a piece of the cake. I pleaded with her to eat a piece, but she kept musing, so I started stroking her. She turned her head, and wrinkles on her neck rippled under my fingers like little streams. For some reason, I no longer wished to tell her I had been to the city.

"Don't worry, Zorka… inside I'm already grown-up and understand everything. This summer I'll tell Mama I'll graze you until I start school."

I told Zoryika that I would pasture her beyond the stream, where the tall grass grew, and at noon during the heat of the day, she would stand in the water at the third pool under the willow bush, where there were fewer pesky bugs and horseflies.

Zoryika's horns shone with a soft lustre in the dim light, and the white, curly hair on her forehead glistened and sparkled at my touch. She stretched toward me, right toward my face, and I saw that her eyes glistened, tears flowing abundantly from them. She heaved another loud sigh, exhaling some kind of homey breath that made me feel not so much small as not quite so grown-up after all.

Jack greeted me faithfully when I left the barn. He immediately spied the cake in my pocket and the piece in my hand, and realised I was not as little as Zoryika had thought. He saw me exactly as I wanted everyone to see me, especially the crutch-wielding old woman Korzhikha.

"You're so smart," I told him, offering a piece of the cake, stroking him, and rejoicing with him in his cleverness while he kept poking his nose right into the very pocket holding the cake, nuzzling affectionately.

I sat on the porch steps while Jack settled on its deck. Mottled, with black-and-white markings on his pricked ears with seemingly broken tips, he gazed at me with such devotion and attention, as if we had already agreed to eat the cake together.

"No, no, we had no such agreement," I protested, turning away to watch the setting sun.

Pink rays slid over the woven fence, and glass jars on stakes glowed from within as if they were electric bulbs. The space of the street beyond the collective farm's water tower expanded, dark haystacks now resembling a herd of elephants descending to a water hole. There was so much open space receding into the sky, and in the sky so many fabulous clouds seemed to graze the earth, that I could not help recalling the city with its garlands of coloured balloons, red flags, and white doves soaring aloft in such numbers that at times it appeared the whole festive city was taking wing.

"Peace to the world!" I cried rapturously, standing tall.

My heart fluttered, but before I could feel myself flying, I saw Jack, who let out a piteous wail and leapt up to fly with me. And I did not fly; I could not leave Jack behind.

I jumped down from the step and, embracing him around the neck, whirled with him. Then I sat back on the step, breaking the cake into pieces, sharing some with Jack and eating some myself, licking the yellow jam that oozed between my fingers.

"No one else has a cake as delicious as this," I told Jack. "The lady doctor gave it to us for our holiday."

I mentioned the holiday and nearly choked on the realisation. To dispel all my doubts, I ran up the porch steps, turned my face directly toward the sun, and found myself once more at the celebration amid the thunderous radio bells, rousing music, laughter, and songs.

"Peace to the world," I said loudly and clearly, as if reading from my ABC.

My heart gave its familiar flutter, but I did not reach for Jack, who was rubbing against my knees. I knew for certain I would not faint, not now, not ever again. I was convinced I had grown, and my malady had let me be.

From that day on, I indeed no longer suffered fainting spells, and blood stopped running from my nose. Of course, I could have forgotten that festive day, but it was precisely then that the understanding came to me: the power of imagination can overcome any illness, and not just illness...

CHAPTER 11

On Saturday night, I dreamt for the first time about sitting in a private office at a pristine white table, and a waiter brought me borscht, steaming mutton with green parsley, and coffee with cream. Swallowing my saliva, I tried my best to show the waiter that I wasn't hungry, but it was still time for lunch. Realising that lunch was a peculiar and insignificant ritual for me, the waiter asked for permission to give the meal to a starving poet who was supposedly waiting behind a curtain. Somehow, I knew that the starving poet was me, Mitya Slyozkin, so I waved my hand with exaggerated nonchalance, allowing the waiter to take the tray away. I assumed that since I was me, there was no one behind the curtain, and the meal would be returned.

The waiter pulled back the curtain, and to my horror, I saw myself dressed in the familiar gown made of a blanket with three horizontal stripes across the shoulders. It was rather unexpected, especially the humiliating scene of Mitya Slyozkin reaching his hands out for the meal.

The waiter looked back in panic, obviously recognising me, and in that same second, anticipating a dirty scandal over a bowl of borscht, I woke up.

Upon waking, for some time I felt a sense of shame, then regret, and finally hunger. Encouraged by stomach spasms, my imagination became so inflamed that very soon I could no longer think about anything else. As lightly dressed as I was, I rushed off to the grocery store.

I ran in my worn underwear and a t-shirt, with a deck of "the tattered" in my pocket. Every cell in my body was screaming out for food. However, I tried my best to maintain the demeanour of just having a routine morning jog. Perhaps I was running too briskly and too purposefully. Jokes were tossed at me, along the lines of: "Hey, comedian, you forgot your pants; they're chasing you!"

Of course, I didn't consider that I has awoken too late for a morning jog. No one in the store was willing to recognise me as a lone fitness enthusiast. Somehow, everyone and all at once unanimously decided that I was a shameless mug and a boor. Outraged customers, sacrificing their place in line, literally carried me out of the store. I almost cried from vexation. Thank God, the ever-closed kiosk at the bus stop was open, and I managed to get two packs of cookies and a can of cod in tomato sauce, as a "burden" to the cookies[45].

I ate the first pack of cookies right away at the kiosk. Well, I did not really notice when and how I ate them. I even rummaged a little in the bag: are they really gone?! I ate the second pack with less haste, controlling my actions. I deliberately walked over to the newspaper display board and munched absentmindedly, as if immersed in reading. In reality, I was enjoying the amazingly tasty word invented by the Soviet milling industry and embossed on my cookies - "Privet!"[46]. Privet! - I mentally responded to each cookie, and only after finishing them did I bother to read the

---

45   In the Soviet Union it was a common practice to bundle highly demanded goods with items that were not in demand yet produced in abundance. However, unlike in the West, these additional items were neither included in the price nor discounted, just added as a burden you had to pay for to be able to buy the desired goods.
46   Very common informal and friendly greeting, "Hi!"

newspaper heading and date: "N City Komsomolets[47], August 20…" "I should call Soyuzpechat[48] and ask why fresh newspapers are posted at our bus stop only occasionally?" - I thought briefly, and in the same second, forgot about my hunger, my failed attempt to look like a fitness enthusiast and just about everything else.

On the front page, just below the article about the Komsomol youth brigade of the suburban state farm "Uzbekistan" titled "Who will replace Aunt Glasha?," I saw the familiar photograph of a smiling high school girl blowing soap bubbles. And next to it there was my poem "Angels of Love," renamed "At the Swan Lake" and dedicated to Rosa Purpurova. (The dedication puzzled me; I didn't know whether to rejoice or to object. The thing is, Rozochka's maiden family name was Purpurik.)

In the line "I started to cherish my dreams …" I found an extra word inserted for some unknown reason: "I started to honestly cherish my dreams…" Good Lord, what a blunder: if one can "honestly" cherish one's dreams, then one can also "dishonestly" cherish one's dreams. "How exactly, will they justify that…?" I mentally protested, with "they" referencing not so much Vasya Kruzhkin, but journalists at the Komsomol life department. Undoubtedly, their hand had also touched the dedication. (Rozochka sometimes called the editorial office accounting department and introduced herself by her maiden name.) Stealthily taking the newspaper from the board, I jogged back to the dormitory. (Incidentally, this time, passersby paid no attention to me.) Carefully studying the publication and the entire front page (the photo essay and the poem, outlined by a single line, were visually

---

47   Member of Komsomol, a communist organization for young adults.
48   Major Soviet newspaper printing and distribution agency.

perceived as a single post), I concluded that the poem was presented tastefully, and looked quite good alongside the picture of the girl, as opposed to being buried among the newspaper snippets. I gradually got used to the new title given by Vasya. Judging by the neighbouring "Who will replace Aunt Glasha?" headline, he didn't skimp, he made an effort and put his entire golden reserve into play. Undoubtedly, he did it in the hope that just as his "Uncle Grisha" was once noticed "upstairs," "Aunt Glasha" would also get attention… Yes, "Vasya the "Little Jew" would give anyone a hundred-step head start," I was happy for him, hoping that my poem would not be overlooked either… and that if Rozochka came across the newspaper, she would certainly read it. And after reading it, she would forgive me and return home to the dorm. In a word, I "honestly cherished my dreams…" and believed that what I wanted to achieve by publishing the poem would become true precisely.

Of course, I regretted that I hadn't come across the newspaper earlier; otherwise, I would have gone to the editorial office long ago and obtained the author's copies. Now I'll have to wait until Monday, but no problem, I'll wait. My imagination obligingly conjured up pictures of Rozochka's joyful return. I didn't even think about Soyuzpechat not posting fresh newspapers since Tuesday for some reason.

In the morning, having left two notes for Rozochka, one on the door of her room and the other at the front desk, I set off for the editorial office. My mood was high, the sun was warm, and the town was fragrant after the night rain. I deliberately went through the Kremlin Park and even sat on a bench by the fountain for a while. Myriads of sunlit sparks merging into a rainbow, the fresh scent of greenery and the delicate aroma of flowers—everything screamed inspiration… I suddenly felt poetic, touched by a poem's close breath.

> A thousand years, a moment's span,
> A planet wide, a grain of sand.
> In all the things God's face revealed,
> The breath of light in all concealed.

The realisation that I too, whatever I am, bear the face of God within me, made me feel so good that I involuntarily laughed out loud and had to leave the bench. Two old women, peacefully conversing, suddenly fell silent and looked at me apprehensively. Feeling their suspicious gazes on my back, I stepped into the rainbow and emerged as if from under a shower. This made me stop feeling poetic. I decided not to go into the editorial office right away, to dry off quicker, but to walk a bit near the House of All Newspapers (HAN) and, purely by chance, I chose the sidewalk under the library windows. The choice proved unfortunate. Two athletic figures leaned out from a second-floor window and ordered me to stop loitering under the windows. This demand puzzled me.

"Who exactly are you; introduce yourselves," I said as politely as I could.

"If we introduce ourselves," the dark-haired one replied, "then you definitely won't be able to pick up your bones. Did you get that, boozer?"

Without waiting for my answer, he ordered the blond one to go down and give the "wet chicken" a good beating. The blond rather skillfully spat through his teeth aiming to hit me, and said lazily, as if we had been talking for half a day already:

"Did you hear, boozer? Beat it, or I'll smear you against the wall."

God, I couldn't wrap my head around them talking to me so provocatively and rudely not just somewhere, but at the HAN, in its intellectual centre, the city's finest library. A thought flashed through my mind: maybe they're plumbers recruited from among convicts?! Quite possible, books are a highly desired commodity…

I made a lightning-quick decision to get to the nearest phone booth and call the authorities.

Meanwhile, the blond continued:

"I'm giving you ten seconds to think it over, boozer."

He disappeared, and immediately a storm ladder tumbled down from the neighbouring window, clattering as the steps unrolled, a real marine ladder made of tarred hemp ropes.

The dark-haired guy poked his head out and without taking his eyes off his watch, threatened:

"You have three seconds left, boozer!"

Never in my life, before or after, have I experienced such strong irritation at being called a name. Picking up the first piece of brick that came to hand, I said I would smash the head of anyone who tried to climb down the ladder.

I stepped back from the sidewalk and, as a precaution, retreated beneath a tree.

This time, four heads immediately poked out of the neighbouring window. I was extremely surprised to recognise one of them as our editor. He also recognised me.

"Mitya, is that you?!"

I came out from under the tree and tossed the brick to my feet. I didn't know what to think.

The editor approached the window where the dark-haired brute was standing, and they began to heatedly discuss something in hushed tones. Then the editor looked out and told me to climb up. I hesitated: was he in cahoots with the "plumbers"? Sensing my doubts, the editor reassured me:

"Climb up, no one will touch you."

"Why by ladder, if it's much easier to enter through the doors?" I asked.

For some reason, he immediately got angry and even snapped at me not to prattle or attract gawkers. His behaviour was more than suspicious. I deliberately played for time.

The blond suddenly asked, indifferently leaning over the ladder:

"Listen, where did you come from?"

He turned his head toward the window where the editor was:

"But what... maybe this wet chicken is really a spy from the GKChP?"[49]

The editor disappeared and replied to something that I didn't catch; warm laughter responded from within the library.

---

49   Russian acronym (pronounced *gekachepe,* stress on the last syllable) for the State Committee on the State of Emergency - a self-proclaimed political body that existed in the Soviet Union from 19 to 21of August 1991, created by the group of communist party bureaucrats in attempt to overthrow Michail Gorbachev.

"Hey you, poet… chronicler… poet-chronicler, come on up, or we'll take the ladder away!"

Jovial benign prodding, or maybe invitations, rained down from above, but the ladder did indeed start to rise in jerks.

"Wait! Ah, what the heck," I said, grabbing onto the ladder.

My sudden resolution elicited joyful approval. I wasn't so much climbing up the ladder as being pulled up by it.

A dozen friendly hands were supporting me when I was climbing onto the windowsill, almost dropped me onto the side-walk in the process.

"If you want something messed up, put the Komsomol in charge," I summed up, causing excessively joyful laughter.

And no wonder, most of the young people (I counted about a dozen) represented the cream of the City of N Komsomol. In any case, I immediately identified the dark-haired one as the head of the industrial and rural youth department and the blond as his deputy. Of course, they didn't recognise me (and who am I to them?), but they did notice that I was wearing shoes without socks. The dark-haired one pulled up my pants and asked me to stand like that on the windowsill. He darted behind a bookshelf and resurfaced a second later with a video camera. Filming my legs, he commented:

"One cannot make a revolution in white gloves (there might not be any). The democratic revolution must be made in white socks, for with just a little imagination, every ragamuffin becomes an arch-revolutionary! However, before us is no ordinary person. An urgent order has come from under the table: for outstanding services in the field of cultural enlightenment, to award the future bourgeois with two pairs of white socks."

Indeed, they handed me two pairs of white socks, after which, to sparse applause, I was invited to the lobby for a snack.

"It's time for lunch, and for some, a lynching," they joked behind my back.

Incidentally, I noticed that everyone, without exception, wore white socks. In general, everything was happening as in a dream, very vividly and very implausibly. Four joined writing tables laden with all sorts of food and lots of vodka bottles. Young men dozing on the sofas. Some shuffling footsteps downstairs, on the first floor, and upstairs, on the third. Constantly ringing telephones and the very atmosphere of some ostentatious, ungenuine festivity caused an involuntary tension in me. If it weren't for the editor, who took me under his wing, I don't know how my visit to the HAN would have ended. I can well imagine that the "white socks," as I mentally dubbed them, could have beaten me up quite easily. Thank God, as he sat down next to me, the editor instructed me in a whisper to answer all questions with "I don't know, I'm seeing this for the first time."

The blond deftly pulled the cork and poured me a full glass of "Embassy" vodka.

"A penalty shot - to the lynching!" he proclaimed.

"No penalty shots," the editor said without raising his voice, and, exchanging glances with the dark-haired one, explained meaningfully: "He has a different assignment."

The dark-haired one nodded in agreement, and someone, one of the latecomers, said that each should determine his own norm. And indeed, everyone poured for themselves. I splashed just a little into the bottom of the glass and felt that my indifference to vodka aroused suspicion. People started asking me in turn: who I was, where I was from, why I had appeared here, and if I knew the editor or anyone else present.

To all the questions I answered succinctly: I don't know, I'm seeing this for the first time.

"So, you don't even know your own name?" I was asked insinuatingly by a young man with a moustache in a dark blue suit, who came up from the first floor and, unlike everyone else, was drinking kefir instead of vodka.

Everyone at the table fell silent, even the editor stopped eating, and only the one who asked continued to chew his sandwich.

"I don't know," I answered. "But I have a guess."

I pushed my chair back, took off my shoes and demonstratively put on the white socks. I put them on in total silence, feeling the heavy, oppressive gazes on me. When I finished, a white terrycloth towel was passed to me across the table. I don't know why, but I suddenly felt afraid. "Well, well, a white towel," I thought in confusion.

Meanwhile, the moustached guy invited me to sit down and, raising his already high eyebrows, asked with interest what this guess of mine was, if it wasn't a secret, of course.

And again, dead silence ensued. The editor rather noticeably stepped on my foot but didn't even glance at me. Just as he was peeling a boiled egg, he continued to peel, completely absorbed by it. In this way, he was warning me: say nothing superfluous.

"I guess some ragamuffin was called the Bourgeois," I said

overly loudly to hide the excitement that had gripped me.

"Nothing of the sort, he's being silly," the editor said impassively and immediately explained: "Poet-Chronicler, with a hyphen, but Chronicler should also be capitalised."

He somehow swallowed the egg in one gulp and froze as if listening to its progress down his oesophagus. The man with the moustache smiled, and many at the table laughed. In truth, I never did understand what the laughter referred to, the Bourgeois or the Poet-Chronicler, or to the egg swallowed in one gulp. In any case, they left me alone. Although I ate little and drank even less, the lunch made me so drowsy that in response to the blonde's casual question (he was sitting across from me and, as the host, was sharing his snacks with me) about what to serve next, I answered that perhaps nothing, because I wanted to sleep rather badly.

The moustached man rose from his seat and guffawed:

"Excellent neural resilience, truly admirable!"

Those at the table smiled at me, and I felt such sincere, friendly warmth, as if I had suddenly, unexpectedly, committed an insanely brave act and saved everyone present from certain death.

The guy with the moustache asked the editor and the dark-haired one to come down to see him after lunch and instructed everyone else to act as per the schedule and proceed with their direct duties. I don't know what captivated me about him: his refined manners, his inner composure, or his Olympic calm, but I felt that he was the boss. He was no upstart, no Swiss admiral, but most likely a military, perhaps a naval officer, specially invited to oversee this enterprise. What enterprise, invited by whom? It remained a mystery which, strangely enough, I didn't want to unravel.

CHAPTER 12

I pulled my chair up to the wall, crossed my arms at my chest, and prepared to doze off. Through my drowsiness, I heard strange conversations about how the House of All Newspapers would evidently be under arrest until the trial; that an enormous number of complaints had come in from both sides (of course, I had no clue which sides or whose) about some literary worker who had styled himself as either a Poet-Chronicler or a Bourgeois, but who was doomed either way. I had a vision of being a Samovar-Bourgeois, fat, potbellied, with a faucet in place of a navel. I stood pompously, hands on hips, in the middle of some huge table, with one and only task: to allow no tea under any circumstance to enter the glasses reaching out from all sides, each set into a sort of a living glass holder. No one knew better than me that as soon as the faucet was opened, I, as the Samovar-Bourgeois, would immediately disappear, because all my chubbiness was in my "unwitting tearfulness…." They pulled me, pushed me, shook me so unceremoniously that I woke up.

"Well, truly admirable neural resilience! Sleeping like a groundhog!" the editor noted cheerfully and told me to follow him. We went through the library, past the bookshelves, through some partitions and found ourselves in a small room with one window, a chair, and a table with a telephone, the receiver off the hook, making short beeps.

The editor sat on the table and put the receiver back, without even looking.

"Make yourself comfortable," he pointed at the chair, "and tell me everything, the whole unvarnished truth: why you came here, what did you need, who sent you? In general, everything, straight up, for your own good," the editor warned with a sternness that suggested he already had undeniable evidence incriminating me.

"No one sent me. I came on my own, I wanted to get author's copies with my publication…"

Suddenly, the telephone rang. The editor stopped me and picked up the receiver just as unseeing as when he put it down.

"Listening carefully, editor of 'N City Komsomolets.' Yes, yes, this is the hotline."

He covered the mouthpiece with his palm and handed the receiver to me:

"Listen, but don't say anything, I'll talk to him myself."

"Reporting with all diligence and responsibility," I heard a distinctly anxious, husky baritone. "On Friday, the fourteenth of August of this year, the head of your newspaper's literary union, Dmitry Slyozkin, acting under the guise of a literary worker, collected seven rubles from each newly arrived member at the meeting. The purpose of doing so was to publish the 'Book of Books' to glorify Soviet totalitarianism and to somehow support Yanayev, Kryuchkov, Yazov, Pavlov, Pugo, and other diehard GK-ChP plotters. Slyozkin plans to arrive at the editorial office on the day of the Assumption of the Holy Mother of God, August 28th. I recommend grabbing him right then and there." A long pause followed, then the question: was this written down?

I returned the receiver, not knowing what to think.

"No, no, repeat the last sentence," the editor asked and whispered to me to move closer and listen with him: the most interesting part is coming now.

After a short pause, he asked the caller:

"Your last name, first name, and patronymic?"

An uncertain cough came through the receiver.

"Well, that won't do. They announced on the radio that one can testify anonymously."

"Good Lord, this is the head of the literary union, my Lev Nikolayevich!"

The editor agreed that in general no names are needed, but in Slyozkin's case it was different.

"He's been caught and taken into custody, but denies any guilt, says the money for the 'Book of Books' was provided voluntarily. So, a cross-examination is required."

Another cough came through the receiver.

"Personally, I didn't contribute any money."

"Well, that's good," approved the editor. "You'll be above all suspicion and that will further aid the investigation of local GK-ChP accomplices," he pronounced the last words as if reading a full case title right from a folder lying in front of him.

In response, the receiver was hung up on the other end. The editor also hung up but put the receiver back on the table. Seeing my confused, even dejected state (I was totally bewildered), he said:

"Don't you see, Mitya, you're surrounded on all sides, there's no use denying it - spill it."

I didn't understand what was happening. My head was

bursting with questions, which precipitated like radioactive salt, destroying my sanity. At times it seemed that I had gone crazy, my brain refused to serve me. The headman is afraid of something – of what? Who are these diehard GKChP plotters and why am I suspected of being their mole? Questions, questions and not a single sensible answer, some total "totalitarianism"! Laughing nervously, I pulled three packs of money from my jacket's inside pockets and placed them on the table.

The editor silently stood up, slowly pulling out the table's top drawer. I saw packs of twenty-five-ruble notes lying in three-layer rows and bound with bank paper strips. "Where had all this money come from and why was he showing it to me?! Could it be a bank… and I'm being set up?! Why me?! 'Totalitarianism'!"

I leaned back in the chair, feeling how the avalanche of new questions made me feel irredeemably stupid. Sensing that I was shaken by what I had seen, the editor pushed the drawer closed just as slowly as he had opened it.

"So, Mitya," he laughed, "I don't take bribes."

The editor handed me the subcutaneous money, which seemed, even though paltry and grubby, so homey and dear, like newspaper clippings of my published poems, compared to money in the drawer. Those sleek, taut packs came with a whiff of cold alienation; they made me almost physically feel the chill of some otherworldly breeze.

"And so, in your opinion, what awaits me?" I asked indifferently and giggled idiotically, surprisingly even for myself. It was the most inappropriate time to remember the letter from the Invisible Incognito, in which he prophesied the Wondrous Genius's march into the Bright Future in shackles. I giggled because I easily imagined myself as the Wondrous Genius.

The editor handed me a glass of water from the decanter he kept on the windowsill. He sensed that I was not myself.

"Mitya, calm down! I give you my word, there's no criminal activity here" (he tapped on the table drawer). "Answer me: why did you come here, with what purpose? And you'll see, I'll also answer all your questions."

After sipping some water, I repeated that no one had sent me anywhere. I had come to the HAN of my own accord. After all, I had the right to come to work and a right to get author's copies of the newspaper where my poem was published. And then, who are these GKChP-ists and why should I be their mole?

"GKChP-ists are the enemies of democracy. And you know this as well as I do," the editor said. "Otherwise, why would they be holding Gorbachev in Foros[50]?!"

My widened eyes, my surprise, and of course my stupid questions, clearly bewildered the editor.

"Mitya, either you're pretending, or you've been living under a rock! Don't you read newspapers, watch TV, listen to the radio? Do you meet people in the dorm, or do you live in a garbage bin?"

Of course, he didn't want to insult me, but that he did. I got angry and told him that he was very perspicacious: yes, I don't read, don't watch, and don't listen! I felt so offended that I appeared such a fool, sitting in front of him, that a lump rose in my throat. So as not to give myself away, I blew my nose and, surreptitiously wiping my eyes, saw that I hadn't blown my nose

---

50   The coup of August 1991 caught Mikhail Gorbachev in his summer residence in Crimea, where he was blocked from any movement and communication by armed forces on coup leaders' orders.

into a handkerchief, but into the bonus, that is, the democratic pair of white socks that had just been foisted on me. He saw it too, and we exchanged glances. Realizing that he would no longer understand anything, I told him to just stop thinking: my wife had left me. And totally involuntarily, I blew my nose again.

The editor believed me. I learned strange things from him: about the GKChP coup, about the democratic revolution and, most amazingly, about my direct participation (on a regional scale) in these fateful historical events.

It turned out that immediately after the issue with my poem "At the Swan Lake," dedicated to Rosa Purpurova, came out, the editor himself received a call from the First Secretary of the regional Party committee, who said, making no effort to sugar-coat his threats, that for publishing the anti-Party poem with soap bubbles, he himself, the editor, and I, the author, would suffer severely due to the state of emergency.

"This is a total outrage, mockery and a direct call to rebellion," he said and promised to deal with us shortly.

Thank God, what happened next was the democratic revolution! But even then, things didn't turn out well for the editor or me. TASS[51] reported that some regions had supported the coup, and the most zealous had put "odes" glorifying the coup plotters on the newspaper's front pages, even citing my poem published in "N... City Komsomolets" as an example. How could I have known that the ballet "Swan Lake," broadcast continuously for three days on all TV channels, would become the calling card of the coup? The editor and I ended up between a rock and a hard place.

---

51   Telegraph Agency of the Soviet Union, the major Soviet news service.

"What about Vasya Kruzhkin?" I asked the editor.

It was he who had come up with the headline for my poem and the innovative page overall. Of course, I didn't explain anything to the editor. I was just curious how Vasya had extricated himself from the mess he had single-handedly created and dragged us into, not out of malice, but purely by chance.

The editor hopelessly waved his hand: what can you expect from the "Little Jew"?!

"He ran off on an assignment and made it in time to escape all this. Went back to his historical homeland… He'll now be chopping wood there, replacing both Aunt Glasha and Uncle Grisha."

The editor laughed somewhat joylessly at his own joke and advised me to urgently leave for somewhere far away too.

I said that for now I couldn't leave, what if my wife came back!

The editor threw up his hands in exasperation:

"Well, Mitya, you're something else! There's a revolution in the country, the whole society is cracking at the seams, foundations of the state are crumbling, any minute a new father of the nation could emerge, and you're like – 'what if my wife comes back'!"

And he started shaming me for being worse than the worst wimp. On one side of the scale is the fate of the world, and on the other is that of the smallest molecule, invisible to the naked eye, and what?! For a person calling himself a Poet, the fate of the molecule outweighs all the fates of the world!

"A joke, nothing more!" the editor summed up heatedly and, making no effort to hide his sarcasm (he was trying to sting me more painfully), mocked me as if in horror: "Can't leave, no way, what if the wife comes back!"

He did it rather amusingly, theatrically convincingly, but I didn't laugh. I felt sad, although I understood that all in all he was right and if I was worthy of anything, it was surely ridicule.

"You see," I said, "it's not a matter of her just coming back. The whole thing is that she might suddenly come back, and I'm not there. You see?"

"I don't understand, and I don't want to understand," the editor answered indignantly.

I reached into my pocket for a handkerchief (I had suddenly got a runny nose, had I stepped into the rainbow so unfortunately, or what?) and, remembering my ill-fated sock escapade, stilled my hand, afraid of making another mistake.

The editor, catching my gaze, smirked (he understood everything and saw through me). He placed the receiver down on the telephone and stared out the window as if thinking about something other than me.

In this situation, it would be stupid to try to prove anything. It's disgusting to be afraid of looking ridiculous when you understand that you already are ridiculous.

Overcoming myself, I pulled out the handkerchief (I am sometimes granted with unlikely strokes of luck) and blew my nose loudly, even triumphantly.

The editor looked at me in astonishment, as if he couldn't believe that someone without care about the fates of the world had a handkerchief. He was put to shame. As if nothing had happened, I asked him why, if the clouds were gathering over us both, he didn't leave too?

I won't go into excessive detail. At that time, I learned things which I preferred to keep quiet ever after. Judge for yourselves: those taut packs of twenty-five-ruble notes turned out to be just a small voluntary donation from the very first "New Russians." Yes, yes, donations for the emerging democracy and reforms. Who were they, the very first? Back then they were called profiteers, bloodsuckers, in short, criminals.

So, what happened? A sort of castling took place: the party elite voluntarily crawled under the table, and the Komsomol elite, nurtured by them, sat down at it. Initially, orders from under the table were followed unconditionally. Only later did the quick-witted students trample their teachers. Luckily, those had already laid themselves down underfoot.

Implausible, you say? I didn't believe it myself.

"You're so naive, Mitya," the editor then told me. "We, the whole country, are all in for democracy, but where do you get democrats from?! That's the paradox, we don't have either democrats or coup plotters. Otherwise, we wouldn't have to put on white socks and shut down our own newspapers for supporting the coup. It's like everyone is playing the military-patriotic 'Zarnitsa' game[52]: we split into friends and foes and we're fighting a mock war. But the victims will be real because in every game, someone inevitably takes advantage to settle long-standing scores and, in this case, for real, with violence. Remember 'Zarnitsa;' here, the game is a revolution on the scale of a great power, no, on a global scale! There will be victims, and they will not be insignificant. And people like you, Mitya, nearsighted, not of this world, overly trusting, overly straightforward, will be the first to fall."

---

52   An open air war game for communist youth.

I remember being offended by being cast the role of the victim, but he said that if it weren't for him, I would have already been lynched during lunch. Because they, the "white socks," were pining for the real coup plotters, and here, according to the testimony of the folk avengers (meaning the informants), the real coup plotter had shown up - Mitya Slyozkin, the mole.

During our conversation, the telephone rang several times, but there was always a mysterious silence on the line. Every half hour, the editor would leave, evidently to see the man with the moustache. Sometime in the afternoon, they ushered me out. They were expecting visitors from the concrete plant, who were supposed to smash all the windows in the HAN, and then in the former Communist Party city committee building, in support of the coup.

As a farewell, the editor gave me a pack of newspapers with my poem and a notebook filled with denunciations from cover to cover.

"Read it, Mitya," he advised me as I was descending the ladder. "It makes curious reading. Maybe Vasya Kruzhkin wasn't so wrong to have run away..."

CHAPTER 13

On the day of the Assumption of the Holy Mother of God, I went to another meeting of the literary union, as planned. I was in a super-combative mood. I couldn't wait not just to give them the money back, but to get rid of it as quickly as possible. But above all, I longed to get rid of the literary union members; I wanted to toss them out on their butts. Yes, exactly that! I mentally rehearsed my throne speech in which I intended to say after handing over the money: "And now, would-be classics, the likes of Pushkins, Gogols, Tolstoys, Nekrasovs, and so on and so forth… I release you to the four winds. Go in peace to your children and grandchildren, but God forbid you ever write again, or I'll tear your arms off!"

Of course, I understood that tearing arms off was a bit extreme… But giving a mere hundred lashes for every misused word, as Leo Tolstoy suggested, seemed to me an undeserved mercy and even an indulgence to all sorts of graphomaniacs. We really needed them incinerated for the sake of Russian literature, I thought while preparing for the meeting, this would be brutal but fair retribution. Everything that had pleased me about the members before now only caused disgust. My U-turn was explained not so much by their false denunciations against me, though by that too, but more by their incurable inability to express themselves. I was gnashing my teeth from the mere thought that the "selected works" in the notebook came not from some trivial scoundrels, but from supposedly gifted people, people of literary talent.

Most of the denunciations began with the words: "Writing to you is a veteran worker, a retiree, one of the Lermontovs on behalf of all the Lermontovs of the regional youth literary union (with the total count of five heads as of August 22nd) ..." Or: "...one of the Turgenevs on behalf of all the Turgenevs..." Or: "...Shakespeare on behalf of all the Shakespeares," and so on. Only the names and the number of heads varied. All twenty-six denunciations were dated August 22nd and 23rd (the "hotline" open for informants by the new authorities was abolished after that). Just by quick counting, I established that each group of would-be classics included three to four people – heads – on average. I wish I hadn't established that. The all-too-familiar reproduction of Perov's "Hunters at Rest" hanging over the dormitory watchman's table, which no visitor could avoid passing, began to haunt me with its sudden metamorphoses. It was right on the day of the meeting that I walked past and was dumbstruck: instead of hunters, I saw long-haired Shakespeares! And they weren't telling each other their tall tales but composing an anonymous collective letter. If only I didn't know who it was about!

However, it wasn't that which upset me, but their clichéd imagination, the epigonism. Of course, I wouldn't have mentioned it, but it was precisely the denunciation of "Shakespeare on behalf of all the Shakespeares..." that finally opened my eyes to what was happening. The thing is, I didn't have any Shakespeares among the literary union members. The newest of them did not dub themselves in any way at all. In my speech, I mentioned that perhaps future classics of world literature were sitting in the assembly hall without even knowing it themselves, but I didn't specify who was who. It turned out that they had appropriated the names of more great writers on their own, without me knowing.

Impostors, Grishka Otrepyevs[53], they still dare call themselves Shakespeares?! The country had barely stumbled, not even strayed from the path, and they had already raised their sabres over Ivan Susanin[54]. Damned Poles, riffraff!

Indignation filled me. At that moment I wholeheartedly felt the selfish baseness of the Time of Troubles[55], or rather, of all troubled times.

Then a thought came to me: since the literary union members had appropriated names for themselves, they had automatically forfeited their subcutaneous money to me according to my tariff. They had spent it on buying literary names, so to speak.

A sudden wave of pleasure made me pause: I had concluded that I had the moral right to not only refrain from publishing the collective anthology but also to not return the money. Of course, I didn't even think of not returning it. I only thought that I had that moral right… But I knew that I would give it back, so that they would really stoop into their greed.

53　　Grigory Otrepiev was an impostor who took the Russian throne in 1605 by passing himself off as Prince (Tsarevich) Dmitry, using military assistance provided by Polish nobility. He was the first so-called False Dmitry, with several other imposters taking the same path later with varied success. Prince Dmitry was the youngest son of Ivan the Terrible; he died in his childhood under mysterious, never adequately investigated circumstances, thus spawning rumors of his survival and, therefore, of the existence of the true heir of Ivan the Terrible who would claim the throne from Boris Godunov, one of the main suspects in the Prince's perplexing demise.

54　　Russian national hero and martyr, killed by Polish invaders in 1613 while trying to lure them into a swamp.

55　　A period of lawlessness, deep social crisis and foreign invasions in Russia between 1598 and 1613.

I walked even faster. None of the newest recruits knew about my tariff and hence, couldn't have taken advantage of it. Most certainly, a hairy hand of some well-informed person was at play here.

I immediately dismissed Mayakovsky and the two Gorkys; they had never been among my inner circle. I had brought them somewhat closer to me at the last meeting purely by chance. But the headman and his assistant, the former veterinary feldsher, were another matter. I remembered the elegance with which the latter had put his silk ligatures on my cuffs, and I almost exclaimed – it was him, bingo! Only he, the veterinarian, could have counted the newly-minted Lermontovs and Shakespeares by heads – a professional habit. But without the headman, he would have never dared; it would have been impossible. Nevertheless, the headman's involvement remained in question.

...So, he had called the editorial office on Monday, informed them in detail, and indicated where and when to get me... He didn't say that he was the head of the literary union; he concealed that, but he didn't call himself Leo Tolstoy either. He and the veterinary assistant had received their literary names directly from me, unlike the newly minted "classics," that's why he did not use that name. Had the investigation considered me a coup supporter, the headman would have inevitably be identified by his literary name. He didn't want to appear as an informer in my eyes, and at the same time, to protect himself, had agitated the union members into filing numerous denunciations, not without the vet's help, and assigned names to them, mimicking my scheme.

I never thought I'd have to accuse Leo Tolstoy of plagiarism!

I began to recall the denunciations, that is, on whose behalf they were written, and discovered a peculiar fact: in addition to the universally recognized and long-deceased classics, there were several foreign names, which I avoided out of patriotic feeling, ours are no worse, and several names of living and working classics, who ranked as scarce with me at an extremely high rate. Here I must admit that this was the result of a trivial self-preservation instinct rather than any considerations of honour.

There was a case when a totally worthless person suddenly wanted to be me, yes, Mitya Slyozkin! That was when I inflated the rate, otherwise I wouldn't have fended the smart-butt off. Seeing a long-deceased classic in a literary union member (nostalgia for spirituality long gone) is one thing, breeding living writers' doppelgangers is another; there is something unnatural, pathological about it. I made exceptions, of course, but only for Nobel Prize winners. But among the denunciations, out of the twenty-six anonymous denouncers, every third was either a foreigner or former compatriot who left to live abroad. Not a single Tolstoy, not a single Nekrasov! It was odd, very odd, that unconstrained by strictly regulated rates, no one would desire to appropriate any of the textbook-famous names! It seemed that despite the freedom of choice, something or someone imposed a taboo on the top-tier Russian classics, like Tolstoy and Nekrasov. Who? Probably those who had kept them for themselves. Bingo! This clearly exposed the headman and his assistant – a rather peculiar use of their official positions for personal gain – and confirmed that they took an active part in organizing the mass denunciations.

Scoundrels! I had elevated them, and they… Well, the harder their reckoning would be! …

Seething with anger, I kept returning to my throne speech. The threat to tear arms off seemed naive, and I replaced it. In the final version, the concluding phrase was: "…but God forbid you ever write again – I'll tear your heads off!"

At first, I was surprised that I had walked the distance from the terminal stop to the HAN without taking public transportation even once. The time surprised me as well: there were almost fifteen minutes left before the start of the meeting. And only then did I realise that the building was closed and abandoned.

All the doors of the HAN were sealed, and the pavement was abundantly strewn with shards of glass, ripped-out window frames, and scattered smashed telephones. If I hadn't known about the visitors from the concrete plant, the planned revolutionary activities would probably have horrified me with their senseless brutality. But I did know about them, and so I noticed that the pogrom had barely touched the first floor, while the second floor was trashed thoroughly: not a single intact window, just gaping empty spaces. It was on the second floor, as in a showcase, where the glaring antagonism of the GKChP coup supporters and democrats, the "white socks," was displayed for all to see. The former smashed the HAN windows with the classic weapons of the proletariat[56] from the street, the latter did the same from within without any weapons. They blamed each other for the overall outcome, and both had their own opinion about what was happening.

I spread out a newspaper and sat down on the porch step to avoid seeing this manifestation of the revolutionary pluralism of

---

56   Famous metaphor for stones.

opinions. Revolution is an astounding invention, truly shocking inside and out. From the criminal point of view, it is brilliant. Everyone is guilty, and therefore no one is guilty. Anyone who touches the revolution is a sinner, and yet you cannot avoid touching it because it touches everyone itself. It is only fair that in the end a revolution devours its own children because the people causing a revolutionary situation are criminals. I don't want to be either a revolutionary or a counter-revolutionary. I don't even want to be a citizen. I want to be an ordinary person. Yes, an ordinary person with direct obligations to his family, to the state if the state respects ordinary people, and a sacred right to decide everything else for oneself. I don't want to be on anyone's side, only on the one that's sunny. Wonders of the world abound: forests, rivers, seas, oceans. And then there's space: stars, planets, all sorts of asteroids! If it's all for a loved one, I understand that. If it's for the revolution, for its heroes, I don't. For near seventy-five years in a row, they admired revolutionaries and revolutionary democrats, collectively fostered some kind of a new human, but when you look closely, you see the "hotline," broken windows and sealed doors. Maybe my literary union members aren't so wrong about their decision to deal with me using the old, essentially GKChP methods? For them, I am (no matter whose side I'm on) a participant in the revolution, and therefore there's no need to coddle me – good for them! They are more honest in their being informers than the real organizers of the revolution. They acted as expected from any ordinary Soviet citizen and cannot be judged for that. The most feasible thing to do was to forget about the throne speech, hand over the money silently and disappear. I still needed to thank them for not rushing to save me; otherwise, they would have ruined me for sure and exposed themselves...

"Sir, what are you doing here, your papers please!" My thoughts were interrupted by a police officer who came out of nowhere.

It was the first time I'd seen a police officer younger than myself, an eighteen-year-old kid, hence the unusual form of address: I was mostly addressed as "you" or "you, young man, yes, I'm talking to you...." But here – "Sir"! I even grew a little in my own eyes, puffed up with importance, and crossed one leg over the other.

"What's the matter, what papers?" I said, defiantly swinging my leg almost under the cop's nose.

At first, he turned pale, then his face became beet red, just like a schoolboy's. Involuntarily, I stood up, attributing his agitation to my careless demeanour, but at that moment he stood to attention and saluted me, clicking his heels.

"Excuse me, no one informed me," the kid cop said apologetically, blushing again like a maiden.

Equally puzzled, we didn't understand each other until the law enforcer hitched up his pants, exposing white socks. He, like me, was wearing white socks, and that explained his apologies better than any words. Taking the initiative, I learned from him that under the so-called youth draft, he had only been enrolled in some reserve special purpose unit the day before and, in essence, the HAN facilities and the movie theatre across the street were assigned to him without any briefing. He even hoped to receive the briefing from me. (Yesterday he was told that his division was being placed under the revolutionary headquarters' command.) When asked directly: "What do headquarters and white socks have to do with it?" – he smiled meaningfully and said that he was hearing about white socks for the first time. You could tell he was very pleased with his answer; little devils were dancing in his eyes: got it, didn't you?! "Good Lord, what's going on?" I thought, realizing that I wouldn't get anything more out of this freshly minted conspirator.

Annoyed, I said that I had put them on purely by chance. In response, smiling just as meaningfully, he saluted again and continued waiting for orders. I felt that I was being drawn back into some dark game, or perhaps a hole from where there is no way out.

"There will be no orders, I am here solely as a private individual," I said. "I'm waiting for people who may not come… understand?"

He understood everything, even got somewhat offended by my distrust, said that he would step away into the shrubbery, observe from there and would come to the rescue if needed.

I agreed. There was nothing else to do: the literary union members were due any minute, and the kid cop would scare them off by his mere presence.

CHAPTER 14

The city of N is remarkable, the finest of the ancient Russian cities. The river, the kremlin, green hills straddled by churches… Golden onion domes melting into the sky, the peal of church bells heard far and wide as if rising from the depths of centuries. It will drift past us, not touching our feelings, because we are, in a sense, not in this world. The bell towers of our churches are empty, a chill of museum halls has swallowed our icons because we are all dead. Dull, grey, bitter, and somewhat unreal – that's what we have become. Dante placed the souls of deceased writers born before the teaching of Christ between hell and paradise, in a city devoid of even a hint of life. We, however, have settled in Limbo on our own accord, having rejected the past. But something has already shifted, is it hell or paradise? Thousands of Russian saints walk and walk in a procession – the day of the Assumption of the Holy Mother of God. Early autumn warmth and silence, sunbeams glide over the leaves, and the sky descends to earth, and the earth rises to the heavens.

Holy Mother of God, make it so that my mother, and all the mothers of the Russian land, are well. Pure Virgin Mary, make it so that Rozochka lacks for nothing, and enlighten me, for I do not want to take part in any lies, but I do not know a single prayer myself.

I began composing a prayer to the Holy Mother of God and suddenly felt how wonderful, quiet, sunny, and spacious were my surroundings and how cramped and gloomy was my internal space: my whole life as a literary worker was one of continuous confusion. Here on earth, the divine breath still glimmers from the depths of centuries. I, on the contrary, have no depth; I feel no height, just dullness, grayness, and worthlessness. In all probability, I am indeed the new Soviet man, nurtured in a collective farmers' barn of communist ideas. For all my mundanity, I am essentially a man of theories, that is, an immaterial one. Only a person like myself could live in the future, to dwell in a non-existent reality, so to speak.

"Uncle, do you have any money?" A boy of about ten in a light blue raincoat interrupted my reflections.

He looked around so apprehensively that I looked around too. There was no one to be seen, apart from something flitting behind the wall of shrubbery.

"What do you need it for?" I asked. "Did someone send you to me?"

"No one sent me," the boy answered, and after glancing at me briefly, became embarrassed, lowering his gaze and starting to poke at the ground with his red sneaker.

There was something vaguely familiar about his face; I felt like I had seen that protruding forehead and those wide-set eyes before... – the union headman?! Most certainly his grandson or grandnephew. I held my breath, as if afraid to breathe.

"Let's do this," I proposed. "You go now and tell whoever sent you that I have money, but it's not mine. Let them come to me, they have nothing to fear, I must hand out the money to each person and get a signature. Tell them the literary union is closed for an indefinite period."

"But everyone knows it's closed."

The boy looked at me inquisitively and immediately crouched down in fright. A whistle came from the bushes, but the boy had already taken off with the agility of a hare. The blue jacket slid between the branches and disappeared as if there had been nothing there. I listened, but instead of the cracking of branches and rustling of leaves, I heard footsteps distinctly approaching behind me. I didn't even need to look back to guess – the kid cop.

This time we established our relationship extremely quickly. I issued a military-style order for him to hide in the shrubbery and not emerge until I called him. In any case, not before 6:20 p.m. I hoped that half an hour would be enough for my business with the literary union members. Alas, at 7 p.m., cursing the white socks, the kid cop, but most of all my promise to "hand out the money and get signatures," I decided to leave. As I was leaving, I went under the trees and discovered a fairly big area of freshly trampled grass behind the bushes. There was no doubt: I had stumbled upon the encampment spot of those who had sent the boy.

Like a professional tracker, from cigarette butts, indentations, and other scattered evidence I established that there had been two adult observers and the object of observation was the House of All Newspapers, not only its porched main entrance but also, the shrubbery with the policeman in it. Knowing that the headman and his assistant lived on Peace Boulevard, I headed for a bus stop in that direction. But they knew that I knew, and so, had probably changed their route. The most vexing thing was that being confident about my connection to the police, which they had witnessed, they would certainly try to inform the literary union, and henceforth all my attempts to hand out the money would be perceived as a provocation. This money was akin to the infamous silver pieces! It was so abhorrent, I wanted to throw it all away. It took some effort not to do so: throwing away hard-earned money, and the subcutaneous money was undoubtedly such, would have been a sacrilege, especially since I had already forgiven the literary union members, who were just being themselves - good Soviet citizens.

I walked home again, and if I had cursed my would-be classics on my way to the House of All Newspapers, now I cursed myself. I gave my word to the Mother of God that I would spend this money wisely: I would live on it and write. Ever since my student days, I had dreamed of sudden wealth that would allow me to stop worrying about my daily bread and cluttering my head with humiliating thoughts of subsistence and just create and produce immortal works. The time had come to fulfil my dream, especially since the immortal works would certainly be published in sizeable print runs and the money would just flow into my pockets on its own. That's when I would have the opportunity to somehow thank my creditors. I was so intent on writing to justify the trust bestowed on me in the form of the subcutaneous money that any possible chance that could prevent me from carrying out my plan would have to be a true hand of God. The thing is, subconsciously I instantly realised that only Rozochka's return could prevent it. But I didn't admit it to myself, I dodged this realisation and asked the Mother of God to protect me from all possible and impossible obstacles, as if nothing had happened.

I immediately felt the insincerity of this pleading and was even afraid that the Mother of God would grant it. Yes, I backtracked. I began to assure the Mother of God that Rozochka's return would not stop me, but on the contrary, strengthen my resolve and thereby expedite the birth of my immortal works. I went so far as to propose a deal to the Mother of God: She would return Rozochka, and I would not take a single kopeck[57] of the subcutaneous money. Except, perhaps, for the publication of the collective anthology?! Despite the authors' lack of talent, this idea must not be discarded, because it will certainly be published when I'm a famous classic, out of reverence. I must concentrate on becoming a classic, and for that, I only needed one thing: I needed Rozochka back home, back home immediately.

Everything for me came down to Rozochka, and I hurried on: what if she had already returned?! Silly?! Maybe for those who have never felt the hand of God.

I was told at the dormitory's front desk that the key to the room and my note had been picked up by my wife, and she had already been home for over an hour.

"At home?!" I didn't understand. That is, I understood what they were saying, but I didn't believe it. I thought the front desk attendant had confused me with someone else or was playing a trick on me at someone's instigation. (She wouldn't have thought of playing a trick on her own.)

"Are you alright? You're pale as death!" The front desk attendant looked genuinely scared.

"I don't believe you," I said. "My wife… Where is she?" I asked, not understanding what I was asking. I only wanted one thing: for this simple woman to finally make certain that we were really talking about my wife and no one else.

---

57   1/100 of a ruble, a Soviet version of penny or cent.

"That's right, I didn't believe her either," the front desk attendant chimed in happily. "I told her: how can it be that you've returned from a business trip? Surely nowadays no one goes on business trips with their own beds, refrigerators, and TVs?"

The woman began to portray how sternly and displeased Rozochka had looked at her. Having taken the key, Rozochka had tossed her head resentfully and left as pompously as if it wasn't she, the brazen woman who had shamelessly removed everything from the room, but rather she had had everything taken from her.

There could be no doubt now, that the front desk lady was talking about Rozochka. My heart fluttered like a waking bird to meet the azure skies and the sunbeams, and I saw the steppe by the Ob River from horizon to horizon, the steppe of my youth, fields of flowers like fields of love. What an interesting woman this front desk attendant is, I thought; she may boil over, get angry, but still shines with joy and even delight. Not feeling my feet, I rushed upstairs to Rozochka.

I don't remember which floor I stopped on. It occurred to me that Rozochka had obviously arrived tired and hungry, and as always, I had nothing. Some stale bread was left by the window from yesterday, but a hardened bread crust for dinner – that's outright barbarism!

I was indescribably happy to have money on me, happy to not have thrown it away. I even felt a chill run down my spine – what should I do? In response, somewhere far, far in the depths of my soul, a little window opened, like that of a cashier. I couldn't make out the face, but the voice sounded like my mother's: "You promised not to take a kopeck of other people's money!" Oh Lord, how could I? Who cares about other people's money when Rozochka is hungry! I rebelled inside me with such fervour that the window slammed shut instantly, and I no longer remembered my requests nor pleadings and flew as if on wings.

As I ran past the front desk attendant, I shouted for her not to let Rozochka leave under any circumstances and to make her stay until I returned.

I got into the first available taxi without much thought and went to the train station cafeteria. It was empty, the counters and display cases oozing a distinct feeling of staleness. Thank God at least there were bread and pyramids of canned mackerel in tomato sauce. Then I went to the "Central" restaurant where I got some sausage, cheese and, most importantly, a two-litre jar of vodka to go, and just as much very good, albeit somewhat thick, port wine. The bartender poured it with a soup ladle from a big flask, praising it the way they praise borscht – fresh, fragrant, eat to your heart's content!

Of course, what surprised me most was vodka to go – this innovation at the time of the alcohol prohibition seemed quite ingenious, but I kept quiet to avoid exposing my ignorance and arousing suspicion. While serving, the bartender was wary of a sudden visit from the control authority. In any case, she asked one of the waitresses to stand by the door to the basement through which I and eight other people followed her. There, she bestowed upon us the desired forbidden goods in glass pickle jars. I spared no expense, the only trouble was that the subcutaneous roubles were difficult to count, and the bartender asked me to wait until she had served everyone. But then she helped: she found a mesh bag of onions and escorted me through the back door. Finally, she advised me against selling the "loose stuff," as she said, near the restaurant, or else I'd get in trouble myself and cast a shadow on her: she had taken me for a small-time "new Russian."

It struck me as funny: undoubtedly the subcutaneous money was to blame; it had created an aura around me through which the real Mitya Slyozkin could not be seen, in the same way as white socks did. The taxi driver, incidentally, took me for a card shark. As we arrived at the dormitory, he said that the most dangerous thing at a party was a son of a bitch with a marked deck and he should immediately be thrown out of the fifth-floor window. This time I wasn't amused but smiled slightly, if only to oblige him. My bewilderment was complete when the front desk attendant greeted me with the question: had I seen two respectable old men with a boy in a light blue jacket, who had just left?

I hadn't seen anyone, but I guessed who she was talking about. The front desk lady handed me a note written in a beautiful student's hand: "From now on, you are no more, you have messed up, do not involve us. We do not need anything from you, please disengage with honour."

"So, do you need witnesses[58]?!" the front desk lady did not hide her curiosity and complained that she couldn't read the note without her glasses.

"What witnesses; what's this nonsense?!"

The lady took offence, saying that I, myself, had told her to hold my darling wife, so she had told the old men to wait and that Mitya had gone for the police.

---

58   In the Soviet Union certain police activities required involvement of impartial witnesses, usually two of them. These could be recruited from virtually anyone around.

"What police?!"

I groaned and even stamped my foot in anger; not at the front desk attendant, no, but at the aura in which I was struggling like a fly in a web.

"Aunt Glasha, please understand…"

"I'm not Aunt Glasha, I'm Alina Spiridonovna," the front desk attendant was outraged at my stomping and calling her by the wrong name.

"Alina Spiridonovna, please understand once and for all that my darling wife is not Aunt Glasha either, but my wife Rosa, and if it comes to it, I won't spare my life and do in anyone who slanders her! I'll go out to the street right now and do someone in," I threatened, and indeed went out onto the street to see if the headman was there with his assistant and grandson in the blue jacket.

Of course, there was no one, but it was still good that I went out and got a little fresh air. The front desk attendant also came to her senses, she had been very scared to see me so enraged for the first time. In the end, we reconciled. I was in such a hurry to go upstairs that I forgot about my mesh grocery bag, and she called out to me and even smirked that because of our quarrel, I had become more upset than she had.

"Take your juices, or you won't have anything to eat," she said and turned away (my mesh bag with jars was standing on her front desk).

I silently returned and took them, she jabbed at me as I left:

"We're protecting our poet Mitya Slyozkin as hard as we can, and look at him?!"

Yes, that's what I'm like and always will be, forget about the former Mitya Slyozkin who wouldn't harm a fly. He'll harm anyone who dares stand in his way, I blustered to myself in the third person, and with a surge of courage hurried back upstairs to Rozochka.

CHAPTER 15

All my courage vanished, however, as I faced her door. I should have just knocked and entered, but didn't dare. I was afraid of seeing Rozochka and yet everything within me trembled with the desire to behold her immediately. Torn and petrified by these feelings, God knows how long I would have remained standing there if the door hadn't suddenly creaked open. That solitary squeaking creak, plaintive like a whimpering pup, resonated in my soul with such desolation that I grew aghast: what if Rozochka wasn't there, what if she had left without waiting for me?

I rushed into the room and sank quietly to my knees. Rozochka was asleep, curled up in a little ball, her chin propped on her tiny fists. It seemed to me that she was gazing at me and smiling ever so slightly, her eyelashes fluttering. I set aside the tray of food and crawled over to her on all fours, trying not to make a sound. I remember ever so vividly her fragrance of spring wildflowers and the trills of larks that I swear I could hear.

"Rozochka," I whispered, gently kissing her brow, framed by shining jet-black curls.

Her eyelashes fluttered slightly but didn't open. Nestling her cheek into her palm, she sighed distinctly, saying:

"Ah, it's you?"

"Yes," I replied, feeling that Rozochka was asleep but had recognised me through her slumber, her half-dreaming bliss.

There's such a natural half-hypnotic state when one is neither fully asleep nor awake. My mother used to say that if you ask someone half-dreaming questions, they'll either wake up or start answering.

I don't know what demon rode me, but I started asking her questions. Leaning close to her ear, I whispered softly:

"Rozochka, my sunshine, tell your Mitya where you've been?"

"I won't!" Rozochka snapped, so distinctly and with such characteristic intonation that I started - had she woken up?

No, she continued sleeping just as before, her breathing steady and calm.

"You won't tell - that's fine," I agreed gently. "Then answer me, my sunshine, were you with some man? Was there a man with you?" I held my breath anxiously.

What a stupid personality I have, to ask and then be petrified of whatever answer might come; what if she said some strange man had been with her, perhaps that very one who turned away when he saw me, maybe it was this Petka Ryaskin fellow? What then? ... I decided I wouldn't ask any more, it was wrong to pry into a sleeping person's secrets, worse than reading someone's letters or peering through a keyhole.

"There was, I had a husband..."

What she mumbled next I couldn't make out, but what I had understood was more than enough for me. My heart ached and I suddenly felt the weight of my body fall on my knees. It took a tremendous effort not to collapse to the floor and I had to grip the edge of the ping-pong tabletop to prevent me from sliding down.

"What was his name?" I forced out hopelessly.

God is my witness, I didn't want to know his name, but why did I ask, why?

"Mitya, his name was Mitya," Rozochka replied with a sigh so mournful as if somewhere deep in her innermost feelings she pitied me.

Lord, how touched I was, how overjoyed by her words: in the year we'd lived together she had never once pitied me while awake. (Of course, one must understand that a woman only pities the one she loves).

I was uplifted and wanted to unpack the tray and run to the kitchen to fry up some sausages, croutons, everything that Rozochka loved. But then it was as if something jabbed me in the ribs: if his name was Mitya, then who did she think I was? Could it be the man she'd been with these past two weeks?

"And what do you call me?" I purred sweetly, then feeling I couldn't bear this torment further, prompted: "Perhaps I am Mitya, your loving husband?"

"No, you're not Mitya, you're a thousand times worse, you - you're a bastard!" she said angrily, her face flushing red.

Rozochka lifted herself slightly and, seemingly, opened her eyes as she started to roll over onto her other side. I say "seemingly" because I'm not certain - her anger frightened me, and I fell prostrate so as not to appear before her, even mistakenly, as this bastard.

I was laying there on the floor, my eyes welling up with tears of anguish for her: she had endured many hardships, returned home, and I… I loathed myself for knowingly doing things that

I should not have done. The worst thing, however, was that I observed myself doing them as if from the outside. Yes, yes, as an artist, I always see myself as some separate entity. I see myself, yet I cannot stop. Then I repent, I lament, admit that I foresaw that I would repent, but in that fateful moment I was seduced by the very idea that everything is permitted to me as an artistic person, as an engineer of human souls.

And then too, weeping beside her bed, I understood that it was through my own fault that I wept, my own fault that I smeared tears over the floor. Understanding made everything seem even more distressing, more hopeless.

Lord, how many unseen tragedies unfold in dormitories! These mere ten square metres saw me choking on grief so many times, so how much of such grief must be scattered across this whole city, this whole country, this entire globe?!

"Mitya, is that you?! On the floor, in your jacket, you'll get yourself all dirty!" I heard an astonished voice above me, and a feeling of mutual recognition poured forth preceding the words as if we had never been parted for even a minute.

Rosa, Rozochka! Is there anywhere in the universe another woman like her, who can lift a man lying helpless with a mere word?

There was a famous student named Valery Gubkin in our school literary club. Everyone knew him. I was in awe of his poems.

The lads go dancing every night,
I worry for them deep inside,
Like brand-new books they're fresh and bright,
But are they good? Hard to decide.

They're still in their schooling days,
And freely swap their belles,
Not charmers on the prowl for praise,
But gauging their own spells.

Some lads take pride in doing that,
This secret I can frankly tell,
But it's not right, they must abide,
For girls are testing them as well.

There was another poem that he sent to our school paper while already studying journalism:

What girls are really made of?
This puzzle I can't crack,
We're not supposed to dwell on it,
And clarity we lack.

Perhaps by them we are bewitched?
Just look at how they dress!
Could they all come from elsewhere,
From lands that we can't guess?

It breaks my heart to watch them cry
When rowdy lads come near,
Disturbing peace with boozy prying,
And causing pain and fear.

What if one night, as we all sleep,
They fly like birds to distant skies,
Forsaking us alone to weep
With heavy hearts and silent cries?

I fear my world would lose its spark,
All light would fade, and shadows grow.
I vow to keep you from the dark,
Just stay with me, do not let go.

Back then Valery Gubkin was a tenth-grader[59] while I was in seventh. Like all older students, he didn't notice me. But one day my poem "The Shepherd Boy Petya" was published in the local paper, and Gubkin told me to come and read him some of my verses. It was a great honour. He listened to me reading my poems while lying on a bench in an empty Russian literature classroom, staring up at the ceiling dispassionately. At some point, he stopped me and advised including those poems along with "The Shepherd Boy Petya" in volume thirteen of my complete collected works. At the time I didn't realise he was mocking me and took his advice as the highest praise for my creations.

---

59   Soviet school system had ten grades, encompassing primary, mid and high school of three, five and two grades respectively.

The only thing that puzzled me was his question: did I know Svetlanka Karmanova?

In our extracurricular reading, we had covered works by various female poets. I was familiar with the poetry by Anna Akhmatova, Marina Tsvetaeva, I even knew of the 17th century Mexican poet Juana Inés de la Cruz and her exquisite verses. But this Svetlana Karmanova, evidently some new rising star, was unknown to me. Naturally, as the author of a prospective thirteenth volume, I felt dreadfully embarrassed and ashamed to admit that I didn't know Svetlana Karmanova and had never heard of her.

"Well then, you and I are not going anywhere together," Valery Gubkin declared, rising to look me over with such a withering gaze that I understood: being unacquainted with Karmanova, I had forever lost the right to write poetry.

Svetlana Karmanova turned out to be a classmate of Gubkin's. She had never written a single poem, and I was offended to the core that he dared place her above the most renowned poets. He fell from grace in my eyes, and I even stopped acknowledging him when we passed. Only later, while studying at the Literary Institute after meeting Rozochka, did I forgive him. Even back in school, he somehow knew that the most exquisite word of all poets, male or female, pales before the word of one's beloved.

Rozochka playfully grabbed me by the scruff and tried pulling me onto the bed. I resisted, dragging her down to the floor in response. Clowning around, we laughed and tumbled together on the mattress, but even before that, uplifted in our mutual recognition, my soul had already taken wing like a moth towards the light. I was fluttering joyfully around the candle flame, whirling in dance, my whole heart delighting in how "Wingletting with the goldenscrawl of its finest veins, the grasshopper loaded its trailer-belly with coastal herbs and faiths. 'Ping, ping, ping!' the zinziver tararached. O, swanderful! O, dawnrises!!"[60]

Rozochka and I were together for ten days and ten nights. On Saturday, 7th September 1991, she left for Moscow. Don't think we had quarrelled or had grown tired of each other, not at all. At the train station platform, Rozochka said those ten days and nights were the best of her life. Need I say how I felt? Laughing merrily, Rozochka begged me:

"Don't be so wise and stern, at least while we're parting!"

But I was wise and stern. Bundled in her lilac sweater, Rozochka clung to me, and I clutched her tightly in my embrace until the conductor announced that it was time for passengers to take their seats.

Pale, with her long slender neck, Rozochka stood at the carriage door like one of the Graces. She waved to me, telling me to remember her instructions. I nodded in reply, wise and silent, for I knew I had lost my voice and could only let out an incoherent wail.

The train pulled away. At first, I walked alongside, keeping pace. Then it accelerated, the wheels clacking faster, and the carriages, softly overlapping each other, swallowed that dear lilac speck from sight. I kept walking though: past the main station building, the kiosks, the water towers, station outbuildings. I turned into the city after passing the ticket counter, without breaking my stride, and felt no surprise when shortly afterwards,

---

60   "Grasshopper" by Velemir Khlebnikov.

I found myself atop a steep hill by the so-called Victory Monument.

I never liked this monument, grandiose in its bad taste. Inflated and presumptuous, straining to be the Bronze Horseman.[61], it embodied nothing but militant mediocrity. Only my fellow literary union members could truly immortalize this edifice in verse - and they did. One of our Mayakovskys wrote: "No noble steed was lying idly here, It sprang up briskly to this very hill, And froze forever in triumphant cheer, The mighty Svyatogor[62], the quelling will!" I remember the headman's assistant (he wasn't Nekrasov yet) applauding enthusiastically. Everyone expected to hear my commentary, but I was bound hand and foot by the presence of several not entirely talentless people and merely asked that anyone commenting on the poem remember the greatness of Soviet patriotism.

Those not entirely talentless rose silently and left the meeting. One lingered by the door, saying he understood "No noble steed was lying idly here, It sprang up briskly to this very hill..." but what did "the quelling will" mean if he was Svyatogor?

Yes, yes, it was so bad it was brilliant! ... To keep from bursting out laughing, I furrowed my brows like a samurai and, without hesitation, professed to find numerous virtues in the poem precisely where there were none whatsoever. Yes, I rhapsodised about the truffles in sauerkraut.

Now though, I was wise and stern, and nothing could deliver me from this morose state, as if to punish me for praising those truffles in sauerkraut. Not Rozochka's pleas at the platform, not even the poems that once made me laugh - nothing. It was a

---

61   Statue of Peter the Great in St. Petersburg

62   Russian mythical folk hero.

state of sudden detachment from desire. At a mere twenty-three, I felt a century old. This must be what nirvana feels like. In any case, I felt that my desires had sloughed off me, while the stream of my consciousness grew more unmoving yet also more all-encompassing.

I sat with my back to "the quelling will." Suddenly the distant river valley opened before me, the far horizon line rising, until somewhere at the very edge of the earth the bell tower of St. George's Monastery stood tall, with the dark onion dome of the Church of St. George the Victorious appearing just to the left. "Russia, Holy Russia! Keep yourself safe, keep yourself safe![63]"

I heard a soft evening sigh, the willow branches below swaying from a sudden breeze as if pondering. "Russia, Holy Russia! Keep yourself safe, keep yourself safe!" Another sigh, the willows nodding in gentle assent, as though the poet's words had been recalled not just by me but were a part of everything around me. A poet is all about his cherished words, and though "We are not granted to foretell just how our word will echo..." one thing is clear: it cannot be a lie.

I gazed into the lilac expanse of the deepening twilight and felt Rozochka's presence as if she had never left and could call out to me at any moment so we could walk home together.

---

63   From "Visions on the hill", a song by Nikolay Rubtsov

CHAPTER 16

The first days of our reunion were very ordinary: she undertook a thorough cleaning and laundry, with me assisting. Afterwards, we rested. She would doze off gazing at the ceiling while I just watched on. The dimples in her cheeks would smooth out, and one could sense her shedding the fatigue amassed during her absence. When Rozochka awoke, I feigned sleep, and it pleased me that upon realising I was with her, she would cautiously snuggle closer before falling back asleep. She felt better and better with each passing day. Only on the fifth day did we start really conversing, though mostly Rozochka just listened and smiled. Then she began lapsing into thoughtfulness more often, her face taking on an empty expression. One day, out of the blue, she suddenly said: "Enough of this kindergarten" and started preparing to return to Moscow, having decided to re-enrol in the medical college and finish her studies.

I didn't argue, instead, I went downstairs to the front desk and called a resort located right by the walls of St. George's Monastery. I requested a room for two for three days. I explained that we were a young married couple who had painted our dorm room and had nowhere to stay for the time being.

During my call, the infamous desk attendant Alina Spiridonovna stared fixedly out the window, snorting derisively and loudly exclaiming in outrage:

"Oh, there is still rascality in some rascals!"

But how delighted Rozochka was when instead of the train station we arrived at the resort! Once in our hotel room, she kissed me and said:

"Mitya, you're a true gentleman! If you still consider Rozaria Fyodorovna your Rozochka, then listen to her attentively and abide by her orders."

She instructed me not to wait for her return, or rather to wait without expectation of her return, for she was no longer that same Rozochka. She wasn't even the same Rozaria Fyodorovna anymore. She had become someone else, no longer an empty shell, but a person with a purpose.

"You and I are still tied together," I mumbled uncertainly (fearing she would remind me that she had changed her passport and family name).

"Ah, so that's what it's about - ties!" Rozochka exclaimed with a smile, her face suddenly growing serious, even stern. "Do you want me to betray my lofty purpose and return to you? Is that what you want, Mitya?"

I sensed not so much astonishment as a threat in her questions.

"No, no, I only want for you to be always with me, for us to live together."

"Oh Mitya! You only say that because you don't yet know about my purpose!" My purpose precludes living with anyone, including you."

She grew emotional and kissed my brow with such poignant bitterness, it was as if I were a deceased loved one. I grew frightened: what did she have in mind, what sort of purpose precluded cohabiting with anyone? Could it really be Chernobyl, some secretive environmental consequences?!

"Rozochka, my blossom, tell me about your purpose!" I implored, suspecting Lord knows what.

"Ah, you're scared!" Rozochka suddenly brightened, cheerfully setting about making the bed as if nothing was amiss.

I must admit, a sense of fear had indeed taken root within me on Rozochka's return. It was morphing into a sort of inexplicable melancholic which I felt most acutely at the resort as Rozochka recounted the hardships she had endured selling our refrigerator, colour TV, dresser, and sofa bed.

"But I arrived back in all-new outfits," she continued, sashaying before me in that now lilac sweater, American jeans, and red-and-white Nike trainers.

"No, no," she corrected herself, "this doesn't count... Turn away!"

She grabbed her purse (also new, with a red triangle on the flap), very similar to a medical bag, and from the telltale rustling sounds accompanying her preparations, I guessed she intended to make an all-new full debut. Sure enough, Rozochka applied lipstick, lined her brows, draped the purse over her shoulder and paraded back and forth like a top model.

"Well, Mitya?" she beamed expectantly.

"Fantastic!" I said.

"And on top of everything... English lingerie." Rozochka pulled it out of her purse - it fit in her palm like a handkerchief - proudly announcing it could easily be fitted in a matchbox.

Never in my life had I seen such accessories. The set consisted of two pieces: a black lace bra and matching translucent knickers which shrunk into next to nothing.

"Where did you get all this?" I asked with no ulterior motive, but Rozochka suddenly grew angry.

"What, you're curious? Very curious?" she asked harshly, then after a pause informed me that she had got it all in Manchester. "Don't you know I live in Manchester City?"

She said it deliberately to pick a quarrel, but I remained silent, swallowing the bitter pill. Yes, yes, it was then that fear tinged with inexplicable melancholy took root within me.

That said, not everything at the resort was bad, in fact, quite the opposite. After making the bed and showering, Rozochka donned the English lingerie. Cosily ensconced on fresh sheets, she said she would deign to reveal her lofty purpose. On 8th September, the day of the Vladimir Icon of the Mother of God, which saved the capital from Tamerlane's invasion, she absolutely had to be in Moscow. Rozochka decided to convert to Orthodox Christianity, to undergo the sacrament of baptism. Upon graduating from medical college, or perhaps even sooner (she wasn't yet fully familiar with church protocols), Rozochka would join a monastery, take vows, and become a nun (a widely accepted practice in the Moscow diocese). Then, and this was the main thing, she would strive to become Russia's Mother Teresa, or rather Mother Rozaria.

"Are you amazed, Mitya, have you understood me?" Rozochka asked, looking at me with that special caution which can't help but betray concealed agitation.

Yes, yes, I sensed this was no idle question. Perhaps the only reason she had come with me to the resort was because, first and foremost, she wanted my opinion about her lofty purpose. It pleased me to realise that Rozochka was agitated about hearing my opinion.

"No, I'm not amazed. I understand you perfectly," I replied sadly.

Indeed, I wasn't amazed. Previously she had often left me baffled by her unpredictability. But ever since she had changed her passport and last name, and frittered away everything of value that we owned in a mere two weeks, nothing amazed me anymore - that inexplicable melancholy remained my only feeling.

"Mitya, but if you understand, why the sadness? Come here, your Rozochka will comfort you," she said, pushing back the covers and extending her arms as if to an infant.

I don't know in what higher realms our happiness resides when it is not with us, but I know for certain: wherever it may be, Rozochka has direct access to it. Only a person like her could seriously set the goal of becoming Russia's Mother Teresa. Only she had the capability for such a lofty purpose. I rejoiced, I took pride, I extolled her purpose to the heavens.

"Don't you agree that 'Mother Rozaria the Russian' has a wonderful ring to it?" Rozochka asked repeatedly, evading my ardent kisses.

"Mother Rozaria the Russian! It's marvellous, it's superb!" I exclaimed rapturously between kisses.

In response, Rozochka laughed merrily, yielding, tossing back her head, and I, taking advantage of her blissful state, would hungrily kiss her lips, her neck… and so on.

"Mitya, you understand that as Mother Rozaria I can't do this, it's a sin," Rozochka would pant excitedly, but we did it anyway…

"Yes, I understand," I gasped in bliss, "it's wonderful - to await something beyond expectation!"

Her next instruction was for me to never lose heart, but to keep writing my poems and plays.

"Mitya," she said, "you're seriously fortunate that I'm leaving you. Every poet has his own Laura, his Beatrice, and every knight his Dulcinea. I want you, Mitya, to embody the poet, the knight, and… yes, the gold prospector and sponsor! Better to die with a leather money belt than without any trousers under a fence." (She was alluding to Rimbaud and Verlaine, whose biographies I had familiarised her with.) "The main thing, of course, is to write your works, to strive for the unattainable. Perhaps I'm even entering the unattainable realm to ignite your inspiration. A new era is dawning, Mitya, all sorts of rock groups in St. Petersburg are already eagerly buying up lyrics for good money, then putting them to music and performing for massive fees."

Rozochka confessed that she had even spoken with some gentleman of high culture selling his folk rhymes wholesale and retail. He had revealed that lyrics "with pictures" sell particularly well, and those meant to be sung as a duet sell like hotcakes, paid for in hard currency.

"Mitya, remember: fame and money go hand-in-hand, and paradise with the beloved in a hut[64] is usually only attained by those with piles of cash. Go on writing your works, strive for the unattainable, and don't be shy about selling your manuscripts. By the way, in the trade they call them 'imperishables," Rozochka informed me.

---

64   "With one's beloved, even a hut is heaven" is a popular Russian saying.

She allotted a year and a half, two years maximum, for me to fulfil her instructions.

"In two years' time, just before taking my vows (after medical college), we'll meet again and resolve any lingering issues."

Yes, that's exactly how Rozochka put it: "Resolve any lingering issues." In just two weeks, so many new words and expressions had entered her lexicon that I didn't know what to make of it. Still, her every word paled in the light of the essence of her instructions and actions to be taken for her lofty purpose.

Meanwhile, I sat there by "the quelling will," the lilac twilight and first twinkling stars telling me I had been left alone, that Rozochka was indeed gone and I would have to carry on somehow. Maybe go stay with my mother? Or better yet, go to Moscow where I might randomly encounter Rozochka. No, she wouldn't believe it was random, she'd suspect it was staged and, God forbid, think I was following her! Then she really would come to hate me…

I shivered and trudged back to the dorm. I would fulfil her orders for now, the so-called striving for the unattainable, and we'd see what happened from there, I decided. My head was pounding, and I could think of nothing except my bed.

CHAPTER 17

I fell ill after Rozochka's departure. My temperature kept fluctuating, soaring to feverish heights when "the thermometer was off the charts," as the neighbour put it, and then plummeting below normal levels.

"Corpses are warmer than you," was Alina Spiridonovna's grim assessment as she came to check on me, wondering aloud whether to call an ambulance or simply have me taken straight to the morgue. I should mention that for some reason, Alina felt guilty towards me and tried to smother her sudden pity with crude jokes. To be frank, I grew to hate her. I could sense that she guessed the true reason for my illness and, blaming herself in some way, pitied me and attempted to ease my suffering. Her breakfasts, lunches, and dinners delivered in a thermos prompted hysterical inner laughter. Such pity doesn't just demean, it kills. Moreover, I saw it as nothing but a parody of Rozochka's compassion. The last straw was when she had my bed linens changed out of schedule.

Without so much as a knock, Alina barged into my room with some hulking plumber who, without a word, scooped me up from the bed and flung me over his shoulder like a sack of pipes and fittings. As Alina stripped the sheets and pillowcases, he stood by like a lifeless statue. I tried to resist, flailing my arms and legs with all my might, but the gargantuan plumber didn't react. He took my fussing for death throes, merely urging the lady: "Alya, hurry up, I think the poor devil is expiring, he's going into convulsions."

He then promptly forgot about me, letting out a cheerful grunt and pinching Alina's backside. She flinched and swung at me hard because the brute deftly used me as a shield, even chuckling approvingly: "That's it, spank some dust out of him!" Then he addressed me with fatherly remonstrance: "You better behave yourself, scaring the lady like that!"

As she made the bed, Alina Spiridonovna kept bending over, watchfully tracking the plumber who kept trying to position himself behind her. I ended up an unwilling party to their vulgar flirtation - disgusting!

"What are you clucking about?" the plumber eventually asked me, abruptly dumping me from his shoulder just as unceremoniously as he'd scooped me up.

"Good Lord, Tutankhamun! There's a table here instead of a mesh[65]," the lady exclaimed in alarm.

"That's why he went thump, I reckon," the plumber said sheepishly. "Don't you fret, Alya, these poet fellows and writers are tough as witches. Look at him rolling his eyes - a natural warlock!"

He then regaled credulous Alina with lore that doing away with a warlock wasn't so simple: you had to smash the nearest timber well shaft or, failing that, the ceiling over his bed.

It wasn't so much the plumber's flat jokes that unnerved me, but my own helplessness. Meanwhile, he went on:

---

65   Some old style soviet beds were made of a metal frame and a metal mesh. Covered with a thin mattress this mesh was sufficiently comfortable to sleep on, often becoming too soft and yielding to body weight over time. It was also very common for kids to use these beds as trampolines.

"Let's go, Alya…see how he's eyeing us and smacking his lips - he's putting a curse on us!"

Alyona didn't believe him, saying my temperature was so high I was blowing bubbles. But when she placed her hot hand on my forehead, she immediately recoiled:

"Look here, he's ice cold like a piece of iron."

She fell silent then pensively offered her theory:

"He's pining for his good-for-nothing little wife, that's what makes him go hot and cold."

The plumber didn't buy it. As they left, he said:

"It's only pipes that burst from heat and cold…The warlock's faking it to get closer to a lady's skirt."

The plumber's vulgar advances and Alina's overbearing solicitude struck me as so abhorrent that I inadvertently shuddered, imagining them mourning my "untimely demise" together:

"Well, curse you, Tutankhamun! Your warlock croaked, and you don't give a damn! … Trying to wriggle under a lady's skirt - you Tutankhamun, how dare you!"

"How was I to know, Alya? I thought he was a real poet, a writer, but I guess his guts weren't up for it…"

"No, no," I told myself, "Anything but that! I won't stand such 'mourners' even in the grave." My revulsion at the scene of "untimely demise" was so intense that, fighting through the headache, I turned to reading the manuscripts. Of course, I could only think about the collective anthology insofar as it represented the striving for the unattainable.

I started with the adventure stories. Though I'd once hoped for an enjoyable read, it was nothing of the sort. The protagonists

- poetic types, philosophers, journalists and so on - were virtually indistinguishable from one another. I marvelled: so much for the creative class! Even more oddly, not content with their primary vocation, all these intellectuals had hobbies too, with rare exceptions.

"…That is, after intense mental labour they liked to unwind, get away from the daily grind and immerse themselves whole-heartedly in meticulous craft: whittling a carriage shaft, polishing some bronze plaque, or brewing Russian moonshine from a German recipe. You'd sit there, whittling away, your thoughts taking shape as does the shaft, all of them of pure gold, just take them and put them on paper – but you can't. Using his poetic intuition, Efim Efimovich sensed that his true artistic timber is not here, it is somewhere on the way ahead, in the subject itself, in the carriage shaft itself." Or: "Efim adored Alla Leopoldovna endlessly, and she loved him uncompromisingly too. Sometimes they'd lie side by side on the shavings, gazing at the toolshed's ceiling, enjoying the warmth, softness, and scent of a pine forest.

'Allochka,' Efim would murmur.

'Yes, Fima?' she'd respond after a pause.

And they'd lie there in silence, as if in a shipyard timber forest. No need for words, everything had been said already, Efim thought joyfully, guessing from her delayed response that Allochka felt the same endless bliss."

After such revelations, I felt a lump in my throat and my breath caught. I readily admit, I too wished I could have lain beside Rozochka on those soft pine shavings.

The manuscript pages kept slipping from my hands. Fighting dizziness, I'd clamber back onto my bed - what was the point of literature, like life, having to be motivated? No, human beings deserve happiness without any justification. My imagination is my own, and no one can rule over it.

At first, Rozochka and I just rested upon the pine shavings, but then my mind painted a colourful picture of my journey to her...

I'm travelling from the City of N straight to the Kremlin. Riding in a special train carriage, I'm guarded by highly trained KGB officers as a national treasure. Of course, I'm unaware of this, I'm a famous poet in a free country, featured in the school curricula right after Alexander Tvardovsky[66]. Waiters bring me various hot dishes at train stops on what seem like ordinary cafeteria trays. But my keen ear picks up muffled exclamations of awe that the trays are pure, highest-grade gold. I pretend some mistake has been made, that I'm not involved, unwilling to flaunt my fame. The information has leaked though, and my adoring readers desperate for autographs mob my compartment with flowers and brass bands in tow. "It's him, it's him!" I hear ringing out night after night. Rapturous sobs drown in spontaneous chants:

"Long live Russia, long live the Poet!"

There's no use denying it, so I raise my hands in surrender to the waiters' and everyone's jubilance. I allow them to leave the tray with cabbage soup and steaming mutton, plus a silver pail

---

66   Alexander Tvardovsky (1910-1971) was one of the most influential Soviet poets. As editor of Novy Mir magazine, he championed works depicting WWII and Soviet life, creating space for critical voices within the system.

with champagne. I need nothing more as the train pulls away amidst a throng in the vestibule and on the platform: some toss flowers into my open window, others throw them underfoot, some heartily wish me a wonderful journey, while others stuff chocolates and chocolate bars into my pockets, urging me to stay a day or two as their guest.

Everything goes fabulously, resonating accordingly in the mass media. I'm oblivious to the hourly breaking news bulletins about the fervour over my person on shortwave - Radio Free Europe, Voice of America, the BBC. Yet the overwhelming public admiration causes serious concerns upstairs. At midnight, a man entirely in black with a wide-brimmed hat appeared and sat across from me, brusquely revealing he'd been sent to thwart attempts by Western intelligence to "neutralise" me.

"They've been tasked," he whispered in my ear, "with eliminating you and pinning this wet job on our gullible operatives."

With an abrupt grunt, he cut it short: "Not a chance."

I nodded contentedly and, catching his meaningful look, opened the champagne. I immediately guessed he was a "knight of the cloak and dagger," but asked who he was, where he was from, and how I could be of service so late at night on this special train.

My question flustered him, and he fidgeted - clearly, knights dislike questions under any circumstances, but he was trapped. He said his full name was Ivan Ivanovich Pronin and he was from the "deaf-mute office."

"Very well," I agreed, filling our flutes, "let's dispense with formalities - Poet Mitya or Comrade Slyozkin will do."

"Pronya or Comrade Major," he offered in turn, proceeding to lay out our plan of action over the champagne.

The plan was extremely simple: as soon as we reached the main St. Petersburg-Moscow railroad, Comrade Slyozkin would immediately cease all contact not just with readers and admirers, but with everyone on board, in other words, disappear completely.

"The international community won't understand my disappearance," I countered modestly yet with dignity, clarifying: "and will voice its profound bewilderment through enemy radio stations…"

"Oh, they'll voice it gleefully, but with funereal mien," the major cheerfully concurred, reassuring me: "That's when we grab them by the gills."

His plan was to indulge the adversary while always staying half a step ahead, not a full step or two, but precisely half a step. While I slept soundly in my berth (the train was due to arrive in Moscow at 9:54 a.m.), he would use his extensive channels to release the official version of events: an acute attack… renal colic, pain medication proving ineffective, Comrade Poet had to be urgently removed for hospital treatment. The authorities remained confident, however, that said Poet would arrive at the Leningrad Station[67] at the scheduled time.

And an utterly baffling remark, inexplicable for the uninformed: those planning to welcome the Poet are advised to kindly refrain from turning up.

"There'll be a mob scene, the place will be absolutely packed!" the major promised, starkly concluding: "You, Poet Mitya, get added public glory, while the state keeps its spotless reputation."

---

67   One of the major train stations in Moscow.

Moreover, he confided, his extensive channels would circulate the most ludicrous rumours about my disappearance, hinting to the international community that the official story was a bald-faced lie, a coverup for the KGB's latest crime - snatching the beloved Poet from his Great People without due process.

Pronya's plan wasn't half bad, not bad from any angle, because awaiting me at the Leningrad Station would be not just flower-bearing, brass-banding readers and admirers, but representatives of the Russian Orthodox Church, emissaries of the Moscow Patriarch himself. We'd arranged that before I proceeded to the Kremlin Palace, I would first visit the Moscow Theological Seminary to read my poetry. Incidentally, the major knew nothing about the Church representatives or my meeting with the clergy - that was where the most delightful, tantalisingly alluring part of my imagined Moscow journey began, the very reason I fantasized about it in the first place.

CHAPTER 18

The train slowed, students and schoolchildren kept dashing across the tracks with flowers and garlands of multicoloured balloons. I listened to the festive hubbub outside, but the music blaring at full volume from the carriage speakers drowned it out.

I opened the window opposite my compartment, and greetings in my honour came raining down on our sluggishly moving train. Smiling shyly, I waved, guessing from the telltale behaviour of my exalted readers (a sea of raised hands, mouths opening in a collective shout then closing again) that they were chanting my name. I glanced around involuntarily to somehow muffle those nasty speakers inside the carriage, and that's when Comrade Major - Pronya?! - came running up. Astounding! ... At first, I didn't recognise him - he was in military uniform with broad navy stripes down his trousers and a single star on his shoulder boards.

"Comrade Poet!" he said confusedly into my ear, the music from above drowning him out too. "Comrade Poet!"

(Clearly, he didn't dare call me Mitya or Comrade Slyozkin after witnessing the Great People's jubilation firsthand)

"Comrade Poet!" he repeated a third time. "They're greeting you like Peter the Great or even the Supreme Leader of the Masses!"

His voice rang with admiration and dread at the same time: apparently, he hadn't anticipated such a grandiose apogee, even having personally orchestrated the welcome via his information channels.

"Come now, my good man, I'm just Poet Mitya," I said modestly, reminding him casually that we had agreed on informality. "Or Comrade General, should I revise our rapport?"

"No revisions!" the cloak-and-dagger knight implored. "To you I was and remain your devoted Pronya, Comrade Major from the 'deaf-mute office' at best."

I said nothing in response, merely giving him a pointed look and raising my eyebrows quizzically at his general's attire.

"Ah…" Pronya groaned with a dismissive wave. "Got a yen to show off." He immediately owned up: "They promoted me just the other day…brand new uniform."

"I see. I understand completely," I said, satisfied, returning my brows to neutral; it wouldn't do to overdo it, especially since I did know military folks are obliged to pay respect to shoulder boards above everything else.

Meanwhile, the general continued sheepishly:

"Truth be told, I never dreamed that you, ordinary Mitya, already rank among the World Leaders and Emperors of literature."

I shrugged, spreading my arms - what could I do if God had gifted me talent beyond measure?

"You don't say," the general agreed, proposing we step into the compartment to coordinate our next moves.

As he explained we'd soon exit the carriage (the doors on both ends were already flung open, the carriage music to be turned off momentarily), I noticed a lilac speck amid black vestments through the drape slit. There could be no doubt - it was her, Rozochka! I'd recognise her anywhere even after a thousand years. The general and I went out of the compartment. The music ceased.

"All going according to plan!" he shouted pre-emptively, because our appearance sent the thousands gathered into a true frenzy, cheers blending into a solid roar.

Dozens of film and TV cameras, incessant flashbulbs going off, clusters of microphones thrust out from all sides suddenly reminded me of a childhood festival.

"Peace to the world!" I cried out emotionally.

"Peace to the world!" the general sobbed no less emotionally.

Oh, what followed! The human sea surged in unison, and the chant repeatedly rolled from one side of the platform to another, like over a stadium.

Pronya and I, unabashedly shedding tears of joy and tenderness, hugged firmly and purposefully held our manly embrace for the press to see. We didn't forget for a second the foreign intelligence machinations, understanding that my appearance before the people, hand- in- hand with a KGB general, would instantly ruin all their vile schemes.

We reprised the scene on the other side of the carriage, too. As the train inched along the crowded rail siding, our carriage drew so close to a speck of lilac that I could easily make out Rozochka's wistful expression in my peripheral vision. She was conversing with the Archpriest. I figured out that this was the Archpriest, from his staff and stole peeking out from under his phelonion.

"Well, I'll be," I thought proudly, "look how far Rozochka has come on her spiritual journey, parleying as an equal with the bishop himself!"

I know not what sense it was, sixth, eighth or twenty-eighth, more likely a spouse's intuition, but not only did I immediately divine that they were discussing me, but I heard, distinctly heard their entire conversation in detail (even though I certainly understood that it should've been virtually impossible amid such a crowd). But listen!

"Dear Master, I still can't believe that Poet Mitya Slyozkin himself is coming to us, the one I told you about in such detail when I confessed before taking communion. The one who recently published a poem dedicated to me, and… and suffered for it, fell from grace in the eyes of the KGB and democratic public?"

"Yes, handmaiden of God, future Mother Rozaria the Russian, it is that very Poet Slyozkin coming to us. But what ails you, what gnaws and torments you? Tell your confessor, unburden your immaculate soul."

"The thing is, dear Master, that this very Poet Mitya Slyozkin is the husband I left to become Mother Rozaria the Russian."

"Lord be with you, Lord save you from blaspheming," the hierarch cautioned piously, regarding Rozochka so abstractedly it was clear he was uttering an inner prayer to forgive those who know not what they do.

"I do not blaspheme, I speak the truth," Rozochka instantly parried, then blushed, remembering that bluntness ill-befitted the future Mother Rozaria, who must instead be soft and prudent.

"Forgive me, Master, but I could never have imagined my Mitya, that dreamy bumbler, achieving anything (she did so enjoy venting any miscalculation at my expense), let alone rising so rapidly to become a poet worthy of inclusion in the school curriculum alongside Alexander Tvardovsky. Inconceivable!"

"And yet it is so," the bishop said gently. "Try to look around impartially, especially over there."

His cuff-clad hand emerged elegantly from beneath his robe and gently gestured at Pronya and me embracing again.

"Mitya!" the general bellowed merrily directly into my ear as usual, striving to be heard over the human sea's roar: "Check out the beauty in the lilac blouse chatting with that high-ranking priest - she's clearly sweet on you… it's making me envious!"

Smiling, he winked at me, and I playfully dealt him a hearty slump upside his head, knowing in advance how delighted Rozochka would be that I was already on such friendly terms with KGB generals, a sort of elder brother free to slap them right before the cameras.

Seeing Rozochka laugh merrily, the priest carefully asked:

"Well, my daughter, what say you now?"

"I'm no daughter of yours nor have I ever been!" Rozochka suddenly kicked up. "I've always wanted to be solely Mother Rozaria the Russian, and nothing more! … So please be careful, holy father, and never forget it."

Her face flushed with familiar red splotches, but she mastered herself, enunciating as if summing up:

"Ne-ver!"

Rozochka's seemingly inexplicable and incomprehensible

anger was quite explicable and understandable to me - she had recognised me and, seeing firsthand my swift and far-reaching ascent, felt angry first and foremost at herself, at her own short-sightedness and underestimation of me. She had dismissed me as a dreamy bumbler, but here I was giving slaps to KGB generals. As for the priest, he'd simply got in the way…

I froze: Lord, help the bishop see the heavenly justice in Rozochka's behaviour as You had shown it to me! And then a miracle occurred, one so common among the Orthodox that some laymen even see it as our Church going too soft. I speak of God's supreme, agonising love which shines upon the Orthodox, making them take no notice of oppression, humiliation, or filthy vituperation against them. Remember in The Brothers Karamazov when Father Zosima knelt before Dmitri prior to his great suffering? As if out of nowhere, the holy father suddenly dropped to his knees before Rozochka, throwing her into utter disarray - what would people think?! Beside herself, she rushed to the bishop, lifted him to his feet and, flustered, fell against his chest:

"Forgive me, Master, for Christ's sake! I have always loved my darling Mitya and now love him more than ever, my azure flower betrothed to me by the Lord God Himself."

She choked on inconsolable sobs, and I, lying on the bed with my hands behind my head, almost physically felt my own eyes well up.

"Pardon, pardon the foolish Mother Rozaria the Russian for refusing to be your daughter! She loved and will eternally love the most famous modern poet Mitya Slyozkin, Peter the

Great of Soviet poetry, but help her, help dispel her final doubts - how could it happen in such a short time?!"

"Oh, handmaiden of God, future Mother Rozaria, you know as well as I what a chosen vessel is," the holy father pronounced with stately deliberation, as if stating an amazing yet long-proven fact. "It descended upon Mitya."

"I knew it!" Rozochka rejoiced. "He could never have managed this on his own…"

And again, the Archpriest gently cautioned:

"Do not be hasty in judgement, 'For to the one who has, more will be given, and he will have an abundance, but from the one who has not, even what he has will be taken away[68]…"

The train stopped.

"Excellent neural resilience, truly admirable," Pronya said meaningfully, leaning in to murmur: "Poet-Chronicler, mission accomplished. On behalf of the 'white sock' movement instigators, you are hereby secretly awarded the highest state honour to be presented in due course."

"I serve our Poetry," I whispered back; releasing his embrace, he stepped away to render a crisp military salute.

"Well, I'll be, it's the young man with a moustache from HAN that I mistook for a naval officer in disguise," I suddenly recalled.

"Comrade Poet, my mission is over, you are safe, the foreign agents have failed. Farewell until we meet again in the Kremlin."

He stepped down from the carriage through the flickering light of relentless camera flashes.

---

68   Matthew 13:12

"Pronya, I recognised you!" I called out joyfully, but he didn't hear - friendly hands caught him and he floated above the cheering crowd.

The chants accompanying Pronya - "Praise Russia, praise the Poet!" - grew more and more distant until they disappeared in the human torrent streaming to meet the train.

I stood stunned and dejected…Surges of frenzied people in search of their idol swept past me with a gut-rumbling roar. Some, craning their necks, asked impatiently:

"Where is he, where?!"

Good Lord, how foolish people are to make themselves an idol! I felt a sort of vengeful relief seeing my readers getting it wrong, having mistaken me for the KGB general. For no reason at all, I waved my arm beckoning several times and yelled at them, pointing toward the rear:

"I saw him, he's there, there!"

Then I came to, unexpectedly discovering that my inner and outer vision had sharpened, along with my hearing.

"Oh Master, I don't mean that…that is, I agree it descended upon Mitya, that he is aided by the Almighty, but then what need does he have of me now?…I thought he would perish without me, perhaps even die, but after his divine deliverance do I have the moral right to return to him, and in so doing sacrifice my high purpose, sacrifice becoming Mother Rozaria the Russian?! That is the question, dear Master."

"Ah, a tricky question. In times past such questions would have meant excommunication," the priest answered sternly.

I'll admit, I sincerely regret those times are now gone. Look around at all the tricky sorts crawling out from among ordinary folk and even the clergy's ranks! Donning cassocks, holding placards instead of icons they progress up the Supreme Councils and other high offices. God's chosen people have risen to be elected by urban and rural caucuses. Excommunicated they must be, all of them must be anathemized, as in memorable times of yore. Or better yet, as in Christ's time, stoned by the masses so they don't dare roil honest Orthodox Christians again.

I never imagined my mental philippic in praise of days bygone would not only be heard by the hierarch and Rozochka, but blight their conversation, too. Yet that's precisely what happened.

"Dear Indira Gandhi!" the priest suddenly boomed like a famous General Secretary, seeming to orate from deep inside his belly. "You are not just India's mother, but ours too."

"What's this about, I don't understand?!" I recoiled in horror.

Rozochka flushed, her eyes flashing: she understood everything perfectly, yet mastered herself, snidely remarking:

"I'm Mrs. Thatcher, Thatcher, got it, eh?"

The priest looked heavenward in amazement, crossing himself widely and zealously three times. He hadn't intended to phrase it that way, his aim was to persuade Rozochka to return home. He was about to say she ought to always remain beside such a remarkable person as Mitya Slyozkin, and then suddenly...

I stood petrified, frozen like a statue. But I shouldn't have frozen, I should've somehow signalled the priest to be silent or at least pause before answering, yet I was flustered, rooted to the spot... And so, he said with that meek insistence that wears stones away, characteristic of holy fathers:

"Free will…! Dear Indira Thatcher, Iron Lady, Mother Rozaria, for crying out loud!"

I crumpled into the human stream right where I stood.

"Where is he, where?!"

"Tromped," my mind replied casually, and I grasped that incidental, secondary thought like a drowning man grasps at a straw.

The crowd came to a halt, froze instantly, and I saw Rozochka. Clutching her breast in anguish, she staggered sightlessly toward me.

"It's all her fault…hers! Mother Rozaria the Russian has doomed our beloved Poet Mitya!" Threatening voices rang out from all sides.

Another stray thought flickered peripherally: They'll trample Rozochka too! Trouble breeds trouble…

I awoke in dread… What nonsense, what gibberish?! That's what you get from reading manuscripts from editorial shelves. That's what unmotivated bliss leads to. Be that as it may, Efim and Alla's endless love simply didn't come to pass for Rozochka and me.

CHAPTER 19

My neighbour, the one who took Doublenose's rifle, was a single mother working as a seamstress in a clothing workshop. I hardly noticed her when Rozochka and I lived together. I knew she had a preschool-aged son named Artur who attended 24-hour daycare, and that was about it. I remembered his name because I gave him a chocolate once and asked what his name was, as adults usually do. (This introduction took place in the communal kitchen.) She jumped up, angrily snatched the sweet away and threw it in the bin.

"He can't have chocolate!" she said furiously, picking up the child and abruptly correcting me that his name was pronounced AHR-tur, not Ar-TOOR.

Dressed in an unbuttoned chequered sweater over a simple blue dress, winter and summer, she didn't invite conversation. Rozochka said her husband Givi (we never met him) used to transport bottled wine from Tbilisi and apparently under-reported only a couple of railcar tankers' worth, but still got jailed. The night before his arrest he stayed up all night partying with friends, then went door-to-door leaving a bottle of Rkatsiteli wine in each room, saying, "With compliments from Givi."

Anyway, we mutually avoided getting acquainted, and I didn't even know her name. But then after the "rifle" case and after I flatly refused Alina Spiridonovna's thermoses, she suddenly showed up herself along with the local therapist[69], behaving as if

---

69   In Soviet Union doctors did home visits routinely.

I were a relative of hers at the very least. It was she who yanked the blanket off me and, pushing me from behind, made me stand before the elderly doctor. The doctor made no effort to hide his admiration, smacking his lips so appetisingly it was as if I was his gourmet lunch. He only addressed her, inviting her to listen to the sounds of him tapping on my ribs, explaining why the saying "thin and ringing" was optimal from a medical perspective. He was so delighted by this "remarkable case," as he put it, that he couldn't resist the pleasure of "counting my vertebrae" at the end, running his bent middle finger down my spine a few times, promising that next time he would be showing me to his intern to amaze her with a textbook case of malnutrition.

I warmly thanked him, but he left no prescriptions. The full extent of his instructions to my neighbour was to start with cod liver oil and semolina porridge, gradually increasing my diet back to normal volumes.

The elderly doctor never reappeared, but my neighbour came every day, or rather every evening. She would bring a pot of semolina porridge and a kettle of boiling water with which she used to brew tea for herself in a half-litre jar. Then she would sit on a stool and tell me the news because I had persuaded her not to do any cleaning or even touch the manuscripts lying on the floor.

From her, I learned that Doublenose's gang was initially going to be sent for "treatment" at a labour camp, but after the coup, they were simply fired from the factory, end of the story.

"But that's not the main thing," she whispered to me. "Now they're selling beer right by the television factory gates, from dawn to dusk. They set up there with cases of beer and charge people an arm and a leg. And the strangest part is they don't drink it themselves - they've been grabbed by the police a few times and let go with apologies. Doublenose bragged that there's no evidence against them, that they're wiseasses."

My neighbour buried her face in her hands, whether from shame or laughter, I couldn't tell, then composed herself and went on:

"They're threatening to bring the factory to its knees, to get revenge on the bosses for all their misdeeds… Now they're driving around on a three-wheeled scooter, and they've roped in the plumber. He's now their procurer, buying up dried fish in the villages for peanuts, which they then resell at an inflated price in the 'Pigsty.'"

She laughed and explained that was the name they had given their little stand.

"Recently Doublenose was bragging that the director of the television factory invited him over and promised to build them a kiosk for free if they moved their beer operation away from the gates and set up shop in Victory Square right across from the regional administration building. Doublenose claims he agreed - he's basically the Pigsty's manager."

My neighbour laughed again and, deliberately to please me as a literary man, marvelled at how such a stupid name could be so wildly popular among the working class. Crowds gathered at the so-called Pigsty all day long.

"We've been conditioned to extremes. You can't spank people into being good. This is a sort of rebellion against enforced 'good,' against mandatory happiness, so to speak."

"Well Mitya, you sure are clever, but just what exactly are you rebelling against?" my neighbour playfully jabbed, giving an eloquent look around at the conspicuous disarray of my room.

There was less cheerful news as well: the stores were empty, their shelves were bare, and anything put up for sale was instantly swept up.

"Where do people even get the money? Prices are rocketing, as if on steroids, and according to hearsay, will be fully deregulated - on milk, bread, everything. As of the New Year the whole country will go on a 500-day 'health leave'[70], subjected to some kind of 'shock therapy' reforms to render us just like Poland: loads of goods and no money..."

My neighbour had visited the market - it was swarming with Poles and Balts selling all kinds of scarce goods: knitwear, perfumes, shoes... Each car had a sign with an address, offering to buy televisions, copper, and bronze in unlimited quantities. They're already scavenging here like it's their place.

She would sigh, but then cheer herself up by saying that a huge country like ours couldn't possibly be picked apart in just 500 days.

I got used to our chats. Her simple blue dress no longer seemed so simple to me. In general, though I didn't feel much better after talking to her...at least I wasn't thinking solely about Rozochka.

When I was on the mend, my neighbour brought me an extra blanket which she used to cover the window.

---

70   500 Days Program – a program of controlled transition of Soviet planned economy to market economy. Even though discussed a lot, it was never implemented.

"You'll catch pneumonia before they get the heating going," she said, then unexpectedly burst into tears.

It turned out the daycare fees had increased twice in just the current quarter, and her Artur had been expelled because the director of the sewing workshop refused to pay the subsidy and failed to give her an advance notice.

"She's getting back at me for insisting that seniority be calculated from time working directly in the sewing workshop as per our new corporate charter - she's only been with us three years."

My neighbour collapsed onto my bed, sobbing. From the very first day she started bringing the porridge and tea, I had been thinking of a way to repay her kindness, and this was a good opportunity.

At first, she protested, but then accepted. She said fifty roubles would be more than enough. I counted out three hundred, asking her to send two hundred to my mother in the Altai region - at least she could buy hay for her goats. My neighbour promised to send it, even writing down the address to avoid confusion. The rest of that evening she was cheerful and rather playful, though admittedly I can get that way too whenever I suddenly come into money.

"You're just as much of a spendthrift as my Givi, Mitya. And your money looks just as beat-up, like it came from a liquor store."

Why did she have to say that?! I tensed. But she kept on talking nonsense, laughing, and comparing me to her Givi in a way that was downright unpleasant... It really stung when she said her Givi wasn't her real husband and had never actually been arrested. He had simply gone back to his family in Georgia after she kicked him out.

And she herself wasn't really a seamstress by training, but an English teacher; she'd even attended a study programme abroad, in Manchester. But then because of that idiot Givi she had had to change career.

Her mention of Manchester just about did me in, leaving me so uneasy that I heaved a sigh of relief when she finally left. She was gone, but I still felt unsettled, as if she had been encroaching on my memories of Rozochka. I didn't eat the porridge that evening, just had some tea before going to bed. The next morning, I fried up some bread so I could say I'd already eaten when she brought dinner.

But she didn't come that evening. I was told she had gone with her son to visit her mother in the village for a vacation. And thank God, I thought with relief, once again losing myself in thoughts of Rozochka, as if daydreaming about her could make up for the guilt I vaguely felt towards her, if not bring her back.

CHAPTER 20

"Hey, over here! Quick, over here! Somebody's been hurt!" …"What a pity, so young, so promising… And that death mask?! Just like Pushkin's, or Napoleon's, or that fellow from Kuprin's 'The Garnet Bracelet,' Mr Zheltkov… Ah, the poor soul should have lived, but fate had other plans…"

"Alright, enough clucking about fate and whatnot… Move aside, let us get the poor wretch from underfoot!"

This was the plumber showing up out of nowhere, unceremoniously flinging me over his shoulder…

I sat up in bed, shaking my head fiercely to dispel the vision clouding my mind. I wanted to dream of something else, but no chance! A trio of "divorced guys" appeared from nowhere, two with a stretcher and Doublenose with a rifle, all businesslike, barking orders in a hurry but only hassling the young women: Pardon, madame! Pardon… The gang's procurer Tutankhamon appeared to be the fourth to carry my earthly remains.

My fellow literary union mates somehow ended up in the crowd too. Mayakovsky was particularly loud:

"A tragedy, a tragedy worthy of an English classic!"

For some reason, his insistent bass voice kept popping up from different spots. And then a sudden hush fell - everyone caught sight of a stunningly beautiful young woman in a lilac blouse and baggy jeans. A piercing, heart-rending wail rent the air:

"I'm not to bla-a-ame, not to bla-a-ame!"

"Well, I'll be… that was just like in the movie[71]!" flashed through my mind, but even before that thought arrived, I opened my eyes and saw darkness, not a glimmer of light anywhere… Where was I? Had I gone mad?! I sat up in fright in the bed, feeling chills of horror. It seemed I was sitting on some kind of wooden stretcher. Instinctively, I reached out and bumped into the wall, into the clammy chill of peeling wallpaper that sighed as if coming alive. I felt relieved - you can't mistake that rustling breath of walls for anything…

My well-wishers, led by Doublenose, jerked the stretcher abruptly and in discord, the plumber overdoing it, though thankfully I managed to grab the bars from below, otherwise they'd surely have dumped me right onto the pavement.

"Easy now, Tutankhamun, don't drop him, you buffoon!" Doublenose hissed in annoyance, then cooed affectionately, as if I could hear him, "And your arms, Mitya, tuck them in, no need for them to dangle."

They called over the headman (I recognised him by his characteristic cane tapping), and after feeling me over, he arranged my arms on my belly as if I were dead.

"Those work boots won't do… Should have been white slippers, or at the very least white trainers," he remarked judiciously, mentioning he'd seen some very sturdy trainers that day at a new department store, sewn on the inside with nylon thread, just seven roubles a pair. "Yes, seven," he repeated with a heavy sigh.

---

71   Indeed, that scream is an extremely famous meme from one of the most popular soviet comedies, "The Diamond Arm" (1969), and the person screaming was played by one of the prettiest Soviet actresses of the time.

My well-wishers shooed him away, Doublenose even slapping the rifle stock menacingly. The headman snapped back but scampered away from the stretcher.

"Spouts such nonsense and still has lip, as if Mitya could have known in advance he'd be stomped to death!" Doublenose sputtered indignantly.

I had to agree with him. I knew better than anyone why the headman had felt me over so thoroughly, my pockets to be precise, and why he had mentioned seven roubles and sighed so heavily. Seven roubles was the fee to participate in the collective poetry anthology which, incidentally, he had never paid. What kind of man was this? Here I am with one foot already in the grave; what was he thinking? He posed as a person of high culture, he was my Leo Nikolaevich Tolstoy, and now look how petty he turned out to be! I felt like spitting down on him from my stretcher, especially since this time they had lifted it up in a more coordinated manner and steadied it at shoulder height.

Suddenly I had an epiphany: the headman was right, right! Maybe I had come to Moscow specifically to have that promised poetry collection published? Which means I must have brought the money… He probably thought I'd been robbed… Hence that heavy sigh. You'd sigh too at the poet stripped bare by his readers and admirers! What kind of readers are they, more like marauders! Well, maybe not all, maybe just one bad apple spoiling the lot.

I felt sorry for the poor headman, genuinely sorry. He could have thought whatever about whomever since he knew and still knows nothing about Rozochka. I wanted to console the poor fellow, tell him, cheer up Count Tolstoy, there will be a celebration on our bright glade[72] too! Alas, I could not even move in my tragic state and indeed, within a moment, I too found myself in need of consolation…

"I'm not to bla-a-ame, not to bla-a-ame!"

I felt a chilling fear permeate through my skin. I jerked violently in bed, smacking my head against the headboard. Well, I had that coming! A sense of doom overcame me: there was at least some semblance of life in my foolish fantasies, but there was nothing but desolation, darkness, and utter uselessness here, between these four walls.

I folded my arms as if lying in a coffin, and it felt so cosy, so restful that I immediately envisioned myself in an open casket right after closing my eyes. I was carried feet-first across a thronged plaza in front of the train station. I could see a sea of bare heads on either side and in my mind's eye I marvelled: heads, heads… so many mournful heads across all of Russia!

The banners were hung at half-mast. I could hear the crowd's steady shuffling tread as it advanced slowly across the square, and then, suddenly, voices bursting with hog-wild joy.

"Well, I'll be… that shriek was the real deal, like in the movie or even better, the shriek to end all shrieks! Gave me chills, I tell you! If Mitya had heard it he'd have been overjoyed, he loved that shrew to the point of madness!"

I smiled inside my coffin. My well-wishers were discussing the distressing news that had caught Rozochka off guard.

"But I'll bet anyone it was not grief that made her scream like that. They've been hounding her - it's always her, her! … She

---

72   Yasnaya Polyana (Bright Glade) is the name of Leo Tolstoy's primary residence, now a museum.

just snapped from the stress."

The plumber peered into the casket, meaning to divine my innermost thoughts from my expression, but I was lying there numb and detached, no longer there though physically present, just a corpse.

The plumber, the fool that he was, had become jealous of Alina Spiridonovna, but his judgment and the whole unsophisticated conversation around the casket put me in a philosophical mood.

Common folks, they're like children. In their mischief they end up causing trouble, then try to blame it on anybody and everybody (it wasn't Rozochka who trampled me to death after all). That's what was happening here. They had even rejoiced that Rozochka, slim, bold, feminine, and charming – in their view exactly the type to bring about a beloved Poet's downfall - had conveniently made an appearance.

That same mournful minute when my lifeless body was pulled up from underfoot, Rozochka had truly been a beauty to behold: anguished arms gracefully snuggled to her breasts; glistening raven tresses slightly dishevelled from crying…" Family people, leave errands aside, Beautiful lady, wipe those tears away…" - lines I had once written in a poem called "Flowers."

More arguing broke out beneath the casket: where to take the bodies? It was high time for everyone to form a funeral procession… But we couldn't very well do it right here at the station's plaza?!

"What 'bodies'? What nonsense is that?" I thought.

"Suits me fine anywhere, anyhow," the plumber said merrily,

then, abruptly meeting a wall of condemnation, he exaggeratedly marvelled, "Well, I'll be damned, this Mitya is a featherweight, a real poet alright!"

"Listen to this jester!" Doublenose jabbed.

"We've no objection to the hero..." I heard the editor's timid, characteristically hesitant voice. "But the word is, poet Slyozkin was a KGB mole, a counterrevolutionary!"

"That's irrelevant," Doublenose firmly objected, unceremoniously telling the editor to take his place by the casket.

Self-appointed master of ceremonies, he strode about self-importantly, purposefully hitching up the rifle, and curtly asked without looking at anyone in particular:

"Did Mitya have any medals or honours, does anyone know?"

Inside, I felt utterly chilled. I did not want to be buried with honours fit for a revolutionary hero or veteran of the Civil War - both went against my principles; I considered both a disgrace.

"He has the highest state honour, but it's completely secret," an unfamiliar Pronya barked in a clipped military tone, producing a dark burgundy velvet cushion from under his general's coat with the glistening Gold Star of a Hero of the Soviet Union resting on it.

"It's all over!" I thought hopelessly when suddenly Pronya said he would lead the procession with the cushion, that we had to go to the Red Square, to the Mausoleum, he knew there were free spots still available, but we had to bury Mitya today, right now.

"Almost like a joke," I smirked deep inside.

Doublenose had clearly been badly spooked by Pronya's general's regalia. He agreed obsequiously and tried to slink away unnoticed into the crowd but failed (hard to miss an armed man after all), as the pliant crowd rippled aside, leaving him exposed. He was reminded of his duties as the funeral marshal and advised inquiring whom exactly Mitya had come to Moscow to see.

I didn't need to see to know it was the headman's assistant who had suggested this. Sure enough, the headman immediately presented his theory on why I had appeared in Moscow. He was just lacking one final detail - the publishing house's address.

"Here we go," I thought, "they want to take advantage of my earthly remains to get their group anthology placed with a top literary publisher…" I pictured the many thousands strong crowd heavily churning as it flooded the street formerly named after Vorovsky, pouring into the publisher's courtyard, and coming to a halt right in front of the grand entrance. Oh, Lord, how many writers' fates and manuscripts lie buried here! It did seem an apt choice to arrive feet first. I inwardly smirked again. Hey editors, meet a celebrated author from boondocks!

Doublenose returned to his duties as the chief marshal, hitching up his rifle and ordering:

"Come on, come on you geezers! No stopping here, we'll take another route: to the Red Square, to the Mausoleum, that's where we'll lay them side by side."

Lay whom side by side? … Surely not me next to the Leader of the World Proletariat?! That's a non-starter, I'm baptised!

I propped myself up and sat upright in the casket, no longer caring what the readers and fans might think, having lost all sense of reality. And then a sudden blow to the back of the head snapped me right back into my senses. What happened was I had abruptly and clumsily fallen backwards from the sitting position, smacking my head against the tabletop serving as the base of my bed. The reason I fell was that riding right beside me on the shoulders of some clergy in a casket identical to mine, seated in the same position, was Rozochka.

PART THREE

CHAPTER 21

All those train stations, brass bands, crowds of admiring readers with flowers and colourful balloons, all those "divorcees" and literary union members with Doublenose and the KGB general to boot - in my fantasies they were all secondary, like set dressing, to really get to Rozochka and make her regret leaving me. But quite unexpectedly for me, these secondary, peripheral people took such a strong grip of the situation that Rozochka and I were almost always reduced to bargaining chips in their hands. Perhaps that's how the Lord God originally created evil, merely as a flavouring for good, but it turned out quite different and became a self-contained dominating force. In short, these secondary people mistreated and abused us so unfairly and sacrilegiously that I could no longer indulge in fantasies - I never, ever wanted to subject Rozochka to any violence, never!

As I recall, I tore down the blanket the neighbour had hung over the window and immediately found myself in an entirely different world. Everything around was bright and festive: pavements, garage roofs, and even the windowsills were covered by snow. The morning sunlight reflected in the windows, painting the frost-covered trees in pink. I was overcome by an inexplicable, unbridled joy and rapture, as if I had truly just crawled out of the grave and come back to life.

I decided to go outside for a walk since not only had my illness made me lose track of the days, but I also hadn't seen anything beyond my four walls for a long time. To my shame, I suddenly realised I was completely unprepared for the winter. I had no coat, no cloak, not even a jacket. Using an awl, some nylon thread and clothesline, I fashioned a sort of poncho robe out of the flannel blanket, sort of military-style poncho but with a double layer over the shoulders.

I first appeared in public wearing it the next day. I knew that my appearance might provoke undesirable gossip, so I shaved carefully and even poured the last drops of my "Chypre" cologne over my head. I hoped smart people would pretend not to notice, while fools simply wouldn't understand. I ventured forth boldly. I still had some money and could afford a proper coat from a department store; my poncho was just a temporary outfit to get me there.

I was mistaken on all counts. I was greeted in an unfriendly way, and where? In my own dorm, my own home! When I peeked into the kitchen to ask what day it was, a neighbour who had her back to me suddenly dropped her spoon and rushed out to the hallway. The other "homemakers," as if on command, fell deaf, until one sarcastically remarked:

"Oh Lord, a rapist?! Not even worth reporting such a pathetic excuse for a man, you could knock him down with a spit, but look at that... a real Manchester dandy!"

I don't know why, but "rapist" and "Manchester dandy" immediately made me think that the neighbour must have spread some vile rumour about me. But why? It was beneath my dignity to investigate it.

At the front desk, I was almost shoved away too: Alina Spiridonovna snorted that the Nativity Fast was approaching and stared out the window demonstratively, in a way that only she could. As I was leaving, she tossed over her shoulder:

"There are still people around - real shapeshifters!"

The neighbour's hand here too, right? However, it was so nice outside that I didn't want to dwell on anything negative. Bundled in my poncho, I walked through the snow with such pleasure, as if my life were only just beginning.

In the Pioneers' Park, I intentionally veered off the path and stopped under a birch tree. I felt dizzy from the snowy, sunlit abundance, the crisp frost and sparkling white dust everywhere.

How wonderful it would be to fall back into the snow and gaze up through the frosty branches at the white sun.

Spreading out my poncho robe, I gently lowered myself down and lay on my back. I didn't feel any chill at all (just a soft cradle of snow) - this is how I could die, quietly and peacefully.

I thought about death and wasn't afraid of it. I didn't think of it as the ultimate punishment for the sins of my flawed life, but as a vast cosmos containing eternal life, in which my "self" exists in endless forms I have yet to experience. Death is the discovery of myself out there, beyond the accessible, where I already was, am, and will always be, a part of some higher reality.

I had never felt so good from understanding such simple and obvious truths before. I couldn't help but laugh at my foolish fantasies: life is death, and death is life. It seemed to me that I was already looking at myself from somewhere beyond, through the white rays of sunlight, through the white birch branches; that

I had already merged with the earth and could feel its vibration.

"Hey you, get up, why are you lying there?" I heard a worried voice ringing with suspicion. And immediately another voice, irritated, pleading that it wasn't worth getting involved: who knows, maybe it's just a homeless bum, more trouble than it's worth…

I sat up. I had the feeling that I had stumbled into one of my new fantasies again.

"Oh, thank God, you're okay!"

"Come on, let's go, why do you need him?"

"That's why… I'm interested, does the guy even have a mother?" The first voice was getting irritated, too. "Hey you, get up, why are you just sitting there?"

I stood up and leaned against the birch trunk, covered with glistening snow dust from head to toe. Two men in canvas work coats and hard hats seemed oddly alarmed, looking around as if I had suddenly dropped out of sight, disappeared. Finally, the inquisitive one seemed to notice me.

"Where are you headed?"

"The post office," I said, because his mention of a mother resonated with a torrent of feelings in me (I somehow already knew, though of course I didn't, that the neighbour had deceived me and had not sent the money), and I decided to take care of the money transfer first.

"Well go on then," the workman permitted hesitantly, "Or we'll take you to a police station!"

I proceeded deeper into the park and soon emerged on a path.

"Hey! Hey!" I heard the workmen's shouts of surprise behind me.

Trudging through the snow up to their waists, they hurried toward me, but when I stopped, they turned back in fear. I don't know who they took me for, but one thing was clear: my walking through the snow baffled them: I wasn't leaving any footprints. Indeed, when I looked back, there were no tracks at all. Apparently, I had walked across a solid snow crust, while my poncho robe brushed away any marks. At any rate, my soul felt so light and bright that I hastened to the post office, feeling as if I was levitating, not touching the ground.

At the post office, I was welcomed warmly and ushered to a free window. When I counted out two hundred "tattered" roubles, someone guessed it was funeral money taken out of a stocking in dire need. Suddenly, I was surrounded by sympathisers, saying what can you do, there's nothing in the stores, and what is available is traded under the counter. And rumour has it that starting New Year's, there will be reforms with old money abolished and new money put into circulation depicting Tsar Boris and even False Dmitry instead of Lenin.

The department store was as spacious and empty as a barn, with footsteps echoing loudly amid the silence. I wandered from counter to counter, and any questions I asked about clothes or shoes was taken by the salespeople as a personal insult.

On the second floor, there weren't even any salespeople. A cleaning lady swishing her mop, shouted upon seeing me: "Shoo, shoo, get out of here!" And muttering under her breath, "Breaking my back here all day, breaking my back…"

Thank God, I found an informal flea market behind the store. I spotted a pair of Finnish ankle boots with red scuffs on their toes. I tried them on, and my feet immediately felt cosy wrapped in the warm fur lining. I had never worn such comfortable fur-lined boots - I paid ten three-rouble notes. Given my dishevelled appearance, the seller was ready to knock the price down and we almost settled on twenty-five roubles. But then, two characters in grimy, icicle-covered fur hats appeared out of nowhere, rudely interjecting in the deal, saying yeah, they're top-notch boots, imported! When they left, my old boots were gone too.

The seller immediately caught on (I even suspected those two odd fellows were his accomplices), instantly raised his voice, and wouldn't let the boots go for even thirty roubles.

"If you don't want them for thirty, take them off, I'll sell them for sixty," he said, and crouching down, began tugging at my legs so vigorously that I had to beg him not to make me go barefoot through the snow.

In my search for food, I ended up at another flea market near the train station, where I ran into a staff sergeant, or rather, he came up behind me and put his hand on my shoulder like an old friend:

"Corporal Obolensky?"

I played along: "Lieutenant Golitsyn?"[73]

We laughed heartily, each at our own witticism. Then he said he didn't need any wine, but some vodka wouldn't hurt. He persuaded me to get a bottle of vodka from a taxi driver and promised to give me as many provisions as I could carry in

---

73   Characters from a hit song of that time.

exchange. The deal was too tempting to refuse. Vodka, though, came to a pretty penny; I had to pay ten roubles.

As soon as we stepped behind the station kiosks, the sergeant ripped out the cap with his teeth and drained half the bottle straight away. I took just a sip to keep him company and immediately regretted it: my stomach felt scorched as if I'd swallowed boiling water. The sergeant was delighted that I wasn't a drinker. He stuffed the bottle with a handkerchief and hid it in his bottomless overcoat. Then he warned me that his merriment was temporary, that in a minute or two (whenever it hit), he might turn sullen, in which case I should shout sharply in his face: "You're getting sullen!" That was his nickname in the unit - Sullen.

"As soon as I showed up anywhere," he confided, "I'd hear snickering behind my back, mocking: 'Here comes jolly Vova Kolobkov!' And such rage would so engulf me that I'd start shaking. But after the Sakha events, the rage was gone."

We climbed into a freight train car converted into a warehouse, with the tiny, barred windows in the ceiling making it look like a chicken coop. Paper sacks of grain and crates of canned goods lined the large shelves. Across the width of the car, like a footbridge from one row of shelves to the other, a wide door, placed horizontally, served as a makeshift bed. The space underneath was used to store firewood and tubs of coal. A welded iron stove by the entrance served as a kitchen counter, on which sat an open can of stewed meat.

The sergeant told me terrifying things. It turned out that besides events in the news, there were unknown things happening in the Sakha region, in which he personally took part on orders from above.

"Sometimes we'd catch an instigator and beat him, beat him with belt buckles until his skin split open. But oh, how they beat us too, stabbed us, killed us from hidden corners!"

The sergeant swore, but not angrily, mechanically, and showed me his disfigured, scarred hand and a very wide, brownish scar across his chest.

"I've got something else here, too." He tapped his temple with his index finger. I thought he was strangely emphasising his remarkable intellect, even more so as the sergeant began philosophising about politics and even prophesying.

"Remember, student" (at the station flea market he had observed me and took me for a kultprosvet student), "Gorbachev's perestroika was foisted upon us from outside. It's only the beginning of a huge international scam against Russians. The real scam is still to come; it will start with Yeltsin's reforms. You'll see… they already have the right people lined up for it, oh yes…"

He turned gloomy, his face darkening abruptly.

"You're getting sullen!" I shouted in his face, as he had instructed.

The sergeant recoiled and smiled as if I had paid him a compliment.

"Good man! Keep doing that," he said approvingly. "Our whole problem is that we marched too much and sang 'Wide is my Motherland[74]' We sang it in the Baltics, the Caucasus, Kazakhstan, and other Soviet republics, while they, the ethnic minorities, took note: how's that, Russians singing 'Wide is my

---

74   Iconic Soviet patriotic song.

Motherland' in their land?! Those Russians are occupiers! And on we sang in our naivety. We thought that since we considered them Russian and wrote their family names and ethnicity into Soviet passports, they considered themselves Russian too, but no! We raised a fifth column[75] within ourselves, our own enemies, our own killers! The 'Russians' from ethnic minorities were the most zealous in bashing their own, bashing them hard to curry favour! And as they did, they caused discontent and even hatred toward us among their own people!"

"You're getting sullen!" I shouted sharply in his face again.

But this time he didn't recoil, but rather leaned his face right into mine.

"What are you yelling for?! I may be getting sullen, yeah, you really get sullen if a stray shell fragment lodges right here."

He tapped his temple again. The conversation broke off. I asked why he wasn't being discharged. He flew into an outright rage, breathing heavily right in my face. Luckily, I reminded him he still had vodka left.

The sergeant caught his breath. Carefully, almost fearfully, he patted his pockets and, finding the bottle, immediately brightened, smiling like an infant feeling his mother's breast.

After taking a few swigs, he calmed down, set the bottle in a visible place on the makeshift kitchen counter, and told me that the shell fragment was pressing on his brain a bit less now, gradually retreating thanks to the alcohol. A sudden sharp shout

---

75   "The fifth column" is a popular Soviet meme, coined during the civil war in Spain in 1936-39 - it was a group name for General Franco's agents who operated behind the lines and undercover, while four of Franco's army columns advanced on Madrid. During World War II, "fifth column" was an umbrella name for agents of Axis powers in various countries.

also relieved the pressure.

"Jerking head motion probably has an effect too," the sergeant suggested, advising me that no matter what, I should keep shouting in his face so the fragment would clear from his brain.

I thought he had already forgotten my question, but the sergeant returned to it himself, without prompting. He explained that they could discharge him right now, but under a provision that would strip him of his disability and injury benefits. A discharge under a proper provision was impossible because the conflicts he was involved in officially never existed.

"You're getting sullen!" I yelled because I distinctly saw that the sergeant had darkened again, even more so than before.

"No, no, it's all right," he reassured me. "The fragment just drifted to a safer area."

He said he knew all about his shell fragment and described the pattern of transformations it caused: first his face would turn dark blue, then the darkness seemed to slide downward, and his face would become normal again, even flushed with the ruddy complexion he used to have before these events.

Indeed, his face soon brightened, and his appetite returned, followed by a flush. He invited me to eat too, but I declined - I couldn't start with stewed meat after my chicken farm rations.

Upon learning about my malnutrition, the sergeant became sentimental, pouring me half a sack of semolina, another of various grains and vermicelli, giving me canned goods, a bottle of vegetable oil… Basically, he armed me to the hilt. And he kept asking if I could have imagined that very morning that I would meet him and have such a wonderful time!

He said he hadn't anticipated it either - he had just gone out to the station flea market when the shell fragment started stirring, to see first-hand what kind of people he had been shedding blood for. And there I appeared in my poncho like some Don Pedro! All I needed was a guitar to play serenades, what a real Corporal Obolensky! That's apparently what the sergeant thought when he saw me. (He meant the hero of the famous romance, though because of the shell fragment in his head, he kept mixing up words, calling me "corporate" or "consulate" instead.)

We ended up staying a good while, talking away... If not for the shell fragment, he would have been an intelligent fellow, despite being a staff sergeant on extended duty! I learned a lot from him. And he had original witticisms.

"I'll give you a special ration of macaroni with meat, so you can cook them sailor-style right away," he said.

He tore open a paper sack, pulled out a few macaroni noodles and, blowing through them, fired out spiders as if from an air rifle.

"There are peoples in Africa who eat spiders, beetles and caterpillars without a second thought," he remarked disapprovingly. And then, quite angrily and without any connection to the previous statement, offered to demonstrate an "automatic burst."

He blew several spiders at a window in quick succession through an extra-long noodle. They landed on the glass like cherry pits. It was only then that I noticed all the windows looked pockmarked.

"I see you don't get bored," I jested, but the sergeant didn't even crack a smile.

"When they put me in the Guinness Book of Records, in my interview for the world press I'll say that some people mocked my hobby. You'll be among those people."

He said the last words as if threatening me. And I wondered: was he getting sullen?

"Everything's fine with me," the sergeant reassured. "Tomorrow this train car will depart in a direction unknown to most, and they'll never know who they tried to spit on!"

Staring like a snake, he slowly started approaching me. And then suddenly shouted: "You're getting sullen!" He shouted so sharply and piercingly that I flinched, bumping against the wall. Quite the joker, wouldn't you say?!

The sergeant helped me lug the sacks of provisions to the taxi stand, and then I treated him to another bottle. He was touched, saying he was taking it only because he didn't know how much longer he'd be stuck here, on the sidings. It turned out last night his warehouse car was uncoupled in Chudovo and another freight car was dispatched to Estonia instead, with nobody notified. The head of transportation explained to him that his car was lost and now he had to wait until it is reported missing, found, and requisitioned.

The sergeant was upset, but I told him not to worry - I would come to visit him the next day. He didn't allow it: the next day he would have to spend all day on the phone at the military commandant's office, looking for his supply officer supervisor.

"It's best if you come around New Year's." (He would leave me an excellent message with the head of transportation.)

We embraced tightly and parted like brothers.

CHAPTER 22

My wanderings through flea markets and second-hand stores, and frequent appearances in the kitchen (cooking vermicelli in beef stew - that wonderful forgotten aroma wafting through the whole floor) gradually restored the respect I had lost. After I volunteered to be the kitchen monitor, supporters and even defenders of my right to use the stove out of turn appeared. Everything fell into place. I had become so accustomed to my poncho that I didn't even consider getting a coat or other outerwear.

On New Year's Eve, when the biting cold winds intensified, I spotted a rather tattered raincoat with a huge almost new hood on a trash pile. It was like a gift from above! I tore off the hood and lined it with a piece of cotton mattress and burlap. That would have been all well and good, but the cotton kept bunching into a lump, and the hood dangled on my back like a camel's hump. I removed all the cotton and inserted a pillow instead. It still bulged, but not as much, and I started using the hood not just for its intended purpose but also as a backpack for snacks. The only hassle was frequent repairs needed by the poncho.

One day, while I was repairing my outfit, there was a knock at my door. Doublenose arrived with Tutankhamun, the plumber. I didn't even recognise them at first, all dressed up in bright winter parkas with all the bells and whistles: drawstrings, zips, and Velcro. They sat side-by-side on the bed: one a giant, the other like an underweight youngster.

"Original! Very original, indeed!"

The typical reaction to anything associated with my (shall we say) universal lifestyle. Though who were they to judge?

Doublenose crossed his legs in a lordly, nonchalant way, but his feet didn't reach the floor, so he relocated to a stool.

The purpose of their visit was to retrieve the rifle. They had a serious conflict with competitors who threatened to kill Doublenose and burn down his kiosk. As the kiosk manager, Doublenose had appealed to the police, but they flat-out told him that no one was going to risk their neck for their Pigsty. Competitors had brazenly relocated the kiosk from Victory Square and dumped it in front of the cinema under construction and even fined him despite Doublenose holding a valid official licence for the spot near the monument to the leader.

While I was talking to Doublenose, the plumber remained indifferently silent. He spoke up only at the direct mention of the rifle.

"I'll saw it off and carry it in my trousers," he said, standing up and lifting his parka to pat the exact spot.

His clarification made quite an impression. Doublenose boasted that Tutankhamun was his personal bodyguard nowadays. For now, he was paying him just for keeping quiet and not interjecting in conversations.

It seemed to me that after Doublenose's remark, Tutankhamun kept silent not so much indifferently as pretentiously.

"You know, Mitya, we can't complain. Within a month of working round-the-clock in the square, they couldn't keep up with clients. We had a clientele of big shots who didn't hesitate in putting in a good word for us on TV and kept the brewery operating at full capacity after a long while. And why? Well, as one insightful traffic cop said, we applied our very well-cured brains to the combination of beer and salted cured fish at an exceptionally favourable time."

Doublenose proudly related that as soon as they painted bright yellow arrows on the kiosk walls pointing toward the monument, and hung equally bright banners underneath proclaiming, "He too loved drinking beer from big mugs!" they instantly crushed all competitors and people from all over the city flocked exclusively to them to drink beer. As the kiosk manager, he didn't hide that the credit for intellectually undermining the competition was entirely his.

Here the plumber abruptly interjected again. Staring at the ceiling, he thrust out his arm sharply and declared loudly and tragically:

"May look puny - pah!" He spat on the floor, grinding it in with his foot as if crushing the manager along with his spit. "But he's a real sharpshooter! A mind of gold, eh! A brilliant noggin that reads people like Scripture!"

His sudden outburst made a very strong impression on me. However, Doublenose objected:

"What brilliant head? Just a bit smarter than some! Now Mitya here really does have a head on him, with higher humanitarian education! Please don't take offence, Mitya, but your brain sits there without a proper application."

He started lamenting that he was totally clueless about poetry, yet now a poetic word was needed for knockout advertising more than ever. Doublenose asked me, the educated poet, to write a worthy poem, for a fee, of course. I delivered an impromptu verse:

> Your path may be obscure and small,
> But do not worry, not at all.
> Go to the yucky Pigsty hut,
> And see your path get wider, bud!

Of course, such "poetry" could never be recognised as satisfactory anywhere but at "Mosselprom" (Moscow agricultural administration). It was meant to just hurry my uninvited guests out the door. However, Doublenose was so delighted, showering me with compliments left and right, that I began to doubt: maybe it wasn't such a bad little quatrain after all?! In any case, I readily obliged Doublenose's humble request to tweak the poem to add some fleur of collectivism. In its final form, it went:

> Our path may be obscure and small,
> Don't fret, my brethren, not at all.
> For those who drink at Pigsty hut,
> It brighter gets and wider, bud!

"Hurray!" screamed Doublenose. "I'll buy it!"

It's hard to explain why I didn't take money for the poem, but I didn't. I said I was giving it as a token of friendship. I also refused payment for the rifle, but Doublenose insisted, saying they had been drinking on credit against the rifle. Like a true merchant, he pulled out a wad from his inner coat pocket and counted out two hundred and fifty roubles in crisp, new twenty-five rouble notes. I was especially surprised they were new bills.

"Dear Mitya, we work directly with the bank! I am the kiosk manager, after all." He rubbed his hands with self-satisfaction. "And for the poem, as long as the Pigsty is in operation, four free daily mugs for you are on the house."

I thanked Doublenose. It seemed to me that although he remained under the sway of old traditions and perceptions of life, a noticeable change had occurred within him. As if it was the same foolishness and primitive boasting, yet also a tenacious grasping and holding of leadership in the niche he managed to occupy. The change was so stark and convincing that I asked him directly:

"Tell me, manager, will I claw my way out or what?"

I had never considered myself an insightful person. And in asking, I was prepared for Doublenose not to respond directly but opt instead for some unexpected form of foolishness. Which is why I felt the directness and candour of his reply even more keenly.

"I don't know, Mitya, you place yourself outside of the realm of money, but now everything revolves solely around it, everyone grabs what they can." (He switched to a whisper. Apparently, he didn't want Tutankhamun, who was busy packing up the rifle, to hear him.) "As for myself, I'll tell you for sure, if they don't kill me before Christmas, then at the very least, I'll open three more additional kiosks. I'm no poet, Mitya, I'm not even an accountant, but I already think in terms of money."

He called out to the plumber, and they left the room without saying goodbye, forgetting to close the door behind them.

"Did you see what kind of outfit he's cobbled together?! A witcher, I tell ya! But no body to speak of…"

"Whilst you being all body, leaves no room for a mind," Doublenose protested, but not angrily, just to show he was protesting. (Perhaps he was pleased that he wasn't the only one lacking a physique.)

I slammed the door shut, set aside the poncho, and embarked on some major cleaning. I wanted to distract myself from thinking about politics, but all sorts of thoughts kept intruding.

Yes, there had been enforced income levelling, and yes, spiritual impoverishment progressed, but some moral values were not subject to revision, those that allowed us to see all this, the lies, spiritual impoverishment, and that one-size-fits-all ideology. Morality, like the nation's health, could not be purchased for any amount of money. If everything but money drops out of our lives, human beings themselves will follow soon. What's the difference between dissent banned by the authorities in the past and dissent hushed as if non-existent in the present? A painting by a talented artist is either immediately perceived to have value beyond the artist himself or remains entirely unappreciated. We haven't learned a thing over the millennia since the creation of the world. We are seduced again and again by that same forbidden fruit - total permissiveness. Yes, total absence of restraints… Seventy-three years wasn't enough to build communism, but five hundred days is supposedly quite enough to establish a democratic paradise. Our leaders are either unredeemable fools or swindlers, for whom Yeltsin's reforms are the beginning of a huge international scam, as the staff sergeant said...

I fell into a funk again, nothing interested me. I don't know how I would have pulled out of my dejected state if not for the meeting with the sergeant. Remembering him, I also remembered my promise to visit the head of railroad logistics. Maybe it's nothing serious? Maybe I'm just getting sullen because Rozochka's departure weighs on my heart like the wandering shell fragment on the sergeant's brain?

On the morning of 31st December, there was quite a snowstorm, so I headed to the train station on foot to test out the hood attached to my poncho. Naturally, I went along the Volkhov River to shorten the path and soon regretted it. The wide expanse of the river let the wind blow so strongly that my robe failed to protect me. My rigging system (clothesline tie-downs) didn't work. Now they were more like the shroud lines of an open parachute or sailboat rigging filled by a snowy whirlwind. To make any progress, I had to lean into the resilient wall of air, which would then suddenly bear down on me from the side, or the rear, or even above. Of course, I fell many times, once particularly badly: a gust caught me, I first ran, then went belly-sliding across the wet ice right under the new city bridge, where for some reason, water never froze. If not for the insulated hood, which by chance, caught on some piece of driftwood frozen into the ice, I surely would have ended up in the river. In short, I nearly lost the poncho, and packed so much frozen snow into my clothes that when I was thawing out under the stairwell at the station, one kind-hearted old man said "it happens" ... and, glancing meaningfully at the puddle I was standing in, told me about a similar case at the Yevpatoria station, where apparently, just like here, there isn't a single restroom anywhere nearby.

The head of logistics turned out to be a young woman, very reminiscent of a flight attendant. Slender and poised, dressed in a dark blue suit and white blouse, she radiated such self-confidence that it struck me as indecent. At first, I mistook her for a waitress from the station restaurant, even more so, as she was standing by the window while the desk was in use by a completely bald, officiously preoccupied younger man, poring over some accounting book.

"You may have a message for me from someone," I said. Feeling the young woman unapologetically scrutinising me, I tightened the clothesline drawstrings and loops to pull the bulging pillow hood tighter against my back.

"Well, behold this typical heatpiper migrating to us for the winter," she introduced me as if she knew me well. She then addressed me wearily as if we had spoken many times before: "If only you'd take that rucksack off when you come into an office since there's nothing in it but filthy rags and fleas."

"Maybe we should check if he has any gold nuggets in there?" the bald man sneered with a smirk, rising from the desk.

I froze, my whole being tensed like a string stretched taut in anticipation. The homeless are still called "heatpipers" in our little town even today. But it wasn't that which stung… I instantly envisioned the bald man rummaging through the hood, through the damp, dirty pillow bunched into a lump, while the young woman, making no attempt to hide her disgust, would say: See, what did I tell you?!

"You have no right... I've never been a heatpiper! I'm a poet!" I blurted out defiantly and felt like some little hook inside me broke and I went hurtling into an abyss.

The weightlessness of the fall induced nausea - I had never stated that I was a poet before. For me it was tantamount to declaring something akin to "I am handsome, and not just handsome, but more handsome than any Hero of the Soviet Union." Of course, I had been called a poet and even the Poet-Chronicler, but never by myself.

And here, standing before strangers in my simple yet now uniquely precious poncho of mine at the train station office, I plunged into the abyss. The deepest and foulest abyss because, having lost my moral reference point, I felt invincible. Moreover, my invincibility grew proportional to the acceleration of freefall with each passing second. The only things that nagged me were nausea and a sense of having traded one evil for another.

Any further details are dull and even tedious. In response to my statement, the young woman said that if I were a poet, then she was the Queen of England. The bald man got up from his desk and professionally ushered me away from the door and told me to consider him the chief of police. He rather sternly demanded documents proving my identity, and if not for my literary worker's diploma, which I still carried in my jacket's inner pocket out of old habit, it's quite possible I would have had to celebrate the New Year in a holding cell.

The diploma made a strong impression. The manager suddenly remembered that she knew the poet Slyozkin - she had read his poem in the newspaper that also published her article about violations in shipping documentation. Having tempered her ire with mercy, so to speak, she asked me to recite one of my poems, flirting shamelessly all the while, to the point that the bald man even took offence at me. He started nitpicking: how did I know the sergeant, and exactly why his car was replaced with another, then lost? Strange questions, misdirected. The manager took my side, saying outright:

"What does he have to do with it?"

She pulled a heavy bundle from the cabinet and read:

"To Corporal Obolensky from…"

She paused for quite a lengthy time until I realised:

"From Lieutenant Golitsyn."

The manager laughed – it matches! She had been thinking the sergeant was nuts. She announced to the bald man that, strangely enough, my amusing attire smelled like violets, unlike some others' clothes reeking of tobacco.

As a token of gratitude, I recited my recent impromptu verse, "Our path keeps narrowing, narrowing, narrowing…", which unexpectedly sent the bald man into rapturous delight, much to the manager's sheer amusement. Not only did he forgive me for "smelling like violets," but he also shook my hand warmly. In response, the manager looked at him with pity, as if saying, "To each their own, I suppose!"

I returned to the dorm by bus and probably would have forgotten about the manager and the bald man if not for one more encounter with them, which turned out to be fateful.

CHAPTER 23

The sergeant left me a priceless treasure – nine cans of meat stew, a gift unheard of in those times. But what touched me most was his message, written in pencil on a thick piece of paper, a label torn from a bag, which I read later in the dormitory.

"Dear Corporal Obolensky," he wrote, "take this ration as a New Year's gift from me! You were in the right place at the right time and saved me. Now I will live because, after meeting you, I was convinced that it is possible to live usefully for those in need, even in the most tattered state. The main thing is not to get sullen. See you later, brother, look for me in the Guinness Book of Records. Shaking your hand, your Lieutenant Golitsyn, and never get sullen!"

The sergeant's simple and silly message, and his nine cans of stew, still with smears of protective grease, his urging to not get sullen, struck me so strongly that I just buried my face in the pillow, like a blushing maiden.

This was not a mournful cry of unbearable loss or unexpressed resentment. No, not even close. I wept from joy and tenderness at my utility, which I had never even suspected before.

If I could help someone without even trying, how many could I help if I made it my goal?! It was at that very minute that I truly understood Rozochka and truly forgave her. I wept from inexplicable luck, which always came to my aid whenever I stumbled and made a seemingly unforgivable mistake, pointing me to the right path. This time it had shone upon me as well, a genuine voice from above urging me to live fruitfully for those in need. I immediately repented that I had not been to a church for a long time, and promised the Almighty that I would visit one before Christmas and partake in the Holy Sacraments[76].

Even a superficial believer who still remembers God will never say in one's heart anything like "Starting from such-and-such a date, I will begin to do good for people." On the contrary, they will try to bring that time closer and will look for an opportunity to do good deeds from that very second. I was no exception and truly experienced great joy from the mere thought of using the sergeant's gift directly for its purpose and doing a good deed for many people.

At first, I knocked on the room of my so-called well-wishers. No one answered. Then I knocked on the neighbouring doors, again to no avail. It turned out that most of the residents had gone to visit their parents for the holidays, and only those still working or totally lonely remained. Doublenose's gang had long since stopped living in the dormitory and only came by occasionally to pay for the room. I was told they had a huge basement in the city centre that they used as both a warehouse and living quarters.

After finding this out, I put all the canned meat into a mesh bag, the one that remained from my first visit to the sergeant, and first knocked on the door of my neighbour across the hall.

She opened it instantly and slammed the door shut just as fast. I only caught a glimpse of her chequered knit sweater flickering by.

76   Russian Orthodox Church operates by the Julian calendar and celebrates Christmas on January 7.

"What do you want?" she asked irritably from behind the door.

"Allow me to congratulate you and Arthur on the New Year," I said as kindly as I could. "Please accept a small gift from me."

"Get lost with your gift!" she shouted annoyedly.

Of course, it was an unjustified rudeness on her part, but her reaction was understandable to some extent. I was flustered, not knowing what to do.

"I'm telling you again, go away! Arthur isn't here, he's at his granny's in the village!"

After a pause, she suddenly asked what kind of gift it was.

"A can of stew," I said.

The neighbour started asking whether it was beef or pork. When I replied that I didn't know, there was no label, she cracked the door open a little, stuck her arm out to the elbow and said "Give it to me!"

The next few rooms were locked, and the neighbour, now standing at the door, suggested I go to the end of the corridor, past the bathroom. Indeed, as soon as I approached, all the remaining rooms instantly opened, without me even needing to knock. Young housewives lined up in a row, and it seemed their long, bouncing shadows were curiously leaping out from behind their backs in the corridor's flickering neon light. Their questions addressed to the neighbour over my head added to the scene of curious fuss.

"Toma, what does he want? Oh girls, it looks like our rapist is finally making a pass at us too! Quick, hold me back, he's already gotten to Toma!" and other indecent things were boldly shouted out in playful agitation. I would have run from them if not for my neighbour standing behind me. I made an effort and stayed, though.

"Dear ladies! Allow me to congratulate you on the New Year and present you with some small gifts!" I proclaimed, and taking advantage of their confusion, quickly went around each of them.

My energetic manner paid off. They thanked me loudly, clearly surprised, and immediately started asking each other what it all meant.

As I headed back, I had already decided that I would give the remaining cans to the neighbour. I felt a baffling guilt towards her. Then a sudden guess made by the ladies struck me – their absurd assumption that tomorrow I would probably be arrested, like Givi before me. They were discussing that he had, too, had handed out gifts. What an awful stupidity was that! Stunned, I paused briefly.

"Toma, oh Toma, what are they arresting him for?"

The neighbour ducked into her room and slammed the door right in my face so violently that the plaster crumbled from the doorframe.

As I lay on my bed later, I decided not to leave my room so as not to ruin her mood or exacerbate my own. Celebrating the New Year at a festive table surrounded by family or friends is great, of course, but one can also meet it while reading a good book.

My library is me, I kid you not. It is divided into three parts.

The first consists of all sorts of dictionaries, reference books and lots of specialised literature: dog breeding, poultry farming, vegetable farming, horticulture and so on.

The second, my pride and joy, comprises works that I liked or was surprised by and acquired to always have at hand. Most of them came to me for free because I got them from libraries as discards. I even took a course to become a restorer-bookbinder, so I could return many of my favourite works to good condition.

The third, smallest part contains scriptures: the Bible, Bhagavad Gita, Buddha's verses (meaning The Dhammapada), the Quran, a few brochures about Confucianism and Lao Tzu – that's the whole list. As I see it, humanity has preserved twelve sacred scriptures for twelve religions that people adhere to. Back in my student days, I was drawn to the idea of writing a story about a Universal God who grew tired of listening to the complaints and praises of people who'd fight each other over their religions and always call for Him as a judge. I remembered the beginning of the work, which I titled "The Twelve Truths."

* * *

"Well, this is becoming ridiculous," God said aloud in exasperation, and angels began to laugh everywhere in the heavenly groves, merrily peeking out and hiding, commanding the divine animals and flowers to behave in truly ridiculous ways. God laughed. "Silly, of course, but good," He thought and concealed His thoughts. "However, earthly matters cannot be resolved here; they must be addressed on Earth."

The Lord God appeared secretly on Earth and approached a group of Christ, Buddha, Allah, and Yahweh sitting around a campfire – Teachers of the twelve religions, already considered prophets, apostles of His Divine Truth by that time. Having taken the guise of a wanderer, the Lord God took off his knapsack, praised the world for having many good and diverse teachers, and suddenly expressed doubt: how could a multitude of teachings all be true, for Truth is one?

"In that case, what is Truth?" God asked the Teachers, but in a spiritual sense, He was asking His own Sons.

Of course, They all answered Him strictly according to their respective teachings, that is, the Sacred Scriptures. So right away I ran into a stumbling block: how could I render the answers of the Sons whose sacred books are missing from my library? In a country of widespread atheism, I hit an insurmountable wall and had to abandon writing "The Twelve Truths" so as not to expose myself as a true heretic.

I squatted down and, taking the collected verses of Buddha, opened it at a random place – it happened to be the Chapter on the Enlightened One, verse 187: "Even in heavenly pleasures he finds no satisfaction. A fully enlightened disciple rejoices only in conquering his desires." I unintentionally pondered: in general, it is also about me. At least, I had no desire to seek out meetings with anyone in the dormitory.

And then came a merry, playful knock on my door.

* * *

I believe in the folk proverb: How you meet the New Year is how the whole year will go. I devised a game to avoid dwelling on how I met it (my soul, like a wound, bled from any careless thought) but at the same time wishing to recall even the smallest details of that past night. I did not reminisce, but rather pondered the narration of my new novel, a novel about my neighbour Toma. I hoped to deceive myself, to numb the aching pain in my heart. Therefore, the more insignificant I imagined myself, the more significant and epically exalted the narration had to be. Moreover, to overcome the pain I had to think of myself abstractly, that is, in the third person, as if of the novel's protagonist hero, one that evokes empathy but is not related to me directly.

Late on New Year's Eve, a young man of about twenty-three years of age left his dormitory room. He was wearing a cotton quilted jacket with a hood thrown back, on top of which randomly glued foil stars and moons glittered festively. The young man's face was hidden by a black half-mask; he was lost in his own thoughts, and it took great effort for him to interrupt his important reading and leave his room. But he left nevertheless because he felt it would be improper to hole up in his room. Knowing the habits of the residents, he was sure that after the third invitation they would take his refusal as a personal insult, as if to say, "Look at your antlers, your wife left you, but hey, you think you're too good for us! He probably digs through trash cans wearing white gloves …" And they would vilify him in all sorts of nasty ways behind his back, so that he would not only enter the New Year drenched in sewage but would proceed through it draped in all kinds of filthy rubbish.

The man in the half-mask strode lightly across the corridor; a chorus of voices responded to his knock. He opened the door and immediately found himself amid a festive gathering. Tables pushed together end-to-end, densely laden with bottles and homemade food, seemed to surge towards him, pinning him against the doorframe.

"Hooray, our Poet-Stargazer! ... Mister X![77]... "Our fortune-teller!" shouted the so-called lonely women, who looked nothing like lonely souls. "Girls, girls, let him tell our fortunes! Kolya, Kolya, let him guess what I want?!" They shouted all sorts of things, not so much merrily or drunkenly as shamelessly. Each of them had their own Kolya next to them, seasoned guys who knew exactly how much their company was worth.

The candour of their intentions so clearly etched on their faces embarrassed the young man. It seemed to him that he had unexpectedly interrupted the very act of fulfilling those intentions. It was so stupid, so vile, so shameful that without a word, he pushed the door to retreat and nearly collided with his neighbour. She shrieked and nimbly dodged aside, for she was carrying a huge, steaming skillet of fried potatoes.

"Ah, it's you!" she announced casually, in such a way that not only those around her, but even he himself, got the impression that they were long-time friends, inseparable buddies.

In fact, it all worked out quite conveniently. He helped the neighbour set the skillet on the table and, reading her palms like a true fortune teller, predicted a mysterious encounter with an enigmatic man who would first abduct her to another planet and then return her happy and beautiful. He even promised that this

---

77   Reference to the main character of a very famous Soviet movie (1956) based on Die Zirkusprinzessin (The Circus Princess) operetta by Emmerich Kalman; he was a very handsome man who always wore a mask.

would happen that very New Year's night.

"He's hinting about himself, about himself!" Kolyas guffawed raucously.

Nevertheless, his predictions found an enthusiastic response. The women vied with each other to extend their hands to him, asking for their fortunes to be told. Yes, it had been a long time since he had experienced such intense interest from ladies. A particular insistence was exerted by the friend of one specific Kolya, who immediately objected: "Lyalka, I'm jealous!" and, swallowing an almost full glass of moonshine, demanded that Stargazer drain the penalty drink. And he did drain it and nearly fell flat on his back from how intensely the booze hit him.

The neighbour caught him and seated him next to her, proceeding to fuss over him as if he were her own Kolya or Givi. The young man laughed joyfully: for the first time in his life, he was being jealously guarded.

"Toma, your Stargazer is sloshed," Kolya continued to complain. "Get him out of Lyalka's sight, or there will be no stopping her!"

Indeed, Lyalka was leaning across the table, knocking over glasses, while he, the young man, feeling an inexpressible joy in his soul, could not even stand up. His legs did not obey, and all objects around him were floating as if in water.

The neighbour came to the rescue again, slapping Lyalka's hands sharply (at any rate, Lyalka cried out) and, shielding Stargazer with her body, pulled off his mask, and then his jacket too. It was all very merry, but from that moment on, there were vast gaps and scattered episodes in his memory that resonated with an aching pain right beneath this seemingly impartial young man's heart.

He clearly remembered that long before midnight, Lyalka and Kolya were kissing in front of the public, and everyone, including himself, was chanting "Bitter!" in unison after each kiss, applauding and even giving them an ovation. Then somehow, the married couples kept switching around, and each new bride was sure to don his jacket and half-mask and would proffer her lips invitingly. He too had embraced and kissed some Lyalka several times, or this could be his neighbour Toma, or maybe not… He vaguely recalled the peak of the party – the chiming of the Moscow Kremlin clock on TV and the pop of a champagne cork. Then suddenly they were outside on a street filled with festive shouts and songs, snow flashing with bright blue sparks. They laughed, snowballed each other and then they were digging him out of a snowdrift and dragging him upstairs, and some prolonged echo morphed into an avalanche with white bursting bubbles popping out – rea-dy, rea-dy, rea-dy…

Rozochka came to him in the middle of the night, and coldly lay down with him, he begged her forgiveness, but she was unyielding. Then in some sudden surge she pulled him to her – he was forgiven, he was filled with overwhelming joy, it seemed to him that now, as in childhood, he would faint again! And indeed, everything blurred, lost its outlines and shapes… And then there was a searing light, and a truly horrific sight: he lay naked (in Adam's togs as the saying goes) on a sort of huge white surgical table, while above him, his neighbour Toma in her famous chequered sweater with her breasts and knees bare, holding a tape measure.

"Easy now, easy," she said, lightly patting his stomach. "Close your eyes and sleep, don't pay any attention."

He closed his eyes, and when he opened them, it was already morning and he lay under a sheet still completely naked, aghast of aggravating the aching pain under his heart. He strained to recall the details of that past night, but in doing so he thought of himself in the third person, as some literary character not directly related to him. Admittedly, he only partly succeeded - and he suffered.

CHAPTER 24

The days after New Year's, I thought of myself and perceived myself only in the third person. Both Stargazer (the fortune teller) and poet Mitya Slyozkin were my good acquaintances and even more than acquaintances – they were a part of me, just as I was a part of them. They knew everything about each other and almost nothing about me. That is, they somehow sensed that there was an "I," but who was that? Indeed, who am I, if I harbour them both within me and am myself their offspring, the product of failed relationships? Moreover, I know for certain (and they fear this in their own guesses) that the discord between them was precisely what brought me into being.

Nevertheless, it was I, some third one, who craved not only Stargazer's reconciliation with Mitya Slyozkin, the poet, but their fusion. Yes, their fusion into a single common "I," resulting in me, the third one, dissipating and vanishing like a fog, like a bad dream - that is, I would yield my place to the new Mitya Slyozkin, enriched by Stargazer's experience. But it was exactly what the former Mitya did not want! To him, this fusion with Stargazer seemed a sort of voluntary insanity, which could only bring him to life as a madman, if at all.

Of course, such a prospect suited no one. The only two options were to run and evade the fusion or face death, which still was a better option than insanity!

In general, all three guises of mine had their reasons to be apprehensive, especially since they all testified to one thing - the terrible disarray in former Mitya Slyozkin's soul, which had reached a critical point.

But let's keep things in order, the discord first.

In the morning, when I (still unaware that I was the third one) lay under the sheet and struggled to understand what had happened, why the neighbour, in Eve's attire matching my Adam's, was measuring me with a tape measure. Then I heard footsteps, light yet confident. They entered the room with no hesitation, as if coming into their own home. Some unfathomable intuition immediately prompted me to recognise the neighbour! Unlike me, she was not concerned about what had happened yesterday, but rather about what should happen today, right now.

The poet Mitya Slyozkin, fluttered in my chest and huddled in terror in a corner like a lump of suppressed scream. (I felt sorry for him. It was at this moment when I realised that I was the third one, merely an observer whose observations did not prevent anyone from acting as they pleased.)

"That's where you belong," Stargazer stated mercilessly. Stretching like a tomcat, he ballooned with pride, filling the space the poet had just vacated.

"This is not your Rozochka, who abandoned you as if you are worthless," Stargazer summed up with proud superiority as the new master of the situation. "Learn, poet, we're now going to act according to our own passions!"

I, Mitya the Poet, and Stargazer could easily hear each other's thoughts and effortlessly exchange them without resorting to speech. For all those around us, we did not exist as individuals; nobody could perceive us distinctly as Stargazer, Mitya the Poet, and me, the third one. No, even though divided, we all existed within the shell of a single "I," and only within this ceremonial uniform could each of us manifest one to others outside and represent all three of us by his separate self. That was the root of the discord, where the reasons for the quarrels lay, but I must avoid getting ahead of myself.

The neighbour entered the room, with loose hair, in a little blue mini robe, full of some ostentatious energy.

"Poet-stargazer (a clear example that in the visible world no one could tell us apart), wake up!" She kicked off her slippers and climbed onto the bed. "Don't you at least remember declaiming poems to me from memory last night?"

The poet Mitya Slyozkin, unlike Stargazer Slyozkin, involuntarily shrank even more: he did remember reciting poems.

"All about love, all devoted to me!" the neighbour reported, radiating with self-satisfaction.

Mitya stirred wearily – not only had he recited poems with hints about Givi, he had proclaimed to all that he was presenting them to charming Toma and her son Artur.

"No way! I don't remember a thing, I overdid it!" Stargazer "confessed," turning to the neighbour. "Although, I do remember, in the middle of the night a charming stranger appeared with a tape measure in her hands…"

He unexpectedly threw off the sheet (Mitya involuntarily shrivelled into a ball) and, embracing the neighbour around the waist, unceremoniously pulled her upon him as he fell back on the pillow.

"She was measuring, who was she measuring, the gentleman perhaps?!" Stargazer asked meaningfully, choking with laughter.

The neighbour also laughed, she understood the ribald hint, but it was precisely the ribaldry that amused her, it expressed Stargazer's legitimate claim on her as his own… Yes, his own woman. Perhaps she had only come to him with her hair loose and in a mini robe to find out how much he wanted to exercise his entitlement over her.

"Not at all, not at all what you're hinting at!" she said laughingly, pretending to fend him off. "I also want to give you a gift." As if wanting to disclose what gift she meant, she pushed away with both hands and then, suddenly yielding to a new inner impulse, pressed herself against his chest and whispered with unexpected ardour: "You, Mitya, you're not so bad at all!"

What happened next?! History is silent on that, as they say.

The neighbour never imagined that by calling Stargazer "Mitya" she would become a source of friction between them. But it so happened, and could not have been otherwise because Mitya the Poet was not merely an involuntary witness to everything history remained silent about, but an involuntary participant and accomplice in that. Of course, for him as the one in love with Rozochka, this sudden dependence on the sensual Stargazer was not just outrageous and offensive but drove him into despair.

In general, everything went extremely badly for Mitya the Poet that day: emptiness, lapses in memory, the neighbour's visit and, most importantly, her disconcerting approachability. He withdrew to avoid any contact with her, while Stargazer took advantage, sparing neither Mitya nor the neighbour. True, she needed no sparing. Flushed and happy, the neighbour lay beside Stargazer in blissful oblivion, while he shamelessly taunted Mitya while staring at the ceiling:

"Learn, poet, to take the bull by the horns! Oh, excuse me, should it be the cow by the udder? Just say 'milky moo' and you'll bleat with pleasure!"

He deliberately groped her bare breasts, playing with her nipples as if they were his personal belongings to show Mitya his dominance. In conclusion, he gave her buttocks a condescending pat, as one would pat a heifer.

"I'll bet she's no worse than your Dulcinea! Well, maybe not quite as curvaceous, but not such a skittish character either."

The neighbour interpreted Stargazer's actions in her own way, snuggling up to him:

"Mitya, how insatiable you are! What if I give you a little snack?"

She giggled and, slipping under his arm, suddenly tensed as if in a sudden pain.

"You must be really angry with me?"

She froze, even stopped breathing.

"What for, why?" Stargazer didn't understand.

"He's dim, stupid, and therefore self-satisfied," thought Mitya the Poet.

"For the money I was supposed to send to your mother, but ended up keeping for myself."

For some time, it was as if she disappeared again: no breath, no rustle, only her heartbeat. Then a sob, plaintive, choking.

She told Stargazer how she had gone to the post office, but it was a sanitation day, how could she have known? She and Artur went to the train station but had no luck there either - it was the lunch break. They wandered here and there, and then the bus arrived. She decided she would mail it from the village. But as soon as she arrived, everything went south: her mother got ill, the cow was hungry, chickens and ducks unfed… she had to buy fodder urgently. But Mitya should know she'll repay him and very soon too.

The neighbour wiped away unbidden tears, and rising slightly, looked at Stargazer's face. God knows what she saw there!

His face was pale and weary, his thoughts were resting somewhere far away… Such faces are seen on athletes, especially footballers who have lost a cup match and are lying mindlessly on the grass, their victory having been so close, so close! However, even this emotion would have been too complex for Stargazer. There was nothing in his soul. He did not know what the neighbour meant and did not want to. He had already decided to ask her whether she would have taken offence in his place or not? And he did ask, blurting it out as he continued to stare at the ceiling.

At first, the neighbour pondered, then quietly began to slide off the "bed."

"I suppose I should go."

She suddenly remembered that today she was going to her mother's to collect Artur and still needed to pack. If everything went as planned, she would return by Christmas, but if not, then she would have to stay longer.

The neighbour assumed Stargazer would certainly react to her saying that, they were no longer strangers, after all. However, he remained motionless. He just closed his eyes, as if falling into oblivion. She could not believe that he could simply fall asleep in a situation like this…

Putting on her slippers, she hesitated to leave. She thought that his anger would be displaced by mercy and if so and since she had the time, she would stay a little longer.

The neighbour was mistaken, her conclusions and assumptions had nothing to do with Stargazer. Mitya the Poet understood this better than anyone - he knew for certain that Stargazer had indeed fallen asleep. Of course, from Mitya's perspective, his behaviour was extremely shameless, impudent, and inexcusable.

When the neighbour realised there was no point in waiting and headed for the door, Mitya's patience ran out. He dislodged Stargazer and deprived him of his pedestal, that is, of his ceremonial uniform.

"Wait, Toma, what grievances could I harbour if you spent the money to help your mother?! There's no difference - my mother or yours, still a mother, right?!"

The neighbour only understood what she wanted to understand, namely, that Stargazer had acknowledged that they were no longer strangers. Still, his sluggishness left a bitter aftertaste, and she decided to teach him a little lesson, coldly saying, "Alright, we'll talk when I get back…"

Mitya had to use all his eloquence and resourcefulness to mitigate the neighbour's ire caused by Stargazer's indifferent behaviour. At first, her resentment even seemed to grow from Mitya's sudden soulfulness, but when he offered her to peek into the iron and take fifty rubles for travel expenses, the neighbour gave in. Perhaps she yielded to a common female curiosity. Nevertheless, cash made a rather favourable impression on her for Mitya's sake, especially Doublenose's crisp new bills.

"Well, well!" she said admiringly. "You could dress yourself in the latest fashion, the very latest!"

She took fifty rubles and hid them under her bra in an almost imperceptible motion.

Stargazer, who had seemed to be sleeping all this time, gave no hint of his presence. But he was not asleep; he was waiting for a favourable moment to reclaim the pedestal. Moreover, he did not doubt his success for a second - as long as the neighbour was here, his power was doubled or even tripled. While feeling sympathy for Mitya, and Toma really did, Stargazer was who she really liked, for it was he who possessed her.

And so, it happened. As soon as the neighbour rushed to embrace Mitya in gratitude, Mitya leapt down from the pedestal with his eyes closed, and Stargazer reappeared in all his glory. He shamelessly threw off the sheet and, spreading his arms wide, responded to each of her kisses with two or three of his own. He blossomed, he shone on the pedestal of the collective "I," like an usurper on the throne. He indulged in taunting Mitya.

"Well, literary worker, have you finally understood who has the real power over a woman? Watch and learn how to enjoy life! Don't like it? Then hide behind your Dulcinea's skirts in your corner and sit there tight, don't come out."

And Mitya did hide and did not come out, not just because he agreed to but because what was happening between Stargazer and the neighbour bewildered him, shattered all his notions of honour and dignity, especially those of a man with a humanitarian university degree, as Doublenose had put it.

"Mitya, you're so good, so kind, so caring!" the neighbour

fervently whispered in Stargazer's no less fervent embraces. "And I, fool that I am, got angry at you! I thought you were heartless. Oh, I'm so silly, so stupid!" she whispered blissfully, kissing him.

"No, Toma, you are smart! You don't let what's yours slip away, and you'll snatch what belongs to others too, if need be!" Stargazer exclaimed quite inopportunely and with somewhat excessive directness.

However, wit as an attribute of cordiality was not Stargazer's trait; it was Mitya's.

"Toma, always and everywhere keep yourself at the centre, in focus, if you're good, then everyone's good. Personally, I only proceed from that, and everything's okey-dokey!"

The neighbour was exceedingly amused by Mitya's sudden avowal. It turned out that he should feel good even if she appropriated this money as well. But then it occurred to her: if he had fallen in love with her or at least had some feelings for her, then his statement was not so stupid after all. Perhaps that's why she went on caressing and kissing him with even more passion. And as she left, she remarked coquettishly, "My little Mitya, your Tomochka will be missing you!"

In response, Stargazer threw his arms behind his head and declaimed completely inappropriately, his eyes still closed, "Toma, they're waiting for you at home."

The neighbour didn't know what to think.

"Mitya, you're such a brute, such a brute!"

"Yep, but you still think I'm cute!" Stargazer replied in rhyme with a hint of offensive self-contentment.

His primitive inclination to construe everything as a compliment to himself suddenly angered her so much that she could not come up with a retort. However, words weren't needed - her departing steps screamed with a promise of swift retaliation.

CHAPTER 25

Toma returned on Christmas Eve. She came back not with Artur but with a huge, tightly tied package in her hands and in a very good mood. All those days before Christmas, she had been sewing a coat for Mitya from a wonderful dark grey fabric and had come with the sole purpose of presenting it as the promised gift. She expected gratitude, for Mitya to try on the coat in her presence so that she could get her revenge.

She was mistaken. He didn't even unwrap the package and behaved oddly, not himself, totally messed up. He fell to his knees before her, confessed to some unimaginable sins, and begged her to spare his highest and one-and-only love for Rozochka.

What did highest love have to do with it?! What were these pleadings and excuses? All she wanted was one single thing - for him to understand that they were even. She didn't care if he tried on the coat or not; the main thing was that she had settled her debt to him. All the fabric, lining, threads, buttons, would amount to the sum she owed him if calculated at current prices. And the labour?! In his usual foolishness, he wanted to give her all the money, but she took only thirty rubles just to emphasize his real loss. Everything looked and felt pitiful, humiliating, and repulsive. She left again that same evening with not a shadow of regret. She no longer wanted to think about Mitya or to meet with him. "He's just totally nuts, no wonder his wife left him!" she thought with pleasure and forgot all about him.

Mitya's apparent beaten-down and unreal state was explained by his being more real than ever before. After days of battling with Stargazer, he had finally won and knocked him off the pedestal. The only trouble was that the success did not bring any relief. The predominance of one guise over another did not guarantee any stability, and Mitya decided to go to the Church of St. George Monastery.

The choice was not explained by the fact that Mitya was Yuryevich[78], even though he was happy about that. It was simply because, for days, the local press had been announcing a historic event—the transfer of the monastery to the jurisdiction of the local diocese, that is, to the believers. A celebration that included a grand service and a procession was to take place in the Church of St. George, and Mitya sincerely believed that repentance and partaking of the Holy Sacraments within the walls of such an ancient church would undoubtedly restore his shattered self, his true identity.

And so, in the morning, poet Mitya picked up the package with the coat presented by the neighbour the day before and set off for the monastery, or rather, in the direction of the monastery; he still had to stop at the market on the way and drop the coat off at the consignment store.

The plan for the coat was excellent—Mitya the Poet wanted to liberate himself from this material reminder of his intimate relations with the neighbour. Stargazer, on the other hand, objected: the coat was tangible evidence of his recent victories.

---

78   Yuryevich is patronymic from Yury; St. George is St. Yury in Russian Orthodox tradition.

Mitya the Poet was heading towards St. George Monastery, gazing at the early passengers hurriedly jumping onto the bus and avoiding any further arguing with Stargazer. Concentrated and businesslike, passengers jumped on board, almost all of them with bags slung over their shoulders or across their backs. The presence of some kind of luggage in their hands was so natural that the rare people without it seemed downright suspicious. Everyone shied away from them warily, guarding their bags. Mitya moved away too, covering his bulky package with the striped edge of his coat. And immediately, as if responding to a password, a slender woman in a yellow fox fur imitation hat spoke up.

"There's some criminal type behind you! Ha-ha, pretend we're old friends, I'm talking to you about some general topic, don't look back, just look straight ahead!" the lady in the yellow hat demanded in half-whisper, leaning towards him. "So, you're saying you were drinking port wine, but it seemed to me it was something stronger! Ha-ha!"

She feigned laughter and, pulling her tightly stuffed bags towards her, rolled her eyes up so naturally that Mitya involuntarily became frightened: was she feeling unwell? However, the eye-rolling which had initially seemed to reference the strength of the drink, in fact, indicated some reprehensible actions of the criminal type at some distance from Mitya.

"Don't worry, I'm keeping an eye on him," the slender woman casually informed Mitya and ordered him, in a tone that brooked no objection, to put his package on top of her bulging bags.

"You've got… some character with a newspaper to your side as well, maybe a habitual felon?! Ho-ho, we're old friends, you watch my guy, and I'll watch yours," Mitya said, deliberately slurring his words in a tongue-twister as he relocated his package, and then announced louder for all to hear: "If I'd had something strong to drink, I'd probably still be sleeping it off, right?!"

The faux fox hat bounced excitedly: Mitya the Poet appeared not just a chance acquaintance of hers, but an ideological companion.

They got off the bus together. Mitya the Poet helped the slender woman carry her bundles to the market, and she undertook to sell his coat in return. She sold it quite successfully—for three hundred and eighty rubles, so Mitya didn't just get his money back but even gained a little. However, this happened already after his visit to the monastery. After handing over the coat to be sold, he returned to the bus stop and went to the church.

St. George Monastery is an amazing place. The tourist hotel where Mitya and Rozochka had spent their best three days together was located just behind its southern wall. At the time, the monastery had been in a terrible state of neglect, having been used by the city municipal services to store coal and broken agricultural machinery, and the monks' cells and refectory used as a vocational school.

But these days, the monastery was completely different: the snow and frosty rime on the stone walls, the entrance to the monastery from the Volkhov river side, numerous people arriving continuously and crowding around the refectory where the bishop was ceremonially accepting the church from the regional administration on behalf of the believers—all revealed the monastery's formerly hidden festive grandeur. Strangely enough, Mitya the Poet did not stand out against the backdrop of the other believers but on the contrary, blended in harmoniously. As soon as he immersed in the crowd, he immediately stopped feeling his threefold self. All his guises suddenly merged into one ordinary self. It was so sudden and so natural that he did not even notice what exactly had precipitated this… and why had he come to the church in the first place?

* * *

I am who I am. This is I, Dmitry Yuryevich Slyozkin. Passing the ranks of old women, I leaned towards one to ask about the plan for upcoming events and was immediately surrounded by them.

"Son, where are you from? Who are you? Are you the one selling little birds near Vitoslavlitsa?"

Silvery-haired, with clear, trusting eyes, they made such a strong impression on me that it felt as if I had suddenly found myself on some heavenly blankets rather than amidst the winter slush.

"No, I'm poet Mitya," I said, and did not feel any pangs of conscience as I had before. I truly felt that I was speaking the truth as if the words were branded on my heart.

The old women examined me carefully with some kind of collective eye and agreed: yes, this is poet Mitya and took me under their wing. Before the procession started, they handed me a robe and a banner bearing the image of the Virgin.

That day, I was wearing old, worn-down half-boots and white socks (my shoes had been stolen and I was saving my Finnish ankle boots for really cold weather; as for the socks, I simply couldn't find any others). The gold satin of the robe and my dilapidated shoes did not really go together, but the old women unanimously decided that I looked "like an angel."

The Church of St. George was spacious and dark; most of its windows and doors were sealed closed with huge wooden planks for the duration of the service. The old women helped me change back into my former attire, and I felt great until the kissing of the icon of St. George the Victorious began. The crowd somehow pushed me into the stream of people exiting the church, so I had to elbow my way quite vigorously back to the icon.

The kissing of the icon had always been a divine act for me, especially here, in the flickering candlelight, when I could clearly see how the face of the Mother of God on the banner turned towards me and she, the Mother of God, blessed me like my own dear mother. Her sudden blessing transformed the surrounding reality. I became obsessed with the idea that St. George the Victorious would somehow respond to my kiss. In short, I elbowed my way to the icon and, overjoyed, began to revel so deeply in kissing it that many around me became concerned: who is this?! And their agitation only increased when I fell to my knees to kiss the cross in the bishop's hands.

"It's Mitya, our poet Mitya!" the old women interceded for me.

I raised my head and saw a row of smug black shoes a little to the side of the clergy. Flashing white socks between them and trousers above, they seemed to be on alert, sniffing…

"It's Mitya, our Mitya," I heard again over my head. "He's a poet!"

They were not introducing me to those around but asking for indulgence towards me as if I were a holy fool. It felt terrible.

I rose from my knees. The heads of the regional, city, and district administrations with their retinues were all present, about a dozen of them or so, all in white socks. I saw my former editor among them. Yes, he stood there in that rank of varnished cockish black shoes and tuxedos, white cuffs, socks, and likely collars too. I did not see the collars though because, having raised my head with pride and holding up my coat with my left hand like a toga, I walked away without looking at anyone. There was something comical about all this, no doubt: by lifting my coat, I had aggressively demonstrated my own white socks. Of course, I did not see any similarity between myself and the authorities. And yet, a black Volga[79] overtook me near the "Vitoslavlitsa" bus stop, braked sharply, and stopped.

"Mitya!.. Owner of the awarded socks, march here at the double!"

My former editor at the regional youth newspaper was clearly in a good mood. He sat sprawled on the back seat and beamed with success and positivity. He looked somewhat excessively refined, like a cross between a lord and a gentleman from KVN[80] with his white cashmere scarf and white cuffs peeking

---

79   Soviet semi-luxury car. Even though sold to public, they were mostly a hallmark of government and party officials and of KGB.

80   KVN is a Russian acronym for the Club of the Cheerful and Witty, an extremely popular Soviet (later Russian) TV show. It is a competition of teams from various universities (later of virtually any origin) in humor, wit and satire; the show took off in sixties, was closed for the most of the Brezhnev's period and revived with perestroika. "A gentleman from KVN" is a reference to the team from Odessa (Ukraine), which earned a truly iconic status in late 1980s.

out from under his black wool coat. His speech was different too, more relaxed, devoid of the party clichés, cracking jokes that made my ears pop. He had never allowed himself such behaviour when the editor of the youth newspaper.

"Mitya! Poet Mityai, never wear white socks again!"

At first, I thought he was drunk, but no, he was just in an excellent mood. He promised that very soon a new regional newspaper would begin publishing, all completely democratic, and he would again become the editor-in-chief. I expressed my doubts, saying it couldn't be; previously, this would have been a position for a candidate member of the regional party bureau, not anyone from the Komsomol.

"Oh, you, poet Mityaika, you've fallen behind the times! All that's left of you… are those white socks."

The former editor almost took offence, but seeing that my doubts expressed nothing but surprise, he asked: did I know who the head of the regional administration was? And then, obviously not expecting me to answer correctly, he explained:

"By former standards, it is a rank of the first secretary of the regional party committee. Do you remember the moustachioed man in the blue suit who always drank kefir? I was standing right by his side in the church."

Leaning over, he whispered in my ear:

"He and I are bosom buddies."

The editor patted me on the shoulder and invited me to work at the new newspaper as the head of the correspondence department.

"Only, Mityaika, you'll have to trade in your patrician's toga for something more mundane, more ordinary attire."

Of course, I immediately understood where all this was coming from. However, the new editor's habit of calling me Mityaika time and again, in and out of season, was so stupid and so irritating that I refused. I said I would only agree to work as head of the newspaper's literary union.

"Mityaika, you're already setting conditions?!"

Well, that was too much for me! I patted the driver on the shoulder and asked him to stop - we were just passing the market.

I made some purchases with the proceeds from the coat sale, loading the packages in my hood. As I was leaving the market I saw a portable "Erica"[81] typewriter on a crate near the market's iron gates. I had dreamed of having such a device all my life: with a beautiful font, line spacing exactly as required for publishing, a very convenient carriage, and a pleasing bell. If it weren't for the encounter with the editor, I wouldn't have bought it; I would have left it for later. But here the thought of a collective anthology occurred to me—I would need this typewriter to prepare the manuscript. While I was testing the machine, the woman selling it (in a grey fur hat and valenki, definitely a former typist) looked at me with a kind of amazed compassion as if I were a Martian. She was surprised and alarmed by my coat, but even more by my professional handling of the typewriter. I typed on the sheet inserted into the carriage: "The typewriter is wonderful, but probably expensive?"

"It costs three hundred and ninety rubles," the woman said, and then, although there was no one around, she whispered that she would let it go for two hundred and fifty.

Taught by the story of my Finnish ankle boots, I didn't bargain. I handed over the money, closed the suitcase, and went

---

81   A German typewriter, very sought for in Soviet Union.

on my way. As I walked to the bus stop (and later, on the bus and afterwards), the black suitcase with its nickel-plated clasps gave me an unexpected surge of confidence. I felt that from now on, Poet-Chronicler wasn't just a nickname but my mission in my life on this Earth, which I had to fulfill, at least in hope of meeting Rozochka again.

CHAPTER 26

January flew by unnoticed. I edited and retyped my own and others' works day and night. The only thing that bothered me was the need to go out for bread and milk. However, I adapted to that too: I set up a makeshift refrigerator between the window frames and stocked up once a week. Everything was going smoothly for me. I prepared a voluminous manuscript of my poetry collection. I edited some of the backlogs for the collective anthology and was already rubbing my hands in anticipation of my spring offensive on publishers when suddenly I learned that prices on all products, including bread, milk, and sugar would soon stop being regulated.

In fact, I knew about this in advance (rumours had been circulating in the kitchen), but I didn't act accordingly. That is, I didn't run with a bag from store to store, as most of the residents of our dormitory did. I hoped that maybe it would work out somehow.

It didn't. As I remember now, I had just finished retyping the "oratorio" (to this day, I am amazed at what prompted me to undertake such a feat). I got up from the table and stretched while looking around the refrigerator space between the window frames, and alas, it was empty. It was dark outside, but the neighbouring house was all lit up like a Christmas tree, merry, shimmering with a rainbow of colours (at least that's how it looked through my frosted windows). I looked at my watch – it was a little past nine pm. I tore off yesterday's calendar page:

ah, February 1st! The birthday of the President of Russia, so it wouldn't hurt to celebrate!

I have never considered myself a revolutionary democrat and do not to date. Breaking is not like making. Dispersing provinces is not at all the same as gathering them back together. The only thing that captivated me about the new president was his courage. Leaving the Communist Party the way he did, publicly slamming the door, required a valiant heart. Just as I had once been in love with Gorbachev as a politician, I was now in love with the politics of Yeltsin. It gave me special pleasure to suddenly declare "My president said so!" during political debates, something no Russian can avoid. What he actually said was of no importance to me because "my president!" was the key message. We were not from the same literary association, no, but from the same dormitory. And of course, I was convinced that my president knew what I needed in life better than myself. Therefore, his appointment of Yegor Gaidar, the famous writer's grandson, as the Prime Minister struck me as a revelation: so that's my president, huh, he appointed Gaidar, "The Rider Dashing Ahead" as the Prime Minister of Russia! It did not occur to me that this direct translation of "Gaidar" begs for an answer to a reasonable question "Where is Yegor dashing to?"

Having torn off yesterday's calendar page and discovered that it was the evening of Boris Nikolayevich's birthday, I marvelled as usual: so that's my president?! And that might have been the end of it, if not for the retyping of the already familiar "oratorio," in which there was no duet of "Gorbachev and Yeltsin" after the duet of "Andropov and Chernenko." By the way, my co-author Incognito had strongly urged me to take a closer look at Boris Nikolayevich, since, in his opinion, Boris Nikolayevich had not yet fulfilled his historical mission, that is, had not died yet.

His request amused me a lot, mostly because I read it not before or after, but precisely on Yeltsin's birthday.

"I will definitely keep an eye on him!" I promised aloud and hurried.

I hurried not because there were only forty minutes left before the store closed (twenty would have been enough for me). It was just that I imagined that somewhere out there in now unreachable Moscow, the president's household had gathered for a festive dinner, had poured out a little shot and had already made a toast to his glory... And I so wanted to "partake" along with them, if only for that minute, to bring myself closer to Rozochka's current dwelling place, that I hurried and rushed.

As I eagerly ran down the stairs and then scurried to the store, I felt like Gaidar, that is, as a rider dashing ahead. At first, the illusion of galloping was aided by the stairs, and then by the speed of my advance - my coat flew out behind me like a Circassian burka.

In the store, without slowing my pace, I headed straight for the farthest corner, to the bread and dairy sections. As I approached, saleswomen rose in surprise behind the empty counters, while one, on the contrary, sat down:

"Good Lord, what is this wondrous marvel?!"

Her feigned fright made me slow down and look around. The store was empty, swept totally clean! There wasn't even the usual canned fish in tomato sauce on the shelves, they were absolutely bare! There wasn't a single customer either, which added to the overall atmosphere of depression. My shuffling footsteps echoed, sometimes overtaking me, sometimes suddenly dying off and vanishing as if I were walking on felt. But the biggest shock I experienced was in the bread section… twenty rubles for a loaf! And this even without any of the promises to improve the quality, as it happened before. The same applied to the dairy section: fifteen rubles for a half-litre… I paid one hundred and forty rubles, that is, a fifth of all my cash, for just four loaves of bread and two litres of milk!

I returned home at a snail's pace, unable to calculate how long the remaining money would last. It turned out that at best - half a month. This seemed implausible, I couldn't believe it, it didn't compute – is this shock therapy?! I really was in shock, and so I kept counting again and again, over and over. There was no hope for even a drop of alcohol to celebrate the president's glory. For the first time I couldn't decide who Yegor Gaidar was, what did he embody? The rider dashing ahead, or our asking in terror: where was Yegor dashing to? Where are we going with him? (Publishing the collective anthology at my own expense was now out of the question.)

My cash did not last until the 15th. I went to the Church of St. Boris and Gleb on the Volkhov River, where the Feast of the Ecumenical Teachers and Hierarchs Basil the Great, Gregory the Theologian, and John Chrysostom was being celebrated - and my soul felt so cosy that, for some unknown reason, tears came to my eyes as I looked at the icon of the Virgin. Oil lamps flickering under icons, candle reflections on childlike yet aged faces, and, of course, the choir of angelic voices under the dome affected me deeply: "Oh, soul of mine, praise the most precious of all Heavenly Hosts, the Virgin Mother of God." Several times the church attendants approached me with a tray for offerings and every time I pulled bills from under my coat and joyfully placed them on the little crumpled pile without even looking. Rapture seized me when I heard the refrain "Oh, soul of mine, praise…." I perceived it as a heavenly behest to praise not only, or rather not so much the Mother of God, but my Rozochka in her image of the Most Precious of the Heavenly Hosts. I understand that there is some confusion here, perhaps even blasphemy, but it was exactly the reason for me to give away my money and to keep pushing my way through the crowd to stand on the path of the charity tray. It seemed to me that this money would somehow help Rozochka, that somewhere high above, too high for a human mind to soar, our Lord God Almighty would see this money and credit it to Rozochka's salvation, and through her, I too would be saved.

I felt so good staying through the entire service, even though initially I had only entered the church to kill time. I had arrived earlier than necessary at the store on Cheremnaya Street (there was a rumour of the lowest prices in the city there) and decided to wait in the church until the store opened. In short, I stood through the entire service and, by avoiding one hiccup, I faced another: the store was closed for lunch. I was upset at first, but when I checked my pockets, I was even glad for there was not a single kopeck.

I made my way home to the dormitory partly by bus and partly on foot. Sympathetic glances met me everywhere—people looked at me as if I were ill. It was all on account of my coat, truly a shock therapy attire, I was shocking people with it. It was amazing: I had worn it before, had ridden buses in it and strolled the streets, but never had anyone felt sorry for me. Yes, the extravagance of my clothing was duly noticed before, but never with an expression of shock or sympathy! It was as if everyone around guessed that I had money, that my attire was just a whim, like so what, he has a coat made from a blanket, who cares? Now, however, everyone acted totally differently: each glance conveyed compassion and pain, there were even mournful sighs heard from some more tender-hearted women. A very large and overweight one (her construction worker's vest looked like an infant undershirt on her) suddenly shouted to the whole bus, nodding in my direction:

"There he is, our woe!"

I don't know how much that mighty woman weighed in her soldier's boots and khaki-coloured canvas skirt, but when she began to move towards me, grasping the handrails, I got scared. For some reason, I suddenly shouted something and belligerently began to approach her. I must have looked like an enraged vulture at that moment. In any case, people surged away from me while I ducked under the stout woman's arms and made my way to the exit.

"Look, look, a victim!" she shouted again.

However, her shouting no longer bothered me; the bus stopped, and I jumped onto the sidewalk without hesitating.

"Look, a victim, a victim of violence!" she lashed out again as if striking me on the back (someone obligingly opened the window to allow the foolish woman to lean out).

I abruptly turned the corner behind the kiosk and waited a bit until the bus left. Then I walked across a vacant lot past the local TV station building under construction (few wanted to walk through pits and excavations). I had been insulted for no reason quite often lately; it even seemed good to be broke and have fewer reasons to go out frequently.

In February, I worked a great deal and learned that work is truly a fortress that overcomes any adversity. Writing poetry and plays at night and sleeping through the day helped me avoid having to go out. I adhered to this routine unwaveringly and liked it until I finally started hallucinating. Staring at the table-top caused large plates with hot dishes to appear suddenly from its depths, as if delivered by a magic tablecloth. There would be homemade cabbage soup and steaming lamb in tomato sauce with little sprigs of fresh green parsley and, of course, coffee with cream. But the finest part of my hallucinations was always the wedding, mine to Rozochka. Yes, those were the most delightful scenes. However, you already know all about this and so as not to repeat myself, I will only clarify some nuances.

On the day of the Presentation of the Lord, I swept up all the breadcrumbs, all the grains, and all the tea leaves. There was nothing edible left in the room, not even a smell, nothing but glass jars filled with slightly salted water (a homemade Ringer's solution). Modesty aside, my fasting experience taught me a great deal, and I spent my energy extremely diligently. For exactly two weeks, that is, until the end of February (I hope the reader remembers that 1992 was a leap year), I was in an exceptionally excellent mood. At night, I would write several poems or one act of a play, or if I set about retyping my works, the usual nightly yield was fifty pages. This fantastic productivity was only interrupted by hallucinations, which, on the other hand, spiced up my life a bit; I even prepared for them, as I mentioned before.

This excellent mood accompanied me through the whole of February and the beginning of March. Starting around March 6th, 7th and then into the 8th and so on, a sinister fate started hounding me. As soon as I imagined myself a distinguished Englishman and took out the pocket watch on a chain adorned with diamonds, everything would become muddled; instead of my wedding to Rozochka, there would be ten trays on my table, each bearing five large plates of steaming lamb in tomato sauce with little sprigs of fresh green parsley. However, what's so special about lamb with parsley? Nickel-plated balls are the real thing!

In my late childhood, I happened to swallow a rather hefty metal ball. As I recall now, I was standing next to my mother's bed, unscrewing it from one of the rods of the headboard with both hands. The ball was not very large but very heavy. Later, in the 10th grade, I learned that my father had filled all the balls on the bed with lead so they wouldn't unscrew, but I had managed to unscrew one of them anyway. As I stood there examining it, I suddenly heard my mother jingling a bucket in the hallway—she had just milked our cow. I quickly put the ball in my mouth and kept standing there. The ball moved very easily in my mouth and clicked against my teeth so loudly that I froze. My mother came in: "What are you doing?" I said "Nothing." At the same moment, I somehow inadvertently dislodged the ball, and it slid off my tongue right into my gullet and all the way into my stomach. I even felt it, heavy and cool, making me feel as if I had eaten and was full. For a long time after that, I didn't eat any solid food, just drank milk and water. My mother kept wondering and even worrying why I wasn't eating anything! I think it was then that my pancreas started reacting to the weight of solid food. Naturally, this reaction became more acute after fasting and I had to watch not so much the calories and proteins in my diet but also the weight of the solid food consumed.

On the 9th of March, I woke up unbearably hungry. All around me, whichever way I looked, there were silver plates with steaming lamb seasoned with little sprigs of green parsley gently parachuting and swaying on their slow descent. Sitting on the bed, I tried to catch one of the plates, but my fingers passed right through the lamb.

"A hallucination, a mirage," I said aloud, because hallucinations would begin spontaneously, out of my control.

Covering my eyes with my hand, I got down from the bed and felt around the windowsill for a jar of Ringer's solution. I drank with my eyes closed, and when I opened them, the mirage was gone. However, I grew even more hungry. The Gospel of Matthew says that Jesus was led by the Spirit into the wilderness to be tempted by the devil and, after fasting forty days and forty nights, he finally became hungry. Unlike Jesus, I fasted for twenty days and twenty nights and became hungry on March 9th, the very first day of Lent.

My hunger was so strong that it took a serious effort to resist the temptation and not steal someone's little pot of undercooked porridge from the communal kitchen.

"Never, under no circumstances!" I mentally commanded myself and began to dress quickly. The decision to go to Double-nose took a mere instant. It was time to see if he would deliver on his promise of free beer for my quatrain extolling the Pigsty's potential. As I was leaving, I took a folder of poems, remembering Rozochka's directive not to be shy about selling my works (she called them "immortals").

CHAPTER 27

When I asked the passengers where to get off the bus to reach the movie theatre under construction, many of them looked at me with undisguised suspicion, while others gazed absent-mindedly as if they hadn't heard the question. It felt like calling into the wilderness—no one answered me. I melted a small spot on the frozen window with my breath and tried to guess our location from the buildings outside. The driver did not bother to announce the stops and did not even stop at them without anyone knocking at his booth. He did not collect fares either, making his showcase of disrespect and lawlessness complete. What was there to collect anyway? Five kopeks?! A laughable price, almost zero amid the soaring daily inflation. Of course, everyone rode for free, and if you ride for free, you can't expect any service or rather, you can only expect what you've paid for.

However, after two months of creative work or (the same thing) voluntary house confinement, I had fallen hopelessly far behind life and was horrified when the driver brazenly announced that he does not stop on request and cursed over the speakerphone at an elderly passenger so foully that I couldn't stand it. I squeezed my way to the driver and shouted indignantly:

"I demand satisfaction! You have insulted not just one passenger, you have insulted everyone! I demand…!"

The bus braked abruptly, and I barely kept my grip on the handrails. The driver killed the engine and, without even looking in my direction, opened the doors and announced that he wouldn't go anywhere, wouldn't move a centimetre until the brawler, that was me, left the bus.

Each of us has heard "extreme audacity" jokes—this was one of them. I was in no mood to laugh, though. I glanced over at the passengers, as if to say, look at this boor! I expected support, moreover, my entire life experience suggested that support was simply inevitable in this situation. I was guaranteed to have it. Alas, most passengers didn't even look at me in response, and those who did grew irate as if it wasn't the driver who had insulted them, but me.

"Citizens, if we leave it like this, he'll remain certain that he can get away with anything," I said as calmly as I could.

"Listen, you cotton-stuffed quilt, you were clearly told to get out of the bus, you cause inconvenience to innocent people," a resounding, husky bass voice boomed from behind me, causing the loose aluminium panels inside the bus to suddenly respond with a rattle.

"I cause inconvenience?!" I said in feigned amusement.

"Yes, you," the owner of the husky bass voice said firmly, rising slightly from his seat.

I had never seen someone so black and hairy, zombified creature with a sullen, muddled gaze. I don't know and won't predict what might have happened if not for the elderly passenger I had stood up for.

"Let's go, it's best we get off here," he said, gently taking my hand.

We walked along the rutted road between garages, and

the elderly man explained to me that the movie theatre under construction had long since been built and put into operation, though not as a movie theatre but as a casino.

"In the evenings, imported cars flock there, flashy, comfortable. As for the ordinary people…" He paused. "What was your name again, young man?"

"Dmitry, Dmitry Yuryevich."

"So Mitya then," the elderly man said with a friendly nod, asking if he could address me informally.

"I don't mind," I muttered, thinking it pretentious to worry about familiarity after the outrageous boorishness we both had just encountered.

Meanwhile, the elderly man continued:

"Ordinary people like you, Mitya, are barred from the place; they won't let you over the threshold because everyone there is in suits and comes with huge, huge amounts of money. And the amazing thing…" The elderly man stopped and seemed to forget about me, looking at the low white sun already grasping at the garage roofs. He took off his nutria fur hat, shaking off the snow dust, and marvelled dreamily: "Where, where do these twenty-year-old kids get such large sums of money?!"

"You must have been a high school math teacher, now retired?"

The teacher chuckled. Putting his hat back on, he said:

"Well now, you're quite the physiognomist, you hit the bull's eye!"

"Interesting, who are they, these kids with lots of cash?"

He chuckled again.

"They're called the 'New Russians.' In the sense that the old Russians had almost everything: jobs, education, respect for colleagues and for elders… The only thing we didn't have was money. And these have the opposite: no respect, no education, but pockets full of cash!"

This "but pockets full of cash!" was uttered with the spirit of a dreamy marvel which seemed curiously familiar to me.

"But surely someone let these kids get cars and money… someone even newer than the 'New Russians'?"

"Are you hinting at the authorities?" he asked very cautiously.

"Yes, at those in power," I said. "And besides, why can't a 'New Russian' be some elderly man without a conscience but pockets overflowing with cash? Or do they not exist?"

I don't know why I suddenly stood up for the young guys, these "New Russians," but I said almost verbatim:

"We have three citizens before us: a high-ranking official, some elderly man, and, as you put it, a twenty-year-old kid. They all have piles of money, they're all unconscionable, but now the question is: which of them is the most unconscionable? Surely not the twenty-year-old kid?!"

The elderly man, who had just been so gentle and refined, suddenly stiffened, and straightened his posture, bristled. (It must have been the nutria fur: no matter how sleek and matted, the fur bristled up on the hat's edges, especially on its front.)

"Well now, Dmitry Yuryevich, you are even more confrontational than one might imagine. I hope I have your name right—Dmitry Yuryevich?"

"Yes, yes… Yuryevich," I confirmed.

The elderly man, referring to himself and his kind who knew life firsthand, delivered a veritable speech that made it clear I shouldn't have got involved in the altercation with the bus driver. Supposedly we, the lumpenproletarians[82] are invulnerable to any revolution or regime because, when you get down to it, we lumpens have nothing to lose. We have no nationality, no land, no money, nothing. It used to be thought that only déclassé elements (criminals, tramps, vagrants, beggars) could be lumpen. But today's life has shown there are also lumpen students, lumpen intelligentsia, and lumpen workers, and it could hardly be otherwise. For generations, the Soviet rule had systematically ensured that no one had anything or rather had just a subsistence minimum.

"But isn't it dreadful," I said, "dreadful if we are lumpens?"

I stopped, but only noticed that when the old man stopped as well. He was looking at the white sun over the garages.

"Why dreadful? If you have nothing, I have nothing, he has nothing, we are brothers, not blood brothers but soulmates, as we could be with anyone, even aliens. Universal human values unite us, and the universal human always trumps the universal national or ethnic."

"Wait, wait," I said, and we started walking again. "You say 'brothers-soulmates,' but what if we don't have enough in common to be brothers? Did you see that hairy black guy?! What universal human values can we talk about with him, when all he

---

82   Lumpen (German: Lumpen - "rags", Lump - "slovenly", lumpenproletariat or lumpenised proletariat, German: Lumpenproletariat) is a term coined by Karl Marx to describe groups of people who have been expelled or excluded from society; economically declassified strata of the population (vagrants, beggars, criminals and other asocial individuals).

needed was an immediate gain—for us to keep going, that's all. He has no interest in why, what for, on what grounds, he doesn't want to know anything about it."

"But maybe the immediate could also be used to build some engaging culture upon it?" He pondered. "Avant-Garde art responds to the immediate moment, and our whole life, the life of entire civilizations, consists of the sum of such time segments."

"If you'll allow me," I said, and we stopped again. "I've thought a lot about this and concluded that the immediate can only build the immediate. But it is precisely this thirst for the immediate that breeds narcotics and addicts, and it is not just about substances. I am convinced that all this art stemming from the immediate is also nothing but an addiction. Tell me, if we are brothers-in-reason, intoxicated by drugs, how deep and lasting is our brotherhood?"

"So that's where you've got to," said the old man, and we resumed walking.

We walked on, but suddenly I felt unwell. I recalled Bulgakov's words: never talk to strangers. I took a closer look at his face—hair sticking out of his nostrils, bristly, exactly like nutria fur.

"And just who might you be? I told you my name, and you should tell me yours."

The elderly man chuckled again:

"Doesn't Bulgakov's advice ring a bell: never talk to strangers?"

I was dumbstruck. At first, I thought he was wearing a coat of dark grey shaggy wool. Nothing of the sort, it was indeed shaggy but not wool and not dark grey, but rather plush, a brownish-mousy colour that hugged his arms and shoulders so tightly that the coat now looked more like a jumpsuit tucked into bluish ankle boots with soles so thick and heels so high that they almost looked like hooves.

"The devil, the absolute devil," I thought in horror.

"Oh, come now! What a typical Russian habit, you've already got aeroplanes, satellites, orbital stations, and space travel, but as soon as you meet an independent thinker, he's the devil!"

"Fair point, fair point, independent thinkers have always been frightening…"

"I propose we change the subject," said the elderly man, stopping by a snowdrift. The rutted road curved sharply to the left, while the pedestrian path skirted the drift and continued straight along an arched structure made of blue corrugated siding.

"Let's change it, but still, what should I call you?" I asked as gently as I could, carefully trying to avoid being rude in my insistence.

"Of course, it's my own fault…but in your place, Mitya, and with your hallucinations, I'd rather settle for a lumpen intellectual…I fear my name and family name might spur your imagination to folly."

He stood half-turned toward me, as if in the same brownish-mousy jumpsuit but now not plush but of nutria fur, with bristly tufts at the elbows and knees. Especially the knees—I kept them in my sight just like his booties (he was looking at his own tracks in the snow with amusement). Now I could see clearly: small and bluish, they didn't resemble hooves at all. Just ordinary booties on a thick platform with high heels.

"No, no, it passed," I said, referring to my hallucinations. "So then, what? By the way, I was told there's a beer bar called Pigsty across from the movie theatre under construction (that is, the casino). It's still far away, isn't it?"

"On the contrary," the elderly man replied. "Just go along the path past the arched structure, and when you round the corner, you'll find yourself on Lev Tolstoy Street and locate the casino right away, it's impossible to miss, all lit up day and night like a cruise ship."

He ushered me ahead and onto the path with an eloquent gesture and stepped back from the snowdrift to let me pass. I was dumbstruck again: it was as if some scorching, incinerating blast had passed through me. The entire drift had been thoroughly trampled, thoroughly—with hooves. If I hadn't known, hadn't seen for myself the elderly lumpen intellectual amusing himself by walking on this pile of snow, I would have easily concluded that some heavy cloven-hoofed animal had tromped all over it. Yes, a heavy one, the cloven prints were deep and distinct.

Struggling to overcome the sudden wave of weakness and nausea, I had to lean against a wall for support.

"And you, Mitya, you are terribly depleted and hungry. And although you reject literature and art that responds to the immediate and mundane, still 'hunger will break through stone walls,' and this morning you set out for Pigsty with one hope—to grab a bite to eat. You have a folder with poems, true 'immortals' under your sweater, right at your heart, but only yesterday you never dreamed (or at least not seriously) of selling them, and now you do. Yes, it happens, the immediate can clutch your throat tightly with its bony hand and have you cry for help with no chance to even think of the eternal."

He silently approached and, gently taking my hand (just as before on the bus), unexpectedly whispered passionately in my ear that he was ready to buy my little lumpen poncho right then and there. He promised a large sum—thirty ounces of gold or exactly nine thousand U.S. dollars at the London Exchange rate.

"No way," I said furiously, "It has never been a 'little lumpen poncho,' it may be a Gaidar's coat, the shock therapy coat, but never 'lumpen,' never! Do you understand—ne-ver!"

I saw astonishingly beautiful shimmering sparks on the nutria fur, and suddenly noticed a massive silver buckle with a blue sapphire on my own shoulder (on my poncho). It filled my brain with radiant morning clarity, and I could distinctly see angels dancing and gliding in its extraordinary flashing light.

"I could never agree to the immediate also because," I said, "it is inconsistent by its very nature, and inconsistency kills everything, including literature and art."

I tore my gaze from the sapphire. I hoped to see its blue sparks on the lumpen intellectual's hand. How surprised I was when I saw him back in his previous spot by the snowdrift on the rutted road. It was evident that the lumpen intellectual hadn't approached me, otherwise his hooves would have sunk into the path.

"Are you unwell?" he called out loudly enough for the distance so I could hear him.

"No, no, I'm fine…But why don't you keep me company?"

"Really…to finish our conversation?"

He stepped onto the path and slowly approached, and all was well (he didn't sink or get stuck in the snow). The symptoms of nausea suddenly vanished, and so did my general malaise.

"So, you didn't answer: what will happen to us or any other people who tear each other apart instead of becoming brothers-in-reason? Especially since an immediate gain, as you rightly noted, could well become the core of an engaging immediate culture, and therefore of an ideology."

I wanted to let the lumpen intellectual go ahead of me, but changed my mind. It's better to just look back at him, I decided, instead of having to grab his coat or go around him through the snow to ask my next question. Incidentally, now that my head had completely cleared, he was again wearing a coat of magnificent dark grey shaggy wool. (Exactly like the one my neighbour Toma had made for me. I even regretted not having tried it on back then. The thought did occur to me: was he wearing my coat?)

The lumpen intellectual didn't answer my question right away. He gathered his thoughts for quite a while, then said that in his opinion people with little to no national consciousness have a proclivity toward revolutions and civil wars, to self-destruction. Consequently, such a people are doomed to become fertilizers for others who have not lost their national feeling.

"Well, I'll be!" I cried out angrily.

For some time, we walked in silence (I heard the crunching of snow behind me).

"In that case, who will guarantee that calls for universal human values are not just calls for self-destruction?! Who will guarantee they are not a provocation or a sort of a call to other peoples to improve their lot, so to speak, at the expense of those who have lost their national identity?"

The path turned the corner of the arched structure onto Leo Tolstoy Street.

"Who would ensure that?!" I repeated fervently and looked back.

There was no one behind nor anywhere around me. The classic was right after all—never talk to strangers.

CHAPTER 28

The Pigsty greeted me with a crimson banner stretched across all three kiosks. It displayed my poems. Written in just two lines, they were perceived as slogans fluttering in the breeze. I felt a whiff of celebration:
PEACE TO THE WORLD! ...
OUR PATH MAY BE OBSCURE AND SMALL,
DON'T FRET, MY BRETHREN, NOT AT ALL.
FOR THOSE WHO DRINK AT PIGSTY HUT, IT
BRIGHTER GETS AND WIDER, BUD!

As I crossed the street and found myself by the kiosks, the sense of celebration grew stronger. It emanated from the table densely set with beer mugs, bottles, and glass jars. Unusually long and covered with a dirty cloth, it nevertheless seemed festive amid the snow, or rather, the snowy whiteness. I was struck by the presence of a police officer by the fence enclosing the courtyard. To be precise, I only noticed him later as he was patrolling back and forth along the perimeter of the so-called summer bar, because at that moment I couldn't take my eyes off the casino building. Pinkish, shimmering with multicoloured lights, it reigned supreme in the depths of the boulevard, a palace from a fairy-tale. Cars, mostly imports, were parked in spaces between the trees. Chrome bumpers dazzled the eyes in the sunlight despite the frost covering them.

"The Splendours and Miseries of Courtesans" - it seemed like a foreign city! I suddenly recalled the lumpen intellectual's warning that the path to the casino was forever barred to the likes of me.

Let it be barred, big deal, like that scares me! The thought had barely taken hold when I was suddenly overwhelmed by fear, fear of alienation and unbearable loneliness. I don't need any casinos or imported cars, I need nothing! Give me back my country ... I had found myself in a totally different country, not at the pike's behest[83], but at that of some Koschei the Immortal[84]. Emelya was a kind soul, and therefore wise. But Koschei?! The more cunning the villain, the more dangerous and hateful he will be.

"Hey Lyokha, you pig, call that guy over, the one wrapped in a blanket," I heard a voice very similar to Doublenose's but more self-assured and confident.

I deliberately remained still, not moving an inch.

The cop approached and stopped in front of me - a snot-nosed kid, but huge, blocking the casino, the sun, the whole wide world from view.

"You're being summoned."

"By whom?! Who may call you, a police officer, a pig?"

"The general director of the summer bar," Lyokha the pig said in surprise, looking rather bewildered over my head towards the director.

I don't know what he saw there, but he immediately squared

83   "At the Pike's Behest" is one of the most known Russian fairy tales, in which the protagonist (Emelya the Simpleton) gets his wishes granted by a magic pike that he once caught and released.
84   One of the most iconic evil folk characters, featured in many Russian fairy tales.

his shoulders, adjusted the belt he wore over his coat, and ordered in a tone that brooked no objection:

"Follow me, citizen!"

I followed because this police officer had returned me to my native country without even realising it, for only in Russia could there be a summer bar in winter!

Passing by the table, my "escort" deftly snatched up an empty half-litre jar and just as deftly "rinsed" it with snow. (Summer bar paths in the snow resembled trenches.)

"Aleksey Filaktich, another one, warmed please," the cop said imploringly, and immediately stiffened, not looking back but nodding behind him, confident that I would surely follow. "What are we to do with this one?"

Good Lord, this Russian servility! He really is a pig; a pig indeed!

Aleksey Filaktich turned out to be Aleksey Feofilaktovich.

"Look here Lyokha, mangle my patronymic just one more time and you can forget about beer, warm or cold! Yes, none whatsoever, and your boss won't help you!"

Aleksey Feofilaktovich stood by the kiosk door like a dresser set out on the street, so bulky and cumbersome he was in his fox fur coat.

"In translation from Greek Feofilakt means 'guarded by God.' Got it?! By God! ... Not by any pig cops."

Aleksey Feofilaktovich apparently felt too hot. He took off his fur hat and began tying up its ear flaps, turning to face me at the same time.

Yes, Aleksey Filaktich turned out to be Aleksey Feofilaktovich, but astonishingly, he also turned out to be Doublenose, the general director of the summer bar.

Of course, we didn't overdo the greetings, just hugged once as was customary. Replacing his hat, Doublenose shouted for four mugs of warmed beer. To save me from trudging through the dirty snow, he slid the fence aside and led me straight across the snowdrift to a packed table, as only the owner could.

"As for me," I said, "one mug is enough, and a bar of some cheap chocolate, if you have any."

Doublenose didn't cancel the order for the beer, but took offence at the chocolate:

"Are you for real, poet?!"

He looked back over his shoulder at Lyokha the cop:

"Grab a couple of Snickers bars too!"

We sat at the head of the table on beer crates, which had evidently been stowed under the table for such occasions. Doublenose, being a true general director, surveyed those present, rapped on an empty three-litre jar with a table knife, waited for quiet at "Kamchatka"[85] (they were arguing over which beer packs a better kick, cold or warm), then announced:

"Today is a memorable day for us…"

Lyokha the cop brought four heated beer mugs at nearly a run. Without foam, the beer steamed like hot broth.

"Aleksey Fil…"

Doublenose strained, and those present fell silent. Lyokha the cop pulled a scrap of paper from his pocket along with the Snickers bars and, openly and unabashedly, read out syllable by syllable: "Fe-o-fi-lak-to-vich!" He explained, "Just so those present don't mangle it."

---

85   At any public gathering an area far from the speaker, the head of the table or any other center of action is informally called "Kamchatka".

The table reacted with an approving murmur. Doublenose, grinning, handed one of the mugs to Lyokha the cop:

"To resourcefulness!"

"To resourcefulness!" the table responded.

It turned into an improvised toast of sorts. It would have been a sin not to drink, so we drank. I downed nearly half the mug in one go! I drank and went adrift, that is, not actually adrift, of course, but drunk. At first, I didn't even realise it, just felt burning in my stomach and started munching the Snickers bar (Doublenose had sliced it into thin, neat pieces). Then a pleasant warmth spread through my entire body, and communicating, mutual understanding and making judgements became as easy as if I had just graduated from the most elite academy in the whole world.

What stuck in my memory was how Doublenose introduced me to the table:

"You all sitting here are drinking your beer with dried fish, but Dmitry Slyozkin (pay attention) is having it with a Snickers bar. And why? ... Because we are ordinary, mass-produced folks, but look how Mitya is dressed? Mitya is bespoke, one of a kind, you could say a piece of jewellery, like a Fabergé egg. He is a poet!!!"

OUR PATH MAY BE OBSCURE AND SMALL,
DON'T FRET, MY BRETHREN, NOT AT ALL.
FOR THOSE WHO DRINK AT PIGSTY HUT, IT
BRIGHTER GETS AND WIDER, BUD!

Of course, there was applause, clinking of glasses, kisses. "Kamchatka" started singing "Glorious Sacred Sea of Baikal..." I felt both embarrassed and pleased. Embarrassed at being compared to a piece of jewellery, let alone a Fabergé egg! In a turmoil, I finished off the beer and Snickers and was about to get up from the table when they pushed another mug over to me.

Doublenose took the floor again.

"Brothers-in-arms! (Why brothers-in-arms? God knows!) Do you know, dear brothers-in-arms, that three hundred and thirty-six rivers flow into Baikal, but only one, Angara, flows out? Well, there are three hundred and thirty-six of us brothers-in-arms too." (Where did that come from?! There were no more than seventeen or eighteen of us present.) "That's a huge number! And Mitya, like Angara, is our sole representative. Today he has come to congratulate us, because today, exactly three months ago to the day, our open-air summer bar came to life and has thrived ever since. Hurrah, brothers-in-arms!"

No one responded to the "hurrah!" On the contrary, those present seemed to cease listening to Doublenose altogether (they started tapping their dried fish and folding it against the table edge). But Doublenose had apparently become the general director of the open-air bar by virtue of his unparalleled intuition. He didn't finish his speech; it was just a pause, after which, without emphasis and said in a completely ordinary voice, as if such things happened every day:

"And now, brothers-in-arms, our highly esteemed Fabergé poet Dmitry Slyozkin is sponsoring each of us with three bottles or mugs of beer (whichever you prefer). All this, so to speak, to celebrate our prosperity."

The table rumbled and the air over the courtyard shook to a rousing "hurrah!" Clinking, kissing, noise, and clamour ensued - three hundred and thirty-six brothers-in-arms were fraternising.

I asked Doublenose amid all this fraternising what exactly he meant. In response, he first submerged himself in the depths of his fox coat, but then emerged pompously from the fur (no Croesus, of course, but quite a merchant of the top guild) and explained that from the moment of our meeting, he owed me for the advertising poem (counting only weekends, Saturdays, and Sundays) thirty days' worth of beer, and thirty multiplied by the four promised mugs came to sixty litres or one hundred and twenty mugs.

"It's all OK," said Doublenose and shared in a concerned tone: "The time has come to pay the dues, I feel we'll soon have to ditch the name 'Pigsty.'"

Of course, we weren't allowed to converse further: the brothers-in-arms very boisterously demanded their free beer. And someone black and hairy (I recognised him, we were on the same bus) started banging his head on the table as if in a fit and shouting that for three bottles he would tear out anyone's throat. He glared at me so fiercely and gnashed his teeth so furiously that there was no mistaking his intentions.

"All right, Renya, enough of that nonsense," Doublenose rebuked him, promising that in a minute or two the directors of the neighbouring shops would treat each one present.

Indeed, Doublenose's former dorm mates appeared, wearing white smocks and bakers' caps. Even his bodyguard Tutankhamun was in a white cap. All of them were carrying crates of beer.

Most of the brothers-in-arms immediately leapt from the table, the rest hastily drained their beers, straddling the long benches.

Lyokha the cop instantly realised that it was time to act and rushed to cut off the horde. He shouted threateningly that anyone who tried to touch the beer would be sorry!

The wave of brothers-in-arms deftly swept away the fence, then floundered. Lyokha the cop and plumber Tutankhamun rushed in and nearly took each other down in the heat of the moment before forming a defensive circle together with the shop directors. Anyone running up got such a hard cuff to the ear that they would inevitably fall or plop down into the snow in surprise. The only one to break through the defensive line was the impossibly hairy bluish-black Renya. Having seized a crate, he dashed behind the kiosk like a yeti, leaping over the snow-drifts. About five brothers-in-arms set off in pursuit.

"Let them run," Doublenose stopped Tutankhamun. "At most, one beer each is all they'll get."

"What a head on those shoulders!" the plumber-bodyguard groaned, and many of those lying down raised their snow-covered faces to look at Doublenose.

Doublenose grinned sceptically and raised his mug as if nothing had happened, proposing a brüderschaften toast. Of course, half-litre mugs aren't shot glasses. I spilt about half of it onto my chest and Doublenose's fur sleeve.

He shouted to his comrades to bring us each another mug and repeated the ritual, this time so successfully that not a drop was spilt while we drained our mugs.

Gradually, the table's revelry resumed. I say "gradually" because the second brüderschaften mug made me feel as if I had graduated from yet another academy. In any case, the ground swayed and events around me lost any sense whatsoever.

* * *

I am reading poems. The low sun warms the back of my head. The table is crushed by my shadow, but the faces of those present shine like electric bulbs.

"Listen, brothers-in-arms, you're being told about love!" Doublenose raps his knife on an empty three-litre jar. Seen through it, faces stretch and contort like in a magnifying glass.

The crunch of snow announces the arrival of shaggy Renya brought forth in his black dog fur coat by Lyokha the cop and Tutankhamun the bodyguard who holds Renya's arms wrenched behind his back.

"For what?!" Renya protests angrily, "Let me go!"

Doublenose nods towards me:

"Only if Mitya allows it, he's the sponsor."

The cop and Tutankhamun dash in opposite directions. Renya falls to his knees, arms raised to the heavens:

"Sponsor, weren't we on the same bus?!"

I look at Renya's upturned, disconsolate face and see that one of his eyes is swollen shut, while in the other, dark purple one, he and I are reflected. (This does not seem strange to me.) Renya approaches sidelong, one hand on his hip while the other is raised as if ready to dance a squatting dance. But he cannot do a squatting dance because I, poet Dmitry Slyozkin, am now sitting on that raised hand. I am reading poems. In my jacket, I have a folder of "immortals" that I planned to sell, but now, as Renya hurriedly carries me around the long table, I take the opportunity to pull them out and fling them into the air above the table.

"Long live the King of Poets!" I shout, meaning myself.

"Long live the sponsor!" the brothers-in-arms shout.

Caught by a light breeze, the white pages scatter, swirl, and parachute down, their sheer abundance dizzying… The lilac pupil went out, the violet speckle dimmed…

* * *

I found myself standing by the kiosks. Wealthily dressed people were emerging from the casino. Judging by their cheery mood, they must have won. Especially noticeable was a stocky man in a fur hat and an excellent fur coat. Next to him was a beauty in a leather coat. Her coat's collar was made of llama, and she wore a deep red turban on which snowflakes seemed to ignite like gemstones.

Lyokha the cop slid out like a shadow from the perimeter of the summer bar. He ran up to the stocky man and reported that all was secure in the area entrusted to him. The man removed a glove, shook Lyokha's hand then immediately forgot about him as other fur-hatted men pushed the cop to the back.

Doublenose then appeared with his shop directors and the bodyguard. They hung back at a distance, like misbehaving mutts, wondering if their master would notice them or not.

"And yet she is in charge here - he is delighting in her!" I sang aloud as I immediately recognised both the head of railway logistics and the chief of the railway police.

To avoid being recognised I pulled the hood with inner lining over my head, turned away and pretended to look elsewhere. My whole demeanour suggested I had no association whatsoever with the "immortals" scattered around me. I was just a guy standing by the kiosks eating a Snickers bar.

The fur-coated man calmly bent down, picked up a white sheet of paper, scanned it, then beckoned Doublenose over. He flew to the man's side.

They conversed, glancing over at me occasionally.

Then Tutankhamun ran up to me, losing his breath in fervency.

"How much do you want for the poem?" he panted.

"Which one?" I asked without much ado, but Tutankhamun had already scampered back.

Incidentally, he seemed to scurry in all directions - his shadow really did scatter every which way in the glow of the surrounding electric lights. I called out to Tutankhamun that he needn't ask – I'd gift any poem free of charge.

But the chief declined my gift and passed me fifty dollars via Doublenose. Then, after the head of logistics read the poem, Doublenose confidentially informed her with the air of a medical expert that I write day and night, with no time even to eat - a talent, a poet of Fabergé quality!

What did Fabergé have to do with it?!

In conclusion, as befits a medical expert trusting solely in the directress's decency, he quite confidentially disclosed (as if revealing a diagnosis):

"Skin and bones - he'll soon be swelling up from hunger!"

"Good Lord, talent in our country is so overlooked, not understood at all! We should be erecting a monument to the man while he lives!"

She sobbed a little, though not for me of course, but for all Russian talent. And that's when the chief unbuckled another fifty dollars, instructing Doublenose directly not to let me die. Or else… Or else what?! In any case, Doublenose promised he'd work himself to a crisp, if need be, but wouldn't let me die…

And one more episode. Doublenose's sidekicks are carrying me through the dorm vestibule when suddenly Alina Spiridonovna notices one of my Finnish boots is missing. They drop me and run outside to stop the cab, surely the boot must be stuck under a seat.

…And now I'm in my room, laid out on my wide bed. Doublenose instructs his people to shove cardboard boxes of food supplies under the bed.

"Well, I'll be, drank himself into oblivion, and he's supposed to be a poet," Tutankhamun tut-tutted, but no one backed him up.

"How much does the man really need?" Doublenose came to my defence, then marvelled unexpectedly, "Just look at the elite company Mitya attracts! Now his poems will sell like hotcakes, and those money bags will be visiting us too!"

He rubbed his hands together, and that was the last thing I can recall. Oh wait, no, there's also a recurring dream, but more on that later.

CHAPTER 29

April 10th was the day when I hoped to lift my fasting restrictions. However, I broke the fast much earlier, and it wasn't an April Fool's prank. On the morning of April 1st someone slid a letter under my door. I thought it must be some joke or other. Can you imagine my surprise when I recognised Rozochka's handwriting?

I quietly lay down on the bed and remained there for a long while with the envelope on my chest. All sorts of thoughts galloped through my head like frisky little horses. Our brief life together, appeared before me truly as if in the palm of my hand.

I can't fathom how long I lay there, caught up in sweet memories, but when I came to, I rushed to the table for scissors and nearly sobbed, giving way to overwhelming emotions. I was trembling, unable to manage even the simple task of slitting open the envelope.

What, what did she write?! Maybe she was telling me she was on her way and needed to be picked up? Or maybe she had already arrived, and the letter was just late? Of course, it was late! Nothing works nowadays, and what works is done so abhorrently that it would be better not done to avoid provoking futile hopes.

With bitterness, I placed the envelope and scissors on the pillow. I felt such an insatiable hunger as I had never experienced even during the fast. "I could eat a horse" was not even close to my overwhelming feeling of relentless craving. Insatiable hunger, by the way, is a main signal that I am about to fall into a tantrum, and in such cases the only antidote is food; solid food.

I hungrily scanned the room: the work desk that often substituted as my workbench, the bedframe, other objects, and various stuff. I was searching for any little metal ball with one sole purpose (yes!) - to swallow it. Oh Lord, anything, even some wretched stale crust, would suffice in that moment. I had completely forgotten (the result of sudden over-excitement) that I had plenty of food under the bed in cardboard boxes, and there were two loaves of perfectly fresh bread on the windowsill in a plastic bag. God himself resolved the situation, as some would say: I spotted the bag. No, no, I didn't remember about the bread! I placed my hand on the bag without thinking and almost jumped in delight - bread!

There's no need to describe how voraciously I ate it. I was devouring it, not slicing it with a knife but ripping the loaf apart with my hands, as any starving person would. (In my nervous shock I was exactly such a starving person, even though I really wasn't).

Thus, ten days before the proper date prescribed by my regimen, I had already started consuming solid food, and in unlimited quantities, too. I must admit though that just after finishing off one rye loaf and setting for the second, I suddenly felt like I had swallowed a lead billiard ball. Still, my hands stopped shaking and emotionally I had calmed down enough to lay back quietly with the envelope on my chest.

This time there were no memories or thoughts at all, not even stray ones: I lay in a kind of primordial emptiness. Only once did a distinct thought emerge: why are you lying here, open the envelope! And I did.

Roza had written on a yellowed sheet of paper, with a faded image of Grandpa Frost[86] and the inscription "Happy New Year 1970!" in the corner. Where had she got it? She wasn't even born until 1972! My thoughts raced: on June 5th she would turn twenty. We had dreamed of celebrating the milestone in Crimea. Oh God, where was all that now?!

"Dearest Mitya!"

(My eyes filled with tears - dear-est! I was dearest to her! … I gazed unseeingly out the window: Rozochka, where are you? How are you, my little flower?! I raised the tattered sheet to my eyes again.)

"Dearest Mitya! I was reinstated at the medical college, but without a scholarship. I had been working side jobs with the ambulance service, but yesterday they started accusing me of stealing a box of morphine and selling it to criminals. They've already turned me in to the police and threatened to expel me. For what? I didn't take anything! They say that you too, as my former husband, will be hunted down. But they're just talking big, this isn't any STD case. I didn't give them your address, and you, Mitya, don't reveal yourself. If possible, send me money, as much as you can, with a hold for pickup. I know you're curious about my goal. Don't worry, my goal shines like a star in the sky, but down here it's just mud. One bishop has already promised to set me on the true path. Every time he sees me, he's all like 'Holy, holy, holy!'… His face is refined, and he is cute, but you, Mitya, even though you're a good slob, you've a cleaner soul than

---

86 Soviet non-religious copycat of Santa Claus.

all of them. In Moscow they're selling poems hand-to-hand, arranging it by phone. If you don't have money right now, I beg you, go sell some of your immortals. I have no one to rely on but you, Mitya. Come here, Mitenka, I'll give you a kiss. We'll meet up as agreed, but for now don't show your face, just send money with a hold for pickup addressed to Roza Fedorovna Slyozkina. I have two passports but live under your family name for now. Send it - your Rozochka."

The letter was distressing. I re-read it several times and concluded that Rozochka's situation was utterly dreadful, she was perishing. And she wasn't just anyone - she was Roza Fedorovna Slyozkina! I even shouted at myself in indignation:

"You're still here?! Money, immediately!"

Preferably in hard currency, I added mentally, because from that second on I was already controlling my actions.

I quickly dressed and threw on my coat. Despite the urge to sell my "immortals" right away, I sat at my desk in the coat preparing almost until noon.

First, I had been writing all these days while exiting my fast, and my newest poems hadn't yet been typed. Second, after the incident in Pigsty and my belated reflections on drinking, I had quite recklessly decided that I would never sell my works again, and because of that, hadn't even made a cursory inventory. Rozochka would not have approved of selling poems without keeping a second copy for myself, essentially forfeiting my authorship. She would be absolutely right about that because anyone trying to become a writer can't help but dream of publishing one's collected works. It's as natural as every soldier dreaming of becoming a general. Boris Leonidovich Pasternak outright deceived us when he said: "There's no need to start an archive, to fuss over manuscripts." Recently I leafed through the fourth volume of his collected works - a brick of over nine hundred pages, which includes Pasternak's very first, earliest literary pieces from his youth. I don't think you need to be a genius to assert with confidence: Pasternak himself started his own archive around the age of twenty and kept it in perfect order his whole life. I know from experience that poets love to show off their wit, to trumpet some new turn of phrase, line, or quatrain. They're drawn to blaze across the celestial sphere like a flaming meteor, dazzling everyone with their brilliance. That's exactly what's happening here… But enough of this!

Instead of just a minute, I sat at home nearly until noon. I was forced to undertake what would eventually become the start of my own archive. Nevertheless, over those several hours, I exhibited true wonders of productivity. The only thing bothering me was the absence of even one new poem dedicated to Rozochka. (Back when it was written, I had typed it in just a single copy - gift poems should be one-of-a-kind). So then… Could it be that the police chief had got that very poem?! Whatever the case, I began my archive with Rozochka's poem. There seemed something symbolic in that. Perhaps that's why, even as I worked wonders, my thoughts kept returning to the recurring dream from that unforgettable yet practically forgotten day of mine.

* * *

Once again I found myself at Pigsty's summer bar with its long table densely set with half-empty beer bottles and cans, faces looming through heavy smoke and haze like they're floating, the buzz of drunken conversation where everyone is talking but no one is listening.

"Mitya, sell your flannel topper for thirty ounces of gold! That's nine thousand green bucks!" hairy Renya shouts fervently, holding me up even higher. I'm sitting on his arm with my legs drawn up, invisible beneath my coat. "Why does he want my topper?" I torment myself.

Renya carries me around the table like a banner, or more precisely, like a tray of food. And indeed, I'm now sitting in an open silver serving dish, poured over with sugar powder. Brothers-in-arms keep exchanging glances as they rise slightly, wanting to see firsthand that of all the promised dishes, I am the one. They're all holding knives and forks, whetting them against each other to show their impatience for me, as if for a cut of meat.

If I take off my coat, which I'd have to do after selling it, I mentally note (with sheer horror overtaking me), the brothers-in-arms will eat anyone found on the table, leaving not a single bone behind. So that's why Renya wants my flannel topper, I realise, and despair gives me strength.

"First of all, it's not a topper, it's a coat, a horseman's coat for riding ahead!"

Renya pulls out a crocodile skin billfold from under his shiny black cloak (he's now wearing a cloak and a top hat like a gentleman), overstuffed with dollars. The billfold is so bloated with hard currency that it won't close, forcing Renya to hold it open before my eyes with the compartments facing out. I cry out:

"Manchester City!"

I do it because I suddenly recognise the Englishman and his billfold. I even noticed the pink handkerchief peeking from his tuxedo's pocket when he spread his cloak wide open in a gentlemanly fashion.

Realising he's been recognised and nothing can be undone, Renya slams the serving dish down on the table with all his might, sending all the dishes (myself in the silver one included) tumbling in every direction, smashing bottles, cans, and jars in a chain reaction. Yes, the last thing I hear is glass shattering. And the last thing I see are knives and forks bearing down on me, about to plunge into my flesh – and this is when I would wake with a scream).

Now that Rozochka's letter had arrived, the recurring dream was a delight: the "Dream Book" by Nina Grigorievna Grishina, brought from the editorial office among other manuscripts, had taught me that getting blows from the living is a sign of family happiness, that all will be well.

PART FOUR

CHAPTER 30

My appearance at Pigsty didn't surprise anyone, it seemed that they were expecting me. Not specifically, but any day now, as they say. The banner with my poem had been replaced (there were just two words "BEER BAR" shining from celestial blue satin). Doublenose told me, as if I were some kind of finance inspector, that offering services to the public was a serious matter, so they should strive for simple but inoffensive forms.

"People must be respected! Homo res sacra!"

It did not surprise me at all that Doublenose had started using Latin catchphrases. It followed his prior attempts at pretension, like "a poet of Fabergé scale." But his emphasis on services offered to the public being a serious matter and mention of the pursuit of simple yet inoffensive forms – raised questions. I sensed these weren't his own words, or rather the words were his, but the thought behind them belonged to someone with authority over Doublenose. Here, I suppose, my prior experience at the newspaper came through, when after a regular or extraordinary Party Plenum I would notice a glimmer of its "great resolutions" in some utterly unpretentious article… It's hard to imagine now, but in those days an author's talent was determined not by a direct compilation of Party decisions, absolutely not, it was defined by the ability to select and arrange facts so subtly that they would convey the paramount necessity of the adopted resolutions on an almost subconscious level. Every paper had compilers of such high calibre, recognised as "golden pens" and even, in a sense, as dissidents (not called dissidents directly, of course, that word scared even the real "dissidents" back then). Not counting Vasya Kruzhkin, I knew two such writers in our youth department. God knows why Doublenose reminded me of one of them! I asked him directly if he had seen the chief of railway police, if it was he who had ordered Doublenose to remove the banner with my poem and who had advised Doublenose to pursue simple but inoffensive forms.

"Him, Mitya, him!" Doublenose exclaimed, and looking around apprehensively, invited me for a confidential chat in his so-called office (he had a cramped enclosure made of boxes filled with empty bottles in his central kiosk).

"Right here, Mitya, right here! On the very chair you're sitting on!"

I was sitting on some kind of barn-like contraption with splayed metal legs that kept springing on their own, giving the sensation that I was constantly riding somewhere, either on a camel or a spider. I even shook my head to dispel the sudden illusion.

Meanwhile, Doublenose proudly shared that the day before yesterday he was visited by no other than Limonych (that's what he called the chief of railway police, always respectfully adding: "hawk's eye and Head with capital H") for an unofficial chat. (Both laughable and lamentable - two diplomats meeting in a closet.)

His obsequious attitude towards Limonych was soon explained, however. It turned out that fortune had smiled on Doublenose: smart people had finally advised him to contact the railway police chief. If not for Limonych - Doublenose slammed his fist on a box, making the bottles clink - the kiosks would have gone up in flames, without a trace. But thanks to him, to Limonych, the kiosks still stood, and Feofilaktovich himself was not only alive and well, but had secured permission to set up a fourth kiosk.

Doublenose began eagerly describing how he would pave the beer courtyard with asphalt, position kiosks at the corners, and string up a rain canopy between them. He had even planned out the fencing - the army was selling anything and everything these days. He already knew where, from whom, and for how much he could get enough camouflage netting to create the best summer beer garden design imaginable.

"Little scraps fluttering in the breeze, light shadows dancing like leaves in an orchard, and the lads already sitting there. Sitting cosily at separate tables, pondering life over a mug of beer; true bliss!"

Doublenose closed his eyes in pleasure, but I brought him back to Limonych:

"But what, the city administration doesn't oversee beer stands now, the chief of railroad police does?"

"Oh Mitya, Mitya, what city administration? There is none, and the shreds that are still left - they hate people like me! They say we're crooks, they won't protect our property because whoever would want to rob us are crooks like us, because we're all just con men, criminal elements; in a word, 'new Russians.'"

Doublenose waved his hand in vexation and sat on a similar multi-legged contraption. He swayed gently before my eyes, as if we both were riding some kind of two-humped spiders.

"I was never a 'new Russian,' I was and remain just a Russian who succeeded solely thanks to my abilities. The difference is I'm a man of new views, a man of the future - Homo Novus."

Doublenose started describing again what efforts it took him to establish continuous production - by which of course he meant beer sales - but this time too, I steered him back to the railway police chief.

"Oh Mitya, Mitya. Limonych truly has the eye of a hawk and the Head with capital H! If I, Feofilaktovich, am a criminal element, then know this: all criminal elements respect Limonych like their father."

And here Doublenose recounted a veritable saga of how, after the latest competitor raid (smashed windows, bottles, and so on), he went to Limonych with a petition, and the man not only resolved all his issues in five minutes but also helped him get a phone.

Doublenose hopped off the "spider" and extracted an ornately designed device with number buttons from somewhere under the boxes (we didn't even have one like that in our editorial offices). He dialled some number.

"Hello, this is a call from the beer bar director... Could I speak to Filimon Puplievich?"

Tutankhamun's gigantic figure barged into the cramped "office" space, and suddenly everything around seemed to shrink.

"You need to speak properly: not 'a call from' but 'this is the beer bar director calling,' and not even 'director' but 'general director.' You're truly "from the outhouse to the penthouse" guy!"

"Alright, alright, I'll call back later myself," Doublenose spoke so gently, as if not to Filimon Puplievich's secretary but to a tiny little girl. After hanging up he flared with indignation.

"You just wait, Tutankhamun! You come waddling in when I have a visitor here! Maybe we're having some kind of official meeting with a stenographer?! And here you are butting in - what do you want, old-timer?! Though what old-timer are you, you're younger than me!" Doublenose raged, "You'll get what's coming, I'll remember everything when issuing your next paycheck!"

Tutankhamun grew flustered and attempted to make excuses, saying Doublenose had warned him to use proper grammar before, but now he gets bashed for mentioning the same thing - why?!

"Oh, shut up!" Doublenose said surprisingly cheerfully. "Did you see that, Mitya, how we're educating each other?! And we've only just begun..." He turned to Tutankhamun, "Well, dear friend, what is it, out with it," he added soothingly, as if apologising for being harsh.

Tutankhamun had come to ask what to do about the accounting school: they were asking for another five crates of beer (they had their graduation at the end of April) but still hadn't paid for New Year's.

"Don't give it to them," said Doublenose, but immediately rescinded his order. "No, no, give it to them, but tell them we'll have our man joining their next student intake. They have too many village bookkeepers there! I may even take classes myself. Some knowledge is worth more than a sack of gold but doesn't weigh you down. Am I right, Mitya, or what do you think?"

I nodded in agreement, though honestly, by then, both Doublenose and Tutankhamun had started to grate on me. Especially Tutankhamun, who had barged in at a very bad time indeed! ... My conversation with Doublenose whilst appearing casual, was in fact highly serious: I wasn't asking about the police chief out of idle curiosity but with a rational purpose, yes, a profoundly important purpose. At that moment, I was tormented by one thought and one thought only: from whom could I borrow money for Rozochka? I needed money, preferably hard currency, as much as possible and as soon as possible.

Of course, I was careful not to reveal my irritation with a careless word or gesture. My prior experience as head of the regional literary union proved quite useful in this respect. Oh, where were my Tolstoys?! In a word, I nodded agreeably and smiled automatically (alas, I would have traded all the world's knowledge right then and there for a sack of gold). The thought of a sack of gold exploded in my imagination like a lightning strike, and just as I had smiled, I remained smiling. Rozochka used to say:

"Mitenka, that sly grin of yours is so becoming, when you smile and seem to just forget the smile on your face. It speaks of a kind of profound absentmindedness and even of piercing demonism as if you're being deliberately insolent."

And so, I nodded agreeably and grinned. I wasn't thinking at all about Doublenose or Tutankhamun or whatever they were discussing. For me, it was as if they had vanished, evaporated, or fallen through the floor. I suddenly saw myself under a triumphal arch of sorts with a sphinx with Rozochka's head and breasts hanging down and gawking at me from it.

"Answer, what is love?" the sphinx asked. Its winged lion body stirred and Rozochka's face and breasts drew so close to me that I rose up on tiptoes and closed my eyes involuntarily. (I won't deny it, I wanted to kiss Rozochka and with that kiss, answer the sphinx's question about love.)

But the kiss never came. I opened my eyes because the sphinx leaned down even further and, with its right wing, pushed me away from a bag of gold that had somehow appeared at my feet.

"Well done, Mitenka, well done! Your non-trivial answer has saved your Rozochka, your wife, Rozaria Fyodorovna. Hurrah, hurrah, peace to the world!"

The sphinx embraced the bag of gold with its muscular paws and, looking back, drew its face and breasts toward me again…

I closed my eyes, more than convinced I would feel Rozochka's kiss on my lips. And kiss me she did, but not on the lips, on the forehead instead. But perhaps it wasn't even her after all - I felt the dead chill of stone. When I opened my eyes, the sphinx beat its wings against the air with such force that I was flung back as if by an explosive blast.

It rose above the triumphal arch (I never understood whose victory it immortalised), tossed the bag of gold over its shoulder like a farmer and beat its wings so vigorously that in a split second it first transformed into a sparrow, then a bumblebee, and finally dissolved into the azure skies.

Meanwhile, the atmosphere in the "office" had grown quite heated.

"Just look at that grin, he's a cutpurse, he must have seduced Alya with that exact same grin!" Tutankhamun was ranting, while Doublenose tried to cool him down.

"Get real!" Doublenose was shouting.

It was so astonishing to hear that archaism from this brute, alongside Doublenose's sudden Latin, that I couldn't help but laugh.

"Look, he's just laughing at us!" Tutankhamun continued his entirely unmotivated fit of jealousy.

Doublenose kicked his bodyguard out, but an air of trust no longer accompanied our conversation. I tried to revive it, but Doublenose didn't play along.

"Could you really be a cutpurse?" he asked, not so much concerned as pensive, almost marvelling, and for the first time he looked at me with a detached indifference that made me feel ill at ease. (such a dry glinting look portends a backstab.)

"Oh, come on," I said to Doublenose. "I have a letter from my wife."

But when I said I wanted to borrow a thousand dollars from the railway police chief, Doublenose was completely flustered, struck dumb.

"Alright, Feofilaktovich, then you lend me money."

In response, he threw up his hands, slapped his knees, and collapsed onto his "humpback spider" which, cushioning the impact, started bouncing along with him as if he were trying to scamper away.

"No, Mitya, no and again no! Where would I get you this money? It's all tied up: kiosks and their repositioning, the canopy, the pavement… Besides, I pay cash for property protection!"

He explained that Limonych helped him sign a serious and highly profitable contract with some bandit security firm for property protection.

He had no money, barely enough for staff salaries. And even then - more capital had to be set aside daily for handling everyday problems. As for savings, alas, none whatsoever!

"Well, Rozochka can't wait either, she's already been detained by police once, and by the way, her passport name is Roza Slyozkin," I said, as if the matter were long settled, "I simply have no choice but to go to Filimon Puplievich."

"You've lost your mind!" Doublenose exclaimed.

He said that just the other day they had met with Limonych and I, Mitya, was mentioned in a positive light. The "Head" had supposedly even praised Feofilaktovich for befriending me.

"You have smart friends, Feofilaktovich, friends with a future. Help them with advice, money, anything you can. It's precisely such help that will create true capital for you, an image that will help you stay ahead in the future."

Doublenose said that because he knew me, Limonych had called the director of the private security firm, some Tolya Croesus, to cut their service fees by half.

Doublenose dropped to a whisper. "And he cut them… The only thing Limonych asked was that I assist you in every way as a poet with higher humanitarian education. And it wasn't just his request - there was another person with him…"

"Enough, none of that matters," I said. (I immediately guessed who this other person was. Her obvious concern for the state of contemporary Russian poetry pleased me.)

"How does it not matter?!" Doublenose clutched his head. "After all this, you'll just show up to Limonych and say: 'Please lend a thousand bucks to a poor poet?' Is that it? Don't you understand how this would affect me, what he'll think of me?! And this Tolya Croesus - have you ever seen a mug with a nose smeared all over his face?!"

"I won't say I discussed this with you. Or I'll say I didn't discuss the money, that guessed he has it, myself. He bought one of my poems for a hundred dollars after all, didn't he?"

"Here, take your remaining fee… I was going to save it for your meals," Doublenose said defensively, leaping up from his multi-legged seat and shoving a fifty-dollar bill at me. "But now he doesn't want to see or hear anything - he wants nothing."

I had never seen Doublenose so upset, so I didn't push it further. I promised not to go to Filimon Puplievich under any circumstances, carefully trying not to sound even a bit menacing. But he, Feofilaktovich, should also try for me - borrow the money from someone else, and not worry, I would leave him a folder with my best poems as collateral.

Even my best poems offered Doublenose minimal consolation, of course, but our situation was at an impasse for us both. He understood I was fully capable of reckless action for Rozochka's sake. In the end, taking the folder, he said, not exactly angrily but still with a rather strong feeling that he probably should not have stopped Tutankhamun from strangling me alive.

"No man - no problem," he said those famous words with such conviction and expressiveness as if he wanted to emphasize some claim to their authorship[87].

In short, taking the folder and demanding that I not stick my nose out, Doublenose went off, as I understood, to visit some resourceful people.

"A thousand 'greens' for little Rose - oho-ho-ho!" he exclaimed, bouncing off the walls of beer crates as he hurried out.

I remained in Doublenose's office, a narrow opening between countless beer crates, for over two hours. Pushing together the makeshift stools we were both sitting on, I tried to nap - alas, unsuccessfully. When put together, those furniture monsters behaved like two irreconcilable roosters viciously charging at each other. There was a sense of some mystical presence of Edgar Allan Poe, or rather, some of his not-so-pleasant literary characters. Still, that trepidation paled compared to the fear Tutankhamun instilled in me when suddenly sticking his head through the passage, he shouted:

"Cutpu-urse! Catch the cutpurse!!"

I admit, at first, I thought this was an attempt on my life at Doublenose's behest. True, I dismissed this thought the very next second. Tutankhamun, enraged like a wounded beast, literally tore apart an empty wooden crate right in front of me. Then, with a drunken hiccup, he went limp and, sprawling on the floor, started snoring blissfully.

Doublenose returned with money - six hundred dollars!

---

87   These words are attributed to Joseph Stalin, even though without any evidence.

CHAPTER 31

I don't want to recall how, stepping over Tutankhamun, Doublenose warned me not to go crazy over my little Rose. A silly comparison: me and Tutankhamun. Imagine a homespun Othello, accustomed to settling everything with a gavel, who always tries to pinch Desdemona's butt while flirting, and then strangles her to death in a fit of jealousy for no reason at all. There you have a sample of Tutankhamunism, and what do I have to do with it?! Light and darkness physically exclude each other. Darkness craves to vanquish light, but this is impossible because the thicker and denser the darkness, the brighter even a little candle burns. And if there is a lot of light, darkness dissipates and flees at its mere approach. Remember the Crown of Sonnets[88] -

"And the light in the darkness, as before, did not die,
And the darkness, as before, did not devour it!"

I don't want to recall how Doublenose self-contentedly counted the crisp one-hundred-dollar bills, how he added my bill to them and then called a taxi to take us to the flea market. There was little interesting in all of this—the waltz of Baltic knitwear in exchange for Russian non-ferrous metals and televisions. The only thing that amazed me was observing Doublenose feeling truly at home amid all these flickering faces and merchandise. Some people he did not just greet fleetingly, but stopped and chatted with them informally. Others, more often Caucasians, he stopped to ask about the kiosk belonging to some Vizier.

---

88   By Vladimir Soloukhin (June 14, 1924 – April 4, 1997)

Amazingly, when talking to Doublenose, they didn't treat him like Doublenose, the owner of three kiosks, but rather as a kind of unofficial representative of the entire Russian people. And Doublenose himself felt his unofficial importance and spouted whatever came to mind, aptly and inaptly.

"Hi Sharzhik! Haven't frozen your balls off yet?! How's business going?"

"Allah be praised!"

"Allah-shmallah, but if you freeze them, I'll have to answer for it!" Doublenose continued spouting merrily.

Seeing me puzzled, he winked conspiratorially and explained:

"The black butts will gobble up everything under the guise of 'Me not understand.' Because it's me who's the Russian here, not them. And everything else, as Tolya Croesus says, is just rubbish!"

Nevertheless, near Vizier's kiosk, Doublenose tensed up, his face grew stern, and rightly so. Vizier stood outside cracking nuts, surrounded by fellows just like him, gold-toothed Caucasians looking more like horse thieves. Seeing us, he said something in his language, slowly came out of the circle, wiped his hands on his thighs, and greeted Doublenose.

For some time now, the faces of people of Caucasian ethnicities (and I am not being Tutankhamunish here) have cast a gloom over me. Why do the owners of these faces hound our girls so shamelessly, while hiding their own from us, even though we won't be chasing them?!

"Vizier, greetings from Limonych. How are things?"

"What things?! Every person is a hostage to what he has acquired. Why does a big man have need of a little one?"

Doublenose nodded at me:

"Need to dress the lad, from head to toe. Underwear wouldn't hurt either." Just as Lekha the cop, he pulled a piece of paper from his side pocket and read it loudly but with no comprehension: "He is a poet for whom we await an adverse turn of fortune."[89]

I immediately understood that written on the paper (by Limonych or someone else) was a verse from the Koran. Even though not Muslim, I felt awkward at this impromptu comedy—what Doublenose read should not be read so meaninglessly, and not at all because it is a verse from the sacred book. No poem should ever be read meaninglessly, it's akin to a deliberate mockery of humanity's eternal yearning for wisdom.

I quietly stepped away from Doublenose, moreover since Vizier's buddies were staring at me like at a scarecrow. In short, I felt the tension and expected a noisy argument typical of offended Caucasians, who, alas, did not differ from Russians with their everlasting desire for respect. Honestly, at that moment I respected no one, not even myself: why was I mingling with these people so different from me?! To my utter surprise, the words read by Doublenose suddenly imbued Vizier with such a high sense of respect for us that he even pressed his hand to his heart.

"In the name of Allah, the Merciful, the Compassionate! I say: 'Wait, and I will wait with you!'"

He barked something to his buddies or henchmen, and they

---

89   Koran 56:30

immediately scattered, nodding understandingly, and hurrying away.

Doublenose pulled me behind the kiosk. I won't go into how our new acquaintances began bringing Turkish leather jackets, jeans, shirts, English scarves, caps, ties, and underwear from all sides. I almost fainted when I saw "Manchester City shorts" on the label of the 100% cotton underwear. Doublenose saved me from freezing by wrapping me in his furry embrace—he warmed me this way during the fittings because, even though the icicles were melting, it was still too cold for being naked.

When the clothes were packaged, the Caucasians, as if feeling their guilt because of Rozochka and trying to cater specifically to me (Doublenose had gone into Vizier's kiosk and was still there), hailed a taxi (a gold-toothed driver, just like all of them, poked his head out of the cabin). At that very moment, an inspiration suddenly came over me.

"In the name of Allah, the Gracious, the Merciful,

By the star as it goes down,

Your friend has not gone astray, nor has he erred,

Nor does he speak out of desire

It is but a revelation from above…"[90]

I looked up at the sky, and as if by magic, all the gold-toothed men looked up too. I felt an unusual power from Allah to command:

"Your Lord knows best who has strayed from His path, and He knows best the well-guided."

Behind me, the door of the kiosk creaked open. Doublenose cursed angrily: he almost fell because he didn't look under his

---

90   Koran 53:1-4

feet but up at the sky following everyone else. The inspiration was gone. I blurted out that I swore by the heavens: all prison sentences would be duly commuted in time for all of us, buttoned up my coat, and got into the car, pushing the packages aside, without looking back.

Doublenose, being an excellent face reader, immediately understood that something special had happened in his absence and asked: "Hey, ethnic minority, Mitya the poet must have been reading poems?!"

The "ethnic minority" nodded in agreement, their faces taking on a sacred reverence. And no wonder, for I had read them verses from the sura 'The Star,' which I really liked back at the Literary Institute, and which now suddenly came to mind.

Doublenose interpreted the reverence in his own way, thinking that it was my own poems that had such a powerful effect. Well, of course, he got excited and began showing off as my best friend. He ran up to the car, knocked on the window, his joyful eyes darting from me to them and back, but mostly to them, and he was just beaming, beaming…

"Well, Mitya, haven't frozen your balls yet?!"

Oh Lord, how sick I was of his balls! I was starving. When Doublenose handed over the money and got into another car near the post office, I even crossed myself in relief.

"Rozochka!" I wrote in a telegram, "I'm leaving tonight. I'll bring what you asked for. Let's meet at twelve on the steps of the Main Post Office. Kisses. Yours until the grave, Mitya."

The telegraph operator receiving the telegram stopped her pen at the last words: "Well, why go that far?!" And she crossed out "until the grave." I didn't argue, and when I paid and got the receipt, when the telegram was already on its way, silver strings sounded in me. Loaded with packages, I felt such lightness that I didn't feel my feet.

In my early youth, I went hunting with my father's double-barrelled 12-gauge shotgun. I also inherited his boots, knee-high 43s that chafed my crotch with their tall legs. My prey was ducks, geese, waterfowl. I had a dog, Almaz, an extremely intelligent Irish setter, and I never returned without a trophy because he would always bring any downed game to my feet within a radius of a mile and a half. Many hunters (especially city folk) would get angry at Almaz and me and even threaten to shoot us both. So, we would go out hunting when it was already getting dark and you could only shoot birds in flight against the light sky. At such a time, no one made any claims against us because only a dog, or rather my Almaz, could find the fallen game in the dark thickets.

Once we lingered especially late. A light spring breeze blew in my face, and Almaz tirelessly walked ahead of me from right to left and back again, like a pendulum. He combed through all the bushes in his unique style, so thoroughly that I had to call him over and hold him back to rest. At first, I could hear water splashing, motorboats roaring, and hunters calling each other to go home (I even thought it was time for me to head towards the railway), but then everything fell silent. In a matter of minutes, Almaz first brought one pintail, then another. I trembled with joy and did not notice that the sky had completely clouded, the breeze had died, and a warm drizzle had started.

While I was hiding the trophies in my backpack, Almaz ran off again. I didn't even notice him disappear; it was too dark to see beyond five steps away. I listened: no calls, no splashing of water—nothing. Everything was saturated with moisture and seemed to stir and swell. A single shot thundered somewhere far, far away on the river, and total silence reigned. I called Almaz, but my voice sank as if into a felt bag. I fired a shot into the air, but the sound of the shot too seemed like it was absorbed into a pillow.

"Almaz, Almaz!" I panicked.

The joy of an easy catch was gone. I didn't know which direction our village was in, which way to go. All along the horizon, for the full three hundred and sixty degrees, there were sparse, shimmering lights flickering. The lights approached, reflecting in the water, stretching fiery spokes toward me, as if I were standing in the middle of an ocean. "Where did all this water come from, where am I?!" I thought, but the thought felt detached, occurring somewhere outside me, and likewise outside me someone started plucking silver strings. I have never heard such amazing music in my entire life! It seemed a stream was ringing, then some fiery spokes, and then it seemed like sunbeams refracted by spring waters were playing with pebbles.

I walked in one direction, then another, and finally tried to follow the silver strings' call. It may seem strange, but following the sweet sounds had led me to the railway, where Almaz caught up with me. Enchanted by the music, I didn't notice that he was rubbing against my knees and getting underfoot. Only when I stepped onto the tracks did I burst into rapture, discovering that he had brought me a goose, an act of extremely rare luck.

My backpack was full, we walked in the middle of the railroad tracks, and the glowing rail lines seemed to permeate me like strings. The music now sounded inside me, bringing along serenity and happiness.

* * *

The first thing I did when I got to the dorm was to throw the packages on the bed and sprawl out next to them. An unheard-of stroke of luck – I had five hundred dollars in my pocket and the music of silver strings in my soul.

"Look, Mitya, keep the money in different pockets, especially the bucks. And don't flash the roubles either – there aren't many, but you'll have more than enough for the trip."

I laughed (Doublenose's advice seemed unnecessary) and, getting up and as before, I put the money into the iron. Then, taking the key from the front desk, I went down to the showers. The music of the silver strings gave way to the music of trumpets. Pompous May Day marches filled my soul, occasionally interrupted by slogans bursting from the radio: PEACE TO THE WORLD! All the holidays of my life were now with me.

I put on my underwear ("Manchester City shorts") to a school brass band playing a fanfare. Each item of clothing felt like another high school diploma awarded to me. I pulled on my jeans and the school band gave way to a military orchestra marching through Red Square with loud drum rolls. Its musicians rearranged themselves on the march as I took the electric razor in my hand. By the time I tried on the brown leather jacket with synthetic lining and tested its pocket zips, the marching brass band began blending in orchestras from all my holidays. The English red scarf of royal mohair and the Caucasian fur cap of grey nutria concluded the review... As I walked to the bathroom to look at myself in the large mirror, the combined military orchestra was heading towards the mausoleum's tribune, and when a green-eyed Caucasian with an intelligent face beaming happiness looked back at me from the mirror, I was not at all surprised that the combined orchestra immediately and vigorously erupted with the "Farewell of Slavianka."

I once read in some newspaper or pamphlet that the proverb "A bullet fears the brave, a bayonet cannot harm them" is as accurate in its essence as the laws of physics, and the proverb is in fact an accurate statement. The author claimed that some unknown psychological energy lurks within us, creating an extremely powerful force field around a person in a stressful situation. This force field distorts space or perhaps straightens it. Bullets cannot find and get deflected from a brave man. The article even featured an interview with a truly brave man, who claimed that as a field communications specialist he clenched severed wires with his teeth and lay like that with the wires in a square in Berlin for about half an hour, while enemy machine gunners fired at him from all sides and snipers took aimed shots at him. He lay there, and everyone thought he had long been killed (just simply lying with non-insulated wires in one's mouth and staying alive is, as you know, not exactly plausible). They lifted him up along with the wires, someone already started prying his jaws open with pliers, and suddenly he opened his eyes – alive, without a single scratch. Of course, everyone was stunned, and then an indescribable joy ensued: bullets fear a brave man! I too was overjoyed. There may be a force field around a brave person, or maybe not, but I swear there is one around a happy person!

I took the key to the showers – blooming and shining Alina Spiridonovna came towards me:

"Mitya, what's up with you, you look so festive?!"

"Alina Spiridonovna, forgive me if I've offended you in any way! God knows it was not out of malice, but purely out of my foolishness," I said, playing the fool a bit.

In response, Alina Spiridonovna blossomed even more:

"Well, Mitya dear, poets are never foolish, they are just unfortunate!"

I told her I know of one person who is deeply in love with her and is ready to strangle anyone in whom he suspects a rival, like some enraged Othello.

"Mitya, that person loves money more than anything. He starts as Plyushkin[91], and only then becomes Othello. I can assure you," Alina Spiridonovna blushed, even her hands turned crimson, "that he will never lay a finger on you, Mitya dear!"

It turns out she extracted a promise from Tutankhamun in my defence. I was flattered and, although I had always looked down on Alina Spiridonovna, I confessed that this evening I was going to Moscow at Rozochka's summons.

"At her summons, she summoned you?!" Alina Spiridonovna was startled and even seemed a bit frightened, but when I happily laughed and confirmed that I was indeed going at her summons, she teared up: "Mitya dear, I'm so happy for you!"

---

91   A character from N. Gogol's "Dead Souls", an epitome of greed.

Almost the same thing happened in my encounter with my neighbour Toma. Unlike Alina Spiridonovna, however, before tearing up she swatted Artur's bottom, then scooped him up in her arms and ran into her room. She paused in the doorway, shouting:

"Look out, Mitya, don't let your happiness slip away!"

Others in the dorm, though not reacting to my force field of happiness as vividly, could still somehow hear the music in my soul.

"What are you beaming about; had some 'happy' weed?! Mitya, I haven't seen you this joyful in ages, I'd bet you hit the lottery jackpot for a car?!"

And so on and so forth… But the main thing was that everyone I chatted with left smiling. Yes, I'm convinced that the force field of my happiness was the sounds of silver strings to which everyone who crossed paths with me in those amazing minutes answered like to a magic call.

A wonderful day, a day like a song. Still, one little thing made it less than perfect, not quite the best day of my life. I alone was to blame for that little imperfection, and that's probably why I didn't immediately feel the bitterness which came to me as soon as I left my room and headed for the station.

I walked along our shuddering corridor and everyone and their brother came out to meet me, as if given an advance notice. They all asked me "What, Mitya dear, off to the station already?!" and wished me a successful trip and speedy return with my betrothed. I don't know why, but this "with your betrothed" grated on me, and I did indeed feel a certain trepidation, which I tried to suppress. Let them stay while I go, that's how I reassured myself, but something had already changed inside of me. And when at the front desk Alina Spiridonovna asked the same thing and likewise wished me a speedy return with my betrothed, I exploded and, without answering, kicked the door so hard with my foot that windows rattled. And it was then that something seemed to slam shut in my soul - the music disappeared. In a fleeting glimpse, I saw the combined brass band approach the tribune, stop, lower their trumpets and, turning 180 degrees, march silently back.

Off they go, I thought irritably, brushing the very thought of the music aside. Striding to the bus stop, I became imbued with minor, perhaps, but necessary cares: getting to the station, buying a ticket (a berth or just a seat?). Waiting for the bus, I weighed all the pros and cons of one ticket type or the other. Time was passing, running, ticking away... I kept glancing at my watch, glad that I had set out for the station with a comfortable time buffer - there was almost an hour and a half until the 10:32 pm train departure. On the other hand, if there is just one bus per hour, this won't be enough. When an "accordion" bus with its glowing windows appeared from around the corner and the people at the bus stop stirred with delight, I felt pleased as well - and then suddenly froze. A sudden thought struck me right through my heart. I even swayed slightly from the pain: the money for Rozochka... I had forgotten the money, just left it in the iron where I had put it.

The sheer horror of what had happened snapped me out of my daze - there were only 53 minutes until the train departed.

Plenty of time if I took the bus now, but I still had to race back for the money - and I took off running.

I ran, calling myself the foulest names, among which "idiot," "moron," and "imbecile" were the politest.

I flew past the front desk and up the stairs. I ran along the corridor, not caring one bit about the residents, whether they were sleeping or awake, it was all the same to me.

The money was still in the iron. I grabbed it and almost cried from an inexplicable bitterness and resentment towards everyone and everything. Then I pulled myself together and, as Doublenose had advised, put three hundred dollars in my jacket, and two hundred, along with the Soviet money, in my passport, which I hid in the pocket of my jean shirt. I stuffed some roubles in my trousers pocket to have it handy for the ticket window. After that I sat on the bed and, taking a deep breath, patted myself down one more time to check for my documents and money. Then I crossed myself and took off running again, mentally reciting the Lord's Prayer. This time the room doors opened as I ran past, not to wish me a bon voyage, but alas, to shower me with abuse as if with garbage from their waste bins.

"I hope this poet finally falls through a hole! I hope he breaks his neck! Damn him, may he burn forever in hell!" (And so on and so forth).

The front desk met me with an ambush: Alina Spiridonovna had locked the front door with a key.

"What happened?" she asked, holding the telephone receiver like a grenade.

"Nothing," I said while still reciting the prayer in my mind,

"I just forgot my money, and now I'm late for my train."

Hitching up her downy shawl (she was trying to pull it higher onto her shoulders), she fretfully cried out that everything with me is unlike normal folks, and, opening the door, urged me to run and run with all my might, but suddenly indifference engulfed me. I was about to say that I couldn't run, however my legs somehow carried me off on their own…

CHAPTER 32

I've always said and still say: "People, don't you ever lose your hearts. Our material world is structured such that God does not give us a burden heavier than we can bear. Sometimes it seems like the end of the world, that we're just going through the motions, ready to collapse, but it's precisely at that moment that we realise that there's no need to fall, at least not yet because angels are supporting us on all sides. Yes, angels! How else can you explain that in a completely hopeless situation, everything fell perfectly into place in your favour? Why in this chain of coincidences your card is suddenly the trump ace, and you find yourself in the right place at the right time? This luck will then repeat itself, you'll straighten your shoulders and forget there was a moment when you were ready to fall. So, I remind you: never despair or lose hope! When times get truly hard, He will surely assist, because His mercy is the foundation of our world."

I rushed to the bus stop - there was no bus. It came within less than five minutes, but it felt like over an hour. It went slowly, with stops, and then got stuck in traffic when exiting onto the bridge over the Volkhov River.

"Don't get discouraged, don't despair, you know better than anyone that the Lord won't abandon you and angels will definitely help at the right time and place," I reassured myself, while inwardly protesting: it's about time they hurried up (there were only ten minutes left before the train departed).

I arrived at the station at 8:50 pm. I walked past the station building and immediately found myself on the platform. Even though there were several people standing by the underpass, the empty platform exuded that special desertedness that a train leaves behind after departing.

At first, like a combined brass band, I turned 180 degrees and marched back. But then a light breeze ran through the strings - I stopped, listened, and something prompted me to go into the station building.

The huge double door only yielded to a firm push. I immediately found myself in a crowd of passengers. Of course, I inquired which train they were waiting for and you can imagine my astonishment when I learned they were all waiting for the Moscow train. The train schedule had switched to the winter timetable since October, so the Moscow train now departed at 9:35 pm instead of 8:30 pm.

Without hesitation, I hurried to the ticket window. It's funny, given my age, I had never travelled in a sleeping car. I'd been in them, but never actually travelled that way. So, when I boarded the car, I deliberately acted nonchalant, as if I'd been taking sleeping cars my entire life. In response, the attendants, two young ladies, laughed rather mysteriously, and one said to the other, loud enough for me to hear:

"What nasty people these 'New Russians' are! They put on their leather jackets and act like they own the train."

The car was practically empty. When paying for bedding, I asked for tea. The attendant lit a new cigarette right in my compartment, took a deep drag and, blowing smoke in my face, asked:

"And why not some brandy in bed with someone while you're at it?!"

As she exited the compartment, she looked at me like at an idiot. To spite her, I forcefully slammed shut the door.

"Lucy, what was that?" her partner wondered in a rusty, cracked voice.

"Wants some brandy in bed," Lucy growled hoarsely and broke into a deep, phlegmy cough from the depths of her chest.

"So that's how it is with you, lying beast!" I thought but when her partner said they'd have to keep an eye on the leather-jacket guy, meaning me, so I didn't walk off with other people's belongings, I felt sorry for the attendants, especially Lucy. It took courage to speak to a presumed thief the way she did. Lucy was probably sick and dishonest, but brave - and as they say, bullets fear the brave. I decided in Lucy's favour and, removing my Finnish ankle boots, climbed up to the upper berth that Lucy had likely prepared in advance according to my ticket.

What a marvellous and contradictory world!

I longed for the music of the soul. Trying not to think of Rozochka, I still attuned myself to her, but there was no music. No, I didn't expect to sleep: the dim sleeping car, the clacking of the wheels, the distant lights of villages disappearing into the darkness - all of this demanded some joyful response from me. At least intellectually I desired music, but my heart remained silent, silent as if petrified.

So, I am the happiest of all! (No strings, as if the comments hadn't even been about me.) Just this morning I didn't even dream I'd be going to Moscow, and yet here I was, going to Moscow, going to Rozochka! (Nothing!) Perhaps my Celestial Powers, my bodiless angels, were travelling with me too?! (I wasn't being ironic at all - it was a thought of a mind despair.)

In my life I've read a great deal of literature on "life after death" and concluded that a brilliant work, one immediately recognized as brilliant, will provide us with an artistic presentation of the real connection between the visible (physical) and invisible (spiritual) worlds. (All religions know these worlds are connected, and we feed on the spiritual world.) All outstanding works of literature and art, all outstanding scientific discoveries, were literally prayed for from God. He has responded and responds to our pleas because He envisions the physical and spiritual worlds not as just converging but penetrating each other, and this penetration is man's door to paradise. I'm not at all surprised by discoveries in nuclear physics and genetics, even the elixir of immortality supposedly sought by all progressive humanity does not trouble me at all. What surprises and worries me is the immortal human being! Immortality will inevitably disrupt the connection between the worlds, the spiritual world will be lost to us as it is more fragile, and the clay from which the immortal is created will reign triumphant on earth.

I dreamed I was sitting in some dirty room, on a hard chair by a window. A well-trodden path in the snow following a prolonged arched structure made of blue plastic could be seen through the window. Rozochka was supposed to come down this path, she knew I was in this awful room. I was watching the path, cautious of missing Rozochka, but I kept getting distracted (I was sure the music of the soul would appear before Rozochka), repeatedly reaching into my inner pockets, first one then the other, checking on my dollars. Dollars were in place, but the path was all dug up (hooved up) by Rozochka's little shoes, or rather, her heels. I thought I had missed Rozochka as she approached.

I heard a soft, quiet knock at the door. Soft fur mittens covered my eyes before I could turn around to the scent of a wonderful French perfume. I pressed her gentle hands to my lips and heard a new, louder, firmer knock. I looked up and froze: the immortal human, the lumpen-intellectual himself, stood behind me. Tufts of reddish hair seemed to billow from his black nostrils. Those fur mittens appeared to be his densely hairy hands. I still hoped I was mistaken and cautiously glanced at the immortal's feet… only to be horrified by his blue hooves!

Yes, yes, it was he who had hooved up the path, cut Rozochka off and shut the door so she couldn't enter. The hair on his head started stirring. I jumped up to grapple with this new Koschei in desperation and nearly fell to the floor.

There was such a loud metal-on-metal knocking at the compartment door that I awoke thinking someone was breaking in to rescue me.

"Hey, New Russian, you in there?!"

"Here, here, Rozochka!" I involuntarily responded, bit my hand, and fully woke up.

"Rozochka?! Maybe I'm Balda Ivanovna[92]!"

Lucy laughed hoarsely and immediately broke into a deep, phlegmy cough. I slid the door open.

"You should go to the hospital for a fluoroscopy. You've got pneumonia," I said sympathetically.

---

92   Informal and ironic for "Jane Doe".

"Yep, bilateral pneumonia," Lucy readily agreed, then announced the toilets would be closed in half an hour – the train was approaching Moscow. And to me: "No big deal, I just switched from American cigarettes to Java[93]."

I parted with Lucy and her partner on almost friendly terms, but knowing them was quite depressing. These girls, without realising it, had the changes happening to the country reflected in their behaviour. What music was there to be heard?!

Lord, my finest city, Moscow! It's where I spent my student years, where Rozochka and I met, visited the Tretyakov and Pushkin museums, hung out at the poetry gatherings by the Pushkin monument. We went on trips to Polenovo, Shakhmatovo, Konstantinovo (I cherish the porcelain shot glass with bright yellow sunflowers on the outside that I bought at the village store and christened with my classmates on the high green bank of the Oka River, to the health of the Great Russian Poet). We visited Zagorsk, Abramtsevo, went out to nature – to plein-air as we called it.

I well remember arriving from Barnaul for the first time: loudspeakers played rousing music, the announcer constantly reported we were approaching the capital of our Motherland, the beautiful city of Moscow, mentioning sports societies, stadiums, parks, and educational institutions. My ear picked out Moscow State University, the one-of-a-kind Literary Institute, VGIK Institute of Cinematography and Patrice Lumumba University. Everything screamed of quality, order, and government's care for the Soviet people.

---

93   Very popular Soviet cigarettes produced for the entire duration of the communist regime.

Where has it gone? Why do dear lips
Feel lizard-cold, repulsive is their sight?
In vases, real blossoms can't persist,
Just paper flowers stay defying blight.

Indeed, where are the cleanliness, order, and government's care?! Where is that Soviet human, where has he vanished to? His upbringing was the focus of all leisure and working time at every workplace, and suddenly there you have it, he's gone, disappeared, without trace! I wonder, if perhaps the new Soviet person didn't in fact disappear, didn't vanish into oblivion, but instantly transformed into the new Russian, new Azerbaijani, Armenian, Georgian, and so on and so forth?!

Moscow! Moscow! As happened in my past, I was immediately swept up in the human maelstrom. In the past, however, it was neat, festively uplifted, yet always politely shy and compassionate. Alas, the maelstrom of today was different, bearing the imprint of all visible and concealed impurities. Overflowing with toppled rubbish bins, garbage, broken glass, shreds of newspapers and wrapping paper trampled into vomit and slush, filth, and stench, it reminded me of the engulfing swirl of a bog belching poisonous gases. I felt I didn't belong in this crowd. Several times, individuals stopped me, winking at me in a friendly way. Furtively looking around, they invited me to follow them to a side alley, promising to bless me with some inexplicable goods at a very low price.

The same dirt and chaos awaited me inside the station building. An impassable crowd stood by the bust of Lenin, listening to chastushki singers. I remember they were mentioning the Mayor of Moscow Gavriil Popov and Boris Yeltsin, and were "with pictures," lots of them. To be honest, I didn't like them. I favour ones that are funny, witty, kind, and definitely not obscene and malicious. Judging by the people's silence, the singing wasn't even for them, it was directed at Lenin's bust.

Moscow, Moscow, how low have you stooped! Russia will be saved by the provinces, which you, the capital, continue to deceive in your side alleys as before. Thank God "the people are silent"!

Political arguments broke out frequently in the fast-food line.

Two solidly built guys in leather jackets like mine approached the fast-food cart. They shoved aside the customers and started loading pasties into a bag. The line became agitated and ordered the vendor not to serve these blockheads. Without hesitation, the blockheads took the cart off the little stool it was leaning on and rolled it to the other end of the hall. The vendor lady simply followed them as if nothing had happened.

"Police, where are the police?! I'm a war veteran!" shouted an unshaven man with a large catfish-like mouth.

I noticed that my mouth also became disproportionately large when I was hungry.

"Keep it down or they'll come back and rough you up," cautioned another unshaven, large-mouthed man, and he explained: "Those are gangsters at work."

The line dispersed. Chaos reigned everywhere, in the Moscow subway, of all places! Cigarette butts and crumpled packs littered the marble floors.

Dilapidation and neglect prevailed even in the once-exemplary dumpling house near the Red Gate, where I went not so much to eat as to revive the music of my soul before meeting Rozochka. I remember always being amused and impressed by the dumpling house administration's request to its patrons, framed like a portrait in a huge oak frame under glass: "Don't dip fingers or eggs in the salt!"

The glass was shattered, and the sign had been torn out, its plywood mount destroyed. The massive oak frame now enclosed emptiness and swayed threateningly, as if warning it was about to come loose from the nail and fall.

The dumplings were different too; more like Ukrainian dumplings, made entirely of dough with no filling.

An unshaven, dirty, large-mouthed man, apparently a "war veteran," was arguing loudly at the counter, demanding to know why there was no meat in the dumplings. It turned out the ground meat had run out yesterday, and a fresh supply wouldn't arrive until tomorrow.

Strangely enough, I liked the dumplings, especially the broth, but there was no music in my soul. I had arrived in a completely different Moscow and we didn't recognise each other.

CHAPTER 33

In keeping with the hussar tradition, I was standing on the steps of the Moscow Main Post Office precisely at 11:45 am. Having arrived much earlier, I had already shopped at the "Tea" store and bought two packs of biscuits, a small bag of sugar, and a can of instant coffee. They put everything in a beautiful bag decorated with an image of the legendary English tea clipper "Cutty Sark" sailing under full sail. Carrying this bag made me feel more confident, and only after getting it, did I head to the Main Post Office. I had plenty of time until noon, so I circled the huge hall with its countless windows twice, even helping an old lady fill out a notice form. (She had money sent to her pending pickup so that her alcoholic son wouldn't know about it, threaten her, and immediately waste the lot.) For a moment, I pictured myself in the alcohol addict's place, next to my dear mother, and I almost cried out from the bitter indignity - it would be better to dive head-first from a bridge right under a train!

As I wandered the hall, I didn't take my eyes off the young girls appearing in the hall or standing pensively at the windows (any of them could be Rozochka). Of course, it took skill and artistry to approach them and then walk away nonchalantly and without attracting attention. In short, time flew by so quickly with all these tactics that I had to run out of the hall to avoid breaking the special Hussar tradition.

Thus, at 11:45 am, I was standing on the steps, watching in amazement as people hurried towards me from all sides. They weren't really hurrying towards me: on the steps nearby there was a money changer enticingly calling out "Dollars, dollars!" while assuring customers he was as "reliable as the Central Bank."

After just a few minutes next to him, my head thumping and I had to move to the other side of the (blessedly!) spacious front steps. Yes, my new spot was less advantageous (the main flow of people from the underground passed by the money changer), but at least here, no one could hush the inner music I had not yet heard but already sensed was coming.

Thanks to the bag, or rather, the "Cutty Sark" on it, I was quite noticeable, but you never know what might happen! Remembering the terrible dream, I didn't let my attention waver for a second. I literally scrutinised with my vigilant gaze each one of the young, beautiful girls who set foot on the Post Office steps.

Rozochka appeared unexpectedly, about five minutes before the appointed time. And not from the direction I had expected, not from the side of the underground. She came from the direction of the telegraph office (maybe she had been making a long-distance call?). In any case, I was almost standing with my back to her when suddenly I heard music - an energetic yet pensive strumming of strings, very reminiscent of how Vladimir Vysotsky[94] would strum at his last performance at the Moscow State University as if wondering what to play next. Just like that, someone smoothly strummed the strings, pausing thoughtfully. Yes, thoughtfully, and I, like a combined brass band, whirled a full 180 degrees and saw with some sudden inner vision - no, I didn't see, I felt - the musicians bringing their mouthpieces to their lips and striking up a fanfare. It lasted a second, maybe even

---

94   Vladimir Vysotsky (1938-1980) - a legendary Soviet actor, poet, songwriter and singer.

a split second, but I already knew for certain that the girl coming from the telegraph office direction was Rozochka.

She was wearing a wing-sleeved jacket just like mine, made from the same rough blanket material. I even made out the three faded stripes of an indeterminate colour on her chest - a distinctive feature of all dorm-issue blankets.

The music cut out. I felt a lump rising in my throat and my eyes grew heavy. My Rozochka in a Gaidar shock therapy jacket?! But what about the fine English lingerie?! What about Mother Rozaria the Russian?! Lord, anything but this, let her have everything better than me! Although, outward appearances meant nothing to Mother Teresa…

The music resumed. Rozochka saw me, nervously shrugged her shoulders, lowered her head, and covered her left eye and whole cheek with her hand like she was embarrassed about something. And the strumming music just went on and on! "Rozochka, I swear you'll be wearing a leather coat with a llama fur collar!" I mentally exclaimed and rushed toward her.

Rozochka didn't recognise me, I was mistaken in thinking she had seen me. As I hurried to meet her, she was glancing sideways at me and then at my bag from under her brow with her right eye. She even moved aside to avoid colliding with me.

"Rozochka!" I called out to her and stopped.

She stopped too and flung up her hands in surprise. I saw a dark plum-blue bruise under her left eye. It looked like a hideous extra eye.

The music began to fade as if I had stopped, but the combined brass band kept marching on, carrying the music away with them.

"Mitya, is that you?!" Rozochka took a step toward me. "Is it really you?!"

I embraced her (firmly, of course, I missed her so much!).

"My face..." she pleaded, patting my back. "Let me go, you're crazy! Let's at least get off the pavement..."

Her voice trailed off as we nearly suffocated - I kissed her the way she had taught me, drawing her lips into mine.

"You're mad!" Rozochka exclaimed again, but not offensively, she even sounded a bit smug recognising her own kissing style.

I took heart completely (feeling big and strong), and demanded she immediately tell me where, when and who, had given her the black eye.

"Ah, this was still during my first stint in the drunk tank," Rozochka replied, asking me not to be upset because the black eye had actually helped her - the cops concerned about saving their own skins, hadn't locked her up like some others.

"Good Lord, what lockup?!" I was horrified, but Rozochka had already grown angry, pulling me by the sleeve toward the underground.

However, we passed by the underground and went down some side street, ending up on Ogorodny Sloboda Street. Trying to mollify Rozochka's angry silence, I said that I knew nothing about this side of Moscow, that Moscow is truly vast, not just a city but an entire state!

Rozochka remained silent. So, I stated directly that raising a hand against another person, a beautiful woman, is at the very least, shameful! ... Of course, I was trying to redeem myself in her eyes.

She stopped and started rummaging under her jacket. Her jacket appeared to be much better than mine, with machine-stitched hems, it could easily pass for manufactured if not for the oval stamp on the shoulder with the handwritten inscription in indelible black ink: "Babushkinsky District, Hospital Number …" Instead of a number, there was just a whitish smudge where it had been bleached out.

Rozochka pulled out a roomy newsboy cap with a tiny, barely visible visor. She cocked it askew over the black eye, so that only her right, dark blue eye shone merrily from under the visor.

"Well, how's this outfit, do I look like my idol?!" she said. "Keep in mind, Mother Teresa started out not even as a nurse, but as a mere nursing assistant."

God knows, all my imagination wasn't enough to picture Mother Teresa in a cap. In her iconic robe, sure, but definitely not wearing both a cap and that robe.

"You know, Rozochka," I said guiltily, "you look more like Princess Diana."

I'm not sure why I said that. I had indeed seen photos of "Princess Di's style" in some fashion magazine. Some top model was advertising various hats, including a big cap. And what I distinctly remembered was that she wasn't wearing a wing jacket or any kind of robe - she was in a sailor-style beach outfit.

"A princess from Manchester City?!" Rozochka exclaimed.

I closed my eyes. Manchester City always stirred up complex feelings in me, and after her meaningful exclamation, I was ready for anything. But Rozochka is remarkable precisely because she's so unpredictable! Instead of the slap I was expecting, she showered me with rapturous kisses.

"What a lapidary sybarite you are, Mitya!" (New words in her lexicon!)

Not a single muscle twitched on my face, even though "lapidary sybarite" was as unacceptable to me as Mother Teresa in a cap, or Princess Di in a jacket made of a hospital blanket. Nevertheless, not a single muscle…

"Mitya, I was complimenting you. Do you know what it means?!"

I shook my head - no, I didn't know. Rozochka laughed and explained that sometimes cool guys from theatre troupes would gather at her apartment, and recently one of these cool dudes (such a sly, handsome fellow) had told her, in expressing his utmost admiration, that she was a "beautiful lapidary sybarite," meaning she surpassed all others with her innumerable charms.

I immediately took a dislike to the sly, handsome fellow, and as Rozochka went on about how talented, resourceful, and unflappable he was, I outright loathed the little rat - the word "handsome" now sounded more like "ratsome" to me.

We walked under the arches of large stone buildings, then through one-storey, almost barracks-like courtyards. Then again under arches and again through courtyards. Our conversation was hard to follow, and at times I didn't understand what she was talking about at all. One minute, Rozochka was asking if my jacket was of genuine leather, the next she was keenly interested in the quality of my jeans, even trying on my fur cap - and just keeping it on.

"You know, Mitya," she said under one archway, "I'm only telling you this because you're Mitya. If you wanted, we could very profitably sell your jacket and jeans through that lapidary sybarite friend of mine."

"That ratsome fellow?!" I jabbed, asking, "And would I have to stay in my underwear?!"

Rozochka reassured me: she knew girls who sewed not just fashionable jackets from hospital blankets like hers, but also proper jackets and Reebok-style parachute pants.

I declined the offer. Rozochka grew angry. She took the bag from me in silence, put her grey cap inside and walked on. I trailed behind - what was she thinking? I was dressed decently, and still, she was being fussy, and if I put on some "DIY Reebok" outfit she'd turn away completely. (Moreover, I suspected she had her eye on my jacket and jeans for that sly rat.)

We entered a secluded one-storey courtyard. Suddenly Rozochka whirled around:

"Listen, Mityaika, maybe you're flat broke - what did you write in that telegram? Maybe you were trying to con your Rozochka? It won't work!"

I had never felt so crushed. And by whom? Essentially, by someone close to me. Me - Mityaika?! She had never called me that before! The houses and courtyard seemed to spin, I felt faint. Rozochka must have noticed… She ran over and hugged me so I wouldn't fall.

"Thank you," I said, pushing her away to show I was OK and the crisis had passed. "I do have money, lots of money! I'm not Mityaika! I'm Captain Pererreau, ebony trader!"

Rozochka understood she had overloaded my ship, my "Cutty Sark," and fussed over me:

"Okay, Mityaika …you're not Mityaika! You do have money, lots of money, I believe you, I do… I'm not even asking you, Mitenka, to show it, no need… We're already here… This is our roof."

It really was a remarkable roof, almost Gothic, covered in tarpaper. Black sheets peeled away from the beams here and there, and the beams joined high above in an arch resembling a wigwam of sorts. It surely would have collapsed long ago if not attached to the neighbouring building's brick wall and welded to it over time. The one-storey structure beneath this grandiose roof seemed almost nonexistent. But there it was: a padlocked door, a small window with a cross-shaped frame and internal iron grating, and lastly, an outhouse attached to the end of the neighbouring brick, hastily cobbled together from whatever scrap materials were at hand: a broken sheet of asbestos siding, scrap plywood, even some old battered cafeteria trays and a heavily worn chess board.

Rozochka and I walked the trampled path through the snow (the snow was only just starting to melt in the shadows cast by the surrounding apartment blocks), the hanging padlock turned out to be fake (Rozochka removed it without a key). What looked truly ominous was the small black "High Voltage" sign with a skull and crossbones nailed above the door.

Indeed, there were some exposed wires strewn about inside the mudroom, and the door to the living quarters was covered in sheet metal with the word "Deadly!" and a red lightning bolt painted on it. In short, the warnings in the entryway looked so believable that I tried not to step on the wires.

Meanwhile, Rozochka inserted a little key into an English-style lock, and the door responded with a disgruntled growl as it opened inward. It was thick and solid, lined on the inside with faux leather insulation.

A waft of medications and hospital warmth emanated from the living space.

"Home, sweet home!" said Rozochka, pulling the growling door shut and turning on the lights.

The neon lamp overhead crackled, flickered, and finally flared, making me squint.

Rozochka tossed her jacket onto a chair near the window and invited me to tour "our chambers" - that's how she put it.

The "chambers" comprised an anteroom, quite spacious (I've already mentioned the furnishings - the chair by the window), and two separate rooms. Rozochka's room was to the left as you entered from outside. Her roommate's (who also worked part-time at the ambulance station) was to the right of a wall mirror and a sink with two cast-iron taps for hot and cold water.

We first entered the roommate's room (Rozochka wanted to start there).

It was a large room, very large, about 20 square metres! The walls were completely bare and yellow (that's how water-based paint yellows over time). The window was a rustic, just like that in the anteroom, but with the glass completely whitewashed like in a public restroom, and the grate was made of rolled wire rather than rebar (the bare bulb on a long cord illuminated the room brightly enough for me to make all this out). Next to the window stood a white, clearly hospital-issue nightstand, its little door ajar. Some medications were lying on it, giving off a mixed smell of phenol and ethyl alcohol. At some distance there was a double bed with a metal mesh base and a naked mattress rolled up like on a rail car berth, with a bare pillow on top. (By the way, I noticed there were no sheets inside the rolled-up mattress.) The only other furnishings were a coat rack nailed to the inward-opening door and a slop pail with a broom.

"Not much to it," I said smugly (my own digs were plusher after all). But Rozochka immediately parried that furniture and such were bourgeois trappings! She didn't need any tables, wardrobes, or even a stove, since her old electric stove had recently burned out anyway, because it was easier just to eat at some diner after classes and a twelve-hour shift, and better to spend that extra hour lounging in bed.

She pressed up against me, and then something unimaginable happened. The thing was, after shedding her jacket, Rozochka was left wearing only a medical gown. I had assumed she had some clothes on underneath, maybe jeans and a top, or if not jeans, then at least some pants - but no such thing.

Except for the gown, all she had on were pumps with kitten heels and stockings that had slid down to her knees. That was it…

"Well, Mitenka?!"

She turned my fur cap around backwards and suddenly appeared so roguishly mischievous with that black eye - the spitting image of a little hooligan! She looked up at me slyly from under her brows, catching my gaze and dropping her eyes, not to the floor, but to the V-shaped opening of her unbuttoned gown, gesturing so eloquently: "Here is your genuine treasure, here are your real furnishings!"

To say that I agreed with her would be an understatement. Her meaningful glance opened my eyes to such depths of true beauty that in an instant I soared to the heavens, came crashing back down to earth, and transformed into the brave young Ivan the Prince. And once you've felt yourself become a brave prince, Ivan the Prince no less, how could you not scoop your princess into your arms?

And I did scoop her up and carried her into that bright little room, onto those silken bed linens, those soft downy pillows, and featherbeds.

That damned door! As I mentioned, it opened inward into the room. I struggled mightily with it, and ultimately prevailed, but at the cost of my princely strength.

Rozochka laughed merrily - it was all fun for her, while I was seeing stars from the exertion. I'd take a step and stumble; the ground no longer supported me. With yet another step, I tripped over the sink and nearly sat down right on the floor. But I didn't let go of Rozochka, God forbid she get hurt, while my own bumps and bruises didn't matter a bit.

Rozochka hopped up, still laughing, hooked the door closed and then tried to help me up – sent her cap flying, kicked off her shoes, her gown opened but she didn't think to cover up. Still giggling, she pulled me by the hand, and then I took flight again, soared up to the heavens like a fierce hunting falcon, and from there I pounced on my little dove, as she herself shed her garments, revealing her beauty.

"Rozochka!" I cried in excitement, "Here's your money!"

I pulled three hundred dollars from the inside pocket of my jacket and placed the cash in her hand.

"Oh!" she exclaimed.

Then she counted the three hundred-dollar bills several times over and hid them away so quickly and deftly that I didn't see where. Not that I tried to see, quite the contrary, as I strived to reach into my pocket for the rest of the money. Doublenose's advice, which I had followed, now seemed disastrous. I was reaching out and failing, my hand just sliding past - the pocket flap was in the way.

Rozochka interpreted my actions in her own way. She helped strip off my jacket and other garments. It was so wonderful, so magnificent, that I asked her in a burst of candour:

"Rozochka, if I become a wealthy man, not a millionaire but well-off, will you come back, will you want to be with me?"

She broke into a merry peal of laughter. "What do you think I'm doing? I've already come back; I already want to be with you!"

We embraced like Ivan the Prince and his princess and were swept away to the faraway realm of fairy tale kingdoms, and sweet madness swallowed us whole.

Sometime toward morning, a terrible pounding on the door summoned us back from the magic kingdom. Rozochka propped herself up, we kissed, and then she said she needed to get dressed and open up - her roommate had returned. She couldn't find her gown in the dim light, so I suggested she put on my jeans and jacket. She did and went padding off in her kitten heels (that telltale tap of the nails). Then I heard female and male voices and general merry laughter.

* * *

Rozochka opened the door. In the beam of light, she was a new Amazon[95]! She approached me silently, slowly bending as if performing some solemn rite. At any rate, when I tried to take her hands, she pulled back. I didn't argue, she just bent again and very pensively kissed my brow. I found it funny and pulled her to me, and we kissed on the lips.

"You are nuts," she said tenderly, then asked me to rest while she spoke with her roommate. "In any case, Mitenka, know that you're the best for me!"

I raised my head to another sight of a new Amazon in the beam of light. The door closed, I dropped my head back and fell asleep, easily, and joyfully, like a saint.

---

95   This is a reference to the first ever theatrical release of an "erotic" movie in the Soviet Union. The polish sci-fi movie "Sex mission" (1984) included mere seconds of esthetically impeccable nudity, but this was still unheard of under Soviet puritan and sanctimonious rule. Still, releasing a title with "sex" in it was impossible, so the movie was retitled as "New Amazons".

CHAPTER 34

I opened my eyes. The paint peeling from the ceiling hung down in folds, creating the effect of a parachute canopy. I lay there smiling as if soaring in the heavens; life was beautiful! Just a minute ago, I had concluded that a person can be not just happy, but infinitely happy. Yes, infinitely… Take me, for example: rested, completely satisfied, I'm not just lying in bed, but striving to hear the music of the silver strings. It seems I've got everything, everything there is to have, what more could I want?! But there is always more to want…

I looked around Rozochka's room; everything was like the neighbour's: the bed, the same nightstand, the window… No, no, the glass is not painted white, the light from the window illuminates the "parachute canopy." Rozochka did not have a bucket or a broom, but she did have sheets! How nice, how wonderful! There is, after all, a reason they say happiness makes you foolish.

I was waiting for Rozochka, somehow knowing she was brewing coffee to bring me right in bed, with cookies, of course. Whatever you say, life at home is made sweet by such anticipation. Why wait for the music? It will inevitably come along with Rozochka!

The front door rumbled, voices – an insistent male's and a pleading female's. Different voices to those that had woken me earlier. And Rozochka's is not among them?! No, it is not, I noted with certainty. But where else could she be? Probably she ran to the cafe for boiling water. That was surely it since the stove had burnt out.

Bliss overwhelmed me again: I'd open the can of coffee, and she would pour boiling water from the thermos and stir it. The anticipation was so vivid, I could almost smell the coffee aroma.

Meanwhile, the voices became muffled. Evidently, the neighbour had invited the guest into her room. However, the female voice became quite different, more piercing! Suddenly the neighbour's door slammed shut abruptly, and retreating, angry, hurried male footsteps drowned in the no less angry roaring of the front door. Then a dense silence reigned. No sound came from the neighbour and I thought that somehow, I had missed her leaving with the angry man. But no, suddenly the door to our room opened (I was lying with my head towards the door).

"Ah, there they are!"

My chest clenched. I had never heard such a joyfully ferocious outcry. I sat up abruptly, ready for anything, but the neighbour had already dashed out:

"Well, Rozka, you missionary of love! You just can't stop - you've taken the sheets again!"

The roaring of the front door swallowed up this enraged cursing as well.

I was left alone. An anxious feeling came over me. For some time, I lay there, waiting for Rozochka, but eventually decided to get dressed. I felt around for my underwear next to the bed with my hand: undershorts (I didn't want to think about it, but the thought came involuntarily: from Manchester City), underpants (bluish, Finnish, with a fine white stripe down the length) and a shirt (denim, with big breast pockets). When I put on the latter, my passport fell out, but I didn't notice and only found it under the bed after thoroughly searching through my pants and jacket. When I found it, I felt like I had been hit like with an electric shock - money! The money, rubles and two hundred dollars, and my passport were still there, in a small plastic bag. I don't know why, but this made me even more certain that Rozochka would return soon. She wouldn't just take off in my cap, jacket and my pants, leaving me with nothing to wear!

I tucked the shirt into my underpants, put on clean socks and pulled on my ankle boots; only then did I go out into the hallway.

Rozochka's coat was lying on the chair by the window. I picked it up, still hoping to find at least my pants beneath it... Rozochka's grey cap fell at my feet. I don't know why, but it was precisely the cap that prompted me to take decisive action.

I pulled the front door towards me, closed, and hooked it, and entered the neighbour's room without hesitation. Here everything was just as it had been yesterday - a bare, pretty much empty room. Nothing to disturb while searching for my clothes. Still, I examined every corner, every nook with such thoroughness that as I left the room, I was sure - my pants and jacket were not in this apartment. My Cutty Sark was gone too. But to hell with the bag!

I threw on Rozochka's coat and hurried out to the courtyard.

It was a magnificent day! The sun shone through the gap between two dark grey, almost dark blue high-rises, and the whole courtyard was immersed in the breath of blueness. No, I didn't misspeak, precisely the breath of blueness, it seemed that way because, touching the shade, the rays seemed to seethe on the shiny blue crust of snow and it shimmered, exuding gently and slowly wavering blueness, so strong that the courtyard was overflown with it as with water.

I was not at all surprised that the run-down toilet was quite clean and comfortable inside. It was pretty much customary to see Rozochka making improvements wherever she went. However, lots of used disposable syringes were scattered everywhere: underfoot, in the bucket, and even in the toilet paper holder. This was quite depressing and even made me nauseous.

Our medical field has taken a wrong turn. Saws, scalpels, hammers, drills, scissors, forceps, syringes, dispensers, shock absorbers and so on, and so on (I'm not even talking about special tables and chairs) - all these objects somehow don't fit within the concept of healing. They may have been appropriate in a torture chamber, but by no means in an operating room. Our surgeons (of course, I'd take my hat off in their honour, if I had a hat) are not to blame - that's just the current level of medicine. But they still resemble butchers more than healers. Unlike butchers though, surgeons deal with living human beings, created in God's likeness.

In the future, medicine will be different, it will follow the path of Christ. No scalpels for you – nothing of that sort… Before any surgery happens, doctors would meet with the patient's soul, and if they recognize each other, feel each other's pain, then healing has already begun, their interaction has begun… The soul is the beginning and end of human health, not the body. If there is a soul, there is a human being, otherwise there is nothing.

It was so good to be outside, so wonderful. The air was fresh, the sun was bright and warm, skies were bottomless and blue, and Rozochka was the one, the only one with whom I wanted to spend my life. We could have gone to some cafe for pastries. Or to the zoo - I love watching animals, especially little ones, carefree and playful. Or just stroll around Moscow, go to an amusement park or movies; anything!

No, all that is impossible. So close, yet unattainable, I suddenly thought with such unbearable bitterness, that the small black sign above the door with the skull and bones enraged me.

I tore it off, struck it against the doorframe several times, and then went and nailed it to the toilet with the same nail it had hung on. This strange structure and this little sign were such a wonderful match, as if they were made for each other. All these broken trays, chessboards, and pieces of roofing are nothing but small offerings (and my little addition too); offerings of unavailing rage. I grinned at the thought of having made my own little offering and even cheered up a bit. Whatever they may say, losing is not as disheartening if you remember: you are not the only loser in the world by far. Why? An interesting question indeed!

I returned to the "premises." Trying to preserve the outdoor freshness within me, I washed up to my waist, drank some water from the tap (it had never been so spring-cold in our dorm), and again, throwing on the coat, sat down by the window.

I could see the thawing path running to the archway and most of the archway itself, and, the sidewalk, cleared of snow, running parallel to the path at some distance from it, and then sharply turning left onto the neighbouring street. The sidewalk was quite crowded, and at times, it seemed that pedestrians were hurrying not to the next street, but to some gathering behind our building.

So, why does a person feel more comfortable knowing that many others have been as unlucky as he, and he is just one of the many?

I firmly set to get to the bottom of it and, in my opinion, had more hope for success than anyone else. Had I spent all night shaking on a train only to end up sitting at this window with no pants, totally perplexed, and not knowing the whereabouts of the person I'd come for, and indeed, my own?!

You must agree, there was something about my situation that makes me stand out from all the other losers, and stand out as much as to make me a truly outstanding person. And like any outstanding person, I, of course, have something to say to my peers.

And then I imagined that those pedestrians hasting to the next street were really gathering behind our building for a meeting, where my edifying speech would be the major highlight.

At first, I'd appear in the crowd incognito, observing. The people are mostly loud-mouthed, unbalanced, so to speak, "front-line veterans," many of them my age. I am gripped by doubt, is it possible that I am the most outstanding among them and deserve unquestioned authority?!

Suddenly, I felt that I did not value my outstanding status and was ready to yield it to anyone, circumstances permitting… For just a split second, I even imagined myself already handing over my laurels - a slightly balding, but truly loud-mouthed little Caesarion bows his head, and I slowly and ceremoniously place my laurel wreath on him… and immediately dive into the crowd, briskly working my arms and legs, trying to move as far away from the new Caesar as possible. Now this is more like a game of tag. However, … I am once again incognito. The audience around speculates:

"Your wife left? Everybody's wives left too. Big deal, poor thing! Oh, she took all the furniture with her, including the fridge and TV?"

The poor thing has nothing to say, because he's not quite that poor. But then another one emerges, even more unshaven and unkempt.

"That bitch of mine (he swears crudely) took all the furniture, including the fridge and TV."

The unkempt one stands with his hands on his hips, legs spread and belly protruding. His clothes are sort of chewed up and shaggy, and his face is shaggy and chewed up. This poor wretch seems unbeatable in his wretchedness.

But the crowd is in no hurry to concede the palm to him.

"Big deal, poor wretch, she took everything! But after she took it all, did he personally give his wife a neat sum for paperwork related to studies or getting a job at the new place?"

The poor wretch is pushed aside. A totally shaggy character appears, with small and unjustifiably piercing little eyes.

"I'm the one, I am!" he declares, losing his balance (they shake him, help him stand upright, but he seems to get even shaggier as a result). "I didn't give her anything; she took a tidy sum herself," he mumbles, tilting sideways.

Matted and tangled, he inspires horror and disgust. In my opinion, this drinking, down-and-out type can no longer be vindicated in any way, and therefore he is significantly more outstanding than I am - a sudden thought flashes in my mind that somewhere deep in my fantasies some little wheel will spin, and my hope will come true.

Alas, the crowd did not yield this time either.

"Big deal! after you gave her money, did you ever visit your wife? And if you did, did you end up in just your underpants in a strange city, in an unknown, strange apartment?!"

I fled, fled discreetly, but still… Then I sat down by the cross-shaped window again to prepare for my edifying speech in earnest.

And here I stand on the raised platform, faces all around me - faces! It's as if I have seen them before, those longing male faces.

"Dear fellow citizens! Did all your wives leave all of you, yes or no?"

"Ye-es!" the many-voiced community sighed, so unanimously that the platform shook as if a tank had driven by.

Many in the crowd had shown off their knowledge by pointing at my Finnish underpants, clearly visible beneath Rozochka's coat, as at the indisputable proof of me being the outstanding one. I felt confident and inspired.

"Dear compatriots! Have you ever wondered why your soul feels more comfortable knowing that many were abandoned by their wives, and you are just one of the many?"

Proverbs rained down as if answering the question:

"Trouble shared is trouble halved!" "There's safety in numbers!" …

"All that is true, but not quite," I interrupted, "Look how many of us out there, left by our wives! And if all of us gathered from all the cities, all the villages in Russia, there wouldn't be enough space for us here, only the Red Square would fit us all! And if all our former wives came too, no place would be enough! We'd become the most grandiose demonstration…"

I got distracted just for a split second, and immediately I saw the orderly ranks of wives who had left their husbands as worthless. I saw them dressed in T-shirts of female athletes from the 1950s, athletic, proudly and firmly marching with raised busts past the Mausoleum.

I wanted their husbands to be athletes from the "Workforce Reserves" society, no less precise in their marching and execution of monumental living figures, even surpassing their wives. Alas, I could achieve nothing with these slovenly loafers, even with my seemingly sophisticated imagination.

And immediately after that I saw the vast fields of Russia, swirling snow, and crowds, crowds of social dropouts, that is, husbands abandoned by their wives, who trudged along in foot wraps to who knows where, their utter demoralization and wraps reminiscent of the routed Nazi invaders, responding to any handout of bread with a happy "Hitler kaputt! Kaputt! Kaputt!"

"What does kaputt have to do with it?!" I lamented my failed entertainment, and in the blink of an eye I am once again standing on the same raised platform and continuing my edifying speech as if never interrupted:

"No, no, it is not in proverbs where we shall find comfort. Death is death, alone or in a company. We all subconsciously realise that when you are one of the many sufferings, this isn't bad luck; bad luck does not torment so many at the same time. This is not a misfortune, we are not the unfortunate, but rather we are chosen. Yes, we are the chosen ones. The chosen are the best, and the best should only have one thing on their minds: how to ease the lives of their neighbours, and even those living far away. So, your wife left, well, she left now what? Should you bang your head against the wall?! Are you supposed to tear open your shirt and roll on the floor in tears?! Or, worse still, shall we fall into resentment and revenge?! Neither, none of that. The chosen would feel a calm relief as she leaves. Her life has become so much easier now that you no longer burden her with your presence, and so you have achieved your goal and improved her life after all. Moreover, it is your sacred duty to assist her in every way from now on, and always answer her every call for help…"

I faltered, faltered not because I had nothing more to say, but because the crowd listening to me had unexpectedly (I did not catch that fateful moment) turned into a single entity, unkempt and sullen and somehow excessively primordially backwards. It was precisely because of its backwardness that I faltered. Yes, I suddenly felt that the crowd did not understand me, that to them I was but a barbarian and they would deal with me as with a barbarian at the first opportune moment…

CHAPTER 35

I'm at the sentry window once again. This time, I felt an unbearable hunger - must have got nervous giving my speech?! The day had passed. Dusk was already settling into our courtyard and lights were turning on in some windows.

I looked at the archway and the well-trodden, muddy path through the melting snow, which appeared churned. I had immediately recalled the lumpen-intellectual, his hairy hands, and the jarring iron knocking against the train compartment. It seems I hadn't even recovered from replaying that terror in my mind when a new knock, though quiet and timid, knocked me off my chair

"Roza, Rozochka!"

"No, not Rozochka or even Lily - it's Katrin!" the neighbour reported. I recognised her voice. Despite sounding cheerful, it also conveyed an underlying readiness for aggression, which I remembered well from the morning.

"Yura, Yurok, come in," Katrin called out, slightly drawling the words, as she turned on the light and peered into the entry-way.

I had barely got a good look at this Katrin in her black suede jacket and man's black beret with a red triangle at the temple (looks like a Marine's beret to me), when a young man about my height, but younger, entered the hallway - a curly-haired, rosy-cheeked (the epitome of health!) blue-eyed brunette. No need to guess - an athlete, some kind of grappler or karateka. The only flaw was his thick, bulbous nose, otherwise, he was a fine young man! Just one glance, and I knew he was that crafty rogue.

Being uneasy is awkward, of course, but his clothes really got to me, and even made me feel ill at one point. A dark brown Turkish leather jacket - the exact copy of mine. Brand new dark blue jeans - another bullseye... His jacket zipper was undone to the navel; clearly, the jacket was tight across the shoulders. No wonder – the bulging muscles twitched and rolled under his tight undershirt, as if living a life of their own.

Maybe I was wrong, but I didn't want to look at him any-more.

"Yurok, meet Rosa's husband!" Katrin said in her drawn-out manner, then suddenly broke into a wild cackle, throwing her head back.

Her bizarre and inexplicable laughter left me flustered. Yurok winked at me and, shaking my hand whispered (his breath reeking heavily of wine):

"She's stoned, and I haven't seen your woman, don't even know her!"

A blatant, shameless lie! I could see his pupils darting around like he was counting something invisible. I turned away.

"What are you two whispering about?" Katrin snapped angrily.

I looked and was stunned, but not because she was big-mouthed and ugly (frontline veteran type). No, no, it wasn't even the beret or her fading youth that shocked me - it was the Eng-lish red scarf I saw around Katrin's neck.

"What are you gawking at, googling your eyes?!" Katrin fumed, stuffing the conspicuously exposed royal mohair scarf back under her jacket.

"Nothing… It just really suits you, that English scarf. Must have cost you a pretty penny!" I said with no ill intent - not trying to be sarcastic, let alone hint at the shady circumstances.

Katrin flew into a rage, nearly lunging at me:

"And who are you?! Why are you here?! Who gave you the right to be in my apartment?!"

When I explained I was waiting for my wife, who had left wearing my clothes, so I had no way to leave until she returned, Yurok quietly went outside. Katrin then threw a full-blown tantrum - running from room to room, inexplicably peering under beds, stripping our bed of its sheets and pillowcases. Each time she ran past me, she screamed that Roza had gone home to Crimea, but that bitch better not think there's no dealing with her, that she can make off with someone else's things. Katrin's mother had Roza's passport, and they'd get the police to haul her in!

That word "haul" did me in, sending me into a daze. In any case, I stopped hearing her running and screaming. I stood staring out the window, watching dusk deepen with every passing second, more and more lights turning on in the huge building across the way.

I snapped out of it when she shoved my shoulder:

"Where's Yurok?"

Not waiting for an answer, Katrin ran outside with the sheets.

I was still staring at the illuminated windows, but no longer saw them. I was replaying what I had heard, or rather, it kept replaying in my mind. It was clear that Roza wouldn't be coming back to this apartment. She had surely left, and the cause was me - my clothes that she had obviously been forced to exchange for her own, pawned with the loan shark, Katrin's mother. After all, it couldn't be a coincidence that Roza greeted me in just a robe?! No, these things don't just happen. I pictured the horror of her situation and felt pain for her (when you're truly destitute, you'll do anything). Then, embarrassed to face me and explain the awkward situation, she simply left. If anyone knew her Mitya was resourceful, that her little Mitya would think of something and fare far better than her, it was Rosa. What a trouper! My heart expanded with gratitude toward Rosa. She had cut the Gordian knot and said goodbye! It was sheer luck that I'd arrived in Moscow in new clothes, allowing Roza to swap them for her pawned stuff.

I heard noise and voices in the entryway. Yurok and Katrin had returned with a fresh stack of bedding. Ignoring me, they went into the room. Then Katrin came back alone, no sheets, dropped a little booklet on the windowsill and said,

"Mama said Roza wanted you to have this."

It was a passport - Slyozkina Rosa Fedorovna. Trying not to betray my feelings, I asked,

"She paid off all her debts?"

"Everything," Katrin replied. "She conned you and paid it all off."

We shared a significant glance.

"She went to Crimea - where exactly?"

Katrin smirked slightly, raising her brows, and I likely grinned back, at least I held her gaze.

"Chernomorsk," she said, then explained, "Seventy kilometres north of Evpatoria."

Pocketing Rosa's passport, I deliberately mused aloud about Chernomorsk, how I'd always thought it was just a fictional town invented by Ilf and Petrov, never imagining it actually existed[96].

I don't know what impression my musings made on Katrin, but she unexpectedly offered to let me stay the night.

"Time I was off," I said, donning Rosa's cap and wrapping her shawl over my shoulders as I headed for the door.

Suddenly Katrin blocked my path:

"What? ... You really do... love her that much?! No explanations, no resentment?!"

I said nothing in response. Honestly, I didn't even understand what she meant. She seemed on the verge of a breakdown.

I silently went out and carefully closed the growling door behind me. Then just as carefully, so as not to get tripped by the wires, I went through the entryway and out to the yard.

It was quite bright in the small yard, and I made my way to the archway. As I walked along the path, I could feel Katrin's gaze on me from the window - an unfriendly look, but her heavy stare didn't bother me. On the contrary, it cheered me and lightened my step. I was sure Katrin envied me for something very important to her, so important that she wished she could trade places with me.

---

96   Chernomorsk is indeed a fictional town mentioned in a legendary novel "The Little Golden Calf" by Ilya Ilf and Eugene Petrov.

At the archway, I paused to consider where to go next and decided I should head to the train station to go back home. As her husband, I needed to be financially secure above all else, so that she could find solace from her horrific poverty with me at any time.

CHAPTER 36

I arrived home at 6 a.m. after having travelled in a tightly packed third-class sleeper car, on the upper bunk. Some passengers didn't even get blankets, and I had given mine to an old lady on the lower bunk who kept putting off going to ask the conductor for one because of her bad legs. By the time she went, there were none left.

The old lady was going to visit her son. He had completed a technical school course affiliated with the Moscow Experimental Jewellery Factory, becoming a skilled diamond cutter. His wife was studying at a nursing school (which touched me deeply). Having just married, they were having a hard time because he wasn't allowed in her dormitory for women, and she couldn't stay in his dorm on the factory premises where all the cutters lived under guard, like in a prison.

The old lady's story upset me so much that I woke up crying several times that night under my little travel blanket. I dreamed of armed men of Caucasian descent standing at iron gates, not letting me get to Rozochka, nor her to me.

"Ro-ozochka!" I would sob.

"Mi-tenka!" she would respond, equally distraught.

And I would wake up in tears.

If it weren't for one minor incident, no one would have guessed I was travelling in just my underwear with no pants. The conductor's poor eyesight and our dreadful era that breeds criminal fantasies did me in.

The conductor suddenly attacked me when we arrived, and I was carrying the old lady's huge, mattress-patterned suitcase to help her off the train.

"Thief!" he yelled, trying to rip my blanket off me.

He thought I had stolen a blanket from the train's supply. I had to explain that I had not, and in fact, I was a theft victim myself, having my pants stolen, and even had to demonstrate their obvious absence.

At the dormitory, no one cared about my attire - that is, no one remembered I had left wearing a fur hat, leather jacket, and so on.

"Oh, it's you?" Alina Spiridonovna said groggily before calmly returning to her couch.

She found nothing unusual in my outfit, nor did the residents on my floor. No one said a word, not about my clothes or my trip to Moscow when I showed up at the kitchen (though I had put on some old wool trousers and thrown my little blanket over my shoulders).

"Please, take these," they said, handing me an entire bag of cheese pies. "It's Parent's Saturday today."

But most astonishingly, even Doublenose didn't react to my old clothes - and we had bought the new ones together!

"Mitya, good you're back!" he said happily, bringing out my folder of poems. "It's cleanup day today, so we have plenty of time to negotiate a mutually beneficial deal."

He proposed a joint business venture: for every poem sold, he would take 15% commission. In exchange, he would:

Provide the author a 10% loan of $700 for the current year 1992.

Ensure the author has an appropriate clientele and provide a table at the beer bar for transactions.

Never disclose any commercial secrets related to this deal.

I liked the terms, especially the loan, which solved a lot of my immediate problems. I decided that after signing the contract (Doublenose asked me to make two copies), I would head straight to the market. With the remaining $200, I would buy some new clothes - it was the Sunday after I returned from Moscow, and I expected to find Vizier and get the same things as before. Yes, for some reason I always expected good luck on Sundays.

However, Doublenose didn't let me go. After tucking away the contract, he said I should spend some time working on the poems while he would run to the casino, and if all went well, he'd return with a buyer.

I looked over the manuscript - it was in order, with poems sorted by theme and separated with bookmarks. The only issue was that I didn't know how to set my prices. If poems were a commodity, there must be some rationale for their value, why one would cost more than another? I bitterly regretted Rozochka's absence: she would surely have advised me what to do... And that very second, I heard her sweet, slightly condescending, and mocking voice in my head - of course, they aren't priced by length. Poems aren't real estate or taxi trips. Poems should be valued for the talent they embody, and talent is a great mystery!

Her vocabulary only puzzled me in that I could have expressed it that way myself, whereas Rozochka typically disdained my way with words.

I was bewildered: we had swapped sides. She took mine - true poems are priceless, while I took hers - any poem can be quantified in monetary terms. Yes, it was I who tried to force poems into the Procrustean bed of some all-explaining price list. It seemed revolting, and I nearly decided against selling poems at all. But then I recalled Rozochka's promise to return to me if I became not rich but sufficiently well-off.

"I want you, Mitya, to be a poet, a knight, and…Yes, a sugar daddy! Better to die with a gold-filled belt than under a fence with no pants on."

That "no pants on" part truly struck me. It made my heart ache terribly, but I resolved not to give up. I glanced out the window absentmindedly and saw Doublenose hurrying along amidst the trees. Several people in multicoloured sports jackets followed him, falling further behind with each Doublenose's step…

"Well, Mitya, it's Tolya Croesus himself coming with his henchmen!" Doublenose said, patting me on the shoulder. "Don't let me down!… Legends about you are spreading, turns out you're the poet of all oppressed street vendors and kiosk keepers, and even more…"

"But are they really oppressed by anyone?" I asked with sincere surprise.

"Of course they're oppressed!" Doublenose assured me. "Guys like Tolya Croesus are our major oppressors," he finished in a whisper, arranging a small table by the lone window, and asking me and Tutankhamun to go outside to greet the guests.

We went out. I put the folder of poems in my hood so I could hide my hands in my jacket, but because the lining had bunched up, the folder stuck straight up out the back, and I couldn't tuck it down into the hood so it wouldn't fall out. My clumsiness made me seem like an insect lying on its back, wriggling its legs, squirming but unable to grab onto anything to right itself. That's how I was with my folder…

"What a rash-ridden tramp is that?" Tolya Croesus asked Tutankhamun nasally as the latter obsequiously invited everyone inside the central, managerial kiosk.

"Ah, that's…that one," Tutankhamun answered, opening the door, and blocking me from view as he ushered the guests inside.

They passed by without slowing. First Croesus in a red-and-black jacket covered in zippers and Velcro, with silver stripes like road signs on its sleeves. Behind him followed two associates in similarly flashy green and purple jackets. Of course, I immediately picked out Tolya Croesus - not so much by his demeanour but by the black fabric covering his smashed nose.

His nasal voice quality and distinct lack of a nose under the bandage sparked associations so unpleasant that I had to hurry around the corner.

I must sincerely apologise to my readers, but I've been allergic to physical deformities since childhood. God knows why, it's beyond my control. My reactions are unpredictable: sometimes I'd be fine, other times I'd plummet like a stone. I was even beaten because of this in elementary school; they thought I was faking. It all comes down to surprise: I'm fine when prepared mentally, but if not, God help me.

Tutankhamun chased after me, practically dragging me into the kiosk. And thanks to him, I overcame my reaction with little effort. Things were made easier by the frame of mind I'd adopted: I wasn't myself, but "that one," the "rash-ridden tramp." And then, when we entered, Tolya Croesus beckoned me over. Well, he didn't beckon me exactly, but seeing me, he exclaimed out loud in surprise:

"Ah, that's…that one?!"

Given my frame of mind, his surprised exclamation sounded like a personal call. I approached the table. Doublenose fussed about, inviting me to sit and meet Tolya Croesus. But I didn't sit. First, I scratched my neck (luxuriously, sticking my tongue out blissfully), then the inside of my arm from wrist to elbow (scratching in sweet, drawn-out strokes until it bled).

"Ah, took offence, eh?" Tolya Croesus smirked.

His eyes, black and shiny, suddenly went dull, as if dimmed by some inner empathy.

"It happens, it happens, I know from experience," he said pensively, seeming to forget about me and Doublenose for a moment as he gazed out the window.

From the moment I saw Tolya Croesus, I wondered why doesn't the black fabric covering his missing nose slip down over his mouth? Now the answer was clear: he had tied two ribbons at the back of his head over his ears, and two more underneath, almost at his neck. But the main anchor was his upper lip, which curled up so high that it not only held the bandage in place but created a weird effect of a low-placed snub nose. It also mirrored the cowlick that hung in the same curve over his sloping forehead. Freckles on his forehead continued onto his copper-red hair.

"Well…had your look, poet? Or are you a rash-ridden tramp?" Tolya Croesus asked, his eyes glinting so piercingly that I felt a bit cowed, sensing a cruel and sharp intellect, merciless if for no other reason than its lack of self-pity.

"No, I don't have any rashes, and I'm not a tramp, I'm a poet," I said, about to sit on the stool Doublenose offered, when Tolya Croesus interrupted me and surrendered his own.

Taking the folder of poems from my hood and placing it on the table, he said he now doubted whether I really was a poet, and he would subject me to a sort of poetic contest in Blois.

"Welcomed gladly, and spurned by everyone!" he declaimed nasally (we'll put it that way) but spiritedly, quoting a line from François Villon's "Du Concours De Blois."

His knowledge (essentially quite understandable - Villon was at odds with the law) was striking and unnerving - watch out, what sort of a scoundrel we have here… they'll strip you bare and make you apologise for it! I responded to him also with Villon, the eight-line stanza from the "Ballade of Countertruths":

> We taste delight in hay alone,
> And find our rest mid toil and moan.
> We laugh but when the pain is sown,
> And only spendthrifts value coin.
> Who cherishes the sun? A mole, discreet.
> The righteous gaze at us with guile,
> To beauties the grotesque beguile,
> And only lover's thoughts are neat.

Doublenose, who had been watching me and Tolya Croesus this whole time with intense interest, suddenly became very bored after I recited these eight lines, seeming utterly distracted by some unspoken concern.

"Bravo!" Tolya said with mock admiration, clapping his hands and laughing to reveal a terrifying number of gold teeth visible beneath the cloth bandage.

I won't hide it; I shuddered. Just that nasal flattery alone was enough! And then the fiery copper hair and molten gold ingots for teeth, alas, not inside a dark maw, but under the "Black Square" of an abyss.

So, my knowledge let me down, quite the contrary, it only made my situation worse. Tolya Croesus said that someone's (yes, someone's) loaded memory now raised not just doubts but legitimate suspicions I was not who I claimed. It was entirely possible I had long been trading in others' "immortals", and so within half an hour I must write a poem on an assigned topic to dispel his reasonable suspicions. He straightaway gave the topic: an address from one poet to another, a monologue to begin with the line:

"Hey poet, honour's captive bind…"[97]

I looked at Doublenose. He remained in that same preoccupied state, but now with his jaw dangling loose and an absent smile on his face. He seemed frozen in contemplation of something remarkable, astonishing. "No doubt he's dumbstruck by his commission from the deal he's dragged us both into," I thought

---

97   The metaphor of a poet bound by honor comes from the poem written by M. Lermontov as a tribute to A. Pushkin after his death resulting from a duel. This poem was a part of the mandatory middle school curriculum in the Soviet Union.

with bitter sarcasm, and I wanted to say to him: "What, Feofili-aktovich, haven't you frozen your balls off yet?!" But instead, I sat on the stool Tolya Croesus had just vacated, took out a pencil (I had no pen), and copied the first line of the poet-to-poet address straight onto the folder. Of course, I immediately understood why Tolya had surrendered his seat - sitting facing the bar counter where his henchmen chugged beer, I was under their observation. As for Tolya himself, he tapped his watch (starting the time) and, taking oblivious Doublenose by the arm, walked with him onto the street. They passed quickly by the window, one after the other. Where they went, why, and what for?... It didn't concern me. Nor did the henchmen and Tutankhamun, staying in shadow this whole time but now loudly arguing who and what I was and why. For me, the key question stood clear - was I a poet or a rash-ridden tramp? I gave no thought to selling poems. But that day (the 5th of April) being a Sunday was no accident - I always came out ahead on Sundays for some mysterious reason.

The thirty minutes flew by in an instant. I realised this from the sounds behind the window, Doublenose's hurried footsteps and Tolya Croesus' deliberate stride. Of course, it was disheart-ening - I had just settled into a genuine, serious poem when, alas, the time was up. I don't know what I would have done if I hadn't studied at the Literary Institute. As a student there, I went through so many "contests in Blois" that to a certain extent, I mastered the winning technique for such competitions.

The first step was to make a draft - complete the task in full in the first five minutes by composing the required piece with no regard for quality. Only then, once you had the draft, could you attempt another, truly serious take at it.

I didn't have that "then". Thirty minutes flew by in a blink of an eye. I had just got into the groove, as they say, when… footsteps. Doublenose was the first to burst into the kiosk with Tolya Croesus right behind him.

"Time's up, time's up!" He tapped meaningfully on his watch, then to his henchmen: "Well?!"

Judging by their confusion, the allotted time hadn't yet expired, but I didn't bother clarifying. Such situations require confidence and the ability to present any text as a divine revelation, rather than the text as such, and I knew that well. I re-read my draft to myself a few times and immediately struck a pose of a prophet who rejected all the worldly and fleeting trivialities of life. I knew my pose would likely be interpreted as a sign of the desperation of a drowning man, especially given the henchmen's responses. One flatly said: "If this Mitya's a poet, then I'm the Pope."

Doublenose surprised me again. Sizing up the situation, he apparently attempted an unobtrusive retreat. He took out a notepad, asked Tutankhamun something officious from behind the counter, then immediately turned to leave, pocketing the pad on the move. However, Tolya Croesus didn't let him - he invited him to join us at the table.

"Hey poet, honour's captive bind…" Tolya recited the opening line half-nasally, though there was a mocking tone his nasality didn't quite capture.

"Time to wake up – approaching New Vasyuki!"[98] he shouted in his peculiar voice, shaking me by the shoulder. "Well, how's our little poem?"

"What does the New Vasyuki have to do with it? I was just thinking," I fibbed trying to not engage his erudition. I was relieved to shift to the "brief poem" which in my mind was already written and even its final version, typed. "One minute of attention," I said, rising. "I'm used to reciting poems standing, including my own."

"And I'm used to listening seated," Tolya Croesus said smugly, reclaiming my - that is, his - seat.

A hush fell. After a pause, I began:

> Hey poet, honour's captive bind,
> Steps of the new Millenium you climb,
> And damn me, it's so obvious to see -
> A bundle of poems accompanies thee!
>
> You bear it for our offsprings' sake,
> With heavy steps your weary way you make
> So, where the fresh new century has sprung,
> Your timeless words would still be freely sung!
> Hey, poet, pause a little while,
> And take along my modest burden pile.
> Please sing it once you are the heaven's guest,
> As I once sang at Muses' sweet behest!

---

98   New Vasyuki is a metaphor for a destination too ideal to exist and only reachable under almost miraculous circumstances. It originates from the novel "The Twelve Chairs" by I. Ilf and E. Petrov, one of the top best-selling and legendary titles in the Soviet Union.

The ending was quite poor: it suggested that the poet marching into the third millennium was essentially heading to God's home, as if to a colleague, to perform his songs. God as a colleague? That's rather something!

After finishing the poem, I slowly dropped my hand, hid it under my little blanket, and slightly bowed my head in a gesture of respect to the listeners. In reality, I was preparing for Tolya Croesus's attacks. Considering his level of knowledge, my piece could withstand no criticism. And sure enough…he asked me to reread the ending. Heart pounding, I did.

"And these Muses - they're women, aren't they?" Tolya Croesus said with an accusatory tone.

I agreed, saying that moreover, they were ancient Greek goddesses, patrons of the sciences and arts. I named each of the nine Muses, which elicited stunned silence from everyone.

"Alright, the ending one more time," Tolya Croesus commanded.

I was almost certain he wouldn't let me read the whole quatrain, that he would cut me off. And he did:

"No, no, not 'sing it,' 'drink it once you are the heaven's guest, as I once drank at Muses' sweet behest!"

Of course, this was unexpected. Tolya's henchmen burst into enthusiastic applause. I joined in too, relieved to be wrong - Tolya Croesus had no intention of attacking my poem. Judging by his erudition and general grasp of poetry, I had set the bar too high. He just dodged it.

When the first round of cheers subsided, the former plumber Tutankhamun spoke up:

"But the redhead, the redhead! Breathing through that rag, but did you see - what a brain! Bright, brilliant, reflective - like Lenin's!"

To be frank, Tutankhamun's statement contained nothing but crude, primitive flattery, along the lines of what he used to say about Doublenose. Nevertheless, everyone, including Doublenose, laughed heartily and applauded again, as if to say, "Well, isn't Tutankhamun something - what a character, hitting the nail on the head!"

I looked at Tolya Croesus: his black eyes were gleaming, crackling with electricity. Naturally ruddy like copper, he had flushed to an even deeper burgundy. And he was breathing, breathing so heavily that the black rag on his face billowed out like a sail, then collapsed inward, clinging to the uneven cavity where his nose should have been, revealing the round pits of his nostrils.

"Alright, enough, enough!" Tolya Croesus ended the outpouring of praise, saying it was time to get down to business. He needed love poems - he intended to publish them under his own name in one of the new local papers to cast an aura of sophistication upon his business.

The moment he said the poems should be about love, his henchmen and Tutankhamun all dropped their heads, avoiding each other's gaze for a while as if Tolya had said something utterly indecent. As usual, Doublenose seemed lost in some unknown daydream.

"What, are you bored?" Tolya asked him with displeasure, urging to conduct the negotiation Doublenose had initiated himself.

"What's there to negotiate?" I interjected, explaining that a good publication required a series of six or seven poems. In a series, the poems were more valuable because the poet's distinctive style had to be maintained throughout - something that ultimately could not be purchased for any sum.

I selected seven poems, some of the best I had dedicated to Rozochka. I also included the "Poet's Address to a Poet" on top as a free bonus piece.

"Well now!" Tolya said, surprised. "And how much will all this set me back?"

"Peanuts," I replied. "Just a thousand dollars total."

Doublenose's jaw dropped again as he drifted back into boredom, while the beer-chuggers at the bar counter choked as if they had swallowed undiluted spirits.

Of course, I had to set a hefty price. I had picked out my very best love poems, every single one dedicated to Rozochka. And when I did that, when I placed the freshly minted bonus piece on top, I suddenly felt pity at the thought of selling my poems with a piece of my sincere love for Rozochka in each.

Tolya Croesus looked at me very attentively with his glittering black eyes, then unexpectedly lapsed into an absorbed daydream no less profound than Doublenose's.

I closed the folder and, gazing out the window, began tying its strings.

"Hold on, not so fast," Tolya said, stopping me. He asked Doublenose's opinion as the middleman.

What Doublenose thought, I could never quite grasp. He droned on at length about how I used to head the regional literary association, had a diploma as a "literary worker," authored the poetic advertising that graced his kiosks all winter, and finally, how Filimon Puplievich himself had bought a poem from me for $100.

"A hundred?" Tolya Croesus asked me curtly.

"Not exactly," I replied.

I explained that on that day, I hadn't been selling poems. I had just got a bit drunk and my manuscript blew open, the pages scattering in the wind. Puplievich picked up one poem himself, read it, and paid Doublenose $50 for it. And I added, for some unknown reason, that his companion, a beauty in a leather coat and burgundy turban on which snowflakes flared like diamonds, had read the poem too.

Here Tolya Croesus started breathing heavily again, like an asthmatic - the black rag inflating with apparent anger, then deflating as if drained.

Silently, Tolya Croesus slid the folder of poems over, took out the eight I had selected, and laid them in front of himself. Still silent, he took out a wad of cash, counted out $750, and handed it to Doublenose.

Doublenose automatically recounted it and agreed just as automatically that it was $750.

"A thousand, a thousand bucks!" Tolya Croesus amended.

I grinned. Then he said that a poet should not love dollars too dearly.

"I'm willing to take my poems back," I said without remorse.

Sensing this, he explained as he stood up that he had deducted $250 in favour of the company, which would henceforth take on the responsibility of providing me with the "roof": protecting my interests from any pickpockets and other criminal elements.

"Right, Feofilaktych?" he asked Doublenose, extending his hand.

"Right, right," the beer bar's manager responded a bit too hastily. To dismiss any doubts, he added, "Without a roof, it's all over!"

Tolya Croesus turned to me - any objections? I said no, and he would drop his when the series was published.

"What's your warranty for the poems - a month, two, three?"

"My warranty is eternity," I said with wounded dignity, for I was indeed offended.

Tolya Croesus grunted in satisfaction. With a nod to his henchmen, he unhurriedly headed for the exit.

Once their footsteps faded outside, I told Doublenose to keep the entire $750 as the loan repayment and his commission. Naturally, he was delighted. He proposed a celebratory drink and sent Tutankhamun to the casino restaurant for hot dishes. I ordered green borscht with sauteed onions, hot lamb with parsley, and coffee with cream.

While waiting for Tutankhamun, Alexei Feofilaktovich paced fervently, proclaiming like a prophet that I could become a great man if I went into business. He had noticed a long time ago that money just scurries right into my pocket.

"You, Mitya, you're literate. You could surpass Filimon Puplievich himself if you just moved a little away from poetry and closer to money. Don't think, Mitya, that big money only goes to dishonest people – it doesn't! Or, at most, only as an exception!"

He leaned in and whispered that he had stupidly thought that too until very recently. But it's not true, money is drawn to honest people, and this is a profound mystery. (Again, it was my vocabulary, but his spirit.)

I did not share Doublenose's optimistic forecasts. After the "contest in Blois," I had sold not just poems, but myself through the poems. This left behind no joyful excitement, only a terrible sense of emptiness and deception. My only consolation was that if Rozochka were there, she would have been pleased.

The green borscht, lamb, and coffee that Tutankhamun brought in special insulated containers, hot and steaming, had a powerful impact on me with their mundane realness. I even secretly dipped a finger in the borscht before taking a spoonful, though the companions didn't notice. However, the borscht, lamb, and coffee made little impression on me then and afterwards. In my dreams and hallucinations, they had tasted far more delightful and, more importantly, appetising. And alas, there is nothing to add to that.

CHAPTER 37

Doublenose's predictions turned out to be accurate: I went into business and money indeed flew to me as if bewitched.

The initial buyers were Lemonich along with the head of railway logistics. Then there was Tolya Croesus, who was apparently in love with a flight attendant, the younger sister of the railway head. Finally, there was the Vizier, a co-owner of many clothing stalls in the city markets, who was courting the older sister - the head of air logistics. After supposedly Tolya's love poems were published, Vizier tracked me down and commissioned a two-act play from me. He demanded that in the first act, the main character, a murid (ethnic Chechen - a kind man, perfectly honest, often moved to tears by any cruel word, even his own) must fall in love with a Russian blonde named Tatiana, arrogant and hard-hearted. In the second act, she was to undergo a transformation, returning to her kind Chechen love and voluntarily converting to Islam before leaving Moscow with him to live in the Chechen mountains.

When I told him I could not write such a play because even a kind murid would never fall for a cruel Tatiana, Vizier became so enraged that I thought he might stab me.

"Alright, I'll try, but I can't promise anything," I said to calm the Vizier down. "After all, there are things money can't buy!"

In response, he randomly selected fourteen of my poems and, with no haggling, tossed three thousand dollars onto my wide bed. It was certainly a large sum, but by that time my iron already held over twenty thousand dollars (it had become prestigious among the affluent to boast about my poems as if they were their own). However, having money had no impact on my lifestyle. So, to amuse myself, I decided to buy what is called a "Gogolian suit."

I had read in accounts about Nikolai Vasilyevich Gogol that in moments of self-admiration (such moments occur for every writer, remember: "Ah, that Pushkin, what a son of a bitch!"), he loved to dress in a sky-blue suit with a bit of a sparkle.

For this purpose, I was drawn to a black suit with a greenish sheen and bought it. However, ever since I had started selling my writings, my pen produced such nonsense that there was no hope of wearing the suit for its intended purpose. So instead, I started thinking of my own reasons for wearing it. The pristine white shirt, greenish tie and black shoes transformed my appearance so much that many stopped recognising me. My new attire made me resemble some kind of foreign creature in the dorms, and women on our floor deliberately evaded me - the homely lasses were bashful about running into a prince.

So, one day (I don't recall the occasion), I decided to go and sell my poems not in my usual coat, but in the "Gogolian suit." I had just entered the central kiosk (I came to sell once a week, on Fridays at ten in the morning, as agreed with Doublenose,) when I saw several buyers already seated there, waiting. These were very wealthy buyers, intent not on haggling but on acquiring poems on the fly, meaning that as I declaimed a poem, they would bid against each other as at an auction, naming higher and higher prices. I had sold poems this way before, with bids skyrocketing five or ten times the initial asking price, which I would establish at the highest "new classic" level anyway, fancying myself a "Fabergé poet." So, seeing these very well-heeled buyers, I rubbed my hands in anticipation of a hefty payday. But what happened instead?

Doublenose led me over to "Tolyas," as I mentally called the wealthy criminal types.

"Meet Mitya Slyozkin, an outstanding contemporary poet! He was considered a prodigy as a child, able to multiply faster than a calculator," Doublenose introduced me in his usual manner (idiotic in my opinion, but unfailingly having the desired effect on buyers).

And then something unusual occurred: the "Tolyas" looked at each other, leapt from their seats and started choking us, then ripped off the collars of our shirts and poured a full mug of beer down our backs. When his mug poured, Doublenose was slapping his thighs and jumping up and down for some reason. After the "Tolyas" left us on the floor and casually exited onto the street, he dashed after them – and returned crestfallen. Apparently, my verbal portrait as an outstanding contemporary poet did not match my actual appearance today in front of these wealthy clients. Doublenose begged me by Christ the Lord to never again wear a black suit with a greenish sheen when selling my poetry.

"Only the coat, only the coat!" he implored so fervently that an argument broke out between us.

"Why do I need money? Why, if I live like a beggar, just not literally under a bridge?!"

Doublenose promised to find me an apartment. It was high time, he said, for me to live like a human being, but on one condition - no matter where or how I lived, I had to come to the poetry sales in my coat made of a dorm blanket. His vested interest was understandable: his 15% commission could sometimes amount to a tidy sum. According to a stray comment he once made, it could equal two weeks' worth of beer sales.

In any case, my objection ("Why do I need money?") held no water. I knew perfectly well that the money was for Rozochka. In fact, she was the sole reason for my embarking upon this whole new, strange way of life.

The next day, I showed up to meet the "Tolyas" in my coat. Of course, I knew that "Thou shalt not tempt the Lord thy God." But when I entered and saw the criminal elements greet me like the participants of the Yalta Conference greeted the Supreme Leader with a standing ovation, I was tempted to get my revenge for the day before, especially on "Winston Leonard Spencer," - my poor ribs still felt the pressure of his bulky rear end. I could forgive anyone, but never "Winston," the Nobel Prize winner in literature! I pulled out my most wretched poems but presented them so pompously as if they were the guiding light of all progressive humanity. I set prices so insanely high I got a bit spooked myself. But everything went without a hitch, "Winston" groaned heavily but paid up… and even left a $5 tip on the table.

That day, Double Nose made $500, while I pocketed around $3,000. But I didn't grasp the value of money.

Once, sending money to my mother, I filled out the transfer order for 5,000 rubles (then equal to about $100). Imagine my surprise when they refused to accept it, citing a government ban on transfers of more than 500 rubles. Good Lord, was I really so well-off?! If only Rozochka knew! ... To thank the Almighty, I went into the local Church of the Apostle Philip and lit the most expensive, most beautiful candles with a golden spiral for every icon. (I didn't know they were wedding candles; to me the main thing was that they were pricey).

Leaving the church, I called over some beggars to give them alms. One of the most wretched approached me on what looked like sticks instead of crutches - a feminine face, a thin beard, and bright blue eyes, clear as a baby's. (The other poor souls froze at some distance.)

"What do you need, bridegroom?" he asked slyly, having noticed that I had lit wedding candles before all the icons.

Seeing my surprise, he laughed mischievously. "It's your wedding to the heavens," he said enigmatically, and that initial off-putting impression from his womanly face passed.

"I want to give you all some money," I said, holding out two 100-ruble notes to him.

His face crinkled up and grew teary, as if I had offended him. "And who are you? Maybe you stole that money, bridegroom, and want to buy your way out by giving it to us?"

God knows why he said that, but other beggars had already surrounded us, expressing their displeasure with the cripple's pickiness - just take it when given, they said. He paid them no mind, staring at me with those clear, childlike eyes. I too did not avert my gaze, and it was as if a little bridge formed between our souls. Nothing like that had ever happened to me before. I never enjoyed lying, though of course, I had to sometimes, but here I felt truly delighted to not have to lie. I told the cripple that I was a poet who composed verses and ditties… and that I had not stolen the money but earned it from my poetry; I wanted to send it to my mother, but could not.

His face smoothed out and he beamed joyfully. "A new Pushkin!"

This assertion amused me. I remembered the literary union, where people were ready to pay me on the spot to be called a new Pushkin. But now the opposite was true: I, myself, longed to pay.

The cripple took the money as if he had heard my thoughts. And then the other poor souls accepted it too, rejoicing and praising the Lord God because no ordinary person would give them money out of the blue. I too was quite astonished, for to make that offering, I had pulled out exactly 1,400 rubles (no more, no less) - just enough to give each beggar two 100-ruble notes. A coincidence, a trifle? Perhaps. But for some reason, I took note of that coincidence, that trifle.

"And you, bridegroom, compose some ditties about us too, your wedding party guests!" the cripple kept urging me, laughing, and joyfully wiping away tears, instructing me not to delay but to compose as soon as I got home.

His naivety and delight were so sincere that I smiled too. As I walked away, he waved his sticks and made it out onto the sidewalk to shout in a thin falsetto voice:

"It's your wedding to the heavens!"

It was an overreach, an overplaying of what had occurred. Everything inside me clenched at his piercing cry. I hurried my pace and disappeared around the corner without looking back.

"Hey, compatriot!" someone called right in my ear.

I turned to see a ruby-red Mercedes moving slowly alongside me, with a young bald man in a yellow leather jacket leaning out the side window, sporting a square, brand-like scar on his forehead.

"Here, take this, brother," he said, holding out some reddish bill to me.

"Ten rubles?!" I thought, surprised.

"Compatriot, where to go, where's the market?" he asked as if he were a foreigner.

"Which market?"

"I don't care which one!"

"How's that?!" I didn't understand. "There's the new market, and the old one."

"Like I said, I don't care… Just as long as it's a market!"

I gave him directions to the old market - it was closer.

The car dipped slightly, then silently took off and soon disappeared behind the buildings. Smirking, I pocketed the money that had been sitting alongside hundreds just a minute before. Say what you will, but Doublenose's predictions about money flowing to me like bewitched turned out to be true.

PART FIVE

CHAPTER 38

I was sitting at a real executive-style double pedestal desk, looking out the window at the square and beyond. Beyond... Above the treetops, I could see the red edge of the Kremlin wall, and behind it the white, sugar-like Sentinel Tower. I could also see the garden next to the wall and the oldest monument to the leader of the world proletariat in modern Russia. Back in the day, Doublenose and his comrades used to run their business right beside this monument. Doublenose did not let me down - in the spring he found and helped me buy a three-room apartment.

I stood up from the desk and began looking around again, as if I had just arrived there for the first time. It was hard to get used to being the sole owner of these remarkable chambers.

The bathroom and toilet were separate. Halogen bulbs stared at me from the suspended ceiling like the eyes of Argus. The tulip-shaped sink and the bathtub were whiter than snow, and the walls around them were tiled with a whitish swirl pattern. Heated floors were installed in the hallway and the kitchen. The toilet was equipped with an electronic clock with a calendar and a fragrance dispenser. All faucets, fixtures, and chandeliers were imported. Doublenose had recently come over and said he'd never seen a kitchen like this anywhere else. The washing machine and refrigerator were General Electric, the microwave and dishwasher were Bosch, the stove was Electrolux. All appliances were housed in a white plastic Finnish cabinet system. Worth mentioning were also parquet floors, double-paned windows, textured wallpaper - in a word, the renovation cost as much as the apartment itself. As for the furniture, there was a mirrored wardrobe, a plastic shelving unit, an Italian sofa and matching armchairs that felt like you were sitting on a cloud. What more could you wish for?! I had furnished all the rooms except for the study. Just the two-pedestal desk I mentioned, a chair, two hooks on the wall (with my and Rozochka's blanket coats hanging on them), and a mattress pad with two sheets and a pillow on the floor. The mattress and linens were a gift from the dorms - a kind of dowry. I remember being overjoyed by this dowry. I put it in the back seat of the taxi - Alina Spiridonovna came running out, kissed me on the cheek, and burst into tears:

"Mitenka, who will we pity and take care of now?! You were the most wretched, the most… God forbid!"

I sniffled too. Silly Alina Spiridonovna, but such a good heart. Better than the neighbour Toma's - she stuck her head out the window in her checked sweater and started shouting:

"Mitya, Mitya…if you ever feel yearning, you are welcome back!"

"Okay, okay, I'll keep that in mind for sure!" I shouted back, quickly getting into the taxi, because more windows were opening, and many residents were loudly wondering: "Is that the one who…? Look at him, all dressed up, in a cab!" (And so on…)

Why was I so happy about the dowry? Why did I take the stupid iron? Why didn't I throw away the blanket coats? I have no idea. I hadn't been selling poems or plays since August - I sold everything, even cleaned out some of the publisher's "backlog." My literary name had risen so high that I was even featured on a radio show, where some young poet was talking about the great poetic constellations: Pushkin, Lermontov, Tukay and, of course, Slyozkin!.. However, it was Tolya Croesus's custom order that prompted me to delve into the "backlog." Out of an old friendship, he asked me to come up with something like a colouring book for children - "Colour It Yourself." He wanted something grandiose with instructions on what to write about, and he would write the verses no worse than any other. I immediately remembered the oratorio of the Invisible Incognito but warned Tolya that my fee would be no less than ten per cent of the price he set for his poems, a major part of the publication. If Tolya valued his work at two hundred thousand, then my cut would be twenty thousand dollars, and if ten, then mine would be a thousand. (I didn't care at all whether Croesus paid for the oratorio or not – I got it for nothing anyway.) However, a week later we met (his bodyguards delivered me), and he pulled out fifteen thousand, which I could hardly believe - I'd never made that much from my work!

I took ten thousand from him and asked a favour: to talk to the drivers who delivered cars from abroad.

"I'll buy cars in Germany, they are duty-free now, and resell here. I feel worn out after the 'Duets of Leaders'," I lied blatantly. (Now that I was mingling with businessmen, I was soaking up their habits and lingo like a sponge.)

Tolya didn't help me because of the discount of five thousand, he helped as one poet to another. By then, I had already surpassed many "New Russians" in business, and it wasn't at all because of any supernatural abilities – I did not develop any. After my encounter with the beggars at the church, and especially after meeting my fellow countryman who gifted me a ten from the window of his ruby Mercedes, I truly believed Doublenose's prophecy of money craving to be mine.

For those who want to go into business, my best advice would be to feel confident that no matter how things go, the money will end up being yours.

I was the first in the city to get the used imported car trade going and did not steer clear of domestic models either (West Germans were selling them for next to nothing). It's just that I didn't advertise myself. A 'poet-businessman' sounds as vulgar as a 'young poet.' Doublenose handled all the paperwork and management, but the idea of a joint venture with the Germans was mine, and so was the financing. I risked everything I had with no regrets, entirely convinced that all the money would be mine in the end. Besides, the risk helped me forget about Rozochka. That is, I didn't really forget her, but the memory of her faded. Deep down, I sensed a proportional relationship: the more money I had, the less Rozochka might need it.

It seemed impossible, but unemployed people somehow self-organised around my money, and within two months we were hauling cars on double-decker trailers around the clock.

The company went bust in mid-September, but I had already sold it to Doublenose by then. I was tired of making money for money's sake. By that time, I already had over two hundred thousand dollars in cash, not counting three cars for sale. I was tired of myself too - money without Rozochka was meaningless; like I said, its underlying meaning was distancing her farther and farther from me over time.

I don't know why, but Doublenose got into trouble soon afterwards. His company was put up for auction, and Feofilaktovich even considered selling his major venture, the summer beer garden covered in camouflage netting and surrounded by a red brick wall reminiscent of the Kremlin wall. I liked that wall. The beer garden without Doublenose and Doublenose without the beer garden would be like separated twins.

"How much do you need to get them off your back?"

"Seventy thousand," he blurted out without blinking, then immediately explained that he needed that amount to buy a building in the park for a restaurant. "It's going for next to nothing, the city needs cash…"

He also had his eye on the abandoned old department store building that had been standing with its windows broken for three years, but that property could only be obtained through the city administration. Doublenose was perfectly in his element in the new era, and with his Kremlin walls he brought his own unique beauty to it.

"Okay, I'll give you five thousand more, but on the condition that half of the restaurant's income is mine."

Alexei Feofilaktovich probably remembered September 22, 1992 for the rest of his life - that was the day I gave him seventy-five thousand dollars in cash, no receipts. I will also remember that day, and not because it was my twenty-fourth birthday. On that day, I finally got a word from Rozochka. She was congratulating me on my birthday and giving me a Crimean address, with "forever yours" written at the end. (This was something new, both scary and wonderful.)

Yes, on September 22nd I was the happiest person. I sent Rozochka a telegram with my (that is, my own, not the dorm's) address and apologised that I couldn't send her any money for now (newly independent Ukraine wasn't accepting transfers). I proposed all kinds of options for meeting up, but in the end, she would have to decide herself.

And she decided. In the last week of November (I had just received my second military draft notice), a summons came with just two words: "Come, waiting."

After that first telegram, I was a bit surprised by the terseness, but she was waiting for me, and that was the main thing. To avoid complications, I bought myself a military deferment for three thousand dollars, certifying me as disabled and exempted from military service for life. The major who sold it to me said that somewhere in the paperwork he would note that I was cross-eyed and missing both legs. I was wondering if that was too much, but he reasonably pointed out:

"A man with no legs cannot be summoned with a draft notice, and your absence can always be explained by treatment at some health resorts."

CHAPTER 39

I arrived in Simferopol at 10 a.m. The plane was almost empty – a terrifying sight, just twenty people or so in the huge airliner. I had a bag over my shoulder stuffed with all sorts of gifts, and three bottles of Armenian brandy packed separately. The customs officer (this was not only unusual but outrageous) turned my stuff upside down, then mumbled that only two bottles of alcohol were allowed. He spoke Ukrainian but mumbled so badly that I could barely understand him. It seemed to me that he was mumbling deliberately to enhance the sense of Ukraine now being a foreign country with a foreign language. He took one bottle and handed me over to two louts who subjected me to a full body search, even counting the money in my wallet. Luckily, Doublenose had suggested hiding the dollars in my underwear – they would have found them under my armpits.

I went outside through a corridor of cab drivers offering their services to take me to any city or village in Crimea.

It was sunny, quiet, a real Indian summer. I couldn't believe it was December. The Lada driver who agreed to take me to Chernomorsk said there had been snow almost all November, and even in recent days the wind was downright squally, and only today...

The two hours from Simferopol to Chernomorsk flew by unnoticed. I was mostly thinking about meeting Rozochka. But I noticed the road from Pribrezhnoye to Evpatoria, wide and straight as a runway, with the emerald sea immediately to the left, sighing lazily, sleepy, and incredibly vast.

After Evpatoria, the landscape changed to brown hills, grey flocks of sheep, lush green winter crops and shelterbelts with lots of magpie nests. Well, that's about all I remember.

I don't know, maybe it was the sea and the weather that affected me, or maybe it was my state of mind, but when I saw the rustic house with peeling plaster revealing the yellow crumbling shell stone underneath, when I saw the sagging roof covered with some greenish, mossy tiles, I thought I was in the wrong place. The dilapidation and neglect were disconcerting. I could not imagine Rozochka living in such an unsightly dwelling. However, the street and house number displayed on the leaning facade left no doubt.

I didn't trust the barn lock (my Moscow experience came to the fore). I pushed the door which opened as if it had fallen into a hole, leaving the hinge and lock on the doorframe. Calling out to the owners, I stepped into the hallway – not a sound. I found the door and entered the hut (it was indeed a hut, not a house or a cottage).

The unpretentious furnishings matched the overall setting. There was a window to my left under which stood a large table covered with a faded oilcloth and supporting a portable two-burner gas stove set upon four bricks, fuelled by a large gas cylinder by the wall. A metal mesh bed sat on the opposite side of the room (such beds were already being thrown away even in villages by the time of my childhood.) On the bed, there was a feather mattress covered with a bedspread and two pillows under a crocheted cover. A light blue curtain partitioned the hut space. The curtain was half-drawn, and in the corner, between the windows, I saw an icon of the Virgin and a little flame in a saucer below it. I involuntarily crossed myself and felt my restraint fade: I was not alone in the hut. Still not sure I was at Rozochka's place, I carefully proceeded behind the curtain, and was immediately enveloped by the warmth of Rozochka's breath. I laughed involuntarily, having guessed before knowing it: she's here, Rozochka is here! It was only later that I saw the magazine clippings on the wall – Princess Diana, Prince Charles, Mother Teresa, and the Queen of England. Below them, was a shining (it literally shone) beaded inscription that already was familiar to me: "Manchester City."

There was another table, this time, covered not with oil-cloth but with a fresh tablecloth, so snowy white and lacy that everything around seemed snowy white and bright. Two hard chairs and an iron bed under a burgundy blanket did not diminish the significance of the icon with its little oil lamp. This part of the room looked almost heavenly neat, maybe because of the sunrays shining through the tulle window curtains onto the inscription and snowy white table.

I put my bag right on the two chairs, and lay down on the bed without undressing (I only took off my half-boots), immediately feeling as cosy and relaxed, as if I had returned home to my mother. Of course, I fell asleep. The night on the train, the commotion at the airport, the flight, the taxi – it all caught up with me, and I slept like a baby.

I woke up to a soft crying, interrupted by Rozochka's hoarse, half-voiced exclamations: "Enough, you've had enough! Better take the syringe; my hands are shaking as if I've been stealing chickens."

A thin, inconsolable lament interrupted the crying: "What are you doing, my dear, making your own mother destroy you?! Lord, what is this?!"

"Quiet, you'll wake him up… Destroy…"

Silence, a rustle, a soft thud of something falling into a bucket, a sudden snap of a released rubber tourniquet and a long, relieved sigh. Silence. And again, barely suppressed sobbing.

"My dear, well what did they diagnose?"

"The medical board?! What do you think?" Rozochka took a deep breath again and began soothing her mother in a gentle voice.

Even for me, who knew Rozochka well, it was hard to imagine that just a minute ago she had been speaking to her mother in exclamations.

"If you believe them, Mum, they already promised me… but here I am, alive and unharmed. Do you want me to dance, or shall I pour you a little drink?"

Judging by the creaking floorboards and the exclamation "Oops!" she actually performed some sort of pirouette pas and laughed almost silently. I too, almost laughed, her laughter was so contagious to me. Then came a gurgling and clinking – Rozochka had poured liquor into a glass.

"Mum, drink up."

"I will, just wait a minute," she blew her nose, overcoming her sobbing, "today is not a bad day for a drink, today is a big holiday: the Presentation of Mary. Today the lamp has been burning since morning, and look, how fortunate – we have a dear guest."

Rozochka's mother rose from the bed. The creaking floorboards revealed her entering the living room and approaching the icon, then apparently crossing herself and standing there for a while, praying silently. Then, already in the hallway, after a gulp of her drink, which provoked a peal of laughter from Rozochka, she said loudly and somewhat melodically, as if pleading: "Holy Lady, be glorified! Virgin Mary, be glorified, be glorified!"

I froze, because I heard the creaking of the floorboards again, or rather, I heard nothing but felt Rozochka's presence. She examined me carefully for a while, and then plopped down on top of me, not caring at all that I was resting.

And then everything whirled and spun and remained forever in my memory: the radiant kindness of Rozochka's eyes, the impenetrable darkness of the windows (half-asleep, I couldn't believe it was already night) and the stoutness of Raisa Maksimovna, Rozochka's mother. I had imagined her as slender and delicate as Rozochka, judging by her soft crying, but in fact, she weighed no less than a hundred kilos. Every time I asked Raisa Maksimovna if I should pour her some brandy, she would nod in agreement and ask (this was her trademark joke) to call her officially Brezhnev. Rozochka would laugh at her failing memory - not Brezhnev, but Gorbachev[99]! Her mother would reply that I should pour her half a glass, regardless.

---

99   Michail Gorbachev's wife's full name was Raisa Maksimovna Gorbacheva.

CHAPTER 40

Rozochka and I lived in Chernomorsk for almost three months. That is, not only in Chernomorsk as such - in Crimea. At first, we stayed at a sanatorium in Yevpatoria, then in Yalta. In all the sanatoriums, Rozochka would somehow establish close contact with male doctors and would be admitted to a city hospital with kidney or liver pains. Then I would visit her, give her money, and the next day take away whole crates of morphine ampoules.

Yes, Rozochka was taking morphine... Yes, after arriving home, she got a job at the hospital with the sole purpose of obtaining drugs by any means possible. Yes, she involved her mother in illegal activities, and because of that her mother was quietly demoted from her position as head nurse to a cleaner, just so she wouldn't be fired, out of respect for her past as an outstanding worker, awarded the Order of the Badge of Honour. Raisa Maksimovna's portrait is probably still displayed somewhere on a long-forgotten District Board of Honour.

Yes, I became Rozochka's accomplice. Yes, I first helped her inject herself and then started taking morphine myself. I did not get addicted though: instead of euphoria, morphine caused me bouts of nausea and drowsiness, and I stopped injecting.

I won't deny that I broke the law for Rozochka's sake. Moreover, I felt no remorse, not even the slightest regret.

By the time I arrived, Rozochka was already suffering from a host of diseases. Worst of all, as I realised later, her chronic myeloid leukaemia (I pronounced it syllable by syllable to get it out) had flared up again. At first, I singled out kidney stones among other diseases. Rozochka was first prescribed morphine to cope with kidney colic. This happened several times and triggered addiction. It's truly fantastic when just a small injection turns your suffering into blissful euphoria. Seeing these terrible kidney colic attacks, I paid no attention to the relapse of her leukaemia. I had disregarded it before, was even thankful for it, for Rozochka once told me that leukaemia brought her to Moscow and to the medical college. Moreover, she never mentioned it after we got married. So, I didn't pay attention to myeloid leukaemia and concentrated on Rozochka's kidneys, and even suggested that Rozochka go for treatment to the "foreign" Truskavets. And then, after Yalta (we were already returning home, to Raisa Maksimovna), she asked me to stop again at any sanatorium or resort in Yevpatoria.

We stopped. Her joints started hurting, she developed a fever, but most of all she was bothered by sweating. I bought five flasks of "Chanel" perfume that looked like shiny brass cartridges at the Simferopol market. One flask barely lasted a day for Rozochka. I assumed she had some kind of flu or a regular cold. But she gave me a pitiful smile - "if only!" - and sobbed softly... It was the first time she had cried in front of me, and the first time I felt that money meant nothing!

Of course, I argued, we had already been through this together once before, the leukaemia got scared and retreated, and it would flee now as well! She liked me not thinking much of her illness. After injecting a dose, as she was falling asleep, she explained that the common name for her disease was blood cancer.

For me, this was the worst of all revelations.

She fell asleep, and I stepped out onto the balcony. The dim glow of electric lights, rain, the honking of harbour tugs and the dense, splashing patter of raindrops on the woven white tabletop met me there. I sat in a rocking chair, not caring at all about the gusts of damp wind and streams of cold water running down my back. I felt shaken: she was my wife, we had lived together, I had embraced and kissed her countless times, yet I did not know of her illness. That is, I knew, but didn't know it was fatal. Myeloid leukaemia - blood cancer! I had never felt death's breath so close before. My heart was sinking - what good were money and prosperity? I didn't want to live. Standing on that balcony, I even thought how good it would be for me to get soaked and pick up some bilateral pneumonia.

I returned to the room completely chilled and shattered, but a hot bath and shower helped me fall asleep instantly, and in the morning my whole body was literally ringing with an excess of energy. Rozochka also felt better, and we left for Chernomorsk without delay. There was a roundabout right at the entrance to the village, where Rozochka asked the taxi driver to turn right, towards the village store. I thought it was to buy something, but instead, Rozochka paid the driver and we made our way through the wet weeds to the old cemetery.

I don't like cemeteries in any form. I was carrying a bag and tried not to fall behind Rozochka. The concrete monuments were greyish green, with polished plaques resembling half-un-folded flags, each with an embossed star filled with red lead. Not a tree, not even a bush - just occasional crosses, also of stone or concrete.

Rozochka led me to a brown little grave with a plaque, as all others.

"You see, this is where my father Fyodor Nikolaevich Purpurik is buried," said Rozochka, stepping aside a little to make room for me too. "Your father-in-law."

She laughed briefly and immediately became pensive. It wasn't a laugh, really, but some kind of sudden chuckle, as if she had heard something from the other side. I felt my hair standing up on my arms, but the wave of sudden fear subsided and ebbed away the very next second. Smiling at me from the portrait was a nice young man, born on May 27, 1950, and deceased on October 28, 1977.

"Now I can see how much I look like him," said Rozochka. "He was twenty-seven, like Lermontov. In three years, Mitya, you'll catch up with him."

"I've already caught up with my father."

Rozochka's feet gave way; I caught her and sat her down on the bag because everything around was damp after the night rain. But Rozochka protested - she did not forget for a minute that the bag contained boxes of morphine. In the end, we sat down on a neighbouring bench, and for the first time, Rozochka asked me, apologetically and sobbing, to give her an injection. No, no, this was not a desecration of the ultimate resting place. Her bluish face showed she was on the verge of fainting.

She told me that her father operated a truck-mounted crane and had hit a high-voltage line at the construction of a greenhouse for the local boarding school. They said that if he had been wearing rubber boots, nothing would have happened to him. But the thing was, no one in Chernomorsk ever wore rubber boots, especially not in the dry autumn.

Rozochka came to after the injection, her face brightened. She pointed out to me that there was plenty of room for her mother to the left of the grave. And to the right of her father, let them bury her. It was distressing to listen to, and then there was another sudden nervous giggle - it ran and faded, but did not disappear, it froze at the tips of my hair.

"You see how much space there is to the right, there will be enough room for you too." I heard yet another hysterical giggle and sensed she could have lapsed into childhood after the injection. "You see, there's a slope towards the fence, I'll be very comfortable looking at the road," she said quite foolishly, as if talking about God knows what, not what she actually meant, and then got up and plopped down on the squelching grass next to a small mound.

To calm Rozochka down (the damp cemetery ground was hardly the best place to roll around), I lay next to her, just a little lower down. What caught my eye was the paved road that ran up from the valley, and right here came closest to the cemetery fence before veering upwards towards the store.

There was a small sidewalk on the other side of the road and several schoolchildren were walking along it wearing bright colourful backpacks:

"...She said it, but he didn't go, and she just gave him an F..."

"No, no, no, she said nothing..."

"You see, Mitenka, what a delightful view opens from here. I always loved watching the road as a child. I kept thinking, stupid me, that a prince from Manchester City would come for me one day… no, not a prince, but some very handsome doctor in a white coat."

I stood up and told Rozochka it was time for us to go. I was in a very determined mood, but to my surprise, she didn't object, got up, and we went back the same way, through the gap in the fence. As we were going down the sidewalk towards the valley, she stopped opposite her father's grave and asked very seriously if I had remembered her request. I said yes, I had remembered. And then, as if thinking aloud, she said that the burial would have to be done in secret or with some very "substantial" permission (that's how she put it), because this cemetery had now been closed for about five years. She also hoped that her father Fyodor Nikolaevich might somehow help with her burial arrangements. Suddenly, hearing her express her thoughts out loud became too heavy for me. Then, with no connection to what she had just been talking about, she asked if I knew that her neighbour in Moscow had called her a "missionary of love"?

"Yes," I said. "I know."

"You probably thought something bad about me?! Admit it, admit it!"

She started to playfully and wholeheartedly tousle me, the way children do. Almost in passing, she mentioned that when Mother Teresa founded the first home for the dying in Calcutta, she dubbed the helpers who joined her "missionaries of love." Rozochka laughed again, with some kind of unspent inner pride, which immediately shattered and reduced to dust anything previously associated with her potential infidelity. It was me - and my understanding of her. We were so close, eye to eye, that even if we suddenly found ourselves on different planets, even the thinnest of blades would not fit between us. Me - and immediately her. Her - and immediately me, even across thousands of light-years…

CHAPTER 41

I told Rozochka about our three-room apartment for the first time after our visit to the cemetery. I was deeply depressed that she didn't envision any future for herself beyond her father's grave and wanted to distract her. But from the very first words, my story captivated Rozochka. Even her mother fell silent, as if she had vanished, only interjecting to clarify details about the hot and cold water.

Rozochka was interested in everything: the layout of the rooms, kitchen, bathroom, toilet, closets, and balcony. She asked about the quality of the renovations, ceiling heights, window, and door sizes, about the wallpaper in the rooms and tiles in the entryway. She demanded detailed descriptions of the mirrored wardrobe and chandeliers several times. I remember when I said the floors in the toilet and entryway were heated, neither Rozochka nor Raisa Maksimovna initially understood what I meant. Only later, when I explained it in detail, did Rozochka admiringly clap her hands and Raisa Maksimovna, pushing aside the curtain, joyfully handed me an empty glass, saying, "Well, you're lying! Okay, fine, I agree, pour me some!"

Rozochka and I burst into laughter. Afterwards, I often told stories about the apartment. These tales seemed to really unite us strongly.

"Tell me, tell me every tiny detail," Rozochka would insist, and sometimes she would fall asleep, without any need for injections, listening to me.

Rozochka turned out to be a strong-willed person; she began to fight her morphine addiction. Unlike me, she controlled her imagination, affected by her condition. She was absolutely delighted when I first told her about my hunger hallucinations; it was like getting to know each other all over again.

"Mityenka, you're my Prince Charles, my real doctor in a white coat! Mityenka, stop, I'm going to cry!" she doubled over laughing.

Our getting to know each other united and strengthened us so much that the resolve and courage of one immediately became the resolve and courage of the other. The same went for lack of will and cowardice, however.

One day, Rozochka felt much better. She was sweeping the clay floor in the hallway and playfully demanded that I turn on the heated floors as she sang, "My darling, take me with you…"

I lay on Rozochka's bed, barely holding back tears of inexplicable happiness and bitterness. Then I went outside (it was late February), the sun was already warm, and white snowdrops had already sprouted and bloomed from under the limestone rocks next to the front door. I presented them to Rozochka, and after breathing warmly on them, she suddenly said I should go to Yevpatoria and buy tickets home for all three of us, to our city apartment. Yes, that's exactly what she said – home, to our city apartment.

I bought the tickets, not for the train as she thought, but for a plane instead. I arranged with the taxi driver who had brought me from Yevpatoria to deliver us to Simferopol airport in a week. And he did, so on the day of our flight, we had time for lunch in Moscow. Raisa Maksimovna hid our undeclared "medicines" in her voluminous clothing – she could barely squeeze through the metal detector. And there was so much hassle with her that in the end, and to avoid keeping other passengers waiting, police officers and airport security alike waved her through without checking.

In Moscow, I suggested getting Rozochka to the Botkin Hospital to see some prominent doctors, but she said "no" so sternly that I didn't bring it up again…

For anyone thinking I spent a lot of money in Crimea, I can only say, absolutely not! The difference in prices in Ukraine versus Russia was astronomical. Even morphine was going for next to nothing. We spent far more in just half a day in Moscow than we had in an entire month in Crimea. True, I didn't scrimp; right after the airport, we checked in at the Sputnik Hotel, and there in the lobby, in front of Rozochka, I exchanged three thousand dollars. I thought the wads of cash would delight her, but to my regret, she looked at them with a sort of frightened astonishment.

"Mityenka, did they really pay you so much for poems?!"

She asked me to read her some poems, for the first time after prohibiting such. I read the dedication – "Cursed be poetic words and rhyme …" Rozochka was stunned:

"Mityenka, I'll never believe you had a woman like that. Admit you made it up?!"

I felt awkward. She suddenly changed the subject, saying I had become a much better writer. This really touched me, and I felt that Rozochka had become different, less aggressive. Before, she would never have let me off the hook, and my awkwardness would only have spurred her on. I admitted that I no longer wrote at all – I had no urge, having bid farewell to my Muse while a guest in Heaven.

Of course, I made a blunder there. But she reacted in a new way again! She smiled and raised her eyebrows quizzically: "Your Muse?!" And then, with soft, cheerful regret, singing the words, she said: "What a sha-ame, such a sha-ame, because now your poems are real, Mityenka, more precious than money."

It was so unexpected and so pleasing that I promised her: there would be more poems, and suggested we go shopping or to some park or zoo. The park and zoo were closed, but we ate pastries anyway and then went to a department store.

She tried on a raincoat, Italian boots with an unthinkable number of buckles and studs, a dress of a mix of dark burgundy and dark blue, and another, patterned with golden polka dots to the waist and alternating green sections in the skirt. She looked like a schoolgirl in that polka dot dress, it suited her so well, she was so beautiful in it that salesgirls from the shoe department brought her a pair of white pumps. (Unbeknown to Rozochka, I bought those too.)

We got Raisa Maksimovna a burgundy raincoat, a Reebok tracksuit, and a pair of brown shoes – a men's size 42 - which had ended up in the ladies' department because of their colourful laces. We also got Rozochka a Reebok outfit and some very nice Nike trainers. I didn't buy anything for myself.

"You'll be amazed," I said, "when you open the closet at home. I used to go to Germany and brought many clothes from there!"

Back at the hotel, Raisa Maksimovna was dead asleep in an armchair, her arm dangling to the floor, and her famous dark brown bottle with the screw cap sitting on the table in front of her. The bottle was empty, and I refilled it with Stolichnaya vodka. Rozochka gave me a look but said nothing.

We arrived home in the morning.

When you come from a provincial town to Moscow, the difference is negligible, but when you come from Moscow, the difference is enormous. No taxis, no porters – nothing. I had to go back to the platform twice for the suitcases and Raisa Maksimovna's little trunk. Everything was cordoned off by the police. It turned out that overnight a fire had gutted the station building. Many of the arrivals took this as a bad omen. Raisa Maksimovna was so frightened that she was ready to turn back to Chernomorsk. But it all worked out fine.

Finally, we made it up to the third floor, huffing and puffing. Raisa Maksimovna sat on her little trunk amidst the bags, packages, and suitcases "like a king at a birthday party..." or even like an ace of trumps. Now it was clear why, despite all Rozochka's pleas, Raisa Maksimovna had insisted on bringing the trunk along – sitting on it she seemed truly invincible. I got flustered for some reason, and could almost physically sense the density of the surrounding silence as I fiddled with the lock. At last, the door opened to everybody's sigh of relief. Raisa Maksimovna exclaimed in astonishment:

"Another door?!"

Rozochka and I exchanged amused glances and began hauling in our belongings, laughing all the while. And then began the celebration of our souls. I don't know what words or concepts could express the joy and timidity, the soaring and plummeting.

No, there are no words for it!

Rozochka ran into the living room:

"Mi-tya! Mi-tyen-ka!" She threw herself into my arms, and all her feelings seemed captured in that embrace. And then – Raisa Maksimovna's voice, somehow frightened and amazed:

"Beau-tiful, beau-tiful… no, more than that – splendid!"

Raisa Maksimovna looked out the window at the golden dome of St. Sophia Cathedral, straightened up slightly, crossed herself and bowed.

"Splen-did!"

She automatically reached for her dark brown bottle, but feeling Rozochka's gaze on her, suddenly became abashed and hid it behind her back with such childlike bewilderment that I felt sorry for Raisa Maksimovna, as if she were my mother too.

"Come on, come on, I double that," I interjected.

"Well then I want some too!" Rozochka exclaimed.

We each took a sip from the little bottle, and then wandered through the rooms, regarding everything as if it all were jointly gained possessions. Strangely enough, I felt like I too was entering those rooms for the first time, and just like them, ran my hands over the curtains and bedspreads and marvelled at the rugs and wallpaper, as if to say, "So this is how people live!" Only in the study, which contained practically nothing except a dormitory bed on the floor and two armchairs against the wall, did we not touch a thing. We all seemed to feel the difference in "temperature" strongly and froze like statues. Good old Raisa Maksimovna came to the rescue:

"Thank God, at least one livable room!"

And then the housewarming began, a truly glorious celebration.

CHAPTER 42

Alexey Feofilaktovich finally found his calling! The once enormous and tasteless one-storey building now looked like something out of a fairy tale with its arches, columns, balconies, a high tiled roof, and pointed dormer windows. An ornamental brickwork pattern decorated the brick chimney stacks.

"Well, poet?!"

"I can't believe my eyes!"

We hugged. Doublenose was unrecognisable in his black overcoat, red scarf, and fancy cap. Underneath the coat, he wore a white shirt and a tie - not Doublenose, but a real diplomat or businessman.

"What did you expect, Mitya? They're putting me forward for the local council! I want you to be part of my team of trusted people."

So, this is the new Alexey Feofilaktovich!

We walked cautiously through the interior halls and rooms, surveying the ongoing renovations. Doublenose reminded me several times that he had been waiting for me, worried about the finishings. But there was no need to worry - he had three crews of Ukrainian craftsmen doing the work, true masters of their trade. In the large hall, I suggested the mezzanine would be ideal for the most prestigious tables, so the railing and main chandelier should be works of art. To my surprise, Doublenose took out a notebook and immediately jotted down my comment.

I was especially taken with the small round room behind the mezzanine, seating thirty to fifty people. The round windows looked like portholes, and the glass doors featured a clipper ship (the familiar "Cutty Sark") just like on the packaging from a Moscow tea shop.

"This will be the Poetry Room," a loud, powerful voice behind me announced.

It belonged to a young man with a huge, furrowed brow and an entirely bearded face. From the shoulders up, he was a copy of Karl Marx, yet with his very lean body, he looked more like a chicken with a lion's head. His eyes glinted with a hungry fire, and he shouted as he spoke, glancing at Doublenose's briefcase (which presumably held wages).

"I'm a professional, and I have paintings I'd be willing to part with for a nice compensation, of course."

We were introduced - Nikolai Tryapkin! No, he wasn't a poet, but a painter and restorer. That was in the past, though; now he was freelancing, working here because he had little children to feed. We chatted briefly, agreeing that he would paint Rozochka's portrait. I felt pity for the lion-headed chick, as he reminded me of my own hungry days.

Doublenose outlined the overall situation: the city council had bought out his company that hauled cars from Europe on very favourable terms. Pleased, he invited me to see the renovations underway at the former central department store. The connection between selling his firm and buying the old mall was a no-brainer, but I don't like counting other people's money, even though Doublenose's money was mine to some extent.

"You mention selling the company, and you invite me to see renovations at the mall, but not a word about the restaurant - what do Lemonich or Tolya Croesus think about it?"

Doublenose was stunned by my sagacity. We immediately went to see Tolya.

To my surprise, Tolya Croesus didn't want to hear a thing about the restaurant business. A controlling stake split into three? Why would he need that? He was busy buying up wonderful poems to publish in a book under the pen name "Dmitry Slyozkin."

"What do you think, Mitya, would they allow a free book launch at the 'Unexpected Joy' or 'Scarlet Rose' poetry club?"

Long story short, not only did he decline our business proposal, but also said (which really baffled me) that a talented person like myself should have been running some respected establishment long ago, one where creative people could at least occasionally gather and expose ordinary folks to their great works.

During this strange conversation, Doublenose kept nodding, agreeing with Tolya and rolling his eyes like Titian's "Penitent Magdalene," clearly playing the role of the ordinary people.

Unlike Tolya Croesus, Lemonich was brief and clear. He didn't beat around the bush, immediately stating that he and his partners had already bought 50% of the shares from Doublenose. But now Alexey Feofilaktovich had the controlling stake in the old mall, which was quite the lucrative deal, so he'd have to cough up some cash too. Soon he'd be ceding the beer bar to his old partners, Tutankhamun and company.

"It's time for a reshuffle. The city council is a place for a proper businessman, the CEO of the mall, not just some bar owner."

Lemonich casually asked my opinion on Doublenose's candidacy, whether he might embarrass himself. I said my opinion hardly mattered. And besides, if they'd already bought 50%, I had no objection to them buying out my share too - for no less than 75,000, the amount I had given Alexey Feofilaktovich six months earlier for this very restaurant idea.

"Ah, so you did invest cash!" Lemonich happily confirmed. "And, as we've discovered, with no paperwork?"

Doublenose immediately did some arithmetic in his notebook and shrugged – yes, that's correct.

And then Lemonich surprised me even more than Tolya Croesus. He said the money issue didn't reflect well on me as a businessman, but what's bad for a businessman is always good for a poet.

"And a poet," Lemonich summed up, raising his index finger, "cannot possibly be a bad guy!"

He noted that virtually every respected person in town, himself included, had bought marvellous masterpiece poems from me. And now the respected people needed a reliable person who knew not just the Orthodox God, but gods too - and the choice fell on me, Dmitry Slyozkin.

"You've been elected as an arbitrator. Once a year, on New Year's Eve, you'll settle disputes like Solomon between the people who chose you, and only you, for this role. And to ensure your independence as a judge, the restaurant in the park will be yours alone. Accept it as a token of society's gratitude…"

He also said society would ensure I had no competitors.

If I hadn't already been involved in the GKChP coup or in the "white socks" democratic movement, I might not have avoided Puplievich's offensive distrust. But I had been involved…so I just took it as information, merely asking:

"Is it possible the arbitrator might have to settle a dispute between, say, the editor of the 'N City Gazette' and some other high-ranking official?"

Lemonich chuckled, wiped his completely bald head with a handkerchief, and stood up from the table.

"Anything is possible, Mitya," he patted my shoulder, "whoever has money calls the tune…But a good person is more precious than money!"

We went outside together.

"You see, Filimon Puplievich, I want to return all the money to society because with this money I've been bought outright. What independence is there?"

"Don't you ever do that under any circumstances, Mitya. As long as the 'obshchak[100]'…as long as society is investing in you, you're safe."

He admitted his own involvement in my selection as an arbitrator, saying he was inclined to help me. I thanked him, to which he replied that I had once greatly helped him too. As he got into his car, Lemonich advised me to come up with a name for the poetry club, have no worries and just go on writing poems.

My talk with Doublenose was no less astonishing. When I asked how he had decided to sell the beer bar, his pride and joy, Doublenose just smirked - his partners had nothing to do

---

100   Collective treasury of one or several organized criminal groups.

with it, the bar's new owner was actually Tolya Croesus. Not that Doublenose cared, Lemonich was right – being a councilman as the mall's CEO is one thing, and as the owner of an around-the-clock beer joint, another.

"I guess you'll be handing over the restaurant construction matters to me now?"

"No way," Doublenose replied.

He had a turnkey renovation contract and didn't intend to end it because thanks to the "obshchak" (unlike Lemonich, he didn't self-correct) he was getting construction materials not just for the restaurant, but his mall too.

Doublenose promised to complete renovations by May 1st, and just like Lemonich advised me to write poems and think of a worthy name for the poetry club.

The circle was complete.

CHAPTER 43

We spent the entire month of March at home. Not literally, of course, but still… Raisa Maksimovna would get up before dawn and, wary of all the kitchen appliances, would wake up little Rosa too. That did not last long, however, and she soon became so adept that she even learned to use the microwave, entering the programme settings herself. She only used the dishwasher once, considering it a waste of money, but immediately took a liking to the washing machine, appreciating its wash quality, drying function, and even the rust-proof steel drum that wouldn't tear clothes under any circumstances. Its glass window especially charmed her, she liked observing the different wash cycles. In short, the "General Electric" appealed to Raisa Maksimovna so much that she even took offence at our Russian engineers:

"Why aren't they ashamed of themselves, inventing rockets, and satellites, but nothing decent for a regular Russian woman! I won't believe they lack the brains; they just drink all day long!"

Raisa Maksimovna trailed off and fell silent, evidently remembering her own dark brown little bottle. Be that as it may, she completely mastered the kitchen appliances and praised me constantly. She was firmly convinced that having such a kitchen would remain just a dream for most ordinary women for a very long time yet.

"Our bosses, whoever was at the top, stayed there," she reasoned. "The GKChP coup stirred them a bit, they circled around for a while, then settled even higher up, because it's most convenient to perch at the very top, closest to the crown."

I never contradicted Raisa Maksimovna about anything. Our conversations in Chernomorsk were mostly about the apartment and other mundane things, but after returning from Crimea I carefully avoided such topics. And it wasn't because I was following some cunning tactic, no, it came from the heart. Yes, "from the heart," and that's not just a pompous, empty phrase! Just think about it, there's an Italian pull-out sofa in the living room, and an extra-wide American bed in the bedroom. Yet Rozochka and I spend our days and nights in my study, on the floor. Why, for what reason are we lying on the dorm bed, happily covering ourselves with blankets, and feeling truly blissful?!

Raisa Maksimovna, on the other hand, enjoyed material things a lot. Once I told Rozochka that it was time for us to visit the artist. She tried to make excuses, as usual, but Raisa Maksimovna intervened:

"Let's go. I'll come along too, I'm tired of the courtyard gossip."

This was a hint at the gatherings near the building. I must say that the yard keeper and a certain circle of retirees (mostly those who earned their pensions by working in the Arctic regions) had welcomed her as one of their own.

"Well, what did you expect?! We've all been through hell and back in our lives, wherever we lived."

We walked through the park along the Kremlin wall, and Raisa Maksimovna marvelled at the knee-deep snow so late in the year. At her request, we sat down on a bench by the silent fountain, and she started talking again about how in Crimea it was already long past time to plant potatoes.

"Oh, come on, Ma," Rosa said; they had gradually started to bicker, not angrily but with the enjoyment characteristic of close people.

I felt good, I was smiling and thinking about the great kinship of souls. Indeed, the damp asphalt was steaming, rivulets were tinkling and shimmering like shoals of small fish, and it seemed to me that I could hear the rustle of porous snow settling under the trees of another park and another spring.

> Beneath the snow, spring lies so fine,
> A tender thing, with snowflake's grace.
> Yet sometimes one can faintly trace
> How life awakens, line by line,
> Through every drop on water's face.
>
> A tiny heart beneath the frost,
> It taps against the icy shell.
> It yearns for warmth and light, but lost
> In cold that casts the pond's ice spell.
>
> Oh, how these drops do vex the frost!
> On roofs and shutters, gardens glossed,
> He hangs them up as icy spears,
> To show his might, provoke our fears.

The harsher winter's cold embrace,
The more the warmth grew in its place,
Until the hour came at last,
The ice gave way, the frost had passed.

In torrents now the water runs,
Reclaims the world in its expanse,
In simpler terms, for all to see,
Spring has arrived for you and me.

We, the members of the school literary circle, sat on the bench and diligently listened to Valery Gubkin, our high school graduate, now a third-year journalism student at the Far East State University. We read him our new poems, and he immediately subjected them to analysis. His assessments are harsh and unsparing; he attentively listened to my poem "Spring Has Arrived" and asked for my notebook – flaws are more visible that way.

"Some people… bring out something that was never there in their feeble verses just with their beautiful voices," he explained, taking the notebook.

The hint was transparent, I braced myself for the worst, but Valery unexpectedly praised the poem and immediately advised me to write prose.

"Your imagery is good for a novel," he said. "Winter embodied in ice. Spring in warmth and water. It's too general, poetry is always concise and concrete. Cold is the executioner, period. 'Oh, how these drops do vex the frost! On roofs and shutters, gardens glossed, He hangs them up as icy spears, To show his might, provoke our fears.' And so on…"

Any hint of abandoning poetry was painful to me at that time, I felt offended. But now I sensed my kinship both with Valery Gubkin and those members of the literary circle who sat shoulder to shoulder with me on the bench back then. Perhaps the genetic kinship of souls can be not just physical, but also spiritual. That spring day of the past did reflect in today's, and did enrich it, after all. And why that one and not any other? There is something in human nature that makes people sympathetic to total strangers far away, with no benefit to themselves sometimes. It's not even my observation that some nations are much closer in mutual understanding of other nations, even hostile ones, than even of themselves of, say, a century ago. I think there is some genetic seed of spirituality in each of us, which possesses a selective memory and responds to just a limited selection of calls. These spiritual genetic seeds are dissolved in the very air we breathe, but are only accessible to us in moments of inspiration, or when we listen to poetry or music, in a word, when we contemplate beauty. Yes, it is when we contemplate beauty that our spiritual genes group together to enlighten us when we heed them. They exist in such an abundance of variations, like in an invisible kaleidoscope, that cloning them is out of the question.

A subtle scent of pine needles and melting snow wafted from the depths of the park. Rozochka nudged me in the side, chuckling:

"What thoughts are you lost in, big guy?"

In response, I recited "Spring Has Arrived."

We were silent for a while, and then Raisa Maksimovna said that even the sun became cheered up by the poem.

The restaurant, or rather, the literary club "Unexpected Joy" seemed to leap out from behind the trees. Its carved window casings, the curved roof, wooden columns framing the veranda and Italian arched windows - everything was in harmony and did indeed give unexpected joy to the eye, a genuine piece of a fairy tale.

Inside, work was in full swing inside. Parquet mosaics were being laid and polished in the halls and on stairway landings. Welding cast flashes of indigo and white on the kitchen walls. In the bathrooms, porcelain fixtures and tiles were being hung. Even for me, a rather frequent visitor here, the pace of construction seemed staggering - everything was changing literally in front of my eyes.

In Doublenose's absence, the construction manager became our guide. He was especially long-winded in the kitchen, showing us where the ventilation shafts ran, where the electric ovens and forced vents would be installed, and where the prep tables would go. Each time, he would glance at Raisa Maksimovna in a way that made me think he had mistaken her for the chef.

In the auditorium reminiscent of a ship's lounge the manager left us in the care of the artist - that same shaggy chicken who had promised to paint Rozochka's portrait. The artist immediately started shouting, which was his normal manner of talking. He handed us a huge folder of sketches of mezzanine hall decorations. Without giving anyone a chance to catch their breath, he seated Rozochka on a low podium and drew her against a backdrop of bright red velvet curtains that cascaded like a waterfall over the luxurious lid of a grand piano, while Raisa Maksimovna and I examined his sketches. Most amazingly, he captured her inner likeness, some subtle wistfulness and detachment. The shaggy chicken had evidently sensed that he had grasped something essential that exists beyond the portrait, yet without which no portrait is complete. He quickly hid the drawing – when the portrait was finished, he would reveal all.

We returned home through the park again, walking in silence until Raisa Maksimovna suddenly stopped and in trepidation, asked:

"Mitya, is the whole restaurant really yours?!"

I nodded.

"And the money the construction workers are paid with? … Well, the manager, for instance… do you pay his salary?"

"I do," I nodded again.

It seemed inappropriate to tell Raisa Maksimovna about some controlling stake, some shadow finances, or my new position as an arbitrator. She had asked directly, without beating around the bush, and deserved an equally direct, straightforward answer. Any references to Limonych, Tolya Croesus, or Double-nose could only confuse and even frighten her.

"That's an ocean of money!" she exclaimed and looked around.

"Don't be afraid, Ma, no one's going to arrest us… Mitya started out selling his poems, and now he's a sponsor goldminer!"

Rozochka and I exchanged amused glances: how perceptive

she was, how she could read me like a book!

"I'm not afraid, but my legs won't hold me - that's an ocean of money!" Raisa Maksimovna repeated, stunned, and then said emotionally and solemnly: "Children, take care of yourselves, with your money there will be plenty of folks eager to worm their way into your family and take advantage!"

And again, I didn't bother explaining that as a poet, I am mostly recognised not just in the criminal world, but in the milieu... or let's say, among the shadow establishment, and that's the most reliable insurance for money, if only because for them, going against recognised poets is far more dangerous than for the official critics, even though the latter can also be pretty ruthless thugs. In short, Rozochka and I only exchanged glances at her fears and burst out laughing, quite inappropriately but wholeheartedly.

We were too careless about her being stunned, being stunned rather than her fears. After this day, Raisa Maksimovna became withdrawn and even stopped mixing with her retiree lady friends. In the following days, it took considerable effort on my part to keep her from communing with her little brown bottle, until I eventually said:

"What are you worried about? The money is in Promstroibank, and to rob me, you'd first have to rob the bank. The real problem is that these days, the most dangerous robbers are the bankers themselves. But to turn out your pockets, they don't need to put a gun to your head or a knife to your throat, for that it's quite enough to make some deceitfully innocent little check mark your financial report."

Strangely enough, my words that one can now rob without knives and guns calmed her down. Raisa Maksimovna came to her senses and started going down to the courtyard gatherings again. I should have moderated my zeal at that point, but no… Seeing that the roads were almost cleared of snow, which now remained only on curbs, I suggested driving out of town for a spin - I had three cars, after all.

Rosa and I went to the garage and, as if in a fairy tale, looked at one car - enchanting, a coffee-coloured Lada model six, just like a toy. We glanced at the second - better than the first, a white Lada model seven, the sun playing on the nickel trim; the car was six years old, but you'd never tell. And when we approached the third, it was a veritable feast for the eyes, beyond imagination: a ruby-red Mercedes-Benz 190E. Rozochka was struck dumb. I pressed the alarm button, the Mercedes blinked its lights, I opened the right door - after you, Roza Fyodorovna!

She rose onto her tiptoes, looked at me in some special, unusual way, came closer and fell into my embrace:

"Well, Mitya, now even I'm scared. You're right behind Tvardovsky, and all other contemporary poets come after you!"

Why she said that, I don't know. And then she apologised for my jacket, jeans, mohair scarf…

"Oh, come on!" I stopped her.

It occurred to me she and I were two peas in a pod. Crude, of course, but that very idiom filled me with delight. Two peas in a pod!… If she hadn't mentioned Tvardovsky and apologised to me, I wouldn't have lost control, I would have suggested that we'd bring Raisa Maksimovna along another time, but as they say, I was knocked for a loop, in my fantasies I had already envisioned myself as the second after Tvardovsky, so without much thought I turned right, homeward. I so wanted to indulge Rozochka, and an orchestra of silver strings was playing in my soul.

When we drove into the courtyard, Raisa Maksimovna was sitting on a bench among her lady friends. Spotting the Mercedes, they fell silent, then burst out laughing in unison: Raisa Maksimovna had cracked a joke, clearly at us. Of course, she had no idea it was us pulling up.

Meanwhile, Rozochka got out of the car and, leaning lightly against the open door, called out loudly:

"Ma, come here, let's go!"

Raisa Maksimovna was dumbstruck, remaining seated as she was. Then she came to and shrugged:

"You mean me, dear? And who's in the car?"

Raisa Maksimovna approached quickly, but became hesitant at the last moment, peering apprehensively into the cabin and trying to make me out through the tinted windows. I opened the door and invited her to get in. Seeing that it really was her son-in-law behind the wheel, she clambered in clumsily, like Winnie-the-Pooh into Rabbit's hole, and plopped heavily onto the seat. The Mercedes sank gently and swayed from side to side, like a small boat.

I didn't notice when Rozochka got in, I didn't even hear the door shut. A gang of kids came running out of nowhere, peering into the cabin and making faces:

"Millionaires, millionaires!"

In response, Rozochka and I just laughed, and I slowly

pulled out onto the main street. We passed the telegraph office, the bridge over the Volkhov River, the Sadko Hotel, then turned onto an avenue of centuries-old linden trees leading out of town. I recalled Bunin: "Crimson rosehips bloomed all around, linden alleys stood dark[101] ..." No, no, rosehips never bloomed here. One could always glimpse the deserted floodplain meadows through the neat rows of trees lining both sides of the raised roadway. The meadows were covered in snow, unusually thick snow this winter. At any rate, whenever I glanced at the shoulder, the flickering of snow between the trees resembled a flurry, a flurry of snow, a white blizzard blowing at the road's edges.

"Good Lord! It's like being on a boat amid a white downpour," Rozochka exclaimed, turning to her mother.

I too looked at her in the rearview mirror. Clasping her hands across her chest and raising her eyebrows in amazement, she stared absent-mindedly at a single point.

"Ma, what's wrong?" Rozochka asked with concern.

"Nothing," Raisa Maksimovna replied without shifting her gaze, and smirked: "Millionaires!"

"Ah, so that's it," said Rozochka with feigned nonchalance.

"Never mind, look: spring, spring is all around!" I said, accelerating.

We were almost crawling as we crossed the "Blue Bridge" and now raced headlong toward the Moscow-St. Petersburg highway. I lowered the window slightly, the tyres hissing on the asphalt like fried eggs on a skillet. The sun was shining, bouncing, and gliding over the treetops, like a head bobbing carefree in the sea.

---

101   From "Dark alleys" by Ivan Bunin

"Yes, spring," Raisa Maksimovna agreed pensively, and for the first time glanced out the window. "Your father also used to drive, and we weren't millionaires either, yet we travelled plenty."

She mechanically patted her pockets searching for her dark brown little bottle, but didn't have a chance to pull it out – I braked near an enormous road sign at the upcoming fork.

"To Moscow or St. Petersburg, your choice!"

We got out of the car. A dark spruce forest stood before our eyes, exuding a fresh, even chilly scent of conifers. The woods lay far below the road embankment, so our gaze fell on the heavy spreading branches, some still bearing drifts of snow. Melting and falling, it crumbled into a powdery residue and the air around seemed to shimmer with the snow dust. The merry peeping of titmice broke the otherwise almost absolute silence, coming from the direction of a village stretching along the road behind the spruces. Somehow it only amplified the sense of hush and sweet shimmering.

"Oh, what bliss, it's like being surrounded by the water of life," said Raisa Maksimovna, inhaling deeply. "Back home in Crimea, it's like this in mid-July. By nightfall, the day's heat subsides, stars come out, the moon rises, you wade into the water, and the sea glows with a still, fiery radiance, and there is a ringing, resounding stillness all around – whatever you touch seems to resonate, to sing!"

She fell silent, and evidently, in an instant, her thoughts swept her right there, to that midnight luminescent sea. Perhaps her habitual pocket patting was the only sign of her presence here.

"Oh, come on, ma," Rosa stopped her. "Just breathe it in. You dreamed of seeing a forest, breathing this piney air."

Raisa Maksimovna agreed that yes, she had dreamed of that, but now she had to go home, it was time to plant potatoes. Rosa and I spoke in unison, trying to dissuade her: what did she need potatoes for, she could buy them at the market. In response, Raisa Maksimovna gave a meaningful smirk – she was no millionaire. Having savoured the effect, she suddenly guffawed, then just as quickly turned wistful, like Rozochka: potatoes or not, by the twenty-seventh of March, the commemoration day or "memorial Saturday" as she put it, she absolutely had to be home.

In the end, the outing along the Moscow-St. Petersburg highway had to be postponed until another time, and we returned to the city to get tickets: a rail ticket to Moscow, and an air ticket to Simferopol.

The next day Raisa Maksimovna left without saying goodbye to her lady friends.

CHAPTER 44

After her mother left, Rozochka fell into a depression, lying in bed for days on end. This was the worst part because she had taken over my study and wouldn't let me in, locking herself inside. All my attempts to persuade her to eat or, at the very least, lie on the couch instead of the floor only led to outbursts of hysteria. She would scream at me to go away, eat by myself, and laze around like the miserable millionaire I was. Then she would cry into her pillow, breaking my heart. I didn't know what to do, remembering her illness all the while, lost in the dilemma of whether to call an ambulance or break the study door, fully aware that either would end our relationship. The only thing I could do was indeed to go to the lounge and fall onto the couch, as if at Rozochka's insistence. "Have mercy, Lord!" I would whisper in my prayers, bitterly regretting Raisa Maksimovna's departure - how good, how wonderful it had been with her around! Her mere presence brought peace and amity to our home.

And then one Sunday, the day after the Saturday of Souls, my phone rang. It happened while I lay senseless, not thinking about anything after another of Rozochka's tantrums. I picked up the receiver mechanically.

"Yes, hello. Poet Slyozkin speaking."

As God is my witness, I had never introduced myself like that before, identifying myself by the family name, let alone as a poet.

A booming voice with a rasp that could not be mistaken for anyone else's answered me:

"Poet-schmoe-et, but my son-in-law is a mil-lion-aire, and who are you-oo?!"

Some words skipped as if played from a scratched record.

"Raisa Maksimovna - is that you?!..." I was delighted and began asking her how she had made it home and how things were, the potatoes, the weather...

She told me in soaring exclamations and interjections that all was well at home and at work, but what about us, what were we up to? I decided to skip blowing smoke and confessed that ever since her departure we had been unable to recover: grieving, missing her, feeling restless. She had left too hastily, should have stayed longer. I added I had left a gift for her on my last visit in a glass coffee jar; she only had to slide the third window from the entrance to get it. There, behind the morphine box, I had left a glass jar with no less than three thousand "greens" masked with some dry seaweed on top.

She probably didn't quite get it about the gift. But she did understand that we were missing her, had been restless, and regretted her hasty departure. She was moved and started paying me rather crude compliments. Listening to them, I too was moved and didn't notice Rozochka dart out from behind me and snatch the receiver. She snatched it, but didn't interrupt her mother, letting her have her say.

Lord, how grateful I was to Raisa Maksimovna for those compliments in my address! However crude, however inarticulate, they were sincere and so timely. Her booming voice made them clearly audible and Rozochka had no choice but to listen to them. There could be no better advocate to defend my shaken rights at that moment … This, of course, was God Himself…

At first, Rozochka looked at the receiver (she held it slightly away from her ear). Since Raisa Maksimovna wouldn't stop and the compliments poured from the receiver like a horn of plenty, Rozochka looked at me. She looked at me sternly, even frowning a little, and then - smiled. Smiled widely, openly, as if breaking free down an icy mountain, sledding down, careening recklessly, daringly, forgetful of any brakes. Everything inside me resonated and rang like the Valdai bells. I don't know what amused her, but to stop the flood of praise, she covered the receiver with a pillow.

"Look at you, enchanted like by a nightingale!"

Here I could no longer restrain myself and lunged for the pillow:

"Let her speak!"

"I won't!"

Rozochka blocked my way, we grappled, fell onto the couch, and wrestled there. Flailing, I declaimed:

> And, like two friends their arms around
> Each other, or two serpents wound
> Into a ball, over the cold
> Dew-sprinkled moss and grass we rolled[102]…

Of course, I declaimed to the best extent possible. At times she squeezed my chest so tightly that I was breathless. But this only boosted the joy. Trying to free the receiver, I strained towards it with all my might, while Rozochka resisted with all

---

102   M. Lermontov, "The Novice", ch.18.

hers. Laughing, we rolled across the couch like madmen. And when I managed to grab the pillow and my advantage seemed undeniable, Rozochka would suddenly jab her chin between my ribs like a sharp elbow, so that I couldn't stand it, would kick out, dropping the pillow - I was ticklish. How long we wrestled, I couldn't say; but I do know that when we lay catching our breath, exhausted, and Rozochka suddenly swatted me with the pillow, the first thing I heard was the voice from the receiver:

"Never been proud of anyone before, but you, son-in-law, I'm proud of. Yes-yes, proud! So, you two, my darling daughter, give in to each other and take care, take care of yourselves. As for me, I'm doing just fine!"

There was a loud crack and crackle in the receiver, as if it had been dropped at the other end. And immediately such a dense hissing groan, as if a squall had blown into the receiver, and then everything drowned in the short buzzer tones.

Rozochka and I reached towards each other, embraced, and felt like we were floating on air. Time stood still, or had we fallen out of time?! It has long been said that the happy do not watch the clock. And we were happy, more than just happy for we did not float on an air, but on the Earth, together with the Sun, together with the other planets, through fields of stars, through nebulae. We floated as one body, for we were one world, in which the beginning of one served as the continuation of the other.

Needless to say, we made up and decided to treat ourselves to a sort of honeymoon - a visit to my mother, and then perhaps somewhere abroad.

CHAPTER 45

Preparations took several days, and what wonderful days they were. In the morning, I would bring the car, and we would drive to stores, markets (looking for gifts for Mum and her friends), and then head out of town. Sometimes we'd stop on a high bank of the Volkhov River and watch the ice drift. I don't know if there is any relation between the words "Volkhov" and "volkhvy" (sages), but I always felt there was; I sensed it by taste, with the tip of my tongue. The very notion of "Hoary Volkhov," as they call it, conjured up visions of vast snowy expanses, the hills on the riverbanks, little churches, and thoughts of the ancient wisdom of Holy Russia. When a breeze would blow from the river carrying the scent of melted snow and icy water, and the setting sun ignited the golden dome of the Cathedral of Divine Wisdom, all doubts were dispelled: "Volkhov" and "volkhvy" have the same origin in delivering the sacred gifts to God. I am convinced that on His Second Coming, which is already "at the door," it is from the banks of the Volkhov River that the sages will bring Him their sacred gifts: hope, faith, love, which will become the new world's gold, frankincense, and myrrh.

Once Rozochka and I stood on a steep bank; the moving ice, the tinkling rustle, and myriads of air bubbles rising from the dark depths seemed to wash over us, creating an illusion of flight. Spray rose in waves and brought about the brightest of rainbows to arch over us and envelop us, turning us into some sort of luminous shadows, shadows of soaring birds. I suggested Rozochka get in the car, but she suddenly whirled around sharply to face me:

"Want to know why I didn't become the new Mother Rozaria of Russia?!"

It turned out Rozochka had devoted considerable effort to move closer to her lofty goal. She had visited all convents in Moscow, but alas, every single one required some incomprehensible recommendations from a spiritual adviser and his mandatory blessing. She tried to follow Mother Teresa's example and took to the streets to help her sisters in need, found in abundance near any subway station. Rozochka started by picking up a drunken woman but was immediately arrested and brought into police custody "on suspicion of robbing intoxicated persons." The most terrible thing was that the police had left that woman, the culprit, right where she was, at the bus stop, propped against a dirty metal trash bin like an inanimate object. And they mocked Rozochka, not believing she had tried to help purely out of selflessness. It was then in the detention centre that she met Katrin.

Memories of Katrin and that Moscow apartment were still fresh and painful enough, but Rozochka still wanted to recount her adventures. Unexpectedly even for myself, I implored her not to do so, to spare us both. Indeed, if I did not have the strength to listen to her revelations, how would it be for her to tell them?!

Love—this is not just you and me… It is also the desire to forgive and be forgiven. It was precisely then, emerging from the rainbow, that I first felt Rozochka and I were one family, one inseparable whole.

Afterwards, we drove in the car. I kept my hands on the wheel, and she sat beside me. Sometimes I would glance at her, and she would place her hand on mine and squeeze with all her might. With all my soul, I praised the Lord for finally enlightening us, finally allowing us to feel one whole, to feel one speed, one road, one destiny together. And this was even more joyous because we were about to visit my mother.

But our trip to Altai did not happen. On the morning of April 23, the phone suddenly rang; Rozochka beat me to it.

"Call from Chernomorsk[103]… Oh ma, surely last time she forgot to mention the potatoes have already sprouted," Rozochka cheerfully announced, and I too smiled.

Then she turned pale and handed me the receiver in fright.

It was the head physician of the district hospital. He said that today, around two in the morning, Raisa Maksimovna Purpurik had died. She had died in her sleep because of a massive heart attack.

The suddenness of the call and the official tone left no doubt.

"But how, she was only forty?"

The head physician fell silent tensely for a while, then, changing from an official to a sympathetic tone, asked whether I knew of her fondness for drink. I said nothing. He then said that from Easter, Raisa Maksimovna, bluntly speaking, had been on a bender.

I had never seen Rozochka so frightened. She began insisting that we should not go to the funeral.

---

103   Some calls were still done throught an operator service in the former Soviet Union at that time. The operator would announce where the call originated from before connecting you.

"We'll tell the head physician that it wasn't us he was talking to, and no one will know…"

"What has the head physician got to do with it? What do you mean 'no one will know'? Your mother just died!" I cried out, shaken.

Rozochka collapsed onto the couch and broke into loud sobs. It seemed she understood the absurdity and stonyheartedness of her words. I did not reproach her, feeling how deep her sorrow was. And when I returned with the tickets, Rozochka was already asleep. I went into the study so as not to wake her, and by some chance pulled back the mattress lying on the floor, and I felt deeply dejected: there were used syringes and morphine ampoules under the mattress.

I quietly lay down on the floor and stared at the ceiling. But I did not see the ceiling, it dissolved and disappeared as if in a haze, as if beyond the distant horizon.

Rozochka! She had started shooting up again. All those days in the study, she had been on morphine and concealed it quite skilfully! I felt sorry for Rozochka and the late Raisa Maksimovna, but most of all, I felt sorry for myself. I didn't know what to do, how to proceed, how to live?! Rozochka had resumed taking morphine, which meant she was in unbearable pain again - a clear sign that her disease returned. And an exacerbation of myeloid leukaemia (I knew that for certain now) always borderlines with death.

I lay there staring… but seeing nothing, everything dissolving and disappearing…

"Mitenka! Are you crying? Why?"

I hadn't noticed Rozochka approach. What could I say?! I pulled my hand with the used syringes and ampoules from under the mattress.

"Ah, that!" said Rozochka sadly and lay down quietly next to me.

God knows how long we lay there… Suddenly she touched my eyes and caressed them. Then I too touched her eyes - and caressed them too, because it's so hard to look beyond the horizon where everything dissolves and disappears as if in a fog.

" Mitenka, I give you my word, I'll quit. Only these last few days… I had a premonition about mama… But I'll get through this and quit, believe me Mitenka, believe me! But right now, I'm terrified I won't cope, that I'll somehow disgrace mama, and that cannot happen… everything must be done properly, mama may have become an alcoholic because of me, because of my damned illness. Oh Mitya, Mitya!.."

She burst into tears, and I felt I was about to sob too.

We arrived in Chernomorsk without a hitch. The chief doctor expressed his deepest condolences, and then said that Raisa Maksimovna's entire working life had been tied to the hospital, so her colleagues have decided to help her relatives organise and conduct the funeral.

"Especially since her daughter, Roza Fedorovna, is one of our nurses."

He looked at Rozochka very attentively and for a very long time. It seemed he wanted to say something more, but didn't. In short, it turned out that all the issues related to the burial had been taken care of. The grave had even been dug next to her husband's, that is, in the closed cemetery.

No matter how much Rozochka cried and grieved, she kept an eye on things, making sure everything went according to her mother's wishes. Without explaining anything to the chief doctor (a true Leninist-communist), the very next day we moved Raisa Maksimovna's body home, and at five in the morning on Monday to the church (by arrangement with the priest). We also arranged for two buses to come there. At eight, after the memorial service, we stopped at the district hospital so that anyone could join the procession to see off Raisa Maksimovna on her last journey.

It's hard to explain now why I ordered two buses. Rozochka was sure there wouldn't be enough people to fill even one. Her relatives on her father's side had long since scattered, and there were none left on her mother's side either. However, Rozochka was mistaken. People filled one bus at the church and four packed buses followed the van with the coffin from the hospital. Raisa Maksimovna's popularity soon became apparent at the civil memorial service, where two collective farm chairmen from neighbouring villages gave farewell speeches. They described the deceased as a person of deep compassion, who could find not only kind words for the villagers admitted to the hospital, but also spare beds, which was always an important factor for non-locals. The chief doctor also gave a farewell speech, but he spoke more about Raisa Maksimovna as an irreplaceable nurse. Overall, everything went properly, and many old ladies at the memorial feast, blushing from wine, told Rozochka that they too wouldn't mind being mourned and buried like that.

On the eve of May 1st, I called Feofilaktovich and asked him to go ahead with opening the restaurant without us: the 9th day after the death was coming up, and of course we wouldn't make it back. Besides, her mother's death had taken a toll on Rozochka. The chief doctor demanded that she immediately get admitted for an examination, but after just three days she was discharged with no explanation. I didn't think much of it and at first was even glad, but became worried when Rozochka was forced to spend most of the day in bed due to pains throughout her body, especially in her joints. However, even more than her pains and bedridden state (after the funeral I had spent a few days in bed myself) I was troubled by Rozochka's silence and detachment upon her return from the hospital.

When I spoke to her, Rozochka would not answer right away, or more often would not answer at all. No, she was not ignoring me, she simply did not hear my questions. Rozochka was absent, or rather, lingered in some far-off realm to which I had no access. And once, sighing and looking around in amazement, as if she had only just arrived in the living room, she suddenly announced with quiet sadness and a singsong voice:

"Ma and Pa are al-ready the-ere, in Par-a-dise!"

Her amazement and sadness frightened me. In them, I sensed a meek envy of a weary heart.

"Ro-zo-chka, today we'll go to Mos-cow, to the be-est doctors," I found myself replying for some reason in singsong.

Rozochka looked at me pitifully, squeezed my hand, and shook her head: her mother's nine days … she would not go anywhere… Then a wave of verbosity overcame her, and she began telling how the three of them, herself, her father, and mother, had gone to the Askania Nova reserve. Her father had been chauffeuring the chairman of the district consumer cooperative and had an opportunity to visit the reserve.

Rozochka suddenly laughed - but she had not been there, because that was in mid-April, and she was born in June. It was strange and implausible to remember so vividly the azure sky, the boundless expanse of land, the scent of a recent spring shower – according to someone else's account.

They had turned off the main road onto some country lane, completely deserted and dark violet, like ploughed fields. The road did not descend but rather dropped as if they were not going down a hill but plunging into an abyss. The windshield darkened, and the first raindrops struck with a thunderous rumble like an earthquake. Her father's hands tensed firmly, and the next second their car began rising upwards like an aeroplane. The cloud cover parted, and she saw a flock of pigeons soaring aloft against the dissolving clouds. She looked again at her father's hands - hairs sparkled like tiny rubies, and she knew her father was smiling.

"Made it, made it through," he said, and somewhere behind them, but very, very close, an iron chariot rumbled by.

She looked again at the windshield and only then realised there had been no pigeons - those were just scattered raindrops overlaying the blue gap in the clouds from the side. And a second later the slope ended, and the boundless steppe lay before them in a riotous blaze of tulips.

Her mother said her father had stopped the truck, spread a tarp, and tossed a sheepskin coat onto it. Then he returned to the truck, while she, Rozochka, remembered well how the sun burst through the clouds and shiny diamonds sparkled in last year's withered grass. One emerald especially amazed her, rocking in a leaf as if in a boat. It burned, blazed with shimmering bluish-green fire, casting its flickering breath even at the red flame of the flowers...

I leaned towards Rozochka; her eyes were open yet they did not see me, that is, she saw me in some other space. I squeezed her hand, and she immediately propped herself up on her elbows. Her forehead was beaded with cold perspiration. I wiped it with a towel, and it seemed to me that her neck and shoulders too were covered in tiny beads of sweat. Alas, I was mistaken. Rozochka involuntarily shrugged off the sheet without interrupting her story for a moment (she was now speaking about their boat trip to Evpatoria), and I saw that those were not droplets at all, but blisters, with some of them turned to purulent scabs. The rush of inflamed blood caused a rash, and her skin was bright red and cracked here and there. Now I saw and felt inflammation in everything, yes, in everything, even in the way she breathed and talked:

"Ma, look, a rainbow! Help me, help me, my hands are shaking like I was stealing chickens..."

I distinctly heard weeping, interrupted by Raisa Maksimovna's thin, inconsolable lamentations: "What are you doing, my darling daughter, making your own mother destroy you?!" Without hesitating for another moment, I took out a syringe and injected Rozochka with morphine. It was amazing, but her vein swelled up as if tourniquet-tied under the needle.

The morphine worked quickly. Rozochka was asleep in a moment.

CHAPTER 46

Of course, I went to see the chief doctor. Of course, he beat around the bush. Of course, he reassured me that the crisis would pass and the malady would recede, and yet when I demanded a referral to some clinic in Moscow or, at the very least, Simferopol, he suddenly shrugged:

"What's the point?"

This was so unexpected and so cruel after all his admonitions. I was flustered:

"What do you mean, what's the point?!"

And then he said:

"Stay strong!"

The chief doctor promised that a nurse would come to see Rozochka every day to give her some very complex injections. And indeed, for a week she did come, but with each passing day, or rather hour, Rozochka's bouts of talkativeness, alternated with silence and detachment, became longer and longer. Finally, these bouts became Rozochka's almost natural state. She already realised that her strength was ebbing away with every hour and the disease was claiming more and more territory. All her strength and thoughts were now focused on the ninth day of commemoration for Raisa Maksimovna, which fell on May 2nd. Every time she woke up, Rozochka would ask:

"What's the date?"

I vividly remember that quiet noon on May 1st, when the sense of spring tranquillity engulfed everything around. I turned on the sprinklers and watched butterflies, "breathing with their wings,[104]" drinking water in the shade of the spreading quince tree. Then I entered the cool interior of the house and quietly stopped by the wall calendar. Rozochka was seemingly asleep, then suddenly woke up.

"When?" She asked.

I was involuntarily startled but composed myself.

"Tomorrow."

"Tomorrow," Rozochka repeated and started coughing. No, no, this was not an ordinary cough. She desperately tried to take a full breath, but something in her chest was tearing and breaking, constraining the already insufficient gulp of air.

I ran to Rozochka and, as before, took her in my arms and sat down on the bed so that, nestled together, we could look out the window. As always, she pressed my hand to her chest with both hands. I tried to reach for the massage brush from under the pillow to brush her emaciated body, but she wouldn't let me. She looked deep inside me with her enormous eyes and kissed my hand.

"Mitenka, I'll probably die soon," Rozochka stated, not asked, and, suppressing her cough, added that all of that would come later, but tomorrow she wanted to commemorate her mother, because her mother died because of her, Rozochka, out of fear… she was so aghast of outliving her own daughter.

Rozochka started coughing, and I tightened my embrace, feeling how her cough tore also apart my own chest.

"Mitenka, Mitenka, don't skimp on the injections tomorrow! As soon as I tell you with my eyes (I understood her with-

104   Allusion to "The Butterfly" – a poem by Afanasy Fet.

out words) get the syringe immediately, don't call the nurse, all her complex injections are just morphine."

Rozochka wheezed, and I, fearing another attack, ordered her to be quiet and not get agitated, while I did everything she asked. In response, she kissed my hand again and, nestling against my chest, said:

"Mitenka, you are my doctor in a white coat, you are my prince from Manchester City!"

She fell silent for a moment as she suppressed the urge to cough brought on by excitement.

"Forgive me, Mitenka… I couldn't become a proper wife… But there, in the next world, I'll wait for you… I'll find you wherever you may be… And you'll say, 'Rozochka and I are one… Roza is the best part of me!'"

She started coughing again, and again I told her to be still, and then she begged for an injection with her eyes. And while I was preparing - breaking the ampoule, filling the syringe - Rozochka looked at me with such penetrating tenderness, it was if I truly were a prince from Manchester City.

After the injection, I knelt in front of the bed and snuggled up to her:

"My angel, I love you! You are the best part of me!"

Rozochka didn't reply, but her eyes became so enormous that they contained more than words could hold - and I wept.

May 2nd turned out to be an extraordinary day, quiet and warm. High feathery clouds, a white radiance of sunbeams sprinkling down from the heavens, the droning hum of wasps amid the wild grapevines - everything lent that day a certain ethereal, even surreal quality. It was soaking in a kind of silvery haze of forgetfulness and sleepiness. On such days, the unreality of the world seems real, and reality seems illusory. Rozochka had pleasantly surprised me that morning. I woke to see her sitting on my bed (actually, not mine - I was sleeping on Raisa Maksimovna's bed). This was so unexpected, so improbable, that I rubbed my eyes in disbelief.

Rozochka laughed with that familiar quirk by which it was immediately apparent that she had taken the drug. This seemed unbelievable in her condition, but indeed she had got out of her bed and given herself an injection all on her own.

"Mitenka, you didn't forget that today is mama's ninth day, did you?!"

She asked with a certain loftiness, as if it wasn't a commemoration but a celebration. Of course, I attributed this to the effects of the drug as well. Alas, I was wrong, but more on that later.

Everything that needed to be done that day, we did. We visited the cemetery and laid a bouquet of fresh carnations on the grave. We went to the hospital to invite the medical staff to the commemorative meal through the chief doctor. We went to the church, lit candles, and asked the parishioners who had prepared the mother for burial to come and commemorate Raisa Maksimovna as well. Yes, Rozochka remembered to invite the parishioners, three tiny, grey-haired old ladies, like the three principal Christian virtues: Faith, Hope, and Love.

"You know, Mitenka, they're so God-fearing, so respectful, so meek, I would entrust myself to them too, let them prepare me for my last journey…"

"Now why would you say such a thing, Rozochka?!" I tried to reason with her.

"What's so bad about it, Mitenka? The old ladies know everything, understand everything, that's why they would prepare me as if for a celebration. And it is, Mitenka, I'll depart from here, and over there I'll meet father and mother. Isn't that a celebration? Alright, alright, don't be scared, I'll talk to the priest myself."

Everything happened as if by itself on that silvery day, relaxedly and effortlessly. I hired a private driver (calling himself a "licensed taxi driver"), and we had no problems whatsoever. Indeed, he had brought the wine and cold appetisers well in advance, and managed to deliver hot dishes straight from a restaurant - yes, really, still hot.

Everything was going well, and many of the medical staff cheered Rozochka's recovery, misled by her upbeat mood. Rozochka slipped away unnoticed a couple of times, as if to freshen up, but I knew the real reason for her absences. And although I knew for sure that she was giving herself injections without my help, when the nurses rejoiced for her, I sincerely believed that it was true, that Rozochka had recovered. The chief doctor, however, brought me back down to earth. As he was leaving, he patted me on the shoulder and said in his characteristic authoritative manner:

"Stay strong, grit your teeth and stay strong!"

After his "stay strong," my strength suddenly left me, otherwise I would have certainly given him a piece of my mind.

Many kind words were said about Raisa Maksimovna during the commemorative meal.

"As far back as I can remember," Rozochka said, "Mother always gave me her very best, she always lived for me..."

Rozochka choked back a sob and then burst into tears, having no strength to speak. I spoke, trying to divert attention from her (even in such moments, despondency is a sin):

"That's exactly how it was, she gave her everything, and then me too. She would prepare something delicious and then give it all to me: 'Eat up, good son, eat!' And I would take it and eat it all."

As she listened, Rozochka wiped away her tears and even smiled at me, showing the size of the delicacies with expressive gestures. Many smiled following Rozochka's lead, and the little grey-haired old ladies looked at me tenderly, as if my words pertained to them personally.

After the commemorative meal, the "licensed taxi driver" took everyone home. Rozochka went with the little grey-haired old ladies herself: both to see them off and to chat, at any rate, she returned feeling at peace and somehow elevated.

"Mitenka, mother would probably have been pleased," she said, and suggested we drive to the sea, just like we had once driven to the River Volkhov.

And so, we went to the fishery (a semi-dilapidated barrack-like structure on a steep, rocky shore that juts sharply into the sea), in front of which the expanse of water stretched out on both sides. It was as if the crumbling building was the bridge of the "Titanic." Rozochka and I went to the fishery quite often during my first visit. In fine weather, waves with their white crests would crash onto the rocks and bounce back like wild rams. On a quiet sunny day (especially at sunset) the white limestone cliffs and the ruins of the fishery appeared pink, and it was very easy to imagine that we were on a detached piece of land -" ...send not for whom the bell tolls: it tolls for thee." I don't know why, but those very words came to mind every time we went out onto the steep limestone shore. They came to mind now as well, and I felt so bitter that I quickly made my way down to the sea, hopping from rock to rock, and splashed water on my face so that Rozochka wouldn't notice.

She did notice. At any rate, when I returned and sat down next to her, and she nestled up to me, and I took her onto my lap so I could feel her entirely, she said:

"Mitenka, I beg you, beg you never to cry for me. I'll die soon" (she nestled even closer and, forestalling my objection, whispered with scorching intensity), "but I won't die, I'll help you from there. Wherever you are, I'll be right beside you. Mitenka, as soon as you bury me... no, no, as you see me off... Well, as soon as you see me off, leave this place right away. I don't like this house, this hut, this shanty. Mommy and I didn't live in it, we just existed, slowly existed. Mitenka, it was only with you that I lived a little, otherwise, I was just dying and dying, but very soon I won't torment anyone anymore... No, no, Mitenka, wait..." (Again, forestalling my objections, she nestled closer.) "There, Mitenka, there, in eternal life, I will always wait for you. I've already asked those little grey-haired old ladies to prepare me, to be sure to dress me in the dress with the golden polka dots… the one with green wedges. Remember, you said I looked just like a schoolgirl in it? And, also, Mitenka, those white shoes that you secretly bought for me… I never got to wear them even once, I just kept saving them and didn't even know what for, but now I understand…"

"Now what are you saying, Rozochka?!" I pleaded. "We'll still go out in them for the opening of our restaurant and to a disco…"

And again, she cuddled in even closer, squeezing my arms.

"Wait, Mitenka, wait… I want to look nice for you in those shoes and that golden polka-dot dress when I run out to meet you. Yes, yes, so that there, in the new life, you'll recognise me right away. Yes, yes, Mitenka, you'll recognise me and love me, just as you did here, and I need nothing more than that. Look, look, those are silver petals raining down from there, from the fields of heaven!"

Rozochka pulled away from me and looked out over the sea with such unnatural firmness that I followed her gaze. Of course, I didn't believe in her silver petals, I thought she was hallucinating, but no…

I was overwhelmed with joy: as if someone had flung open the windows over the sea, letting streams of white sunbeams touch the water, and the rippling surface sparkled and shimmered, like ringing silver petals had indeed been scattered down from the heavens. Yes, yes, ringing… In fact, what I saw weren't petals, but rather silver coins raining over the sea.

"Lord, how beautiful!" Rozochka exhaled.

And it truly was beautiful. Spellbound, we couldn't take

our eyes off this magical spectacle. The heavenly windows kept closing, then opening again in a new place, and glistening silver meadows reappeared before our eyes immediately in the sunbeams beneath them. The rain kept ringing and ringing and the sea kept shimmering and shimmering in gratitude.

Yes, it was indeed a silvery day!

And suddenly, coming to herself, Rozochka cuddled close to me again.

"Do you see, do you see the rainbow?" she asked and fell silent, as if giving me time to see and appreciate it.

Impressed by the silver rain, I was ready to see anything. I craned my neck, turned my head, looked all around, but didn't see any rainbow.

"What a pity you can't see it, and it's so big—from horizon to horizon, we're already sailing under it. Do you see?!"

As if to meet the rainbow, she lurched forward so abruptly that I could barely hold her back.

"Do you see, do you see?!"

I saw nothing except that Rozochka was having an attack while still on drugs, and it turned into a full-blown waking delirium; perhaps she imagined us on a Yevpatoria-bound steamer.

"Yes, Rozochka, yes, I see the rainbow," I agreed.

Then I embraced her and, feeling the heat of her feverish body, said we needed to go home.

I took Rozochka in my arms and couldn't help but be amazed once again by how light she was. She probably weighed less than a small teenager.

In the car, she seemed to calm down a bit and even dozed

off briefly, only to be gripped by new coughing fits. Utterly exhausted, she looked dreadful (a living corpse), and her eyes cried out—no, no! —in a scream for help.

I gave her two injections: intramuscular and intravenous. After a while, Rozochka calmed down again and even tried to hum a tune. However, within a minute, she fell completely silent and drifted off to sleep.

I went outside and told the "licensed taxi driver" to go for dinner, then remain on duty until morning. The driver objected, clearly fearing that I might disappear without paying him. I gave him fifty dollars, and he drove off.

He drove off, and I started listening to the sound of the wind in the treetops, and watching enormous green stars rise and sway above the horizon, like the masthead lights of some drifting ship. My soul felt desolate and lonely, so lonely, as if I were on an uninhabited planet where I was destined to die.

The thought of death frightened me, not directly, but through Rozochka. I remembered the leukaemia, the ampoules of morphine, that today was the ninth day since her mother's passing, and I felt a grave chill inside—there was no life on this planet without her.

I hurried into the hut and had only just reached Rozochka's bed when she said it wasn't a rainbow, but a bridge supported by angels.

"Yes, yes, Mitenka, by angels and missionaries of love."

She spoke these words with her head lifted from the pillow and without moving her lips, but so distinctly, that I glanced back over my shoulder.

"No, no, I won't return, I'm tired, we'll go together, mo… ther…" Rozochka said again, as if from behind me.

I took her in my arms, and together we gazed out the window, in which I saw a star streaking across the glass, while Rozochka saw a rainbow in the rays of the rising sun.

God knows how long we sat like that! Rozochka's talkativeness suddenly gave way to prolonged lapses of unconsciousness, or she would suddenly rouse, pull slightly away, look searchingly at me and, having remembered everything, cling to my chest:

"Mitenka, my angel, don't hold me back, let me go! It's good there, Mitenka, we'll all be together there."

I didn't understand what she was asking and only held her tighter.

"Rozochka, my little angel, don't go, don't leave me alone," I whispered.

Rozochka raised her enormous eyes, and in them I saw the spiritual anguish I was causing her. And so, as not to torment her, I fell silent and closed my eyes to better keep my silence. In one of those moments, likely at dawn, sleep overcame me.

I dreamed of Rozochka and myself standing by a spring, the sun shining over it. Its ringing waters fell onto the rocks below and blossomed into a rainbow.

"Where are we?" I asked Rozochka. "It's so nice here, so beautiful, so marvellous, just breathtaking!"

"Guess!" said Rozochka, and, laughing, ran from me, inviting me to play chase. "You're the prince, aren't you, my prince?!"

She stepped right to the very edge of the cliff, but there wasn't enough time for me to get scared. Rozochka waved her wing-like arms like the Swan Queen from Swan Lake and flew across the stream.

"I know, I know… we're in Manchester City!" I joyfully exclaimed and asked: "Right, right?!"

"Right!" Rozochka answered merrily and, descending gently on the other side of the stream, waved her handkerchief at me playfully: "Goodbye, Mitenka! Goodbye…"

But then a light breeze began moving the rainbow her way, and I suddenly saw that the handkerchief in her hand was silk with golden polka dots, like the dress with green wedges, and on her feet were the white shoes that I had secretly bought for her in Moscow when we were travelling home with Raisa Maksimovna.

The thought of Raisa Maksimovna (that she was gone, had died) troubled me. I thought: but why is Rozochka here in those white shoes and that golden polka-dot dress? I thought it, and Rozochka immediately read my thought and said so tenderly, so tenderly, as if apologising:

"Guess, Mitenka, guess, my angel!"

The realisation was sudden and simple, like an electric shock. I awoke, but even before regaining consciousness, I already knew that the irremediable had occurred.

"Forgive me, Rozochka, forgive me!" I said aloud, not fully understanding what I was asking forgiveness for, but completely certain that she could hear me and would forgive me.

Carefully, as if carrying a sleeping child in my arms, I stood up and just as carefully, as if laying a sleeping child down, placed Rozochka on the bed. As I straightened her limbs, still warm, I thought Rozochka had become significantly heavier. The whole time I was laying her down, I avoided looking at her face, but when I did, I rejoiced for a split second (it seemed to me that Rozochka was alive). Then hit by reality, I grew sad.

Rozochka lay with her eyes open and with a pitiful, pitiful smile settled on her face. It was as if she asked me for forgiveness—well, at least for having become significantly heavier for me.

Involuntarily, I extended my palm and closed her eyes. My actions were mechanical, I felt I was guided not by my own, but by some universal human experience, more useful than mine. Still, there was something hurtful in how it now applied to Rozochka and me.

"No, no, you are not to blame for anything. It is I who should ask your forgiveness, because I am so very lonely. Yes, very…"

I lit a lamp under the icon of the Holy Virgin, approached Rozochka, kissed her forehead and crossed her and then myself. Then I took out a bottle of vodka and two glasses, and went out to the "licensed taxi driver."

The driver was asleep on a fully reclined seat. I tapped on the hood, he awoke and turned on the parking lights. Then, stretching, he got out of the car and asked, seeing me filling the glasses:

"It's over?"

I didn't answer, just handed him a glass topped by a sandwich.

"May she rest in peace … so young," the driver said sympathetically, and we drank without clinking glasses.

Then I poured again (less for him, a full glass for myself), emptying the whole bottle.

"She said not to grieve for her, not to weep over her, that she'll be good over there…"

The driver shivered, but not from the cold; I let him go.

"Come back around ten," I asked and went back into the hut.

I lay down on the floor next to Rozochka's bed, without looking at her. I wanted to dream of a sunny spring that Rozochka and I could admire together, but instead, over and over, I dreamed I was going out to the driver, and he was asking:

"It's over?"

This "it's over?" multiplied endlessly and echoing in my mind, tormented me so much that I would wake up: yes, it's over… Everything had lost its meaning. I was left alone on an uninhabited planet.

CHAPTER 47

I didn't linger in Chernomorsk after the funeral and was back in Moscow the next day. The following morning, I found myself standing in the square near the bus station in Barnaul, waiting for a shuttle bus to my hometown of Cheremshanka.

I hadn't been home in six years. Nothing for Barnaul, but a quarter of my life for me. And yet, I felt like I was the same while everything around me had changed. Kiosks, kiosks, and more kiosks – they were everywhere... And the music... It seemed like some kind of never-ending celebration was going on, but it was all but a veneer. Sometimes you could see the lost faces of villagers in between all the kiosks and stalls overloaded with foreign goods. They tried desperately not to notice the gaudy abundance, tried hard, but couldn't... Their own sacks of goods for sale looked like beggars' satchels.

At noon, I sat on my brand-new suitcase in an overcrowded van. Men and women, tubs and buckets and all sorts of clattering utensils gradually settled into a uniform mass. Even I had become a part of it with my foreign suitcase.

The van livened up once the city was left behind. Conversations ensued, revolving around prices and purchases, but more often about who saw what. Men, as if on cue, encountered nothing but drunks, mostly at the railway station or under a fence, but a case at the passport office doorsteps was reported as well. Women saw homeless children: scrawny, dirty, with bobbing little heads on slender necks, cursing viciously at each other, as if in a state of derangement. (People didn't tell such tales even after the war.)

I asked the driver to stop at the turn towards home, by the famous, truly regal ash tree. When I was little, Mum and I often rested under it. As I grew up, I'd climb it and catch cockchafers in its sap-filled crevices. After my graduation from high school and before leaving for distant Moscow, I stood under it, as if to commit it to memory.

The ash turned out not to be so big and regal after all. One part of the tree had dried up. Its lifeless bark hung in tattered strips, exposing aged wood covered by insect marks.

I sat on my suitcase. Of course, I could have taken a taxi, but it has been the custom since the time of Odysseus to return to one's father's home in rags. Early May, yet an icy chill in the shade – I sensed the scent of autumn, yes, late autumn and sorrow too. I felt sorry for this withering ash, for my lonely mother, and for myself. Her only son, all I had managed was to send home five hundred roubles.

It was bitter and shameful, but not because I had plenty of money while my mother didn't, or because the ash had been enormous in my youth but had now dried up. No, of course not. Those things were present, but they weren't the main issue. The main things were the offence and bitterness over something beyond me, something I had missed, failed to absorb, and keep in my heart. Indeed, couldn't Rozochka and I have come earlier?!

The head of the vegetable brigade, Ivan Ivanovich Ogorodnikov, gave me a ride home – he was going on his horse cart to get seed onions. Learning that I was Evdokia Slyozkina's son, he remarked thoughtfully:

"Well, there's no arguing with what nature has decided: this is a vegetable, this is a fruit, and this is an industrial crop."

I didn't follow his logic, so he explained that at first Evdokia shed tears over her husband, now over her son – that's me – because her family name is Slyozkina[105]. Had she a different surname, her actions would correspond accordingly. Take his – Ogorodnikov, meaning "vegetable gardener," - he became the head of the collective farmers' vegetable brigade; almost the entire vegetable gardening rests on him. He used to do carpentry, battling his nature, trying to overcome his destiny – you assign me one thing, he'd say, but I, Homo sapiens, will take another. He didn't. As he grew older, he ended up doing vegetable farming anyway.

In their brigade, there's a Matrena Baklushina[106]. She can sleep while walking and is first-rate at slacking. She'll swim across a freezing river to escape from work, stealthily, alerting no one. Or there's Cleopatra Evlampievna, a former dairy worker from the Altai Mountains. A snake would always bite her as soon as summer hit. There were never any snakes in Cheremshanka, yet (he witnessed it himself) as soon as Cleopatra arrived, that same summer snakes appeared under her porch.

"And it's all because her name is Cleopatra," the brigade leader philosophized.

---

105   Last name Slyozkin is derived from a Russian word meaning "little baby's tear".

106   Last name Baklushina comes from the word baklusha – a wooden blank for carving a spoon. Russian saying "to chop baklushas" means to do nothing, or nothing meaningful, as doing that at workshops was the easiest, least skilled work.

Last summer, some Mardonius Khryushin[107] visited them, wearing a hat and carrying a briefcase with two locks. "You've got bedbugs in your office's guest room." Such a neat freak and so literate: inspection, disinfection, action, machination… Everything ending in "-tion, -tion" … And everything lil' - lil' disputies, lil' agreementies, lil' cucumbies, lil' tomaties…

The collective farm chairman was flustered, afraid to sign a contract for the future harvest with this unknown man. He says:

"Ivanych, you're my only hope, what's your opinion?"

"Best to wait. We'll see if he lives up to his name or surname."

"Watch out, Ivanych, for your theory not biting our butts: he'd conclude his lil' dealies with all our neighbours and turn his back on us!"

The next morning at daybreak, he went to the stable, and there, behind the cattle sheds, found a man in the middle of a large puddle lying there so pathetically, with his hat and briefcase next to him. Ogorodnikov pulled him out and was staggered to see not a face but a pig's snout. Terrified, he couldn't get a word out – did he find a mangled corpse?! He wiped the man's face with some hay and saw him breathing. Thank God, not drowned, just drunk, hat full of mud, briefcase caked in manure, and filth in his pants. He pissed on the poor fellow a bit to clean him off and gasped: under the snout, there was not even a face, but a puffy little countenance – none other than Mardonius Khryushin.

They opened the briefcase together with the chairman and found stamps and seals of all kinds, forms, government documents – the guy was a real crook! Vodka became his downfall…

---

107   Khryushin comes from "khryu," Russian for "oink".

"But why the fuss?" the brigade leader relented. "Everyone drinks nowadays. They refused to sell Mardonius their beets, and now we brew moonshine. And our local cop Efim Probnikov[108] is like a taster – gets the first bottle of every batch. Yesterday was the Feast of the One Hundred Saints. Tomorrow is the Annunciation. The day after, Palm Sunday... Then a thousand years since the Baptism of Russia ... each day on the calendar is a holiday. So, if you've got your health, you can stay drunk all year long..."

He recounted how he'd already suggested at the collective farmer's meeting to rename Cheremshanka, Mardonia. Everyone got angry with him, but why?

Near the house, Ogorodnikov helped me with my suitcase and suggested going out to the fence in the evening, and stand there, listening to the village.

"You'll hear a drinking song from almost every single house, and why? Well, because up there," he pointed a finger to the sky, "our village has already been renamed – we're Mardonites!"

I set my suitcase on the porch step and looked around. Chickens foraging by the leaning fence. The summer kitchen cobbled together from unimaginable scraps of plywood and thin wooden planks. A wicker fence dividing the inner courtyard. Everything reeked of extreme poverty.

I approached the poplar tree and marvelled at the smoky freshness of its bark and the fact that I had already seen all this poverty before. Yes, yes, of course, I had seen it all in Crimea. But over there all the neglect, poverty, veggie garden, trees, all the surrounding nature had independent significance. They had

---

108   Probnikov is derived from the Russian word "to try" or "to taste".

always been there and always would be, without me. But here, everything – the log cabin, summer kitchen, little sheds, leaning fence, this awakening poplar, and everything, everything I saw through my or my mother's eyes – was mine, was with me, was a part of me. Much, of course, had changed, had become different, but we recognised each other. We did. If the brigade head Ogorodnikov is right and Cheremshanka has already been renamed up there in the heavens, then it happened in part through my own fault.

I didn't take out the stick that secured the cabin door. I remembered the "electric" glass jar lamps of my childhood, the smart and friendly Jack, the hunched old woman Korzhikha with her scary crutch, and as in my childhood, I sat on the porch, sure that wherever Mum was, she was thinking of me, and I just had to wait a bit: she was hurrying home.

And indeed, just as I sat on the porch, just as I looked at the setting sun, at the glowing glass jars on the fence, just as I gazed down our collective farm street, I saw her hurrying. Following her were a bluish goat with a white underbelly and two snow-white yearlings. I also saw Jack, or rather a spotted mongrel very much like Jack, running ahead and occasionally woofing towards the house, clearly sensing my "alien" presence in the yard.

Mum passed the well and approached the gate to the live-stock yard. At the gate, a little coal shed blocked her from view, but it was clear she was herding the goats inside. Then her head in a dark brown kerchief with red apples along the edge appeared above the gate.

The mongrel retreated to the middle of the street and started barking loudly.

"What is it, Sharik[109]?" Mum asked in bewilderment, but the dog's unease had already passed on to her.

Opening the gate, she carefully scanned the little front garden over the fence, ready to find someone else's goat or other uninvited creature there. She even raised a little stick to deal with the trespasser. And then she glanced at the porch.

"Ma-a?!"

She started and backed away, hiding the stick behind her back like a child, and sat on a bench that I hadn't noticed, by the fence.

"Mi-tya!" Mum exhaled, and nodded her head so quickly and finely, as if she wanted to say something else but couldn't get enough air.

Bubbling with emotion, I flew off the porch; Mum leaned her forehead against my shoulder while I firmly, firmly pressed it closer.

"Ma, easy, easy ma!"

I carefully sat her back on the bench.

"Nothing, nothing." Mum stared blankly at her feet in rubber boots. "How, how could I?!"

"It's okay, Mum, I only just arrived. Ivan Ivanovich Ogorodnikov gave me a ride."

I crouched down and tried calling Sharik over. But he looked at my empty hands wisely – and didn't come.

Mum continued sitting silently, mechanically fiddling with the stick. Good Lord, how tiny she is in that huge dark brown shawl, that broad plush jacket, those big rubber boots. And that stick in her hands makes her look like a teenager. Good Lord,

---

109   A very common, cliché dog's name in Russia.

how much she has aged: deeply sunken eyes, wrinkles crisscrossing her face – yet she is only forty-four. I remembered how Mum took me to hospitals in Barnaul when I was little… And then, when I was in 8th grade living at the dorm, she never missed a chance to send me dry biscuits and homemade jam…

And now I hunkered there, straining with all my might not to see how she helplessly fiddled with the stick. I felt my own guilt in her helplessness – Rozochka and I never even sent our address. No, more than that! I never managed to! …

"Sharik, Sharik!" I called in a breaking voice.

Sharik's silhouette melted into some mottled blur. A terrible hopelessness, frustration – I felt like a Mardonite. And then gentle, gliding touches: Sharik had come over after all and began licking my hand.

I burst into tears.

CHAPTER 48

Izba is a traditional Russian peasant wooden log house. However, one wouldn't say "my izba is my fortress" and in the same way, we don't say "a house isn't good for its walls, but for the pies." This immediately sounds off, not genuine, it gets stuck on your tongue. But when we say "my home is my fortress" or "an izba isn't good for its walls, but for the pies" it feels right, izba and pies go together naturally and just shine[110].

Mum pulled away the lid - a whiff of half-forgotten wood smoke came from the oven, immediately reminding me of real homemade cabbage pies. Yes, cabbage pies.

Speaking of pies was not timely… But Mum was delighted, fired up the oven and ran off to the neighbours. While she was gone, I examined the house, starting with my room.

The same trunk stood by the heater, the same sheepskin coat on top of it. The same table by the window and the same chair. The same bookshelf in the left corner, and on the right the same iron bed along the wooden partition wall. The same old wardrobe grandly called an armoire, and the same little rug made of colourful scraps. Everything was as before and yet completely different, like museum pieces. And not at all because the room looked uninhabited…

I quietly sat down on the trunk. What surprised, or rather shocked me, was the portrait gallery of classic writers on the

---

110   The centrepiece of an izba is a Russian stove, which explains why the Russian stove (called stove even though it is actually a huge oven) and everything cooked within are so important for the traditional Russian culture.

wall: Pushkin, Lermontov, Gogol, Bunin, Dostoevsky, Tolstoy, Sholokhov, Yesenin, Bulgakov, Shukshin, Chekhov, Blok. And naturally, my own portrait was standing on the table.

It caught in my chest, like when Sharik had licked my hand again.

Dry birch logs blazed with a white, almost smokeless flame. Only as it bent and spilt into the chimney did the flame darken at the edges, in curling black tendrils. The "murmuring of the fire" is indeed an apt description.

The kitchen. A stove was attached to the oven. First, you'd put your foot on the edge of the stool upon which sat the dough trough, then onto the stove. One step up onto the footstool by the cauldron and you were on the heated top platform, covered by an old, tattered sheepskin coat. It was always cozy and joyful to sit on top of the Russian stove. From there I'd watch the steaming pots, the red-hot stove, and craning my neck I'd spit onto it. The spittle would instantly curl up into a ball and evaporate. It was so fascinating that I'd get carried away, lose my guard, and receive quite a stinging slap on the lips.

"There you go, you rascal," Mum would say, brandishing a towel. I'd let out a merry snort, hide away, and observe from the depths of my "den," Mum kneading dough and humming a tune. Every time she leaned back from the trough, she'd manage to glance my way, provoking a burst of laughter. It seemed her main focus wasn't the dough, but this cheerful way of interacting with me. Good Lord, it's been twenty years or more, but it feels like I sat on that oven only yesterday.

Beyond the kitchen partition (with a wide opening instead of a door) was the hallway. It was a proper room with a large table in the middle and a bench pulled up to it. This is where we'd receive guests, so the hallway served as the living room, too.

I approached the yellowed family photographs hung on the wall. In one, I'm in my mum's arms, wearing a sailor suit and a beret with a pompon, my smiling father with an accordion next to her on a stool. I flinched inside – I'd already outlived my father; he couldn't have been over twenty-three in this photo… and we looked identical…

A coat rack hung on the partition, loaded with all sorts of quilted jackets. Next was the heater – tall from floor to ceiling and wide from wall to dividing wall separating the living room from the main room. A bench stood by the heater, covered with a camel wool blanket. I used to love lying there, reading books.

The main room. Perhaps it was the main room because it had three windows all facing the garden. Or because of the Chinese roses in tubs that looked like trees? Or was it the double bed with its shiny nickel knobs winding around equally shiny bars? (Incidentally, one of those knobs is missing, swallowed accidentally …) Above all, this was the main room because of the huge mirror hanging over an antique chest of drawers.

I peeked into the mirror. With a barely perceptible delay, it reflected my "salamanders[111]," the chest of drawers, and part of the bed with its headboard. But the most amazing thing was that all the objects in the mirror seemed more curved, and therefore even more real. I remembered once lying down by the chest and falling asleep.

I dreamed of a little white house deep in the courtyard, a path strewn with fine pink gravel, a low picket fence with crim-

---

111   Brand of shoes popular at the time.

son rose bushes draping over it, morning sunlight, and diamonds of dew glistening on the dark green leaves. And there was a sound of light arpeggios played on an accordion.

I looked toward the little house (afraid someone might appear and stop me from picking a flower), but it was quiet and deserted. Choosing a red rose, I gently tugged - a fiery shower poured over my head. I awoke.

"Lord, where were you?!" Mum whispered fearfully. "Thank goodness something shifted in the mirror, or I would have stepped on you..."

She lifted me up and looked horrified - my whole body was feverish, my clothes damp on the shoulders as if I'd just emerged from the shower.

After changing my clothes and wrapping me in a blanket, Mum started preparing all sorts of medicinal concoctions while I lay on the wide anodized iron bed, staring at the ceiling. A dark spot above me widened, and from it, like a stone dropped in water, ripples spread down toward me. They seemed viscous yet elastic, as if this was all happening on a sheet of rubber. I had a distinct sense that the rubbery ripples were pulling me in, swallowing me up. Suddenly I saw Jack, a German shepherd I'd never seen before, flying around me.

"Jack, Jack!" I called, and he smiled at me in response, stuck out his tongue and wagged his tail.

Then Mum called out to me, and told the nurse from our village clinic, "He's delirious."

But I wasn't delirious. I was conversing with visions that Mum, the nurse, our visiting neighbours couldn't see, which is why to all of them it seemed I was raving. No, I wasn't delirious, I understood well that I wasn't. I existed simultaneously in two dimensions: here with Mum, and there with them, with visions as real, as my own flesh and blood. What's more, just as I saw Mum, the nurse, the visiting neighbours, all the people-visions saw them too, even better than I did, because it was they who told me who was approaching my bedside, so that I could identify the visitors without turning my head.

What I remember most vividly were the people between the ceiling beams and the ones in the mirror. They were dressed in light white robes and looked very beautiful. I took them for doctors. The woman in the centre was especially beautiful, I couldn't take my eyes off her. Her face was Rozochka's face at the climax of inspiration. Her beauty radiated not just from her face, but her entire being.

She stretched out her arms toward the little boy lying in the bed. "So, this is how you grew up?"

In response, everything inside me fluttered. I heard the light tinkling of an accordion and felt that I was that little boy.

"You're so beautiful," I said and grabbed her robe with all my might.

The people around her smiled - I felt a sense of security beyond measure.

"Listen, Mum has brought in the doctor, so try and respond," she said, making a breezy gesture over my forehead.

I looked at her intently, but there was no little boy, neither in her arms nor in the bed, and no bed at all. She held a red rose in her hands, the same one I'd wanted to pick in the little garden by the white house.

"Respond," she repeated, beckoning over a knight from her entourage. He was dressed in some scaly garment, with a camouflage-green sleeveless cloak draped from his left shoulder and down his arm. Were it not for the spear in his hand, I would never have recognized him as a knight (he looked more like a Second World War guerilla).

In any case, I didn't take a liking to this knight, his dark moustache, reddish beard, mop of hair with a middle parting, but most of all, the strong sense of his direct connection to me (I noticed red rose petals in his hair).

The beautiful woman turned toward him, and at that very instant I heard the clanking of instruments in the doorway and a man's voice stating it was now a crisis situation - either/or...

Mum, lamenting softly, came up to me and, as she changed me into dry clothes, suddenly noticed a red rose blossom tucked in the folds of the blanket.

"How did this get here?!" she marvelled, straining to listen. "And that - the sound of an accordion!"

She glanced over at the potted roses, as if expecting some explanation from them. But our houseplants never bloomed in winter.

I told Mum this flower had parachuted down on me from the ceiling, that a gorgeous lady had given it to me, and the bearded man she called my guardian angel and knight - he was very sullen, a pilot with a head of a tadpole ... It was he who dropped the flower.

I reached out my hand, and Mum handed me the blossom. I looked up at the ceiling, between the beams, and saw that the beautiful, beautiful lady and all those people who'd been with her had shifted over toward the wall above the mirror, while my guardian angel stood in the mirror like a portrait in an enormous bronze frame. He resembled a very stern Russian prince, his hands resting on the hilt of his sword, drawn from its scabbard but with the tip lowered toward the floor.

I closed my eyes and heard my mother's wailing through her sobs - she thought I was delirious again. I wasn't delirious… But so as not to frighten her, I buried my face in the flower and immediately fell asleep, or rather dissolved into the fragrance of the garden. I don't know how long I slept. When I came to, I was still lying there with my face in the blossom, still engulfed by the fragrances of the May garden.

I raised myself up. The windows were blazing with such an extraordinary sunrise that I thought they must be wide open, and I'm in a little white cottage, with the scent of roses wafting in from an enchanted garden. And indeed, I suddenly saw a neat little white house, paths covered in pink gravel, a low picket fence draped with flowering rose bushes and the approaching soft roulades of an accordion.

> A thousand years, a moment's span,
> A planet wide, a grain of sand.
> In all the things God's face revealed,
> The breath of light in all concealed.

I looked around. I expected to see my father but instead, saw Mum, gently shaking me by the shoulder.

"Mitenka, son, we're going to bake some pies!"

CHAPTER 49

For over three weeks at sunrise, the men from the collective farm carpentry brigade would gather on our porch and leave only at sunset, as if obeying a shepherd's horn. I decided to repair the fence and re-roof the house, and served as their expeditor, foreman and, of course, the client. They happily followed me to the construction materials market in the city, examined logs, boards, slate tiles, and nails, and then discussed their impressions up on the roof. They very much liked the way I responded to all their advice, which was by opening my wallet and buying the recommended materials on the spot.

One day, when Silanti Plotnikov, the brigade chief, and his men were dawdling by some stacks of beams and boards, either a guard or a superintendent of Caucasian origin came running up to them.

"Come on, come on!" he gestured towards some used boards lying in an untidy pile like firewood. "Over there, you'll find what you can afford over there," he said, as if striking them with something heavy, causing the men to hunch over and immediately flow towards the indicated pile.

Silanti jerked as if to go too but hung back by the stacks, outraged by how simple Russian guys are bossed around by just about anyone these days. That's when I intervened, asking Silanti to select at least two cubic meters of beams.

Like a mountain eagle taking flight, Silanti soared up.

"Over here, men," he called sternly, and seeing their hesitation, spurred them on: "Come on, come on, we have someone to give us orders, while certain others" - he looked straight at the Caucasian guy - "should be commanding their many wives back home."

The guard smirked contemptuously but didn't leave, watching to see what would happen next.

Now Silanti looked straight at me: "So two cubes then, Yurievich?"

He had used my patronymic for the first time (he and my father had once worked together as youths).

"Perhaps two isn't quite enough - two and a half," I said, and it was as if an electric spark passed between us, levelling the tension instantly.

The men immediately cheered up too, enthusiastically measuring the beams and setting aside those required with such zeal they might well have struck the guard. He spat at their feet and walked off. The men then really let loose, teasing their chief.

"Yurievich, we'll just have to marry Silanti to your Mum – he's a bachelor after all! We'll drink to it, eh? … Then you won't have to travel half the world to patch the roof, your stepdad will take care of it… You can count on that!" The men joked merrily, while Silanti stayed silent, occasionally glancing over. He only spoke up when the talk turned to "your stepdad."

"Alright, enough of your chatter," Silanti suddenly flared up angrily and went to the other end of the store on the pretext of still needing to select slate tiles.

For those three weeks, I had to scurry about like a squirrel.

My Mum was also kept busy, running the kitchen from morning till night, preparing lunch and dinner for the five of us men. The collective farm chairman and board members would drop by, friends too, and everyone had to be catered for with tea and a spare minute. Luckily the neighbour, Cleopatra Evlampievna, came to help, otherwise Mum wouldn't have managed such an influx of what the chairman called "unaccounted mouths."

My Mum seemed to grow younger, despite bustling about from dawn to dusk. The cheerful knocking of axes and hammers in the yard, the chatter and laughter - all entranced her, made her life full, made her feel indispensable. She basked in that bliss of being needed, especially when she climbed up the scaffold and onto the roof to treat everyone to kvass.

Silanti, overcoming his shyness, would drain his glass and grab his axe to continue trimming the logs rather too hastily. The men would exchange glances, while Mum stared off blankly with a half-forgotten inward smile. Then she'd catch herself - "Why am I standing here idle when there's so much work to be done?!"

Silanti would set down his axe again: "Evdokia, be careful!" He would follow her solicitously with his gaze until she descended to the ground.

I don't know why, but Silanti's solicitous look irritated me, provoking some inner harshness. I couldn't control myself and would go behind the fence to the stacked beams that had already become a hangout spot for local youth coming from the city on weekends.

On one of those occasions, I met a former classmate. We started catching up on where everyone was. Most of all I was interested in Valery Gubkin, the school poet, the prodigy, and later a journalism student at the Far East State University. It turned out my classmate had seen Valery a couple of months earlier - he was going as a volunteer to the Balkans. He said Valery had lost his taste for life, that his life, like Vronsky's in Anna Karenina, was worthless and he was only too glad to give it for the small but proud Serbian people.

I could sense my classmate disapproved of Gubkin, saw him as a Russian superman type, oblivious to what he was doing. But I immediately felt happy for Valery, as if a blindfold had been removed from my eyes.

"You know," I told my classmate, "I'm being conscripted and I'm also going as a volunteer to the Balkans to fight for the Serbs. But please don't spread that around - we volunteers must sign a non-disclosure statement." I lied, and it seems I believed my brazen lie even quicker than my classmate did. In any case, when the repairs on the house and fence were completed, and we set up tables in the yard with food to celebrate, I wasn't at all surprised when the first toast was raised to me as a future warrior, a soldier-internationalist.

My Mum sobbed, raising her apron to her eyes, and Silanti immediately stood up, placing his hand on her shoulder to say on everyone's behalf:

"Just stay out of harm's way whenever possible, don't seek trouble, but serve with honour." He paused, then summed up: "And we'll all await your return here - may your guardian angel watch over you." (Then to everyone) "It's actually his guardian angel's day today."

Not everyone perhaps, but he and my Mum would certainly await me, I felt it keenly, and in an impulse of filial gratitude I kissed them both and assured them it would indeed be so - I wouldn't seek trouble and would return in due course. Then we would all build a new house together, just as we had re-roofed this one.

The celebration cheered up considerably after that, really hitting its stride.

Why did I agree with Silanti? Why did I mention a new house? Was it only to overcome the harshness within me? No, no, and no. There was no harshness. Yes, it melted away in me forever in that very moment when I learned Valery Gubkin had gone as a volunteer to the Balkans. In that moment, I sensed with my whole being that it was only there I could transform myself for a new life or failing that, still gain something more important than my current life. And if I kissed my Mum because I was going to part from her, I kissed Silanti because he transformed that parting into a name day celebration for me. Without realizing it, he had not only shown me my path, but blessed it, too. That toast to my guardian angel made me suddenly remember the recurring dream of the beautiful lady and the sullen knight from whom I received the symbolic flower – my cherished Rozochka. My knight, holy martyr Dimitry, whose hands rested on his sword – that vision on the day of my arrival was for me and about me. So how could there be any harshness? It passed, melted away.

I arrived home feeling dejected but left encouraged. I had found hope.

On the night of June 2nd, I was in Moscow, and that very morning I found myself knocking on the administration door of the "Unexpected Joy" restaurant. Doublenose and his comrades emerged - we embraced, patting each other on the shoulders.

"Accept our sincere condolences on the loss of your wife," Feofilaktovich intoned in exaggerated mournfulness. (Coming from someone triple-divorced, the condolences came across as sly irony, even mockery.)

"Okay, okay," I said to observe the proper formality for the occasion, and immediately changed the subject: "The mail sure worked fast though!"

Feofilaktovich explained that the mail had nothing to do with it - my "licensed taxi driver" was a local cop keeping an eye on me at Limonych's request.

"So, he was afraid I'd flee and not pay the promised fee?"

"He got orders to do it discreetly, so you wouldn't become suspicious," said Feofilaktovich, and they all laughed together, as if to say, see how tightly we have everything under control here.

"So, you were watching me in Altai too then?" I asked irritably.

"No, no, we didn't even know you were in the Altai! Limonych assumed you'd gone home to your mother's - but where are you from, Manchester City?"

Why did he mention Manchester City? It made no sense. But my irritation immediately passed.

Feofilaktovich demonstratively went to the desk and pulled open a drawer.

"Here's the missing person report…we were about to file it."

The report was written in a lovely feminine hand on a notebook page.

"So, it is…you even enlisted outsiders."

"No outsiders," Tutankhamun spoke up. "My wife wrote it of her own accord, and I brought it…"

"Ah, so you didn't know!" Doublenose marvelled. (Somehow, he instantly became unlike Feofilaktovich - same suit, same tie, but not a shred of pompousness.) "Remember the lobby attendant Alina Spiridonovna? They got married, so Tutankhamun here is now a married man. We even had a wedding, combined it with the restaurant's launch party - what a crowd, the whole beau monde of the city!"

Picturing Alya and Tutik (surely, she can't call him Tutankhamun) discussing my disappearance, all I could think to say was:

"Congratulations, I never expected it, I can hardly believe it!"

But my congratulations didn't delight the former plumber - he grumbled it was no big deal, what was so unexpected about it and so on. To avoid starting a quarrel, I asked Doublenose to show me around the restaurant.

The restaurant was certainly luxurious; from the coat check and restrooms to the dining halls and kitchen, it had been completely renovated. The elegance of the wallpaper and mirrors, chairs and tables, sconces and lighting left no doubt.

"But what about the Poetry Hall or the captain's quarters of this vessel?" I said, looking down from the mezzanine at the diamond-sparkling chandelier.

In an instant, Doublenose became Alexei Feofilaktovich again. He stopped, buttoned his jacket, adjusted his tie, and strode decisively towards the rear of the lobby to a burgundy velvet curtain covering the wall next to the orchestra stage. He pressed some buttons, and the velvet parted to reveal glass doors with the familiar image of the tea clipper Cutty Sark, but in its Russian rendition, that is, as Grin's Seagull going full speed under crimson sails.

Of course, the captain's quarters were modest compared to the ground floor and mezzanine halls, seating about thirty. But all the cosier it was, with ornate ceiling mouldings like elegant parasols over each table. Yet some force seemed to draw me like a magnet, not letting me focus and look around.

I raised my eyes. There was a portrait hung in the centre of the room, right above the stage, and a white, elegant grand piano stood slightly off to the side. Everything clenched inside me… Yes, it was Rozochka, Roza Fyodorovna. She wore the faintest smile, her gaze piercing me before sliding past. The painter (lion-headed chicken) was unquestionably a brilliant artist: he had captured Rozochka in the golden polka-dot dress and white high heels she had never got to wear. But most striking were the eyes, alive, full of unspoken mystery. Alright, the polka-dot dress, fine, the white heels, alright, the piercing look - but the reflection of red velvet turning into a rainbow seemed to me a materialization of the artist's truly superhuman vision. It was one of those cases where the mystery taken from life manifested itself in full as the mystery of art. That very minute I experienced both the joy of reunion with Rozochka and the bitterness of parting with her again. I stood petrified, choking with tears that would not flow.

CHAPTER 50

My decision to participate in the war in the Balkans may have surprised some, but it didn't upset anyone. June 10th marked 40 days since Roza Fyodorovna's passing, and we commemorated her in a small circle in the cabin lounge. After that, there was nothing to keep me in Russia. At the secret patriotic gatherings organized by Doublenose and Tolya Croesus through proxies, I and a few other criminal romantics (delusional military-age dimwits who had seen nothing but penitentiaries) were presented as top-tier patriots. The organizers probably believed our Pan-Slavic patriotism to some extent, but I didn't. Like Valery Gubkin, who compared himself to Vronsky from Anna Karenina, I had lost my taste for life and was going to the Balkans with one hope – to give meaning and purpose to my life and death. As for my subordinates (being the eldest, I was elected the group's leader), they had no concept of patriotism whatsoever. Their chicken-sized brains drove them to the Balkans for a baptism of fire, after which they all hoped to return to their brethren as tougher, more authoritative men. The thought of dying never even crossed their minds. That's probably why they so eagerly cherished the gifts showered on them at these meetings, to the point of feeling jealous over whose trinket was flashier. The only thing that could have delayed my departure was the so-called arbitration court convened by Filimon Puplievich (Limonych).

On June 15th at 10 am, on return from the Church of Boris

and Gleb, Alexei Feofilaktovich called and, with an unusually respectful tone, asked me to come to the workplace, specifically reminding me to wear white socks.

Intrigued, I didn't keep him waiting, and the first person I met on the porch was Filimon Puplievich.

"Come on, Mitya (correcting himself), Dmitry Yurievich, let's go," he said worriedly. As we walked to the private office, he explained we would be holding an extraordinary arbitration court session. "Beau monde has gathered… You'll see… Make sure no one has cameras or video equipment - we have an artist for that purpose. As for the rest, decide as God lays it on your soul. No one really knows anything - it's a totally new, unestablished tradition," Filimon assured me. He then retrieved a dark crimson robe and a headpiece, akin to a fez without the tassel, from a closet.

The robe was roomy and comfortable enough. Donning it like a cassock, I felt quite confident and cozy. As for the fez, I put it on and instantly forgot about it.

Filimon scrutinized me from all angles, and once satisfied, handed me a folder: it was time!

Alexei Feofilaktovich and company joined us on the mezzanine, also in robes but no headpieces. Judging by how Tutankhamun rushed ahead of me to the cabin lounge doors, flung them open, and bellowed at the top of his lungs "All rise, the arbitration court enters!" this brand new, unestablished tradition had been rehearsed extensively. For some reason, this booming "All rise, the arbitration court enters!" almost set me into fits of Homeric laughter. Especially "arbitration"! Indeed, Doublenose and company could hardly pass as ordinary judges. There was something almost over-the-top parodic yet precisely on-point about Tutankhamun's cry in relation to what was happening. What difference did it make whether we were arbiters or mardonians, if we'd already been renamed in the heavens? I recalled the vegetable brigade foreman Ogorodnikov, then instantly forgot both him and my urge to laugh.

The captain's lounge hall was overflowing with tables but there weren't enough seats and people crowded the aisles - a motley, picturesque crew, some in white socks.

As I proceeded to the stage, I spotted my charges, the so-called romantics. One of them, grinning mockingly, reached out to clap me on the shoulder, but a blow to the ear immediately knocked him to the floor.

"No touching the arbiter!" Tutankhamun barked imperiously.

Many in the aisles respectfully made way for me. No one showed displeasure at the violence; in fact, the "romantic's" face registered a complex mix of astonishment and admiration.

Our appearance in robes, the strict subordination, the unquestioning obedience were all reminiscent of the Politburo of the non-existent USSR, the summit of a sunken Atlantis' hierarchy. Filimon Puplievich and company were seated in the cabin lounge like the top clergy, priests invisible to ordinary mortals. And we, the archons, kings of inherited lands, decided human fates before everyone's eyes, but only insofar as it benefited the priests.

As the eldest archon, I took a seat at the centre table on the stage, whilst my retine occupied side tables positioned slightly to the rear.

Tutankhamun struck a gong, commanding everyone to sit and drawing mild laughter from the audience. Then, after another strike of the gong, Alexei Feofilaktovich gave a brief opening statement, explaining that this was the fairest court in the world because it was elected by the interested parties.

"So, paraphrasing the famous words, one could boldly say this court is in every respect our court!" he concluded with pathos.

Alexei then began reading out the case briefs. He would place each case folder before me, and the plaintiffs would come to the podium, accompanied by four thugs (obviously Tolya Croesus's people). Some would occasionally add extra details to their case. I carefully listened to the defendants and, after announcing my decision, would strike the folder with a wooden gavel, closing the case with no possibility of appeal.

All cases generally followed the same storyline: someone borrowing something from someone else, then either not returning it or returning it without upholding previously agreed terms.

My decisions proved unerring, as I proceeded from the universally accepted postulate that a deal is more binding than money. Money, however, was no trivial matter either. The hall would hush when the dispute centred on thousands of dollars or an expensive foreign car. But it reacted quite differently when the same primitive storyline involved petty cash. It was over just such a small sum that Bobchinsky and Dobchinsky[112] (as I dubbed those insignificant humans) petitioned the arbitration court. Good Lord! They could have spoken forever about their utterly worthless case. Of course, I heard them both, then brought

---

112   Characters from "The Government Inspector" by Nikolay Gogol.

the gavel crashing down on the plump folder with such force it exploded in a cloud of dust. The hall burst into hearty laughter. Bobchinsky and Dobchinsky however, failed to grasp the closure of their case and demanded I articulate my decision. In response, I slammed down the gavel yet again. Catching my displeasure, the thugs promptly booted Bobchinsky and Dobchinsky off the stage. Despite being a true circus stunt, it gave life to another aspect of the ritual: for any foolishness, the arbitration court should respond not with profundity but with the gavel and firm kicks up the culprit's butt.

By way of distracting myself from the repetitive case storylines, I began to observe the audience and particularly, the artist (the lion-headed chicken) and the journalist (formerly editor-in-chief of the "N… City Komsomol" paper, now of the "N… City Gazette").

The editor-in-chief looked quite respectable in a tuxedo, white shirt, bow tie and, naturally, white socks. He sat in the gallery surrounded by similarly dressed young men, close to Filimon Puplievich and the chief of the railway police who appeared to be part of that circle (Filimon wore a tuxedo, a bow tie and white socks too). Strangely though, I felt this didn't concern me as much as one might expect.

The artist, on the other hand, piqued my curiosity intensely. Unlike the editor, he was dressed unpretentiously, in a black t-shirt and grey knit vest, and sitting slightly apart in the front row, alone, appeared fully immersed in his work. For all my preoccupation, I kept glancing his way and meeting his piercing gaze, got the impression he was making sketches, perhaps not just of the court proceedings (as Filimon told me in advance) but also of me personally. Naturally, this couldn't help but intrigue me after his brilliant portrait of Roza Fyodorovna. I resolved to insist on seeing his sketches after the proceedings were over, using my arbiter's authority against any possible objections.

Meanwhile, the time had come for the final case: "The Emerald."

A certain Mr. X had somehow acquired an extraordinarily large and beautiful emerald worth $100,000 from an unknown English lord in Manchester.

Placed before me on chocolate-coloured velvet in a jewel case, the emerald's oval shape and glowing green brilliance resembled the bright grassy field of Luzhniki Stadium[113]. (But I'm getting ahead of myself.)

So, Mr. X brought the emerald to our city and, being uncharacteristically careless, showed it to Mr. Y, who had exhibited an even greater sleight of hand than the former's by taking possession of the stone.

Having been relieved of the emerald, Mr. X didn't suspect Mr. Y of the theft and didn't even entertain the possibility. (People in power usually employ other methods.) But facts are facts.

It so happened that a fire broke out at Mr. Y's home during his prolonged trip abroad. The family's valuables and jewellery were saved, but to accurately assess the gems and jewels, an unmatched expert was employed - none other than Mr. X. He immediately recognised the emerald but couldn't repossess it as it had already been entered into Mr. Y's family's treasure registry. With no recourse, Mr. X appealed to our arbitration court. Mr. Y accepted the summons. However, neither appeared in person, and their representatives declined the judge's invitation to elab-

---

113   Largest stadium in Moscow.

orate on the case, thereby allowing him to rule on the parties' fates - or rather, the fate of the stone - based solely on the above.

I stood to announce my decision and felt an unprecedented tension in the room. I sensed the tautness of the silence like an archer feels the drawstring. Any word from me could be a slaying arrow for Mr. X, for Mr. Y, for myself most of all!

I took up the jewel case and raised it for all to see the emerald. More than anything, I wanted the artist to see it. Why? I don't know - I just wanted him to capture its beauty. For what purpose? No idea, but I had the subconscious sense that if beauty belonged to everyone, it could indeed save the world[114].

And the artist did see it. For once, I didn't meet his gaze - his pencil was flying as he sang his ode to the emerald.

I then pronounced: "I could now give this precious stone (surveying it again), worth \$100,000, to Mr. Y, but I will not." (It seemed half the room exhaled in relief.) "Mr. X has convinced us all, myself included, that this gem does not belong to Mr. Y." (The half that had exhaled burst into applause.)

"I could now give this emerald to the prime culprit in the case, Mr. X, but I will not." (And the other half exhaled in relief.) "Mr. X has convinced us all that this emerald is not his but belongs to a lord from Manchester!" (And that side applauded in turn.)

"I could now give this emerald, worth \$100,000, to its true owner, but I will not, because that is just not possible."

"From now on, this emerald belongs..." (I strained to lift the case again - the silence thickened to pudding, its swelling

---

114   "The world shall be saved by beauty" – an iconic quote from Dostoevsky's "The Idiot".

weight pinning everyone and everything down.) "From now on, this emerald belongs" (I repeated to gather strength to overcome that all-subsuming silence, then forcefully exhaled) "to society as a whole!"

A shrill, wholly inappropriate cry of "Bravo!" and the artist's fervid but solitary applause shattered the dead silence.

"To the 'obshchak' then?!" Tutankhamun boomed in astonishment, speaking up after a lengthy silence.

I closed the case and struck the table with the gavel - so be it! The room suddenly came alive, many rushing for the exits while others swarmed the stage to escort the emerald-laden case that Tolya Croesus and his men were carrying away.

"Wrong decision, the '$100,000 gem' should belong to Mr. Y!" shouted the editor-in-chief from the noisy gallery, smirking as if remembering something.

His entourage applauded the remark, and as one of the black suits was leaving, he said loudly enough for all to hear: "The judge must be removed."

Many turned to laugh. Unexpectedly, I met Filimon Puplievich's questioning gaze (he had opened the door for the departing editor-in-chief like a doorman). In response, I just shrugged indifferently.

A few minutes later, the artist and I were seated in a private office. No matter how much I asked to see his sketches, he refused - unfinished work is never shown. I was about to invoke my arbiter's authority when a mobile phone rang.

The unfamiliar caller claimed to be representing Filimon Puplievich (I instantly believed him for some strange reason).

He asked about the time of my flights to Moscow and Budapest. I remained silent, so he chuckled and inquired if I had any requests – I wasn't heading to a wedding after all, anything could happen. I thanked him for the thought and asked that all proceeds from the Poetry Hall (the cabin lounge) be donated to widows and orphans. He chuckled again, saying it would be done, but what about a final, personal request? And it came to me, and I answered each word carefully:

"I request that my wife's portrait be returned to its former place, and when that happens" - I made a significant pause - "I request that my portrait by the same artist be hung beside it."

The lion-headed chicken got agitated, insisting he wouldn't have time to paint my portrait so quickly.

"Tell him he'll have enough time," the caller said, sounding surprised. "And that's all? You're a brave man…"

I didn't let him finish… I hit the "End call" button with the finality of putting a period on a novel that could never be rewritten.

A minute later, I parted ways with the artist, no longer wanting to see his sketches. I offered him money as an advance for the new portrait. He took offence, remarking he'd been paid too much already for the previous one. Then, already at the doorway, he shouted he would paint me for free, God willing.

Yes, God willing…

IN LIEU OF AN EPILOGUE
FROM THE PUBLISHER

Recently in the City of N… on the Volkhov River, the "Unexpected Joy" restaurant has placed a portrait of a youth with an angelic, pure gaze and rose petals in his hair in its mezzanine room beside the portrait of "The Lady by the White Piano." The young man is dressed in chain mail, like a knight, with his hands resting on the hilt of a downward-pointing sword. At first glance, he appears to be is holding an emerald, the size of an Easter egg and glowing with extraordinary beauty in his right hand. This, however, is but an illusion created by the emerald mounted on the tip of the sword's hilt.

Looking at the portrait, some claim that emeralds always bring woe to their owners, while others say they bring joy. But all unanimously agree on one thing: the young man and woman depicted in the portraits are truly lucky people.

THE END

Viktor Slipenchuk

CROSSROADS

Novelettes and stories

CROSSROADS

Vladimir Yalikov, the driver from the Korostylyovka motor pool, hit an elderly woman with his trailer. It happened like this. He left the motor pool around noon as they were preparing a lumber truck for a journey. Before reaching the district store, he turned onto Kolkhoznaya Street to go home and pick up a gun, since the hunting season was open. Kolkhoznaya was the main road. Yalikov slowed down, looked left, and saw no one. He started to turn, and then a woman came out of nowhere. The truck was moving very slowly. Someone more agile would have jumped into the ditch, and that would be it, but what can you expect from an old woman? She hesitated, and the trailer caught her on the roadside. Yalikov jumped out and people parted to let him through. As soon as he saw what had happened, he felt shaken. He leaned his shoulder on the cab door to stop himself from falling and closed his eyes. When he opened them again, he couldn't believe what he saw. Aunt Pasha, Zhenka Kolotov's mother, was lying on the ground. What had he done, what had he done? Doctors at the hospital diagnosed deep shock, and an X-ray confirmed a spinal fracture. She died that same day without regaining consciousness. She had just died, but the rumour had already spread from yard to yard: "Vovka Yalikov ran over some granny on Kolkhoznaya Street!"

The first thing drivers want to know is who was the culprit, where and how it happened—only then do they ask about the victim, whether it was a man or a woman, young or old. They rarely, if ever, ask about the name because it doesn't change the court case. Therefore, it wasn't surprising that Zhenya Kolotov learned everything about the incident on the same day, right after returning from the sawmill. Well, not exactly everything! Ivan Onatsky, the Medvedka-to-Sawmill line bus driver, met Zhenya thirty kilometres from the village. He honked from afar, and they stopped cab to cab. He and Ivan had known each other for a long time and had played together in a brass band prior to serving in the army.

"What's up, trombone?" Zhenya asked, leaning out of his cab.

"Oh, that's, um, you didn't see anything, did you?" Ivan flexed his index finger, which meant controllers among the drivers.

"Why would they go that way?" Zhenya wondered.

"They would have busted you at once, drums!" Ivan rejoiced. "They're smart bastards nowadays: they hitchhike out, and then get you where you least expect them."

However, Ivan was not happy that they would bust Zhenya at once. What he really meant was, "Look at him, we played in the same brass band together. He's also a driver, but clueless about the details of my work." Zhenya understood this too and laughed.

"Lots of fare dodgers?"

"Yep, seen some."

"Then… why don't you sell them tickets?" He suggested, still laughing.

"Can't really push those babushkas!"

Ivan lied blatantly. He took no fare dodgers. Ivan charged every stowaway a rouble, including people he knew—this was a sort of his own fare, but he didn't talk about it and changed the subject.

"Did you hear Vovka Yalikov ran over a granny on Kolkhoznaya?"

"Ran over?" Zhenya didn't understand.

"Yep, hit her with the trailer while making a turn."

"Get out of here!"

"Out of here? Me?" Ivan took offence. "It's all I've been hearing about lately. It's all they talk about on the bus. Out your butt!" He swore, offended to have his words questioned when he wasn't lying. They parted. Or rather, Ivan went first. "So much for a good chat," Zhenya thought with annoyance. He wanted to know the details, but not by grabbing Ivan by the sleeve. Zhenya couldn't bear it and shouted after him:

"Bye, crybaby!"

He pulled the gearstick and sped off.

"I'll go to Vovka's first thing and hand the wood over later. The foreman, of course, won't say anything, but Lilka Khalyuto will grumble; she might make a fuss. What a rare idiot. Gossip is always the first thing on her mind, so much for a dispatcher." Zhenya opened the window and spat. "Let her fuss, I'm ahead of schedule. Okay, enough of that, but Vovka, poor Vovka. His wedding is on the seventh. What a present. Ivan says a granny, so probably old, may have outlived her time. And Vovka's life is just beginning. Oh, damn!" Forgetting himself, Zhenya floored it and somehow froze, turned off completely. Even the smoothest of roads would still remind him of itself with a pothole from time to time.

He saw a mound, which looked like the skullcap of a giant, shining with gold embroidery under the sunset, and felt the inexplicable joy of nearing home. The mound heralded home from afar. The road led to the asphalt highway connecting the village with the newly opened health resort. Zhenya had memories of this resort, nothing special, but he gave way to them just to relax before seeing his friend.

Zhenya returned from the army in early May. He arrived in the evening, and opened the door, without knocking, of course: everyone was at the table having dinner - his mother, father, brother, sister. Mother jumped up from her stool and groaned, clutching her lower back. She had suffered from brucellosis her entire life, having worked as a calf herder for as long as Zhenya could recall. Even back then, she would fall ill, but didn't make much of it at the time. Her mornings would be accompanied by moans of discomfort, but the pain would generally subside for most of the day, allowing her to bustle about before the aches and pains made their unwelcome return in the evening. Zhenya embraced his mother and helped her back on the stool. Embarrassed at appearing frail - it's hardly the right time to be unwell! - she wept. The others around the table grew animated too, leaping up, his sister clinging to his neck and peppering him with kisses. Unaccustomed to such affection, Zhenya felt a deep gratitude stir within him as the entire welcome ceremony played out properly, allowing everyone to be seated once more. He said:

"They've built a health resort by the hill, it's a palace!"
"That's right," their father agreed, while the sister ranted:
"What did you think, they only have palaces abroad?"
"Have some borscht," mother said.

His elder brother, Leonid, went to the pantry and fetched a bottle of wine. Living separately, it just so happened that his wife had sent him to ask Zhenya's father about that year's hay situation, as they wished to purchase a cow - Tatiana was pregnant again and would be unable to cope if she had twins again. "You can laugh all you like, but a cow's a necessity with such a brood." Leonid remarked. Everyone gathered, was drinking, and as always, and for as long as Zhenya could recall, conversation turned to an argument about their sister. The sister was nearly twelve years older than Zhenya but four years younger than Leonid. The age gaps meant they scarcely even looked related. Whenever they all convened, even in the past, their father would typically keep silent while their mother took charge, bossing everyone until she noticed the disagreement between her children, prompting tears and wails:

"It's not my fault you were born so far apart. Your father and I wanted you all at once."

"All right, Pasha," father would placate.

A hush would then fall, so quiet you could hear a fly battering the windowpane.

These arguments about his sister had been tiresome before conscription, but now the bickering somehow warmed Zhenya's soul, evoking that familiar scent of kinship binding their family of five. Zhenya unbuckled his belt and hung it on the back of the chair.

"What's all this fuss about Raika?"

"She bought a trip to a resort but doesn't want to go… Threw twenty roubles at it yet still not happy, rich girl!"

His mother started berating Raika, while Zhenya sat listening with a smile. He felt content, he was home. He loved everyone here, and everyone loved him, though it went unspoken. And why? People tended to dwell on the negatives most of the time. If that's truly how life works, it's a pity. Take Raika, a teachers' college graduate who plays piano - a genuine artist, yet she considers herself a fool. She suffers from headaches, but these days, who doesn't? It's just a sign of the times. Leonid's right: it's high time she got married, but she simply won't heed the advice. Now she's off to Crimea. Zhenya tried to follow the flow of the conversation.

"Let her go, maybe she has a boyfriend there." Leonid flushed from the wine and, as her brother, was determined to get involved.

"No way! I just want to see Crimea."

"See? She's going to waste her money; could have bought a piano. She plays well and brought everyone to tears at the kindergarten matinee."

Mother pulled her apron to her eyes, ready to cry.

"You won't listen to your mother! I'm uneducated; what do I know?

"Pasha, what's the big deal? Let her go. Yalta is popular now, maybe you and I should go too.

There was a look of surprise around the table.

"What nonsense."

Mother waved her hand in annoyance.

"We'll slaughter a boar by New Year's Eve, Leonid will take it to town, and then there's our pension."

"That pension won't get you far, so just be quiet…. Yalta! This one's thrown away twenty roubles, and you're heading the same way."

"Why not, Mum?" The idea seemed to have grabbed everyone's attention. "Five hours by plane and we're in Yalta."

"Oh, yeah, let's go make fun of our old age. What are you thinking?" Mother suddenly smiled. "If Nikiforovna found out, she'd have much to gossip about!"

She and father laughed, and the children smiled too.

"Raika, let me go on your resort trip," Zhenya suggested.

"Oh, Zhenya, I'll buy you sweets if you do!" Raika rejoiced.

"No way, he just got here and is heading away already…"

"Why, it is just twenty kilometres away," Leonid interceded. "I pass by it every day on my way to Pokrovka."

The health resort was constructed on the banks of Crooked Lake, and Raika had booked a stay immediately after its grand opening.

At any rate, it was settled that Raika would go to Yalta, while Zhenya would visit the new local resort. It would allow him time to ponder where to apply himself after the army, so that he could complete the ninth grade, for at his age there was still much to learn.

It was now after midnight and Leonid was ready to go home.

As he waited at the gate to see his brother off, Zhenya asked:

"Lenya, is Raika pretty?"

"She's got everything. But she shoos everyone away. She doesn't like anyone; this one has bad breath, and that one's legs are too crooked…"

"She says such things?" Zhenya marvelled.

"Yep, and laughs at them. Otherwise, she's just fine apart from her headaches."

"She's exaggerating, isn't she?"

"I don't know. You see, the one she likes doesn't like her. Got it?"

"What's the matter? She's thirty-two, she'll find someone."

"Kolka Savateev asked her to marry him, but she refused."

"Who needs him? He's too tall and walks like a goose." Zhenya interceded.

"That's exactly what she said – told the matchmakers we don't need that goose here."

"That's our Raika!" They laughed.

"So how are you? Why didn't you come home on the holidays?"

"They sent me to combat troops, and then there are these events."

"Yeah, Mum and Dad were worried. I said he isn't alone there, but with the troops. Raika turned as pale as a wall; we talked little in her presence.

There was silence.

"How's your work going?"

"It's okay. It's fine for now. Join us. They've found coal in

Pokrovka; there will be open-pit mining, and we're already hauling timber there. Okay, we'll talk later but now I must go or else my wife will take me over the coals for coming in late."

They parted…

The next day, when Zhenya opened his eyes, even before he moved, the ceiling was already shaking, floating in front of his eyes. "Hangover." he thought. He moved his eyes; it hurt. He calmed himself, thinking, "It's all right, it'll pass." But by evening, it hadn't passed and the next day, he felt cold and realised that he was ill. His mother gave him oatmeal and bilberry broth, to no effect. At first, he tried to joke and laugh, but after lunch, he crawled to the lavatory and back, feeling utterly exhausted. Nothing to be proud about, so much for a soldier.

Raika came home from work with a thermometer and measured his temperature. Thirty-nine point nine. Zhenya remembered nothing. He would see a black dot, look at it, look at it, look at it, and then suddenly it would start making ripples like a pebble thrown into the water. Or Ref, the sheepdog from the outpost, crawls to the car and whimpers, whimpers, and he can see through the tank's visor how it leaves a bloody trail on the grass. He must open the hatch and help Ref, but he can't, there are bandits somewhere nearby, hiding. God forbid, Ref will crawl under a caterpillar. Zhenya rushed out of bed. Raika was terrified.

"He has cholera!" This thought burned through everything like lightning. Raika dashed out as if the ceiling were about to collapse.

"Raika!"

His mother followed her but could not catch up. Dad looked up from the hog feeder he was fixing.

"Pasha, what's up?"

"Oh, just felt like running around like crazy. Why?"

Mother walked to the barn, sat down on the overturned trough, and dropped her hands onto her lap. Father sighed, sat down beside her, and quietly put his fists on his knees, the weight of them still in his hands. They just sat like that, two rapidly ageing parents. "Heh, Yalta, Yalta…" The old man thought sadly. He felt sorry for this nearest and dearest, easy-to-read woman. Her son had just arrived, Pasha had come to life, and he had taken to crafting this feeder. Oh, who could have known how much he would like to take Pasha to Yalta. She'd lived her life, and what had she seen? He had got around during the war and visited VDNKh[1] before retirement. He could have done something for her, but never found the time, and now their health is fading. The old man sighed again: no one was privy to these thoughts.

He was mistaken. Yesterday, at dawn, as he awoke to resume working in the barn, he realised the old woman had understood everything. The cheerful clang of the hammer resonated within her soul: "Yal-ta, Yal-ta!" She didn't know how, despite the pain in her lower back, she managed to extract a basin from beneath the washstand and splash the water into the yard. "I must prepare breakfast before my son wakes up," she mentally justified her actions, as if someone were reprimanding her for rising too early. "Breakfast… I should have peeled the potatoes over the basin first and emptied it only afterwards." She was also

---

1   Russian acronym for the Exhibition of Achievements of National Economy in Moscow (pronounced ve-de-en-kha).

impatient about another matter: was the old man truly crafting a feeder for the boar? "Yes, he is," she affirmed after spotting the new white timbers in the blue twilight. She saw them and dashed to the hut, noting, however, that he had used the timbers initially intended for the gate. At any other time, she might have quarrelled about it, but now she merely thought to herself: "The old man's gone mad."

Now they were sitting side by side, watching helplessly through the gaps in the old gate as their daughter dashed frantically towards the bus stop.

"Oh, children, children!" Raika spared no thought for her aching feet. Consumed by a dreadful premonition, she was beside herself. She couldn't shake the morning visit of the infectious disease prevention team from her mind. They had inspected the entire kindergarten—the kitchen, the food stores, the toilets. It was like previous inspections, but far more thorough; before, they had simply taken the staff's word for it. This time, they scrutinised everything personally. Overall, they were satisfied with their findings and commended the hygiene in the kindergarten. The team's head was talkative:

"There's a flu outbreak in Priobsk and in other places too… It's spring, and it's scorching! And then those tourists from different countries are flocking in."

The news was alarming. Priobsk was far away, and there were no fatalities yet, but it was still frightening. Nevertheless, the disease prevention team departed, and the kindergarten staff discussed their visit. They were somewhat anxious, but their agitation was short-lived. Soon, the whole incident was forgotten.

They trusted Soviet medicine to protect them.

Raika had also paid little attention until she put the thermometer on Zhenya, and it suddenly struck her like an electric shock: "God, some kind of flu... And diarrhoea." Her legs carried her to the hospital. She was running, dithering in her head: "There's flu in Priobsk... Tourists from afar are coming, and Zhenya served abroad... I'm such a fool; I won't make it in time!" Raika was ready to burst into tears. "Poor Zhenya, he's calling for some Ref, probably a foreigner."

At the hospital, she rushed straight to the chief doctor's office, trying to save every second. The chief did not interrupt, listened, and calmly said, "I don't think it's a big deal. Take it easy."

"Maybe he has cholera?" Raika sobbed.

"Wha-a-at?" The doctor seemed to catch on; Raika must have planted some doubt in his mind. He stood up. "All right, then, I'll examine the patient myself, even though it's not part of my job description. Let's go."

He stressed his last words. Raika didn't understand; she could not know that the chief was twenty-eight today, and he had only been in charge of the district hospital for a month. Besides, he had worked as an attending physician in the infectious diseases department before his recent promotion.

So instead of the resort, Zhenya ended up in a hospital, and what a hospital! The infectious disease ward was located at the edge of the village. It looked like an ordinary peasant's hut from afar. It would have been impossible for any villager to build such a hut, however, and why would they? "Twelve rooms, no less,"

Zhenya thought. That was all he thought. Perhaps someone else in his place would not have thought of it. Everything was floating before his eyes, wobbling as if submerged in water.

"A soldier's been brought in," a voice rang through the wards. This alone would draw attention to Zhenya, but he was also the first seriously ill patient in a week, and the first to be brought in by none other than the chief physician, so all the interest in him was justified. Strangely enough, the interest did not diminish from day to day but, on the contrary, increased more and more—Zhenya's ward mates were to blame.

All three days, while Zhenya lay in bed, they discussed him in public. The girls asked, as if by chance: "Who's he? Where did he come from? How did a soldier end up here?" The guys would answer, and not without intent, as they had their own interests, too. A tank crewman, he had always been a healthy man, but he's still here. It justified them, in a sense.

"The soldier was swabbed again today.... Tomorrow they'll take a blood test. He was delirious, calling for some Ruth... He'll be sunbathing here for at least two more weeks."

In short, when Zhenya left his ward to watch TV for the first time a few days later, he was already the centre of attention. When the girls saw him, they moved aside, and Zhenya got confused at first. One of the girls looked at him from below, slightly slanting her eyes. The sun had crept into the hall through the thickets of bird cherry trees and pushed the hall apart. Zhenya heard the murmur of spring waters from within the shining columns of air. He turned away at once, as if his eyes had never met the girl's. But the moment gushed so vastly and powerfully that

Zhenya lost himself, penetrated by its blaze, caught off guard just for a split second—she laughed. Her eyes were enormous, grey with some elusive speckles of colour. Her forehead was straight, but the roundness of her dark eyebrows made it seem to bulge. The strands of hair flowing softly down her cheeks elongated her face and gave it an expression of shyness and sadness. However, her decidedly upturned lower lip and her eyes that radiated with myriads of gold speckles as if snatched from another, tirelessly cheerful character, lit her face with a glow of coquetry and mischief.

When their gazes met, the girl looked at him, without realising it, as if to say, "I understand that you are looking at me, not me at you. Well, that's fine; let this be you then." This probably could have cheered Zhenya up at some other time, but not now. Now the shock was too deep. Staring at the TV screen yet still seeing the eyes full of mischief in front of him, Zhenya became worried.

"She's laughing at the fact that I ended up in this hospital." He was embarrassed by that, regardless. He hadn't looked at the girl even once for the rest of the evening.

"What's there left to talk about? There's nothing more to say…" And yet, if Zhenya had known back then that Valya, the girl from the hospital, was friends with Vovka, he wouldn't have got so close to her. No, he wouldn't have. The thought pained him and made him angry. "How long can I go on like this for the rest of my life?" He rummaged in his pockets, took out a cigarette, lit it, and checked his watch. "I should make it back by eight. There's the river, the mill, and the village outskirts beginning right from the health resort."

Thinking of the hospital, Zhenya's mind drifted back to Valya. Her family name was Korbut, which is quite famous. That's how our acquaintance began. Zhenya smiled. It sort of happened naturally, he didn't plan for it and it was wonderful even though it was in the hospital, and then Vovka came to visit. Zhenya lowered the car window but decided against tossing out the cigarette and took another drag. Vovka went to see her first, only then did he remember Zhenya, his friend. When Zhenya saw them together, he understood everything instantly. She also understood that they were friends. Later, Vovka caught on too. They hugged tightly, but both felt a certain chill.

Remembering the quarrel, Zhenya no longer felt the same hatred for Valya. He didn't know how he would have acted if it had happened. Afraid to admit it to himself, Zhenya told himself twice: "I've cooled down about her, I've cooled down. Six months have passed, that's enough…" He threw out the cigarette butt and, raising the window, berated: "I wish I could just shut myself off like that… once and for all… But you can't shut it off, it all feels as if it were only yesterday!"

One day, the three of them went to an abandoned watermill and sat down on a large, flat stone. Zhenya felt awkward, like a third wheel next to Volodya and Valya, but he couldn't leave. He wasn't held back. On the contrary, at the very beginning of the walk, Volodya gave him two expressive looks with an easily recognisable meaning, but something happened to Zhenya.

He quipped and told funny stories of army life, feeling a deep disgust for himself. At first, it was hard to comprehend, as if it didn't even apply to Zhenya. Vovka wanted him to leave. Zhenya knew it but decided he would stay, stubbornly, with a gloating satisfaction that somehow cheered him up, unexpectedly even to himself. He noticed Volodya seemed puzzled by his cheerfulness. Zhenya looked at Valya longer than usual, but she did not seem to share Zhenya's joy. Volodya felt reassured and stopped jealously watching her, laughing several times as Zhenya told his stories. Strangely, this made Zhenya angry. Yes, the more Volodya laughed, the more Zhenya's dislike for him grew. He furtively glanced at Valya, not yet realising what was happening to him. Zhenya hoped to see at least a shadow of resentment towards Volodya on her face, but Valya seemed absent. Zhenya hoped for anything: remorse, awkwardness, shame... He and Valya had kissed, after all! Vovka doesn't know that... There was neither shame nor remorse, all Zhenya saw was a distant concern. Suddenly, he realised the ambiguity of his behaviour with utmost clarity.

"I need to leave, leave now..." He stood up.

"Anyway, you two stay here, and I'll go."

Zhenya hesitated a little but didn't expect to be stopped. "As soon as I leave, they'll be kissing. If Vovka left now, she would kiss me, that's how she is... she doesn't care who's with her," Zhenya thought and felt such a strong squeeze under his heart that he had to slow down a little, buying time to gather his strength. "I've got to rise above it, rise above it." Zhenya walked away with an exaggeratedly firm step. Not even a hundred steps away, he felt relieved. "Vovka will be lost with her, lost…"

"Zhenya, why are you leaving?"

Zhenya felt as if he'd been hit in the back of his head. "Really, why?" He looked back and saw them standing on a rock. Valya had her arms crossed over her chest, probably so Vovka could hug her more comfortably. If they had stood apart, Zhenya would have thought of some excuse and left after all, but now he decided to come back. He wanted to look into her eyes; he just couldn't comprehend how it could be like this! "Now I'll speak my mind, I'll reveal all! I do feel sorry for Vovka, but…" Zhenya put his hands in his pockets, approached closer and stopped. Valya beat him by just an instant. Slipping out from under Vovka's arm, she jumped down from the rock.

"Zhenya, I told Volodya that you love me too."

"Wha-at?"

Zhenya felt dizzy.

"What did you say?"

Zhenya felt as if the ground would open and swallow him. Fortunately, Vovka was staring intently at the river, as if he had noticed something interesting in its murky waters.

"I told Volodya that you said you loved me," Valya began. "I told him that you said that you love me. But he didn't believe me. He said I made it up! I must be terrible at making things up, because anyone can make up anything, right, Zhenya?"

Valya laughed sharply, nervously. Zhenya felt her eyes on him, anticipating his response. It was no laughing matter; he had to answer.

"Oh God! Did he think it would be so ridiculous?"

"Yes, I told you so," Zhenya mumbled, his tongue feeling numb.

"Zhenya, what were you saying? Say it, please. Say you love me, Volodya didn't hear!"

"Yes, I said that," Zhenya almost shouted. "So what?"

Valya laughed again, a haughty sound as if she was running in unnaturally small steps, and suddenly stumbled.

"Volodya, Zhenya also said that he could do anything for me, just like they say in books! He'd swim across the river if I told him to."

"Stop it, Valya, what's the point?"

Vovka's words carried such longing and pain that everything turned upside down in Zhenya's soul. "My God, she's going to ask Vovka to swim now, and he can't swim!" Zhenya muttered as he saw Vovka sitting down awkwardly without taking his eyes off the river.

"Come on, Vovka, it's just a free concert." Zhenya looked at Valya with hatred. "I also told her she looked like some actress."

He dashed into the water.

"Ah-ah, it's cold!" he screamed, though he felt no cold at all; on the contrary, he was burning inside.

"Zhenya, Zhenya, come back!" Valya screamed.

Zhenya sensed she didn't expect him to do that.

"You've been sick recently; you'll catch a cold. Come back, I was just kidding!"

Her words, with their begging tone, only spurred him on.

The river wasn't wide. As he climbed to the other bank, he shouted, "Vovka, I swam for you, tell her!"

Zhenya lay on his back and poured water out of his shoes without taking them off.

"I'd better leave, or she'll make you fly for her. What's in your script, drama queen?" Zhenya shouted, feigning joy, and left without looking back. He was cold.

Why is it that sometimes there is no reason to love a person, and everyone knows it, yet they still do? Or there is no reason to hate a person, yet they are despised and tormented? Why? Just because. Scientists, of course, try to explain everything through the number and arrangement of chromosomes, through combinations, but so far, they have not succeeded. They are still working on their facts, facts are everywhere, in the army, at workplaces, and from ancient times, too. Lyonka Gvozdyov, the regimental poet, told him that Jesus Christ had suffered the same fate. He sat under a fig tree with Judas Iscariot. Zhenya was amused by the fact that Judas had a surname and remembered it. They started talking. Iscariot had lots of questions, mostly about Jesus' beliefs. His eyes were burning; he was excited, such a passionate young man. "What's your opinion of Rome?" he asked, "What do you think of Caesar? Jesus didn't sense any trap. Render unto Caesar what is Caesar's…?"

They had a conversation, and then what? Jesus liked Judas because of his deep knowledge, lively character, and inquisitiveness. Jesus spoke of Judas as a remarkably handsome and inquisitive young man.

And this handsome man went and sold the one he admired as the son of God to the high priests for thirty pieces of silver.

So much for his chromosome combination. And what happened next? They brought Jesus to Governor Pontius Pilate, who had a custom of granting amnesty to one prisoner on a holiday to please the people. Pontius Pilate saw that Jesus had no guilt, only accusations, and was put on trial purely because of the envy of the chief priests for his intelligence and excellent healing abilities. He said to the people:

"These are the prisoners, Christ and Barabbas; which of the two do you want me to release?"

"Barabbas, Barabbas!" the people shouted, even though Barabbas was jailed for killing two fellow citizens while drunk, and they knew it.

So much for another combination. Or take Zhenya's foreman, for instance. Who did he wrong? No one. He's just demanding and fair. Who loves him? No one.

But take Vanka Onatski. He won't give you a free ride. He charges his fellow teammates, yet most people respect him, even admire him:

"What a rascal, well done."

Zhenya broke into a sweat. The scale of the world had opened up to him. He had forgotten about Valya, about Vovka, even though in considering all the "combinations," he meant them.

"Well, well." Zhenya whispered gently, as if luring a bird and trying to look at it from all sides without scaring it away.

An oncoming truck sped by. "From the state farm, probably hauling beets. We have licence plates with the letters 'AD' in our motor pool," Zhenya noted automatically, but this didn't distract him.

"Comrades scientists!" – even in his thoughts he made a pause, imagining an audience of thousands. "It's not about chromosomes." Zhenya looked around once more. Yes, according to his conclusions, it was all about human conscientiousness. He felt shame. Wow, he contemplated God knows what, and it turns out consciousness is key. Not much of a conclusion, just disappointment. "Schoolbook truth. Okay, whatever."

Cheerful lights flashed at the railway station. Zhenya decelerated and switched to low beams. He drove into the village, where everything was familiar. He knew those lights - the bakery, the state farm, the medical school, the health centre, all of them. The village could well be called a town. Zhenya remembered how Vovka Yalikov had appeared on Kolkhoznaya Street wearing a white shirt and shorts, running, and rolling a bicycle wheel in front of him. Zhenya recognised him immediately as a city boy. Vovka stopped.

"Is this the street you live on?"

"What's it to you?"

White shirt, shorts… he was showing off.

"I'm going to live here too, nice street, better than the city."

He knew what to say. True, starting off by praising his city instead would have been unwise.

Zhenya reached Kolkhoznaya Street. He didn't like to drive past the house without stopping, but this time he had to get to the grocery store before it closed. He switched back to full beams; it seemed darker on the street than in the field. He saw a group of people near the house, mostly women and children, with the windows dark. He was surprised.

"What's going on there? Everyone else has their lights on. Maybe a power cut?" He thought nothing of the people. What was wrong? Perhaps some neighbours had come to visit. He looked back; it seemed to him someone called his name from the street, or was it just his imagination? It sounded just like his mum's voice.

The shop was crowded as usual. Zhenya greeted everyone, making sure he was loud enough. He had to be extra polite before trying to skip the queue to buy vodka; people wouldn't be happy. Men were likely to be more understanding, but women might even kick him out in a fit of class hatred for a man buying vodka. Zhenya stopped. Yes, all women, all knew him, all stared at him. "No luck today," he thought. The salesgirl was also looking at him, Lyuska Paramonova. "At least she won't judge; she's even sympathetic, and she has a sales quota to meet. OK, let's try…" He thought.

"One bottle, please."

Zhenya held out a five-rouble note, regretting he didn't have the exact change; the queue wouldn't forgive a delay. But everything seemed to be all right. Lyuska took out the bottle without even looking. When Zhenya took the change, the queue even parted a bit to let him through. This was puzzling. "My impudence surprised them, or I've got them hypnotised, or maybe both. Well, impudence wins, as they say…"

Shoving the bottle into his pocket, Zhenya hurried out, still not knowing what to make of this unexpected courtesy.

… Aunt Pasha passed away an hour ago. Volodya sat devastated. The expert assessments, countless explanations, and protocols were all done for the day, yet it felt like there weren't enough of them. Volodya would have preferred to keep busy, explaining how everything had happened for the millionth time, rather than sitting idly. But the day had ended, and Volodya was left alone. "Perhaps I could even go to the cinema," he thought and immediately shuddered. "How can I, when Aunt Pasha just died? I should have taken a sharper turn." He sighed intermittently, as if gasping for breath. Suddenly, for the first time that day, he felt the full weight of his misfortune. "I could go to jail! I could, in a snap." Volodya felt uneasy. "No wedding, no Valya, nothing at all… Why me? Why did this whole thing land on me?" Volodya almost cried in a rush of self-pity but held himself together. His grandfather and grandmother were watching him now. Grandfather had said that Granny had been ill since lunch, since the moment she learnt… Creaking with his crutch, he followed Volodya into the hut, but Volodya forgot. He sat down by the table and forgot, and they were watching. He looked in the corner, there was a bed, Grandfather's round spectacles glittering. He did not see anything else… "How quiet it is! Sometimes they would talk and moan so loudly that I would wake up in my own room, and now there's total silence," he thought with dislike. He realised that he ought not to speak now ("I better not… granny's heart isn't good"), but he couldn't bear it ("Ah, what the hell…"):

"Aunt Pasha passed away."

Grandmother groaned, the spectacles stopped glittering, and Volodya heard his grandfather's unnaturally cheerful voice: "Don't be silly, old girl, don't be silly."

Volodya thought: "Look at him, how strong he is. He dropped his crutch, but pretended he threw it himself as if he was angry with the old woman… Come on, come on. To them, this is perhaps even harder than it is for me." He smiled a strange smile, as if he had suddenly discovered some odd pleasure. He buried his face in his hands to hide his smile, afraid they might see it.

"Maybe you worry too much, and she'll survive."

Volodya almost jumped with anger. It would probably have been better if he actually did jump up or shout, but he prudently hesitated. They always find a straw to grasp. No, Volodya would not let them have it. To hell with it. He was drowning in the first place. He clutched his head and exhaled.

"Oh, I wish it were so. She died and won't come back to life!"

It was dark in the hut, but it was as if he saw himself in the window's square of light. He felt impressive and sure that if he'd announced that from a stage, the audience would have roared. Volodya felt he had an innate thespian flair. Sometimes, while watching a film, he would catch an actor not performing well - "No, not like this, you are doing it wrong," knowing in his mind how it should be. This talent helped him a lot at work. He would approach the foreman and say: "Kuzmich, I can't drive today, I need to stay at home," and the boss would immediately agree. Zhenka Kolotov couldn't do that. He would argue with the foreman and still wouldn't get his way. Remembering his friend, Volodya grew nervous. "He'll come back and we'll meet." Volodya didn't want to meet him; he'd had enough of Zhenka's brother Lyonka. They met, and Lyonka yelled "How could you?" and snarled in disgust, as if he'd touched dirt: "Get out of my sight!" That "get out of my sight" still rang in Volodya's ears. Woe onto him, it would be better for Volodya never to have been born, let alone live! "Gotta turn the lights on." He got up, and searched around on the wall with his hand, but forgot what he was searching for.

"Yes, the lights!" The room lit up, he saw his grandparents and almost shrieked. "Why am I messing around? They feel hurt; how they look at me! They catch my every move… I wish I could say something encouraging to them, but there's nothing to say." Volodya rushed to his room and plumped down on the bed, still dressed.

Volodya did not feel the tears immediately. A streak of light through the door lit the pillow, and for a moment its beam reached Volodya as if not from the kitchen, but from his most distant childhood.

Volodya stretched out his hand, and the strip of light slid across his palm. "Just like from the sun," he thought. The whirr of a manual sewing machine came from behind the door—his mother was making him a white shirt. Volodya felt good, very good. Perhaps he had never felt so good. The machine stopped, and Volodya heard a newspaper rustling. It was Uncle Misha. Volodya hung off the bed and pulled up a fireman's helmet. The metal came to life under the strip of light, sparks flashed on its rough edges. "Like the stars that came alive," Volodya rejoiced, testing the strength of the steel welt with his fingernail. "A real helmet… perhaps no one else has such a helmet," he thought contentedly, and almost heard Uncle Misha. It was very important for Volodya to have such a rare thing—a true jewel for a suburban boy. "I'll let everyone play knights," Volodya decided, and immediately imagined setting an order to offer the helmet to his friends. He would be the last to put it on, saying, "I've worn it a thousand times already." And everyone would believe it. Volodya got excited. "Because the helmet is mine." He went to bed longing for the morning—he didn't want to sleep at all. On the other hand, he didn't want to make Uncle Misha angry, especially now, after what had happened. Uncle Misha was perfectly fine, of course. Volodya wouldn't mind if he lived with them, it wouldn't have been a problem, but no, he had to mess around with his mum. She called out to Volodya: "Son, save me!" She pleaded jokingly as Uncle Misha tickled her. Volodya rushed at him, tore his shirt, and beat him with his fists: "Here, take this, take this!" He got heated up. Uncle Misha laughed at first, but when Volodya bit him, he groaned and let Mum go. Oh, how proud Volodya was! He had dealt with Uncle Misha on his own; he had protected his mother. He was waiting for praise but suddenly saw his mother worried:

"Oh, my God, did he bite you?!"

"It's nothing, Nadia," Uncle Misha replied.

Volodya felt ashamed, and for the first time, he wasn't ashamed of himself but of his mother. "She was pretending. She's fine with Uncle Misha. He knows that, he knows she feels good! She can't deny it now." Volodya jumped out into the yard and hid in the vegetable garden. The new discovery shocked him. "Uncle Misha is not one of their kin; Volodya has a daddy, he lives with Granny and Grandpa. Volodya was deliberately not told about it, but he knows, he knows everything now, don't think he doesn't!"

He lay in the potato haulm, listening to the growing and receding noise of passing cars. He wanted to go far, far away to his father. And he would go. Once it gets dark, he would get on the bus and leave them all behind. He cried and fell asleep on the soft, warm ground. In his dreams, he was travelling on a big red bus. His father sat behind the wheel; he looked back at Volodya and nodded to him.

Volodya woke up instantly as if leaping out of a dream. "I've forgotten and fallen asleep." He wiped his tears with the corner of his pillowcase, turned the pillow over, and listened. The outer door slammed. Volodya froze. "We surely have a visitor." It sounded like his grandfather had let someone in. A thought pricked him: "Could it be Zhenka?" An inexplicable fear whispered: "You're ill and can't go out. You should have taken your clothes off, pulled on your blanket, and that would have been it." He heard muffled voices and his grandfather's crutch approaching.

"What's come over everybody? Any other day they would have chased me out of the shop, and scolded me, and deservedly so, but not today. Today, they even moved out of my way!"

Zhenya stood on the porch for a while, as if waiting for someone, then slowly descended the steps. The door slammed, and a man in an unbuttoned trench coat jumped out. Zhenya hadn't noticed him in the shop. Overtaking him, the man was pushing a half-litre bottle into his trouser pocket. Obviously, the queue had parted for him too. Of course, he doesn't even think about why they did... It's all right. When he drinks with his friends, he will probably say: "Lucky me, I got it without queuing."

Zhenya smiled.

"These people, they were offered to release Jesus, the Lord God himself, but they asked for Barabbas, the lush."

Holding the bottle, Zhenya walked around his truck and kicked the tyres for no reason, just out of habit. "Still, something moves people; I just don't see it. And it is important to see it; otherwise…"

Zhenya wanted to climb into the cab but stopped and leaned on the wing.

"That's why I separated myself from Vovka and Valya. I don't get it. It won't end well… There should be some grand purpose for a man to fulfil. There is. There must be!"

Zhenya felt a vague, lingering anxiety, a heavy feeling like a premonition of imminent trouble. It had happened before: anxiety would fly into his soul like a lost bird but would never materialise. It would fly in, circle, create confusion, and fly away. Where from? Why? What did it try to convey? Probably nothing. But Zhenya would already be worried, thinking it was a sign, a signal, that there was a reason for everything. He would search for it and find a hint of something.

Volodya graduated after ten full years of high school, not without difficulty. He wasn't a good learner, but could not allow himself to drop out. He did it for his grandparents. They dreamed of his high school certificate as if it were a magic cure for all life's problems, and Volodya tried his best. It started with a letter from his mother. Volodya wanted to enrol as a mechanic's apprentice in a car repair shop right after eight years of school, like Zhenya

Kolotov. He had already taken care of the paperwork when the letter came. His mother wrote:

"Congratulations on finishing your eighth year. Your brothers, Tolya and Gena, send you greetings. Mikhail Gavrilovich, your stepfather…"

Volodya read aloud but stopped here, looked at his grandfather and asked:

"Is she afraid I've forgotten who is who?"

From this point, he felt annoyed but went on.

"Mikhail Gavrilovich, your stepfather, asks you to move in with us now."

"Now!" Volodya stressed it.

"He will help you get into the railway school to become an assistant diesel locomotive driver (he has connections)."

Next, his mother wrote that she would not come on holiday because of the children and the distance.

Volodya answered at once: "Thank you for offering the railway school. I'll do all ten grades…That's it!"

His grandparents were delighted. Grandpa took out a small bottle of vodka and, drinking it all by himself, shouted, probably expecting his daughter to hear him in Saratov:

"You, Vovka, are no longer hers! Prove yourself and make us proud! What's Granny to her? And who am I? Well… Think about it! Look at that princess, it's too far for her to come, but who made her go there? Stubborn girl… But you, Vovka, you must respect her; she's your mother. And prove yourself, we'll help you…"

Grandpa used to become noisy after drinking, but Volodya

was never afraid of him. This time, he even cheered up. "Grandpa always supports me… He loves me the most." Most of whom? Volodya didn't specify. It was "most of all," and that was enough.

He sat facing his grandfather, lowered his head, and sighed. Volodya had a gut feeling that Grandpa would not miss this sigh and would respond. And he did.

"What are you doing, eh?" The old man was worried but immediately feigned cheerfulness, trying to hide his anxiety. "Hey Granny, look at that, our Vovka is not a boy anymore, he's a man!"

"You bet!" Grandmother agreed and chased Grandpa away from the table.

Volodya was not a little boy anymore indeed. Among other things, he knew that his grandparents had spent all their money on their vegetable patch in spring, and only with young potatoes would the situation improve. But his patience failed him. This "most of all" urged him to put it to the test. He pleaded piteously:

"Grandpa, I'd be better off with a bike, an adult-size bike."

Volodya's grandparents were good, kind people. With difficulty, they bought him a bicycle.

"Ride it, grandson!" But Volodya hardly ever rode it, just from time to time, but he admired it a lot. He would go into the storeroom where the bicycle was, turn it over, spin the rear wheel, sit, and look into the silver flickering of the spokes. It seemed to him the cooling breeze from the wheel blew right into his soul, caressing it. It felt so pleasant and good, as if Volodya was running his fingertips over silk. And he heard some lark far away, ringing, ringing.

No, no, it was not a bicycle he needed; it was something

else… That's why he befriended Zhenya Kolotov—Volodya realised Zhenya would never cross that something, he would go down in flames but wouldn't step over it. And so it happened there, by the mill. Volodya sat down on a stone, staring at the water, his friend was still near, but he already saw the silver blinking of the spokes. And then—the silk and the lark's call, pouring from the very depths of his soul, making his every vein freeze in languor.

So, Valya was in love with Kolotov. What of it? What of his own love for her? Kolotov left; he was gone. What a moment that was! Volodya tried with all his will to revive the sensation. He froze, waiting for the lark to sound again. It did not. He noted that with regret, as if from a distance, as if about someone else. "Grandfather, grandfather did not let him. Though no, not grandfather—the friend. Why did he come, why?!"

Volodya felt anger as poisonous as rabies. Perhaps he would get up now. Outside the window, someone shouted, a short call: "Vova!" He shuddered, and raised his head. "Did I really hear that?" The room brightened, filled with watery ghosts. A window appeared on the wall, stood there, dashed up, spilt all over the ceiling, and then dropped down as if a mysterious projectionist could not adjust the frame. "Cinema at home," Volodya thought unhappily, and the blinding light from the door to his side blew away the shadows. Squinting, Volodya turned around.

"There's someone here to see you!" Informed his grandfather. He didn't close the door, waiting for Volodya to get up.

"Who?" Volodya asked, still squinting, though of course he knew who.

"Romka."

"Romka who?" Volodya thought his grandfather was confused.

"Ugh! Onatsky; old Dmitry's nephew," grandfather recalled the last name of Roman Ilyich, the safety engineer. Volodya smiled sceptically and uttered, "All fur coat and no knickers." He didn't like Roman Ilyich at all and yet, was as glad to see the "engineer" as he would a relative.

Roman Ilyich sat on a stool, half-turned towards the table. He looked like a bird with a thick, extended beak and flapping wings. Just having a long nose and a spreading cloak is not enough to look like a bird. One must be able to turn their head slightly upward like Roman Ilyich did, as if looking at his own back. It also requires keeping one's gaze directly in front of one's nose, like wondering whether to peck or not to peck.

Volodya came out into the kitchen, and Roman Ilyich perked up.

"I've just returned from a hunt," he put out his boots and showed them, not to Volodya, but to his grandparents, "I didn't even have time to change. I'm running all over the place amidst the usual comments that Romka is doing nothing; he's our motor pool's professional slacker.'"

Roman Ilyich turned his head towards Grandfather, thinking whether to peck or not to peck. He got distracted. Grandma groaned, "Uh-oh, it's all in God's hands."

"Not true," replied Roman Ilyich. "Everything is in the hands of the public prosecutor."

He looked at everyone. "All these people, eh?" By all accounts, Roman Ilyich felt himself the master of the situation. Subconsciously, he was proud to be involved in the court case. He considered it his official duty to exploit the moment to compensate for all the indifference to his position and to prove his social utility, and maybe even his importance. The situation seemed favourable. The word "prosecutor" caused Grandmother to freeze, while Grandfather reached out to move his chair, then changed his mind and remained standing, leaning on his crutch. Volodya, on the other hand, slammed the hallway door with deliberate loudness. He pretended it had cracked open even though it was closed. Silence quickly overwhelmed this distracting slam. It was Roman's moment to act. He asked:

"Why am I here?" His eyes narrowed as if looking at a maggot on the tip of his beak. "That's right. I was at the prosecutor's office."

He said that then boasted as if he had indeed eaten the maggot:

"We know each other through hunting, but are not exactly friends," Roman Ilyich began, about to mention something concerning the prosecutor before halting himself abruptly. "However, that's beside the point. I recounted everything to him exactly as it occurred, though he was already well informed. He mentioned that we needed to determine the extent of culpability. I responded that what culpability can there be? Our driver was sober, he's a member of Komsomol, a Communist Labour Champion who exceeds his quota by half, having achieved his annual personal target as early as September.' I presented a printed character reference. He read it, smirked, and asked if I were nominating him for a medal or something. I said that medal or not, champions like him are rare. He understood and told me they have no reason to imprison an innocent man. Told me to compile a detailed accident report with assessments from experienced drivers… could he have taken a sharper turn? Ultimately, he requested such a report, indicating that an investigation would proceed, albeit without our involvement. I thought alright, we shall discuss this promptly."

Roman Ilyich returned to examining the maggot again. Grandmother took advantage of the pause, got out of bed huffing and puffing. Grandfather moved a chair and said:

"Romka!" He tapped his crutch. "Help us out, please?"

Volodya grumbled but did not object. He sat down on the bench with his back to the window. Roman Ilyich completely ignored Grandfather's words, as if they had never been spoken. He clicked the lock and opened the folder.

"I hurried to the office to see the chief, Pal Sergeyich. He was already there with Partorg[2] Nikonov, deep in discussion. It seemed the socialist competition bonus was all but lost. Nikonov lamented, 'What a holiday present for us!' Pal Sergeyich, more composed, demanded an update from me. As I began to explain, Nikonov kept interrupting. 'Roman Ilyich, has everyone been enrolled for the briefing in October? He really picked his moment to ask."

Roman Ilyich swore and looked at his "beak" as if Nikonov were right there at its tip.

---

2   Party organiser – a member of enterprise management whose duty was to make sure all activities required from the Communist Party perspective were performed properly.

"Well, that's beside the point... So, I asked Ivan Ivanovich, how can this be? Pal Sergeyich had no choice but to request a log with signatures for the briefing by tomorrow morning. He then suggested that I sit down with Yalikov and draft the document.

"Exactly, exactly," Nikonov interjected. "Yalikov is a member of Komsomol and a school friend of Kolotov; he won't lie and will assist the investigation... They have concerns about the turn and speed." Roman Ilyich smirked. "Look at him, so ideologically driven; he probably sees that socialist competition banner in his dreams! Well, never mind that... So, they instructed me to take action, and we'll find some public figures to endorse the document."

Roman Ilyich pulled a stack of paper from a folder, flapped it closed and put the papers in front of Volodya. For the time being, the safety log was set aside.

That evening, Valya was still unaware of the accident. She overheard a snippet of conversation in which the girls from the third group mentioned "Surgeon Vasily Mitrofanovich Sabutsky was called straight from class because some granny was admitted in shock." However, she paid it little attention.

"Tomorrow I'm on duty (Valya was interning at the hospital), I'll find out everything then." The girls didn't discuss it further; by their final year, they had seen plenty of deceased people. It wasn't that they had become indifferent to it, but they no longer expressed their feelings openly - it was somewhat embarrassing for graduates.

Moreover, that evening Valya did not wait for Volodya. He had promised to visit the next day, saying, "I'll definitely bring some game." He emphasised, "Game." Valya was indifferent to his promise, but her dormitory friends were excited and had a bottle of alcohol ready. Oleg Alpeyev, the only lad among the graduates and the Komsorg[3], had also promised to come. "Why, just five roubles each, and we have a Komsomol wedding," he joked. Valya laughed, yet she suspected that tomorrow Oleg would have more to say. He would speak, indeed, but Valya, despite having agreed to Volodya's proposal, somehow didn't believe the wedding would actually happen. Why? She simply didn't believe it, perhaps because the holiday was still nearly three weeks away, or perhaps for another reason she couldn't pinpoint. That evening, left alone whilst her friends were at the cinema, Valya wrote a letter home to Priobsk and mentioned nothing about the impending wedding:

"Mum, I send you many, many kisses. The suit is gorgeous. The girls saw it and commented it was a trouser suit, but they all agreed it was beautiful. I haven't worn it yet. What's new? How is Lada? (A stray, hay-coloured mongrel that lives with them). I can take her with me. She'll have more fun in the village; I've already found a place and made arrangements." (Valya didn't mention with whom; it was Volodya). "The girls are over the moon: fourth wedding since we started school. Father hasn't written anything."

Valya pondered this and heavily smudged her last sentence, making it illegible.

Three years earlier, she had visited her father in Almaty, considering a university degree in journalism. Mum had slipped a bottle of "The Old Castle" into her suitcase, repeatedly stressing, "No matter what, he is your father." He indeed welcomed

---

3   Almost identical to Partorg but dealing with affairs of the Young Communist League.

her warmly. Aunt Lida, his wife, was also hospitable, and they had a nice dinner together. However, the evening soured when Father became drunk, and he and Aunt Lida began to quarrel over money. Valya can still recall the hushed, whistling whispers escalating to full volume.

"You said eighty roubles plus a fee… where's the fee?"

"Did you forget about the alimony?"

"Quiet, turn on the TV!"

"Two months to go, she's eighteen in September."

Valya heard him rubbing his hands as Aunt Lida requested: "Lyosha, turn on the TV!"

Valya left them that same night.

It had been two years. It was naïve to think all journalists were prudes just based on that. But Valya didn't simply take pride in her father's essays; it was more than that; every one of them was a celebration. They were published in central newspapers, and she used to cut them out, labelling them: "My father." No, Valya had no regrets. She wasn't trying to prove anything to him. Like her mother, she would be a paramedic, nothing more, nothing less.

Valya set the letter aside, draped a knitted pink sweater over her shoulders, and hurried to the library. Although she had agreed to Volodya's wedding proposal, she felt far from ready for it. Why did she feel unprepared? It was simple: a wedding dress was necessary, a veil was essential, and white shoes (preferably platformed) were required. Goodness, a bride needs an entire array of things! Yet strangely, her confusion about the wedding wasn't what spurred her sudden urge to dash to the library to borrow a collection of stories by Alexander Grin. But that's exactly what she did.

"Hurry, hurry…" she urged herself, as if fleeing from pursuit. In the whole world, with all its oceans and continents, there was only one heart now - hers, Valya's. It was beating with such force that every beat seemed to make the world shudder.

"Hurry up, hurry up, I must get there before the library closes. I need to get this story and show it to Volodya, let him read it… And then the dress, the shoes, and everything else." Valya thought. It's a pity she couldn't remember the title, but she was sure she would find it. In that story, two friends both love the same girl and are equally in love. They both court her, and she chooses the more deserving one, but then one of them slips and is left dangling over an abyss. The other offers his hand, yet in a moment, the first one sees a hidden desire in his friend's eyes; it's horrifying. Realising this, with the words "You wanted this," the lad lets go and plunges into the abyss. The girl had chosen him. "And it's fair, one cannot secure love through death, even consensual. Love must come voluntarily, or not at all. Everyone must understand this… But Zhenya doesn't get it. He just gave up, surrendered… How could he? She's also a good person; it's not her fault that she was fond of them both. It's more of a trial for her than for them… And Zhenya yielded too soon, just gave in. How could he? I'll marry Volodya just to spite him. No, he won't understand." Valya thought with pain. "If he did, I might have acted differently, but he won't understand. And that's not even the point…"

Valya couldn't comprehend why exactly, but she intuitively felt she needed to show Grin's story to Volodya. She might consider marrying him, but first, he needed to read it. After that, she believed she would know what to do next, but he must read it.

Valya successfully found the right story just in time. She clutched the book gently to her chest, feeling a sense of calm wash over her. Tomorrow she would finish the letter. Everything would happen tomorrow. And that tomorrow, Valya hoped, would resolve all her questions and doubts once and for all.

Zhenya Kolotov parked his truck near the water pump; it was easier to pull onto the road from there. He thought to himself, "Have I got everything? The bottle is here… have I got matches?" He opened the glove compartment and rummaged around for a box. "This must be it…" He glanced at the windows. "They are probably in the kitchen…" Climbing out of the cab, he jumped down, the bottle in his pocket making a gurgling sound. He clutched his pocket in alarm, checking the neck of the bottle - it was intact. Zhenya marvelled: "Well, it's true what they say, you can't mistake vodka for water, it even gurgles differently, and it burned my stomach when it did." He slammed the cab door shut. "That's it, time to go."

He hesitated at the gate and looked at the windows again. "I haven't been here for six months." A surge of memories bubbled up from deep within his soul: Vovka, their childhood together, the incident by the mill. It welled up, threatening to turn his soul inside out, but Zhenya forcefully suppressed it, and the wave receded. Only in the depths from where it had arisen did it still ache, so much so that Zhenya thought, "That's how remorse hurts." However, the pain quickly eased; he had mastered it. Zhenya opened the small gate. A luminous rectangle from the window lay directly in front of the porch. The cross frame and Vovka's head behind it seemed to be carved out of ebony. Zhenya wanted to step over the image, which faintly reminded him of a theatrical prop at the Regional Palace of Culture; when he did, the shadow moved. He involuntarily jerked his foot back, as if he had injured someone, and leapt onto the porch.

In the hallway, he trod cautiously, as if feeling his way, but caution failed him. Someone opened the door; Zhenya lost his balance and, tripping over the threshold, collided with Roman Ilyich, who was sent reeling. Zhenya didn't recognize him at first. The light blinded him. He grabbed Roman Ilyich, preventing him from falling, and steadied himself.

"You?!" Roman Ilyich exclaimed in confusion.

Grandmother gasped. Grandfather jumped up, his crippled leg twisting inward as if it was not his own and had been borrowed, complete with the felt boot. His glasses shone, and his crutch was raised; it was unclear whether he was defending himself or preparing to strike. Vovka remained motionless, pale, and tensed like a taut string.

As his eyes adjusted to the light, Zhenya squinted and smiled. Approaching Vovka, he grew serious, extended his hand across the table, and greeted him.

"Don't work too hard… what's that?"

"Well, the log," Volodya replied, somewhat embarrassed.

"Ah, the safety log," Zhenya joked. "Don't sign it yet."

Roman Ilyich didn't seem to appreciate the joke. He bristled and tapped away like a woodpecker:

"What are you laughing at?"

"No, it's not that. I'm just saying. You drink?"

Zhenya placed the bottle in the centre of the table. He was about to propose a toast to 'a sinful soul,' but something held him back. Instead, he said:

"The old biddy has had her day."

His tone was uncertain, hovering between inquiry and complaint, but it was enough to make everyone pause. Silence fell as they waited. Zhenya couldn't understand what they were waiting for, and it frustrated him.

"No need to overthink this, you know; yes, it was all very unfortunate, you know."

Zhenya expected some reaction, a movement, anything, but they remained static, as if in a daze. Then, Roman Ilyich suddenly sprang into action, grabbed the log, stuffed it into a folder, zipped it up, and headed for the door.

"Where are you going?" Zhenya asked, nodding towards the glistening bottle.

"I can't stay, Pal Sergeich is waiting in the office," Roman Ilyich replied with dignity. He rustled his cloak just like wings, passed by the window as if gathering momentum for takeoff, and disappeared. To Zhenya, Roman Ilyich seemed like a man of little worth, but his departure left a tangible heaviness in the air. It grew quiet - too quiet. The silence seemed to thicken like pudding, making it almost frightening to turn around. Suddenly, the door creaked loudly. Everyone looked around instantly, and it felt as though someone had entered the hut. Who? The air was charged with an eerie feeling as if haunted by a presence.

"Here's the thing, my boy," Grandfather said, stepping up to the table and handing Zhenya the bottle. "Take this and hurry, hurry home."

Grandfather's words were cryptic. Zhenya hesitated, looking at Vovka with a perplexed expression. Grandmother, worried, interpreted it in her own way:

"Go on, go on, my dear, don't let a sin weigh on your soul."

"Vova?" Zhenya called out in bewilderment, almost pleading, "Can you at least explain what all this means?"

Their eyes met. Volodya couldn't bear it, tilted his head, and coughed.

"Have you been home?"

"Why?" Zhenya asked, then dashed to the door, propelled by a sudden premonition.

"What is this… Can it even happen like this?" Zhenya felt feverish. Initially, he had started running home, then remembered: "The truck." He returned, climbed into the cab, and took out the ignition key, but his hands were shaking so much he couldn't insert it. He leaned heavily on the steering wheel. "What am I doing? Time is running out! Oh, you bastard!" he cursed, as though he had found the source of all his troubles hiding in the cab, but it brought him no relief. "Wait," he whispered. "Oh, if this is true, I wouldn't want to be you, Evgeny Kolotov." After murmuring that, he suddenly felt as though he had been reborn. His hands steadied, and the fever dissipated. Zhenya felt a chilling determination within himself. He started the ignition, turned on the headlights, pressed the clutch, shifted gears - methodically, without rushing, without panicking. "Oh, let it not be true…" He released the clutch and drove as if heading not to his home but to an accident scene, as if it wasn't him, Evgeny Kolotov, but someone else entirely, someone wielding higher power over the former Kolotov.

At the end of the street, the lights caught a hurrying figure in a cloak.

"What are you laughing at?"

"Oh, if it's true," Zhenya muttered, chilled by the sensation of another entity speaking through him. He understood all too well what it meant. These words were unsettling, yet somehow not entirely, not completely, as if this feeling had been usurped by the one with the higher power. "You're scared. The old biddy has had her day." The words struck mercilessly, making his soul bleed. Zhenya groaned, stopped the car, and dropped his head onto the steering wheel, waiting for the pain to pass. Or maybe it wasn't pain. Zhenya felt something profound and subconscious stirring within him. It would give him strength, it surely would. But it seemed that someone else was leading the way. Zhenya would pay dearly for using this path, but now he had no strength left to wait. He took it and repaid the one with a higher power for his cruelty. "And if it isn't true? Yes, what if…" Oh, how relieved Zhenya would be, how easy his life would become. A feeling of jubilation washed over him like an echo from an unprecedented parade of human happiness, and Zhenya thought: "I will go home, I will kiss my mother, and I will tell my father: the director of the state farm sends his regards, he says there is no other foreman like you. That was three days ago, but I forgot."

And again, Zhenya headed home, his soul free of discord, harbouring just one small, very possible wish. "Mother will be surprised, of course, and say, 'Why are you sweet-talking like this?'" And he'll sing to her: "That's because, that's because we're pilots."[4] That's it, from now on he lives anew, in a new way.

Here is the grocery store, his home is next...

Yakov Maksimovich Kolotov was on the state farm chief accountant's record as a pensioner for five years already, but he did not sit idle. Just before Zhenya returned from the army two years ago, the director of the state farm appointed him as the "bridge train" supervisor. He arrived in a jeep, entered the hut, sat down on a bench, and said:

"Help me out, Maksimych, the bridge train is being dismantled, ten barracks are being left behind, we've bought them, and already transferred the money to the bank."

"Pasha, something for the table." Yakov Maksimovich hurriedly prepared for the director's visit, which was quite an event in those times. However, Vyacheslav Zakharovich, the director with city education, declined, as he had to rush off for a field inspection with the chief agronomist - spring was around the corner. "That's OK, no problem," Yakov Maksimovich settled down at the table. "What's up?" Paulina joined them, sitting next to her husband while she continued to select seed onions, not interfering with the men's conversation.

"You see, Maksimych, we're expecting migrants from Ukraine this spring. We need to tidy up the barracks. We'll renovate some, rebuild others, and put up sheds. We need a supervisor - a commandant."

"My army days are long gone!" Yakov Maksimovich laughed; a sentiment echoed by Paulina; it was an unusual role

---

4   A line from an iconic early Soviet song "Planes First" praising the Air Force and its pilots.

for a villager.

"He isn't a commandant type anymore."

"Well, you were a foreman, you managed, and there are only ten barracks here. We'll provide you with a team, you'll just oversee them."

The director brightened, smiling broadly and warmly.

"Well, it's not that simple," Yakov Maksimovich grew serious. "And when the people arrive, that's how many—fifty families?"

"Thirty-five."

"That's pretty much the same. If anything, they'll be a headache; people these days are not considerate, they are overly demanding."

"That's right. Utilities and comfort are a priority now," the director agreed.

There was a moment's silence.

"Why don't you give this job to Shalom? He likes authority; let him take charge," Yakov Maksimovich suggested, remembering the foreman from the second brigade, also a retiree.

"No, we need you here, your gentle approach to our conditions."

"Yeah, and someone to saddle the entire work upon!" Paulina interjected.

"Pasha!" Yakov Maksimovich stood up. "I'll come over tomorrow."

That settled it. There was some swearing, of course, but not much. "It was my own doing," Paulina thought. "If I hadn't intervened then, perhaps he would have refused. Now he'll sign up, against his own good, but he will." She conceded, but said:

"Don't come to me complaining; I warned you."

The role of the commandant was challenging, but it was not without value. In his brigadier times, Yakov was passionate about machinery - harvesters, tractors - and he had now taken up carpentry. Naturally, a person in charge needs to know the job well before ordering around. Over two years, Yakov Maksimovich mastered a planer and chisel, and most importantly, found a purpose at home. He set up a workshop in a shed and spent his time there. Long after the barracks were demolished, and he wasn't a commandant anymore, he still found work for himself. "The gates are old, I used up the materials on the pigpen, otherwise I would have renewed them long ago," Yakov Maksimovich mused while working with the planer. "Good, hard, tinkling wood, but if you work smart, it's pliable," he told himself. "I used to scold Zhenka, but he's right: it's not my calling to be a foreman, it's just not. It's easy for youth now, we could not choose back in our time. They'd just say go, you'll manage, and you go because there isn't anyone else to do it."

Yakov Maksimovich heard someone banging on the gate. "Is Pasha back already? That was quick," he thought as he looked out. It was his daughter. He wanted to tell her about the lunch in the oven but wasn't quick enough; she dashed past and into the house like a meteor, likely already rolling the rugs to beat them clean. "Mother's blood," Yakov Maksimovich nodded approvingly, "A hard worker." Before he could gather his thoughts, she was already on the porch, rushing towards him as if chased. He left the barn and stood by the woodpile.

"Raya, the cauldron is in the stove."

His daughter paused.

"Daddy, let's go inside."

Yakov Maksimovich sensed some unease in his daughter. He was concerned, but didn't question her and led the way inside. She let him go first.

"Don't worry too much, Daddy," she said.

"It's something serious, she's going to cry," he thought as he hurried along. "Calm down, calm down..." They entered the hut.

"What's wrong?" he asked, pulling the cauldron out to give himself something to do.

"Dad, they called from the hospital; Mum was hit by a car. I went there, and our Lyonka sent me to you. He said she was alive, but they wouldn't let me see her... I don't know what to do!"

Her shoulders shook; she was on the verge of tears. Yakov Maksimovich carefully placed the cast iron on the cooker and muttered:

"Lunch."

He sat down, holding a black cloth - grief washing over him. He gazed distantly at his daughter and asked:

"Was Tanya with Lyonka?"

"Didn't see her," she replied, falling silent.

"Zhenya will come, and you can go with him... I'll go now." He got up, still clutching the black rag, and headed to the hospital.

Paulina Grigorievna lay on the wooden couch, her face etched with concern as if lost in deep maternal contemplations.

"How are the children, Yakov?" she lamented. "Look after the grandchildren… Let Raya manage the household, and make sure Zhenya kisses his mother goodbye; he's the type to forget… I do feel for him, he's so young." She added apologetically, "I'm leaving you all so unexpectedly…"

The head doctor entered, coughing and looking away.

"You can collect the body."

Yakov Maksimovich glanced at Pasha. "I'll take her tomorrow, no need to frighten the grandchildren… I'll have time… Lexeevna will help, we got through the war together… I should get that polka-dot dress from VDNKh… I loved seeing her in it… I need to go home, go home."

He covered Pasha's face with a sheet and whispered, as though he might awaken her:

"She's had a hard day so I'll collect her tomorrow morning."

"Of course, of course," the doctor agreed, locking the door and handing the key to Yakov Maksimovich. "You can leave it with the head nurse afterwards."

The doctor led Yakov Maksimovich into a small hall with chairs; his older son was already there. They left together.

"Go, bring Tanya and the kids, we all need to be together…"

"They're already with Raika, let's go."

"I'll walk, and you go park your truck. We'll pick up Mum in the morning." The old man turned and shuffled away, burdened with grief.

The evening was quiet, the twilight's fading glow still visible in the deep blue sky, and the stars' light felt not yet distant and empty. In contrast, the blinding flash from a lorry's headlights seemed distant, almost unreal to Yakov Maksimovich. All around was silence. Nature seemed attuned to sorrow… and life itself was one of endless sadness. Yakov Maksimovich walked along the wooden boardwalk beneath the poplars, hearing the leaves screech as they touched the ground. The trees listened, listened until one seemingly couldn't bear it anymore and sighed like a human in pain. "It is human… everything around is human," Yakov Maksimovich realized, and it felt natural to him. What puzzled him was why people refused to notice it. "It would make living too uncomfortable if anything you did might hurt another human being… But it all comes down to that. A new heaven and a new earth are perhaps when everything and everyone is human. That's when joy will rise; of course, sadness will remain, for a human is not human without sadness. But then, everything will be complete: both inhaling and exhaling, and God would be near, and where there is God, there is no death, only eternal life," Yakov Maksimovich thought. Yet, grief clung to him: "Who will you tell now about what you've seen? The children, the grandchildren? How can you explain what words can't explain? How much of life must we share before we can truly communicate feelings? Of course, there will be a new heaven, a new earth, a new humanity, but I am all alone, bitterly alone… I can't do it without you, Pasha… I'll die."

He paused at the crossroads with Kolkhoznaya Street. "… But the children, Yakov, and the grandchildren… look after them." The streetlights flickered on. He noticed a girl with a pink sweater draped over her shoulders, a book in hand, walking absorbed, oblivious to her surroundings. Yakov glanced around anxiously to check for cars. "Thank God, no cars. I suppose it takes some misfortune…"

He exhaled in relief as the girl reached the pavement and continued safely. "I will, I will keep an eye on them, Pasha."

From a distance, Zhenya saw everyone had dispersed, yet the hut remained dark. This unsettled him. "It's not without reason," he thought, feeling as if a piece of his heart had shattered, flared briefly, and then turned to ashes. No pain followed immediately, but he waited for it to emerge from within. It never did.

As he turned the truck, the new gate crossbar caught his eye, glowing as if imbued with an inner light. Realizing his father had replaced it that day, he braked, turned off the headlights, and darkness embraced him.

Artyomka opened the cab door and announced, "Uncle Zhenya, Grandpa said we're staying at your place tonight."

"I'm scared," Oksana added. "Korovkina says that our granny will return at night."

"She will come," Zhenya replied absently, then suddenly alert, pulled Artyomka close.

"Where, where's our granny?"

"She died," Oksana said solemnly, and Artyomka added in a whisper, "Vovka Yalikov ran her over with his truck at lunchtime."

Releasing Artyomka, Zhenya leaned back in his seat. The surrounding darkness was complete. He barely noticed the stir at the door.

"Uncle Zhenya, why doesn't he let me in?" Oksana complained.

"Where's your dad?"

"He's with grandpa, they're all sitting on the porch," Artyomka replied, then asked, "Uncle Zhenya, ask dad, are we going to school tomorrow? Go to Mum, why are you following me?" Artyomka protested, but his sister had already squeezed herself into the cab.

"You go, I'm scared."

"You're not a real pioneer."

"Are you real? You're a worse student than me."

Left on their own, the children grew restless. They could have roamed and played freely, yet they chose to stay close, sensing that something mysterious and unsettling had occurred. The adults appeared absent-minded; their confusion was palpable. They would have hidden their turmoil from the children if they could, but humans are mortal, and there is no escaping that. The realization was daunting, yet confronting this reality, and remaining human in the face of it, was the true challenge. Nature had trustfully revealed this law: everything from the beginning to the very end was bestowed upon humanity, for humans to have dominion over it.

This wasn't the reason for Artyomka's agitated state, of course. A premonition overwhelmed him: this temporary lack of discipline would soon end with his grandmother's burial, and then school would resume as usual. Granny would not be there anymore, but he did not yet fully comprehend it. He was eager to enjoy his freedom here and now and explore its limits.

"Uncle Zhenya, tomorrow you'll go to dig a grave with my dad, and I'm going," Artyomka declared, informing rather than asking, surprised by his own audacity. "Would they allow it?" He was awaiting his uncle's response.

"Yeah, like they need you there," Oksana interjected.

She struggled to accept Artyomka's newfound assertiveness, which she had had to tolerate all day. How was he better than her? Yet, it appeared he was. Artyomka had taken on a role that elevated him to the level of the adults, a change Oksana couldn't quite understand, but sensed that from that day forward, Artyomka would progress so significantly that she might not be able to keep pace, despite sharing the same birthday. Uncle Zhenya didn't reprimand Artyomka for his insolence - Oksana found no other word for it - but indulged him.

"You must ask Grandpa, Artyomka." What would he say? Oksana felt oddly unsettled.

Zhenya opened the door and climbed out of the cab. As he jumped to the ground, he felt the bottle in his pocket again. "Here's the thing, my boy, take this and hurry, hurry home." he recalled and recoiled in fright: "What have I done, Ma!"

That night, the brothers got to sleep in the attic. From the porch they could see Tanya standing on the ladder, holding the flashlight for her sister-in-law. The light pulsed through the cracks in tune with Raya's sweeping motions. The ladies chatted as the simple task engaged them, momentarily distracting them from their thoughts. A chuckle sounded. Zhenya felt as though Lyonya, too, was smiling there on the porch. Perhaps his thoughts were with them, and Zhenya mused that it wasn't by chance his brother had suggested making a bed in the attic, nor was it coincidental that their father had instantly agreed, saying:

"Raya, take the canvas from under our mattress."

He had brought a bedspread and a cotton blanket himself. "It's not for nothing," Zhenya murmured to himself, his attention quickly drifting elsewhere.

As the moon rose, its shadows marched across the courtyard like soldiers on parade. As the faint sound of an aeroplane spilt from above, Zhenya suddenly imagined it as a distant rumble of tanks at a testing ground.

He immediately envisioned himself in a tank, even feeling a slight shiver in his body, reminiscent of rotating the simulator with his right foot.

"Where's Kolotov?"

The third squad was on a smoking break under pine trees, and now Zhenya seemed to notice cigarettes flickering in the black void.

"Why do you need him?" The deputy platoon commander inquired; Zhenya recognised his voice.

"It's about yesterday; just for a minute."

"Pulgrebyak, Sergeant Pulgrebyak," Zhenya identified the second voice. He heard several people point out simultaneously:

"He's there in the PT area."

Yesterday, during the driving exam, Zhenya distinguished himself: he completed the test course in record time in his new tank. He was accompanied by a test driver, sergeant Pulgrebyak, who sat in the commander's seat as an observer. However, as they approached Mount Sapun[5], Pulgrebyak instructed Zhen-

---

5   A place of legendary fierce battles during the siege of Sevastopol (Crimea) in 1941-1942.

ya to tighten his throat mike and ordered him to ascend the mountain in seventh gear, and then proceed without stopping or shifting not to the right, along the river, but straight ahead onto the ramp-shaped ledge and then along the smooth sandy old riverbed. Everything was executed flawlessly. They soared from the ramp for about twenty meters, snapping the pine tops. Naturally, Pulgrebyak became a hero among the cadets. Zhenya recalls how the battalion's deputy commander exclaimed: "I can't believe it…" And how Pulgrebyak, looking down at the cadets, strolled leisurely along the tank's track, exuding an air of field marshal grandeur.

There was no grandeur in the sergeant now. He pulled Zhenya aside and grabbed him by the button of his overalls, breathing in his face, leaving Zhenya breathless.

"What's with the onions?" asked Zhenya.

"Ah, got a parcel," the sergeant waved dismissively, shifting from foot to foot, the spot of moonlight slipping down his sleeve as if trying to hide in the folds. "We flew, the deputy chief engineer calculated that we should have landed the turret down from that ramp. It was our lucky day, perhaps the trees saved us, understood?!"

The sergeant spat and immediately laughed ingratiatingly.

"You're an ace, even though you're a cadet. You outperformed all of us test drivers."

Zhenya became wary. What was Pulgrebyak implying? He asked:

"OK, maybe, but what about your order?"

"Don't play dumb."

Pulgrebyak smiled, the gold teeth of his upper jaw gleaming brightly, and Zhenya suddenly realized: "His teeth were knocked out by a direct blow, it's a dead cert." Prompted by a hunch, Zhenya sharply drew his right shoulder back as if preparing for a strike. It was an involuntary action, but Pulgrebyak had recoiled. Zhenya did not hide his grin.

"What's the matter with you?"

"Nothing," his voice sounded strained, "Do you know what I'll get for that manoeuvre?" Evil lights flashed across his eyes and immediately extinguished, making them seem vacant. Of course, Pulgrebyak was ridiculed for suggesting taking on Mount Sapun via the ramp.

"Don't confuse courage and stupidity," said the battalion's deputy commander.

But when was that? The ramp was now conquered, and not even by a test driver, but by him, Zhenya, a cadet, essentially a rookie. That's how Pulgrebyak proved himself to the major! But what else? Zhenya didn't understand.

"You see, the deputy commander is angry and threatens me. Nothing good can come of it now…"

It was the first time Zhenya had seen Pulgrebyak confused. Confusion did not suit him. People like Pulgrebyak do not give up, Zhenya thought, and the leap from the ramp had convinced him of that, but here…

"Listen, Kolotov, when they start investigating, you say: I did it on my own accord, driving through the ramp was a mistake, they won't do anything to you." The sergeant looked pleadingly, like a teenager, into his eyes; a gesture which reaffirmed Zhenya's suspicion: "His teeth were knocked out with a head-on strike, when he looked at someone just like this... And he's got gold teeth instead..."

It's hard to articulate how such a thing could occur. Pulgrebyak had distanced himself from Kolotov, pushed him away. Zhenya disliked those who could not see others in themselves and only saw themselves in others. Such people are dangerous, but also pitiable. He had nearly been expelled from the Komsomol, but he stood up for Pulgrebyak and took all the responsibility upon himself. He believed it was justice, yet now justice was catching up with him in the moonlit gloom, scorching his soul. He had missed something back then. Today, wasn't the right time to dwell on such concerns, but his heart overpowered his thoughts. "He who doesn't pity himself must not be allowed to use that as an excuse to not pity others. How arrogantly must one regard oneself above others, to think that any sacrifice made in his honour can be justified by his own sacrifice, even his death..." Zhenya knew he was no better than Pulgrebyak, no different at all. He saw he was reaping what he had sown; he had taken the blow, and although he realized the blow would be not as scorching for him, that wasn't the reason to take it - he nonetheless embraced this factor as his primary motive. "Pulgrebyak had embarrassed himself, and you pity him. You pity everyone, what a pitiful soul you are..."

Zhenya glanced at his father, who sat with them on the porch, feeling so distressed inside that his body seemed foreign, too overwhelming to bear.

His father inhaled slowly and deeply, gazing at the gate in mournful anticipation. This sorrow was compounded by pain, and by the fact that Zhenya had sort of wasted himself and might not even be worthy of this pain now. Yet the pain persisted, and in the attic, as the scent of bitter hay filled the air and he had almost heard milk sprinkling from a cow's udder into a metal bucket, the pain intensified. "Mum's not coming back, she's gone forever," Zhenya wept. He felt small and defenceless. Then, with a childlike fear, he listened to the silence, held his breath, and exhaled with relief. His brother was close; he could reach out and touch him, but there was no need to interrupt his rest.

Zhenya longed for sleep to deliver him from his thoughts, but slumber evaded him. "We are born, we arrive on this earth, and then everything crumbles. If only there were a bond between people, a sort of umbilical cord! When one person suffers, everyone will feel it. Bound together, unified, whole. Would he then have no pity..."

Zhenya groaned. His brother, already awake, came to his side and nudged his shoulder.

"Dreams?"

Taking a deep breath and settling himself, Zhenya replied:

"Yes, a dream." He paused.

"Lyonya, what if people were connected to each other as if with an umbilical cord? If one person was hurt and everyone felt it, if one person was well and everyone felt well, wouldn't people think differently? They wouldn't harm each other but only do good, and those not connected wouldn't survive..."

"Did you come up with that yourself?"

"Yes, why?"

"So," Lyonya paused, his voice reflecting his contemplation and a sudden awareness of his seniority. "It's impressive that you thought of it on your own, although maybe not entirely on your own—but that's beside the point," he mused, as if speaking more to himself. "The umbilical cord exists." He paused again, searching for the right words. "Do you know Tolka Karikh? During the war, his father, still alive at the time and working at the stables, found a millcake as big as a millstone, and just as hard. He dumped it on the porch, and Tolka invited all of us street kids round. We started breaking pieces off it, some using chisels, others with hammers, nibbling away, feeling music in our bellies. I sat next to Tolka by that millcake. What a find! I barely had time to look around, but I did anyway. Tolik found a nail embedded in the cake and ate around it like meat on a bone. His ears moved as he chewed, him being so frail, skinny, near transparent." Lenya paused. "He didn't chip off even a small piece before calling us over. Ask Raya, she remembers it too. You youngsters live in such times of abundance, you make a fuss over everything."

Lyonya's voice trembled, cutting through its roughness.

"Look at your father…"

He reached for the board nailed at the head of his bed and, pushing it aside, whispered:

"Look, look!"

Zhenya's throat tightened. His father sat on the porch, still facing the gate, smoking, waiting, not giving up.

A tiny drop of emotion trembled in a corner of Zhenya's soul, where human suffering resided. It shimmered like a distant star, but it was enough for all the warmth of his unspoken love for his mother to surge forth, causing a muted, shoulder-shaking sob.

Before dawn the next day, everyone was already up and about. Zhenya's father remained at home, waiting for Leonid, who had gone to fetch the car, taking Tanya and the children with him.

"You make lunch, then send Artyomka to let us know when it's ready. Oksana, help your mother," Lenya instructed, subtly hinting to Artyomka - just as the boy was about to ask to join the trip - that he and Oksana were needed more at home. As he drove out of the courtyard, he told his wife:

"Don't overdo it."

Tanya was in her last month of pregnancy, nearly due.

In the dim early light, Zhenya drove the forestry truck to the motor pool. From there, he planned to walk to the hospital. On route, he dropped his sister off at the home of Inessa Alekseevna Oparina, a single, elderly woman known for her busy chatter. Her nickname was Lekseevna the Commander because of her bossy demeanour.

"You did not have to come to get me, darling, I would have come on my own. I had been talking to her all night... I was wrong, thought she would be seeing me off, what a disaster!

She cried alongside Raya, and then as if suddenly realizing, she chided herself:

"All right, all right, dear, off you go. Klava and Froska Gridnev are waiting for me. Pasha will scold me for not hurrying when we meet. She'll say 'Why do you let your eyes go wild before it's time, we had an agreement...' Let's go, my dear, let's go," urged Lekseyevna, stopping Raya from succumbing to her grief.

"You, my darling, are the chief helper and I'm the old one now; remember that and follow my lead," she said. "Stay strong for maybe someday, you'll also have to see me away."

The gravity of Lekseyevna's words didn't frighten Raya. It was as though the old woman had unlocked the links of a vast, living chain and inserted her, Raya, as a small but essential link.

The sad day proceeded smoothly. They brought the body home from the hospital, dispatched the lumber truck, and dug the grave. Everything was done properly. Yet, a premonition of a new misfortune had clung to Zhenya's heart like a tick since early morning. He sensed that trouble was near, already upon him, observing him silently, getting ready to seal his doom with one swift blow.

He and Lyonya went to the cemetery to show the lads where to dig the grave. Lexeyevna had advised them that on Parents' Day she and Paulina had selected the spot. "It's dry, shaded by two or more birch trees chatting with their light-coloured leaves..." Zhenya had noticed them from the back of the truck as they approached. Birches seemed to hold hands, surrounded by a serene silence, their leaves drifting through the golden air as if dissolving into it.

Zhenya surveyed the area, and counted the graves - everything was correct, the spot was right here. He picked up a shovel, careful not to damage the roots, and started marking the contour of the grave, not intending to dig, but the other guys stopped him: "Leave it, leave it, relatives should not be doing that."

Zhenya felt a pang of guilt, as if he had indeed tried to overstep a boundary. That was an important rule. Had it not been for the misfortune and his depraved thought, "the old biddy has had her day," he might have ignored the warning. But now, he paled and bent over in a rush to clean the shovel. It was the first thing that came to his mind, and he felt the gaze of someone behind him. No, it wasn't the guys nor Lyonya - it was too scary to even consider that it might be the one who had peered into his heart and frozen his hands. And though Zhenya knew there was no one, he couldn't help but look back. A cloud passed over the sun, and for a moment, he imagined that the shadow of the one peeping at him flickered, rustled with leafy garments, and vanished, perhaps within Zhenya himself.

Zhenya told his brother about the unsettling sensation he had experienced, hoping for a laugh, but Leonid's response lacked any hint of amusement. He regarded Zhenya with a serious gaze and said, "It's your conscience that's torturing you. Even though it resides within us, Zhenka, it seems to observe us from the outside. Did you say anything unkind to Mum?"

"I didn't," Zhenya replied.

"It's okay, it'll pass," Leonid reassured him.

True to his word, the feeling dissipated, but only temporarily. After lunch, when Lyonya had left for the motor pool, the shadowy feeling returned. "It's some kind of witchery" Zhenya thought, yet there was nothing supernatural about it. He was being haunted by the tangible shadow of a real, pervasive gossip.

The previous day, after Onatsky parted ways with Eugene Kolotov, passengers on the bus had noticed something amiss with Ivan. He hadn't driven a kilometre before he stopped again.

"That's the life of a driver, guys, not exactly sweet. Accidents are bad, but there are worse things in life!"

He opened his bag and commanded:

"Fair dodgers, come here!"

His passengers were mostly women and schoolchildren, who worried he might drop them off mid-route and possibly withhold a portion of their fare. Surprisingly, Ivan distributed tickets to those without them for the first time in memory and sighed deeply as he finished, "That's right…"

His resentment towards Kolotov reignited. The absence of any fare inspectors on the way to the forestry farm only strengthened it. The passengers puzzled over Ivan's deep sigh, wondering, "Why did Onatsky turn down the fare?" They contemplated his remark, "That's the life of a driver, guys, not exactly sweet." Women often appreciate being addressed as men, as their equals in resilience, and they sympathised readily when a man shared his troubles.

"We're gossiping here about the accident, but he's only human. He expects people to empathise with drivers and tries to be considerate… Drivers have souls like everyone else," the women concluded. They wished Ivan good health as they disembarked. Ivan remained silent, his reproachful silence speaking volumes, suggesting an unknown grievance. The passengers, feeling guilty, were prepared to apologise, especially those who got free tickets. But Ivan was emotionally far away, overwhelmed by a grudge against Zhenya Kolotov, or perhaps even against the whole of humanity (he went from being disliked to appreciated just for saving them five rubles). That was yesterday. Today, according to the dispatcher Lilka Khalyuto, "Ivan is talking bollocks." It was no longer Ivan, however, Ivan went home to rest, it was his uncle, safety engineer Roman Ilyich, who was stirring things up.

"Yesterday, I was at Yalikov's. The younger Kolotov came in, a bottle in his pocket, and declared, 'The old woman had her day, let's drink to her memory.' I thought he was out of his mind, and he replied, 'What's the point of getting upset?'"

"Oh, Roman Ilyich, really?" Lilka asked, peering out curiously, her body barely fitting through the window.

"Fyodorovna," Roman Ilyich retorted, giving her a sharp look. "I wanted to confront the scoundrel... But then I thought maybe his shift just ended, and he did not know what happened, so I let it be. And my nephew, he told me he'd explained the accident to Zhenka himself when they met on the road..."

"Oh, Roman Ilyich," Lilka responded, shocked. "He and Yalikoff love the same girl... that's probably why, oh, what a story, he came on his lumber truck late in the evening, came to see Vova without even knowing what happened – and we know what really happened!" Lilka realized.

"That's right," Roman Ilyich concluded meaningfully, as if leaving it to Lilka to connect the dots. "Fyodorovna, I must run," he said, pointing at his folder, "No rest for me, day and night, I'm like a hamster in a wheel..."

He left, but Lilka Khalyuto remained. The shift was due to change at ten - how many would she share details with then? True to her nature, Lilka, shrewd as she was, would not trust such information to just anyone. There went Zavalishin; Lilka kept her silence. "From rags to riches, a foreman… a fluke in the middle of nowhere."

"Hello, girl. Did Kolotov bring in his truck?"

"Yes, before dawn. He was like a ghost, neither a hello nor a goodbye; I had to go and sign off for him."

"Cut him some slack, it's a terrible time for him."

Pavel Kuzmitch sighed, and Lilka was tempted to say, "It is a misfortune indeed that Yalikov's girl is all he thinks of, what the shame, they hold nothing sacred." Yet, she held her tongue, and it turned out to be a wise decision. Zavalishin was to use Kolotov's lumber truck for his shift.

"I'm heading to Pokrovka, and will be back by four." He pocketed his waybill.

"See, he wants it more than anyone, I see that in his eyes," Lilka thought.

"Do you know what my maternal family name is, girl? Remember it: Shaipov. I have Chechen blood in my veins. If I hear you speaking ill of the boy, you'll have only yourself to blame…"

Pavel Kuzmitch thrust his hand through the window, causing Lilka to shriek.

"No need to be scared just yet," he said as he opened the window latch. "But mark my words, for I'll put your tongue right here and trim it with this frame," he declared, pulling the latch back with force. With that, he climbed into the truck and drove to Pokrovka.

"You wretched convict!" Lilka fumed. She was still scared, however, and rushed to Nikonov, complained, and reluctantly confessed to the party boss because Zavalishin was angry at her. So, in the afternoon, Lenya's legs shook when he stopped by and heard about the gossip going around Zhenya. He did not believe it but was furious all the same. You can't silence liars. Lenya realised it wasn't the right time to deal with the gossip. Perhaps that was why his anger ignited so intensely. He went home thinking that it wouldn't be right to bury their mother feeling like this…

Lenya found his brother in the shed. Zhenya stood with his back to the door, fitting carpentry tools into their sockets. He tried to distract himself from the anxiety that plagued him, but this simple task only deepened his introspection. His hands moved automatically, and when his brother called to him, Zhenya startled, dropping the chisel onto the soft wood shavings below. This minor detail, though seemingly insignificant, was enough for Leonid to suspect Zhenya's guilt. He had overreacted and said something he did not mean to say.

'Why are you scared of your own brother?'

Lenya bent down, picked up the chisel, and threw it towards the socket, but missed. The chisel bounced off and fell silently onto the shavings again. Now Zhenya bent down, picked it up, and methodically placed it back on the board. His unhurried actions only further confirmed his guilt, which now seemed blatant to Leonid, yet brazenly unacknowledged by Zhenya. Lenya, on the contrary, was far from calm. God forbid if he were to learn of something similar about Artyomka… Leonid's legs trembled.

Mustering his resolve, he waited until his brother turned to face him.

"Look how calm he is! Mum's had her time, huh? Why won't you say something, anything?

Unable to contain himself, Leonid shook Zhenya by the shoulder twice. Zhenya did not react or push him away. Lyonya slumped onto a crate.

"Zhenka, is it true?"

Leonid's voice broke, a surge of indignation rising within him:

"Do you have a heart of stone? Strangers show more compassion."

Overwhelmed with anger, he stood up abruptly.

"It's disgraceful!"

He threw himself at his brother in a fit of rage, but Zhenya was already enraged too. "He calls himself my brother, but readily believes the gossip!" Lenya was a little shorter, stocky, his back broad, bulging muscles showing even under his leather jacket. Zhenya was taller and thinner, but also the more agile of the two. He sprung aside and, not expecting it, Lyonya stumbled on a crate and flew out the open door. At first, they were both too confused to do anything. Then Lyonya got up slowly, with a terrible expression on his face. Zhenya was afraid, but not of what was about to happen. He was afraid of not having time to tell his brother the truth.

"Lyonka, I didn't know about Mum... do you understand that or not?!"

Everything in Zhenya was screaming, but he couldn't hear

himself, and it seemed to him that his brother couldn't hear or understand him either. Zhenya braced to defend not himself but something much greater, something that might not be worth living without.

Lyonya heard him and understood everything. But the shock was so great that he could not stop on the spot. "Well, could he have said it right away, bastard, could he…?" Lyonya looked at his brother furtively.

"Come out, don't be afraid."

"I'm not afraid."

At that moment Zhenya feared nothing. His brother understood him, he truly did, Zhenya's heart told him so. Lenya felt offended… but wasn't Zhenya offended too?

He went out into the courtyard and, standing behind a stack of logs to avoid being seen from the house, asked:

"Are you gonna fight?"

"Why couldn't you, you bastard… why didn't you tell right away?" It was as if Lyonya had let a spring unwind. He struck Zhenya on the shoulder with his right hand. Zhenya swayed, barely keeping his feet, and shaking his head, wheezed:

"So, you believed it? Yes?!"

From the outside it looked like they were having fun – that's until Zhenya knocked the wood stack down with his shoulder and rose with his face covered in blood. The brothers did not notice their sister jumping into the yard until she started yelling,

"What-are-you-do-oing-what-are-you-do-oing?!"

She didn't scream, she begged in tears. Confused by her unexpected appearance, the pair rushed to rebuild the woodpile.

Then Lenya whispered:

"Drive to my place, clean yourself up, but don't say a word to Tatiana …"

Zhenya ran across the yard to the street. His father came out and called:

"Son!"

Zhenya stopped, unable to look back, but his father called out to his brother.

Valya met the next day to the fanfare of her alarm clock, its relentless trill piercing the morning silence. Fumbling impatiently for its off button, she woke up. The noise ceased, and the stirring girls fell back into a blissful semi-slumber. That last precious minute of sleep hovered within reach, just close your eyes… But no, it was futile; the door at the end of the corridor would shortly slam. Valya smiled in anticipation. The door slammed, followed by the echo of long, limping footsteps drawing closer. It was Oleg Alpeyev, and as expected, he knocked at their door.

"Girls, get up!" Oleg's voice bellowed down the corridor before he quickly stomped downstairs. At the bottom, there was a washroom. Silence followed the slam of the door - a deceptive quietness. Within fifteen or twenty seconds, he would call for them again. Unable to bear the suspense, Liza Sveshnikova donned her dressing gown.

"Girls, you know what he's up to!" she exclaimed, clutching a glass filled with water from the previous evening. Her voice, tinged with righteous indignation (her patience finally worn thin), rang out: "Well, let that parasite try something again; I'll teach him a lesson!"

Liza stood by the door, anticipation lighting up her eyes. Seconds ticked by, but no knock followed. It appeared that Alpeyev wouldn't return.

"Looks like he's finally caught on," said Liza, a sigh of relief escaping her lips, though a shadow of disappointment crossed her face - she had waited in vain. But her eyes sparked anew with determination; now truly infuriated, she resolved not to let him off so easily next time.

This morning ritual was customary, yet today, it struck a different chord with Valya. A pang of envy towards her friend stirred within her, a surprising and unsettling revelation. "Unlike you, I'm stuck…" But in what? thought Valya. The sight of the book of stories by Alexander Grin on her bedside table reminded her: "Today, everything will be decided."

Valya headed to the hospital dressed in a dark burgundy Crimplene trouser suit, her mother's gift. She hoped Zhenya would see her in it. Today, she and Volodya planned to visit him, hoping for reconciliation. It was her influence that had cooled Volodya towards his friend, and this realisation warmed her soul. She tried chastising herself for selfishness, but her heart responded with a surge of tenderness. "Volodya is a good lad, though a bit reserved," she mused, equating 'reserved' with 'in love.'

People on Kolkhoznaya Street followed Valya with their eyes, and she overheard two girls debating the availability of imported goods. "No way they'll send us those; they're all sold out in the city," one argued. "Of course, they're sold out!" Valya silently agreed, involuntarily taunting them with the moves of her youthful body.

When entering the hospital, Valya hoped to show off her outfit to everyone at the registrar's office. However, her arrival went unnoticed; the head doctor was talking to the head nurse by the glass wall.

"You see, Maria Afanasyevna," said the head doctor, "how deeply it affects them. He's been like family since childhood, working alongside them."

"Yes," Maria Afanasyevna, an elderly woman with dyed blond hair, sighed, "the poor woman was heading to us for treatment... Such is life," she gestured resignedly, and Valya understood they were discussing the previous day's accident.

Noticing two large X-rays in the chief physician's hands, Valya asked for a look.

The doctor handed her the X-rays, and suddenly, she felt the room's focus shift to her attire. Yet, this was the last thing she wanted at that moment. Hiding her unease, she straightened the photos, spotting a legible ink inscription in the corner: "P.A. Kolotova."

"A fatal outcome, I'm afraid. Even Vasily Mitrofanovich could not do anything to save her," the chief physician's voice broke through her thoughts.

Valya didn't inspect the X-rays in detail, fearing her reaction might betray her inner turmoil. Despite her efforts to remain composed, Maria Afanasyevna approached her before lunch, her tone brooking no argument, "You need to rest and promise no more pills; they're not what you need."

Hesitating as their gazes met, the head nurse softened: "Valechka, can you tell me what's troubling you?"

Valya was taken aback, initially mistaking the attention for interest in her suit. "What a fool I am!" she thought, her eyes filling with tears. Maria Afanasyevna offered her a handkerchief and a comforting smile, lifting Valya's spirits and making her smile as she wiped away the tears.

"Well done," Maria Afanasyevna encouraged her. "And no more pills. May I join your gathering tonight?"

Valya nodded, almost moved to tears again.

Siberian autumn is brief and capricious, its beauty is intense and unpredictable, so each cloudless day is cherished. The vibrant gold of the leaves and grasses begins to fade, and even a sunny day is softened by a pinch of gentle melancholy. A woodcock's whistle breaks the silence, a tit calls out, and a mouse rustles in the stubble. The air carries the subtle scent of smoke from the vegetable gardens, evoking memories of spring and transforming the sadness into a delicate, dreamlike anticipation of rebirth.

Valya paused mid-step. "No, I must not go to the dorm… I need to see Zhenya, and ideally with Volodya." As she raised her palm, a leaf drifted past her, its movement almost echoing with a soft chime. Listening to this gentle sound, Valya felt a sudden, sharp pang of sadness: this leaf had its own life, and it ended. Then, a thought struck her, "Volodya has arrived, perhaps he and Zhenya are already together… Yes, that must be the case," she reassured herself. And so, eager to not miss them if they were indeed nearby, she approached Volodya's gate.

* * *

Volodya lay with his hands behind his head. The morning calm spread quietly across the windows like a vast lake, only blue shadows still harboured the last drops of the night's powers. Volodya sensed them as woven with an invisible, taut mesh of strings that tinkle softly when the morning light starts breaking through them.

Out of the corner of his eye, Volodya noticed his own shadow. The clothes draped over the back of a chair merged into a strange shape on the wall, fused with the shadows from his elbow and chin. "Inanimate," Volodya thought and shuddered at the sudden feeling of being at one with this shadow shape. He was now hesitant to move; this peaceful connection was strangely alluring. Time seemed to stand still. "What a bliss … nothing's going to happen… and that ringing, it's like music." Volodya revelled in this sensation, feeling something within his soul started moving, slowly at first, then picking up speed, spinning faster as if propelled by the soft breath of a purring breeze. He couldn't recall how long this moment lasted, a minute, two, or perhaps only a second. The music ceased abruptly. "All I had to do was think of Valya, but there you go…" The lingering annoyance gave way to bitterness. "Is that so?" Just yesterday morning the mere thought of Valya's smile would have filled his soul with lark's trills; now, something had shifted unfavourably within him, and it was terrifying. "What if it were always like this… Valya, but no music?" He forced himself to try and dismiss the thought, but it didn't vanish. It hovered distantly, like a frightened bird perched just out of reach, its beak pointed accusingly at him. It did not fly away just because Volodya yearned to keep it in sight. "It's a chain of events. Valya pulls Zhenya, and with him, everything else..."

Volodya froze. The 'bird' unfolded its wings without taking flight, and drew closer, holding its wings raised behind its head like a cloak. It paused and settled, its wings folded, waiting. What joy was there for Volodya in all of this? None, only bitterness... Even if something works out, Valya will leave him as soon as she finds out why Zhenka came to see him yesterday, and there won't be any 'ifs' about it. Kolotov's soul, you see, is such that he feels responsible for everyone. Volodya wanted to think of Zhenya with scorn, but ended up feeling envious and angry. "Your Zhenya got what was coming to him yesterday!" Volodya smiled, and because he didn't need to hide his smile, it was genuinely sweet. "He'll stumble into even more trouble," Volodya thought vindictively of his friend, and again, feeling afraid, he believed it. "She's come back... he can't drive her away... From now on, it will always be like this."

He glanced at the window; it was time to get up. He grimaced. "The radio is silent... I'll wake the elders," he muttered as a pretext, as a new, inexplicable anger welled up within him, overshadowing all other emotions. "They aren't sleeping, but they let me sleep, their dear grandson, poor thing. They've turned off the radio for the same reason." Volodya got up, deliberately making the bed creak as loudly as possible and moving a chair for the same reason.

His grandparents, who were indeed awake, stirred when they heard him rise.

"Vova, you should get some more sleep," Grandmother suggested, but Grandfather objected:

"Get up, Vovka; pay no attention to her and go to work."

"What work? How do you expect him to work?" Grandmother interjected. Grandfather silenced her:

"Quiet, he is not exempt from it."

"Oh-oh," Grandmother sighed, and Grandfather peered into the room, tapping his crutch.

"Did you write the report?"

"What report?"

"Onatski's from yesterday."

"Yes, I did."

Ignoring his grandfather, Volodya dressed, making it clear he didn't want to talk. Yet, the old man lingered, wanting to ask something else but unsure where to start. He finally blurted out:

"Vovka, make sure you report everything as it happened, hiding nothing."

Grandmother sighed loudly again, and Volodya halted in astonishment.

"You're still young, with your whole life ahead of you," Grandfather said.

"And how am I supposed to live?" Volodya blurted out.

Grandfather sniffed and, tapping his crutch, headed for the hayloft.

"Live like people. With decency."

"Not one of them can even begin to understand," Volodya

seethed, but his anger quickly gave way to such bitter resentment that he sank back onto his chair, half-dressed. "Not even my own dear grandpa…but it's all become clear… I'm sure his gun is still in the pantry." Invigorated by the thought of the gun, Volodya felt an urge to head straight for the pantry, but instead, remained seated, entranced by a faint call of a lark wafting toward him from far, far away.

* * *

Having slipped through the gate, Zhenya jumped into the truck and drove off while wiping his face with a sleeve. "No, not to Leonid's, Tatiana might guess, or the kids would spread the word… Maybe to Vovka's…" The thought came unbidden. Pain clutched his heart and then slowly sank into his stomach. "No, that won't do…" Zhenya said aloud and remembered the bread factory's bathhouse. He glanced at his watch and perked up. "Perhaps it's best to head there. I'll wash my shirt, and besides, it's on a completely different side of the village—nobody would know, nobody," Zhenya reasoned, feeling his logic was sound and everything would go as planned.

The bath attendant stopped him. Suspicion flickered across her face, causing her eyelids to flutter like reeds on a rolling lake.

"Are you drunk?"

"I fell off my bike."

"Breathe!"

Zhenya exhaled into her face.

"Come in," she said grudgingly and turned away.

Zhenya looked back and saw a naked man sitting behind the clothing cabinet, his scrawny legs dipped in a basin.

"We sometimes get drunks," complained the attendant.

"Just don't let them in," commanded the man.

"But they buy tickets…"

They discussed Zhenya, ignoring his presence as if he were an inanimate object. This offended Zhenya, but also oddly comforted him. "Nobody would know, nobody…"

As he was about to enter the steam room, he overheard:

"I have a feeling… he's drunk." The man and the bath attendant scrutinised Zhenya so intensely that it took some effort for him to pull the door towards himself. "Look at you, so sensitive," Zhenya brushed off the comment and entered the steam room. The vigorous lashing of birch whisks beckoned him into the murky depths of the hot steam. Initially, Zhenya sat on the lower bench. He didn't listen to his body; it made itself known on its own. Crossing one leg over the other, Zhenya noticed that his right big toe felt numb. "I must have hurt it when tripped near the woodpile," he thought and massaged it involuntarily.

Later, Zhenya climbed to the very top, puffing heavily in the dry fury of the steam. It felt like bliss. However, only now, experiencing a slight trembling in his muscles, did he fully grasp the absurdity of the fight. "Vanya Onatski!" It all became clear and to quell his blazing fury, Zhenya started to yank his toe back and forth, as if trying to break it off. "Scoundrel, such a snowflake… exactly like his uncle." The source of rumours was obvious and Zhenya's anger flared even more. He was ready to confront Onatski, but then someone on the neighbouring bench stirred:

"Hey, lad, what are you doing there, clipping your nails?"

Scalded by the remark and recognising Ivan Onatski, Zhenya almost cried out, "Look at you, drama queen!" but restrained himself and pretended not to hear. Ivan, however, felt slighted by the lack of attention (he didn't recognise Zhenya) and said:

"Why do they even let such people in?"

"What people?!" Zhenya knew without asking. After that, he remembered nothing, as if a wall of fire had risen before his eyes.

* * *

Valya opened the gate and immediately saw Volodya in the depths of the yard near the cellar. He was sitting on the logs facing the house and appeared to be reading a letter. She opened the gate silently, but now, as she closed it, the latch clicked loudly. Volodya turned sharply. He appeared to jolt, although Valya wasn't entirely sure. He was sitting in the shadow, and she was looking directly into the sun, so she could have been mistaken. "Hello."

Volodya nodded and, as Valya approached, hastily stowed the letter in his trouser pocket. Valya interpreted his hurry in her own way: he was being considerate. He had even run into the house to fetch a newspaper to lay it out for her to sit on.

"Sit down, Valya."

He remained standing. Valya smiled.

"Why are you behaving like that… Why did you put the letter in your pocket, it will get mussy."

Noticing Volodya's embarrassment, Valya suggested:

"At least fold it neatly and put it in your breast pocket." Volodya was wearing a blue sports shirt with epaulettes. Valya thought he looked absolutely stunning in it.

"Come on, let me do it for you," she said, reaching out her hand out confidently, expecting him to hand over the letter. But Volodya stepped back, nudged a log with his foot, sat down, and looked away as if he hadn't heard her.

Blushing, Valya lowered her hand. She couldn't explain Volodya's lack of interest, or rather, she tried to explain it by anything but what it should have been.

That morning, after locating the shotgun, Volodya had discreetly moved it under the logs where Valya was now sitting. Convinced that it was now securely hidden, he had been quite active. He fetched water, chopped wood, ran to the police station to give a statement. He didn't go to the truck park though, fearing they might send him off on some urgent tasks when he needed to be at home. In his statement, he noted that he had not been speeding and that he could have made a sharper turn had he been more attentive. He felt as if he had flown back from the police station on wings. On his return, watched by his grandparents, he sat down and started writing. After that, he asked for nails, telling them, "I'll fix the fence, it's getting loose, and the wire along the garden is hanging over the weeds." Assisted by Grandfather, work went smoothly, and when the wire was repositioned, Volodya genuinely regretted that the job was over. A burning sensation immediately displaced this regret: it wasn't, after all, his intention to enjoy the work, no; he wanted with bitter sorrow to leave something to be remembered by, that was the goal. Volodya tried to rekindle a recent grudge against Grandfather, but it didn't work; it seemed too petty compared to their shared, albeit small, task.

He waited for Grandfather to go inside the house and took out the letter: he was saying goodbye to his grandparents, brothers, and mother. He even apologised to his stepfather for the bitten finger and thanked him for the fire helmet; he knew such things are not forgotten. He had thought everything through and written a line to everyone. He asked Valya and Zhenya to pick snowdrops by the old mill in spring – "they smell of lark's trills," and to Valya separately: "I love you, forgive me, with deep respect, Vladimir Timofeevich Yalikov."

It was a bitter letter, written with tears. Something had happened to Volodya: he read it and couldn't hardly believe he had written it. How could anyone stoop so low as to cut everyone off in such a calculated way? What villain would do this? Volodya shuddered. Someone like that did not deserve to live. He would burn the letter, destroy it without a trace. Then, just as he reached into his pocket for matches, he heard the gate click. Valya saw him jolt.

Seeing her, Volodya was overwhelmed by self-loathing. Each extra minute of life was unbearable and the desire to end it grew stronger. Volodya felt some old, yet different strength of spirit return to him as his decision firmed. Perhaps this strength was driven by despair, but what did that matter now?

Volodya nudged the log with his foot, sat down, leaned his hands on his knees, and looked to the side. "Afraid to show your guts? Show them, do it! You were preparing the biggest gift for her." Volodya turned sharply towards Valya, elated by the mere fact that he could look straight into her eyes. He smiled wickedly, vengefully. He knew how inappropriate and terrifying his smile was, yet didn't hide it and truly let go of the brakes.

"Why have you come here, do you know what I am? You don't know what I am!" Volodya's eyes blazed angrily and, stunned by his sudden anger, Valya recoiled.

"Volodya, I came…" Valya started anxiously. "At Zhenya's… they have been struck by a disaster … haven't you heard?!"

"I haven't heard… I!"

Volodya lowered his head, and his shoulders began shaking.

"You're laughing?!" Valya cried out in disbelief.

"Yes, I'm laughing!" Volodya raised his head up sharply, full of hatred, and exhaled, "Yes, I'm laughing!"

Valya gasped in fear.

"It was me, I killed Aunt Pasha! And I'm now supposed to go and comfort them?" Volodya's face, suddenly illuminated by a sunbeam, looked so terrifying that Valya couldn't take her eyes off him.

"Vo-va!?"

"And yesterday, yesterday," Volodya shook his head, "Zhenya came to comfort me, to comfort me! He didn't know, you see, he didn't yet know."

Laughing hysterically, Volodya didn't hear Valya scream as she covered her face with her hands. She didn't want to know or see anything. Her whole being revolted, resisted, refused to believe what had happened, and yet she didn't miss a single word Volodya shouted.

"I was scared, I was a coward, I didn't tell him…"

Valya uncovered her face and stood up. She looked at Volodya as if for the first time, not hiding her disgust. She stared at him intently, as one would at a tiny insect, trying to understand how such a small thing could contain so much venom. Her eyes were dark; when Volodya met them, he faltered, stopped shouting, and said in a barely audible voice:

"No, Valya, I'm not an insect. I'm worse, a thousand times worse, look." Nervously clutching the edges of his pocket, he pulled out the crumpled letter. He handed it to her and smiled mysteriously, incomprehensibly, as if in response to someone's treacherous deceit. "Read it, but it's all nonsense, lies, and about you, too… I just wanted to cause more pain, that's all…"

Volodya was certain that Valya would rightly condemn him, perhaps even be frightened by him, and run from him as if he were plagued.

"Vova?!"

Valya sat down from where she stood, not noticing whether there was a newspaper to sit on or just bare logs covered in sap. This somehow caught Volodya's attention.

"Vova, you're sick, don't you understand? You're sick!"

She bit her lower lip and then, covering her face with her hands, cried quietly and angrily.

"What on earth were you thinking, you fool… what am I supposed to do now?" she muttered, leaning towards him.

Volodya was confused. Then, jumping up, he snatched the letter back.

"I lied about everything, I lied…"

But Valya wouldn't stop.

"You don't love anyone, not even me. And without love, how can it be? How can it be without love? What would people say!... Vova!..."

Valya raised her tear-streaked face; she felt she had found and grasped a lifeline.

"Vova, do you want me to marry you right now?"

She leaned onto Volodya, and he heard music coming from somewhere far away, and as if responding to it, something deep inside him shifted, turned with unbearable pain. Unable to control himself, Volodya clung to Valya, and now their grief and tears were shared.

* * *

Zhenya came to his senses on a hard bunk. He was alone. An electric light bulb flickered coldly in a barred niche under the ceiling, and the sun slowly cooled on the iron bars in the window. "It's all right," thought Zhenya. "This is how it should be." Turning towards the window, he groaned, but not from physical pain. His soul ached, having nothing to rest on, nowhere to find solace. "Everything, everything is bad!" Zhenya felt hurt: everyone around seemed to have conspired against him, no one wanted to understand him, no one... "That's why I'm here, that's why." He bitterly surveyed the empty, grey walls, as if confirming his downfall. "And Onatsky... Let the bathhouse attendant and that other guy... The bastard played the victim!!"

"Officer, if everyone starts beating us up, what kind of

bright tomorrow will we have with faces like this?" Drawing a circle around his face, Ivan seemed to invite the officer to assess what kind of future he could now expect. The officer smiled, it was hard not to: a black eye and the idea of a bright future didn't quite match. Yet the smile hurt Zhenya, and he decided that the officer had taken Ivan's side. No matter what Ivan was like, he was good at winning people over and gaining their trust. He had cunningly portrayed himself as a wronged simpleton, but Ivan was no simpleton, he was playing the system.

Zhenya didn't regret the fight; it seemed necessary, not so much for him as for Onatsky. "He needs to be taught a lesson… sure, we were interrupted, but Ivan must have got something out of it, he must have… He thinks he can get away with anything," Zhenya thought and felt as if he had hit an invisible wall. "He's playing the system, and what about you? What are you trying to achieve? You don't know, you don't know!" Zhenya mentally triumphed, as if it wasn't he who was confused, but someone else, someone unpleasant to him.

He heard wings fluttering. Two pigeons landed on the windowsill, one after the other. Black with white specks on their wings, they peered in the window. The male pigeon opened its beak, and the female stopped grooming her feathers, sidled up and peered curiously into his beak. Then, as if pecking at something, she gently tugged at the male's tongue. "They're kissing," Zhenya realised, and his irritation vanished.

"Animals, birds, insects, even trees - every living thing communicates its purpose: look, look, this is what I am. They don't realise it, but they know their purpose. Why don't humans too? Probably because they only see with their eyes, while their hearts remain closed. One must look and see with one's heart. The human heart is the guide to higher meaning, to the deep connection between everything that was, is, and will be. Or maybe there is no connection, and everything around is just a bunch of scattered children's blocks, and people only imagine this connection out of fear of their insignificance?"

Zhenya became truly frightened, feeling like he was falling into an abyss. Then he remembered his brother's words: there is a connection, there is - and saw his father sitting on the porch. His heart leapt, and through the pain rising from somewhere deep within, he felt that there was indeed a higher meaning.

The pigeons seemed to have been awaiting this from him; flapping their wings, they rose and left. The sunlight followed them, rolling across the ceiling into the window, leaving Zhenya feeling utterly lonely.

"Mum!" he whispered, trembling, and gasping for breath. "What am I to do, Mum? I wanted good for everyone, for everyone!"

Zhenya didn't feel the tears; they fell inward, and they could never be wept out. "How frightening it is to be and to leave without fulfilling yourself." Would neither his mother nor father be fulfilled in him? Those who believed in him... "What are they keeping me here for?!" Zhenya grew agitated. "They had clearly understood nothing!"

Zhenya jumped off the bunk and froze at the metal-clad door. He heard approaching footsteps. The lock clicked, a heavy chain clanged, and an elderly Kazakh sergeant opened the door.

"Not good, not good, you slandered yourself, you cursed, you got drunk!"

Zhenya interrupted the sergeant:

"My mum is there, you understand, my mother!"

"I do understand, so why are you in such a state? Come, your father is here…"

From afar, Zhenya saw his father, and again an unbearable pain struck his heart, taking his breath away. His father stood in the alley, leaning on a stick. Zhenya saw him with a stick for the first time, and everything inside him tautened, like a string about to snap. The sergeant helped. He walked ahead and spoke to his father about the truck.

"No, we'll go on foot, my older will collect the truck."

His father turned and his soul opened completely to Zhenya, and Zhenya understood his father's great suffering, not with his mind but with his heart. He realised that his father not only knew everything about him, but he also knew much more than Zhenya could ever know about himself.

"Let's go, son," father said quietly, and they slowly walked home.

The evening was quiet, the blue sky was melting away, and the rustle of fallen leaves sang their farewell to the retreating autumn. Zhenya walked beside his father; he walked home knowing that at home they believed in him, and that this belief would sustain him through the years; otherwise, life would lose its meaning.

"You'll kiss your mother…" His father sighed and explained after a pause: "It was her wish." Then, as if emerging from somewhere, he added: "Volodya Yalikov and his fiancée have come, they're waiting."

They encountered a herd of horses near the house. Tolya Karikh, standing in his stirrups, shouted:

"Hello, Yakov Maksimovich! Hello, Zhenya!"

He guided the horses from the water hole, and they calmly obeyed.

"You see," said his father, and sighed again, touching Zhenya's shoulder. They walked home, and his father's forgiving heart was beating in Zhenya's chest.

1975

LITTLE LAUGHING DOLL

… It's always joyful to realise something big, explain it to someone else and have him understand it too.

Do you know where that came from? Do you think it's from one of the greats? No, not at all. It's an extract from my diary, 'Notes of a Young Naturalist.' I realise it's not the best title for a diary, and I'm no naturalist anyway, but I started it a long time ago. One day, I heard on the radio: 'From the notes of a young naturalist,' so I grabbed a notebook and wrote: 'Notes of a Young Naturalist.' It wasn't even a notebook, but a massive book in a thick dark brown binding, and its pages were white, thin, glossy, with red stripes curving across them. Above each stripe at the top there were small hieroglyphics, like little spiders. It was a beautiful book! I found it near the airfield where the Fifth Army was stationed. I was in the third grade then, and often grazed cows near the airfield after school together with Edka Voskoboynikov, my best friend. The grass there was good, knee-high.

When Edka saw the book for the first time he said, 'What a find! You could do your homework in it for the rest of your life.'

I let Edka read my diary until the sixth grade, and then I stopped; stopped after September 22nd. That was a special day. A lot of poems appeared in my diary after that. I remember the first one by heart even now:

> *With a couch on my shoulders, not on a truck,*
> *Sweaty and tired, I crept.*
> *Then I saw you strolling with another shmuck,*
> *I sat on the couch and wept.*

I wrote it on September 22nd and never read it to anyone. It came to me instantly and I liked it, although I neither carried a sofa that day nor cried on it. On the contrary, I felt wonderful that day.

At one o'clock in the afternoon, I packed my textbooks in my bag and went to school. I walked through the garrison because our school branch was located behind it, not far from the airfield - our new two-storey school hadn't yet been built. The branch was in a U-shaped house, with barracks for pilots on one side and our classrooms on the other.

I took my time; I knew I'd make it. And even if I didn't, I wouldn't have been reprimanded that day anyway. It was my birthday: so, nothing bad could happen! I hadn't finished my homework. I had only dealt with geometry and physics, but not Botany or Russian, but thought, "even if I get a 2[6], they won't say anything at home either."

I got to school early. Edka saw me and shouted, "Did you solve the geometry problem?"

"Sure," I replied.

I was pleased to see everyone immediately interested in me. But honestly, if I'd known that the whole class wouldn't be able to solve the problem, I wouldn't have done it on such a day. I'd rather have ridden Genka Rogozinski's bike. But that's not the point.

---

6   Grades at Soviet schools were 1 to 5, but the de facto lowest was 2, with 1 reserved for something exceptionally bad, more often related to behaviour than anything.

Everyone copied my answer, even Svetlanka Karmanova, an excellent student. When Ivan Andreevich entered the classroom, he commanded: "Open your homework notebooks and place them on the edge of your desks."

Everyone complied, and Ivan Andreevich went around to check each personally.

"Yes, you've all solved it," Ivan Andreevich chuckled. "Unlike the sixth 'B'[7] where no one succeeded."

Everyone protested, "So what, Ivan Andreevich? Don't compare us to them! They're all slackers in that class."

Amidst the commotion, Svetlanka Karmanova looked at me as if I were a famous artist. I got a bit embarrassed and started rummaging through my bag so she wouldn't notice.

I should mention that Svetlanka was very beautiful and tidy, like all excellent students, but she wasn't a tattletale, troublemaker, or suck-up. Dimples appeared on her cheeks when she laughed, and she was very smart.

"And not everyone solved the problem themselves. Some…" Ivan Andreevich paused, and I felt his gaze on me. "Some of you cheated. Most of you, in fact."

I looked up and met Ivan Andreevich's eyes. He was looking at me with such intensity that my heart missed a beat. It seemed he had guessed why I was rummaging through my bag. I looked away, but he kept looking at me, saying, "Be honest, Gubkin; did you cheat?"

As soon as I heard that, I was so relieved. I stood up, smiled, and said, "Yes, I did."

"From whom did you copy your work?"

---

7   Classes typically were of 30-40 people. There were usually more of the same-aged children attending the same school, so they would be split into parallel classes, say, 6A, 6B, 6C and so on; Cyrillic letters were used though. Most schools operated in two shifts to accommodate more children.

"Whom?" Of course, if I'd been in a bad mood, I might have said nothing. But it was my birthday, so I just said, "From her."

Svetlanka shrieked and jumped up as if she'd been scalded. As soon as I saw her reaction, the fun was gone. The class fell silent. Everyone knew I hadn't cheated, and they all wondered what she'd say about it. But I felt terrible. I felt I had humiliated Svetlanka.

"Ivan Andreevich, he's lying. I copied it from him."

"You?" Ivan Andreevich's glasses nearly flew off in surprise.

"Yes," Svetlanka blushed even more and sat down with her head bowed. The class fell silent.

"I don't understand! Gubkin, can you at least explain who copied from whom?"

What could I say? I raised my head and looked out of the window. Let Ivan Andreevich be indignant at my behaviour and punish me! But he suddenly smiled:

"Ah-ah-ah-ah-ah. I see, I see!"

I looked at Ivan Andreevich. He was looking at Svetlanka, smiling softly, and not just smiling, but with some secret significance. Embarrassed, she blushed even redder.

"I see, I see," Ivan Andreevich said again and studied the class register for a long time. Then he opened the task book and, still smiling, asked, "Who wants an A or a B?" There was a murmur in the class:

"Me, me!"

"I think we should let Gubkin be the 'birthday boy'."

The class erupted. It was all quite fascinating. He didn't know that it actually was my birthday.

"Gubkin, the problem you solved at home, assuming you did so, can be solved in two ways. One way is what's written in your notebook, which is the more difficult, by the way. Solve it in the second, easier way. If you do, you'll get a 5. If you don't, you'll get two 2s, an extra one for cheating. That will be the promised 4." Ivan Andreevich put his hands behind his back and walked slowly around the classroom. "And the first to solve the same problem on the spot gets a 5, I promise."

The lesson flew by without a hitch. I solved the problem during recess, and Ivan Andreevich counted the recess as a lesson. Svetlanka solved the problem too, but she didn't get an A. She didn't get it because she never told Ivan Andreevich about it. In fact, Svetlanka solved the problem even faster than me. Edka told me so: he was sitting at the same desk as her and saw it with his own eyes. At first, Svetlanka drafted everything but didn't rewrite it. When I put a perpendicular on the tangent and got an additional isosceles triangle, she became happy and said:

"He's going to solve it!" And she laughed but didn't write down her own solution, so that Ivan Andreevich wouldn't think that I had somehow learnt the solution from her.

Then, during the last break, Temka Khudyakov started playing zoska[8]. He had a piece of fluffy white fur and a lead plate with four holes in it, like a button. Temka had sewn it to a piece of fur with copper wire, and it turned out to be a magnificent zoska! Temka could strike it three hundred times non-stop. He played with it in a classroom, which was strictly prohibited since it caused dust and other problems. Lidka Yag-

---

8 Similar to the game of footbag, but played with a specially made shuttle-cock, more similar to jianzi.

nysheva, the student on duty, grabbed the zoska, and threw it away! The zoska flew across the classroom like a small parachute. Svetlanka Karmanova gave it a flying kick, and it hit me square on the forehead. Everyone laughed, but Svetlanka turned away as if nothing had happened. I pretended not to have noticed who hit me, jumped up on a windowsill and hung my hand with the zoska out of the window:

"Who did it? I'm counting to three. One, two…"

Temka dashed to me: "Valera, don't throw it out. It was Karmanova!"

I shouted menacingly, but held fire. I couldn't attack Svetlanka, even as a joke, after everything that had happened that day. Svetlanka ran away from me to the girls. They scrambled to protect her, shrieking, and then we boys jumped on them, making faces like pirates. I untied Svetlanka's bows, and the girls tore off my white collar. The botanist entered the classroom and saw us pig piling in the corner.

"This is an outrage! Who's on duty? Yagnysheva, who are the instigators?"

"I didn't see, Lyubov Sergeyevna!" Lidka had tears in her eyes.

The botanist was surprised and then using a pedagogical trick, said, "Calm down, Yagnysheva, I'm sure the instigators will confess of their own accord."

"Of course, they'll confess." I stood up at my desk. Svetlanka stood up too right after me, which cheered me up a lot.

"Go out and laugh in the corridor." The botanist wasn't joking.

We walked quickly through the classroom and out the door. Svetlanka went first, and I could see her shoulders shaking with barely restrained laughter. We rumbled in the corridor, and many in the class laughed too.

Then we heard, "I'm surprised at Karmanova falling under the influence of that slacker Gubkin!"

I walked home with Edka Voskoboynikov. He was making faces the whole way, imitating the botanist's indignation, especially at me. Then Edka told me that Svetlanka had solved the geometry problem before me. I praised Svetlanka, "She's good, really good!" However, I stopped letting Edka read my diary after that. On that day, September 22nd, I composed my first poem. And I also titled my diary 'Notes of a Young Naturalist':

"I turned thirteen today. I feel that I … Svetka Karmanova. In five years, I'll replace the dots with a word. I swear I won't let anyone hurt her. She must not know anything about the word. This word is still a secret, even to her."

Nothing came of this secret, although my diary from the sixth grade has not been read by a single living soul, not even Edka. But everyone knows how I feel about Svetlanka Karmanova today.

It happened this summer. Our cow Rozka had finally calved, and Mum said:

"Lida Yagnysheva will look after Rozka, and you will go to your father."

So, I went to my father's, to the first brigade. There, with little conversation, he took me to Uncle Vasya, the headman, and Uncle Vasya offered me a job as a second loader on a ZIL[9] during the harvesting season. The ZIL stood by a warehouse, and I did not immediately recognise the first loader. Only when I stood on the wing did I see that the first loader was a girl. And not just any girl, but Svetlanka Karmanova.

"You?!"

"Me," said Svetlanka and sat down on a spare tyre. "Are you my second loader?"

"Yeah," I replied, still amazed.

"Then get in." She must have been amused to see me so surprised because she laughed and repeated, "Get in!"

There was nothing special about Svetlanka being on this ZIL. She had long wanted to work on a collective farm but had never had a chance. Every summer she went to her aunt's in Arzamas, and only now, after full eight grades and starting the ninth[10], she finally insisted on her wish.

"Get in, the sun is already up." She pulled her headscarf with two fingers, stretching it out like a visor. Svetlanka now resembled a village woman used to hiding her face from the sun.

"You look like an actress."

I climbed into the back and watched the driver carrying water. He approached the truck, set the bucket down, lifted the bonnet, unscrewed the radiator cap, and threw it sharply under his feet.

"Oops!"

"Is it hot?"

"Yep, burning," he confirmed. "You're the second?"

"I am."

---

9   Soviet brand of trucks and other heavy machinery.
10   Eight grades of school were the minimum, after which teens could choose to go to a trade school or stay in high school for two more years.

"Sit down; there's no reason to stand." He poured in the water and handed me the bucket. I turned the bucket over and sat on it.

"Do you want to sit on the tyre?" Svetlanka moved, but I didn't leave the bucket.

"Valera, so you lost a whole year just because of twenty days?"

"What year?"

"Well, you were born on the twenty-second of September."

"It was all down to Galina Pavlovna... She was the head teacher before you came to school. She did not care if it was short of one day or twenty; you had to be seven to go to school."

"I was born on the tenth of June." She grabbed the side of the car as it took off, then reached for her bag. "Do you want me to make you a Panama hat, or are you okay about getting a sunburnt nose?"

"Please; but how?"

"With a newspaper?" She opened the household bag with a broken zipper and took out a newspaper. "I was going to wrap bread in it, but I forgot the bread." She pushed the bag aside and knelt to make a hat.

"You'll be sent rolling when it shakes!"

"Then don't jinx me!"

Her pigtails crept from under her headscarf onto her face, and she brushed them away with her hand. When Svetlanka put the hat on me, I said it was more like a helmet.

"Okay; a helmet it is! Just hold it on with your hand, or you'll lose it." She stood beside me, and I felt her light dress tickling my knees. Svetlanka kept adjusting her dress with her hands, and I looked away, tensely staring ahead – not caring what she thought!

The ZIL stopped next to a harvester, and its operator shouted from the bridge:

"Look, the girl's got the right guy!"

We were both embarrassed. The grain started pouring and we did our job scattering it diligently over the truck bed without looking at each other. Svetlanka scattered it with her hands. Her bare feet sank into the grain and seemed as golden to me as her hands. When the wheat got under her dress she laughed, and then I worked alone: I wanted her to laugh longer.

"Wow, you're working hard!" Her admiration did not distract me. I rushed to the top of the pile and felt the hot grain pouring down my back before spreading across the bed.

Shoveling at the barn was much harder. Svetlanka stopped competing with me after the tenth trip.

"What's your sport?"

"Skiing," I said.

"Ah, that's right," Svetlanka remembered. "I have a second grade in gymnastics."

"Oh, sure!" I blurted out.

"You don't believe me?"

Svetlanka turned away, threw away her shovel, swung her arms, and her legs made an arc in the air. She stood back on her feet so suddenly and so close in front of me that I had to catch her. In response, she laughed in my face, so close to me, and I laughed too.

"Svetka, are you showing your knickers to everyone?" Sashka Tsygalnyuk was smiling cheekily, holding his bicycle with one hand. He smiled so that we could see his gold tooth. Svetlanka was ashamed, and I couldn't stand it. Everything that happened next, happened in an instant.

"Here!" I exhaled, jumping out of the truck. Sashka jerked his left elbow, and my blow ricocheted off the top of his head. In the next second, he threw down the bike and hit me in the face with all his might. Tripping over the bike frame, I fell on my back, rubbing my shoulder on the ZIL's tread. Sashka jumped at me, but I managed to push him away with my foot.

"You're screwed!"

Just as he grabbed the shovel, the driver jumped out of the cab.

"Don't you mess with the boy!"

Sashka immediately shuddered.

"What did I do? He started it. Svetka, hold it!" He threw the shovel into the back of the truck and, picking up the bicycle, jumped on the saddle and rode off. He looked back at the gate. "We'll talk at the club. You, Svetka, come too, I've already got tickets."

"That's enough, now be off with you!" The driver turned to me and for some reason added in a whisper, "You watch out for him. His dad was jailed for a year for battery." Spitting, the driver climbed back into the cab, and I went under the truck to retrieve my helmet.

As we drove to the harvester, I wiped the dust and blood off my shoulder with my T-shirt. The abrasion was not deep, and I stopped thinking about it.

Svetka was squatting on her knees with her legs covered by her skirt. It was embarrassing to wipe the blood on my lips, so I licked my lips and swallowed it. Then Svetlanka stood up, and I felt her dress tickling my knees again. I didn't look in her direction until she said:

"Maybe he'll apologise eventually?"

Then I looked at her and saw her eyes full of tears.

"Of course, he'll apologise!" I rejoiced. "You heard him, we're going to talk about it at the club."

My battered helmet didn't protect me from the sun, but I didn't mind. It didn't matter, I didn't care about my nose, that wasn't the point.

That evening, I put on a khaki zip-up jacket with slanted pockets on the sides and went to our collective farm club. It was a gorgeous jacket; my older sister Olga brought it from Vladivostok. Many people in our street envied me, and some guys from the rice plant even bullied me at first, thinking I was a city or garrison boy.

At eleven o'clock, I was outside the club. The high moon was already shining, and night was settling under the trees. The frogs were croaking in the pond, and the fireflies, the last fireflies of August, were flickering through the gardens, adding their own song to the night.

"Come here!"

I approached the group of guys and recognised them all at once. We greeted each other, and Edka Voskoboynikov said, "They're waiting for you by the dance floor."

"The rice plant guys?" I asked.

"Who else? Sashka Tsygalnyuk arrived with a stake and is asking for you."

A harmonica shrieked, and we saw Lyonka Khudyakov surrounded by girls and lads. Lyonka was in a soldier's uniform, looking sharp.

"What's up, fellas?"

"Hi, Lyonya. How long have you been here?" Genka Rogozinsky asked as he came up to Lyonya, and they shook hands. Then Lyonka stretched his harmonica, and the waltz 'On the Hills of Manchuria' got everyone swaying towards the dance floor. Genka Rogozinsky came back to us.

"He's a tanker, a sergeant."

Edka asked me: "Is it Karmanova?"

"Because of Karmanova? Yes," I replied, firing a match, and tossing it upwards.

"What did I say?" Edka said.

The guys perked up, and Genka Rogozinsky frowned at me: "It's your own fault! He wrote notes to Karmanova last year."

"Besides, Sashka says you hit him first." Tolik Rada looked at me, and everyone fell quiet. I shoved the box of matches into my jacket pocket and shook it there for no reason.

"That's true."

"I say it's your own fault," Genka repeated.

Of course, I didn't have the right to be angry with Genka, but I was. The rascal knew everything: who was to blame, who had written notes....

"Ah!" I waved my hand dismissively and went to the dance floor.

"Valera! Wait!" Edka Voskoboynikov caught up with me. "Shall we just go home?" Edka said it delicately, so that I wouldn't take offence, and then I exclaimed:

"He insulted her!"

We didn't talk about anything else, but Edka walked close beside me. Tolik Rada caught up with us near the dance floor.

"Rogozka is coming now; he ran after Vitya Voronkov and Kolka Altabayev."

"Cheers, mate!" Sashka Tsygalnyuk was already waiting for me. He dashed out onto the moonlit spot, looking as happy to see me as if we had been friends for a hundred years. The group of rice plant workers followed him.

"Need a ticket? Just a rouble for a special guest." Sashka passed the stick into his left hand and pulled out a ticket. I stepped closer to him, and we found ourselves circled.

"What, using a stick to drive up the price?"

"Yeah, the price!" Sashka said with a cheerful sulkiness.

The ring shrank… He'll tear the jacket. The most important thing is not to miss and stay calm. Edka Voskoboynikov will engage at once… And Svetlanka didn't come…

"Give me the ticket. Just drop the stick."

"It's not in the way."

"You look like a wuss with it."

Sashka Tsygalnyuk laughed and threw the stake away. Then, turning to everyone, said:

"Do you mind if he buys another ticket for the last night's show then?"

The circle grew noisy, and Sashka started approaching me

slowly. I took my hands out of my pockets and heard Lyonka Khudyakov switch from waltz to foxtrot. I imagined everyone dancing and Lyonka's fringe bouncing from under his cap.

And Svetlanka didn't come…

Sashka jumped on me, and I kicked him with all my might while falling. We got up at once.

(Lyonka plays chords… It's easier that way… Not a proper way to play…) Sashka stretched out his hand, and I saw him being handed the stake.

And Svetlanka didn't come…

I ducked and felt the stake touch the top of my head briefly. Sashka spun around, and I punched him in the jaw…

When Rogozka came running to our aid with Vitya Voronkov and Kolka Altabaev, we were already sitting by the well. The moon was floating in the bucket, and we took unhurried turns touching it with our lips. The moon was cold. For some reason, I thought that it was August already, and soon I would be sixteen. My grandfather got married at sixteen. That's strange. Everyone married so early before the revolution.

"You know, I'm never getting married."

Edka Voskoboynikov looked at me strangely with one eye, the other one swollen shut, and we laughed.

"Edik, they won't recognise you at home," I told him.

"Look at you!" He pulled a flap from my jacket, and Tolik Rada smiled, gently touching his shoulder.

We lay down on the grass and kept silent for a long time. I was thinking about all sorts; about running to the barn at dawn the next morning. And on the next one, too.

"Shall we go home?" Edka Voskoboynikov stood up.

"Go home." I shook hands with everyone, and the moon walked me all the way to the hayloft.

Going to bed, I thought again that it was already August. "No, I'll never get married." When I closed my eyes, I saw Svetlanka. "Do you want me to make you a hat, or are you okay about getting a sunburnt nose?"

That night, I thought a lot, but only about good things. About Svetlanka, about never getting married. I tried not to think about Sashka Tsygalnyuk writing notes to Svetlanka.

On the second of March, we were all still studying at the school branch near the airfield, since the new two-storey building wouldn't open until the seventh.

There was a chemistry test. Edka, Kolka Altabayev and I solved the two-period test in just one period. During the second period, we sat on a bench near the school and watched the snow melting and the streams running by. The sun glistened in these little streams, and they flowed, flowed like molten silver. Maybe it wasn't like silver at all, but it seemed so to me.

We were sitting on a bench, and suddenly heard the roar of planes.

"The engines are being warmed up for flights," announced Kolka Altabayev. His father was a colonel and the head of a refuelling motor park. Indeed, ten minutes later, the first plane took off, and then the second soared over the airfield. We couldn't see them speeding along the runway, blocked from view by the officer's canteen, but when we saw them already airborne over the canteen, Edka remarked,

"It's like they are flying off the roof."

Kolka Altabayev reacted immediately:

"Yeah. Another one's about to take off. Three planes make a flight."

It was at that moment that I remembered my frequent trips to the canteen when I was in the fifth grade. Uncle Vanya, a pilot in the rank of captain, lived with us for some time. He flew green LIs, and we called them 'Douglas'[11]. Uncle Vanya, who always had plenty of coupons for the canteen, would call me over and say:

"Valera, be my pal, redeem the coupons for me."

To redeem coupons meant going to the cafeteria to have breakfast, lunch, or dinner instead of him. I did this a lot, and not alone; four of us, Edka Voskoboynikov, Tolik Rada, Genka Rogozinsky and I, went there together. Leaving our cows grazing behind the airfield in a ravine, we'd head to the canteen. We'd go in, take off our caps (we all wore military caps with blue crowns), and sit quietly at a table somewhere in a corner. One of the waitresses would then come up and ask:

"Do you boys have coupons?"

I'd give her enough coupons to feed everyone. I remember the first time Genka Rogozinsky came with us. I handed over the coupons and waited. I've always liked waiting, perhaps even more than eating. We sat there as if we were real ace pilots. They served us all sorts of food. They brought us plates of sweet rice with butter, not much rice, just a little at the bottom of a plate. Genka Rogozinsky saw it and whispered, "Ew, it's not enough for our cat." We all just smiled; it wasn't our first time in the canteen.

---

11   Li-2 was a license build version of the legendary Douglas DC-3.

We already knew that sweet rice was meant only to stimulate the appetite. Then we each got borscht with meat, a chop with fried potatoes, cocoa, chocolate, and biscuits in packs. Genka Rogozinsky didn't finish his borscht; he grabbed his biscuits and chocolate and ran outside. He was afraid we'd been mistaken for someone else. We didn't follow him, of course. We ate as much as we could, put the chocolate and biscuits in our pockets, and sat there. The waitress came to us for the dirty dishes, we stood up, thanked her, and headed out without hurrying. We only put our caps on once outside.

Genka was waiting for us by the cows.

"Well, how was it?"

"It was great!" We lay down on the grass, took out our chocolates, and ate them in small bites.

By the time we were done with chocolates our anger at Genka had subsided. Tolik Rada gave him a talking-to. We had coupons for everyone this time. But what if we didn't? Running away from the table without a warning – that's just rude! We sometimes went to the canteen with just one coupon between us. We'd get rice, soup, a chop, and cocoa for everyone, just a pack of biscuits and a chocolate bar had to be shared. Technically, the waitresses weren't allowed to give out three portions for one coupon, but they did, and they'd even ask sympathetically:

"Are you boys full?"

Back in their time, after the war, even bread was scarce… But that's all behind us now. Now we sat on a bench near the school and watched the planes take off.

"Yeah, another one's about to take off. Three planes make a flight!" Kolka said.

We kept watching, waiting for the third plane to take off, but it didn't. Kolka started making excuses.

"Seems like it wasn't cleared for the take-off. Perhaps there's an emergency."

And then we saw it: the aeroplane appeared over the dining room, then its tail went up and its nose down and – bang! - it fell on the roof (as it seemed from our vantage point). Then it tumbled several times, black dots and dashes flying off it like sparks, and white smoke obscured the crash site. The smoke was dense and white as a cloud.

"See, I told you it was an emergency!"

No longer listening to Kolka, we ran towards the aeroplane. A few more schoolchildren rushed after us. Soldiers appeared from somewhere. Military fire trucks and an ambulance overtook us. There were many runners like us, and the smoke, dense and white, kept coming and coming. Then it started drifting towards us. It had a bitter flavour, but it wasn't at all frightening. It felt like we were taking part in an exciting game.

We didn't make it far before patrols stopped us. The plane had fallen into the ravine where Edka Voskoboynikov and I had often grazed cows. We were stopped, but we didn't turn back. We stepped back a little and watched the plane burn. Several soldiers were standing with us, also watching, and one of them said:

"The entire military district is now in trouble!"

The smoke just kept coming and coming. Now, however, flames started breaking through. The smoke grew thicker, then darker – and then bang! We even ducked!

"The tanks exploded! End of story!" The soldiers looked at each other, and one of them jumped on us: "Get the hell out of here!"

Without taking offence, we walked back in silence.

We arrived at school just before the bell rang. After such an incident, we weren't afraid of being late, even though we had a history lesson with Mikhail Mikhailovich, the headteacher. We took our time and sat down at our desks. At first, we sat quietly. Mikhail Mikhailovich was late, and we began talking about the aeroplane. Everyone asked us, the eyewitnesses, what had happened, everyone except Svetlanka Karmanova. She sat up straight, too straight, staring fixedly ahead as if petrified. I immediately sensed something bad.

"Svetlanka, what's wrong? You've gone pale!"

But she didn't hear me; she just kept staring at some point ahead. Her forehead was dripping with sweat and her cheeks were red. Everyone fell silent and watched Svetlanka. She bit her lower lip and didn't notice that the class was quiet, and everyone was watching her.

"Guys!" Svetlanka said quietly, barely moving her lips. "I'm scared. It's my, my…"

We understood. We tried to calm her down, but she kept staring at some damn invisible spot. My skin chilled, and I felt uneasy. And then Mikhail Mikhailovich came in. He told us to sit down even before we could stand up to greet him. We all sat down, but Svetlanka stood still, unable to tear her gaze from that invisible spot, and as white as a sheet. Mikhail Mikhailovich cautiously approached her and whispered:

"Sveta, your mum's waiting for you at home… Go home."

Through the window, I watched a green 'Pobeda'[12] drive up and take Svetlanka away.

---

12   Pobeda (Victory) was one of the first consumer cars mass-produced after WWII in the Soviet Union, also used by various organizations.

Mikhail Mikhailovich started talking about the Great Patriotic War[13], without opening the register. At first, it made me angry. "Look at him, what about the curriculum? He wants to calm us down... Now he's going to talk about the heroism of the Soviet people."

Mikhail Mikhailovich did indeed talk about the siege of Leningrad. Our eyes met. Mikhail Mikhailovich averted his eyes, and I could see sympathy in his gaze.

"What else can Mikhail Mikhailovich do?" I thought. "He's just like us, only he's lived more, seen more. It's no bad thing that he's decided to calm us down."

"Mikhail Mikhailovich, can I go home?" Everyone looked at each other, making me feel embarrassed.

"Go, go, Gubkin," he answered readily as if he had already decided to let me go and was only waiting for me to ask.

However, I did not go home right away but headed instead, to the garrison park. The poplars were not yet green, but a bluish haze already covered their fresh branches. The snow was soft and not at all cold. It made good snowballs, but I didn't feel playful. I put some on the branches and they looked like peeled apples. Then I sat on a bench by the summer dance floor. The wooden floors, devoid of the snow, breathed damply of sunshine. Spring was in the air, and I thought: "How is it so? There's me, there's Edka, there are all the people I love. But Svetlanka doesn't have all of hers." I imagined what was going on at Svetlanka's and felt it with my heart – and it wasn't pretty. "Everyone loses a dear one at some point. That's not quite the issue. Every loss takes a piece of love away from someone." Did I read that, or did I make it up?

13   The name for the war between the Soviet Union and Germany, which was overwhelmingly emphasized over WWII as a whole.

Who cares! It was true, and there was nothing anyone could do about it.

No, that's wrong; it is not true! We must love more with every loss. Then there will be no less love on earth. I felt the urge to do something good for Svetlanka. Now, immediately, so she knows. But what? What should I do? Maybe get her a doll, that laughing toddler figurine we saw together in the shop.

"Valera, look, what a funny little guy. He'd make anything feel joyful."

Eyes sparkling, Svetlanka had run off and when I caught up with her and hugged her by the shoulders, she almost didn't pull away. And in the evening, at home, this poem practically wrote itself:

> *Beside me sits a tiny friend,*
> *A tiny friend.*
> *He shines with quiet peace so bright,*
> *It's pure delight.*
>
> *An open book of fate he holds,*
> *In little hands*
> *Our thoughts have coiled in a dance,*
> *In moment's trance.*
>
> *When bats of night take daring flight*
> *In velvet height,*
> *The gates of moonlight set him free*
> *To come to me.*

I've long expected his advent
To stop my fall,
To teach me 'bout life well spent
And duty's call.

So, what about the doll? Shall I give it to her? Of course! And the poem too. I'll write it on a card and put it in a parcel because she's not likely to come to school tomorrow. Yes, in a parcel, that's the right thing to do!

I returned home at three o'clock in the afternoon. Rex wagged his tail in greeting and stamped his front paws twice on my coat.

"Get out!" I had to push the dog away from the porch before opening the door.

Rex took offence and hid in his kennel. I went in, found my piggy bank behind the mirror, and within a quarter of an hour, was in the shop. The lady at the post office helped me wrap the doll. I asked her to put a postmark on the parcel immediately, and she did.

"Will it get delivered today?"

The telegraph operator looked me over from head to toe.

"It may if you deliver it yourself."

I was not too fond of her joke, so I ran outside. A warm south wind made me unbutton my coat and remove my cap. The Garrison highway was dry; I got to it and stomped with all my might, knocking the mud off my boots. Spring, early spring had sprung. This day could have been wonderful if not for the plane crash. If not for the plane… If not for the plane…

I had to do something; my homework, at least. I came home, took the collar off the dog, and stroked him. But I didn't feel like doing homework.

That night, I had various dreams. We were all walking together, holding hands, all of us, the whole class, the teachers, my father, my mother, my older sister Olga. The sun was high above the meadow, and larks were basking in it. The meadow was full of flowers. Suddenly, the sun grew darker, darker… We looked and saw that it wasn't the sun, but a crashed plane. The forest in front of us grew dense, and everyone asked me:

"How can we walk together, holding hands, through the woods? We can't. With the aeroplane gone, there's less love, any way you slice it!"

"I don't care," I said.

Some people got angry with me. Genka Rogozinsky reproached me:

"You're a daydreamer, you just make things up."

I didn't agree with Genka. I stepped forward and said:

"Nothing's gone! Let's follow each other but still hold hands so no one gets lost. I'll go first, let Edka follow me, and let Svetlanka follow Edka."

I set them all up, and we went through the forest, and no one got lost. Then the sun reappeared, and the larks, and the meadow, and the flowers…

Edka woke me up. He came running to me at first light and said:

"Let's do our homework together."

"Why, all of a sudden?"

"Nothing in particular. The year ends soon, it's better to get some good marks."

I smiled. Edka was funny. It had nothing to do with the homework, he was just worried about me, that's why he came running at dawn.

"Edka, stop pretending. Let me just copy your algebra and physics solutions right away."

"Huh! Look who's the cheeky monkey today!"

Smiling, Edka pulled notebooks from his bag.

"Where were you yesterday?"

"Nowhere."

"Tell me! Who was in the shop, Pushkin?"

"I bought Svetlanka a present."

"Ah…" Edka became serious. We were silent.

"Look, I'm not going to school."

"You what?"

"I'm not going to school. I don't feel like it."

"Where are we going?" Edka asked at once.

"We could go to the river. Or the garrison park."

"Let's go to the river and get some willow twigs, the girls will be jumping with joy tomorrow."[14]

We walked through the slushy mud, holding onto the wattle fences. The puddles and streams were murky and deep. I carried Edka several times. Edka chuckled:

---

14   In Russian Orthodox tradition the Palm Sunday is Willow Sunday; Orthodox Christians cut and present each other with willow twigs with furry buds on them.

"Come on, big brothers, help me out!"

Edka called my rubber waders his "big brothers." We reached the river near the rice plant. An orange mound of chaff stretched right to the water, and Edka, making a spyglass with his hands, declared:

"All clear, they are coming on white boats. Chief Petty Officer, do you recognize the invaders from the Iron Star?"

"One moment, Captain."

I quickly opened my bag and, grabbing the first notebook I found, rolled it into a spyglass.

"Take my radiation detector, Captain. I have a feeling they'll bombard us with alpha particles."

"Don't worry, CPO, I have already activated the shields. Put your detector away; you're not in a physics lesson."

I looked at the notebook; it was a physics notebook.

"Captain, I am impressed by your intuition."

"Nonsense!"

Edka dropped his bag and began taking off his coat.

"When I was training on Centaurus, I had a similar case. Our major task now is to capture one of their boats."

Edka carefully laid down his coat and started descending to the river bend.

"Captain, allow me… The scientific council will not approve such a risk."

Edka stopped, so I halted too and took off my coat.

"I was just as eager at your age. Look!" Edka pointed to the moving ice floes accumulating in the bend; they seemed alive.

"I understand. Shall we seize the largest boat and head out to the ocean?"

"CPO, the scientific council was wise to replace your biological brain with an electronic one." Edka assumed the role, and his voice took on a metallic tone.

"Yes, Captain, the scientific council knew with whom I would be working." I approached the water and nudged an ice floe with my foot; it drifted slightly before brushing the shore again.

"Captain, we'll need grappling hooks."

"You mean steering cannons, CPO?"

We pulled out two suitable poles from a pile lying near a brick chimney, and Edka said:

"We'll leave the cannons here after Operation 'Blue Anabiosis' succeeds."

"Yes, Captain!"

Jumping onto a floe, we pushed off from the shore, and Operation 'Blue Anabiosis' began. Smaller floes crashed into our 'boat' and shattered with a tinkling sound. Edka stood on a protruding section, the ship's bridge.

"CPO, the aliens have sent armoured turtles at us… Keep your cannon ready!"

Our poles bent dangerously under the weight of the hefty floes, and their tips started breaking off.

"Captain, the monsters are cumbersome; we need to manoeuvre."

"Let's do it," Edka agreed, and we began steering our floe into the fast current.

"Captain, we must not miss the 'blue forest.'"

"Nonsense, we'll gain speed, turn at the bend, and we'll be in the forest."

We pushed away a dark 'turtle' that emerged on the left side and caught the current. The 'boat' slowly turned, and Edka ended up at the rear.

"Captain, I'll take the helm; gauges have failed."

"Don't rush, CPO; we need to use inertia."

I tested the depth with the pole. It didn't reach the bottom. The water bubbled and hissed at the edge of the floe.

The floe picked up speed. Operation 'Blue Anabiosis' was entering its critical phase.

"Listen, Edik, let's brake. If we hit a snag at the bend, we're done for."

"Exactly, CPO."

We started paddling with the poles. I tried reaching the bottom again, but it was still too deep. Our ice floe was picking up speed ominously.

"Stop!" Edka said. "We need to save our strength. Let's rely on luck."

"You're right, Captain. Let's sit down."

We pulled out the poles and squatted. Our feet were ankle-deep in water.

"Should we take off our boots? It might be difficult otherwise." I unbuckled my waders.

"Let's wait."

Now we looked ahead as the floe was turning. Holding our poles ready, we prepared to fend off any snags. I looked at the hill; it was slowly drifting away from us.

"Keep your eyes forward!" Edka awaited the turn. The water bubbled around the floe like it was boiling.

The sun peeked out from behind a cloud, making the water shimmer, and Edka said:

"In the worst case, it's about sixty meters to the bushes."

"Who knows, maybe there's a snag there too."

"There shouldn't be."

Our legs were getting numb. I thought of standing up, but at that same moment, something shifted and scraped under the floe. The right edge lifted out of the water. The floe tilted, and Edka, unable to keep his balance, fell forward on all fours and hit me in the chest with his head.

"Steady!" I grabbed Edka's shoulder. We started sliding off the floe. Something moved again under the floe and there was a loud crack behind us.

"Get down!" Edka's eyes were wide with fear.

Thick slush poured into our clothes and boots. The floe, or what was left of it, levelled out and slowly drifted away out of the fast current towards the bushes. Edka was the first to recover. He looked around and solemnly declared:

"It seems we've dealt with the aliens."

"Yes, Captain, the steering cannons… Edka, it's cold."

"I'm shivering too… We'll reach the bushes, and at worst, it'll be waist-deep."

"Maybe we should hop across the floes… Are we still collecting willow branches?"

"CPO!" Edka tried to snap at me but lost his breath.

"Alright, Edka, forget about the aliens. Stand on that edge."

I sat down, dangled my legs, and reached the bottom. Pushing our 'boat,' now more of a hexagon, I jumped on it and slid off immediately. We crashed into ice-filled bushes.

Breaking off some willow branches, we easily hopped across the floes to the shore. I started shivering.

"Quick, or we'll freeze solid!"

At home, we hung up our clothes and sat by the stove. The fire crackled, and occasionally the logs snapped, sending pink sparks up the chimney.

"Valera, you don't have to answer if you don't want to… Did anything ever happen between you and Svetlanka?" Edka threw a log into the fire. A burst of sparks licked the bricks and disappeared up the chimney.

"Why do you ask?"

"Oh, nothing… The janitor Kapitonovna painted quite a picture of you."

"What picture?"

"Do you remember I went to get chalk during the lesson recently? I walked into the staff room, and Kapitonovna was there cleaning the windows. 'It wouldn't be a problem if they didn't make such a mess in the classrooms in the evenings…' And you know Mermaid, she was there… 'You should tell us who's making all this mess, Nadyezhda Kapitonovna.' 'How can I remember? There are so many of them. Just yesterday, I went to the 9B…' Mermaid froze because that's our class… 'It was locked; I had the key… And they were inside with a bench against the door. I asked, why are you in the dark, why the bench? And this one, what's his name, the red-haired one who always recited poems in your class…' 'Gubkin?' 'Yes, exactly. He was trying to hide her behind himself, and when I looked, she had spots on her face, and her apron was crumpled. I told her she was shameless. She ran away. And this one, what's his name…' Then Mermaid saw me. 'Voskoboynikov, what's going on?' So, I grabbed the chalk and left."

I felt Edka wasn't telling me everything. But even what he did share infuriated me. To be honest, I never thought I could get so mad over such a trivial story.

"Oh, I'd have a lot to say about Kapitonovna, but wouldn't bother." I felt so uneasy that I stood up and started pacing. "That's not how it was at all… We were doing geometry, and the first graders were peeking in and distracting us… I didn't even notice it was getting dark."

"Did you kiss her? Be honest!"

"Yes, but not in the classroom, in February… on Soviet Army Day."

Edka sighed.

"Don't you mind Kapitonovna. Just ignore her! She's not all there."

"That's not the point… It's Mermaid… The day before yesterday, I greeted her, and she said, 'Gubkin, could you walk with me?' And she smiled and nodded. I said, 'Let's go!' We walked, and out of the blue, she started telling me she'd just been talking to Svetlanka's mother."

"Valera, don't pay attention!"

"It's not that… I'm not worried about myself… If Mermaid… Svetlanka already has enough to deal with…"

"Don't worry about it. Just give her a nice gift for the 8th of March."

"I already sent a parcel yesterday."

"Good!" Edka pulled his trousers off the line and started putting them on. "If anything happens, I'll send a love letter to Yagnysheva."

"What?"

"Just that… And if Tolik Rada and Kolka Altaev send theirs too, it'll be great. Then no one will bother you. Eight people is almost half the class, and where there's half a class, it's no longer an isolated incident but a trend." Edka picked up his bag and added, "Mermaid will be scared and sweep things under a rug. After all, as the class supervisor, she'll be the first to get in trouble." Edka winked and said, "Shake on it, CPO!"

We shook hands, and Edka went home. As he closed the gate, he said once more:

"Don't worry, it's nothing! And tomorrow, bring the willow twigs, and I'll bring six or seven bottles." Edka winked again, and we shook hands once more.

My mood improved a little, and I decided to work on the birdhouses. Mum returned from work at around six. Seeing what I was doing, she said:

"Mark my words; it'll snow again!" She sat on the bench by the summer kitchen while I worked on the porch. "Did you take care of the cow?"

"What's there to take care of? I cleaned the barn and gave it some hay."

Mum sighed and watched on as I repaired the birdhouse.

"Even sparrows don't live in your birdhouses," she teased, trying to provoke me. "Maybe you're doing something wrong;

you should ask your father."

"I can manage fine on my own."

Out of the corner of my eye, I saw that my words had an impact on her. I put down the hammer and did a few exercises. What was Mum thinking? That I'm all grown up now?

"You've caught up to your father, just not with your brain," she concluded unexpectedly.

"How can you say that? I designed these birdhouses!" I protested, just for the sake of it. To be honest, I was pleased to hear that I'd caught up with my father.

Mum smiled, and I suddenly noticed how small and fragile she looked, in her oversized rubber boots and a quilted jacket. Her scarf had slipped back, revealing her thin, grey hair and wrinkled face.

"Mum, you're become so tiny!" I exclaimed in surprise.

She immediately, and very obviously, saddened and would probably have cried if I'd said anything more. Mum's nerves were weak. I grabbed the barbell, lifted it over my head once, and threw it to the ground. A wheel from the combine clanged off, but I shouted cheerfully:

"Don't worry, Mum, you're small, but I'm strong. I'll grab some hay with the pitchfork just once, and it'll last the cow all night." I vaulted over the fence separating the yard from the hayloft and ran to the stack.

Do you imagine I didn't know what Mum was thinking? By saying, "You've caught up with your father, just not with your brain," she was warning me not to get too proud. How could I possibly catch up with Dad and gain wisdom in just one day?

Parents imagine their children can hear their thoughts. Or at least, Mum thinks I can.

Dad came home from work at around nine. Delicious smells of dinner wafted through the kitchen, even reaching my room, but I paid them no mind. I pretended to be studying. After washing up, Dad peeked into my room, and when I didn't look up from my book, he left, thinking, "Let him study, we'll talk after dinner."

I really can hear both Mum and Dad's thoughts. I just pretended not to.

Then, about ten minutes later, I overheard a conversation in the kitchen. I went to get some water to see who was visiting. As I stood up, I heard:

"You know, he can study well; he's smart, but lately..."

It was Mermaid!

"...started being late. I think there's a fascination..."

Mermaid lowered her voice, and I couldn't hear what fascination she was referring to. At first, I wanted to go to the door and eavesdrop but decided against it, simply on principle. I opened Anton Chekhov's "The Man in a Case" and started reading aloud. I was reading and thinking to myself: "Is she going to tell them the Kapitonovna's story? Would she mention the aeroplane... she probably should talk about the aeroplane, it's important... But what about Kapitonovna? I'm not afraid for myself, no, not for myself..."

"Valera, come, eat," my father called out.

I could tell from his voice that he wasn't angry with me. I sat, as usual, on my father's right hand, my mother on his left.

The table could seat five more people. It's a big table but still not enough when relatives visit us on holidays. We take another table out of my room on such days.

I tasted the soup and said:

"White rooster, huh?"

Dad said nothing, and Mum replied:

"Yeah, the white one; eat up!"

And so, I gorged myself on the soup. Then my father cut an onion and gave me a quarter. I didn't refuse, but Mum said onions gave her chest pains.

"It's not the onions but the change in the weather," said Dad.

Remembering the conversation with my mum, I asked:

"Is it really going to snow again?"

"It shouldn't," Dad replied. "I was at Grandpa Dubovik's; he plans to unwrap apple trees next week."

Dad and I didn't talk again until after dinner, until after Mum had cleared the dishes and wiped the table. That's the way it is with us. Dad and I talk, and Mum sits next to us, knitting. Mum pretends not to listen, even humming something under her breath, but in fact, she's all ears; she likes to listen because our conversations are always interesting.

So, my dad and I started talking about starlings and early spring, and then he said:

"Raisa Konstantinovna came by."

Honestly, I was waiting for him to mention her but had no idea it would end before it started. My dad changed the subject immediately.

"Mikhail Mikhailovich went to the district centre, with the chairman... the new school opens on March the tenth... Your school is..." Dad chuckled, "it's like a university; it would take more than a day to get around all the classrooms."

"Did you see the gym?" I rejoiced.

"The gym! Why, the Lobodan church with all its domes would fit in there!" Father put his elbows on the table and wiped his forehead with his handkerchief. For some reason, Mum gave Dad a disapproving look, but he gazed at me cheerfully and added:

"Well, go and do your homework. Mum and I must go to the field at dawn tomorrow." He got up from the table and went into the bedroom. Mum, unhappily laying her unfinished shawl on the chair, followed him.

"Alexei, I told you to talk to him."

The door of the room slammed shut abruptly. The Mermaid had told them everything after all. Now they were going to argue...

I turned off the lights and went to my room, lay down on my bunk without undressing and thought about myself, about Svetlanka, about the disaster in her family...

A plane crashed. When a plane crashes, dreams crash with it. I read that in a book. When you see it in real life, you need no books to think the same. The plane was silvery, and the sky was clear and blue that day, and the sun was bright, and the streams flowed and looked like silver in the sun. When I saw them, I thought: just like molten silver, flowing, flowing...

On March the fifth, all mirrors in the main hall of the House of Officers were covered with cloth. Three closed coffins stood there with banners bowed over them in reverence. Trimmed with black ribbons, the coffins held human ashes mixed with soil. Human ashes are inseparable from the soil and from the Earth. The planet is six billion years old (so say scientists), and people have lived on it for millions of years. All these years people lived, died of old age, in war, by accident, and all of them were buried in the ground. And so, human particles in the ground amassed, more and more of them every year. Perhaps every little pinch of soil has our particles in it.

I used to lie in the grass while herding cows and watch ants fussily running around. When I got bored, I'd watch the larks. Suddenly, out of the blue, joy would rush into my heart, and I'd spread my arms and hug the ground, then jump up and shout:

"Earth! Life! Life!"

The cows would raise their heads and look at me, and our Rozka would shake her head and return to grazing.

I remembered all this somehow when they buried Svetlanka's father. He wouldn't see grass, larks, or ants anymore. It was scary. I didn't go close to those who buried him; I stood at another pilot's old grave with a propeller set on a pedestal. The pedestal was welded from iron railings; it was painted in blue and seemed airy. A solemn platoon raised their carbines and shot three salutes in reverence for the brave aviators lost; in honour of Svetlanka's fallen father. At the cemetery, Klavdia Ivanovna, Svetlanka's aunt from the city of Arzamas, joined her family. The aunt and Svetlanka's mum were wearing black, and Svetlanka, as usual, was wearing her green teddy coat with a hood. I kept my eyes on Svetlanka. Her face was stern, and there were no tears. She and her aunt were supporting her mother under her arms. Svetlanka's mother was crying inconsolably and fainted several times, and when the mound over the grave grew, her cries turned into wails of visceral, primal anguish. I couldn't stand it and squeezed my way to Svetlanka. As soon as she saw me, she fell on my chest and cried, too. Everything after that was like a dream. I don't even remember how I got home. I remember travelling on a green bus, sitting alongside Svetlanka. I held her hands; they were soft and hot. And I don't remember stopping at the entrance to her house. Everyone walked past us. We noticed no-one.

The flat door opened, the aunt called for Svetlanka. Svetlanka sobbed and, kissing me quickly on the cheek, ran inside. I didn't like the way the aunt looked me over from head to toe before closing the door, shaking her head judgementally. "What did I do wrong?" I thought and looked down at myself. My coat was clean.

That's all I remember clearly. The rest of it was like a dream.

When Svetlanka came to school the next day the girls immediately surrounded her, chit-chatting. Edka and I told them strictly:

"Hey you chatterboxes, let the girl put her backpack down."

I was actually quite pleased that the girls sympathised with her so much.

Svetlanka smiled at the girls, and when she saw the willow branches on the windows, she exclaimed:

"Girls, how lovely!"

Everything was fine that day. The only person I didn't like being there was Mermaid. When she asked Svetlanka about Anton Pavlovich Chekhov, she looked at her as if she were ill. This was Mermaid's way of showing her deep empathy for Svetlanka's grief and her great attention to every one of us.

"Sit down, Svetlana, excellent."

She took a long time to write the grade in the journal, and then, looking at me, said:

"Gubkin, did you understand anything?"

I was surprised and answered without standing up:

"What's there not to understand?"

"Stand up when talking to your elders!"

"Well, I might as well get up." I answered and stood up reluctantly.

"You think very highly of yourself, but you don't get above a satisfactory grade in all your essays." Mermaid was talking to me, but was looking at Svetlanka: she wanted to humiliate me in Svetlanka's eyes.

"Satisfactory seems a positive evaluation. It says I can understand the basics."

"Exactly; the basics!" Mermaid smiled, but she didn't feel like smiling.

"Raisa Konstantinovna," I smiled too, "you recently mentioned the poet Nadson, but we haven't studied his work. Do you know any of his poems by heart? Probably not, because the curriculum doesn't require it of you."

This would have stirred a storm, but the bell rang, and Mermaid only said:

"We'll talk more about your extracurricular knowledge, Gubkin. I see that I was not wrong to burden you with this conversation."

She picked up the register from the table and dashed out of the classroom.

During the second lesson, Edka nudged me and nodded at the window. I looked out and saw Klavdia Ivanovna, Svetlanka's aunt from Arzamas, enter the schoolyard through the wicket. She walked around a puddle covered in glistening ice and headed for the entrance. She wore a black hat and a dark all-season coat and was clutching a burgundy lacquered reticule in her left hand.

The second lesson was physics. I love physics: we had recently assembled a receiver with Vasily Petrovich and several tenth graders. Vasily Petrovich asked me about the electron tube, but I didn't even hear the question.

"Gubkin, are you asleep? Go to the blackboard and draw a diagram of an electron tube."

I stood up, but I didn't even make it to the blackboard. The door opened, and Mermaid came in. She apologised to Vasily Petrovich for the intrusion and asked me to come to the staff room.

I drew a diagram and only then, went to the staff room. The door was open, and I heard:

"Of course, I wouldn't turn to you if it was a small matter," (that means to Raisa Konstantinovna, our Mermaid), "but we had a similar case in Arzamas. And it all ended…"

Klavdia Ivanovna saw me in the doorway and faltered. Mermaid turned to me.

"Ah, Valery, sit down."

"It's all right, I'll stand," I said, and suddenly I saw the doll. It was sitting on the teacher's desk near the inkstand, laughing merrily, either to cheer me up or, on the contrary, to mock me.

Mermaid noticed my gaze and asked:

"Gubkin, tell me frankly, do you consider yourself an adult?"

I pretended I hadn't heard the question and asked:

"Raisa Konstantinovna, did you call me?"

Klavdia Ivanovna was the first to speak:

"Yes, we called you … Valery," she addressed me affectionately and tenderly as if I were a five-year-old girl. "We need to speak to you about your relationship with Svetlana."

"Sit down." Mermaid moved the chair, and the doll, now facing me, kept laughing. "Gubkin, we know everything and, in some sense, are happy about your friendship."

Raisa Konstantinovna paused, and Klavdia Ivanovna continued instead:

"But we'd like to know about the depth and purity of your relationship. Do you think we're entitled to that?"

I remained silent. Klavdia Ivanovna sighed.

"All right, well, tell me, why did you lock yourself in the classroom one night?"

I raised my head and did not avert my eyes. Mermaid and Klavdia Ivanovna were waiting.

"It wasn't like that. You were told a lie."

"What was it like?"

"Raisa Konstantinovna, I don't even want to talk about it!"

Perhaps my tone was unnecessarily harsh, but, honestly, it just happened of its own accord, beyond my control. Klavdia Ivanovna looked worried.

"All right, all right, Valery, don't answer." She opened her purse and took out a written sheet of paper.

> *Beside me sits a tiny friend,*
> *A tiny friend.*
> *He shines with quiet peace so bright,*
> *It's pure delight.*
>
> *I've long expected his advent*
> *To stop my fall,*
> *To teach me 'bout life well spent*
> *And duty's call.*

In her reading, the poem sounded odd. She somehow gave it a completely different meaning. I didn't even recognise it at first. Klavdia Ivanovna put the poem aside, and Raisa Konstantinovna said:

"Beautiful!" She smiled, and I liked her smile. "Here, Valera, you wrote about duty."

"Yes, yes, Raisa Konstantinovna, that's why I read…"

"I think it's your duty now to study hard. That comes first and foremost."

"Valery, you've invested too much in a relationship, too soon." Klavdia Ivanovna said it gently, but her expression was harsh, and I felt her scorn for me.

"Can I go now?"

Without waiting for permission, I went to the door.

"Stop, Gubkin! Klavdia Ivanovna and I would like to ask you not to meet Svetlana after school. And do not tell her about our conversation. Otherwise…"

"Otherwise, what?"

Mermaid was embarrassed, and Klavdia Ivanovna from Arzamas replied, no longer hiding her contempt:

"Otherwise, I'm taking her away with me." She pressed her lips tightly.

"Gubkin, you realise it's the end of the year, I'm against her leaving. Do you realise how much depends on you now?"

A technician came into the staff room and took the bell. I couldn't take my eyes off the aunt's lips.

"Raisa Konstantinovna, I'll do as you ask."

I followed the technician out. The bell rang, and the kids poured out; I stepped aside, and they spilt out into the street.

Back in the classroom, my mates surrounded me.

"Vasily Petrovich gave you a 5." Genka Rogozinsky was curious, he pushed everyone away. "What is it? Why were you summoned?"

"It's nothing really," I said.

I packed my textbooks, and Svetlanka came over.

"Anything serious?"

"No!" I smiled.

 Edka dragged me down the corridor.

"Honestly! Because of her?"

I nodded, and Edka said:

"Don't get discouraged, we'll write messages today."

"What kind of messages?"

"Love letters." Edka gave me a sly wink.

"No messages! Anyway, we'll talk after school."

The boys surrounded us again, and Edka said:

"Be brief, and not a word to anyone else! He's under pressure for the same thing."

Everyone understood Edka at once, although, frankly speaking, I did not fully get what it was all about.

After lessons, I went off with Edka. Svetlanka wanted to come too, but I said:

"Svetlana, Edik and I need to talk… Goodbye!" That stupid "goodbye" came out of my mouth all by itself.

Svetlanka turned abruptly and ran towards the group of girls without saying anything. I could hardly control myself. I wanted to stop her and explain everything. "No, I must not!" I immediately stopped myself. "It's better this way. Better for her…" I turned back to Edka. He was strolling towards the garrison park and stopped when I called out his name.

"Gub-kin, Vo-sko-boy-nikov, tomorrow's the seventh!" girls shouted in chorus.

Edka raised his cap as if to greet them, and the girls, laughing, waved their bags.

"Valera, what are you doing? Let Svetlanka come with us."

"No, she should not."

Edka was surprised, and then I told him word for word the whole conversation in the teacher's room because it was a conversation I would remember for the rest of my life.

"She should not… And no messages, either."

"What then?"

"It's okay. Let's just leave it as it is."

"And you won't go near Svetlanka, not even once?"

"No, I won't."

Edka and I walked in silence for a long time, and then he said as if to himself:

"Or maybe you're wrong about how you feel."

"Who's wrong?" I stopped.

"Don't get angry." Edka adjusted his bag.

"I'm not mad. I'm not going to school anymore."

Edka stopped as well.

"Are you out of your mind?"

"That's the thing, I'm not. Tomorrow I'll hide in the attic and will tell my father after the holiday. I just don't want to ruin my mother's eighth of March." The decision came unexpectedly, but I immediately felt it was just what I needed and cheered up.

"Why? I'll go to evening school. I'll work as a trailer driver... My dad will take me on his tractor."

"Maybe, you'll have second thoughts?"

"No, it's settled." I patted Edka on the shoulder and said, "But I'll do my homework anyway. You can bring me the assignments and tell everyone in class that I don't want to go to school. But not a word about Svetlanka!"

"Valera, maybe you should reconsider and think of something else?"

"Look, a car!" There was a new Moskvich[15] parked outside the House of Officers. We went over and touched it.

"Wow! Not like the old one!" Edka walked around the car.

"If I go to school," I said, "I won't be able to resist talking

---

15 Moskvich (Moscovite, a resident of Moscow) – a Soviet brand of consumer cars.

to her."

"Do you like it?" The car owner in a brown hat and a blue all-season coat opened the door and got behind the wheel. Then he rolled down the window and stuck his head out:

"Where do you want to go?"

"The collective farm club," replied Edka.

"You mean the new school? Get in!"

When we were already on the motorway, I asked:

"How do you know our village?"

"Oh, I know everything. I even know that your new school will open tomorrow at fifteen hundred hours local time."

"Nah. The school will open on the tenth."

The man in the brown hat corrected the mirror, and I saw his laughing eyes.

"Wanna bet?"

"I'll bet!"

"Your friend is a witness." He adjusted the mirror again, and I realised that now he was looking at Edka. "Where should I drop you?"

"Over there by the billboard." Edka pointed to the fence near the tailoring shop, and the man in the brown hat stopped sharply. Saying goodbye to us, he said:

"So, keep in mind, tomorrow at three. Tomorrow's a holiday, and school's not a bad present."

"It's gorgeous!" Edka confirmed.

"Agreed!" The man in the hat laughed, and the Moskvich sped further down the motorway.

"Edka, who was that?"

"I have no idea! Someone from the district centre."

"Is tomorrow the day? Why didn't anyone tell us?"

"Could be a surprise. Valera, what about you? Are you coming?"

"You can tell me about it later. That's it, I'll go through the garden." We stomped around for a while and parted ways.

The real celebration of the Eighth of March begins on the seventh. Men say: "Happy coming!" and women answer, "Thank you, thank you," and smile.

On the morning of March the seventh, I stood in our shop at the gifts showcase and witnessed it all with my own eyes. Most of the men who ran into the shop rushed to the cash register. Then I saw them run out with boxes of perfume. Sometimes the men in the queue would quarrel. Then an elderly saleswoman would say:

"What's all the fuss? You're not at a booze shop."

The queue would fall shamefully silent. Someone at the counter would confirm "Exactly!" then affectionately shout "Happy holidays! as he handed over the receipt and dashed out smiling blissfully.

The morning of the seventh was warm though not sunny. Not knowing what to do, I wandered towards home. In case my mother had a short workday, I would hide in the attic. It was a holiday, after all...

I lay down in the attic on an old worn coat. At my feet lay a bunch of last year's garlic and several yellowed books. I had thrown both out of the box when searching for my "Notes of a

Young Naturalist."

I wondered if there would be a school opening today, or if that Moskvich guy had been playing a trick on us? They would probably invite the brass band from the rice plant or use our collective farm band. At the end of lessons, guys would be congratulating all the girls and Svetlanka would ask for me... Of course she would; she'd ask Edka why I wasn't there...

The wicket creaked and I woke up.

"Valera, hurry, where are you?" Edka called softly, but his voice alarmed me.

Something must have happened...

I peeked out the attic window and shouted:

"What's the commotion, Captain?"

Edka shooed Rex away and walked towards the summer kitchen. When he saw me, he got angry.

"Get down!"

I rushed away from the window, ducking to avoid the rafters. My every leap echoed throughout the house. A cloud of dust rose above the floor from under my feet. I sneezed twice as I ducked into the attic opening.

"What's wrong?"

"Get down." Edka lowered himself onto the porch and waited for me to sit next to him. "The school opening is about to start. Yesterday's guy in the brown hat turned out to be from the district centre, and he arrived with a whole delegation."

Rex, jingling his chain, squeezed between us, and Edka and I petted him.

"We only had two lessons, and then we went to the new

building." Edka stopped talking and stroked Rex again. When petted, Rex pressed his ears and pointed his nose upwards, he even closed his eyes in pleasure. And I felt very uneasy because Edka started stroking Rex again and stopped talking.

"Have you seen Svetlanka?" I couldn't bear it.

"I haven't seen her. Kolka Altabayev went home after the second lesson, and then came running back, saying she'd been poisoned."

"How?!" I jumped up.

"She drank vinegar. Valera, sit down!" Edka grabbed my arm. "She's at the district hospital, and you know they've got excellent doctors there! Sit down; I've got my motorbike. Twenty minutes and we'll be there."

"Don't tell me to calm down! Do you hear me?!"

I was angry, so furious at everyone and everything in my life, that I'd have howled at the top of my lungs if Edka hadn't been there.

"Don't calm me down; tell me why she drank vinegar!"

Suddenly I laughed unexpectedly to myself. Edka's eyes widened, and I was terrified, why, why did I laugh? I was shaking; just one more second and I would have burst into tears. To prevent that, I hopped up and ran to the wicket. The motorbike was there.

Edka, looking pale, blocked my way:

"Valera! Valera! You're not going anywhere in that state!"

"I can and I will! I'm OK now." I pushed Edka away.

"Why did she do it? Go ahead, talk. I told you, I'm alright." I sat down beside the motorbike, picked up a twig and started drawing circles and triangles on the ground with it.

"She had some kind of quarrel with her aunt yesterday." Edka took a rag out of his sweatshirt pocket and squatted down. "Anyway, Svetlanka's mother went to Vozdvizhenka after the funeral. They had relatives there, so Svetlanka and her aunt stayed. As soon as the mother left, the aunt started to assert her authority. She kept asking why you were locked up in the classroom and why you had given her that doll instead of something else." Edka stopped talking and, folding the rag, started wiping his palm for no apparent reason.

"Then what?" The twig broke, its tip hanging helplessly from the peeling bark.

Edka dropped the rag and stood up. "The situation continued for several days, until yesterday unable to stand it, Svetlanka confronted her aunt, saying: 'You're interfering with my homework, auntie!' And her aunt went like: 'Oh, is that right? So, that's what it's come to! Tomorrow you'll come with me… what's that city name… to Arzamas.' She got on the phone and started calling long-distance. Svetlanka said, 'Auntie, if you say one word to Mum, I'll—' She locked herself in her room. And the aunt screamed, 'I'll tell the neighbours too! You want to pop one without tying a knot?!' After that, she raved noisily about various things while she collected the laundry from outside. Svetlanka saw through the window that her aunt was surrounded by neighbours and went to the kitchen. The neighbours came into the flat, and the aunt continued raving madly: 'I'll take her away tomorrow, she'll thank me for it!' But Svetlanka would thank her for nothing, for by then she was already on the floor, poisoned by vinegar. When the aunt saw her, she fainted… But nothing happened to the aunt; she left for Arzamas this morning. Nobody saw her off, not even Svetlanka's mother."

Edka took hold of the motorbike's handlebars and raised the kickstand. I threw down the twig, got up and asked:

"Got it from your uncle?"

Edka nodded and turned on the bike using the makeshift key, not the original one. A red light flashed on the headlight.

"It's one heavy bastard!"

Edka pressed the start pedal and tried the throttle. The engine roared. He sat on the bike and I leapt on behind him.

"Edik, full throttle!"

He nodded silently and shifted gears. Out of the village, we hit the asphalt, and after two kilometers, Edka went full throttle. We met only two or three cars on our way to the district centre. There could be more though – I kept looking at the speedometer. At junctions, the arrow slid down to sixty, and it felt like we were crawling.

"Edik, full throttle!"

Edka nodded and maxed out the revs. The arrow went up. Somehow, I thought it'd drop the moment I took my eyes off it.

"Edik, faster!"

Edka shrugged, the arrow froze, and I saw Svetlanka's sparkling eyes in the speedometer.

Before entering the village, Edka turned onto a country lane. We made a detour to avoid passing the traffic police station.

On the main street, Edka gained speed once again. We flew past the shops. Suddenly, a girl ran out of a front garden around the corner. Edka dropped the throttle and slowed down. The girl, seeing us, stopped on the curb. Edka chuckled, pulled the accelerator, and picked up speed. At the same second, the girl ran across the road. I don't remember how I grabbed the handlebars, reached out, shoved the girl aside, and rolled on the asphalt. The motorbike caught up with me and painfully smacked my shoulder…

When we got up, the girl was already running into the gate of a house by the road. The motorbike roared, peering out of the ditch with its rear wheel still spinning. Edka ran to the bike and turned off the engine.

Rolling it up to the fence, we inspected it. The headlight and the front mudguard were smashed, and the right footrests were bent. We examined the tank - it was intact.

"It's alright." As Edka bent over, I saw wisps of cotton wool. The sleeves of his black cotton jacket were ripped at the elbows, and one trouser leg was torn to the knee.

Gawkers started surrounding us. A woman with a bucket of water ran out of the nearby house.

"Would it start?" I asked.

"I don't think so…" But just in case, Edka inserted his homemade key and cranked the ignition. The motorbike sneezed and rumbled.

"They will catch you! You can't drive it!" a woman with a bucket shouted, but Edka had already shifted from the first to the second. Avoiding the main road and sneaking along the fences, we finally reached the hospital. The gate was open, and we drove into the courtyard. I jumped off immediately, and Edka drove the motorbike towards a jeep with a red cross. I didn't wait for Edka to park the bike and rushed to the door.

"Where to?" the elderly woman looked me over carefully and concluded, "Ah, the trauma department… Third door on the right."

Afraid that I might be turned away, I followed her directions and almost ran into Svetlanka's mother. She was standing in the corridor with a man in a white coat. I froze.

"It's nothing, it's just a nervous breakdown. We'll discharge her in two weeks." The man closed his notebook, and Svetlanka's mother asked:

"Doctor, and what about the move …"

"No, no, that's out of the question! For now, she must be protected from anything that might cause her further anxiety."

The doctor looked around and saw me. "Who are you here to see?"

Svetlanka's mother, shrieking, ran up to me.

"Valera!" She hurriedly opened her purse and took out a handkerchief. "Doctor, look, he's covered in blood." She clutched my head with both hands and cuddled against me, crying.

"It's nothing, it doesn't hurt a bit."

"What happened?"

"Ran into a little trouble on a motorbike…"

"On a motorbike, well, well…" The doctor said it like he was establishing a diagnosis.

The nurse came over: "Come with me, young man."

When Svetlanka's mother wouldn't let me go, I told her:

"I want to see Sveta."

"No way!" said the doctor. He wanted to add something else, but Svetlanka's mother gave him such a look that he immediately softened:

"All right, but he's coming with me."

The nurse threw a white gown over my shoulders, and we walked down the corridor. Then we went up to the first floor. The doctor opened the ward door, and I saw Svetlanka. She was asleep. Her face was pale and serious. There was a white night-stand next to the bed. I looked at the bedside table, and my heart burst with agonising longing and infinite happiness.

There was a familiar little man sitting on it. He looked at me and laughed...

1971

WINGED WAR STEED

My heart fluttered and started racing, jolting me awake. I had been sleeping on quilted mats laid on the floor. Upon rising, I immediately spotted two sweets, real ones, in transparent wrappers. I tucked them under the waistband of my pants and dashed outside. Usually, my mother and I were the first to arrive at the collective farm's kindergarten – she was the headmistress, and I was too young to be left alone in the mornings.

Today, she did not wake me up, so I went to kindergarten by myself, feeling quite grown-up. Everything felt marvellous. The sun had already risen, and the street lay bare before me. The two candies sparked a torrent of unexpected thoughts. They exploded my mind with suddenly revealed possibilities. Dozens of ideas buzzed in my head, and I finally decided that I would give one of the sweets to Pavlik Bashta, a boy from the older group who ran faster than anyone but refused to play with us, the middle group boys. I devised a plan to win him over. The plan was splendid, but Pavlik might not agree to become my winged war steed for just one candy.

He certainly wouldn't resist two candies, I mused, but I wanted to try one myself. I had only once tasted such a bonbon in a clear wrapper. It was incredibly, incredibly sweet. Much sweeter than sugar. I felt an urge to make sure those I had were just as sweet but paused.

But what if he doesn't agree to just one?! The thought scorched me, and I sprinted down the road. If he doesn't agree to one, I'll tell him: take the second one, damn you! Just like the cook curses when the water carrier demands a full day's wage for one extra barrel.

As I approached the kindergarten, I saw many boys from the older group perched on the fence. Pavlik wasn't among them. My mother stood near the summer kitchen, surrounded by teachers. They were all in white gowns (we easily distinguished them from other workers by this). To avoid attention, I ran to another gate. I didn't want to draw attention and be teased as a "mummy's boy" later: my mother was the headmistress of the kindergarten.

Maria Vasilievna, our group's teacher, called out to me. Opening the gate, she told me to wash my hands. We'd be having breakfast on the veranda, and then the whole kindergarten would go to the river for a swim. The news that we would go to the river after breakfast sparked a bonfire of excitement in me.

I ducked down so no one would think I was a mummy's boy and dashed to the main building. I only glanced at my mother once (she had her back to me), but still, other teachers' faces told me she was silently smiling at me in her thoughts.

On such a day, I wouldn't mind giving up the second candy as well. I imagined Pavlik racing across the green floodplain meadow, and me keeping pace because I was holding onto the reins, the sturdy parachute cords he brought from home as his personal harness. A sudden joy engulfed me. Just as I was thinking that no sweet was too dear for such a strong steed as Pavlik, I ran into him, face to face, in the washroom.

"Oh, it's you!" said Pavlik.

He warned me that if I rushed into him like that again, he

wouldn't care that my mother was the headmistress and would trip me so I'd break my nose.

He mentioned my mother deliberately to hurt me, knowing that no one liked it when everything they did had something to do with their mother.

"Where's your harness?" I asked.

"What for?" Pavlik was startled.

"Because I want to ask you to be my winged war steed."

"You?! Me?! A winged war steed?" Pavlik mocked me.

"Who do you think you are?" he asked. "Do you think I'll agree just because your mother is the headmistress?"

He struck me hard, but I remained silent. I knew Pavlik would say such things because, in his place, anyone would, for Pavlik was the best winged warhorse of all.

"Do you know who my father was before the war?"

Pavlik paled, and I thought everything had fallen apart because long ago, before I was even born, Pavlik's father had been the chairman of our collective farm, and now he could barely walk with crutches. And then, to my relief, the bell for breakfast rang.

"Don't rush off! We'll have breakfast on the veranda," I said, and proposed that for each of his runs from fence to fence, I'd be Pavlik's horse as many times as he wanted.

"You've gone mad," said Pavlik and ran to breakfast.

While we were washing, I heard him announce to the older group that we'd have breakfast on the veranda. From Pavlik's tone, I guessed he had forgiven me and was proud to be the bearer of the good news. Time permitting, I'd tell him we were going to the river after breakfast. I imagined us running through the grass and golden dandelions and daisies that wedged between our toes and got so excited I had to stick my head under the tap. The cold water refreshed me, and I hurried to the veranda.

Luck was on my side again. Pavlik was waiting for me.

"Look," he said, pulling out the side pocket of his short trousers with detached braces.

The pocket was stuffed with parachute cords.

"But I still won't be your winged horse; you're too poor a runner," said Pavlik, boasting that the space between the kindergarten's fences was too small for a winged steed. "Fence to fence is for water-carrying horses."

"We're going to the river after breakfast," I said. "And look!"

I pulled two real candies in transparent cellophane wrappers from under my waistband and promised to give one to Pavlik if he agreed to be my winged horse. He saw the sweets and immediately swallowed.

"Real ones, in wrappers!" he marvelled, and I hid the sweets again under my waistband as Misha Rubanyuk ran up to us.

Misha was fifteen days older than me but being much shorter, looked like he belonged to the younger group. He was interested in everything that interested me. He even sat next to me at the table, and yesterday had asked if he could sometimes tell the group that he was older than me. I didn't allow it. I told him he should outgrow me first, then talk. Misha blushed as red as a boiled crab because he realised, he'd been caught trying to be taller at others' expense.

"Look," Misha said, running up and pulling out his pocket just like Pavlik.

I saw a bundle of crumpled hairy twine tied with coarse thread and deliberately covered the pocket because I immediately guessed it was a pathetic harness for a war steed. Of course, it couldn't compare with a harness made of real parachute cords with strong silk threads inside, which many fishermen used for lines. I didn't want Pavlik to see Misha's harness, but he did and immediately began mocking us.

"Oh wow, what a great harness!" Pavlik laughed exaggeratedly. "Just right for a water-carrying dobbin."

He ran to his table in the older group. I told Misha not to sit with me – I wouldn't sit with him. Misha hunched over, becoming even smaller. He blushed again, like a crab. Serves you right, I thought. I walked away from him and deliberately sat in the thick of the boys, leaving no free space nearby. Misha Rubanyuk had worn out his welcome with his friendship.

After breakfast, we headed for the river. The older group had their own teacher, and Maria Vasilievna was with us. We mixed with the older kids on the highway but after that separated again: the older ones were heading for the second pit located further down the river, while we went to the third, on the nearest river bend where the river was shallow because of the lack of rain.

I didn't see Misha Rubanyuk; he avoided me after breakfast. But Pavlik Bashta approached me himself after we left the highway.

"Give me your sweets, but don't cry if you fall and break your nose."

I reminded Pavlik that we had agreed on one candy, but he said that once he put on the harness, we'd run straight to the second pit, skipping the third.

"This isn't just from fence to fence."

We both looked out over the floodplain meadow dotted with golden dandelions and then he pulled out his magnificent harness with two cross-grab ropes and said:

"From the second pit to the third, you'll be the winged war steed."

It was an incredible stroke of luck. To gallop as Pavlik's winged stallion in front of everyone! But I didn't show my excitement and, pulling the sweets from under my waistband, said:

"Here, damn you!"

I had never seen Pavlik's harness up close. Now it lay on the grass and was much better than I had imagined.

If you're a winged war steed, you need to throw the strap over your shoulders, pass it under your arms, and the first cross rope closest to your back becomes the saddle girth, and the other, closer to the rider, forms the reins-holder. It keeps the reins from falling apart and tangling. If it's the rider's turn to become a stallion, he doesn't have to wait, but immediately harnesses himself from his end.

This magnificent harness had lots of other uses. But as it lay on the grass, I examined it well and realised that given some time I could make one myself, maybe even better. The revelation filled me with joy, and I couldn't stand still. My whole body trembled with impatience.

"Pavlik! Let me help!"

"No way," said Pavlik, mentioning that the sweets were suckers.

He put one sweet in his mouth and the other, still in its wrapper, in his pocket. But I was no longer interested in candies.

I burned with impatience. Finally, Pavlik got harnessed as the winged warhorse, and we dashed off.

Joyful faces, the laughing sun, and the expanse of sky and meadow – not feeling my feet, I had a bird's eye view of everything around me.

"Gubkin! Bashta!"

I heard the call, but my heart was too full to respond, and I felt too alive to stop.

Behind the wall of willows, Pavlik slowed down, and I almost knocked him over.

"Enough!" he panted. "We're already at the first pit."

Only then did I see the river bend behind the willows and adults diving like swallows from the steep bank.

"Now it's your turn to be the horse," said Pavlik.

I didn't wait for him to unharness and quickly donned the harness from my end.

"You must have seen somewhere that it's double-sided!" Pavlik was surprised.

I kept silent. I didn't want to waste time talking.

"To the second pit. Then we'll have run far enough," warned Pavlik, before offering, "Do you want me to bite off half the sweet and share it with you?"

"No, it's fine thanks," I replied, because no sweets could compare to what had just opened to me.

"I didn't know you could run so well," said Pavlik, and I laughed because now I knew it was true.

We ran again. And again, the expanse of the green meadow and sky filled me and overflowed my heart. Pavlik couldn't keep up with me. The straps would tighten and loosen, but that only gave me more strength. I galloped like a real winged war stallion. As soon as I felt Pavlik was about to pull the reins, I leapt forward with my whole body.

Boys from the older group emerged from behind the willows.

"There they are, there they are!" they shouted, parting to make way for us.

Pavlik let go of the reins, and I shed the harness without stopping. I saw little Misha Rubanyuk stepping away from a solitary willow. I could recognise him from a hundred miles away. He began descending to the river, and from a distance, it looked like he was sinking into the ground. Pavlik Bashta and the other boys shouted something to me, but I heard nothing. I didn't want to hear. The expanse of the sky and meadow filled me, and I dissolved into them.

When I reached the third pit, everyone was already busy with their own activities. Some were building sandcastles. Some were jumping frog-style, belly-flopping into the water. Most were running back and forth, splashing each other. The water and sun, the noise and joyful commotion were everywhere, and I decided to leap into this jubilant world.

I dived like a bird, like an untamed winged horse. To avoid crashing into anyone, I veered right of the bathers. I aimed straight for the wide, lush willow bush. I knew I would soar over it and cannonball into the open space of water and sun.

I nailed it! I didn't crash into anyone and soared over the willow bush like a winged warhorse. I purposely kept my legs bent until I touched down at the bottom. And when I did, I instantly uncoiled like a tight spring.

The bottom was muddy and sticky. I thrashed my legs and hurried to get out of the water. I had never been taught to swim, and started floundering. I flapped my arms like a large bird, but my every attempt to rise was involuntarily stifled by my wings moving upward. I couldn't surface but wasn't scared. My eyes opened, but the stirred yellow murk dimmed the light, and I started drinking it to avoid choking.

A shimmering silver streak flickered just above my head. I knew I needed to touch it, at least to catch sight of it with my eyes. Then, I would see the sun again, the whole jubilant day. But I couldn't reach it. The yellow water kept pushing it away with every flap of my wings. Desperate to get closer, I drank the water with my eyes, my wings, my whole body. The water poured into me relentlessly. The tearing pain made my eyes bulge, and to help them, I drank and drank. But the yellow water kept coming, pushing out the vast expanse of life I had just discovered within myself moments ago.

I slowed my arm movements and stopped flapping them like wings. I contracted and sank slowly to the bottom; its muddy stickiness embraced me, but I never forgot about the bright streak above. Gathering all the remaining expanse of life within me I searched for it through the yellow murk. I collected all of it into a silver ball of life, and something inexplicable lifted me.

I saw the shining streak and felt the little ball stir under my heart. Silently, I whispered to it: wait, it's still too early, the yellow murk might still get us. And we stayed still. But the bright, shimmering streak had already heard our silent conversation and glided towards us slowly. It came closer and closer, and the living ball, drawn by it, moved inside me towards my eyes. At some point, I sprang open as if from an electric spark and flapped my wings with all my might, like a winged warhorse. I struck with such force that the streak burst and rang like thousands of sparkling splashes.

I saw the sun, the jubilant children, and the lone Misha Rubanyuk, pointing fearfully at a shiny ball. The ball floated up slowly, lingered under a bush, and then slowly sank again. It did not even cross my mind that this ball was me.

No one paid attention to Misha until Maria Vasilievna suddenly sprang up, throwing off her gown. She rushed into the water, right where Misha was pointing. I still didn't realise she was coming to my aid.

I thought of my mother and immediately saw her because my eyes were now as large as the sky and the vastness of endless day. She was sitting in the summer kitchen with the cook, drinking tea. She raised her glass, and the teaspoon suddenly slipped from it.

"Oh, my God!" my mother shrieked and dropped the glass.

It shattered against an iron bucket with a clang. I wanted to pick up the teaspoon, but everything disappeared and got forgotten.

I didn't remember how they revived me and brought me back to the kindergarten. I only remember that during naptime, we sat on the steps of the main building's secluded porch in a shadow of enormous trees. The trees gently rustled their leaves, and everyone spoke in hushed, spooked voices. We talked about evil divers living in the water and dragging down drowned people. Some argued if it weren't for Rubanyuk, I would have drowned for real. One girl, Olga Volkina, who knew all the alphabet, hoped that next time Rubanyuk wouldn't be there, the divers would drag me down and everyone in the group would get to watch.

Someone said drowning was very painful, and everyone immediately hushed Volkina and promised if she drowned, they wouldn't save her but hand her over to the divers straight away. Volkina started whining that she was afraid of them. And Misha Rubanyuk said she wanted to know everything at others' expense. And if she remained like that, no one would sit next to her. He looked at me, but I kept silent.

My mother came out from behind the building, glanced quickly, and left. No one prevented us from sitting on the porch during quiet time. I asked Misha:

"Where's Pavlik Bashta?"

"He's sleeping," Misha replied. "Pavlik said if you had drowned, he'd have given you a cuff on the head."

I fell silent again, understanding everything, everything to the very bottom. I got it why Misha spoke like that and why Pavlik did. And why my mother came running and left in a hurry. And why Volkina wanted me to drown. I understood everything, but this understanding didn't bring me joy, only the melancholy of the life that had revealed itself to me.

29.06.2012

THE MAGIC OF THINGS

One day, I noticed some things could grow larger and become bigger than they are. A small bolt, nut, or valve needle could suddenly become so big as to obstruct other things behind them.

The first time this happened was in the shed attached to our house, where we stored bent bicycle frames, wheels, and all kinds of other stuff my older brothers had scavenged from the military junkyard near the airfield. Many times, my mother told my father to haul this scrap metal away on his cart so she could finally tidy up the shed. My father remained deaf to her pleas as if he didn't hear her at all.

My eldest brother Vovka (six years older than me) was always very afraid that one day our father would pay heed to our mother. At Vovka's command, Edka, our middle brother (two years younger than Vovka), and I would immediately drop everything and start cleaning up. We would stash the scrap metal in the corners, hang the wheels on special wall hooks, and push the huge box of miscellaneous items, which Mum called the junk chest, under the workbench with its vise and a large metal toolbox containing wrenches, hammers, chisels, and files.

My role was insignificant. I either handed things over or stood somewhere to the side, putting items that Vovka and Edka might need that day into a canvas bag. Most of these items came from the big box. He would squat over it for a long time before pushing it back. My brothers would pick out things they fancied, while I just watched. The box contained all sorts of things: various nuts, tubes, empty jars, pieces of copper wire, small wheels, bearings, ugly gas masks with corrugated tubes and canisters, and many other items we didn't even know the names of. During the clean-up, it was usually from this box that most items ended up in the bag.

One day, Vovka picked out an empty Vaseline jar but didn't put it in the bag. Instead, he pulled a reddish bronze medal from his pocket and placed it inside the jar.

"Look," Vovka said. "It fits perfectly, snug as a bug."

Edka and I looked, and I saw the embossed portrait of a leader, surrounded by a thin rim, and a small bump in place of a ring for the ribbon hook to attach the medal to the metal plate wrapped in a beautiful multicoloured ribbon. The ribbon was missing, and someone had removed the ring with a file. Vovka used the medal as a striker in a game of Penny-Up.

"That's probably Dad's medal, isn't it?" I asked, and my brothers froze, even holding their breath.

"Who told you that?" Vovka asked sternly, standing up, and the medal in the jar suddenly appeared so big he couldn't close the jar with its lid.

"No one told me."

I explained that I had seen a similar medal in our parents' bedroom, in the top drawer of the dresser under the large mirror. My brothers exchanged glances.

"Did you rummage in the dresser?" Edka asked reproachfully, standing up as well.

"No, I didn't. It was open. I saw it in the mirror. There were several boxes and one of them had a medal just like this."

"That medal is Mum's. It's called 'For Valiant Labour'," said Vovka and scolded Edka for not closing the dresser.

"I didn't have the strength, the drawer was stuck," Edka defended himself and then attacked me as if I had spied on him to peek into the dresser. I repeated that I hadn't peeked, just saw the medal in the mirror.

"Don't you dare tell anyone, don't blab," Edka warned.

"Of course, I won't," I said, but Vovka waved his hand, as if to say, let him talk, Dad will find out eventually anyway.

"He won't find out," Edka retorted. He said that neither Mum nor Dad wore their medals because they had already been photographed for the Honour Board and the newspaper. It didn't matter whose medal was whose, since the medals were the same, but the medal papers were different.

"What, they're going to pin the papers to their chests?" Vovka said.

We laughed heartily, imagining Dad with numerous documents pinned to his chest.

"That's enough," Vovka interrupted. "Silly laughter can bring bad luck."

He squatted, and we did too. Vovka started looking for a metal tube for Edka and told me to bring the biggest raw potato from the summer kitchen. I brought one, and they were still struggling to find the right tube. Finally, Vovka said he found it. He reached so deep into the box that he had to rise slightly. We strived to unblock Vovka's hand so he could pull out the tube. It slipped several times, but he finally got it out.

It was a tube from a school pen with an ink nib on one end and a slot for a pencil stub on the other. Caps and nib were missing, but I recognised the thing immediately. Straight and smooth, it seemed cut short at both ends.

Looking through it towards the light, Vovka said:

"It shines like steel, like a hunting rifle (and the tube immediately seemed huge). Bring the cartridges!" Vovka demanded.

But I didn't know where they might be. I searched around with my eyes. Then Edka jumped up and snatched the potato. I clearly saw it had also become different, much larger than before. Vovka stuck the tube into it and when he broke it free, it contained a lump of potato.

"Look, a bullet," Vovka said, showing the tube's hole stuffed with potato. "Not ready yet though."

Using a nail, he gently pushed the lump of potato deeper into the tube.

"Now the gun is loaded."

Vovka ordered Edka to stand in the doorway, facing the yard, so the bullet wouldn't hit his eye.

"You're not a squirrel. They only shoot squirrels in the eye to avoid ruining the fur."

He asked if we knew this. I didn't, and the tube seemed to become even larger. Vovka blew into it from the other end, and the bullet hit Edka's ear with a pop and, rebounding, fell at my feet. It looked like a snail that had emerged from its coiled shell.

"Throw the bullet in the rubbish bin, it's used!" Vovka said and stuck the tube into the potato again.

He prepared another charge, but I didn't throw away the used bullet. I tucked it under the waistband of my pants and quietly broke off two small pieces of copper wire while standing as a target for Edka.

"Valerka, don't move – you're disturbing my aim," Edka complained, and I told him he had moved too.

He started arguing, but Vovka said:

"If you hadn't moved, I would have hit your head, not your ear."

Vovka allowed us to shoot wherever we wanted, but the bullets had to fly into the yard where the chickens would pick them up. Otherwise, he said, we'd have to sweep them out of the shed because a crushed bullet looked like a spit if stepped on.

After each shot, Vovka loaded the tube again, so he chose who got to shoot. Mostly, of course, he and Edka shot, but I got to shoot a few times too. The potato became completely useless.

"Alright, that's it," Vovka said, placing it on the workbench.

The potato now looked like a pockmarked ball. But we had never seen balls covered with round holes before and Vovka said that now the potato resembled a hedgehog.

"Then we should stick pins in it," Edka noted.

"Oh, come on," Vovka disapproved.

Then I took out the bullet that had fallen at my feet from under my waistband and stuck two prepared wire ends near the end with a small piece of dark potato skin.

"Now guess what this is?"

Our first potato bullet had dried and curled slightly, and with the wires, it looked exactly like a snail without its shell.

"It doesn't look like a snail, snails have horns, and this one has antennae," Edka said. "There are no such worms anywhere."

Which is good, I thought, and wanted to throw my creation in the rubbish bin because I couldn't stand worms, even the useful ones like silkworms. But then Vovka intervened, saying that if a snail shell was lying nearby, he would immediately think it was a real snail.

"It even has a dark face, like a real one. Look how clever you are!" Vovka marvelled, and the snail in my palm became a huge diamond.

My brothers leaned in to get a better look at my treasure, and Edka said:

"Vovka, you just don't know our Valerka; he can sometimes make something so good that no one else could ever match it!"

My heart swelled. My brothers had never said such things to me. And I couldn't stand it. Unexpectedly, I squeezed my hand with all my might, my treasure crunched and was crushed. I immediately unclenched my fist, but it was too late, the damage had been done.

"Well," Edka said. "What have you done? You've turned the snail into spit."

I was ready to cry in frustration but then Vovka placed the remains of the potato in my hand.

"Go scrape off your spit with the hedgehog and throw it all in the rubbish bin. And remember: the main thing is not what you made but what you can make, and because it's in your head, nothing bad can happen to it."

He looked at how neatly we'd cleaned up the shed, then put

the box with the medal and the tube at the bottom of the canvas bag. He folded the bag like an old boot's shaft and placed it in the corner of the huge box. He stood up, took a long look from above, and just in case, weighed down the canvas bag with the magneto casing.

"Alright, let's push it back!" Vovka announced, and he and Edka started pushing the box under the workbench.

I managed to help a little too. When we stood up and were about to leave the shed, Edka said that if the medal's ring were intact, they could replace it.

"Oh, come on," Vovka said. "Do you think I filed it off on purpose? No, it was an accident."

He explained that he wrapped the medal in a woollen cloth to protect it, clamped it in the vise, and took up a file.

Vovka fished a three-sided file with a wooden handle from the tools and showed us.

Vovka only meant to file a small notch near the loop to see if it was painted red or made from a rare red bronze. He carefully set the file, but when he pulled it towards him, the medal unexpectedly spun in the vise, and the file slipped, shearing off the loop to the very hole. Vovka threw the file onto the tools.

"It's a beast, almost like a cold weapon."

The file had always seemed very big to me, and now it was even larger than the rusty Japanese bayonet we used in the autumn to cut corn stalks.

After my experience with the snail, I deeply understood Vovka. So deeply, it was as if I had accidentally sheared off the medal's ring myself.

We fell silent, and Vovka, looking at us, suddenly cheered up.

"Don't worry, if Dad goes for the belt, I'll run away from home."

"How will you run away?" We didn't understand.

"Very simply, I'll sleep in the attics of collective farm barns or empty rice mill warehouses."

"Forever?" Edka asked in horror and awe.

"Forever, if Dad doesn't forgive me."

"And if you were him, would you forgive?" Edka asked.

"No, I wouldn't. This medal is more valuable than some military ones, and Dad's nerves are all frayed because of Graves' disease."

We started asking Vovka where he would eat or if he would go begging from yard to yard, and what about school? Would he not study anywhere?

Vovka answered reluctantly because he himself didn't know what would happen to him. For the time being, he would take a handful of change from his piggy bank, and then he would see. Edka said that all the money in the piggy bank was Vovka's, he had won it playing Penny-Up, so no one would mind if he took the whole piggy bank. Vovka disagreed:

"Just a handful, otherwise it will look like we saved money for me to run away from home."

"Oh, Vovka, now no one will play Penny-Up with the pilots like you did," Edka said sadly and asked, "Will you take the medal with you?"

"No, it's not mine," Vovka said, and we fell silent.

I remembered how the military pilots would come to play Penny-Up. They were always cheerful and neatly dressed in city-style silk shirts. Happy and laughing, they came to our street as if to celebrate something. And for us, they were the celebration. The pilots could beat any of the boys at Penny-Up, except Vovka. When Vovka threw the striker, he concentrated so much that everyone fell silent. He never missed. He hit the striker on the stack of coins, and they scattered like splashes in all directions. Edka and I rushed to collect the change, while Vovka stood and pointed at coins that rolled farther away with his bare foot.

The pilots felt that Vovka played Penny-Up not just for the money, but as a demonstration of his skill and sharp eye. This piqued and provoked the pilots. They got excited, dreaming up ways to beat the Ace, as they called Vovka. But he stood there, hands in the pockets of his tattered trousers, looking into the distance as if the conversation were not about him. He even became a little alienated from us, Edka and me. At first, when we rushed to collect the money, the pilots stopped us. But when they learned that we were Vovka's brothers, they apologised, realising that someone like Vovka couldn't have bad brothers.

When Vovka wasn't there, Herka Voronkov and Vitka Grebenyuk (our neighbours, high schoolers from our street) would come running for him. They reported that the pilots were calling for him, the Ace, to empty their pockets.

Our elder sister Raya, who studied at a technical school in Vladivostok, ruled our home during holidays. She never let

Vovka go until he finished his chores – fetching water for the cow and chopping wood. To help Vovka finish his work faster, the boys would often help Vovka, and even the pilots sometimes chopped wood.

Raya sat on the porch in a shiny black hat with a veil sprinkled with white stars falling over her eyes and read the newspaper "Chernigov[16] Kolkhoznik[17]." She observed the process to ensure everything was done well. Only then did she let Vovka go. As they left, the pilots always asked: "So, what do they write about?" – "They write that our military pilots are the best in the world," Raya replied, and they all laughed heartedly.

Vovka laid down the rules before starting: fair game, no cheating. No one could beat him fair and square. He was always chosen as the captain in dodgeball, too. Everyone knew that wherever or whatever our Vovka played, he would emerge victorious.

It pained me to think that Vovka would run away from home and become a beggar. So, I said that should he run away, he would not have to beg because Mum cuts bread for everyone in the morning, and Edka and I would bring Vovka's portion to him. And I would even break off some of my own.

"How do you know Mum will cut bread for Vovka when she knows he's run away?" Edka wondered.

"I know," I said. "Mum will never accept that Vovka isn't with us, and so will always cut bread for him."

Vovka came over and gave me a hearty cuff upside my head. He looked into the distance as if he were alone and we weren't there. I also started looking the same way because tears welled

---

16   Also Chernihiv – a city in Ukraine.
17   Worker at a collective farm (kolhoz)

up in my eyes, not from the cuff, but because Edka and I would never find a brother like our Vovka.

Vovka was away from home for five days. He appeared early in the morning in the deep ravine behind the garden; we brought him bread.

Dirty, tattered, covered in burrs and weeds, Vovka asked, "How's Dad?" We said Dad was silent, and Mum was crying. Raya was scolding all of us, saying she would tell the pilots to drag Vovka back by force.

"No, they won't," Vovka said, smiling to himself. "As long as you come to the warehouses, they won't touch me, they think you're guarding me."

It was surprising to hear that because after Vovka left, all the boys from our street and the station began to hang out at the warehouses. Edka and I would go there as well, but never too close. We understood we were not needed now. We thought no one saw us watching Vovka. Little did we know we had become such big objects that we could be seen from everywhere.

"Look what I have," Vovka said.

He pulled out light round stones from his pockets, the kind used to strike sparks, and started juggling them. He did it skilfully, very skilfully, like a real juggler. (Vovka was still the same big brother, interesting to be around). And then Edka said he had seen Vovka's medal in the Vaseline jar on our parents' dresser. Vovka dropped the stones.

"You know, Vovka," Edka said. "Tomorrow morning, Valerka and I will ask Dad for forgiveness."

"What are you going to say?" Vovka asked, gathering the

stones, and putting them in the pockets of my jacket.

"We'll say we won't do it again."

Vovka said we had nothing to do with it. He added that he couldn't forbid it, but later, after Dad punished us, we shouldn't come to the warehouses, or we'd get some from him too.

The next morning, we waited until everyone gathered in the summer kitchen. Edka instructed me to ask for forgiveness because the youngest is always forgiven more easily.

When I started talking, Dad put down his spoon, and Mum immediately sat on the stool by the stove. Raya didn't even look at us and instead, gazed out of the window, as if bored.

Dad listened, paused, and slowly took the jar with the medal out of his breast pocket.

"Take it," he said to Edka. "Give him this medal and tell him it's his now."

We had already bolted out of the summer kitchen when Raya, opening the window, shouted after us not to drag Vovka to the table right away, but to take him to the summer shower. She had once seen him from a distance – he was as dirty as a pig.

Vovka was waiting for us in the ravine. Huffing and puffing, we told him that Dad had forgiven him, and that now, the medal was his. Vovka listened seriously and distantly. There was something in him, something chiselled like the medal. Only when he opened the lid did he laugh. And Edka and I grabbed his arms from both sides.

We walked through the gardens, and I was bursting with joy. We were going home with Vovka, our big brother.

I had never felt such great joy before. But Raya ruined everything. She said Mum had cried while watching us through the window.

12.06.2012

VICTORY DAY

Leaning on his left leg, Yakov Antonovich paced back and forth near the truck, both awaiting and dreading the train's arrival. The train didn't come, or rather, it did arrive but didn't bring any children. He felt a weight lift from his heart. As he got into the vehicle, he saw the relieved faces of the milkmaids, but how could he blame them? He asked Gennady Pushkarev to stop by the collective farm club and felt the silent gazes of the women on him until he turned behind the brick building. That day, with the painter's help, he transcribed the entire telegram onto the back of a film poster and hung it on the wooden fence opposite the kindergarten.

"In the coming days, children from the Dmitrievsky orphanage will be dispatched to you by express train from Kabarovsk. Ensure reception and dispatch. Adoption by the population is not to be prevented. Polkovnikov."

The telegram was from Vladivostok on the eve of the holiday, and thus its somewhat confusing nature was justified. At least, it was understandable to Yakov Antonovich Khvosh, a solitary man, former headman of the "Path to Socialism" collective farm and currently the village council chairman.

"…not to be prevented." He envisioned the bustle of large train stations, trains delayed, the confusion, the station's aluminium-tasting hot water, passengers on roofs and footboards of the carriages, all determined to celebrate the first anniversary of the great victory at home. He realised that the telegram was sent in advance with the hope of universal understanding: children must be given priority boarding. He sighed deeply. It was entirely possible that not a man named Polkovnikov, but some colonel, had sent it[18]. Nevertheless, if there was no confusion, it was even better that the sender had such a resonant military surname. Yakov Antonovich was confident that even the collective farm chairman would abide by it and would not refuse the vehicle. "Of course, he wouldn't refuse anyway – the children… and still, a military surname is quite handy these days," Yakov Antonovich thought, mentally outlining the plan for his forthcoming tasks.

On the first day, they left for the station after lunch. Unexpectedly, it was reported that some Moscow train, running late, was arriving from Spassk. Yakov Antonovich limped to the dairy farm and fortunately caught Gennady Pushkarev just arriving from the midday milking. Yakov Antonovich only had the milk cans unloaded and ordered the milkmaids to stay put.

Climbing into the back of the lorry and throwing his stubborn leg over the bench closer to the cab, he took the telegram out of his jacket pocket, read it aloud, and waved for Gennady to drive.

"We'll discuss everything, girls… the express train from Spassk takes just forty minutes to arrive, we must not miss it."

The milkmaids, who had been cheerfully watching their former brigadier a moment ago, grew sombre: for many families, this meant another mouth to feed.

"Ah well," Yakov Antonovich sighed loudly, as if for everyone. "Adoption by the population is not to be prevented."

---

18   The family name Polkovnikov has its root in the Russian word for colonel.

He adjusted his leg: how could one hinder it? Two days ago the orphanage director came, they scraped together some flour and soy cake to last until July, the elevator promised to provide more in the third quarter, but now it wouldn't be enough… Yakov Antonovich sighed deeply again, and the women, sensing that their former brigadier was now deeply worried, started talking about the bountiful wild garlic, the radishes that would be ready to pick by the twentieth in this warmth, about nettle soup – in general, they could manage.

Yakov Antonovich left the lorry on the station square by the candy-striped horse pole and went to see the station master on duty; Ignat Voronko, a prickly and quarrelsome man.

That day Ignat was astonishingly polite, seating Yakov Antonovich in his chair like a dear guest, while he sat on a bench. He allowed the lorry to be driven right up to the platform and announced his willingness to hold up the train if necessary.

"Let them telegraph later that Chernigovka delayed it. Otherwise, you see, the stop is just three minutes. These passengers don't understand that Muchnaya station is Chernigovka, and it's the district centre. But if we hold it up a bit…"

Yakov Antonovich had never witnessed Ignat's reasoning before and was very surprised – such a man as Ignat should not be given power, all his restrictions and concessions would always be illegal. However, he took advantage of his permission and drove the lorry to the platform so the children could see and rejoice at the vehicle right from the train. Besides, this was a comfortable parking spot.

At home, involuntarily feeling ashamed of the relief he had experienced at the station, Yakov Antonovich mentally reproached himself: it was still not clear if it was for better or worse that the children hadn't arrived today. Maybe tomorrow he wouldn't bring the milkmaids.

And so it turned out. They stood on the wooden platform together with the orphanage director Dmitry Ivanovich Kolombin, and slightly below, behind the disorganised row of traders, all of them women, also waiting for the train, stood the empty lorry with a pre-war bicycle leant against its side. About two hours remained before the midday milking, and noon was just beginning to assert itself. Winged musicians, ant-like insects, buzzed languidly in the fresh young greenery. The day seemed to languish, to suffer in their plaintive whining. Sometimes, the wind would blow in gusts from the river, as if washing this sound away. Dmitry Ivanovich's jacket sleeves would puff up, and his round glasses would sparkle, making him look like a long-legged intelligent bird. His glasses and long sharp nose gave him a bird-like appearance, as if he were always peering and peering for something with his nose.

But again, the children did not arrive. Helping to load the bicycle into the lorry, Yakov Antonovich told the director not to come tomorrow: making this way on a bicycle would be inconceivable. It was better to prepare for the meeting; tomorrow was Victory Day, perhaps they could organise some amateur performances, a festive table of sorts. He and Gennady Pushkarev would manage it here at the station. Yakov Antonovich also didn't want Dmitry Ivanovich to come because he hoped the children would be brought tomorrow. Children are children, but people would still try to take the bigger, prettier ones. Those who remained… They needed to be welcomed at the orphanage, especially by the director, Dmitry Ivanovich; his feelings needed to be preserved, not squandered.

"If anything, come on the tenth. Even then… call me in advance," advised Yakov Antonovich.

During the night, he was awoken several times by the heavy drone of bombers on training flights. He went outside, looked at the gleaming runway, then at the starry black sky – the Milky Way lay slightly tilted, like a lake within a lake. The rustling leaves, the sweet smell of apple trees, and the cold well water with a hint of fresh logs, suddenly evoked a painful longing for his past failed life. Yakov Antonovich returned to the hut, lay down on the broad, hard bed, and fell asleep. Again, the drone of planes would seem to hang over him, slowly blending into the roar of tractors, as only happens in dreams. For a while, Yakov Antonovich would hear the rattle of a hay mower and keep moving further towards the river with his scythe, looking for Polya. There she was, running with a saucepan: "Yasha!" They sat by the tent. The grass wilted in the day's heat, it was fragrant and languorous, and in the clearing sky, the endless blue seemed to be their souls merging.

"Kolya! Where's our Kolya?" he asks, and Polina suddenly steps back and retreats, retreats farther away. Now they are in a military town. Heaps of ruins, a fire site. Broken trees lie around, the bark hanging like torn clothes, the whiteness beneath it, frighteningly human. Yakov Antonovich saw a fence, a torn-off section tangled in telegraph wires, his heart leapt and gasped as if someone had stepped on his chest with a lead boot. A pink sock caught on a broken fence flapped in the wind, crying, calling: "Daddy!" Yakov Antonovich would wake up in a cold sweat and go outside again…

By dawn, the flights had ceased.

Leaning against the fence, Yakov Antonovich gazed at the broadening sky. Just as the night had brought him unexplainable sorrow, now he felt a benevolent premonition. This new feeling frightened him a little – what was he to expect? Then the old woman Klanya, who looked after his modest household, came and set out a glass of homemade liqueur for breakfast. He was genuinely surprised: what was it for? And then he remembered: it was a holiday, Victory Day. The feeling strengthened, and hour by hour, his confidence grew that something would happen today that would drastically change his life. Though he tried not to think about it, upon arriving at the station, he was not at all surprised to see many more women meeting the train than the day before, and almost all of them had registered with him to adopt a child. Right there on the grass by the station water tower, which resembled a silo, the beggars had spread out bread, onions, and lard on their rags. "Surely, they've got a bottle of vermouth as well," Yakov Antonovich thought pointlessly and nearly collided with Renka Voronko, the stationmaster's brother, a legless man, black and shaggy, fused to a wooden cart resembling a scooter, which he swung forward as if it were part of his body.

"What's up, Yakov, called out the people?" Renka asked in his thick, hoarse voice that frightened children and dogs alike, and skillfully swerved towards the water tower, carrying a bottle that glinted in the sun in his apron.

At any other time, such a meeting with Renka or any of his gang would hardly have pleased Yakov Antonovich, but today it somehow elevated his sense that everyone is human. Watching more people approach from the direction of the grain plant and the elevator, he straightened up, tugged at his tunic, and brushed the dust off his breeches: he should thank the old woman for the fresh uniform, she had prompted him well. Hearing the lively strains of the accordion, he smiled: the day was shaping up into a real holiday. He walked to the car, holding his head high with dignity, trying to put less weight on his left leg – he was, after all, some kind of authority here. However, that sense of authority evaporated as soon as the stationmaster announced that the express from Spassk had departed and the orphanage was in the fourth carriage. Time and again, he pulled out his notebook to check that he had the list of parents wishing to adopt a child, with him. Coming across his own name first, Yakov Antonovich not only forgot to maintain his composure but also forgot himself. When the train stopped, everyone rushed towards the fourth carriage, suddenly creating the need for a person of authority. It then took Yakov Antonovich a while to battle his way to where two conductors, waving their rolled signal flags, were holding the crowd back from the carriage. It was they who had demanded the presence of a person with authority.

"Where's the person in charge?" one of them impatiently asked, and the crowd, as if it were a single face, silently looked around and produced Yakov Antonovich. Now he was representing all of them. And yet, he remained Yakov Antonovich Khvosh, a resident of Chernigovka, a solitary man who had lost his wife and son in the war and had decided to adopt a child today; right now.

He saw a young woman in a brown jacket and black hat descending the steps; the veil adorned with stars, covering her face, gave her an absurd, masquerade-like mystery for the occasion. Stepping onto the platform, she lightly nodded and held the veil with her hand. The high, padded shoulders of her jacket, raised as if wings were folded beneath them, caught the eye.

"Comrades, who here is from the Dmitrievsky orphanage?" he heard a ringing, excited voice but did not immediately realise it belonged to the young woman because the people around also became agitated and moved away from the carriage. He then saw Renka Voronko falling from his scooter, having a fit. To be honest, it was frightening to look at Renka – a living stump, and terrifying when in a fit. "Oh, what a misfortune!" It's anyone's guess how things would have turned out if the city teacher, as Yakov Antonovich mentally named her, hadn't been so firm, so sweet, so resourceful.

Although her cheeks flushed, she did not get flustered, addressing the crowd loudly and clearly. It was especially good that she spoke loudly because it was important for everyone to hear and process it themselves. Beginning with the secondary details, she pressed a purse to her chest, pulled out papers and began listing the clothes and shoes being transferred to the Dmitrievsky orphanage along with three boxes of toys, as well as forty sets of bed linen and blankets.

While Yakov Antonovich, licking his pencil, signed the necessary papers, Gennady Pushkarev, not succumbing to the general confusion, carried the boxes and chests onto the platform, along with the conductors. The last one, with the bed linen (a heavy and bulky redwood chest with old monograms on bronze plates), had to be dragged with frequent stops, hindered by a twelve-year-old girl named Olka, who clung to the handle next to Gennady. Skinny, in a washed-out yellow-grey dress, bald and barefoot, she evoked a feeling of frustration and pity. She frowned at all requests to let go, her bulging, pale eyes turning blank, and stiffened even more, gripping the handle tighter. But when they started dragging the chest, she appeared to wake up, helping with all her might, her shoulder blades visibly protruding from the effort. "Wait, wait, you'll strain yourself," Gennady tried to stop her, but setting to work, she became agile, resourceful, and a bit fussy, like any woman forced to compensate for a lack of physical strength. Outpacing everyone, she darted here and there, adopting the role of mistress of the train. Before dragging the chest down the steps, they sized up the best method. Olka jumped onto the footboard, and waited, realising that more strength would be needed. Her zeal did not go unnoticed; the women watched affectionately and sympathetically: what help could she possibly offer the men? Unable to reach the chest, Olka jumped onto the platform, grabbed its side. "Look at her, a real trouper," the women loudly marvelled, and the men, grinning, looked at Olka anew. Buoyed by their appreciation, she tried even harder. Yakov Antonovich also noticed her light, fluttering figure, but was distracted by Ignat Voronko. Ordering the men to carry the revived Renka into the station, he rushed to Yakov Antonovich intending to delay the train. The city teacher, hiding the signed papers in her purse, intervened:

"Why delay it? The documents are signed, the goods are here," she said, pointing at the chests and boxes on the platform. "And the children… Olka!" she called, but since no one responded, she resolutely walked towards the chest, where a barefoot, bald girl in a yellow-grey washed-out calico dress stood petrified. Within minutes, the shrewd and nimble girl had transformed into someone else entirely. Stamping her sturdy, massive heels, the young woman confidently approached the girl, staring blankly at the bronze edge of the chest.

"What's the matter? Why are you standing there like a statue?"

She took Olka's hand rather sharply, but the girl unexpectedly recoiled, grabbing the chest. The young woman was taken aback, her face flushed, and even her hands turned pink. Suddenly afraid she might cry, she turned pale.

"Comrades, Happy Victory Day!" her voice trembled.

The pre-prepared phrase the city teacher intended to deliver with pathos, faded away. She felt a hot prickling in her chest and a sense of resentment in the silent estrangement of the women, who seemed to edge away from her. Rising above it, the city teacher suddenly began complaining, hastily and incoherently, that she wanted the best, but … It transpired that she wasn't supposed to travel with the orphanage; she was going to Vladivostok on her own, but they had asked her. Today, the stations were crowded. In Iman and Spassk the children were taken, but the provisions and Olka were left behind because Olka had hidden… Of course, she was complaining, not hoping for sympathy; she was hurt, but oddly enough, the other women now seemed to draw closer to her.

A sudden sharp whistle of the locomotive drowned her out, and the train started moving. The young woman rushed to her carriage, asking everyone as she ran to deliver Olka to the orphanage along with the documents and property. In parting, from the vestibule platform, she shouted: "Olka!" She waved a crepe-de-chine handkerchief, pressing it to her lips to stifle a cough, and was gone. Nothing was left of her, except for the shout that struck Yakov Antonovich straight in the heart: "Olka!"

Responding with a wave, Olka straightened, holding the crepe-de-chine handkerchief with her gaze, and then slumped again, clinging to the chest as if it held all her salvation. "And so it is," thought Yakov Antonovich, involuntarily imagining himself in Olka's place. "It must be awful when they take your comrades, and you somehow know you won't be chosen, won't be taken, and have to hide in advance from the insults in this mighty chest."

"Step aside, girls, make some room," he asked, and approaching Olka, placed his large hand on her shoulder. "I want to show her our hills."

The women continued to stand motionless. They had been told about his plans to adopt, and suddenly the girl, and alone at that, seemed incredible. "They'll come to their senses now," thought Yakov Antonovich, mentally rejoicing in the course of events that had fallen into his hands. He just had to hold on.

"What do you want, Yakov?"

The throng of women parted, forming a ragged corridor, to reveal the blind beggar Sasha Bezverov with his two-row accordion on his knees, sitting cross-legged on the grass, facing the sun.

"Our Sasha, the musician," said Yakov Antonovich and, feeling Olka's body tense, reassured her: "Don't be afraid of him, he's half-sighted, and he throws his head back for effect when begging."

Grinning crookedly, Sasha spat, but the women scolded him: "Mind yourself, you're being shown to an orphan."

"What, I'm not doing anything!" Sasha jerked, turning his head to follow the gaze of the crowd.

"See there, behind the roofs, the blue ones?"

Carefully lifting her head, Olka gasped: "Oh, so near!"

The women nodded in agreement: yes, yes… But Yakov Antonovich objected: close, but not much; if seen from his house, the view would be different. Olka didn't even have time to blink as he lifted her and put her on the chest.

"Look a bit to the side, see the trees – that's the collective farm garden. And to the right – the airfield. And on this side of the garden, towards us – the whitewashed house with zinc roof – that's mine!"

Sensing where the chairman was pointing, the women split: some sided with Yakov Antonovich, others grumbled – is that how you welcome someone? He would have been better giving her a pie, some candy to comfort her, but instead, he put her on the chest! What would she see there? A man is a man, she needs a mother. Yakov Antonovich also realised that perhaps it wasn't the right way, but it was the only way he knew. Should Olka choose him, the old Klanya would help, but otherwise, he would be both father and mother.

"Gennady, there's a bundle on the seat in the car, bring it,"

Yakov Antonovich asked, wiping sweat from his forehead. "Well, Olka, did you find it?"

"Yakov, you're like a child," women scolded him, but he knew very well that it was impossible to see the house from here; he needed this conversation with Olka for its own sake, simply as a conversation. But she suddenly stood on tiptoe.

"What about the chimney, is it the brick one?"

"Yes," confirmed Yakov Antonovich.

"And does the roof slope?"

"It does indeed."

"Then I can see it, over there, by the garden," said Olka.

Yakov Antonovich, not hiding his proud superiority, looked towards the grumbling women, who hushed reluctantly.

"Right, by the garden," he happily agreed and took her down from the chest as quickly and easily as he had put her there.

Yakov Antonovich was sure Olka hadn't actually seen the house. Yet he had no doubt that it existed in her mind.

"You know, Olka, I'm alone too, just like you, completely alone."

He suddenly became agitated and fell silent, searching in vain for the right words.

Gennady Pushkarev returned with granny Klanya's treats. Catching Olka's cautious glance as she followed the bundle, the women got flustered, remembering their own supplies. Yakov Antonovich wanted to get ahead of them but, unfortunately, couldn't find the ends of the cheesecloth tie. "Ah, granny, granny," he thought sorrowfully, placing the bundle on the chest, and trying to console himself with the thought that a man is a man.

The women pulled out their own pies, sugary fried dough, home-made biscuits, and honey, and offered it all to Olka: "Take it, child, try it." Frightened by the abundance of food, she retreated closer to Yakov Antonovich, who, no longer hoping for anything, wiped the sweat from his face absent-mindedly. Suddenly, Olka grabbed the bundle with her characteristic explosive energy and using her teeth, quickly loosened the ties. Pleased at Olka's initiative, Yakov Antonovich told the women strictly:

"Wait… we have everything."

He unwrapped the cheesecloth, revealing the same pies, the same homemade biscuits, and the same honey, the colour of cow's butter.

"Honey!" Olka exclaimed in surprise but immediately became serious.

"Take it, take it," demanded Yakov Antonovich, "as a reward for your hard work. I noticed you right away, I thought: who is this helper, who's everywhere on time? I'd like someone like that, otherwise…"

He suddenly fell silent, paused. And then, out of nowhere, got angry:

"I'll tell you what, women, if Olka decides to stay with me, I give you my word, I'll be both her father and mother. It's up to you to decide."

He waved his hand not quite contemptuously but still rather rudely. Yet in response, as if out of unexpected tenderness, the women's hearts softened: What about us, Yakov? Let the girl decide for herself.

Olka was very pleased that Yakov Antonovich said he'd noticed her right away. So pleased that she almost laughed out loud. To be honest, she expected to be noticed. That's why she almost laughed, realising she wasn't mistaken. Therefore, when Yakov Antonovich demanded she take what she wanted, she took not the honey (she wasn't little), but a small pie. The anger with which Yakov Antonovich suddenly attacked the women didn't surprise her. Olka didn't know why, but she also got angry at them. So, while they were deep in discussion, she, without hesitation, quickly gathered the treats into the cheesecloth bundle and pulled Yakov Antonovich's sleeve as if to say, let's go! He got flustered, and hobbled to her, wanting to stroke her boyish head in a burst of emotion, but Olka thought it was out of clumsiness, ducked and slipped through. Then she looked back, ran to the chest, and lowered the end handle she had been holding, gently pressing it down and returned.

"You, Gennady, look after the luggage and take it to the orphanage. Empty this chest and bring it back, Olka will take it; it's hers," Yakov Antonovich said firmly, looking at the chest intently as if hoping the chest would somehow appreciate his words and remember. "Tell Kolombin: I'll ask them for dimensions later and provide a replacement."

Unexpectedly for Yakov Antonovich, Olka nestled her head against him, and they walked off. The human corridor parted, Sasha the musician habitually raised his blind face to the sky, pulled the bellows, and started playing "The Little Apple[19]." His military cap with the red band lay overturned, expectantly, on the grass. Yakov Antonovich stopped and rummaged through his pockets, at which Sasha suddenly shook his head violently:

"Go on, go on, I don't need anything," and as Yakov Antonovich continued searching his wide breeches, Sasha swore

---

19   A classic Russian folk song and dance, mostly known as Russian sailors' dance.

and broke off the music. "I said I don't need anything; I'm playing for the holiday."

After walking a few steps, Yakov Antonovich turned, as always, turning his whole body, and Olka looked back too. Yakov Antonovich was curious: why wasn't Sasha playing? However, encountering the living human wall of silent gaze, he forgot about him, straightened up, stood for a while, feeling an inexplicably strengthened faith in himself, and looked down at Olka.

"I'll show them..."

Why he said this, who knows? In response, she furrowed her brows and likewise muttered:

"I'll show them..."

And, hiding her head behind Yakov's arm, she quietly laughed. He smiled, and they walked off. Strangely, people heard this almost silent laugh. Sasha pulled the bellows, the women stirred, sighing, and bringing the ends of their faded peasant scarves to their eyes, and the men, as if nothing affected them, started shouting all sorts of cheerful curses, very similar to threats, in which the women read only helplessness and vulnerability. And so, they silently joined in, moving in time to Sasha's lively "Little Apple."

Yakov Antonovich and Olka crossed the station square and went along the street. They walked from one yard to another, and every time someone emerged from behind the fence, Yakov Antonovich would stop and announce:

"We're going home; me and Olka, my little helper."

1982

SMALL VICISSITUDES

This happened in Cannes at Villa Du Soleil. His wife was sitting under the canopy on a light mesh lounger, covered with a terrycloth towel, while he was swimming in the open pool. More precisely, he was lying on his back on a foam noodle, arms outstretched.

"Look, look!" he exclaimed in surprise, pointing at a bluish-green snake resembling a bent cut of wire. The snake floated above the pool towards a sprawling Cannes pine, which looked more like a small forest.

No, she saw nothing.

"Perhaps it's a visual phenomenon, like floating black spots," she suggested. "Or some other small vicissitudes?"

"What vicissitudes?"

"Small ones," she chuckled and explained, "They appear to be there, but they're not really. Or vice versa—they're there but appear not to be."

"I don't understand," he said and explained, "As it flew, the snake first disappeared behind the extension roof, then reappeared and got lost in the dense pine foliage. It looked all watery. A hungry seagull could easily snatch it up."

"Still, I didn't see anything," his wife said and went back to her lounger under the canopy. He leaned onto the noodle again.

"It's always like this with her," he thought. "She'll say something nonsensical and then stick to it as if there's something so important in that nonsense that it can't be compromised… We've raised our children, they're grown, soon we'll have grandchildren, and she's still on about these small vicissitudes that seem to be there but aren't, or vice versa."

What does she mean? He didn't even want to think about it. Maybe they've been together for too long and grown weary of each other. "We should part for a while so she can experience these small vicissitudes for herself," he thought arrogantly.

A fluff, much like a dandelion puffball but significantly torn on one side, floated slowly through the air. He peered inside. Long seeds, attached to light parachute umbrellas, resembled construction trusses…

He climbed into the fluff. It noticeably swayed but remained steady thanks to its ingenious stabilisers. The fluff's interior, quite spacious, resembled the structure of a spherical ship, where the construction trusses, though piled up on the torn side, formed a garland tied together with a transparent cord.

"If desired, the damaged part could be easily restored," he thought. "The fluff would become less airy and transparent, but its hidden properties would be revealed."

What properties? He felt a growing unease, as if on the verge of an unplanned journey. Moreover, the thought of hidden properties seemed strange, arriving from somewhere outside himself.

He sat on something resembling a small smooth box and suddenly felt everything around him moving; the trusses started to grow and evenly fill the torn part of the sphere.

He looked at his wife, who had jumped up from her lounger.

Her frightened cry, though unheard, was clearly readable from her searching gaze that scanned the pool and then darted under the canopy.

His wife hurriedly disappeared into the extension.

"Oh my God, what's happening?"

He didn't know what to do. Long black seeds, the trusses, were rising in sparse rows, spacing themselves at arm's length in a calculated sequence.

"Oh my God, what's happening?" he called out again, but didn't hear his own voice.

Thank goodness the trusses had gaps between them. He looked up and realised the futility of any hope. After all, these were seeds from an unknown dandelion, not real trusses.

Detaching from the garland, they released their parachute umbrellas upwards. Umbrellas merged and have already covered a part of the gap with their billowing cloud.

He felt uneasy. The fluff was about to restore itself – he saw the inevitable future.

"Oh my God, what's happening?" came his wife's frightened cry, and rushing towards the cry, he felt himself splashing in the water, with the foam noodle floating nearby, and the completely restored dandelion-like puffball floating in the air along the noodle, almost touching it.

The puffball rolled towards him, and he maliciously thought, "Gotcha!" and raised his hand to swat it. The puffball then suddenly stopped and slightly crouched as if braced for the inevitable. Unexpectedly, he changed his mind and, taking a deep breath, blew on the puffball as hard as he could, noting absently that his lungs weren't the same after COVID.

His angry breath caused the umbrellas to tremble hard, and a breach appeared on the puffball, reminiscent of the one he had entered through.

Is this an invitation to resume the "small vicissitudes"?

A chill ran down his spine. He looked inside the puffball. It seemed to him that behind the pile of seeds resembling trusses, someone was there, sitting on the smooth box he had previously sat upon. For a moment, he saw the end of the terrycloth towel hanging down—but that couldn't be!

He carefully examined the inner space of the so-called dandelion, hoping to identify who might be there by any direct or indirect signs.

There was a round room resembling an isolated cab, its floor lined with soft bluish foam. In the centre, a round glass table with a monitor was hovering in the air, apparently kept in place by magnetic force. Telescopic antennas extended from the monitor, with glowing LEDs at their ends like fireflies. There were three chairs fastened to the floor (or rather, the deck) by the table, facing the damaged part of the fluff.

It was probably a spaceship bridge. But he had never been on a spaceship. He saw a notebook and a steel-grey "Parker" pen on the soft floor. He had owned such a notebook and a pen about twenty years ago. They were scattered on the floor as if someone had just dropped them.

He was overwhelmed with excitement – how could this be? He looked under the canopy and saw his wife was looking around in confusion. Seeing him, she exclaimed:

"Oh my God, where have you been?! I almost went crazy - you just vanished into thin air."

"Come here," he said, trying not to show his agitation.

Without hesitation, she jumped into the pool and grabbed his arm firmly just above the elbow.

"Do you see?" he asked, pointing to the crumpled and torn puffball. "I was just there… Inside."

She looked at him intently. He knew that look—it didn't relate to the subject of conversation because the subject and the look were incompatible. The subject always seemed too insignificant. But it wasn't insignificant!

They were speeding from the village of Chernomorskoye to Yevpatoria. He was driving, and she was dozing beside him. When they hit a bump, she let out a small yelp, and he asked:

"Aren't you afraid to sleep? What if we get into a deadly accident?!"

She looked at him very carefully, patted his shoulder and, resting her head on it, gently said:

"We will die together."

He felt there was nothing to worry about now - sometimes, the worst isn't so bad if seen through her eyes. And yet, her priorities drove him mad sometimes. On the other hand, thanks to them, she was more understandable and dearer to him. And in the past, she used to get dolled up, unrecognisably…

She let go of his hand. The splash of the water suddenly pushed him. He tried to grab the noodle but slipped. Surfacing, he asked:

"Where are you?"

"Where could I be?" she said, peering out of the puffball through a gap.

"You're there?!" he was surprised.

"Where else would I be? Get in!" she demanded.

He tried to climb in but couldn't, despite the puffball's stabilisers. The vessel behaved like a rodeo horse. Watching the water splashing out of the pool, he thought the water was disturbed by the puff.

No, the puff had nothing to do with it.

He suddenly felt that some foreign, invisible force was causing the water's erratic splashing, something even the ingenious stabilisers couldn't compensate for. He felt this acutely when he found himself inside the puffball.

She was sitting on the smooth box, having laid a towel on it, the same one with which she sat on the lounger. Where had it come from?! A thought flashed about the vicissitudes and priorities she couldn't seem to give up—a kind of fate. "If only this mysterious dandelion would seal her in," he thought absently with some satisfaction. And then he suddenly got scared. "No, no, if that happens, it's best we're together."

The thought seemed so endlessly long that he felt his thoughts were stretching time by stretching themselves. That would explain the lagging, delayed reaction of the fluff's ingenious stabilisers to everything around it.

He stepped towards the nearest chair by the table and suddenly froze, remembering the notebook and pen on the floor. The entire space of the fluff lunged forward, and the fluff itself suddenly stopped sharply, as if it had run aground. He noticed that the notebook and pen were gone. But then, when the space played back with some delay, he saw the pen gleaming in a soft fold of the foam, with the notebook beside it.

"Tell me, why are we here?" she asked.

"I don't know, it's inexplicable."

He sat in the farthest chair, placing the pen and notebook on the table before him.

"You always had an explanation for everything. Remember, after visiting the excavations in Veliky Novgorod, you said that there were several civilisations on Earth before Atlantis. We don't find their traces because those previous civilisations were environmentally clean and, being more advanced, left no traces. Then you insisted that we're forever looking in the wrong place because our perception is based on material objects. We should be looking for accompanying bodies of thought, which are plentiful, yet they elude our perception."

"I think there's someone else here besides us," he said.

"Don't scare me! Can I sit in your chair? What if someone is already sitting in the one next to it?!"

They exchanged glances.

"Sit here," he said, moving the notebook and pen to the centre of the table, and stood to switch seats.

Again, the fluff's vibrations didn't match his movements, and again he thought it was his wife's fault for getting up from the smooth box too soon. But she hadn't got up. He knew this for sure but blamed her for some reason. Why?!

"Be careful," she warned, watching his clumsy movements. "It feels like someone invisible is interfering."

"You noticed too?" he asked involuntarily, holding onto the back of the chair he intended to sit in.

"Of course!" she said, and they exchanged glances again.

He thought he had given himself away, and now all his efforts were futile. Before whom?

"Your place is free," he said, sitting in the central chair.

"I'll wait," she said. "And you sit between them."

"Why 'between them'? Are there two of them? There are three chairs."

"There are three of them, and the third one causes discord - you took his place."

"Listen," he said, feeling the same unpleasant chill running down his spine. "Sit next to me. We need to stick together because your small vicissitudes don't bode well."

"Why mine?" she said, not hiding her displeasure. "It seems you were here before me. Do you think I don't remember the 'Parker' pen and your buckram notebook from twenty years ago that you lost just before going to the army? I remember perfectly how we turned the flat upside down and found nothing."

"And now it's all here," he said thoughtfully. And they exchanged glances again.

He opened the notebook.

"All objects, both animate and inanimate, have a name and an accompanying thought. An object can be destroyed, but the accompanying thought cannot. The time will come (and this time is not far off) when we will learn how to find and extract from the surrounding ether the bodies of thoughts that once accompanied material objects. Civilisations of the past have left these thoughts on Earth. Keywords spoken at the right time and place will reveal great inventions to be used as our own. Just saying 'Open, Sesame' will expose the lodes of wealth, concealed not in dungeons but here in the Earth's noosphere. We need to find the keywords, like the magical 'Open, Sesame' that will reunite everything that was and is into a single solid civilisation, the civilisation of Homo Sapiens."

"Wait, wait," she interrupted. "I remember why we were looking for the notebook and the 'Parker'! You said some keywords had opened to you and you wrote them in that buckram notebook. That's why we turned everything upside down."

"You remember that exactly?" he doubted.

"How could I forget?! They were conscripting you, and I was six months pregnant. You were hugging me with one arm and writing in that buckram notebook with the other, saying the keywords had opened up to you. And you kept repeating that you loved me, and I was crying out loud…"

"Did I say these keywords out loud while writing them?"

"I don't know. I had other things on my mind…"

"Please, sit next to me and, please, try to remember," he cautiously asked, afraid to disturb the invisible presence.

But everything had already happened. She didn't have time to switch seats. The surrounding space stirred and moved. The seeds that resembled construction trusses rose one by one, matching the fluff's oval and forming a semicircle. It reminded him so much of his first entrapment in the fluff that he believed everything would settle now.

"Yes, yes, it will settle," he said cheerfully, loudly in tune with his feelings and, not hearing his own voice, smirked smugly.

He expected her to cry out in fear: "Oh my God, what's happening?!" and they would find themselves back in the pool. Everything would return to normal. Impatiently, he turned to her and froze in shock—an expression of horror was etched on her face. She was looking through him.

Following her gaze, he turned around and felt petrified.

The seeds arranged themselves not to restore the dandelion's damage but to form a semicircle behind the chairs. They covered themselves with their parachute umbrellas, dissolving into them. A jagged sponge-like loop of watery rings appeared on the screen; it resembled a bluish-green snake. The perspective shifted, and he saw, as if under a microscope, the division of the dandelion, very similar to the division of a single-cell organism. Everything around cracked and screeched with the deep sound of ripping strings. He turned to her again, absently noting that the puffball's tear wasn't repaired and they could leave it together.

His thoughts were now brief and fast and somehow preemptive. No, no, they couldn't leave the so-called puffball together. A glass wall with airy rings, reminiscent of the watery rings of the bluish-green snake, stood between them.

They simultaneously rushed to the dividing wall and both felt its impenetrability at the same time. "Here are the small vicissitudes for you," he thought with the same unexplained pleasure and, feeling no fear of the invisible presence, but rather flaunting himself before it, said very loudly:

"I'll get out of the puffball now, and she can stay here, in this dandelion."

Of course, she couldn't hear him. He didn't hear his own voice, but he felt her growing anxiety. She urged him to open the buckram notebook and find the keywords using her gaze and gestures. She believed that would undo the locks and shatter the glass wall.

He flipped through the first and second pages, which explained the possibility of a single solid civilisation of Homo Sapiens. All other pages contained the words written in all capitals: "I LOVE YOU"!

Twenty years ago, leaving for the army, he had indeed loved her with all his heart.

He placed the open notebook upright and propped it with the 'Parker' pen so she could easily read the repeated words. And, without caution, he stepped firmly towards the break in the fluff. Deep down, he hoped some inexplicable unknown force would stop or at least delay him.

Nothing stopped or delayed him. Already in the pool, hearing the hungry cries of seagulls overhead, he felt he was falling into an endless emptiness. Yes, he now knew for sure that without her, his life had no meaning. He looked up at the sky, and in the same instant, she was in his arms.

"You?!" he was surprised.

"Yes," she replied.

"You read the keywords from the buckram notebook?"

"Why read them?! They're here," she lightly tapped his chest with her forefinger. "And please, ask nothing, I didn't see anything anyway."

28.01.2023, Moscow

GLOSSARY OF DIMINUTIVE NAMES

Edka, Edik - Edward
Fedya - Fyodor
Gena, Genka - Gennady
Goga, Gosha - Georgiy (George)
Herka - Herman
Kolya, Kolka - Nikolay
Lenya, Lyonka - Leonid
Lilka - Lilia
Misha - Mikhail (Michael)
Mitya, Mityenka, Dima - Dmitry
Olya, Olka - Olga
Pasha, Pavlik - Pavel
Petka - Peter (Pyotr)
Raika, Raya - Raisa
Rozochka - Roza (Rozaria, Rose)
Sasha, Sashka - Alexander
Temka - Artemiy
Tolka, Tolik - Anatoly
Valya, Valka - Valentin (male) or Valentina (female)
Vanya, Vanka - Ivan
Vasya, Vaska - Vasily.
Vitya, Vitka - Victor
Vovka, Vova - Vladimir.
Zhenka, Zhenya – Yevgeniy (male) or Yevgeni

REVIEWS

'*Zinziver*' is a masterfully crafted story that immerses readers in a vivid and enchanting world. From the beautifully descriptive prose to the profound philosophical reflections, every page brims with emotional depth and literary elegance.

— Gareth Stamp, The Guardian
of the Eurasian Creative Guild, Journalist, Writer

* * *

'*Zinziver*' fits seamlessly into the tradition of Russian literature that explores the intersection of reality and fantasy. Its use of surrealism and hallucinatory experiences draws comparisons to Mikhail Bulgakov's The Master and Margarita. Through meticulous detail and rich symbolism, '*Zinziver*' offers a compelling and deeply human story that resonates long after the last page is turned.

— Maria Bregman, editor-in-chief of Creativitys. UK

* * *

In his novel, Viktor Slipenchuk adheres closely to the essence of things, weaving delicate patterns of meaning, colour, and light.

— Tatiana Sokolova. Literary critic, Russia

* * *

Viktor Slipenchuk's much loved and revered novel from 2000 takes its title *'Zinziver'* from that cheery-songed little woodland bird the tit, and the lyrical song of the bird is reflected in Slipenchuk's own lyrical, poetic voice. The story is of a successful young businessman and poet's pure love for a woman. But it explores what creativity and imagination is for, through fantastical dreams that are in some ways more real than reality. "In order not to frighten her, I buried my face in a flower and immediately fell asleep, that is, as if melted in the fragrance of the garden. How long I slept - I don't know". Yet Slipenchuk's novel is also an acute observation of a turning point in Russian history in the 1990s, as the Soviet Union broke up and a new Russia struggled to emerge.

—John Farndon, author, poet and translator

* * *

'Zinzever' is a cornucopia of one man's witness testimony in the face of an impoverished writer's daily transition through the collapse of the USSR and decadent rebirth of Russia.

— Bruce Gaston, France

* * *

Slipenchuk has written a beautifully interwoven novelette that shared the hopes and dreams as well as the reality of family politics.

What '*Crossroads*' shows beautifully is that duty and family can be integral to one's life. The characters in '*Crossroads*' are raw and show an honesty that can sometimes be overlooked in novels to portray a glamorous exterior.

Love is never easy, indeed nothing of true value can be said to be smooth sailing and we see this in '*Crossroads*'. "Why is it that sometimes there is no reason to love a person, and everyone knows it, yet they still do?". This is one of the many truths spoken in this novelette that absorbs every one of your senses.

Introducing many readers to late Soviet and early post-Soviet Russian culture, this novel is a masterclass in writing a novel that shows humanity but also lets the reader explore a moment in history perhaps they are not now familiar.

With a glossary that guides the reader but never patronises with the Russian terms, '*Zinziver*' will enthral the reader and take them in to a world that really does seem another era.

Understanding the past is so key to our future and learning about key events that have shaped our future is vital and Slipenchuk seems to maybe unknowingly light the fire of interest with the reader to keep on discovering history.

— *Francesca Mepham, Editor and literary critic*

ABOUT AUTHOR

Viktor Trifonovich Slipenchuk - Is a Russian poet, prose writer and publicist. He was born on September 22nd, 1941 in the village of Chernigovka, Primorsky Krai, USSR. Before taking up the pen, he led a thoroughly 'seasoned' and experienced life. He worked as a geological prospector, zootechnician, sailor, fish farmer, builder and journalist, all of which provided rich material for his literary creativity. He has great knowledge of life, an inquisitive mind and an original view which is reflected in his works.

He is an author of more than 30 books (poems, short stories, novels, essays, journalistic articles), many of which have been reprinted many times and have also been translated and published abroad (in Mongolia, China, Japan, Vietnam, France, Serbia, Ukraine).

The author's works include the poetry books: 'The Light of Time' (3 reprints), 'Journey to the Empty Space' (2 reprints), 'Genghis Khan' (2 reprints), 'The Thirteenth Feat of Hercules', 'Zigzag', as well as the prose books: 'The Fire of Silence', 'Zinziver' (2 reprints), 'Bright Resurrection', 'The Golden Box', 'Star Spas', 'The Flash of the Blade', and the play: 'The Governor'.

Five radio plays were created on 'Radio Russia' based on the works of Viktor Slipenchuk, including 'Genghis Khan', 'Bright Resurrection', and the 'Journey to the Empty Place'. Popular songs and romances were written based on V. T. Slipenchuk's poems, and award-winning music videos were shot.

He is a member of the Union of Writers of the USSR (Russia) since 1982 and the Corresponding Member of the Academy of Russian Literature since 2009, he had been awarded the Golden Yesenin Medal 'For Loyalty to the Traditions of Russian Culture and Literature', he has also been awarded the Diploma of the Moscow City Organization of the Union of Writers of Russia 'For Faithful Service to Russian Literature' and presented with a medal in honour of '55 Years of the Moscow City Organization of the Union of Writers of Russia'. In 2013, he was awarded the Mongolian Order of Glory of Genghis Khan and was elected as an academician of the International University named after Genghis Khan.

In 2023, the 'Khudozhestvennaya Literatura' publishing house published a collection of the writer's works in 8 volumes.

These are Viktor Slipenchuk's works available internationally in their original languages:
Japan (2007). In Russian and Japanese: "The Laughing Baby-Doll". 'RONSONYA' Publishing House. Tokyo.
China (April 2009). In Chinese and Russian: " The Laughing Baby-Doll". 'Modern Press' Publishing House. Beijing.
China (October 2009). In Chinese: 'Zinziver'. 'Modern Press' Publishing House. Beijing.
China (April 2011). In Chinese: 'Star Spas'. 'Narodnaya Literatura' Publishing House, Beijing.
China (2014). In Chinese: 'The Fire of Silence'. 'Narodnaya Literatura' Publishing House, Beijing.

Ukraine (2011). In Ukrainian: 'Zinziver'. 'Treant' Publishing House, Kharkiv.

Vietnam (2013). In Vietnamese: 'Star Spas'. Hanoi.

Serbia (2013). In Serbian: 'Star Spas'. 'Treči Millennium' Publishing House. Belgrade.

Serbia (2013). In Serbian: The poem 'Genghis Khan'. 'Treči Millennium' Publishing House. Belgrade.

France (2012). In French: 'Zinziver'. 'L'age d'Homme' Publishing House. Paris.

France (2013). In French: "The Captain's Smile". 'L'age d'Homme' Publishing House. Paris.

Mongolia (2014). In Mongolian: "Star Spas". 'ARILDAL' Publishing House. Ulaanbaatar.

Mongolia (2015). 'Genghis Khan'. A bilingual edition of the poem in Cyrillic and Old Mongolian script. 'ARILDAL' Publishing House. Ulaanbaatar.

The novel 'Zinziver' was published twice in Russia. 'Soviet Writer' Publishing House, Moscow, 2000. 'VAGRIUS' Publishing House, Moscow, 2001. The novel 'Zinziver' was published in the Roman Gazeta №9-№10, Moscow, 2024.

Foreign publications of Zinziver: 'Modern Press' Publishing House, China (Beijing), 2009. 'Treant' Publishing House, Ukraine (Kharkov), 2011. 'L'age d'Homme', France (Paris), 2012.

The play 'A Novel Without Remarks' by Sergei Korobkov was written based on the novel 'Zinziver' by Viktor Slipenchuk. It was staged by director Gennady Shaposhnikov at the Theater of Nations (2004-2007).

CONTENTS

FOREWORD 5
FROM THE TRANSLATOR 7

ZINZIVER *Novel* 11
PART ONE
CHAPTER 1 13
CHAPTER 2 21
CHAPTER 3 35
CHAPTER 4 46
CHAPTER 5 56
CHAPTER 6 64
CHAPTER 7 77
CHAPTER 8 87
CHAPTER 9 99

PART TWO
CHAPTER 10 107
CHAPTER 11 118
CHAPTER 12 130
CHAPTER 13 140
CHAPTER 14 149
CHAPTER 15 159
CHAPTER 16 169

696

CHAPTER 17   176
CHAPTER 18   184
CHAPTER 19   194
CHAPTER 20   200

PART THREE
CHAPTER 21   208
CHAPTER 22   220
CHAPTER 23   230
CHAPTER 24   241
CHAPTER 25   251
CHAPTER 26   261
CHAPTER 27   271
CHAPTER 28   282
CHAPTER 29   294

PART FOUR
CHAPTER 30   301
CHAPTER 31   312
CHAPTER 32   326
CHAPTER 33   335
CHAPTER 34   348
CHAPTER 35   358
CHAPTER 36   364
CHAPTER 37   381

PART FIVE
CHAPTER 38   388
CHAPTER 39   394

CHAPTER 40 399
CHAPTER 41 406
CHAPTER 42 413
CHAPTER 43 419
CHAPTER 44 432
CHAPTER 45 445
CHAPTER 46 459
CHAPTER 47 467
CHAPTER 48 474
CHAPTER 49 482
CHAPTER 50
IN LIEU OF AN EPILOGUE
FROM THE PUBLISHER 491

CROSSROADS 495
LITTLE LAUGHING DOLL 581
WINGED WAR STEED 635
THE MAGIC OF THINGS 646
VICTORY DAY 659
SMALL VICISSITUDES 675
GLOSSARY OF DIMINUTIVE NAMES 687

REVIEWS 688
ABOUT AUTHOR 691